THE COMPLETE KOSKI & FALK
Volume II

A. G. Hayes
with Raymond Gaynor

Savant Books and Publications
Honolulu, HI, USA
2020

Published in the USA by Savant Books and Publications
2630 Kapiolani Blvd #1601
Honolulu, HI 96826
http://www.savantbooksandpublications.com

Printed in the USA
Edited by Daniel S. Janik

Cover design by Daniel S. Janik
Cover image "Armageddon" by Pete Linforth from Pixabay
Cover image "Silhouette Agent" by Mohamed Hassan from
Pixabay
Cover images reproduced with permission

ISBN 9780999693841

First Printing April 2020
Library of Congress Control Number: 2020936674

NOTE: *Quantum Death* was published before its prequel, *Finding
Kate*. For continuity and clarity, however, they are presented in
order of their storyline in this collection.

TABLE OF CONTENTS

Book Four:

Dedication

To my wife Connie who sailed aboard the Queen Mary from Southampton to New York in 1948; we were married in Los Angles, in December.

Chapter 1

Angina pectoris. Dr. Gordon Metcalf ground the heel of his right hand into his chest. He was a chemist, not a medical doctor.

For weeks he ignored the shortness of breath, the slight pauses in heartbeat. But this...he was dizzy, on the verge of losing consciousness when the chamber in his heart finally pulsed.

He waited. The spindly fingers of his left hand gripped the rail of the outdoor veranda that ran the length of his home. He sucked up air until his reed-thin body, down to less than a hundred pounds now, straightened, then sagged with deflation.

It was eleven-thirty when the news flashed across the television screen. He quickly calculated the time: eight-thirty in California, three hours behind Panama. Metcalf's heart had literally paused when he learned that the *Queen Mary* was in danger of being destroyed.

Dear God! What have I done? I never thought...

It hadn't occurred to him that the ship, so big and so seemingly indestructible, might one day be in jeopardy. What could he do? An old man, weak, maybe even at the end. There was only one thing to do.

He took a piece of paper he had kept in a drawer and dialed the 202 area code number written there, breaking his fourty-seven-year silence.

A live woman, not a menu of choices, responded: "FBI headquarters."

"I need to speak to an agent. Hurry, please."

The Bureau believed him to be dead. Of course, he'd planned it that way in 1967. It bought him these peaceful, nearly guilt-free years on Contadora. But now, there was so much he felt he had tell the Bureau and so little time left. How can a breathless old man compress so many years of distorted reasoning on his part into a few minutes of telephone conversation?

After being transferred from extension to extension, he was

connected to an agent.

"I can't go into my rationale at this time," he said, "but when I disappeared in 1967, I took with me a briefcase containing the results of a scientific experiment I had been working on at Neogenetic Conveyance Industries in Middlesex, UK division. I boarded the *Queen Mary* on her final voyage to Long Beach, California. I didn't think anyone knew I was on board."

"Obviously, no one did, sir," the agent said crisply. "You eluded the FBI, the National Security Agency, CIA and British Intelligence. We, in fact, instigated a futile worldwide search."

"Then you're familiar with the experiment?"

"Familiar with its existence, not particulars, sir."

It was obvious to Metcalf that he was talking to a veteran. But the man sounded nervous, eager, and probably unable to believe what he was hearing. After all this time, years after the trail went cold and his predecessors deemed the file inactive, here was the principal player, calling to say he was alive.

"You were quite clever, Dr. Metcalf," the man added.

When Metcalf made the decision to board the ship, he knew that, despite his attachment to the scientific community, he was the type of person who could easily fall through the cracks of civilization and be lost to the world.

"Not clever enough," Metcalf wheezed. "Someone, a Latin unknown to me, followed me on board the ship. He attacked me one night," he paused, hearing his breath sound like dry whistles. "I fought him off and I...I believe that I disfigured him for life. I couldn't let him get hold of the briefcase, you understand."

"Yes, sir. I know."

"Before I left the lab in England, I placed the compound in a specially constructed container."

He stopped abruptly, his feelings about the receptacle stung his mind. Secretly, he had dubbed it The Devil's Crucible, because he considered the contraption as a vessel whose depths seethed and boiled with a flesh-eating mixture that would grind through bone as surely as a chain saw. It was conceived by a part of his brain that must have been under the spell of Satan himself.

"Well," he said, once he was able to go on, "I put the compound in its container that, in turn, went into a briefcase reinforced with steel, and I took it onto the ship." He stopped again, a series of raspy coughs eating up ten seconds on the line.

"For reasons I don't have time to explain now, I'd intended to hurl it overboard. But I underwent a change of heart and decided to relinquish it to the United States' authorities in Long Beach at the end of the voyage."

Another pause and more gasps followed by a deep, punctuating sigh.

"Of course, once I knew the Latin was after it, I had to hide it. Somewhere where it could not be found, and would remain safe until I summoned the courage to notify the authorities. I had no *choice* but to hide it. Don't you see?"

The agent seemed to be holding his breath. "Hide it, sir?"

Metcalf heard the horror of his own words. Sweat moistened his face and he swiped a hand across his wet upper lip. "Yes, I hid it, then jumped ship in Panama. I've been living here on the small island of Contadora off the southeast coast of Panama ever since."

"Then, the briefcase containing this compound is..."

"Yes. On the *Queen Mary*, in Long Beach, California. God forgive me."

Sickeningly, he sensed the agent's mind ticking off some of the deadly combinations of volatile chemicals that must be in the briefcase. The chemicals themselves were harmless, inert, so long as they remained undisturbed and were not exposed to extreme temperature.

Metcalf's voice was a soft rattle now. "I imagine that you heard the news about the *Queen Mary* on television."

There was stunned silence on the other end of the line. Metcalf knew that he did not need to tell the agent about the madman on the ship and the firebombs he planned to detonate. The bombs would burn the tinder-dry decks at a temperature as high as four thousand degrees Fahrenheit. Steel melted at three thousand degrees.

"Are you at home, sir?" the agent finally asked.

"Yes, but let me tell you exactly where on the ship the briefcase is hidden."

"No!" the agent stopped him, "Not on the phone. Look, Doctor, please, just tell me where you are. Give me your address and don't call or talk to anyone. We have people at the Consular Section of the U.S. Embassy on Panama Bay in Panama City. They'll fly out to the island and should be there within the hour."

But, if he had to wait for the agents from Panama City to arrive, he was afraid either he wouldn't last or, worse, the Latin might beat them. Somehow, now that he'd broken silence, the Latin would know and find him.

"Hurry," Metcalf wheezed.

Chapter 2

"Click." The sound of a tape recorder being turned off.

"That concludes a phone call that's thirty-five years too late." Agent Falk muttered to himself. "We've all been living on borrowed time." Pushing back his chair he stretched his six-foot frame admonishing himself, "Get to work."

The recording had been sent to Cerberus HQ and had been forwarded to him; that action itself indicated the urgency of the call. The FBI was not in the habit of passing anything to anyone. Glancing at his watch, Falk knew there was still one very important factor missing: Agent Susan Koski, his partner in the everlasting battle against international corruption and the destruction of the United States. There was no time to waste.

Chapter 3

"Wait, Frank, hold on a second," Joseph Falk said. He was on the phone in his parents' home in Studio City, California, and the caller, his Washington Bureau Chief, was new on the job and fair game for second-guessing. "How can we be certain this guy has in fact planted bombs on the Queen Mary?" Falk didn't want it to be true. "It could be a hoax. After 9/11, everybody's ready to believe anything."

Frank Heeley was breathless with excitement. "No way, Falk, no hoax. The guy left a note in his apartment flatly stating his plans. And the local authorities found evidence of explosives there. And he was sighted on board earlier by one of the ship's personnel. This guy, Jack Bonecutter's his name, was a reluctant but expert demolition man when it came to personnel mines and explosives in Nam, and is now a Hollywood screenwriter. He's also a certified schizophrenic who has obviously gone over the edge."

"But why does he want to destroy this ship?"

Heeley sighed. "That, I don't know. Look, my information from Long Beach PD is sketchy, but it seems that today is the anniversary of the ship's maiden voyage, back in 1936. Bonecutter has been obsessed with her since he was a boy. He has something like eighty websites bookmarked on his computer describing every detail about her, from her tonnage to how many freakin' rivets it took to put her together.

"His note said that he resents her being permanently docked in the Port of Long Beach and 'prostituted,' transformed, I suppose, from what he saw as a majestic, seagoing castle into a floating tourist trap, hotel and shopping mall. He says he wants to 'set her free', so to speak."

Falk knew the situation was serious, but he had arrived in California only last night. "I don't know, Frank."

"Look, Joe," Heeley interrupted, "we're talking about a mammoth ocean liner, the Queen Mary. The ship weighs almost eighty thousand tons, and is over a thousand feet long, one hundred feet longer than the Titanic and twelve decks high. It's permanently docked in one of the busiest ports in the United States. Cruise ships leave there every day for Mexico, Alaska, you name it, destinations all over the world." Heeley talked fast, hurrying to get the facts out.

"Our alleged bomber is hidden on board and plans to blow himself up with the ship. He's planted ten homemade incendiary devices at various locations only he knows, to be ignited at eight o'clock tonight by a remote-controlled detonator he has on his person."

Healey paused. Falk offered no response. "It's a nightmare," Healey continued. "I just spoke to LBPD, and they're already evacuating the ship, but there's one thing they don't know."

"Frank, it's only nine a.m. local," Falk broke in. "Negotiators have eleven hours to locate, engage and subdue this individual."

"We *could* detail a team on this end or scramble one from the local field office, but that would take more time than we want to spend. Moreover, we want our involvement to be as minimal as possible; one or two people, tops," said Heeley, continuing, "Joe, you're one of the best agents the Bureau's got. And you're less than fifteen minutes away by military chopper, which, by the way, is on standby at Van Nuys airport." Heeley took a deep breath. "We need to get someone on that ship immediately."

"On the ship. You can't communicate with this guy from dockside? You want me to board a vessel that you're telling me is about to be blown up?"

Heeley may have been new to his position, promoted when Falk's previous chief was murdered during a Bureau investigation, but he was quick with the standard vernacular. "Did anyone ever tell you, Agent Falk, that working for the Federal Bureau of Investigation was a picnic?"

"Hey, Frank, I'm with Rover Division. My job is to sniff out terrorists, thugs, rogue militia groups and the like. This is not my station. For this assignment you need a good man from a First Response unit with..."

"We need *you*, Joe. When you and agent Koski literally saved this country's ass by uncovering those responsible for the serial killing of all those lawyers in Nevada, you merited the commendations you received."

Falk groaned.

Heeley's voice saying, "Hey, come on, Joe," recalled Falk to the present emergency. "Frank, why us? Can't the local authorities handle this?"

"Because there's more to this situation than we can risk with the locals. My orders were to assign you."

Heeley's tone had risen a few decibels, and Falk heard him clear his throat to bring it back under control. He knew the last remark was no argument. Heeley held the title, but they both knew who the superior agent was.

Then he added, "And because we are already involved."

Falk leaned toward the kitchen table and set down the mug of coffee he'd been holding in his left hand. "To what extent?"

Heeley sighed. "Eighty years ago our government bungled a top-secret assignment connected with the Queen Mary. The assignment involved a scientist who was working in England and is now in Panama. British Intelligence has its panties in a bunch and is threatening to get involved directly this time if we can't resolve it."

"British Intelligence. Shit! This is going to be a fucking circus!"

Until last year Falk had always been a loner. He preferred to live the roaming life in the field as part of the FBI's elite Rover Division. There he was free to make his own decisions. He had proved himself to be dangerous by the long list of convictions he amassed.

But the Nevada assignment that paired him with Special Agent Susan Koski changed all that. He thought it was possible that his developing feelings for her made him a better man.

Professionally, however, Falk secretly felt diminished because he was forced to work with someone as a team, making him one-half of a successful effort, one-half of what he once was. And now he wished she were here. He sighed.

"Okay, tell me about this so-called bungled assignment and the scientist in Panama."

Heeley's voice dropped to a harsh whisper. "Are you alone?"

"Yes, I'm alone."

"And this is a secure line?"

"Damn it, Frank, you know it is!"

As Heeley explained, Falk knew that Jack Bonecutter was about to destroy more than himself and an old ship.

Chapter 4

Jack Bonecutter fell into a black abyss, his legs and arms flailing furiously, hands thrashing, grasping for something, anything, to stop his wild descent. He grabbed at the madness of empty air, twisting from side to side, clawing for rungs of the ladder he gambled was there. His temples throbbed, and the beat echoed in his ears, his arms, his chest.

One hand, then the other, finally caught a rung. His feet, too, found support against the blind darkness that sucked him downward. He clung to the ladder, gasping for breath, nerve endings prickling and adrenaline pumping. Gradually the thumping in his chest subsided, and he breathed normally again.

For only a moment he released one hand to wipe a dense gauze of cobweb from his face. He was right; the wooden ladder his grandfather helped build was still intact, after over seventy-five years.

In 1934, the ladder was bootlegged as a convenience for the original builders in Scotland. It was a means by which they could stay inside, protected from the raw winds of the Clyde as they moved from top deck to the bottom of the ship. Bonecutter was thankful for their ingenuity.

He was convinced that no one but himself remembered the shaft and the ladder, unless the grandchildren of others who worked beside his grandfather were aware, which seemed improbable.

Hits to the Queen Mary web pages were from the curious, not the well informed. Her seductive secrets were forgotten as surely as her freedom was abandoned to crass commercial captivity.

The bridge was the nerve center of every ship, where the helm and other navigational equipment were located. The chartroom was small and spare. It contained a long, low bench built into the wall, a floor heater, wall panels for voltmeters and control lights, stacked wall cabinets for maps, and a large oak chart table where navigational maps had been laid out when the ship was at sea. Beneath the table that was more than waist high and built to accommodate a standing man, was a cupboard three and a half feet high and three feet wide and deep.

When the Queen Mary was in service, this cupboard was used for miscellaneous directional materials, but it had stood empty for years, its wooden floor gathering dust. The cupboard floor contained a flat trapdoor, the access to the long, vertical ladder to which Bonecutter now clung. He originally planned to carefully explore the shaft and test the ladder. However, the earlier appearance of two evacuating personnel on the bridge obliged him to rip open the wooden door on the floor and drop, feet first, into the darkness.

Now he slid one leg from the wooden rung and rotated his foot, relaxing his leg muscles, then repeated this movement with his other leg. He planned to balance on the ladder for many hours.

Here, in this dark shaft, he must remain hidden until it was time to go back up to the chart room and depress the small red dot on the remote in his shirt pocket.

He was safe here. Security, in their evacuation efforts, had checked the chart room. They would check the bowels of the ship hundreds of feet below. Bonecutter was suspended between the two.

He saw nothing; the cool dank blackness of his surroundings clung to him like shrink-wrap. He was aware of a hollow roar, like the sound of the ocean one heard in a conch shell, but loud and piercing.

Above the roar he heard the wail of sirens. Good. That meant everything was proceeding according to plan. His agent, Pete Powers, had called the police after finding the note Bonecutter left in full view in his apartment. The evacuation had begun in earnest.

His design was for the police to have plenty of time to get everyone off the ship. He didn't want to harm anyone.

Oh God!

He suddenly remembered he'd forgotten to take down the printout he had tacked above the desk in his apartment. His scalp prickled. Printed from one of his websites, the paper displayed a cross-section of the ship, on which he circled in red marker the exact location he chose for each bomb.

Damn! At least I remembered to delete the page from the hard drive, so the police won't find it when they confiscate the computer, he thought. *Meant to bring the printout. Could be a costly mistake unless Pete Powers and the police miss it. Things in plain view are often overlooked. Who am I kidding?*

But there was no turning back. For one agonizing moment, he feared one of his spells was about to overtake him. His skull seemed to shrink, and pressure built in his temples, a sign that he needed the medication he had decided to discontinue weeks ago.

Sounds, not voices, not words, but discordant music as if from a warped dulcimer filled his head. He did what he usually did: He waited. He concentrated on the eternal peace he expected when this day and night were over. This time the spell did not materialize and the shrinking feeling passed.

He mentally retraced his steps. Had he forgotten anything else? Had he chosen the best possible locations for his bombs? It had taken him nearly an hour to hide them on board, just before he dove into this shaft.

He was proud of his bombs. He'd spent days constructing the nests of explosives. He was surprised at the ease with which he obtained the needed materials from Internet sources. These included the powerful transmitter that allowed him to trigger the bombs prematurely, should an unfortunate circumstance arise to make that necessary.

Each bomb resembled a meat pie approximately eight inches in diameter. The "meat" was a sticky mixture the grunts in Nam called "foo," because that was the sound it made when ignited. As he put the bombs into place, he inserted electronic fuse-receivers in each.

Now, with their deadly potential in check, the receivers awaited his command. They would respond to a transmitted signal, spark each bomb's explosive, gelatinous core, and splatter liquefied fire in every direction. The firestorm created would burn with an intensity of four thousand degrees Fahrenheit. Because the wooden decks of the Queen Mary were more than seven decades old and combustive as kindling, they would quickly ignite and the result would be unstoppable.

A mental vision of a torrent of flame flashed across his mind like an inferno, caused a momentary sense of misgiving. He was about to take from the world what he considered to be the ultimate ocean liner: the quadruple somersault, the grand slam, the quad axel of ocean-going vessels. In the past she routinely crossed the North Atlantic, carrying nearly two thousand passengers in graceful, felicitous splendor.

The Queen Mary had rare, almost human character that Bonecutter felt certain would never again be captured in a vessel.

Despite the fact that on her maiden voyage she crossed the Atlantic in four days, twenty-three hours fifty-six minutes, Bonecutter insisted that she was much more than eighty tons of massive power.

Her lavish interiors were superior to all. While built to endure, one had only to envision her spacious ballrooms and salons in different lights to concede she was, in fact, a palace. Marble columns, rich thick Brussel carpets, ornamental paintings and lustrous draperies left an air of magnificence.

By night, all windows were ablaze with light, her broad, long ballrooms brilliantly illuminated by enormous crystal chandeliers.

A sudden deep involuntary sigh jolted Bonecutter's chest. He let go the vision of her glory days. she, like so much Bonecutter prized, had been devalued.

The green glow of his watch face told him it was nine o'clock. In eleven hours, the sea, like a pack of wolves leaping at the ship waiting to devour him, would have its way. No trace of Jack Bonecutter or the poor, beloved Queen Mary would survive.

Chapter 5

In Panama, Metcalf walked slowly from his living room into the kitchen. He had acquired doctorates in biochemistry, human anatomy and cellular physiology. He was a thinking man.

He never considered himself brave. Never. Yet he knew that, if the Latino got to him first, he would never tell where the briefcase was hidden.

The mysterious Latin man was doubtless aware of the mercenary potential of the chemicals and would auction the weapon to the highest bidder. He would be tenacious, determined.

Back in 1967, Metcalf was sure he had done the right thing,

A. G. Hayes

taking the amalgam, literally stealing it from his lab where he was commissioned to work on the top-secret scientific military experiment under the auspices of the United States and British governments.

"Never do anything against conscience, even if the state demands it." Einstein's words haunted him. By developing the mixture against his better judgment, Metcalf had done the exact opposite, and had ever since been paying for it.

After long, agonizing hours of analysis and self-reproach, he decided there was only one viable course: The world would be better off without this weapon. It was then that he took the briefcase, boarded the Queen Mary, and headed for the United States. As he told the FBI agent, he initially planned to drop the briefcase overboard. But something stopped him. In the end, it was as much to save himself as the compound that Metcalf concealed the briefcase and jumped ship in Panama.

In the intervening years, he gradually concluded that the reason he didn't toss the experiment into the ocean was that he was a servant of science. How could he ignore the fact that once one deliberately formed elements into a creation with global consequences, it no longer belonged to you; it belonged to the universe. For better or worse, the compound existed.

Initially, Metcalf had wanted no part of the experiment, but the British and American military convinced him that it was for the "good of his country." Simply the knowledge of such a weapon, they argued, once they were ready to reveal it, ensured that the western super-powers would remain in a position of strength from which to negotiate peace while the Cold War raged, threatening Eastern countries.

Metcalf poured another cup of weak coffee and eased back into a kitchen chair. Until this morning, when he learned of the threat to the Queen Mary, he had been successful in pushing thoughts of the experiment from his mind.

As a scientific experiment, it proved successful well beyond everyone's wildest imaginings. It failed miserably, however, in human terms. Occasionally, he would promise himself that one day he would go to the ship, retrieve the damnable thing, and turn it over to the U.S. Defense Department. But time passed. And now his heart was failing.

Despite his unconscious mind's best efforts, a growing sense of unacknowledged responsibility intermittently returned, and that the amalgam, if unfound, would someday decay. He had no idea how long it would take before that happened. The process could have already begun. At some point, the propellant itself would tend to spontaneously ignite. He had not had time in the lab to adequately address shelf life and the hard questions concerning the compound's ultimate impact, were it allowed to age naturally.

Now, however, the potential for natural decay over a period of years was no longer a factor. The window of opportunity he had in which to deal with the danger had shrunk, a saboteur on the Queen Mary reducing it to hours. Hours he did not have.

Then, of course, there was the man who had assaulted him on the ship. Metcalf recalled the attack vividly. The man assailed him at night in the shadows of the promenade deck. Metcalf, thirty-four years old then and physically healthy, fought wildly, managing to avoid the steel blade as it whipped toward his belly. Twice he was nearly gored.

Then a quick, lateral lunge let him dodge the man's third charge and caught his attacker off guard. The aggressor pitched sideways. Trying to regain balance and avoid the airborne, spinning blade, his assailant stumbled and fell on the knife. Metcalf saw the steel enter the man's face just below the cheek bone, and bury itself to the hilt in the *zygomaticus major*, that muscle which angles the mouth upward when smiling.

Metcalf turned and fled. As he slipped from the ship before first light the next day, he envisioned his attacker's wound, one he knew would forever affect the man's ability to smile, leaving a grotesque, one-sided, painful stretching of lips against a show of teeth.

Metcalf swallowed the last few drops of cold coffee from his mug, and with a shudder tried to rearrange the protrusion that had gradually, over the past few years, developed between his shoulder blades. It was symptomatic of his severe respiratory ailment, emphysema, and its potential for congestive heart failure.

Suddenly he was aware of a din of silence. From the kitchen, he could hear even the slightest sound from the front of the house. But now it was unnaturally quiet; even the quetzals in the guava trees were still. Metcalf winced as another angina pain gripped him. He coughed as the pain increased and stabbed his chest.

This time it was really bad. If only the federal agents from Panama City would hurry. He rubbed his left arm, and simultaneously, a board on the veranda groaned.

Chapter 6

Captain Benjamin Booker Marshak, Long Beach Police Department, was on his house throne when the phone rang at 8:35 a.m. He was smoking an unfiltered brand and studying the subject of this month's centerfold, a prone, ebon-skinned sister with one hand resting between widely parted, nude thighs. He cursed the phone, which he managed to reach before it woke his wife, and he heard the news about the Queen Mary.

Now he was in one of the two construction mobile offices on the pier beside the threatened ocean liner. Using these as his command post, he quickly completed his on-site assessment, and the evacuation of the ship began.

The First Response units and Major Incident vehicles were arriving. All civilian access, including media entry, to the ship, pier and "A" parking lot was prohibited. The press was all over the situation. By now there was not a city on earth that wasn't carrying the news of Marshak's nightmare.

He jumped as the ship's forward klaxon let loose an ear-shattering blast, announcing nine o'clock. He'd forgotten that the horn sounded every hour. Keyed to lower bass A, it was called "the voice of the Queen Mary." Here beside the ship it was unnerving, suddenly an intolerable assault on Marshak's ears. He grabbed a phone and punched in a number.

"Sergeant Bowyer!" he bellowed. "See that the horn gets the delete key. Now! And for the duration of this crisis." He dropped the phone back into its cradle.

Man, he didn't need this. His twenty years of service had been relatively quiet, his performance as captain of the precinct exemplary. Like his chief, he was tough on all criminals. As he was a fair-minded, second-generation African-American with an African-American-Asian wife, accusations of racial bias seldom plagued his department.

"You carry a big stick," his officers said, referring to the political clout his mixed ethnic background afforded.

Marshak always grinned, his large features loosening into soft folds, and grabbed his crotch in a slick, Michael Jackson move. "You got that right."

Yes, his was a kick-ass department, but he believed solidly in every man's rights under the Constitution of the United States. Unless of course, he was some son of a bitch about to torch the Queen Mary on his watch.

Incendiary bombs. Man! Fire and water was every mariner's nightmare since the Phoenicians set sail in the seventh century. Now they had become his. He remembered when the Queen Elizabeth burned and sank in Hong Kong harbor in 1972. He read about what happened in New York back in the '40s, when the French liner Normandie burned at its mooring. So much water was pumped into her belly that she rolled over and kissed her career goodbye.

"I'll get this guy," Marshak said aloud, "even if I have to storm the ship myself and carry the bastard off by the balls."

If the vessel ignited, the chances of extinguishing the fire with hoses and on-board sprinklers were nill. Her wooden decks, aged and filled with tar strips, would respond to the flames like a hungry infant to its mother's breast. Marshak ran a hand over his head. A few tight, gray-black rings still clung to the rim of his otherwise smooth crown.

"Did you know," he often asked of people who tended to note his increasing hairlessness, "that the head grows bigger as the brain gathers intelligence?"

In fact, he really didn't know if it was true; he never actually read it. But it seemed a fitting prelude to the statement with which he inevitably followed. "As I grow older, I look at it this way: I don't have less hair, just more head."

Flicking a button to respond to his suddenly alive intercom, Marshak thought back to the woman in the centerfold. "What?" he barked in the direction of the speaker.

"Ja...Ja...Jack Bonecutter's agent and his analyst are here, sir," stammered the timorous officer at the desk in the front office. He had been through incidents with his captain before and learned that the heart of a fuzzy teddy bear beat beneath that burly hide, but the bombastic exterior still made him nervous.

Good, Marshak thought. He wanted to talk to those two bozos, get a fix on where this asshole Bonecutter was coming from. "Send them..."

Before he could finish his sentence, the door burst open and a short middle-aged man dressed like a well-heeled cowboy propelled himself toward him. "Captain Marshak? I'm Pete Powers, Jack Bonecutter's literary agent."

He stopped abruptly when the metal tips of his Texas-born boots thudded against the side of Marshak's desk, and turned back toward a thirtyish, gnome-like gentleman who came up beside him.

"This is Jack's therapist, Norman Chaum," Powers went on without losing a beat. "Captain, you've got to let us talk to Jack. We know him. We know what he thinks and how he feels. He's obviously disturbed right now, and what he needs more than anything else is to talk to someone close to him."

"Oh, yeah," Marshak said under his breath. "Since he's holed up on a fuckin' ocean liner that he plans to blow up tonight, along with himself, I'd say he's disturbed, all right." What Marshak said to the men, after compressing his lips for control, was, "How do you do, Mr. Powers, Mr. Chaum?" Without getting up, he offered his hand. "I'm Captain Benjamin Booker Marshak, LBPD. Happy to make your acquaintance."

It was always good to start things off on the right foot. Busy or not, one didn't want to seem inhospitable. "Won't you gentlemen have a seat?"

He indicated two pre-formed plastic, hunter green chairs facing the desk. Chaum took a seat, but Powers paced between the desk and the chairs, running his mouth. "Captain, Jack Bonecutter's not some overly sensitive, high-strung author. He's a sick man who needs to be treated with kid gloves. I'm an agent; kid gloves are my specialty." He paused and leaned over the desk, peering into Marshak's face. "Beyond that, I'm a taxpayer, and as such I've got certain inalienable rights."

"Hold it, Powers," Marshak said, being inhospitable. It was that old my-taxes-pay-your-salary inference that did it. "Let's get this straight: What's really bothering you is that fifteen percent you see going down the tubes."

Marshak immediately regretted the harsh remark. On closer scrutiny, he saw what might be genuine concern in Powers' eyes.

Power's let the comment slide. "The point is, Captain, this whole thing can be stopped right now if you'll only let us talk to Jack. He's a pussycat who wouldn't harm a fly."

Marshak stood up and grinned. Six-two with a large frame, Marshak made another chin as he peered down at Powers. He wanted to quote Mencken: "It is a sin to believe evil of others, but it is seldom a mistake," wanting to add, "In my twenty years in law enforcement I've made few mistakes." But he said only, "Yeah, right."

"Captain Marshak," Norman Chaum, the short, padded, confident man with a full head of hair and sharp, handsome features, said softly, "I can appreciate your position. But if you will only allow me to talk to Jack. He's got a lot bottled up inside. I might be able to make him aware that he can achieve the catharsis, that is, the emotional release, he needs in other ways."

"Phhfft!" Marshak snorted. "I'd say he's emotionally relieving himself pretty nicely out there right now."

Powers stepped in again, switching to a more supplicating tone. "Look, Norm can talk him out of this. I know he can. He's used to dealing with people on the edge."

Marshak walked to the window, giving them his back, and looked out toward the ship. "Ah, yes, the resident shrink, invested with the responsibility for Freudian hocus-pocus."

From his view in the command post near the entrance to the ship, he could see that the evacuation was proceeding in an orderly fashion. There were no signs of panic. In fact, a pocket of chaos at the "A" parking lot entrance seemed to be due not to hurried evacuees but to new arrivals. They were bottom feeders who generally watched reality TV shows and who bee-lined here when they heard the news that the ocean liner might be in delicious jeopardy. What a world.

The pier was cordoned off, and dozens of press vehicles and network news vans circled the perimeter, looking for the best spots in the "B" lot. Marshak heard the phones in the front office ringing incessantly.

Chaum smiled slightly, less than nonplused by Marshak's slur. "I'm a professional psychoanalyst, Captain. I'm not asking you to approve my methods, merely to arrange for me to speak to Jack. My professional opinion is that, in addition to other problems, he still suffers from a form of post-traumatic stress disorder as a result of his experiences in Vietnam in the '70s."

"Oh, great." Marshak turned around and flung up his hands. "As if we haven't all had it up to here with assholes who can't cope and who blame it on their childhoods, their parents, the war. Maybe we should call in Dr. Ruth, who'll no doubt tell us that all of this is due to the fact that Bonecutter failed to masturbate as a child."

He ran a hand over his smooth pate and returned to his desk, lighting up.

Powers waved at the smoke. Inhaling deeply, Marshak exhaled two imperfect rings that wafted in Powers' direction.

"I've smoked all my life," he said slowly. "I'm in perfect health, and my wife of twenty-five years has lungs that inflate like Dizzy Gillespie's cheeks used to." Marshak's brown-eyed gaze stayed on Powers.

"Getting back to the subject at hand," Chaum interjected, "there's also Bonecutter's war wound, which adds to his emotional distress."

"I know about that," Marshak said, on top of things. "I had the Army fax me a copy of his war records."

Chaum was a piranha. "And he is also in transition to mid-life at a time when his marriage is dissolving. His wife…"

"Oh, so now he's having a mid-life crisis, too." Marshak grinned sardonically. "Man, this guy's all fucked up."

"That's just the point," Powers chimed in. "That's why you've got to let at least one of us go aboard, find him and talk to him. I'm his closest friend, for God's sake."

"I don't care if you're his father. You can't go on the ship."

Marshak sighed. If he wanted to get any truly useful input on Bonecutter from these men and get rid of them, he'd better change the tenor of this meeting. He stabbed his generic cigarette into the ashtray.

"Look, fellas, I was out of order. Maybe once we establish communication, I can let you talk to him on the phone. In the meantime, you might as well go home. I've got a job to do. If he wants to off himself in a big way, maybe none of us can stop him. But I am trying. I have men outside who are trained in crisis management. If there's nothing more you can tell me that is helpful..."

"Captain," Chaum said pointedly, "that's what we've been trying to do. Are you familiar with schizophrenia?"

Marshak's eyes flickered skyward. "Split personality. Don't tell me. The voices are making him do it."

Chaum's smile stopped just short of condescending. "In point of fact, multiple personalities are a very rare form of schizophrenia. I'm referring more to a split mind, a splitting from reality, a more common form of the disease, though no less serious. Jack Bonecutter suffers from a severe thought disorder, a serious alteration of perception, emotion and thought, as a result of schizophrenia."

Powers seemed to be into the subject. "Do you think it's genetic in Jack's case?" he asked Chaum. "His father and grandfather were just as obsessed with the Queen Mary as he is."

"Schizophrenia can be heritable," Chaum replied, "but it can also be the result of psychological stress. Or both. You see..."

Chapter 7

Pete Powers suddenly turned away and walked to the window. The mention of Jack's family made him recall a cross-section of the ship and a photograph of Jack's grandfather he found in Jack's apartment an hour earlier. He had stuffed the two items into a manila envelope. However, since he had left the envelope in the glove compartment of his Porsche when he arrived at the pier, he decided not to mention it.

Powers tuned out Chaum and Marshak as he wondered if there had been a clue to Jack's present behavior that he missed when he stopped by his client's apartment last night.

Jack had been nervous as a bull at a new gate. Maybe, Powers speculated, it was because Lew Blasingdon, CEO of Daystar Studios, impatiently awaited Jack's rewrite of an overdue script.

"Jack," Powers had said, "you know I'm your friend as well as your agent. Your problems are my problems, babe. Tell me, how's the script coming, really?"

Jack hedged. "It's…coming."

"Yeah. Well, maybe I can stall Blasingdon a little longer. Tell you what. I'll go with you to that meeting at the studio in the morning at nine."

Jack did not protest; in fact, he seemed to expect Powers to make this offer, and actually made Powers promise to be at the apartment exactly at eight.

"Okay, I'll be here," Powers agreed. "We'll talk, do coffee before we meet with the big guy."

In a stunning reversal of his usual method of operation, Powers arrived at the Sunset Strip apartment this morning at eight sharp. When Jack didn't answer, Powers let himself in with a key the author had given him a few months earlier. Jack had moved into the apartment when he and his wife separated.

Pete's mind froze for an instant as he read and re-read the note Jack left on the desk, saying he planned to put himself and the famed ocean liner out of their misery.

"Holy shit!"

Pete snatched up the phone and dialed 9ll. It was busy. Was there anyone else he could call? Jack had no family. Melissa, his soon-to-be ex-wife, was on an extended vacation cruising somewhere in the West Indies. The studio, of course. Lew Blasingdon. It was certain that Daystar Studios would want to know anything affecting the future of one of their screenwriters.

Powers knew a good property when he saw one, and the movie

Jack was scripting for Daystar looked in every way to him like next summer's smash. The studio's last few releases had gone straight to video, multimillion-dollar special effects' bombs. Jack's poignant, mainstream drama could very well save Blasingdon.

Not that Powers gave a damn about Blasingdon, but maybe the studio's clout could help Powers get on the ship and talk Jack out of the madness he was contemplating.

Loosening the collar of his striped, Garth Brooks-style shirt, he dialed Daystar Studios and read the entire text of Jack's note to the machine that answered Lew Blasingdon's phone. Next he re-dialed 9ll and, getting through, relayed the essence of Jack's words to a jaded, infuriatingly pragmatic woman on the line.

Finally, Powers called a close friend who also knew Jack. Norman Chaum, in-house psychoanalyst for Daystar Studios, had an office in the Daystar tower and was retained to be there for the burgeoning number of stressed-out, Type-A executives. This arrangement saved company time and money, as these administrators no longer had to travel to Beverly Hills' higher-priced shrinks.

Waiting for Chaum to answer, Powers scanned the room. The apartment was neater than usual, neatness with a sense of finality that he hadn't noticed last night. On the desk was an advertisement ripped from the Los Angeles Times, depicting the latest renovations to the Queen Mary. Blatant commercialism, Powers thought. He knew the idea would devastate Jack, whose interest in the ship was gradually reaching obsessive proportions.

On a shelf above the desk was an old photograph of Jack's grandfather, Angus Bonecutter, standing in a section of the Queen Mary's wheelhouse, under construction at the time the photo was taken. Without knowing why, Powers picked it from the shelf, slid it from its frame, and stuck it into a manila envelope from the desk. He tucked it under his arm.

Last night Jack mentioned that the photograph was taken in the mid '30s, when his grandfather worked on the ship. She was not a name then, but a number: Hull 05340, a skeleton in a misty harbor in Scotland. Jack grew up with stories his grandfather told about her. That was how he came to know every detail of the ship's design.

As years passed, the stories, together with models he constructed and brochures and newspaper clippings he collected, became integral to his sense of family and self. After World War II, his family emigrated from England to the United States, finally settling in Los Angeles, where Jack was born in 1948. They were all dead now; Jack was alone.

"I once made the five-day North Atlantic crossing on her," Jack said last night. "In nineteen fifty-one, when I was three. With my grandfather and parents. It's my earliest childhood memory."

"I don't remember mine," Powers quipped.

Jack seemed not to hear. He said, "That trip was the most exciting yet the most terrifying experience of my life." He turned away, looking at nothing. "Exciting because my grandfather took me up to the crow's nest, that barrel on the mainmast support high above the deck. Terrifying because it was so bizarre and frightening to a three-year-old. He dangled me with his arms outstretched beyond the edge of the crow's nest." Perspiration gathered on his upper lip as he went on.

"I wondered about the ocean. How big was it? Where did the Queen Mary end and the ocean begin? And why did the wind up there above the ship, above the world, it seemed, take the breath from your lungs, press and stifle your mouth and nostrils? I remember looking down and feeling my body freeze with horror. Then I began to scream for grandfather to hold me close, to bring me back from the abyss."

"Jesus." Powers finished his second double scotch. "If that was my experience on the ship, I don't think I'd give a rat's ass about her."

Jack continued to stare into space, his eyes glassy and un-answering, so Powers got up to go. "Terror has its own particular irony," Jack went on. "Once put into perspective, it's comforting, knowing you've faced and endured it. And not only survived it, but played it out, over and over, a thousand times, in your mind and senses, until it became part of you."

He was silent then, as if slowly floating up to the present. He got up and patted Powers on the shoulder. "Don't forget, Pete. Tomorrow morning, eight sharp."

Sadness washed over Powers when he stood in the apartment this morning, remembering. He had suffered dysfunction in his own past. His father left when Pete was just a kid, and he grew up in "La La Land" with few dreams. Before meeting Jack, he was convinced he had to take advantage of everyone in order to survive, to obtain something that seemed due.

Jack had changed that. A writer with great sensitivity, he gave a vulnerable, human edge to even the most terrifying characters he created, and his scripts sold and gave Powers success and self-respect. With these came respectability.

Now, in addition to the million-dollar home, the Porsche, the other trimmings, there were people, from network and studio heads to stars and scenery pushers, who were always in when Pete Powers called.

Still waiting for Chaum to answer the phone, he looked up, and something caught his eye. Tacked to the corkboard above the desk was a sixteen-by-twenty-four-inch cross-section of the Queen Mary. It depicted her interior viewed broadside, details of all inner areas clearly delineated. Penciled alterations indicated the latest structural changes when she was turned into a hotel. Bold red circles were inked in various locations.

Preoccupied, his mind registering the item's importance on a subliminal plane, Powers mechanically removed the tacks from the drawing, folded it, and tucked it into the envelope with the aged photograph of Jack's grandfather.

Finally, Powers heard Norman Chaum murmur a sleepy hello into the phone.

"Listen, Norm, I've some kind of wake-up call for you: Jack Bonecutter's in trouble, big time. I'll explain when I get there. I'll pick you up in ten minutes. We're going to Long Beach."

After hanging up, he crossed to a well-stocked bar and swallowed two fingers of Bell's straight from the bottle; hair of the dog. He bent and wiped away a spot of the amber liquid that spilled onto his genuine reptile boots, straightened and adjusted a silver belt buckle the size of a saucer, and hurried out.

Chapter 8

In Captain Marshak's mobile office beside the ship, Norm was still pitching his position to Marshak.

"As I said," Chaum concluded, "My diagnosis was subtype undifferentiated schizophrenia. Pete has told me of Jack's occasional lapses into odd speech patterns, something we call clang associations. He rhymes words that make no sense and are totally out of context with the conversation he's engaged in. This is a classic symptom of a severe form of schizophrenia."

Marshak scowled. "Now you're saying the guy talks to himself?" He got up from behind his desk and started toward the door.

"Not exactly. Rhyming words comfort him. They come unbidden to his mind, and sometimes he verbalizes them, wittingly or otherwise."

Marshak noticed that Powers followed him to the door. The police captain opened it and turned back to the therapist. Chaum finally got up, grasped the lapels of his own jacket and leaned forward with an I-know-better-than-you expression.

"Remember, Captain Marshak, that despite your personal opinions on mental illness, you are dealing with a man who has lost contact with reality. He's having delusions about himself and the world in general. Hence, he lives in a mental world quite different from ours. This thing with the Queen Mary is a form of hallucination, the result of disordered thought processes."

Chaum stopped in the doorway and held Marshak's gaze. "Take care, Captain. When the human mind, dealing with a built-in defense mechanism, a psychic compulsion to suppress a traumatic experience or to subconsciously hide from past trauma, suddenly consciously confronts it…well, the first bomb that goes off may be in Jack Bonecutter's head. You may get your explosion before you expect it."

The buzz of Marshak's intercom stung the air, and he stormed back to his desk. "What?"

The voice of the officer at the desk in the outer office quivered as it filled the room. "You…you have a stat call on line one, sir. It's…the Pentagon."

Marshak rubbed a hand through the small patch of hair at his left temple. "The Pentagon? Calling me? You mean THE

827

Pentagon?"

"I believe...yes, that Pentagon, sir."

Marshak punched another button. At the door, Chaum and Powers waited, as if hoping the call might somehow change his decision to ban them from the ship.

Marshak took a few notes as he listened intently. Once he said, "Say *what?*" Finally, he snapped, "Yes, sir," and hung up the phone.

Marshak felt a flush creep up his neck to his face and turn his dark cheeks burgundy. He sank into his chair, suddenly aware that his two visitors were still standing in the doorway.

"Goodbye, gentlemen. Thank you for coming. I'll call you if we need you."

When they did not immediately move, he darted his eyeballs in their direction.

"Goodbye."

Powers mumbled something as they left, leaving Marshak figuring he had not seen the last of them. He swallowed an antacid tablet from a plastic container on the desk and noticed that his heart was pumping hot flashes to his ears.

He couldn't fucking believe it. A colonel no less. A fucking, full-bird army colonel was flying in to take command of his operation.

"We've already spoken to the Governor, the Mayor and your Chief," the Pentagon spokesperson had said, "and you'll be briefed by the colonel on a need-to-know basis. All I can tell you with specificity at this juncture is that national security is at stake, and the United States Army has autonomy in matters of this nature."

"Yes, sir," Marshak had said.

There was more involved than an old ship and a sick dude who wanted to deep-six her.

Chapter 9

Rufino Jose Quintero was in his late-sixties, of medium height with a thick, powerful body kept in shape by punishing daily exercise. His teeth were strong and even, his dense hair like the mature growth of a chia pet, with gray tufts gaining on their deep brown predecessors.

Quintero was born in the tiny hamlet of Camoruco in the interior of Venezuela in 1947. At age fourteen he left Venezuela, never to return. He traveled as far as limited resources allowed, to Chile, where he took up residence and joined the CLB, the Chileans por Libertad Brigada. The CLB saw to it that Quintero was trained by the best.

In 1972 he reunited with many CLB associates at the Baddawi refugee camp in Lebanon. Here Quintero first took a man's life.

From then on he sold his services as a hired killer to the highest bidder, until, in 1999, he was contacted by a well-organized drug cartel operating behind the facade of a luxurious tourist resort on Pinos Bay, in the Darien jungle of Panama.

The head of this cartel, a man Quintero knew only as el Patrón, had heard of him and employed him exclusively for the past several years. Quintero handled only certain assignments for El Pulpo, his employer's octopus-like network of crime with tentacles in many countries. Quintero's latest kill had been in Loja, Ecuador.

He had just returned home to Pinos Bay, three days before el Patrón called to send him to Contadora.

One of el Patrón's many sources in Panama City informed him of a phone call that would interest Quintero. For many years rumors trickled down from various Washington, D.C. informants about the product of a British-American experiment in biochemical warfare that went missing in 1967.

Now, almost five decades later, the scientist responsible for that product and its disappearance had made a strategic phone call and been located. He was residing almost directly under Quintero's nose.

Today, as he stepped cautiously onto the verandah of the old house on Isla Contadora, he considered this killing with relish, inwardly smiling at the prospect. Quintero, of course, did not smile outwardly, since any such attempt produced an unnatural pulling back of his lips on the right side of his face, resulting in a ghoulish, toothy grin.

Now, at last, Quintero would repay the gringo who was responsible. This prospect was one of the singular pleasures for which he had lived. Slowly he stepped to the screen door of the old man's home. He knew the gringo was alone. His El Pulpo contact had informed him.

Thanks to slipshod governmental security, El Pulpo had penetrated the headquarters of the FBI in Washington and learned of the gringo's phone call minutes after it was completed.

Because Quintero was nearby (Contadora was a short plane ride from Pinos Bay) and because he had a personal stake in the matter, Quintero was given the assignment. In return, he accepted no pay.

"It is my pleasure," he whispered as much to himself as those who'd called him.

He slipped into the living room and slowly made his way toward the kitchen. He would first extract from the scientist where the secret briefcase was hidden, in exactly what part of the ship. Then he would kill him.

The man represented Quintero's one failure. Quintero had been commissioned by the Chileans por Libertad Brigada at the time.

His failure on the Queen Mary was Chile's failure, a circumstance that nearly caused his death and was why he left the CLB. If he failed this time, it would be El Pulpo's failure, and el Patrón was not as lax in his discipline as was Quintero's previous employer.

He fully understood how badly they wanted the briefcase. It could mean world domination to whomever possessed it. But none yearned for the conclusion of this matter like Quintero. He had waited more than forty years for this moment.

Chapter 10

They scrambled into Lew Blasingdon's office and scurried to be advantageously seated: Directors of Publicity, Public Relations, Legal, Production, and various other departments of Daystar Studios.

Anyone there might have though Lew Blasingdon was Gary Cooper incarnate, with his silver hair and dark horn-rimmed glasses, wearing a neat pin-striped suit. He stood straight and tall behind the desk, silhouetted against partially drawn vertical blinds.

His office was plain and functional. On his desk were a phone/fax, a PC, and several photographs of children, grandchildren, and a salon-tanned wife with expensively sculpted bee-stung lips.

The executives might have described Blasingdon as the picture of reserve and dignity. He made four times their salaries. His four-million-dollar helicopter always remained ready on the helipad two stories above. But the man seemed relaxed to the point of being less than status conscious, as if at his level of stratification there was no necessity for show.

His lean pink face with its tolerant smile furthered that impression. These executives might have thought they heard incorrectly when he addressed them in his smooth, melodious voice.

"I called you all here because I'm happy to announce that one of our scriptwriters has gone berserk and is about to blow up the Queen Mary in Long Beach harbor. I want as much mileage from this serendipitous event as possible.

"And," he went on, "if he somehow gets out of this, I want his ass when it's over. The motherfucker owes me."

The executives were careful to not act surprised by any of this. They knew that Lew Blasingdon's Donna Karin two-thousand-dollar suit never dared wrinkle. They knew that his once-black hair had turned lustrous silver rather than risk his disfavor with a flat, matte gray. His ruddy complexion was not attributable to inner warmth, but to blood pressure pharmaceutically controlled but volatile. The perpetual smile that strangers read as tolerant was proof of the depth of his determination to publicly appear so.

Questions piled upon questions, from the group in his office.

"What writer?"

"Have the police been notified?"

"Do you think he means it?"

"Why the Queen Mary?"

Some, like Blasingdon, never cramped by the tyranny of conscience, began to contemplate the movie that could be made, and who was available to direct.

Blasingdon sat down at his desk and held up a hand with slender fingers and subtly manicured nails. "This is the message that was relayed to me in my car on the way in, patched through from my machine here." He tapped a button on the fax phone, and Pete Powers' unsteady voice was heard reading Jack Bonecutter's message.

When it was completed, Blasingdon nodded. "Now you know as

much as I do. Assume the police have been notified. Your single consideration should be how we can milk this thing from every conceivable angle, no matter how remote. I'd like to see our man draw this out as long as possible, take hostages, make public threats, build public interest."

He cleared his throat and nodded in the direction of his publicity head. "If there's anyone nearby with a video camera who catches any of this, I want his or her tape, no matter what the cost, before the FOX news hounds get hold of it. Questions?"

Maggie Culina, Vice President of Post-production, ventured, "It sounds like Jack Bonecutter needs help. Most of us know him. Isn't there anything we could do to help…"

Blasingdon interrupted her by standing, and gestured for an all-rise. "I have another meeting." He checked his watch. "It's nine-fifteen. We'll meet here again at ten-thirty. I'll want your suggestions, legal considerations, the works."

His minions slowly filed from the office.

By the time the door closed behind them, Blasingdon already knew what he was going to do. He planned to wait for their input. Let them earn their preposterous salaries. He earned his. He worked hard at making millions, and even harder at making it appear that those millions were immaterial to him.

He replayed Powers' message, and thanked the fates that it was not his responsibility to find Bonecutter and the bombs. Blasingdon had taken the Queen Mary tour on several occasions when certain of his bourgeois relatives came to town and needed to be entertained.

Being slightly familiar with the ship, he thought of thousands of places where Bonecutter could hide, and millions of nooks and crannies into which the explosives could be secreted.

Chapter 11

Agent Susan Koski ran with long easy strides, breathing the fresh morning air. Six-thirty a.m. and the streets of Reno were already beginning to fill with early morning traffic. Her cell phone chirped and she slowed to flip it open.

"On your fourth mile yet, Koski?" It was her boss, Frank Heeley.

"Almost at the end of the fifth and final. What's up?"

"Plenty. I want you down at the military section of Reno Airport ASAP. Report to the C.O. He'll fill you in. Pack a small bag. You're going for a fast ride in a small plane. I'll be in touch."

The line went dead. Koski increased her pace.

Chapter 12

Sharp, nauseating pain grabbed Gordon Metcalf's heart and squeezed.

"Oh God!"

He slumped against the table. This time it was much worse than before. This time…in some dimension of his stuttering senses, he heard footsteps in the house, approaching the kitchen…the angina struck again, and he clutched his left arm, his chest. Breath left him. He looked up the moment the stranger entered the room. No, not really a stranger.

Quintero's eyes glistened. His half-smile twisted into a grimace as he reached into the sheath that held the unusual blade that was his signature. Metcalf was ten years older than Quintero, stoop-shouldered, tall but thin as a heron, his skin paler than white. The scientist knew that this time there would be no contest.

Pain blurred Metcalf's vision, yet he was able to make out the glint of steel.

"Finally, gringo."

Quintero's thick, powerful body inched forward as if this was a fortunate day, this minute too sweet to hurry. Metcalf assumed his killer would use the blade first as persuasion, to extract information about the briefcase's location, then do the final deed slowly.

Grasping the knife handle, which itself was noble, cut from the beak of *el pico de pez espada*, the mighty swordfish of the sea, Quintero's face suddenly took on a contemplative look, as though he were imagining the blade slithering first into his victim's gut, in and out, over and over, leaving Metcalf to die in as many parts of his body as possible.

"Forgive me, Padre, for I have sinned," Metcalf easily imagined Quintero meekly confessing tomorrow. "A man with a suitcase filled with bad scientific magic sought to murder many thousands of innocents. It was my place, my duty, to kill him, Padre."

Then Metcalf wheezed and doubled over, struggling for a single breath.

Metcalf could already feel the death of his organs. Oblivious to any human presence now, he was cosmically aware of oxygenated blood returning from his lungs to the left atrium of his heart, where a valve opened, allowing the flow to enter the left ventricle, which prepared to contract, but paused.

"No!" Quintero leapt beside him. "No!"

He grabbed the front of Metcalf's shirt and pulled the limp man to his feet as if, though there were others on the ship in California that he would kill before this day closed, only this death was *muy importante*.

"*Basta!*" Quintero screamed.

Metcalf's body let go and slumped before Quintero's blade could find it, his last thought of the Devil's crucible, and his dying wish that somehow someone would find it in time to redeem him.

Chapter 13

Marshak heard a commotion in the outer office of his command post, but kept his eyes on the window as a wide, squat, Army UH-1 Iroquois helicopter, better known as a "Huey," thundered in his direction. Muscular and minatory, the olive-brown craft thumped over the water, flying low and slow, allowing full view of waist gunners on either side of its open doors.

"Definite command presence," Marshak thought aloud, turning his attention to a chopper from a local television station, circling like a blue-fly above the Queen Mary. "You're about to get your marching orders," Marshak mumbled in the fly's direction.

The United States Army would soon remind the media insect that air space above the ship was restricted within three miles, altitude two thousand feet.

The floor of the command post shuddered with deafening vibration as the Huey swept past the TV chopper at six hundred feet. The media pest, getting the word, turned tail and left the restricted area.

After one more menacing pass over the ship, the Huey put down on the helipad adjacent to the parking area opposite Carnival Cruise Lines lot "D," bordering Ocean View Avenue and the exit ramp from the Harbor Freeway. Within minutes a field-uniformed mini-Schwarzkopf marched into Marshak's office, flanked by two crisp aides.

"Colonel J. Manley Beard, United States Army Rapid Deployment Forces," he said and gave Marshak's hand one solid jolt.

He was a short, neat man with buzz-cut, carrot-red hair dappled with gray. His eyes were small and very blue, clear as a boy's, his face emanated straightforward expression. He automatically seated himself behind the desk Marshak considered his own.

"We understand that evacuation of the ship is nearly complete and proceeding in textbook fashion. Good work, Captain. We like that."

Marshak was silent. *And if we don't, tough titty.*

"We've been in touch with FEMA and the Office of Homeland Security, the Navy, Air Force. The CAB, FAA and NTSB have assured us of their full cooperation, if such should become necessary." He turned and gave the room a quick, but thorough appraisal.

"We'll use this office while we're here at Com Cen, Captain. The outer office is being equipped with computers, television and radio equipment, to be interfaced with the ship's existing security system. We'll have a state-of-the-art digital umbilical cord, so to speak, tying us into the ship's internal closed-circuit communication network."

So that was the buzz of activity Marshak heard in the outer office; his command post was already being converted into Com-Cen.

"In fact," Beard went on, "the first areas of this floating hotel will be beaming back to monitors here very shortly. Miller and Nakamura," he indicated his two aides, who silently nodded and adjourned to the outer office, "should get us clear, sharp definition in both color and black and white."

He quickly whisked Marshak's overflowing ashtray from the desktop and tossed it into the small "round file" in the kneehole of the desk, never missing a beat in his speech.

"Broadcast quality digital video will be on continual 'record' to relay anything they see on the ship." He stood and reached for Marshak's hand again. "Between us, Captain, this Bonecutter fellow and the whole business scares the living hell out of me."

Marshak noted that he abandoned the royal pronoun for this little heart-to-heart.

"I know you don't like it, Captain. Certainly, I don't enjoy it. But, in a sense, it's war, isn't it? And one doesn't expect to enjoy war, does one? In a war, neither side knows who will win, only that their job is to kill people."

Marshak tipped him a bogus "right on" and was silent. *No fucking kidding! You must be some kind of fucking Rapid Deployment genius.*

"However," Beard added, "we're going to win this one. And we won't concern ourselves as to who gets the credit, will we? So long as we get the job done."

Beard gripped Marshak's right shoulder with his free hand. "Right, Captain?"

Marshak felt heat rush up to his ears and wished he could control the flush of frustration and anger that he knew was evident. But he had to stifle it, at least for now. It looked like he was going to be stuck babysitting this self-aggrandizing Army egoist for a while.

"Right," he finally replied, and was released from the colonel's grip. "We still call the Queen Mary a ship, sir. Not a hotel."

"Whatever. We'll need to talk in a few minutes," Beard said, checking all the drawers of the desk to make certain they were empty.

Turning and heading for the door, Marshak said, "We'll take the smaller office, the one down the hall adjoining your outer office. Sir."

When Marshak got to the diminutive office, workmen were busy connecting his phone, and there was a note on the otherwise barren desk, stating that a manila envelope addressed to him had been left with the guard at the "A" parking lot gate. It would be delivered to his office presently.

He called the guard and learned that the envelope was left earlier by exiting Hollywood agent Pete Powers. What the fuck could that be? Well, Marshak didn't have time for Powers or his mystery envelope right now.

Chapter 14

Clinging to the old wooden ladder in the dark shaft, Bonecutter could make out faint syllables as the ship's PA system lisped the repeated evacuation order. It instructed personnel and guests to leave the ship immediately, giving no explanation and emphasizing the fact that there was no imminent danger.

To relieve stress on any particular part of his body or limbs, Bonecutter had turned around, his back now facing the ladder, heels downward for balance, dug into position on the horizontal rung. His arms encircled the two-by-four vertical sides of the ladder, using them like suspenders to prevent him from the unthinkable: toppling to his death before the appointed time.

He had chosen eight p.m. for a reason. To be sure it was dark, precluding his seeing the ocean from the chart room above, where he planned to be at detonation. He preferred that the wolf waves not be part of his final vision.

His eyes were closed, and he re-envisioned the sight that had brought him here this day. He allowed that those who owned her had kept the ship in excellent superficial condition. Glossy new red-and-black paint adorned her three smokestacks. The bulk of her hull was painted black, except for the marine red anti-rust area at the waterline and the wide band of white that covered the exterior of the top three decks: the sports deck, the sun deck, and the promenade deck.

But that slick new facade was the only virtue Bonecutter ascribed to those who currently possessed her. She was landlocked and abused, profaned and exploited. Portside and amidships, elevated walkways and up and down escalators leading to the gangways marred the perspective of her beauty.

Sprawling, spider-like scaffolding was continually needed to maintain stairways, handicapped access, additional restrooms and the other trappings of tourism. They all scarred her former majesty. Constant refurbishing and renovating to accommodate paying guests gutted her authenticity.

Bonecutter deeply resented the way she had been handled. Every decision in her past should have been undertaken glacially, and only those intimately familiar with her past should be allowed to tamper with her future. Well, her future was his now.

When he had arrived earlier with his carryon containing the bombs, he was not challenged. He might have been a terrorist, but security personnel only randomly checked belongings; he paid his admission and walked past the checkpoint with a nod and a smile.

On the escalator, his gaze fell on the wooden railing of the promenade deck where a long line of dew had gathered and become moist jewels that winked in a sudden shaft of sunlight. Swallowing against a sense of sadness, he stepped onto the elevated amidships walkway, turned right and went down the stairs to the lower decks.

He began at the stern, the planned location of his first incendiary device being one of the two sites where once the mighty engine rooms were located, the very bottom of the aft portion of the ship. The engine rooms once housed four-thousand-horsepower steam turbines that propelled her through the stormy North Atlantic in excess of thirty knots.

It was early, not even eight a.m. when he came aboard, yet tourists by the dozens were everywhere, chattering excitedly in various languages. Whatever happened to English? He might have been Magellan putting into an inhospitable port.

During the next forty-five minutes, Bonecutter worked his way forward. He stealthily found eight of the predetermined locations and covertly secreted an incendiary explosive in each. They now rested ominously in the old engine room, Ye Olde Bakery Shoppe, the QM cinema, the wedding chapel, the QM History Museum, the long table in the Country Cottage Room, the Trafalgar Square gift shop, and a first-class stateroom suite on the promenade deck near the bow.

His two remaining units were to be placed in the Churchill Lounge beneath the navigational bridge, and in the signals and flag cabinet in the wheelhouse section of the bridge itself.

When he had entered the lounge, he counted less than a dozen people, most focused on the surrounding glass windows facing the foredeck, and preoccupied with the panoramic view of the bay and the gathering gray clouds above it. Gingerly fingering the two explosive incendiaries in his pants pocket, he walked to the far end of the bar.

"Water, please," he told the young waiter who raised his head and eyebrows in receipt of the order.

Fighting impatience, Bonecutter was forced to wait for the right time to position the explosive. Precious minutes ticked away.

He had finished his water when a waitress came up and, leaning against the bar, put in an order for a Bloody Mary. While her body shielded his hands from the patrons' view, Bonecutter slipped the next-to-last nest from his pocket and pressed the wax adhesive to the underside of the thick, polished mahogany lip of the bar.

As he walked out, he sighed with relief. Only one bomb left, and that would be placed in the flag cabinet in the wheelhouse. Then he would enter the adjoining chart room and open the trap door to the shaft below the chart table. He slid the remote firing unit into his shirt pocket and headed for the staircase leading to the bridge.

Chapter 15

Bonecutter felt inspirited, alive for the first time in months. He knew that the wail of sirens swelling in the distance announced the arrival of ambulances, SWAT teams, probably a Haz-Mat van, and other emergency vehicles.

As he climbed the stairs, he glanced up and his vision was captured by the crow's nest perched more than halfway up the forward main mast. When out at sea, all the sailors felt sorry for the whoever was assigned lookout duty there. When the bitter North Atlantic winds raged around the vessel, a man could turn to ice in ten minutes or less. A shudder passed over Bonecutter, as if a cold, metallic ribbon was drawn across his spine.

Four decades earlier, Bonecutter's grandfather had taken him high above the deck and into that round metal lookout, placing three-year-old Jack on the rim with his stubby legs dangling against the side, air alone between them and the sea. At first he felt no fear. He laughed and pointed to the sun, a giant peach sinking fast into a gray sea, much larger than he imagined and whose surface rippled with gold.

From down on the deck, the ship was so huge, unending and immense that the distant waters would never see a three-year-old above it. Yet high in the crow's nest, little Jack saw it was the sea that was immense and never-ending, looking like a pack of wolves constantly leaping up at the ship, threatening to drag her down to destruction.

With the sun rapidly descending, Jack soon could not distinguish where the vessel ended and the pack began. He quickly switched his vision back to the horizon just as a final gleam of sunlight blinked and faded. Thin drafts of icy air rose around him and he shivered. Suddenly he wanted to get down, and he turned his upper body back toward his grandfather, outstretching pleading arms.

"Whee," Grandfather cried and scooped him up into his arms with such swift strength that Jack let out a little shriek of startled, breathless shock.

At first he did not know what happened or where he was. He thought he was riding high against his grandfather's chest, but his body lost its weight and he seemed to be floating in space. Then he knew he was on his back, his head draped over one of his grandfather's arms, his legs over the other.

"Whee," sang Grandfather again, extending his arms far out over the edge of the crow's nest and swinging young Jack back and forth, back and forth, until Jack's eyes dizzied and hurt.

The wind roared past his stinging ears and stole the breath from his chest. What felt like a gale pressed against his face and forced his nostrils shut. He felt nauseous, giddy, at the mercy of great, uncontrollable gulps, his eyes running tears, his nose bubbling with mucus. Kicking his feet and flailing his arms did nothing to stop the terror; in fact, he felt certain he would fall.

On and on it lasted, the old man's voice like eerie music that the child heard but did not hear, repeating, "Whee, little Jack, whee!"

Finally, his child's heart beating thunderously, he found himself again against his grandfather's chest, back on deck, trying to close his mouth against a scream, seeing his own terror in his parents' faces as they raced to him.

For years Bonecutter tried to push thoughts of that day away. Ultimately, he found that reliving was a tactic, not of forgetting, but of forbearing. Yet it left his feelings confused. Abused and violated, yet cuddled and loved, driven to strike out while compelled to submission. And there was no one to blame.

He loved his grandfather. Had they not gone to the edge of life together and survived? Did they not have a bond stronger than death?

Balancing on the ladder in the shaft below the chart room, Bonecutter yet again paid the price of remembering.

The shrinking feeling that was the precursor of what he had come to think of as a "spell," began to tighten against his temples. The roar of air in the shaft pounded in his head and the involuntary growl that gurgled in his throat like deformed dulcimer music escalated to a din that pressed unbearably against his eardrums. He could not think clearly. He felt his eyes roll around in their sockets.

Losing the fight for control, his mind went outside his head, taunting its empty shell, and yet the pressure built, his head pulsating. Releasing one arm from its grip around the vertical post of the ladder, he slammed his fist once, twice, against his forehead.

"No! No!" he rasped.

But it went on and on. Finally, gradually, the pressure slipped away, and the only thought he could collect from the dizzying vortex in his mind was childish and disjointed.

"Tinker bell, Tinker bell, go to hell, you smell," he heard himself say in a foreign, lilting tone.

Chapter 16

Seated beside the pilot in a helicopter sporting army colors and flashing toward San Pedro, Joseph Falk thrashed through thoughts of his earlier phone conversation with Frank Heeley. Falk's new bureau chief tended to overstate a situation. This, it seemed, was not one of them.

"Back in the nineteen sixtie," Heeley had said, "in an experiment never written up in any journals or disclosed beyond a small circle of high-level British and American scientists and statesmen, a powerful step had been taken. Dr. Metcalf had built into his infusion the chemical means by which a vital human gene, p53, would mutate.

"Gene mutation is a molecular change in the structure of a single gene inside a cell. Mistakes in DNA replication can cause mutation, some of them inheritable changes. But the application of chemical agents, called mutagens, induce or at least greatly increase the rate of mutation. Depending on the mutagens, it could happen over a lifetime or immediately.

"For purposes of his experiment, change was dubbed 'lethal' if it eventually resulted in the death one way or another. Certain chemicals in Metcalf's witch's-brew mixture killed immediately. Other's took their time or simply increased overall likelihood or efficacy.

"The mixture was developed for military use in war, so a propellant was added to disperse and disseminate the lethal properties into the air. There were other chemical additives, like a binding agent and preservatives. And a retrovirus with a natural homing instinct to find its way into the exposed's stem cells in the bone marrow.

"Even worse was what Metcalf resisted including, but upon which the military insisted. Like a number of mutagens. One, for example, an industrial waste product, did two things: when it moved into a cell, it mutated the p53 gene, a critical growth-regulator. This gene normally attached itself to a cell's DNA at specific locations, and bound onto questionably activated genes whose proteins controlled cell division."

Falk had taken copious notes and studied them carefully. He had difficulty writing, as Heeley quickly became breathless, and began to talk faster but more softly.

"A mutated p53 gene lacks the ability to bind to the DNA and thereby fails to turn on the gene involved in turning off cell proliferation. Therefore, not only would the cell experience frenzied, uncontrollable growth, as do cancerous cells, but the mutated gene also would induce the production of an enzyme rendering other toxins in the cell more potent.

"Thus, the mutated p53 gene would result in death by multiple mutagen-caused diseases. And if it did not kill directly, it ended up contaminating the individual's gene pool for generations."

Falk said what Heeley was about to say. "A cloud of these chemicals released over California by the explosion when fire reached the briefcase would start a chain reaction of death and deformity, moving rapidly, threatening populations across the Western United States for decades."

"Yes," replied Heeley simply.

Falk had been held up at Van Nuys airport, a congressman

having commandeered the chopper originally scheduled for Falk, so he began his search of the Queen Mary forty-five minutes later than planned.

A cool slither of water dropped onto his hand and he reached up and swiped at an errant strand of still-wet, chestnut hair dangling over his forehead. After Heeley had hung up, Falk had only enough time to jump in and out of a cold shower, dress, and strap on his 9 mm Beretta before the car arrived to take him to the airport. Now he shivered, as much from the overwhelming weight of his mission as from the dampness of his hair and the cool morning air.

On Heeley's orders, he advised no one of his assignment. He couldn't phone Koski. She was on a routine assignment in Reno, doing timed surveillance on a racketeer the Bureau was interested in. Agents watched the suspect in stages, each assigned to a particular part of his day. Knowing Special Agent Susan Koski, Falk felt sure she was bored to tears. Here in Long Beach was the kind of assignment she craved. And speaking of cravings, he missed her.

Joe's senses suddenly filled with her essence. He loved the fresh, lingering scent of Savon Doux Place des Lices Pivoine, the peony soap with which she bathed, but it was her natural scent he most savored. And the tactile silkiness of her hair that complimented the translucence of her skin that glowed with pale peach undertones. Beyond the physical and emotional response her mere presence evoked in him, she was simply comfortable to be around.

Her IQ slightly exceeded his own, something he alternately admired and resented, which occasionally caused some friction between them. When there was time and they got together, they usually talked a lot. But even Koski's silences were good company.

To Falk's way of thinking, too many of today's young women were tough, sneering, ball-busting wonder women who had bought into their own publicity. He was weary of the stereotype, of faces afraid to register primness or frailty.

He liked that he had witnessed both in Koski. On her first assignment, he saw her kill a man, then momentarily fall to pieces, like a broken sparrow, from the heart-wrenching pain of that ungodly act.

Joe straightened and looked out of the chopper at the landscape that was fast-reeling itself under the nose of the aircraft, and nudged his thoughts back to his phone call from Heeley.

Once Falk knew the facts of the situation, Heeley didn't have to spell out the consequences of failure. The irony was that Jack Bonecutter himself could not be aware of the real horror he would unleash if the Queen Mary exploded in flames.

The poor, sick bastard had no idea of the chain reaction his personal vendetta against those who enslaved his ship would cause because of a mixture of chemicals fashioned into a biochemical weapon of war and hidden aboard the ship long ago.

"Thousands, maybe millions of unsuspecting people are in imminent danger of exposure to the deadly chemicals," Heeley had explained before their phone conversation ended. "And you are their only hope of survival, Falk."

Falk was ordinarily an optimistic person, but he knew he needed all the help he could get on this one. "You said that the briefcase containing this chemical fusion was put on the Queen Mary in 1967 by the scientist who created it. And you said that you have located this man in Panama, right?"

"Well, yes."

"And you'll get the exact location of the briefcase from him and relay it to me, right?"

"Right. And we will tell you, the minute we know…"

Falk was uneasy about putting stock in Heeley's words when he let his sentences dangle in that fashion, but he had no choice other than trusting Heeley now.

"I'm no chemist, Frank," Falk had said, "but I understand basic human cellular physiology. Tell me again what these gene-altering chemicals do."

"Here's the way it was put to me by a scientist who knew something about this experiment," said Heeley. "When exposed, cells making up those tissues and organs would be overrun by these pernicious compounds. Depending on the degree of exposure, they'd kill their hosts immediately or kill them slowly over time, or mutate their genes irreversibly, altering the entire protein-producing mechanism of their bodies and affecting them and their offspring for generations."

"Is there anything you haven't told me that could possibly make this situation worse?" Falk asked.

"It's December, and the freakin' Doppler radar shows a red storm cell offshore that's being driven east in the Pacific by thirty-mile-an-hour-plus winds with gusts expected to reach seventy miles per hour by nightfall.

"The cloud that would be generated and rise as a result of Bonecutter's incendiary bombs exploding and igniting the hidden container of toxic chemicals would destroy all human life within an undetermined radius in the way I just described. And, this is the worst part, the wind would at the very least, carry that toxic cloud inland, over all of Long Beach, a city of approximately 71,000 people, and from there LA and beyond."

Falk experienced an icy dread. "Frank," he asked, "what degree of exposure does it take?"

"As little as three hundredths of a milligram inhaled would be lethal. Those who do not die instantaneously will see their cells, diseased by mutagens, begin to grow uncontrollably. As I understand it, one of the many deadly aspects of this mixture is that it contains a retrovirus designed to find its way into the bloodstream and, ultimately, to the stem cells in the bone marrow itself."

"God! So not only will cancerous cells form, and proliferate, there would be a total breakdown of the immune system as well."

"Correct. Death would be a certainty once membranes strangling the lungs triggered respiratory paralysis."

It was Falk's nature to grasp at straws. "Frank, wouldn't at least some of the elements in this stuff have a half-life of some specific duration? You said the container was hidden on the ship in the late 1960s. Wouldn't some properties have altered, maybe even been rendered ineffective to some extent by now?"

"I asked the same question, and was told that, contained as these properties supposedly are, in a hermetically sealed container inside a reinforced steel briefcase, they could probably remain unchanged and lethal for a hundred years."

Falk's thoughts darkened. Chemicals, it seemed, were to be the theme of his day. Wasn't that a perversion of exactly what chemotherapy was? A bombardment of chemicals into one's body to kill the cancer cells. Falk fumed as he pondered the scientist in Panama. What kind of monster would concoct such a mixture?

The helicopter banked left and descended to five hundred, then four hundred feet. Falk looked out at the western sky, which was slate gray with thunderheads like fluffy sheep piling up against one another. Wind ruffled the sea like the feathers of a herring gull.

A storm was forming, headed in the same direction as he. A light fog swirled beneath them, broken and web-like, then Falk caught the smell of salt, fish, diesel fuel and humanity, and glimpsed the Queen Mary below.

Viewing the ship's three monumental smokestacks, he thought she was majestic, even in captivity. A shrine to lost opulence, to the pampered leisure of pre-World War II transatlantic ocean voyaging. In the more than sixty years since her maiden voyage in 1936, she had hosted now-deceased presidents, dignitaries and other celebrities from all over the world. Churchill once held press conferences and over-drank in her Art Deco bar.

Falk imagined her at sea, the soft wash of water caressing her bow. But now she was permanently dry-docked in Long Beach California. Maybe he understood some of what Jack Bonecutter must feel. The moan of her old wooden decks could be construed as a cry for help, for peace, as tourists who lacked the sense of history to thrill at her legacy trekked through her. They sought the only prize a desensitized, under-educated, violence-overloaded, flagging civilization could conceive: ghosts in her galleys.

Falk sighed deeply, sighting the large, blue X on the helipad located on a raised platform just east of the outer parking lot. Three hundred feet away were two construction trailers that appeared to be a command post, a buzz of police activity around them.

The pilot roared toward the helipad without any sign of decreasing his speed. Falk turned to him.

"What's up?" His voice crackled into the pilot's helmet.

"Up, sir?" The pilot asked.

"The helipad." Falk pointed as the large X vanished beneath them and was quickly left behind. He had expected to deplane there.

"My orders are to deposit you on the ship, sir. Astern, on the sun deck, next to the Ye Olde Bakery Shoppe, sir."

"On the…"

Falk had assumed he would first meet at dock HQ with the colonel Heeley had mentioned. He shrugged. Probably there was nothing Colonel Beard could add to those professional, precise orders Heeley had given Falk on the phone: "Until we get a location from the scientist, all I can tell you, Joe, is to get on board and follow your instincts."

Falk checked his watch. It was ten forty-five. Was it really less than two hours ago that he spoke to Heeley? It seemed more like days ago when Heeley solemnly pronounced, "Joe, you understand that at this point we can't let the public, the media, or even the police, know the truth.

"That would open up a can of worms we definitely don't want opened. Especially since we failed to get our hands on the briefcase back in '67. As far as everyone is concerned, you're there only to locate Bonecutter and his bombs."

Heeley lowered his voice conspiratorially. "And, of course, a man is a lot easier to find than a briefcase, so your primary search will be for Bonecutter. If you happen to get your hands on the briefcase first, before you're able to apprehend Bonecutter or locate his bombs, get the hell off the ship." Even the Bureau viewed the old girl and the schizoid who obsessed over her as expendable.

As the chopper continued to descend, Falk tried to concentrate on strategy, or his lack thereof. He reminded himself that uphill battles were his specialty. Falk had learned early on that he alone was accountable for his actions, which made him a tough, independent competitor.

On the other hand, finding an unbalanced man and his bombs

and a one-foot-square briefcase hidden on an ocean liner nearly a thousand feet long and twelve stories high was not going to be easy. And time was moving on relentlessly.

Heeley had held out one ray of hope: the chemist in Panama who originally hid the briefcase on the ship. The only clue Heeley ascertained from the Bureau agent who spoke to the man was that he had hidden it somewhere no one would find it.

"The scientist is sick, old, maybe even feeble-minded," Heeley muttered, "but as soon as we have him, we'll have an answer for you, Joe."

Chapter 17

Falk was given exactly four seconds to jump from the helicopter onto the sun deck astern, before the pilot's collective pitch change required a burst of power, and the chopper lifted and disappeared over the bay.

Quickly sighting his cover, Falk bolted across the exposed deck toward amidships, vaulting over a long, low bench, running full-tilt, hoping the bomber was not nearby.

Reaching Ye Olde Bakery Shoppe, he rammed a shoulder against the push-bar door and burst in, turning and slamming his back to the wall just inside. He scanned the room. He had worn one of his weighted jackets: two small, flat weights like those used in shower curtains were sewn inside the left front lower lining. The weights flipped it out and away if he were required to simultaneously twist, bend to become the smallest possible target, and reach for his holstered Beretta.

The precaution of inserted weights could save a second in opening his jacket, and therefore his life. He instinctively felt, more than saw or heard movement, as his weapon cleared leather.

"Don't shoot me!"

The voice came from behind the coffee counter, just below a sign on the wall that read "Espresso, Freshly Baked Pastries, Desserts & Other Sweets."

A sensational, tanned blonde with brilliant green eyes and a smile that certainly could be described as sweet stood up, empty palms uplifted in his direction.

"Koski!"

"Hi, Joe." Her tone was almost timorous.

He could not believe it. His heart seemed to float at the sight of her, as always. But she shouldn't be here. "What are you…how did you get here?"

Susan Koski rolled her eyes, swung her petite body around the counter, and sauntered toward him. The timid demeanor disintegrated, replaced by her usual confidence, which presently included an edge of sarcasm.

"Glad to see you, too."

He watched her take note of his charcoal blazer and black pants; then she looked down at her own outfit—jeans, oversized beige sweater, and J. Crew jacket, white socks and high-tops.

"My invitation said casual," she quipped, handing him a Bluetooth phone ear bud. She indicated the earpiece. "Cutting-edge, latest issue from Quantico."

She pulled back her hair and revealed a similar, small flesh-toned earpiece fitted snuggly into her ear. "The microphone is built in and picks up our voices from vibrations in our heads."

Falk didn't like this development one iota. This mission was dangerous enough for one, let alone two. One person might escape Bonecutter's notice, but he would surely spot two. He held up a hand to signal her to silence and went to the window. It looked like a ghost ship out there; the stern section quiet and totally devoid of movement, indicating that the evacuation was no doubt complete, and that Bonecutter probably was not in the immediate vicinity. Falk re-holstered his weapon and ran a hand through his rich brown hair.

"What are you doing here, Koski? How did you get aboard?"

Her full lips pouted. "Last question first. I got here ahead of you and the ship was still being evacuated, so I played the part of an official herding the people ashore. No time for amenities, I guess."

She shrugged and continued, "Heeley pulled me off the Reno surveillance gig. Said he had talked to you, maybe twenty minutes earlier. Said his intention was to fly me here where I would meet at dock HQ with the local yokels and this Army Colonel Beard. I was to stand by in case you needed two more hands. And, by that time, he would have word from agents in Panama as to the location of the briefcase, which I, being the only other person to know about said briefcase, would pass on to you."

She paused to take a breath. Falk was silent, wondering when her needle would hit empty.

"So," she continued, "he sent a jet-powered chopper out of Reno-Tahoe to fly me here, which took less than forty minutes. I should have been here after you, except I heard you got held up at Van Nuys Airport. Just a few moments ago, Heeley called me at headquarters dockside, and said I should get aboard at the stern. Like I said, I played an official evacuator."

Falk had to interrupt. "So Heeley figures I can't handle this one on my own. Is that the bottom line?"

"No. It's not that at all."

"It's not? What is it, then? You tell me."

She straightened, and her glowing green eyes pierced his.

"That's what I'm trying to do." She paused and sighed. "I was told to tell you that, unfortunately, we won't get any help from the scientist in Panama. When the agents arrived at his home on Contadora Island, he was dead; stabbed several dozens of times, although it appears as if he died of a heart attack before the stabbings."

"Jesus!"

Falk eased back against the wall. As Koski approached him, he caught the warm aroma of peony soap on her skin and the fresh scent of her hair.

Her tone was softer and more empathetic. "Heeley decided that, given the new circumstances, you might appreciate an additional someone to help you in the hunt. So here I am."

She combed a hand through her thick blond hair, and it furrowed between her slender fingers, then fell back into place.

"So, where do we begin, Joe?"

He looked down from his six-foot height at her five-one, a tad over a hundred pounds. A deep sigh washed over him. He placed a hand on her shoulder and let it slowly slide down her arm to her warm hand, where their fingers entwined.

"I am glad to see you," he said truthfully, quickly looking away, avoiding those eyes he could so easily get lost in.

A brief touch was all there was time for. That seemed to be their lot in life: jumping from one assignment to another, never having enough time to properly explore some of the deeper, important conversations of life.

"Look," he said, moving away from her spell. "Here's how I see it. Logically, if I were this guy, Bonecutter, and I was obsessed with the ship and planned to die with her tonight, I'd feel like I was in charge of her now. Like, finally, I was the captain of her fate.

Where would the captain be?"

Koski raised her eyebrows, as if she had not already thought of it. "On the bridge."

"Right. But there's no good place for a man to hide on the bridge, as far as I know. When the police and security personnel evacuated the ship, surely they checked the bridge, the wheelhouse, that entire area. Nevertheless, I think he'd be as close as possible to the navigational nerve center of the ship, possibly positioned to move to the bridge once darkness closed in."

"Assuming that's true, giving us his possible general location, we're left with the bombs and the briefcase."

"The location of the bombs is something we'll have to hope we can persuade Bonecutter to tell us, if and when the time comes. As to the briefcase, which is our secondary, but more important mission, if we find Bonecutter and his babies, it won't matter where the case is, at least for the moment, and that'll become another story."

"I have a hunch," Koski said.

Female intuition, Falk thought disparagingly. Even so, one had to consider it's origin. If it was Koski, it was never without merit. He and Koski had worked together on one assignment in the past year, the serial killings in Nevada and California. Koski's hunches had proven generally accurate throughout; he had to give her that. He decided to project an interested look.

"What hunch is that?"

"The scientist, Metcalf, kept a low profile when he took that voyage back in 1967, so he obviously was not in a stateroom. He stayed hidden. His access was limited to places where a lot of people congregated where he blended in unnoticed or places where there wasn't anyone around, where others could or would not go, where he'd not be seen."

Falk raised his eyebrows and gave her a slightly impatient bottom line gesture with his hand.

"My guess is someplace like the gym. Or, in the other extreme, a lifeboat."

Falk's brow furrowed. "Remember, the ship was torn apart and rebuilt into a hotel since she's been in Long Beach. Wherever it's hidden, it's not going to be easy to find."

Koski rolled her tawny-speckled green eyes. "Well, that doesn't necessarily rule out the gym, or any other location that has lots of hiding places for that matter."

Falk's male intuition told him that Metcalf had to choose a never-disturbed, almost inaccessible place; a location where maintenance, cleanup, and refurbishing crews had no reason to set foot. He sighed. Which could admittedly be a gym.

"Okay," he said, "we'll check out the gym and other rooms that offer hiding places, and work our way toward the bow."

"Oh, by the way," Koski reached into a pocket of her jacket and produced a three-by-five envelope, "Beard gave me this." She opened it and carefully produced a folded sheet of plastic.

Falk wrinkled his brow. "Looks like plastic kitchen wrap."

"Does, doesn't it? But it's a chemical wrap developed by R and D at a lab here in California. It was initially intended for use in high-risk chemical experiments. It's designed to neutralize leakage. We're supposed to immediately wrap it around the briefcase when we find it."

She slid the wrap back into the envelope and replaced it in her pocket. "If we find it."

"We'll find it."

He pulled opened the back door of the bakery shop, which led to a long passageway amidships, and turned to look back at her.

"At the end of this corridor is an elevator. We'll take it down to an area once used for baggage storage. From there we'll take a stairway to a disused, horizontal conduit that runs the length of the ship, stem to stern. We'll follow…"

"Wait," she said. "How large is this conduit?"

Falk drew back with an exaggerated look of appraisal, as if calculating Koski's petite frame in relation to the size of the pipe.

"You'll make it."

She didn't laugh.

"I was thinking more of my…well, trouble with tight places." She shrugged. "Okay. Forget it. I'll survive."

Falk cocked his head and looked down at her. "Sure?"

She glared. "I said I'd be okay."

He gestured toward the long corridor. "We'll follow the conduit about half the length of the ship, until we're over the number three boiler room, aft of the forward turbo generator room. Then the stairs to R deck and the elevator to the gym."

Koski sighed heavily. "If you could make this any more complicated, you would, right?"

"Koski, we can't just stroll through the damn ship. There's supposed to be no one left aboard. If this guy sees us, he's liable to decide to detonate." He broke off, not wanting to go there. "Look, believe it or not, it's the quickest and maybe the only way to get forward without his seeing us, in the event he's somewhere besides the bow, which he might be."

"It sounds as if you know this ship pretty well."

"Information delivered to me at Van Nuys Airport. I memorized as much as I could during my delay."

As sense of imminent danger ticked at Falk's brain. "Koski, did

Heeley say who stabbed Metcalf?"

"He suspects a Panamanian cartel that's using hotels in Panama as fronts for drug running."

Falk did some quick calculations. "Panama is three hours ahead of us, same as the East Coast." He checked his watch. "It's eleven here, so it's two p.m. in Panama. The news of Bonecutter holding the ship hostage was on FOX at eight-thirty this morning, California time; that would be eleven-thirty in Panama. If somebody had access to a private jet or even took a commercial flight out of Panama, they could get to California in ten to twelve hours."

Koski shivered and hugged herself, rubbing her upper arms. "Metcalf's killer could have left Panama as much as two and a half hours ago and be here by, say, seven o'clock tonight, our time." She shook her head. "That's cutting it close. He'd have only an hour. And no way could he get on the ship."

"If someone wants to steal your car badly enough they will, despite the number of auto-theft devices you install, right? Well, a clever person could get aboard and create total havoc here in one hour."

She nodded. "So if we don't find what we're looking for soon, we may acquire some serious competition."

Falk started down the corridor. "Yeah, the operative word being 'serious'."

Chapter 18

In his soon-to-be-over lifetime, Jack Bonecutter had often quoted Samuel Johnson. "Curiosity is one of the permanent and certain characteristics of a vigorous mind." Bonecutter believed it. It was the result of curiosity, satiated daily by a virtual mountain of books and life experiences, planned and unplanned, lived and relived, that filled the stories he wrote with the ring of truth, the voice of authenticity. It was a blessing; also, a curse.

After several hours on the ladder in the dark shaft, he began to wonder what was happening topside. He tried to stifle his curiosity, but without being aware, he had turned back to face the ladder and moved up several dozen rungs.

Earlier, despite the roar of air in the shaft, his ears had picked up a familiar, heavy, steady thumping—the deep, guttural growl of a Huey. The sound was reminiscent of Bien Hoa. It filled his head, turning him inward to a memory he was powerless to dispel. It flooded every crevice of his brain with that remembered day. A day when three of his buddies had died in a minefield and he, unfortunately, had lived.

They had been doing long-range recon and were walking through a seemingly innocent field when suddenly several nearly simultaneous explosions ripped the air. A piece that might have been the heart of one grunt was hurled through space and splattered onto Bonecutter's chest. A chunk of flesh, some part of another friend, fell at Bonecutter's feet. Another nearby soldier was so disintegrated as to leave no visible physical trace of him on earth.

With shards of shrapnel lodged in his crotch, Bonecutter left Bien Hoa, mentally, long before the Huey that would evacuate him put down in the field. And on the litter that carried him away from the carnage, he was heard singing a rhyme, an inexplicable source of solace.

"Simple Simon met a pie man going to the fair..."

Bonecutter was living proof that those who survived suffered deeply and long. All that remained of his friends were scars in his mind. And the circumstances following his return from that tour of duty had done nothing to alleviate the pain.

It was almost comical now to think that for years after he had returned, he and Marissa had actually tried to pretend that he had not changed. Outwardly, he was unaltered, unless you took into consideration the raised, six-inch slash of pink scar tissue that began where his scrotum once was and continued down his right inner thigh. But inside there was always the lingering sense of inadequacy. Army doctors had explained that the degeneration of his sperm-developing tubules was due to too much body heat; what remained of the testicles being forced to reside in an altered section of his lower abdomen.

"We can't guarantee that surgical rearrangement would produce the desired effect," the doctors had said.

The desired effect was reproduction, of course. Marissa wanted children. Bonecutter, too, longed to procreate.

"I need whole genitals," he had screamed at the doctors, "with gonads and a sustained erection. And I must have sperm with any distribution of chromosomes whatever, so long as the suckers can swim upstream."

But nothing was produced. Except for a palpable void in his and Marissa's togetherness. For years they continued to make love, but it was like prying passion open. Each time became a main event.

Gradually, he relinquished the need to fill her. They fought bitterly, and the cycle of vicious verbal battles ended last week when she gave their relationship its death blow, the announcement that she was pregnant and wanted a divorce to marry her lover.

Bonecutter's thoughts jumped to the present, and he realized that he had taken the remote from his pocket, that his thumb hovered, quivering over the red detonator button. He shuddered and quickly returned the mechanism to his pocket.

He looked at his lighted watch.

He had been on the ladder for three hours. A muscle in his left calf had tightened into a knot, and he maneuvered a hand down to his leg to massage the cramp away.

He was curious, and wondered each minute what was happening on the ship above him and on the dock below. Certainly, everyone had been evacuated, as his note instructed. He had warned that he would begin the fireworks early if a bomb squad came aboard. Had they conformed to his demands? Or were they out there now, waiting for the chance to pick him off?

He wondered what it would be like on deck now, alone, with no other human footfall echoing through the ship. How would it feel to wander in uninhabited staterooms, or the silent cinema, or the grand ballroom when no music echoed from its brocade ceiling?

What was that?

His head suddenly hit something hard. He released one hand from the ladder and felt the object above him. A board. It was the underside of the trap door beneath the chart table. When had his feet covertly carried him upward to the very top of the shaft he had plunged into earlier?

Well, as long as he was here and because he was curious, he would take a quick look. He touched the pocket of his denim jacket once lightly to remind himself of the courage there, the remote and its small red button he could depress at will if he encountered evidence of betrayal.

Slowly he pushed up the slab of wood and looked around the chart room. It was a small area, with only one window, starboard, facing the bay. If he chose to linger here for several minutes, he would not be seen by a dockside sharpshooter. Good. Then the sudden jangle of a phone. A phone! A phone on the ship was ringing!

He froze.

It was the phone on the bulkhead wall in the wheelhouse, just outside the chart room, not twenty feet from him. Was it possible they knew where he was? But, no, other phones at various, apparently random locations were also ringing, resonating in near unison throughout the otherwise eerily silent ship.

No, they didn't know where he was. They were ringing all phones in hopes he would pick up one, allowing them to pinpoint his location. Or they wanted to speak to him. Either way, he would ignore them.

Looking forward through the open door of the chart room and the panoramic windows above the steering and navigational equipment of the wheelhouse ahead, he had a captain's-eye view of the bow. He watched a gull glide to the deck and perch there, preening itself.

The phones continued to ring, a continuous, stereophonic jangle harsh and persistent. Their ringing was urgent and irritating. And Bonecutter was curious. So what if they pinpointed his location? They wouldn't dare send anyone to search the area. And if they did, they would not find him because he would be back in the shaft, and they would surmise that he had left the bridge.

He stomped past the bulkhead, careful not to let himself be viewed from the dock hundreds of feet below, and stood, staring at the insistent instrument. He reminded himself that he was, after all, in charge and could afford to relax his guard somewhat, enough to see what they had to say. They wouldn't dare kill him. He alone knew where the bombs were. They might, if they had the chance, fire to disable him, but it would be tricky from this distance.

Finally, he scooped the phone from its cradle on the wall.

"Jack Bonecutter?" a deliberate, nasal voice asked. Bonecutter was silent, only his nervous breathing transmitted across the line. "Listen, Mr. Bonecutter, this is Colonel J. Manley Beard, United States Army. There is something you need to know. Despite our best efforts to evacuate everyone, you are not alone on the ship."

Not alone. What did he mean? Bonecutter managed to remain silent, a flush beginning in his cheeks.

"We are not to blame. You've got to believe that. We followed your instructions to the letter and evacuated all tourists, hotel guests and ship and security personnel in a timely manner. Moreover, I can assure you that there is no police presence on board at this time. None whatsoever."

Beard paused as if summoning courage. "However, there was a Girl Scout troop on the tour early this morning, and one of the girls, a helpless little child only ten years old, apparently got separated from her troop and is presently unaccounted for."

"It's not true," Bonecutter said harshly. "What kind of gimmick is this?"

"No trick. I swear. She is, I'm told, a precocious child, very inquisitive and bright. And we have reason to believe that she is deliberately hiding on the ship somewhere."

"You must think I'm an idiot!" Bonecutter exploded. "Don't tell me this. I don't want to hear it!"

His head began to ache and throb. He had planned everything so carefully, given them more than ample time to get everyone off the ship so that no one would be hurt.

He shuddered as his spine prickled icily. If they did not find her by eight, she would be killed. No! Oh, God, no! He was not a killer.

He felt pressure building against his temples, the too-familiar shrinking feeling of a spell, but Beard's voice, now seeming to come to him through a long hollow tunnel and carrying unthinkable implications, kept him momentarily in the present.

"Mr. Bonecutter, I'm a soldier. I agonize over every decision I make, especially when human lives are at stake. I've read your war record. You were a brave warrior. My decision to make this call was in the earnest hope that you are reasonable and will agree to let us send a team aboard to search for the girl."

"No!" Bonecutter screamed. "No, Goddammit! I'll find her." He slammed down the phone. He would find her. He had to. He buried his face in his hands. Oh, God. It was supposed to be just the Queen Mary and him.

He set his mouth grimly, turned and headed for the interior stairway leading down to the officers' quarters. He'd start there. He knew the ship like the back of his hand. There wasn't a place on it where one could hide from Jack Bonecutter. He looked at his watch. High noon.

As he left the wheelhouse, the phone made a sorry jingle, as if it suffered a shock, and then died. In the same instant, he felt a shudder from deep in the belly of the vessel; the lights dimmed and flickered, suggesting that somewhere on the ship the electricity was failing.

Chapter 19

Willie Dill purposely got separated from Girl Scout Troop 892 in the Trafalgar Square Gift Shop during the chaos that followed the order to evacuate the ship. The pre-teen girls, ages eight to eleven, utilized the buddy system, but Willie had sworn her partner to silence. She insisted that she simply must go back to the old projection room adjoining the theater she had glimpsed earlier, where a bank of television monitors maintained surveillance of the ship's interior and exterior, and several computers sitting on a desk had caught her eye.

"But why do you have to go back to that room?" her partner asked.

"Because it's there. Because it's a cool place. Because we're being evacuated and who knows what's going on. Because, well, I'll bet those computers are full of tons of information."

Her friend nodded her agreement, concluding that Wilomena Jean Dill had to uncover the dark secrets that undoubtedly existed on the attendant hard drives.

"Even though the police didn't give a reason for making us leave the ship," Willie's companion argued, "and even though most bomb threats we hear these days turn out to be bogus, there might really be a bomb somewhere." Willie pooh-poohed the idea, but the girl persisted. "Besides, the projection room is way back in the cinema. You might not be able to find your way to the exit."

But Willie's insistence had prevailed, and the girl agreed not to report her buddy missing until the Scout troop got down to the dock and were back on the bus.

While the other scouts were shuffled out of the gift shop, Willie huddled behind a rack of T-shirts in the corner. She was small for her age, and the top of the tiered rack stood a foot above her head.

In her green Girl Scout skirt and a white sweatshirt nearly covered by her green Girl Scout sash, she blended perfectly with the tees on the rack. Patches and pins adorned her sash, including the "Point, Click, Go Try It" award she earned in Brownies.

Her most recent accomplishment was the troop's web site. She had designed it, replete with Scout songs, yellow smiley faces, and recently added a chat room. She had plans for a chat schedule to be up and running soon, so that her troop could talk electronically to girls all over the world.

Willie was in fifth grade, having skipped fourth in the private school she attended. She did not consider herself a nerd. Soon enough, more girlish issues would have to be confronted, even by Willie. Presently, however, other considerations occupied her mind.

For example, when two of her friends' computers recently crashed, they pleaded with Willie to restore them, because their parents said it was too expensive to hire a technician. Both computers, Willie suspected, had simply fallen prey to an internet virus. She told the girls that her own computer was not prone to such trivial nuisances as viruses.

"How come?" they asked.

"I have an on-line e-mail filter that deletes ninety percent of questionable mail, and I keep both a virus program, IPE, and an e-mail bomb catcher running at all times to warn me about any mischievous mail before it ever gets to me," she explained.

"Then, of course," Willie went on unasked, "I have my own modified browser that is not as vulnerable to bombs as others. Moreover, I have a backup system that consists of two hard drives in both of my computers. The second hard drive checks the first and eliminates any intentionally damaging insertions, and every week I use a special backup program to save a full, clean backup."

"Okay," one of her friends interrupted, uninterested in her friend's technobabble. "So can you just come over and fix my computer?"

"Sure," Willie promised, and she planned to do so tomorrow.

When she had ducked behind the T-shirt rack earlier, she

pinched her eyes shut behind her thick glasses with their large, dark frames, not wanting to see the moment of discovery if it came. But it didn't.

Soon the shop was silent, clerks having been forced to leave hurriedly with the rest. She stuffed three packages of cheese and crackers and a candy bar into her backpack, left five dollars on the counter, and split, eager to find the old projection room and computers.

She made her way down a long, thickly carpeted corridor. After testing various passageways and doors, Willie Dill, techie genius, had to concede that she was hopelessly lost.

Chapter 20

Marshak learned of the partial power outage aboard the ship when he returned to Beard's outer office following a trip to the can. He resented the fact that Beard had talked to Bonecutter without letting him know in advance.

Damn! And another thing: Beard still had not seen fit to share with him the reason why the military was involved in what Marshak considered a local problem. Not even a reliable rumor stirred as to the military's interest. And Marshak would be damned if he'd ask.

Beard was standing by the computers that were manned by his young communications experts, Miller and Nakamura. Together they awaited the conclusion of a printout, and Marshak deduced from Beard's expression that it was not good news.

Beard ripped it from the printer and sighed, then handed it to Marshak. "What do you think, Captain? Bonecutter's work?"

According to the data, a generator shutdown had caused loss of power to a large portion of the ship, mainly the lower level decks and holds; the PA system and phones in some areas were out.

"The next best thing to knowing the answer to a question," Marshak said smugly, "is knowing where to *get* the answer. At my earlier request, the chief engineer has been standing by in the next trailer in case we need him. Looks like we do."

Within minutes the four were standing before a startled engineer. He was a middle-aged man in conservative blue slacks and short-sleeved white shirt with Bob stitched in dark blue thread on the pocket. No doubt his job had been routine and mundane until today, and his uneasy body language said that while engineering might come easy to him, conversation did not.

After considering the specific areas of power failure, Bob said, "As you know, or you may not, umm, portions of the ship have their own power plants, fitted with steam-powered generators. There are several, well, all kinds of built-in safety devices, some computerized, some not, to prevent a generator from exploding."

"Yes, yes." Beard was noticeably impatient.

"Well, it appears that a generator must have registered a fault."

"A fault?"

"So the protective equipment kicked in," the engineer said with a slight "duh" tone in his voice.

Marshak, like Beard, was antsy for the bottom line, but seeking Bob's input being his idea, he was patient. "Yes, go on."

"Errr, I guess I should start from the beginning." Bob's vision flickered to the floor then back up. "You see, if a fault occurs in a generator, or between it and the first circuit breaker, then the generator has to withstand the short-circuit current until its field is automatically switched off by computer. After this short-circuit occurs, automatic equipment disconnects the generator, isolating it from the rest of the system."

He paused to see if they required further explanation, and Marshak, who did not understand at all, looked at Beard. Beard's equally quizzical expression told Bob to go on.

"This reduces the generator's excitation so that the terminal voltage decreases instantly." Another pause. "This shuts down its prime mover and takes the generator completely off-line."

"Look, man, just tell us how this could happen. What caused the fault to begin with?" Marshak asked.

Again the engineer's eyes momentarily sought the floor. "Might be a mis-set. We were told to leave immediately."

Beard cleared his throat. "Since so much of this operation is computerized, can we get the generator started again by computer, from right here?"

"'Fraid not. I can't chance it without going to the site itself and checking out the equipment. It could be as simple as a sticky valve, but it could also be a fault in the feed-water pump."

Beard stopped him by gripping his shoulder and jolting it in the same way he shook hands. "Thank you, Bob. We appreciate your input." He turned the man toward the door and patted him on the back. "We'll let you know if we need you again."

Beard paced his office then eased into his chair. Marshak stood in the doorway. "Why would Bonecutter knock out only one generator?" Marshak wondered aloud.

"Why would he knock out any generator?" Beard asked.

"Colonel, shouldn't we have explored with that engineer the reasons why the backup generator didn't kick in?" Marshak asked.

Beard dismissed the policeman's curiosity with the infuriating vagueness that was getting under Marshak's skin. "Our operatives can figure it out."

Yeah, right, Marshak thought: the blonde female agent and the guy flown by chopper to the stern earlier. He also wondered how the two "operatives" would operate this evening, about six, when the clouds that were gathering ushered in the storm and early darkness, and they were still searching frantically for bombs while trying to apprehend a maniac. Well, it was Beard's call.

Earlier Marshak suggested they try to locate Bonecutter's wife, who was on vacation in the West Indies. It was possible, Marshak speculated, that she could talk her old man out of this. Marshak's woman could talk him out of, or into, almost anything.

But Beard had countered, "No need involving some hysterical female. Besides, she's divorcing the guy. Having somebody else's kid, I understand. I doubt there's any love lost between the two at this point."

Marshak wasn't so sure. He'd been married previously, three times, in fact. He figured he probably didn't have the world's biggest heart, but a piece of it still throbbed with some affection for every woman he had ever loved. He shrugged. But this wasn't his operation anymore.

The phone rang. "It's for you, Captain, the Chief on line three."

With a phone to his ear, fielding questions from the Police Chief, Marshak suddenly thought of the unopened envelope literary agent Pete Powers had left in his office earlier. No doubt it was buried under reports, printouts, and the swimsuit issue of a sports magazine he picked up from the kiosk when he went for cigarettes.

Whatever was in the envelope, which might be an offer for the movie rights to his view of this fiasco, he conjectured, would have to wait a few more minutes. Right now he needed to remain here where the action was.

The little girl on the ship bothered the hell out of him. He had a granddaughter about her age. *Damned kid, gumming up the works*, he cursed mentally, and popped an antacid tablet into his mouth before blatantly lying to his superior on the phone. "Not to worry, Chief. I can say with specificity that we should have this wrapped up by, say, three o'clock, latest."

Miller, on one of the other lines that was insistently ringing, put it on hold and looked up at Marshak. "It's Willie Dill's parents, Nancy and George Dill, on line four, Captain."

"Great!" Marshak thundered and punched the flashing white button.

Chapter 21

The Bondesque thrill of the chase that was so romanticized, the notion of dashing agents capturing foreign spies passing highly classified secrets in exotic locales—that was mostly fiction, Koski thought. This was what it usually came down to: crawling on hands and knees like a sewer rat through an old pipe in the bowels of a ship, your lung capacity seriously reduced by the close, stagnant air.

It would help if she could see. Just ahead, Falk's body swayed from side to side, alternating hip and knee joints as he made steady headway on all fours.

But no light penetrated the forty-eight-inch, circular conduit they were worming through on their way to the forward section. Koski's open eyes might as well have been closed. There were no grays, no shades of black on black, simply depthless, solid ebony that she felt pushing directly into her, attempting to smother her. *Just keep moving. And don't think about it. That's the key.*

It was at times like this Koski appreciated her prior employment as a videographer for the Nevada Bureau of Land Management.

Trained at the FBI Academy at Quantico, she was an excellent markswoman and held a degree in criminal science. Originally she had turned down the FBI, taking the BLM position. It was in that capacity that she had worked with Falk, uncovering a foreign plot to take over the United States from within while pinning it on Native Americans.

Because they had worked so well together, and because she wanted to pair with Falk again, she was here, feeling the walls of the dark conduit close in on her.

A trickle of perspiration ran down her forehead and settled in the corner of her eye. Each breath took its time coming now. "How much farther?" she wheezed.

"Not far." The reply echoed back, muffled but in Falk's usual, optimistic tone.

At this moment she thought it insufferable at the way he always looked at the "bright side." Were they heading out of the conduit or going farther into it? Falk would reply with the most positive response.

He was so different from David, her ex-significant-other. David was a moody, cynical, Reno vice cop who had been busted with cocaine he'd confiscated from a perp when he decided to keep and use it. He was serving time in Susanville prison and Koski seldom thought of him now.

Something else nearly died then: Koski's confidence in her own instincts. She had totally trusted and believed in David. And had been totally wrong.

Working with Falk had helped her regain a portion of her self-confidence, and, with him, she felt she was on the way to full recovery. Not that Falk himself fostered that in her. On the contrary, when they met, he was a loner who obviously resented having a partner.

Yet, while she had proven herself on their previous assignments, some of that nagging self-doubt remained. And what of the emotional tie that she felt slowly developing between them? Both stretched like strings of catgut on an old guitar, ready to twang if properly strummed, yet capable of snapping at any moment.

Koski again became aware of the encircling walls, the stifling, still air, the coal black darkness. She thought she tasted a cool water, like an ice cube in her mouth, and mentally crunched them into wet jewels; the false sensation, however, merely heightened her anxiety.

Then, suddenly, the darkness switched off. Koski saw an orange glow in a recess ahead, revealing Falk in silhouette. When she realized it was a flashlight in his hand, she moaned.

"You mean, you've had a flashlight all along? And here we are, fumbling our way in the dark!"

"Preserving the batteries," he said, his voice resounding off the close curvature of the walls.

"For what?" Koski was working hard just to breathe.

"An emergency."

"Shit! What could be more of an emergency than this?"

"Anything that might unexpectedly come up. Don't talk, Koski. Save your breath."

The light died and Falk crawled on as if unconcerned. He did not want to tell his anxious companion that he thought he had heard water. It occurred to him then that when the ship was fully operational, this conduit would have been automatically flooded in the event of breech, fire or explosion.

Having found no evidence of moisture on the dusty but otherwise nearly clean surface in front or behind, Falk speculated that the automatic safety device that would have likely triggered a flood had been disconnected during the ship's original refitting. Or it was down due to the temporary power failure.

Realistically, he could not discount either "what if." Or others, like, what if the automatic safety device was not disconnected and awaited only a second, confirmatory sensor command to fire? What if one of Bonecutter's bombs was to go off at this minute? Would the explosion trigger the flooding? He envisioned a rush of dark water spiraling toward them. There might be regular intersecting "safety" pipes, and, if so, he would need the light to find it. The pang of unease at the thought started to rise in him, but it quickly passed.

Falk knew himself. It was when a situation seemed most out of his control, that he felt the most confident. At this moment, the challenge was enough to supercharge his capacity to deal with it and he felt a full measure of concentration, inner strength, and—it only happened when he was in high gear like this—a groove. From the day an assignment began until it ended, the rhythm of his life was automatic and harmonious. When fully activated, he was propelled by an instinct that was at once delicate and feral.

Falk's marriage to Meg had been good, but did nothing to help him make order out of this undomesticated aspect of his psyche. Meg. It was nearly five years since she died, but it seemed like yesterday.

A full investigation proved that the stray hunter's bullet found her by accident; there was no one to directly blame, the police report said. Yet there were still days and nights when Falk blamed himself, despite all the therapist's words to the contrary.

It was one of the reasons he had became a loner. One of the reasons he felt out of step with life when an assignment, which kept his mind busy, was over.

Now he had met a woman whose mere presence at a mission's conclusion tended to smooth the transition so that the distinction between feral and domestic blurred without diminishing the strength of either. And he unconsciously vowed in this minute that if they got through this assignment, he'd find the time and the way to tell her.

Chapter 22

Koski was fighting for air again, and furiously. She thought of only one thing, and it froze like a block of ice in her brain: She could not turn around. If something happened ahead, she would have that long, black eternity to retrace, crawling backwards, because she could not turn around. If something happened behind her, she would have to scramble ahead. To what? How far? No up, no down, no sides. She could not turn around!

Anxiety rose to a panic that heightened the certainty of suffocation. Her heart seemed to swell in her chest. She was about to scream. She had to scream. She had to beat her fists against the walls, to trample Falk, to do anything necessary, anything to get out.

Abruptly the terrifying sensations and compulsions receded, and an exquisite dizziness prickled across her brain, bringing a rush of heat. Now hot water seemed to fill her, bathing her from the inside out, soothing, lulling her away to a black depth that promised a perverse peace. Some small part of her relinquished to it before, finally, from a seemingly vast distance, a voice, Falk's voice, recalled her.

"This is it. This is where we get out." He flashed the light ahead, revealing a side-chamber with four steps built into a steel wall.

Koski lunged forward, crowding him, scrambling up the steps to the freedom of a lower deck, hungrily gulping and gasping for air.

Falk, following, grabbed for her. "You okay?"

She straightened and breathed easier, pulling away. "Of course," she said with obvious irritation. "I'm fine."

Falk watched color return to her pallid cheeks, then bent and brushed off the knees of his pants.

"Classic."

"Pardon?"

"Classic," he repeated, "Panic, a sense of suffocation, near loss of consciousness. All typical of claustrophobia." He straightened and smiled. "But you were a trouper; I'm proud of you."

He knew that she was still shaken, and he was certain that that, more than anything he could do, his words would cause her to pull herself together. One thing he had learned about this woman: When threatened or made to feel vulnerable in any way, she reacted by getting royally pissed off.

She looked dead into his eyes and demanded, "So where are we going now? What are we waiting for?"

He wanted to hug her, but answered simply, "We take the elevator to R deck. It opens to the gym."

They fell silent then, hurrying to the elevator where he punched the "Up" button. There was one other thing he desperately wanted to tell Koski, but would have to wait. Aside from the fact that he preferred to work alone, and despite her claustrophobia, in any life-and-death situation, he felt most comfortable with her, above all people, at his side. They entered the elevator together.

When the elevator eased humming and the doors slid open, they started to move, then froze. Falk's finger went to his lips. Was that which he heard a slight shuffling of feet? Were they lucky, or unlucky, enough to have found Bonecutter already?

Falk slipped the Beretta from its holster seconds before Koski's automatic cleared her waist. Silently they fanned out of the elevator, weapons leveled.

Falk let his vision sweep the room, which was high, long and broad, with gleaming wood floors and windows on both sides. There were several free-weights, treadmills, bikes, stair machines, aerobics gear, a juice bar, and a cardiovascular center, a full line of health and fitness equipment. Falk moved slowly into the room, Koski to his left.

At the far end of the room, near the entrance to the spa, sauna and pool, a punch bag suspended from a beam was swinging, its movement causing an almost imperceptible creak...creak...creak at the juncture of its connection to the chain from which it hung. Otherwise the room was silent. Someone, only moments earlier, had...a flash...a girl bolted from behind the juice bar to their right and raced for the elevator.

"Whoa!" Falk, re-holstering his weapon, swung around and caught her waist as she tried to escape to his right and behind him. "Hold on!" he shouted.

She was a small, wiry bundle of kicking, screaming juvenility.

"Ow," Falk hollered as she sank her teeth into his left wrist, and he released her.

"Wait!" Koski said. "Wait." Returning her 9 mm to its waist holster, she gently but firmly restrained the girl, squatting to make eye-level contact. "Listen. It's okay. We're not going to hurt you, I promise. It's okay."

Reluctantly, the girl stopped wriggling and adjusted her green Girl Scout sash and dark-rimmed glasses. She had a pretty face, with large hazel eyes that were serious and not afraid.

"Everybody was evacuated," the girl said in an irritated voice. "What are you doing here?"

"What are we...?" Falk stuttered.

Koski, rolling her green eyes up at him, their tawny specks flashing, smoothed the girl's sash around her shoulders. "We're police officers, assigned to be sure everyone gets off the ship safely."

She stood but retained one of the girl's hands in a friendly way. "What happened? Did you get separated from the others? Are you lost?"

"I came here on a field trip with Girl Scout Troop 892."

When she offered no further explanation, Koski said, "I see. But they've all left the ship and gone home. How did it happen that you didn't leave with them?"

The girl met Koski's stare proudly. "I hid in the gift shop."

"You hid," Falk said, incredulous. He thrust his hands into the air and turned away in frustration, then moved toward the windows on the bay side of the ship.

"You didn't want to leave?" Koski asked the girl.

She shook her head from side to side but remained silent.

Koski sighed and led her to a nearby bench. "What's your name?"

"Wilomena Jean Dill. People call me Willie."

Koski offered her hand. "Pleased to meet you, Willie. What a nice name. I'm Susan Koski. That's my partner, Joe Falk, over there. How old are you, Willie?"

"Ten. I'm in the sixth grade. I skipped fourth."

Falk had heard all he needed to hear. He pressed gently on his phone ear-bud. "Colonel, Agent Koski and I are in the ship's gymnasium, where we've encountered a ten-year-old Girl Scout named Wilomena Jean Dill. Was there something you forgot to tell me?"

Beard's harsh, nasal voice answered. "Ah, yes, I was just about to call you about her. Good, I'm glad you found her." Beard paused as if attempting to figure out what he should say next. "I wish I could get word to Bonecutter that we have her in custody, so to speak; might ease the trigger finger on that remote of his."

"You wish what, sir?"

"Ah, yes. Well, you see, he has no means of communication, and the damned phones and PA system on the ship are temporarily out, as is electrical power in certain portions of the vessel. We don't know yet what caused the outage, but we're told that it could be a generator in the amidships boiler room."

Falk gnashed his teeth. He was about to say that the ship's generators were not exactly his responsibility when Beard went on.

"We need that generator on line, agent Falk. It controls our video lifeline to the interior and exterior of the ship. We need it to maintain full surveillance capabilities." His voice tapered off.

"I have some general knowledge of generators," Falk said, "but I'm no engineer." He looked at his watch; it was past noon. "And we need to find..."

He glanced toward Koski and the girl and knew by the way Koski ignored him that she was paying close attention, probably hoping he would not say anything that might scare the girl.

He lowered his voice and moved farther away.

"Time is running out for us to carry out our primary assignment, sir."

"Yes, yes, of course." Beard paused on his end of the line.

Falk took a deep breath and listened while Beard conveyed the essential information regarding the generator and boiler room.

"Okay, I know where that boiler room is located. I'll take a quick look."

"Good man. When you return to the gym, call us. We'll have a plan worked out to get the girl off the ship."

Falk knew that the chances of Bonecutter, wherever he was, learning that Falk and his partner were on the ship were increasing with every passing minute. And the crazy bastard had made it crystal clear in his note that he would detonate his bombs sooner than eight o'clock if his instructions were not precisely followed. Falk ended the conversation with the colonel.

"Look," he said to Koski, rejoining them, "I've got to check out one of the generators. It'll take a few minutes, maybe ten. It might not hurt for you to scope the gym for the…for my briefcase, which I foolishly forgot when we were here earlier." He pointed a finger at the girl. "You can help us by…"

"Oh good!" The youngster was instantly on her feet. It seemed that her resentment at their intrusion into her plans had passed and now she was ready to play detective.

Falk put a hand on each of her shoulders and gently pressed her back down to the bench. "I understand that it's part of the Scout promise to help people at all times. You can help us by staying here with Koski for a few minutes, right where you are. That means you don't move from that spot until I get back, understand? Promise?"

He gave Koski what he hoped was an optimistic look, but as he turned and hurried to the elevator, a prickle of frustration danced through his nervous system. For the first time since he started this assignment he had some doubts as to its successful conclusion.

Chapter 23

When his second meeting with Daystar executives concluded at noon, CEO Lew Blasingdon had heard no suggestions for exploitation of the Queen Mary situation better than his own, which he declined to divulge. This, then, would be his show, and his alone.

Blasingdon learned long ago that the reputation of power is what ultimately gave one power, and he had both in abundance. But power bred isolation, and isolation slowly broke down the channels of communication he once relied on to create his reputation.

More and more, he had to keep strategic corporate information to himself, and this made him less apt to rely on the judgment of others who, he naturally concluded, lacked facts. This, his wife said, made him capricious. Perhaps that was so, for he was about to commit the most capricious act of his life.

He phoned his pilot, telling him to be at the helipad atop the Daystar tower and ready to fly to Long Beach. Now. Sooner, if possible.

The intercom buzzed, interrupting his mental selection of the best remote camera operator for the job. Pete Powers here to see him about Bonecutter, it advised. Blasingdon recalled that Powers was considered a first-rate cameraman before he turned agent. It wasn't as if the shots he wanted had to have cinematic excellence; Computer Graphics Division and Post could fix up almost anything. The important thing was to get something live.

Less than two hours later, Powers was cramped in the silver chopper to the side of Dan Hansen, the pilot, and Blasingdon. The CEO didn't care about Powers beyond his camera skills. In fact, the man looked sick. He'd gone to Blasingdon to persuade him to call Marshak, to bring Daystar's clout to bear on the uncooperative police captain.

Blasingdon had smiled benevolently. "I'll do better than that, Pete. I'm going to Long Beach to talk to this Marshak asshole in person." As if it were a gift, he added, "And I'm taking you with me."

Powers had thanked Blasingdon for the response, especially since his and Chaum's earlier attempt had failed. It wasn't until they were in the helicopter that Powers learned what his role was to be. Blasingdon would not approach Marshak until he'd obtained enough on-the-spot footage to pre-sell "Death of the Queen Mary," Blasingdon's working title for the upcoming big-screen version of today's events. If Bonecutter lived to pull off the bombing, Blasingdon's minions, who were now racing down the Harbor freeway toward Long Beach to be there for the eight o'clock main event, would capture it from a dock's eye view.

If the explosions were as spectacular as Blasingdon hoped, mountains of film would be ready for "Death of the Queen Mary," and what was not immediately used would swell the vaults of Daystar's stock footage library. The scenes Powers was about to film would add a sense of richness and the personal touch that Blasingdon so coveted and sometimes managed, in his impersonal way, to attain.

As they approached San Pedro, Blasingdon tapped Powers, who he saw was still trying to make sense of innovations in remotes since the last one he had operated.

"Listen, Powers," Blasingdon said, his usually soft voice sounding loud and brayish, "get me some good footage, and your entire stable of writers will be working for a long, long time."

Chapter 24

Pete Powers fiddled with the camera, examining its menu of

shooting modes. Ordinarily, he would have salivated at the prospect of Blasingdon throwing work his way. But he lived by his hunches, and, years ago, when he read Jack Bonecutter's first script, he had a hunch that here was someone who could make an agent proud, and substantially rich. Well beyond that, he felt as though he had found a friend in Jack, and he was right.

His mind suddenly formed a black silhouette of the Queen Mary inside a red circle with a red slash through it: NO FILMING, his intuition warned. Instead, they must get the hell out of there. Yet, his compunction to help Jack plus the power of Blasingdon's offer edged out his inner voice.

He turned back to Blasingdon and shouted, "Don't forget. The deal is, I get you some live footage, and you'll get us on the ship afterwards to talk to Jack, right?"

The mogul gripped Pete's shoulder from behind. "You have my word on it."

Pete steadied the camera against the side of his face as he caught sight of the magnificent ocean liner in the distance. Could Blasingdon be trusted? In a far corner of his mind, he heard Sam Goldwyn say, "In two words: im-possible."

Leaning close to the pilot's ear, Blasingdon shouted, "When we get there, take her in low, Hansen. Let's begin by going along the length of the ship, a couple of times on each side."

Powers could see that Hansen was edgy. They were informed at take-off that no aircraft were allowed near the ship. How far were the authorities prepared to go to keep air space clear since September 11, 2001? Also, the chopper was already fighting some vicious crosscurrents due to the storm that had stalled off shore, but was now moving in.

"I don't know, Mr. B.," Hansen said haltingly. "There's a strong wind out there. Dock side may be okay, but it could be dangerous on the weather side."

"Don't worry about the weather," Blasingdon shouted, as if it, too, were under his control. "We'll only be here a few minutes." He rephrased his earlier order more firmly. "Stem to stern, port and starboard, Hansen. I want it all. That's what you get the big bucks for."

Chapter 25

Falk left the gym and hurried back through the long conduit through which he and Koski had crawled earlier, to the amidship boiler room. Fortunately, rewiring an obviously malfunctioning switch in a glorified fuse box was all it took. The backup generator immediately hummed to life, the tick of his watch on Falk's wrist reminding him that the side trip had cost valuable time from his main mission.

When the elevator to the gym ground to a halt and the door opened, he saw Koski and Willie seated on the bench, chatting, even laughing. He marveled at their casual manner, as if they had always known each other, as if their world was not hours from potential destruction.

Willie seemed particularly at ease. When Koski abandoned her sometimes hard-shelled exterior, she had that effect on others.

"You mean that you, yourself, have actually crashed your own computers?" Koski was asking. She shot Falk a glance as he advanced, and he gave her a thumbs-up to signal he had successfully accomplished his side-mission.

Continuing the charade, she opened her arms in the empty gesture that told him she had searched the gym and found neither briefcase, explosive charge nor Bonecutter.

Willie wiggled her nose to readjust her large glasses, and then pushed a chubby finger at them just above the bridge of her nose. Her expression was luminous.

"Oh, yes, I crash them once or twice a year, trying new hardware or attempting to customize new programs to my needs." She smiled, and her hazel eyes brimmed with amusement. "My mom and dad say that I'm much more dangerous than any computer virus."

Falk flipped open his cell phone as he walked up to them.

"Hi, Joe," Willie said, as if they were old friends.

Falk nodded. "I'll call Beard," he told Koski, "and we'll get our little Brownie here to safety."

"Brownie!" Willie protested. "I got my wings a long time ago. I'm a second-year junior."

Falk was about to communicate with Beard when he glanced toward the window facing the bay and saw a helicopter heading straight toward the ship. He stumbled across the gymnasium, his vision focused on the silver aircraft that was ignoring the air space restriction around the Queen Mary. The sight of it, nosing directly at them, so mesmerized him that he was hardly aware that Koski and the girl had come up behind him.

The chopper dipped and swayed against a strong westerly wind and came in loud, low, and fast, three men clearly visible behind the glass bubble of its cockpit. In that moment, the din of its motor reached a deafening pitch and it seemed the machine would burst through the window where Falk stood riveted. The pilot made a last-minute lateral maneuver, sweeping the craft up and to the right, out of sight, the clatter of its rotors veering with it.

Koski articulated Falk's thought. "Who are those idiots?"

Chapter 26

Bonecutter was separated from the gymnasium by one deck and the second of the three funnels as he continued his search for the Girl Scout. He entered a room originally called The Cinema Box, the room that projected movies through the famous unicorn carving into the amidship ballroom. He thought how once a projectionist, ancestor of today's video jockeys, had spun his magic here with clumsy, clattering reels of film, unraveling moving pictures that were now being digitally restored for late-night television.

Crossing the room, he examined a bank of functioning television monitors along one wall. They were running on backup batteries. Like hazy photographs, they displayed interior and exterior images of the ship, in color, but with less than up-to-the-minute clarity. He eased into one of the chairs and surveyed the layout. Had he discovered a means of scanning the ship without leaving this room?

He'd spent enough time in projection rooms, watched enough movie and television dailies to have a working knowledge of a console. Slowly he moved a slide switch and the pictures dimmed. Returning the switch to its original position caused the images to come up to near-normal brightness. He turned a large, notched knob, and filled the room with the screech of feedback before he quickly reversed it. So now he knew where the master volume control was.

One by one, he gingerly tested the controls, ten remote cameras in all, each operated from the console where he sat. He was euphoric. If he could observe large portions of the ship from this closed-circuit television system, then sooner or later, the girl likely would show up on one of the monitors. And then he could get the little pain in the ass off the ship.

He was about to shift his glance from the clear, amidships shot that he supposed was being furnished by an exterior camera high in the superstructure, when he saw the silver helicopter come into view. He gasped. He knew that aircraft. Hadn't he and his wife Marissa once flown on one like it? At once he wondered where Marissa was, unable as we was to remember why she wasn't here with him. With the greatest effort, he forced himself to concentrate back on the console.

Clumsily at first, then quickly getting the feel, his fingers manipulated the camera control, tracking the helicopter. He followed the erratic, weaving machine, aware of the pilot's difficulty controlling it in the high wind as he repeatedly buzzed the ship.

Fingering the zoom lens control, Bonecutter was able to zero in on the picture, closer and closer, until he could see the familiar face of Lew Blasingdon peering out through the expanse of glass. Blue letters emblazoned on the chopper announced Daystar Studios. Then Bonecutter recognized the nervous pilot. And seated beside him, trying to maneuver a remote camera was Pete Powers.

"What the fuck?"

Bonecutter watched in disbelief as the aircraft yet again swept the area, swung into a tight turn as if to attempt another run, then vanished from one monitor and entered another. It made its way along the opposite side of the ship, the wind nearly tossing it when it cleared the bow. Trying to give Powers a pick-up shot, Bonecutter figured. He slammed his fist down on the console. "Crazy sons-a-bitches. You're gonna kill yourselves!"

Chapter 27

When they made their first swing down the side of the ship, Powers' camera did not find the one male and two female faces peering out of the gymnasium window. On the second pass, however, it caught them and might have preserved their surprise for "Death of the Queen Mary" and posterity.

"Wait!" Powers shouted when his camera's unblinking eye saw a blur of the trio behind the window.

"Wait?" Hanson screeched. "Wait? What the hell are you talking about?" He was fighting an updraft that had caught them when he tried to nudge closer to the side of the ship.

While Powers shouted what he'd seen to Blasingdon, Hansen ignored them, and, skillfully avoiding cables and fore-rigging, swooped back over the three majestic smokestacks, and down the weather side of the liner.

Suddenly the cockpit was filled with harsh static, and a voice barely loud enough to overpower it announced, "This is Army Patrol, Skymaster three. You are violating restricted air space. Climb to two thousand feet immediately and identify."

The three men whipped their heads to the right as—WHAAH— the Skymaster helicopter burst into their vision then thundered by.

"Holy shit!" Hansen said. "The Army." The chopper hadn't shown up on his instrument screen. "It must have come up straight from the pier. It has armed waist gunners. After two tours in Nam and one in the Gulf, I'm not going to be shot down in California by my own countrymen."

"Powers," Blasingdon barked as if he had not heard the Skymaster's order, "be sure you get a good shot of those bozos when that chopper comes by again. They're our tax dollars at work, trying to prevent three working stiffs from doing their job."

Pete couldn't believe what he was hearing from Blasingdon, but there was no time to consider. The military was calling the shots; the plot had just significantly thickened.

"The Army thinks we're terrorists, Hansen!" Pete shouted over his shoulder. "Get us the fuck outta here! NOW!"

But Blasingdon was poking the pilot, probably having seen the twitch that said Hansen was about to obey Pete's order.

"Hansen," the CEO said, "don't let these assholes scare you. The military's involvement only means that Bonecutter is now writing the most important story of his life." He leaned closer. "There's a twenty-thousand-dollar bonus, payable in cash on our return to the studio, if you ignore that restricted horseshit a few minutes longer and let Powers get a little more footage. What do you say?"

Hansen was silent as he fought the stick for control against the winds buffeting the craft. Pete could sense the pilot considering Blasingdon's proposition, calculating how risky one more pass might be. They could insist that their radio was out, that they didn't hear and were not aware of the order. Hansen could use the money; he had a wife and kids.

"What the fuck are you doing, Hansen?" Pete shouted. "You're not going to let the prospect of twenty thou' and that ready-when-you-are-C.B. routine make you do something we'll all regret, are you?"

Powers knew that money could cloud a man's thinking, make him lose sight of the difference between need and greed. "Look, I want outta' here right now! You'd better…"

He didn't get a chance to finish, to warn the distracted pilot that the mere act of considering might cause him to misjudge the ferocity of air turbulence that waited for a chance to thrash them. Hansen hesitated one second too long.

The small craft fluttered as a violent gust of wind rocked across its airframe.

Pete's camera fell to his lap. His fingers were a vise on the hand supports as he felt the helicopter writhe to one side, his main concern no longer the camera's eye. Behind him, Blasingdon made a wheezing sound.

Too late, the reflexes rooted in the grooves of his mind that impelled Hansen to try a corrective maneuver cut in. The engine revved as he asked it for power, but the cockpit bounced out of kilter, its weight shifted, and the chopper attempted to lift away, but instead stuttered and froze.

Chapter 28

What happened next tingled Bonecutter's nervous system array. He felt as if he was there, in the cockpit with his friend and the other two men rather than simply viewing them on the monitor in the old projection room. It felt as if his body was there, suspended along with them as the chopper hung in mid-air for that eternal second. He saw the aircraft dip and do a crazy quarter-turn. Like a swimming fish, it swayed from side to side until the motion grew as violent as a fighting marlin thrashing its tail. Then the tip of the tail rotor assembly made a kiss of contact with the mainmast cable of the Queen Mary.

Careening out of control, the aircraft narrowly missed the upper decks, dropped and slid down the steel side of the ship, leaving a streak of blazing gasoline along the hull. The chopper erupted into a dazzling ball of orange light as its fuel tank exploded an instant before it met water. Flames and chunky metal shot from the aircraft. What little remained of it and its occupants sizzled into the bay.

Bonecutter could remember the scene in split-second images.

Pete Powers' lips moved silently, then opened wide in a silent scream. Blasingdon clawed for support, desperate for some alteration of fate. Hansen's fiercely straining grip on the throttle was still trying to make right what would be forever wrong.

Emotion paralyzed Bonecutter. He was shocked, sickened, sad and angry, though surprise was the overriding sensation. Surprise that, at this terminal point in his life, he could still experience other emotions.

Bonecutter's nature was to mourn life's conclusions as the death of dreams. He hardly knew the doomed pilot, but the man must have had hopes and aspirations. Blasingdon, certainly, had his. In fact, his were grandiose, probably too much so and responsible for the deaths of all three men's dreams.

Pete Powers. There was a dreamer, and not only for himself. He had a wife and six kids. And now Pete's dreams for his family and theirs for him were dead.

This last realization draped itself heavily over Bonecutter, and his resolve to die heightened. There were no fantasies that would die with him. And now, more than ever, no one's dreams were contingent upon him. He laughed a little twisted laugh. On one monitor he noticed the debris from the helicopter, bobbing on the water's surface amid a slick of black oil.

He tried to swallow the lump that was constricting his throat. Pete Powers' friendship was Bonecutter's last worthy connection to the world and tonight Pete was already asleep in the sea.

Chapter 29

Someone thrust a hand mike at Marshak's face.

"It's being reported that the Army shot down the civilian helicopter in which three people died. Is that true, Captain?"

It's about to be reported that Captain Marshak delivered a neat, sound karate chop to the side of a reporter's head, Marshak silently said. It bothered him enough that the chopper had crashed, and that Powers, the gutsy guy he now wished he had granted access to the ship, was dead, along with two others.

But now the media hyenas had started doing what they did best, and what Marshak felt was ruining this country: making the news fit their own definition of the public's thirst. Pushing it, squeezing it, bearing down upon it, until fresh news—their interpretation, that is—was born.

He shoved the phallic-looking instrument away from his mouth and growled, "That is not true."

He had left his office minutes earlier to make another of his frequent visits to the john, and been accosted on his return by a dozen members of the press. Somehow they'd gained entrance to the hallway of the command post, where they now surrounded him, pushing in tight, screeching like a cave of startled bats.

Where was security? *If one of these, just one of them gets on that ship...*he dodged another microphone. Damn! Somebody's ass was going to burn for this.

"But, Captain, what's a military aircraft doing patrolling the air space above the Queen Mary?" a young woman, a clone of all the others, persisted. "Do you still maintain that this is not a terrorist attack?"

"This is not a terrorist attack!"

"Have you located the bomber yet?"

Marshak brushed them aside. "No comment." But, like water in a muddy stream, others immediately displaced them.

Someone else's voice managed to isolate itself from the rest. "Will you be holding a media briefing soon?"

Marshak saw a handful of his officers coming to the rescue from the other end of the hall, but he couldn't wait. Elbowing the overzealous men and women from his path, he ground his size fourteens down on toes and propelled his weight against the sea of bodies.

As he reached the door to his office, he turned and, in as controlled a voice as possible, said, "This is a domestic bomb threat, not a world war. When the Chief thinks a media briefing is appropriate, we'll let you know. In the meantime, I suggest you all go home and take cold showers."

Marshak was not a media darling.

Slamming the door behind him, he swore, picked up the phone, and punched at a number. "Get Sergeant Wilson in here, now!" Somebody's ass was going to burn for this.

To be honest, Marshak knew what his problem with reporters was: patience. He had none. He never saw fit to cultivate it. Not with the fourth estate or anyone else. Giving in to the basic premise of patience went against his grain.

Oh, he knew about patience being rewarded with delayed gratification, about taking one day at a time. All of those were, in his view, pseudo-psychologies. When you got to the bottom line, patience was not a virtue, but a subtle, insidious disease, an atom-sized form of desperation masquerading as high-mindedness. He'd have nothing to do with it.

He lit a cigarette and took one long drag, then placed it in the small, shallow, aluminum foil faux ashtray he'd lifted from the restroom. He began rummaging through the clutter on his desk for the one thing that gnawed at the back of his mind now, the unopened envelope Pete Powers had left for him. Before he could locate it, his intercom sounded, and he was summoned to Beard's office to "go over what we have."

A young Army lieutenant sitting beside Beard's desk rose as the colonel introduced him.

"Captain Marshak, this is Lieutenant Smothers, one of our top-notch PR men." Marshak shook Smothers' hand and took a seat. Beard sighed almost imperceptibly. "Captain, how did the reporters get into Com-Cen?"

Ordinarily, Marshak was cool on the defensive, but it was not his favorite position, especially in front of a green lieutenant. "I was about to investigate that when you invited me in here, Colonel. Sergeant Wilson should be on his way to my office as we speak."

"We agreed to use your personnel, for the most part, in order to attempt to maintain a low profile. However, maybe it's time to call in…"

Marshak stopped him with a palm up. That was all they needed, more bodies to keep track of. "Since the chopper accident, and our subsequent need to investigate it, nothing is low profile anymore, Colonel. We've got boats out in the bay collecting debris and pieces of dead bodies and the NTSB people are flying in. There's no way this situation will ever be low profile again." He paused and straightened. "However, insofar as my responsibility extends, everything is now under control."

Beard pointed to the small portable TV set on his desk. "You were on the news a few minutes ago, Captain. Live and in living color."

Marshak chose to find no racist intent in the last part of that remark, a prerogative he thought underused.

"Pond scum," he said, feeling inclined to air views on the media he generally kept to himself. "Generally," he went on, "people all over the world are getting fed up with the media's intrusive tactics, particularly those of the broadcast media." He shook his head. "At least some of the public is finally starting to put faces on the term 'the media', which the journalistic community uses as if speaking of someone other than itself."

He stopped, suddenly doubting that Beard and the green lieutenant were on the same page as he on this subject.

Beard set his pencil down and leaned back in the chair, his usual clipped, nasal voice taking on a rambling, philosophical tone.

"We once read about a small bird down in Africa that spends its entire life perched on the back of a rhino or hippo. We don't recall which. You would think this would drive the animal mad, but he agreeably abides the pest. As we understand it, the bird survives by pecking away at minuscule creatures, vermin which, in turn, feed on the larger animal's flesh. The bird is also sensitive to its host's predators, apparently, and squawks to warn him of danger."

Marshak, himself a fan of the Discovery, National Geographic channels and Wild Kingdom reruns, sat quietly, containing his impatience. Beard went on, turning at times to include Smothers for affirmation, which the lieutenant provided with short, brisk nods of his head.

"We see the media as the bird," Beard said, "and the rest of the population as the rhino. Or hippo, whichever. They drive us mad sometimes with their pecking and scratching and squawking, but they have their usefulness; they, too, are a part of the big picture, of the system, and maybe we should be more understanding of them."

Marshak, rankled, listened to what he considered to be an outdated, condescending lecture, then answered. "Nevertheless, when the bird takes a dump on his back, the rhino—or hippo—doesn't have to like it or can't be wholly blamed if, after an endless number of pecks and dumps that begin to fester into a sore, he decides to eat the little bastard."

Smothers looked as if all of this went over his head, while Beard cleared his throat and sank his gaze into the papers on his desk. "The helicopter crash was dreadful. Highly unfortunate. And we will downplay it as much as possible."

The compassionate Marlin Perkins demeanor was gone, Marshak noted. We're all business, now. Beard gestured toward his young companion.

"We've assigned Lieutenant Smothers to handle all future news releases. We, Captain—you and I—will hereafter be *persona non grata* as news sources. Smothers will feed the media the positive stuff: The ship was evacuated without incident. Thanks to the efficiency of the Long Beach Police Department and the security skills of the Queen Mary's personnel, a potential disaster infinitely worse than the helicopter accident will be averted. We have been in communication with Bonecutter and are making every effort to negotiate with him. That sort of thing."

He turned to Smothers for confirmation and was rewarded with, "Understood, sir."

Beard turned back to Marshak. "Did you have anything further to suggest to Lieutenant Smothers, Captain?"

He had a suggestion, all right, but decided it would better keep. He did, however, need some questions answered.

"Since the press has decided to feed the rumor that the Army shot down the studio chopper, it might help clear things up if we told them exactly what the Army is doing here, some hint as to why the military gives a damn about this whole affair."

"Smothers has orders on that." Beard turned to the young man again. "Correct?"

Smothers nodded, stating, "Correct, sir," then directed the rest of his reply to Marshak. "A certain amount of federal involvement is standard procedure where bombs are concerned, especially since 9/11. Also, several foreign countries have recently been in negotiations with the Queen Mary's owners regarding possible acquisition of the ship.

"Because Mr. Bonecutter's threat could put such possible acquisition in jeopardy, these countries have requested that the military oversee this situation, thereby precipitating the army's presence. Their role, however, is merely an advisory one at this juncture."

He stopped and it was his turn to look to Beard for confirmation that he had correctly presented the rhetoric.

Before Marshak could blow holes in their spin, Beard thanked the lieutenant and dismissed him.

"Now then, Captain," Beard said calmly, leaning back in his chair, "recapping the situation on the ship: We have Bonecutter, two FBI operatives, Falk and Koski, and the Girl Scout, right?"

"Right."

Beard leaned forward again and reached into an In basket on the desk. "In point of fact, there will be one more person arriving this afternoon who, if this situation is not resolved, we'll be obliged to maneuver onto the ship."

"What?" Marshak sprang from his chair. "Man, I don't fucking believe it!"

Beard didn't seem that surprised at the protest, as if he shared Marshak's opinion, but he simply went on. "An agent with British Intelligence is already here in the States, I understand. You see, the Brits have a stake in this."

"It's beginning to look like everybody and his fucking brother has a stake in it, but that doesn't mean…"

"Captain," Beard said, stopping him with a palm up. He slipped the note into the Out basket with its predecessors and eased back again. "What I'm about to tell you can never leave this office. Understood?"

Marshak sighed quizzically and sat down. "Understood."

Beard picked up and fingered his pencil. "I guess it's time I filled you in as to what's really happening on board the Queen Mary."

Chapter 30

When the aircraft exploded in full view of Falk and his two companions, Koski's protective instinct caused her to grab Willie and fiercely bury the girl's face against her chest, away from the sight, but not before the girl saw much of the disaster. Several minutes of intense consolation followed. She masterfully handled a reassuring talk with Willie.

What signaled the initial stages of disaster syndrome—dazed disbelief, distraction, numbness—was already progressing naturally as Koski soothingly repeated the girl's feelings about what she had witnessed. If indeed any of them lived to get off the damned ship, Falk would recommend that both Willie and Koski talk to a therapist to assimilate the whole shipboard experience. But now, he had to go.

"Koski, call Beard and tell him that we've got Willie and that she's safe, and that you and she are leaving the ship." He adjusted his stance determinedly, setting his feet firmly apart. "I've got to find Bonecutter." He turned and started to move away as if his mere pronouncement had settled the matter.

"Hey!"

Koski was on her feet, in his face. She glowered, then turned back to Willie, whose face mirrored her disappointment at what Falk had planned for her. "Stay there a minute, sweetheart. I need to talk to Falk for a second."

She took his arm and led him back toward the windows, where fire and rescue crews were at work with the wreckage in the bay.

"I'm not leaving this ship, Joe," she whispered firmly.

Falk looked into her resolute eyes, faceted with fiery light.

"Koski, there isn't time to talk about this." He glanced at his watch. "It's almost one o'clock. I don't have…"

"All the more reason why you need an extra pair of eyes and hands, and you know it."

He glared. "Okay, then, stay on the ship. Both of you. But you're on your own. She's your responsibility now. *You* can have yet another pair of eyes. I don't need or want them."

He knew as soon as he said it that it was insane. It would be worse than criminal to deliberately leave the two alone.

Koski turned toward the bench, and paled, but Falk did not need to follow her gaze to know why. He knew, with the sickening intensity of a rock hitting bottom in his belly, that Willie was gone.

Chapter 31

Marshak still didn't like the idea. There was a briefcase on board with chemical properties so lethal that the very disclosure of its existence would cause irreparable damage to the United States and Great Britain. It didn't change the fact that Marshak was against putting another person on the ship. And what about Beard's two so-called 'operatives', agents Falk and Koski? What were those two hotshots doing?

He headed for the outer office. His day was complicated enough. Minutes before the helicopter crash, as Miller and

Nakamura, Com-Cen's communications officers, manned the bank of electronic equipment, Miller had turned to Marshak, his cheeks red with sudden excitement.

"Captain, look. I think…yes. We've got visual back."

Beside him, Nakamura hollered, "Yahoo!"

Marshak turned to the equipment that had been little more than static since the generator had shut down and power and phones failed in select areas of the ship.

"The backup generator has finally kicked in?"

"Affirmative, sir. We're visually hooked into the entire ship again." His elation dimmed as he continued to fiddle with knobs and switches. "However, audio's still out. The PA and phones, too; I don't understand it. The phones should be operational. It doesn't make sense."

Nakamura, nevertheless, was elated. "At least we've got a picture."

Marshak had leaned between the two, so close he could feel the blink of Nakamura's eyelids.

"Never mind pumping your 'nads, Nakamura. Just get the fucking phones working." He straightened. This was a lucky break. Or was it luck? "Who could have restarted the backup generator?" he wondered aloud.

From behind his right shoulder came the level, nasal reply that signaled Beard's entrance. "One of our operatives, of course."

Marshak had no comment. He had to abide the little pests who lived on his back and pecked away at him. Now the phone rang.

Miller picked it up.

"Yes, he's right here," he said and handed the phone to Marshak. "Security at the main gate," he explained.

"What now?" Marshak growled.

"I've got a Mr. and Mrs. George Dill here, Captain," the guard reported. "They say you told them to come."

Marshak swore. "No, I did not tell them to come."

What he had said to Willie Dill's parents, in fact, was that they should stay by the phone at home, and he would contact them as soon as he had any word about their daughter. He sighed. He, himself, was a parent to five grown children. Were it his kid, he wouldn't have stayed at home; he'd want to be as close to the scene as possible.

"Send them to the office adjoining mine," he grumbled. "I'll talk to them there."

As he walked toward the office, he looked out of the window and glimpsed the Dills, hurrying toward his mobile command post. In their forties, they looked like most mothers and fathers looked when their child was in jeopardy: heartsick, bewildered, filled with foreboding. On an ascending scale of one to ten concerning what Marshak hated most about his job, dealing with distraught parents was right up there.

Chapter 32

In the subsequent hours, Falk and Koski threw every skill they possessed into their search for Bonecutter, his bombs, the briefcase and Willie. Leaving the gym, they first scoured the amidships portion of the vessel, ever cautious, always hoping that they would spot the saboteur before he spotted them.

Falk sweated every corner he turned. Like a triple black diamond ski slope, unmarked obstacles were everywhere. But Falk's mind was focused; he was in his groove, heading forward in optimal drive.

In late afternoon, they found themselves in a galley and

reluctantly gave in to hunger, halting long enough to devour slices of turkey from the refrigerator and some fruit.

Falk was tormented by the fact that they had let Willie get away, a misstep both he and Koski would regret all of their lives if they did not find her.

Chapter 33

"It's him!" Miller's voice cracked, as if articulation of what he saw on the monitor would make it vanish. "It's him," he repeated, softer. "We've got him."

Marshak and Beard rushed to the console.

Pointing to the monitor, Miller adjusted the image and whispered, "I discovered a feed that must have been deactivated at the time of the evacuation, but I've got it back online now. It's a hidden security camera in the projection room of the old theater. And there he is."

The four men stared at the figure seated before the monitors in the ship's projection room.

"It's Bonecutter, all right." Marshak, too, found himself whispering.

It seemed appropriate that the camera allowed them to secretly observe the man. Marshak whipped a large, white handkerchief from his hip pocket and wiped it across his forehead. Bonecutter looked to him to be in a trance, as if he'd been sitting in that exact position for some time.

Beard put a hand on Nakamura's shoulder. "Good work."

On the screen, the man's head nodded forward and then came up and back, until his distorted face paralleled the ceiling. His eyes were feral and his jaw slack and distended; his mouth cavernous.

It hit Marshak that the poor bastard had probably watched his buddies die in the chopper crash hours before. Maybe he was only now having a reaction to that horrifying event. Or maybe it was something else, something no one could guess, that tortured the man.

Miller's little finger automatically whirled up the audio knob, forgetting it was out of commission. Had they been able to hear the sound, it would have hurtled through the command post, the force of its report strong enough to make them shudder.

Begun like a growl, the sound rose to a piercing, orgiastic howl that held interminably. Then, in cracked and with collapsing notes, it fell to a pitiful whimper, then to a second of utter silence. Then Bonecutter straightened and, in a voice unheard by anyone else, cooed, "Flea, flea, let me be, bloodthirsty busy, busy bee flea."

Bonecutter jumped up and stumbled from the room.

Chapter 34

There was something in the way the man calmly strode into the command post that instantly decided Marshak. He did not like Simon Drummond. In their little chat earlier about what was behind British Intelligence involvement with the Queen Mary, Beard had told Marshak more than he cared to know about the man from MI6.

"He was hand-picked by the Prime Minister himself," Beard said. "Not only because he happened to be in the States, but because his experience and credentials are impeccable."

Marshak nodded. He'd not lived under a rock for the past fifty years. He had seen the James Bond movies, read some novels in the genre, and he knew all about The Firm.

"Drummond joined British Intelligence after taking his degree at St. John's," Beard went on, "and was called in on the terrorist scare with the QE2. Apparently, he became familiar with every oceangoing vessel exceeding one thousand tons, which includes the Queen Mary, of course, speculating that any one of such ships might one day be the target of a terrorist attack. Such conscientious investigation included keeping abreast of configuration changes in this ship since she was acquired by your city, Captain."

It wasn't any shortage of qualifications that decided Marshak against Drummond. He simply saw him as a wimp. Over a traditional tattersall patterned hunting shirt, he wore a dark wool jacket, and his dark trousers looked like sixteen-wale cords. He was close to sixty years old, Marshak judged, and about five nine, with a well maintained build. His complexion was florid, and he had the sort of face that aged obligingly, gentle folds developing around his mouth where Marshak wore harsh parentheses.

Oh, he knew the type. Drummond retained a look of old English traditionalism, a kind of tweedy uniformity that went out in the '60s and projected a sense of extraordinary self-control. He would be reserved, overly analytical, slow to react...and utterly useless. Besides that, the exceptional thickness of his hair, the color of a walnut shell streaked with gray, caused Marshak to conclude that this tidy Yorkshire-type would only add to the curse of his day.

In the outer office, Marshak watched Drummond as he studied the blowups of Bonecutter, Willie Dill, Falk and Koski on the wall, the principal players in this drama. Drummond blinked once, his intelligent blue-green eyes like shutters, opening, exposing only as long as necessary to permanently record, and closing.

"I'll need to scan what you have on these individuals," he said as he headed for Beard's office. Behind him, Beard tried to fill him in on the few facts he had, including the news that they now knew that Bonecutter had been in the projection room.

"Then the FBI agents have not yet found the briefcase or explosives, Colonel?"

"No, not yet, but…"

"And they have not found the missing girl?"

"Well, no, but…"

"And do you know where the two agents are at present?"

"Not exactly. Communication is spotty from certain confines of the ship."

Walking beside Beard, Marshak muttered almost inaudibly something about how unpleasant it was, how difficult to have patience, when little insects on your back pecked away at you.

As they entered the office, Beard changed the subject by outlining what Marshak thought was an inane, elaborate plan to get Drummond on board by deploying a team of Navy SEALS he had summoned.

Marshak wondered if the Brit would see through what he himself saw as a blatant delaying tactic. Like Marshak, Beard apparently wasn't comfortable with intelligence personnel from another country—friendly or unfriendly—going on board. But, unlike Marshak, it was possible that concern for the man's safety was only part of Beard's reservation. What if the man did accidentally stumble onto Bonecutter? Or worse, found him, and the man would not relinquish control of the briefcase. A Brit would be responsible for defusing the situation, taking charge, credit and stealing Beard's thunder.

Well, Marshak decided, there was little chance of such scenarios as these playing out. Drummond would not find anything. The man would get his tidy clothes dirtied if he tried to do much digging around on the old ship.

Thumbing through the bios Beard passed to him, Drummond

abruptly dismissed Beard's SEAL plan. "I'm afraid that won't do, Colonel."

Marshak, seated in a chair beside him, was silent, but he allowed that he had expected a more pussyfoot approach on the Englishman's part.

Beard, apparently unsure he heard Drummond correctly, said stiffly, "Excuse me?"

Drummond leaned forward. "With all due respect, Colonel, what you suggest would take, I estimate, at least a couple of hours to accomplish. I don't have time for such bloody shenanigans."

Marshak looked at Drummond. He had delivered that last line like Maggie Thatcher saying to the first President Bush before Desert Storm, "Economic sanctions are all well and good, Mr. President, but when do we bomb the bastards?" Marshak kept a stone face, however, not ready yet to declare his position, though he enjoyed seeing Beard redden.

"But I have my orders," Beard blustered. "And I'm afraid I must insist."

"No, Colonel." Drummond stood. "I must insist." His eyes turned cold and stormy. "Several hours ago I received a phone call from the Prime Minister. I was at an important counter-intelligence conference in San Francisco but was obliged to abandon it and fly here. I have only a few hours in which to perform the almost impossible task of finding and neutralizing a small briefcase of chemicals on a very large ship.

"I was told that you and the local authorities would have the potential bomber and his bombs in custody and have the situation in hand, but nothing seems to be in hand."

Beard opened his mouth but didn't get a word out.

"I understand," Drummond went on, "that the ordnance is set for detonation at eight o'clock tonight." He turned and marched to the door. "Frankly, I don't give a tinker's damn what your orders are, Colonel. Mine are to do whatever is necessary to accomplish what I have come here to do."

Beaming his icy blue-green eyes on Marshak, he said, "Captain, may I have a moment of your time?" and left the office.

All right!

Marshak was out of his chair and out the door before Beard had a chance to close his mouth. Marshak mentally swallowed every derogatory thing he'd ever said or thought about misplaced British reserve. Here was a Limy with balls who just might get something done.

In his office, he offered Drummond a seat, but the man declined.

Drummond reached into an inner jacket pocket. "I have something of yours."

An odd, uneasy feeling crept through Marshak as Drummond produced a large, familiar manila envelope. Its front bore Marshak's scribbled name, and he recognized it immediately as the envelope for which he had earlier turned his office inside out.

Drummond handed it to him, explaining that he found it in the restroom he had visited when he arrived. "It was sandwiched between two strikingly pictorial magazines," Drummond said matter-of-factly.

Two burning emotions flooded Marshak, a sense of relief so profound that his entire upper torso inflated and deflated with it; but also underlying panic. He had an intuitive feeling about Pete Powers' fucking envelope, but he had not paid it proper attention early on. One should listen to the whisperings of intuition. He must have inadvertently scooped up the envelope with his magazines when he made an earlier trip to the can. Damn stupid unprofessional oversight.

"Are you aware of its contents, Captain?" Drummond asked.

Marshak didn't answer, but went to his desk and eased into the chair. Taking the envelope in his hands, he pulled the two attached metal fingers up and flipped open the flap.

Stuck to a large, folded, white paper was a small, yellow note imprinted "From the Desk of Pete Powers." Scribbled on it were a few sentences:

Captain Marshak: Sorry you couldn't see your way clear to let Norm and me on the ship to talk to Jack. I hope you don't regret that decision. In any case, here are two items I found in Jack's apartment this morning. I hope they will be helpful in some way. Have a nice day.

Powers' signature on the bottom was a distinctive scrawl beside a hastily drawn smiley face.

"Shit!"

Marshak's stomach tightened as he remembered the chopper crash. Man, he was not having a nice day. Not at all.

He removed the stick-on note from the large sheet, and as he unfolded it, his day got even worse. It was a cross-section of the Queen Mary. Spasms in his gut told Marshak that the circles in red ink were the locations of Bonecutter's bombs, pinpointed so clearly that all but a blind man, or someone who was letting the little pests on his back get to him, could have seen. He might have had bombs and bomber in custody hours ago.

He was almost afraid to look up at Drummond, but he had to know. "Has anyone else seen this?" It would be the end of his career if the Chief or Beard knew of this negligence. He had reamed Sergeant Wilson a new asshole just for allowing reporters into Com-Cen earlier today.

"No." The blink of Drummond's eyes as he replied was compassionate, but there was steel behind it.

Marshak's mind raced ahead, trying to imagine a way to salvage this situation, but he could think of none, however, he regarded the fact that the Brit had not revealed the knowledge to anyone else as another plus for the man. He had a hunch, however, that he was about to pay the price of that conspiracy.

He glanced again at the note. "Powers indicates two items."

Drummond dipped into his jacket again. "Yes, this was also in there." He offered a slightly bent, sepia photograph.

Marshak glanced at, then turned the picture over and read the notation there: Angus Bonecutter, 1934. He flipped it back to the obverse and studied it. There seemed nothing extraordinary or unique about the photograph.

Jack Bonecutter's ancestor stood on a partially constructed section of the ship's wheelhouse, obstructing most of the view of the chart room behind him. The floor of the small room in back appeared to be in mid-construction, since only the upper torso of a worker in the background was visible, the lower part of his body disappearing beneath the floorboards.

Drummond reached and retracted the picture. "I need this, Captain. It's trying to tell me something."

It flashed across Marshak's ever-expanding mind that hunches frequently played a part in the everyday lives of most individuals he met in his line of work. Oh, they would deny it, probably. They would insist that they dealt only in cold, hard facts, and that unreliable, unscientific intuition was the softer gender's domain. And yet, daily, they gambled their lives on it.

"Captain Marshak, you must help me get on that ship, straight away."

Marshak wasn't sure he had heard correctly. "Me. But, I can't get you on."

"Yes, you can." Drummond leaned forward, spreading his hands on the desk.

"But how can I?"

"Just do as I say." He turned and started for the door.

They hurried from his office and down the hall, where they stopped briefly at the photocopy machine to duplicate Bonecutter's cross-section of the ship. Drummond described his plan as it seemed to spontaneously form in his mind.

Marshak couldn't believe he heard right, and that he was actually abetting the man, but he waved away a couple of police officers that came up to them. Too late he saw his years of service, the pension and 401K going down the drain.

"Drummond, you can't do this," he whispered.

Holding a wide black marker he had lifted from Marshak's desk, Drummond flipped over a two foot by two foot desk calendar and printed something on the back in huge, heavy letters.

"Do what?" he asked.

Marshak's mouth spewed out a spray of spittle as he let go an exasperated exhalation. "You can't just walk onto the ship like this."

Drummond finished printing and handed Marshak the pen. "Why not?"

As they walked across the dock toward the escalator leading to the main deck, one of LBPD's finest made a move to challenge them, but then pressed his hand-held radio to his mouth. Marshak cringed. Checking with Beard, no doubt. Man, at a time like this, one could count his friends on one middle finger.

"Because," Marshak whispered through a false, toothy grin as another policeman headed toward them, "our loony friend with the bombs has threatened to press the big button if anyone goes on board or tries to stop him. And he already knows about the kid."

"Then he should hardly care if I go on board." Drummond seemed calm, confident, insufferably G-man. "I'm not planning on trying to stop him. He's not my responsibility nor my concern."

"But he doesn't know that," Marshak insisted.

Drummond held up the sign he had crudely printed: I AM A SCIENTIST SENT TO FIND VOLATILE CHEMICALS ON SHIP.

Marshak felt sweat trickling down his face, despite the fact that the wind was gusting and dark gray clouds streamed like phantoms across the cold sky. He whipped his rumpled handkerchief from his hip pocket and swiped it across his face.

"But that's just it, Drummond," he said. "According to Beard, these are not your ordinary, run-of-the-mill, HAZ-MAT volatile chemicals. And you have no idea where in the belly of this old battle-ax they're hidden. It would take days."

He continued to grin nervously as he spoke, unsure as to why he felt compelled to try to impart a sense of normalcy to the insanity that was unfolding. And it struck him that it was just that: insanity.

"Drummond, it's too dangerous. I can't let you."

"Just keep walking." Drummond, too, smiled unnaturally at the policeman who neared.

Marshak waved away the officer with rising irritation.

"Look, Drummond, I can't let you put others in jeopardy just because you think you're some kind of hotshot."

Drummond stopped abruptly and turned on him with only slightly controlled ferocity. "You owe me, Captain. Big time," he stated, and resumed his brisk stride.

"Shit," Marshak hissed through gritted teeth. "I'm a dead man."

He sighed resignedly. But no matter; they were at the Up escalator now, which was still, having been deliberately disengaged earlier. There was no going back.

"This is Agent Simon Drummond," Marshak told the police officer and the quizzical security guard stationed at the base of the unmoving stairs. "He's an expert in various systems on the ship. I'm clearing him to go aboard."

The guard frowned. "But, sir..."

Marshak turned to Drummond, talking fast. "Don't forget, Bonecutter will pick you up on a monitor when you reach the gangplank at the top of the escalator. He may not be able to read that sign of yours, but if he is in fact watching the monitors, it may make him curious enough to hold off on any snap judgment."

The agent nodded impatiently. "Right."

"And you'll be sure to give Agent Falk the photocopy of the cross-section so that he can begin to look for the bombs."

"Yes, yes." Drummond patted the breast pocket of his jacket. "It's here." He turned and marched up the escalator to the gangplank.

Turning to the still protesting guard, Marshak grumbled, "Officer, it's a done thing. I take full responsibility." Turning back to where Drummond stood, he watched.

Holding up the handmade sign, the Brit stood still for a beat, then turned slowly, to be certain Bonecutter, if he did observe this bizarre proceeding, could have several views from which to read it. Then Drummond tossed the scribbled sign over his shoulder. It zigzagged down to the dock, coming to rest at Marshak's feet just as Drummond stepped off the gangplank onto the deck.

After a moment of benediction to the man's courage, Marshak

bent, picked up the sign, folded it, and stuck it into his jacket pocket. Suddenly he was heatedly conscious of the media's eyes on him, their videophones and cameras and zoom lenses atop the vans behind the barricades, straining to see him. Beard's Lieutenant Smothers would have his hands full, fielding a new round of questions from the press people who saw Drummond board the ship. Better Smothers than Marshak.

A gust of wind whipped across his face and he realized that the it had abruptly risen, thrumming wildly through flags lining the rigging of the ship behind him. The sea had turned gray. Boiling swells began sucking at the pier.

Looking up, he noticed how dramatically the sky had changed from earlier in the day. At eight, maybe ten, thousand feet above sea level, a layer of stringy cirrus clouds had formed and streamed overhead. Over the next few hours, they were entirely replaced by dark, foreboding cumulonimbus clouds taller than the width of the horizon. An early darkness would fall soon. He said a silent prayer for those on the ship.

Approaching the command post, he wanted to call his wife, but decided the call would have to wait; two of Beard's elite crew were heading his way. Maybe once he produced the original cross-section that was in his hip pocket, Beard would be forgiving enough not to bring him up on charges of negligence. Maybe. He almost laughed out loud. Who the fuck did he think he was kidding?

By the time he got to Com-Cen, darkness engulfed the ship and a cold, driving rain begun.

Chapter 35

Quintero had received four commands from his patron in

Panama City. He planned to obey three.

"Si, Senor," he had replied when commanded to go to Isla Contadora to discover the hiding place of the magical briefcase, and kill the gringo once the secret place was known.

Unfortunately, he didn't learn the hiding place, but he had a plan to do so. At least the gringo who had stolen Quintero's smile was dead; that alone warmed Quintero.

"Si, Senor," he repeated when told to fly to California and to get on the big ship, no matter what measures that required, and to find the important briefcase.

El Pulpo, the octopus that curled into every eddy of every major civilization throughout the world, had many tentacles and controlled a jet plane that regularly flew legitimate businessmen associated with various Panamanian corporations from Latin America to North America and back. Quintero had availed himself of this expediency in the past and did so this day.

He left Panama City by ten in the morning, landing at Long Beach airport at six p.m. Pacific Standard Time. He drove a rental to Long Beach, arriving at the dock at six-forty. He had done what it took to get on the ship: Overpowering a security guard in the "B" parking lot, he donned the man's dark blue jacket and cap and stuffed the guard's body into a shed at a remote corner of the lot, then slit the guard's throat.

Quintero draped his own flight jacket over his arm and tucked his beret into a pocket. The area was dark enough between spaced light standards to allow the shadows to obscure his face. He slowly, casually ambled through the "A" lot and headed in the direction of the ship.

For several minutes he mingled among the maze of other security personnel and police officers on the dock, few of whom seemed familiar to one another.

It was then that the young woman positioned in the glare of one of the parking lot floodlights screeched for attention, yanked up her tight sweatshirt, and bared her breasts.

Quintero had chosen her quickly but carefully several minutes earlier. The coed with a USC shirt had initially refused Quintero when he humbly approached her in the outer parking lot, in which she and a female companion were sitting in a black Isuzu Trooper. Quintero did not attempt a smile. The resulting grimace would surely have spoiled his plans. His manner was unthreatening, even ingratiating, and he peeled off three twenties from a roll in his pocket.

"I am a reporter. Care to make a public statement?"

At first she ignored him, but he said, "I require only three harmless seconds of your time." He slid two more Andrew Jacksons and held them before her. At this she stopped and listened.

Quintero knew about American college students. He followed the news on television. He did not claim to understand it, but he knew that many young women in universities in America embroiled themselves in causes. Many demonstrated endlessly, passionately, against what they viewed as this or that injustice. Lately it had become the fashion to bare one's breasts in public, either to make a statement, to punctuate the *cause du jour*, or just to exhibit oneself.

When Quintero had scanned the crowd in the outer lot for exactly the right woman, he fixed on this loud redhead with a mischievous face. Small of frame, she nevertheless had the endowments Quintero required at the moment: large breasts that could be easily exposed because she obviously spurned bras. Two more bills later, a bargain was struck.

"Give me two minutes lead time," he had instructed the woman, then he surreptitiously disengaged the latch at the gate separating the front from the "B" parking lot and sauntered toward the ship, the security uniform jacket allowing him to blend unchallenged.

The student's perfectly timed screech caused all heads to turn in her direction as she ran through the gate into the nearer lot, faced the ship, and raised her shirt above her head.

Quintero saw the jaw of the guard closest to him slacken, then the man's mouth fall completely agape. *En boca cerrada no entra mosca*, silently quipped Quintero. A closed mouth catches no flies. Quintero had a sense of humor.

The girl's breasts were only visible for the three Mississippis for which Quintero had asked, which he thought she counted off in her head. Blanched beneath the fluorescent lights, her breasts were glorious, large round mounds that Quintero thought, to the touch, would resemble two silken sacs of mercury. She re-covered herself, turned, and raced back to the Isuzu, which leaped forward as her companion hit the gas, and they were gone.

Police and security personnel in the area probably looked at each other, raised their eyebrows and grinned. Some may have shaken their heads at what seemed a harmless college prank. An attempt at fifteen seconds of public notoriety. But Quintero did not see the aftermath of the redhead's expensive stunt. During the distraction, he swiftly slipped onto the staircase astern and darted down below to an old engine room.

"*Si, Senor*," Quintero again answered with instant accord when given the third command from el Patrón in Panama earlier today.

Two American agents on the ship must not be allowed to take possession of the briefcase, and must not live to identify Quintero, who could be traced to El Pulpo. One of the agents, he knew, was a woman. Quintero would have to find steel in his belly to do that deed.

"Finally, *compadre*," el Patrón had said, for Quintero was at this time still his friend, "you must come directly here to Panama City with the briefcase. Bring it directly to me. Remember, do not open the case. Only find it and bring it straight to me. *Entiendes?*"

Quintero needed the passing of six heartbeats to solidify his resolve.

El patron did not like waiting. "*Entiendes?*" he repeated.

"*Si, Senor*," Quintero finally said, but his true intention was not embodied in his reply to this last command.

In 1967, he had tried to snatch the case from the gringo on the ship. Back then, Quintero had not known, had not cared to know, what was in it. He was young and full of the fire of adventure and blindly obedient to his employer. The details of why he must do a thing were beyond the purview of his curiosity; he must simply do it.

Intervening years, however, had rendered Quintero more cautious, hence more curious, and had honed his resources. El Patrón and the two American agents were not the only persons who knew the potential of the magic weapon inside the case. Quintero, too, knew.

For more than twenty-five years Quintero had been an exemplary operative, doing as he was told, devotedly, and well. But good workers eventually come to understand the ways of those who employed them. An informed worker knew that one day he would be asked to do what he alone could do. This was the point after which he was expendable. Quintero knew that once he made his delivery in Panama City, death would await at the first corner.

He smiled inwardly. El Pulpo was unaware that there was great cause to mistrust its wandering tentacle. Quintero would not go directly from the ship to Panama for two reasons: One, he must go to confession, to the first Catholic Church he could find. Two, he knew enough about the briefcase's secret to have an idea as its international market value. Quintero had decided to become a momentary capitalist. Then he would retire.

In the engine room now, he shed the guard's jacket and cap and slipped back into his comfortable flight jacket with its warm aroma of lamb, and donned his dark beret. He decided on a simple plan to locate the case. He would follow the American male agent, who would be the most persistent searcher.

He had the man's photograph in his pocket, along with the woman's, given to him by el Patrón at the Panama airport. He would let the government man do the work and then pluck the prize from beneath his nose; that was how Quintero would play the game.

First, however, he must find the man. Nothing and no one would stand in his way.

Chapter 36

Marshak stood beside Beard and silently cursed. For all the so-called operatives, the electronic miracles and layers of visual communication at their disposal, they were getting nowhere. Sure, he and Beard looked over the shoulders of Miller and Nakamura at screens, some of which revealed the ship projection room's bank of monitors which, in turn, were trained on various areas of the ship.

Trickle-down technology. It was amazing. But where did it get them? Bonecutter, the bombs, the little girl, and the briefcase were no closer to their grasp. And, despite Beard's earlier command to

Miller and Nakamura to "Get me shipboard audio if you have to rig together two cans and a piece of string," the phones and PA system had remained silent all day.

Bob, the chief engineer, relinquished all responsibility for the audio failures, offering the opinion that this outage was not directly connected to the generators; that something must have gone awry in the high-tech area of electrical operations. Miller and Nakamura concurred, but as yet offered no solution.

The monitors they watched had picked up Bonecutter several times at various places on the ship, and Beard immediately called Falk to report the sightings. However, each time Falk and Koski reached the designated location, Bonecutter had left the area, continuing to run, helter-skelter, through the vessel, still searching for the girl.

His movements became more frantic and erratic with each passing hour. Now he had returned to the projection room. When Beard reported this to Falk and Koski, who were in the process of searching the forward sections, they started backtracking on the run.

"What's that?" Miller asked. Something had moved on one of the projection room monitors.

Marshak had seen it, a blur of movement at the bottom of the screen.

Bonecutter, too, had seen it. He leaned forward, frantically adjusting the camera angle on one of his remotes. The picture remained fairly clear as the camera dipped, revealing a long shot of a large room. Nothing moved.

"That's the First Class Grand Ballroom," Nakamura said, checking a detailed deck plan that hung on the wall by the console.

"Get me a tight shot of that room," Beard ordered, his hand on

Miller's shoulder.

"No can do, sir. We don't have a camera there. We have to rely on Bonecutter's monitor in the projection room."

"There it is again," Marshak said. This time it was clearer. It was a man. Marshak turned to Beard. "Which one of your operatives is that, Colonel?" he asked, knowing full well it was neither.

Beard shook his head and remained silent.

Visible for less than ten seconds, and only from the rear, the broad figure in dark pants, brown leather flight jacket and dark beret dashed from behind one column at the perimeter of the dance floor to another. And something else became clear: this man was stalking.

"There's the girl," Beard said, his voice falling in dejection as Bonecutter's camera picked up Willie on the dance floor.

Unaware she was being followed, the girl stepped slowly, cautiously onto the stage and disappeared behind a floor-length, emerald green curtain.

"The stalker looks Latin," Marshak noted aloud. "Expensively dressed." He turned to Beard. "You have no idea who this asshole is?"

Beard shook his head negatively again, but his expression said what he didn't want to acknowledge. Marshak knew he had an inkling.

Miller said, "How in hell did he get on the ship?"

"Could have been on from the start," Nakamura speculated. "They might have just missed him in the evacuation, like they missed the Girl Scout." He paused for a second then asked, "But why would an adult want to stay on the ship?"

It was natural for Nakamura to ask that, Marshak thought. He and Miller were unaware of the "various chemical properties" on board. But that was not what pinched at Marshak's brain.

"A more important question," he said, "is what Bonecutter will do now that he knows this new guy's on the ship."

He looked at Beard and nodded and the two walked away from the console.

"So," Marshak asked softly, "you think he's from the Panamanian cartel that's after the briefcase?"

Beard sighed. "No doubt."

Marshak nodded. "It looks like he's about to detain the girl."

He saw a spasm in Beard's Adam's apple. Marshak, too, wondered just how far the stalker's definition of detain would go.

"Nakamura," Beard said as he and Marshak returned to the console, "exactly where is that ballroom?"

"It's on the deck just below the theater and the projection room, where our friend Bonecutter is, sir."

Marshak noticed that Beard was finally showing nervousness, aware of how much more precarious the situation had just become while sand continued to sift through the hourglass.

The colonel passed a hand lightly over his forehead. "Then, on their way to the projection room, Falk and Koski will pass the ballroom?"

"Well, they're one level below the ballroom right now, sir. Two levels below the theater and projection room. If, once they're in the area, they took the elevator up one level, it would open in the corridor right outside the ballroom and, up one more level, open in the corridor outside the projection room." Nakamura looked like he was onto something.

"Of course, they probably won't take the elevator, too noisy. So they'll be relegated to the stairs from their present level to the ballroom level."

He paused and studied the blueprint on the wall, then looked back at Beard. "However, due to access to the amidships funnel at that location, that particular stairway doesn't go directly to the next, the projection room, level. They'll need to go through the ballroom, to the opposite side of the room, to catch the stairway there to the theater and projection room, sir."

"Sounds like a fire safety violation to me," Marshak mumbled.

Nakamura nodded. "I'm sure it actually is, sir. However, no one has ever..."

"Nakamura," Beard interrupted, "you're saying that Bonecutter can't go to lower levels without using either the elevator or that stairway down to the ballroom?"

"Which is where the girl and the new player are," Marshak put in, being unhelpful.

Nakamura again consulted the deck plan and answered Beard. "Actually, no, sir. Bonecutter has another option. He could go from the projection room, through the theater, out the double doors into the corridor where the elevator is, go down that corridor to a room at its end, which has a stairway leading both up and down."

"Damn! I need to let Falk and Koski know what they're up against." Beard pressed lightly on his left ear. "Falk, come in. Damn!" he repeated. "Damn it all to hell!"

"What?" Marshak queried.

"Too much static, unreliable reception, too much iron and steel." He exhaled noisily. "Let's hope that he and Koski get to that room soon."

"Hope is good," Marshak muttered; it was barely audible.

By doing everything by the Army's book, they were now reduced to hoping. Marshak was irritated and enjoying watching Beard sweat. He returned his attention to the monitor and

Bonecutter's back.

"What is that bastard thinking?" he said. "If only we could read his mind. Now that he knows his demands were not complied with, that there are who knows how many others on the ship, how long will it be before he presses the button on that transmitter?"

No one spoke, and Marshak felt the energy in the room coil up a notch, winding up everyone's nerves.

"I could order bomb sniffing dogs and a SWAT team aboard," Beard growled.

Marshak cut in, "According to the note he left, he's a purist about the old ship and would be a stickler about the exact time of her demise. Sending dogs and others could prompt him to trigger his bombs. It's possible the only thing stopping him at this point is having a kid on board."

He let his words trail off and headed back to the small office where Willie Dill's quietly whimpering mother and alternately cursing and praying father awaited his latest report. What could he tell them?

He looked at his watch. It was six forty-five. If Falk and Koski didn't do something quickly, in little more than an hour Bonecutter would change the Dill family's world forever as well as his own and that of thousands of others. The ship would become an inferno, and the briefcase and its chemical properties, given the imposing storm, would be mushrooming not just over Long Beach but over half the western states.

Chapter 37

"He's as dangerous as a second lieutenant with a map."

It was an expression Bonecutter's fellow grunts in Nam had applied to people who were fuck-ups. As in any war, Nam had its share of fuck-ups. This was how Bonecutter felt about the Long Beach Police Department.

He almost couldn't blame them. The bastards were simply inept, he thought, when he saw the Girl Scout and the man whom he took to be a plainclothesman sent to extract her from the ship.

Well, the rest of the world would soon know about the police department's incompetence. Bonecutter would do so by way of the media. He'd call a local TV station and tell them who he was; that he ordered evacuation of the ship at eight o'clock this morning; how LBPD had not complied; and how their negligence put the life of a little girl and others in jeopardy. The news networks would eat it up.

One phone call disclosing the contents of his note, which he was sure the police had withheld from the press, would put the pressure on, big time. But would it end up being too much pressure? With the press, things could fly completely out of control. Maybe it wasn't such a good idea after all. Once the news hounds got some fresh meat, the situation could change drastically and rapidly. Bonecutter had seen numerous incidents in the past that were adversely affected by media involvement.

Those situations were no longer able to play out naturally. No matter how broad their spectrum may have been, media accelerated, exaggerated, compressed, dissected, and finally distilled events into the worst that was in them. No, leaking anything to the press right now wouldn't do. What was he thinking? He wasn't thinking straight.

Then suddenly he forgot about the girl and the man and became increasingly conscious of an eerie feeling that had plagued him since he returned to this room, an inner sense that he was being watched. As he concentrated on the notion, the feeling intensified, prickling the back of his neck at first then hammering with metallic percussion on his spine.

He scanned the computers on the desk, the facing walls, rows of narrow shelves containing a radio, schematics, and miscellaneous electronic equipment. Nothing. Pushing away from the console, he hurried around the room, surveying the back wall, pausing only momentarily to note the barometer that hung there. It read twenty-nine-point-nine and dropping. He had no exterior access, but several of the external monitors indicated that rain was falling. Hard.

Moving on, he detected nothing suspicious until he glanced up at the ceiling, and there it was. Cleverly concealed where the molding met the wall opposite the desk was a slit of lens, wide-angled, capable of taking in the entire room. Obviously, part of the first-class security system, a monitor monitoring the monitor.

"*Quis custodiet ipsos custodes?*" he quoted. Who shall keep watch over the guardians? That camera must have cost them a bundle.

Snatching a marker from the desk's surface, he climbed onto a chair beneath the lens. He uncapped the thick felt tip and tested it on the wall. Then, stretching up, slowly and deliberately, enjoying the screech of felt on glass, he smothered the recessed lens with moist, black bands of ink. He couldn't help but smile at the irony of it all: a million-dollar surveillance system rendered useless by a ninety-nine-cent marker.

He jumped down. What was it he had planned to do next? He couldn't recall. Why, now when he needed to think clearly, was his mind trying to wander? Should he go back to his safe place, the bridge and the chart room? There he could forget the girl and the man who pursued her and pass the rest of his life in the womb of the ship where he belonged.

Jesus, that sounded so Oedipal. It was good that the end was near; he was beginning to sound like a fucking psycho. Marissa, who never missed an appointment with one of her analysts, would say, "You're so anal, Jack."

Marissa. He pushed aside the sliver of fear that had intermittently dogged him, that even death had not the power to cure the torment of being without her. How had all that was right gone so wrong? He put a hand to his forehead and scrubbed. A jackhammer was at work behind his right temple.

Then a glance across the monitors arrested thought and motion. A camera set up to capture close-ups of dancers in the ballroom looked directly into the Girl Scout's face. The picture was of poor quality, but it caught a curious, innocent face with huge eyes like dark brown planets of water.

His breath caught. And then it seemed she looked straight at him. Her lips were slightly parted, and he imagined he felt her warm young breath, smelled the sweetness of it, like heather warmed by the sun, breath like that of the daughter he had wished for but would never have.

His hand went to his head again. Wait. What was this in his hand? The remote. When had it jumped from his pocket into his hand? He could have accidently set it off!

His head swam and, as if it were afire, he dropped the remote back into his pocket. He felt control slipping away, his life rushing on too quickly, turning a corner he could not allow it to turn now. His eyes squeezed shut. A ringing in his ears began and rose to a roar, and he smashed his fist into the center of the console, sending shards of plastic flying in every direction. He stumbled around the room, his body ricocheting from one point to another, writhing in agony.

"Aaagh!" he screamed, his mind bruised and aching.

Flesh exploded around him. A piece of a buddy fell at his feet. Another splattered across his chest.

"No! No!"

The responsibility was not his. The Army shrink had said so. It was not his fault. But Bonecutter knew better. He knew the remorse of which he never spoke to anyone, the guilt of gladness.

Yes, he was glad, despite himself. Pleased it was not he who died; implicit in that, happy they did? That it was not his heart strewn across the minefield. Joyful, then, that it was theirs? He had never, *could* never tell anyone about his secret guilt of gladness.

Above all, he didn't allow himself to feel it. Never again, not even for an instant. To feel anything meant to be touched, to face judgment. And to face that judgment was to be forced to do something about it. They did something. They died. They gave their lives. And he, he was here. Goddammit. Alive.

His eyes closed involuntarily, opened wildly, and his mind went somewhere beyond the moon. A lyric that fell pleasantly on his ears filled the air. "Piping down the valleys wild...on a cloud I saw a child."

A child.

Jesus, God! How could he do it? What kind of monster was he? What kind of fiend kills a ten-year-old?

There was only one thing he could do. He must retrieve the bombs, all of them. Take them back to the chart room. It was not the way he'd written the last chapter, but an experienced author went with the flow. An expert did not feel the need to adhere to an original story outline but let his characters to some extent dictate their fate.

He and Pete Powers had often discussed the fact that a good writer wanted that spark, that surprising, spontaneous element that happened in the process of the race to the finish.

Bonecutter would die with his bombs in his arms. This altered means would bring him to the same end, and cure him of a life which, like that of the beached Queen Mary, lacked dignity.

But where were the bombs? His head buzzed like a chain saw.

Think. Think.

He fought the shrinking feeling, the loss of eye control.

Think, you bastard.

Then he remembered. One was in the flag cabinet in the wheelhouse of the bridge. And one was in the wedding chapel. One was in Ye Olde Bakery Shoppe. One in an engine room.

Yes, he remembered now. He spun and propelled himself from the room, out into the corridor, down to its end, and into a room where he knew a stairway led to the lower decks, where he would start a rewrite, before he met a sharper grief than death.

Chapter 38

Double-timing up the stairs to the ballroom level, Falk stopped abruptly on the landing, and Koski rear-ended him, knocking her back against the railing, her high-tops squeaking against the top stair.

"Ssh," Falk cautioned, an index finger to his lips, breathless from the race here. He looked around with obvious disappointment. "Damn."

The landing faced a blank wall; the only exit was a door to the right.

"The stairs don't continue up from here. We'll have to go through the ballroom. There's bound to be stairs leading from there up to the next level, where the projection room is."

Koski was silent. She didn't think there was bound to be anything, but her partner always looked on the bright side.

Falk put his hand on the doorknob and slowly opened the door, his Beretta at the ready, and as he did, he felt a vibration in his jacket pocket. He shut the door.

"Damn."

"What?"

"I'm getting something but it's impossible to make out with all the static."

Koski pressed her ear mic. "Yeah, me too. Say something."

"Like what?"

"That'll do. No static. We can still stay in contact. Seems distance and surrounds have gone crazy. Beard must have been trying to convey some news."

"It'll have to keep a while. Once we're inside," he whispered, "if you hear a sound, any sound, drop. Right?"

She nodded and he reopened the door. He dashed inside, positioning his back against a large marble column. At his left, Koski dropped to her knees, her pistol drawn.

There was a half-second of hesitation before Falk followed suit. He, too, heard something. His weapon fanned the room. Nothing moved. He rose slowly.

Later he admitted to himself that he didn't like that Koski had heard the sound before he did, but now he heard and concentrated on a series of faint, muffled, thumps emanating from somewhere in the high, broad, seemingly empty room.

He signaled Koski to the left and he took the right, the two nosing cautiously into recessed areas and around the large, Italian marble columns positioned several feet from the walls.

Then the sound repeated: a thumping, louder now, like two feet simultaneously pounding the hardwood floor, yet he was still unable to pinpoint its location. Hugging the wall, he edged toward the stage he knew was behind the long, heavy green curtain. Something looked wrong. Yes, the green drape was askew, one panel had been torn away. He was close to the sound now. Slowly he pulled aside the curtain.

The stage was bare, except for a wooden, six-by-six-foot, breakaway musicians' platform at its center. Falk crept closer to the structure. The sounds were coming from under the three-foot high platform. But there was something else: a moan, a choked cry.

"Koski, " he started to call.

A faint footstep to his right made him aware that she had already skirted the room and was there at his elbow. He re-holstered his weapon and quickly examined the platform. Two metal handles were folded into a recess on one side.

"Hurry!"

Pulling the handles down, they were able to lift the framework slightly, and a fold of green curtain tumbled out at their feet. Straining with the structure's weight, they hiked it higher and yanked it back, away from the twisted, mangled mound of emerald drapery, which came to renewed life at the sound of their presence. Crouching beside it, they began tearing at the material.

The large hazel eyes were what Falk saw first, and they shimmered with a circus of emotions. Then the rest of Willie Dill was revealed. Gagged with a stiff peach-colored linen napkin from the adjoining galley, her lips were cracked and slightly bloodied at the corners. Koski started loosening the knot, while Falk untied similar linens that bound the girl's wrists and ankles.

Her mouth finally free, Willie's chest expanded convulsively, her lungs enveloping a great draft of air, then expelling it with a groan. She flung her arms around Koski's neck and cried hysterically.

"It's okay," Koski soothed. "You're okay now, Willie." She rocked the child in her arms.

Falk reached over and patted Willie's shoulder as her tears began to subside. "Are you hurt?"

She touched her lips, still breathing spastically. "Only my mouth, from the napkin."

Falk looked at Koski. "Why would Bonecutter do this? It's uncharacteristic."

"What happened, Willie?" Koski asked.

She shook her head and dabbed at her lips. "I didn't see much. A guy grabbed me from the back. He was a huge dude."

Koski nodded. "Good. Anything else?"

"I saw his wrists. The hair was dark, almost black." She shuddered, remembering his harsh touch. "And his skin was darker than mine, like my friend Maria. She's Hispanic."

Falk and Koski exchanged glances.

"Not Bonecutter," Koski said. "I saw his photo in Beard's office when I arrived. Caucasian, blond, medium build."

Falk nodded, but his skin creeped in various places on his body. "The 'serious competition' we spoke about this morning. That must be why Beard called, to warn us that he's here on the ship."

Koski ran a hand through her hair. "Oh, God."

Falk's eyes narrowed as he thought hard. "The good news is that he, whoever he is, did not want to critically harm her, merely to keep her out of the way." He paused, and his eyes twinkled as he leaned close to Koski and whispered, "Not a bad idea, really."

"Yeah, right." Koski rolled her eyes. "But, seriously, what do we do now?"

A sharp flash of lightning strobed the room and the floor reverberated with the storm's first thunderous display. Willie closed her eyes, and made an almost imperceptible shuffle closer to Koski.

The next moment a piercing, animalistic "Aaagh!" resounded directly above them and echoed through the neighboring rooms and corridors.

Falk shot Koski a look of stunned disbelief. "Come on," he shouted and ran for the stairs he hoped were there.

Chapter 39

As Bonecutter raced through the ship collecting his carefully constructed explosive mounds, he grew calmer, his determination now funneled and focused solely on his collection effort.

He no longer ruminated on reconciling the past, no longer questioned whether death would cure him of the disease called Marissa. Indeed, the very speculation as to how much of the poor, dear Queen Mary he ultimately took with him no longer entered his thinking.

He no longer even considered the Girl Scout's presence, although minutes earlier, this had impelled him on his present, altered path. In all but the narrow, concentrated effort of amassing his bombs, Jack Bonecutter had "left the building."

He halted now in the Trafalgar Square gift shop area. "Somewhere…," he said aloud, "somewhere here. But, where?"

Then a bench caught his eye and memory returned.

"There."

He rushed to the bench, reached down and extracted the explosive from its underside. He quickly, too quickly, yanked the electronic fuse receiver from the device, as he had done with the others, unaware that the receiver had snapped, leaving half of it embedded in the mound's core.

Without examination, he slipped the device into a large plastic souvenir bag he had discovered earlier and slung over his arm. Now, he believed, he had seven unarmed bombs in the bag, their disconnected receivers in his jacket pocket. There were three bombs left. But where were they? He tried to concentrate. His feet must have moved because the squeak of his shoes jarred his thoughts.

"At the bow."

He looked around. Had he said that? He must have because, yes, he remembered clearly now that one of the last three bombs was in a stateroom at the bow. The others were in the bar below the bridge, and in the wheelhouse of the bridge, tucked in with the small, square flags used in the past for signaling in accordance with International Code.

As he ran down the wide aisle between shops, not a conscious thought, but some mechanical mode of thinking decided what to do once he had all ten explosives in hand. He would make a cake. After all, today was the seventy-first anniversary of the Queen Mary's maiden voyage. It was the event he had initially planned to celebrate. He'd combine all the little gooey mounds into one large, perfect round. There were candles: the electronic fuse receivers in his pocket. He would take this cake to the very core of the ship and, embracing it, light the wicks that would begin the celebration.

Chapter 40

Falk had to face the fact that there was no time now to get Willie off the ship. Maybe later, once he got his hands on

Bonecutter. But for now, God help them, he, Koski and Willie were a team.

Frustrated by time, they scrambled into the elevator, abandoning any real hope of silent surprise. When the lift stopped and the doors opened, Falk leaned out and checked the corridor in both directions, then headed for a door with a small window, behind which he believed was the projection room.

He peered in, a quick scan of all four walls revealing that Bonecutter, if in fact he had been there and discharged the scream they heard minutes ago, was gone. Falk silently cursed. It must have been him. He pushed open the door. Maybe their prey would show up on one of the screens on the desk.

Willie followed him in, but Koski stationed herself in the hallway to sound the alarm if anyone approached.

Quickly, Falk swept his vision across the screens. None of the cameras recorded movement. He noticed that a portion of the console was smashed, and shards of plastic littered the floor. Bonecutter had been here, all right. And something he saw had sent him over the edge.

A large portable radio with short-wave bands stood on a shelf at the back of the room. Falk mechanically switched it on and kept walking. Tuned to the British Overseas Service, the station filled the room with the strains of Grieg, a selection from Peer Gynt Suites. Peer Gynt, a man who went through life with no grasp on reality. Leave it to the BBC to come up with appropriate music.

Inadvertently, he moved the dial as he went to turn off the radio, and picked up an announcer forecasting the local weather: storm warnings from Point Conception to the Mexican border. Thunderstorms, unusually violent, expected to bring a fierce electrical display and torrential rains, causing high tides and winds gusting up to seventy miles per hour along the California coast and as far south as Baja.

Willie, sitting at the desk that supported three computers, seemed to be paying little attention. Falk switched off the radio, but a thrill of excitement ran through him. Finding it might have been a stroke of good luck. Here was a not just a workable receiver but a potential transmitter.

He was familiar with short-burst transmissions, a system used and perfected by the British during the Falkland Islands War. If the radio could be tuned to the frequency of Bonecutter's remote detonator, he could have someone at dockside arrange a jamming signal to respond to the same phase, and broadcast it throughout the ship.

No one would know. The signal would be pitched beyond the range of human hearing. It would allowed the entire ship to function as a tuning fork, jamming all other signals on the vessel, and rendering Bonecutter's remote useless.

Falk sighed. There was one big problem: He didn't know the frequency at which Bonecutter's remote was set. Moreover, in attempting to discover that frequency, it was possible that he might trigger the bombs. He cursed silently as he discarded the idea.

"Willie, what are you doing?" He realized that she had booted up all three computers.

"Don't get tweaked," she lectured. "Didn't you say that the phones and PA system are still not operational?"

"Yes, but…"

"This will only take a second." She had already determined the last function performed on each of the first two computers and was working on the third. "This might help us."

Her fingers flew over the keys, yet she maintained a steady

stream of chatter as she alternately clicked her way to various windows and admonished the tortured machine for being too slow to respond or for not obeying her commands.

"Settings," she ordered as she tapped a key. "Drive converter," she directed, striking several others.

The entire operation took place in mere minutes, during which time Falk unsuccessfully protested.

"Aha!" she exclaimed as she kept tapping. "This is basic, elementary, Computer 101 stuff. Looks like they were in the process of converting the file system when the power failure occurred, or when they had to evacuate. What a nightmare for them."

She paused as if she expected Falk to ask her to explain further, and when instead he tried again to protest her actions, she ignored him and answered the unasked question as she worked.

"To save information on files, a computer uses a filing system to control how the files are stored on the hard disk."

She punched another key and several windows opened simultaneously, cascading down the screen. Falk could not have understood them if he tried, which he did not. He had an old desktop computer at home on which he played video games for dexterity, but he knew little of the machine's mysterious inner workings.

"Aha," Willie repeated. "This machine went into hibernation mode."

Again the pause. Enthusiasm compelled the technician to explain, but Falk was too frustrated to stroke a ten-year-old psyche.

"Hibernate features," she went on indomitably, "allow the computer to enter a suspend state, with all power turned off. I'll bet they tried to restart about the same time the external power failure occurred, or, more likely, when the power was restored." She paused, in deep concentration. "Still…"

Her furious clicking of keys pushed Falk to his boiling point. "Willie," he said, "you have exactly one minute, and we're out of here."

"Yes," she said, not in response to his threat, it seemed, but to some function of her work. "It looks like this hard disk is between two gigabytes and two terabytes. It could accommodate the conversion to a file system compatible with the other computers in the network.

"It'll be more efficient because it uses a smaller cluster size, which makes better use of disk space. It can relocate a root directory with backup copies, making the computer less susceptible to crashes. Goofy," she suddenly exclaimed, as if reproving the machine.

"The computer knows what it's doing," she explained to Falk. "It's people who screw things up." She talked fast as she began a final series of keyboard commands.

"So, during the system conversion, the anti-virus software detected that the boot record had changed. It offered to repair that situation. The silly person who was doing the conversion told it to go ahead and perform that repair, which he or she should definitely not have done. This changed the boot record, and the hard drive and all of the information on it became inaccessible."

She turned to Falk with an expectant, suspended expression.

"And that data included the operational codes for the PA system and most of the phone lines, which, if I'm correct, should now be…" she turned back to the keyboard and with an index finger gently tapped one key, "operational."

The phone on the desk did not ring but gave a slight half-jingle as if goosed. Falk picked it up, and, getting a dial tone, stared at the girl, his mouth open.

"It's working."

Willie smiled broadly, her small, even teeth a toothpaste-commercial white, the crinkle of her cheeks partially closing her hazel eyes behind her glasses.

"Willie," Falk felt compelled to ask as he took hold of her arm and gently dragged her from the machine, "what kind of books do you read?"

He expected her to name computer manuals, or maybe Einstein's special and the general theories of relativity. He wouldn't have been surprised if she said she was too busy surfing the Net to find time to read.

Instead, she gave him a what-do-you-expect-a-kid-to-read look? "'Attack of the Talking Toilets'," she said. "And 'Winnie the Witch'. And I just finished 'Just as Long as We're Together' for the third time." She added, "I also like jokes and riddles."

Falk let go of her arm and she followed him toward the door that led back to the corridor and Koski.

"Can you say this tongue twister fast three times?" she asked as she walked. "Upon an island hard to reach, the east beast sits upon his beach. Upon the west beach sits the west beast. Each beast thinks that he's the best beast. Which beast is best? I thought at first the east beast was the best and the west beast was the worst. Then I looked from west to the east, and I liked the beast on the east the least."

Falk raised his eyebrows and silently kept walking. At the door, he turned and shot a final glance at the surveillance screens.

"Hold on."

Where there had been no movement earlier, several cameras now recorded a flurry of motion. A blond male dressed in jeans, a black turtleneck sweater and denim jacket, raced down a long hallway bordered by souvenir shops, heading toward the front of the ship.

"Bonecutter," Falk whispered, and his heart leaped. Now he'd get the bastard.

"That's Trafalgar Square," Willie squealed. "That's where I hid in the gift shop behind the rack of T-shirts."

She paused only for a second, then asked, "Who's that other guy?"

Falk had seen him. The camera angle was poor and the interior area ill-lit, but Falk made him out to be late fifties, with a tweedy, conservative look. He was definitely not Hispanic. He was in the officers' quarters, diligently checking lockers and old chests of drawers.

The man moved smartly, nimbly, with the quick thoroughness of a pro. A practiced burglar who enters one's home must hustle to locate the greatest number of treasures in the shortest period of time.

He never opens the top drawer of a dresser first, because he would then need to close that drawer in order to inspect the contents of the second, and so on. He opens the drawers from the bottom up, leaving each open as he moves on to the next one above it. Yes, this man was professionally trained.

The MI6 agent, Falk concluded. But how did he get on the ship without Bonecutter seeing him on a screen in this room? Or maybe he had. Maybe that sight had precipitated the agonized scream they heard earlier.

Surely, Bonecutter, that poor, deranged son of a bitch, was now on his way to the place where he would detonate his bombs. He could have done it with the remote from here, but no. Falk's original hunch may have been right.

To the extent possible, Bonecutter would stick to ritual, carefully choosing a particular room in which to die, a symbolic place.

Falk grabbed Willie's hand. A glimpse at one monitor had let him see the dark, wind and rain they would encounter once they reached exposed portions of the promenade deck on their way to the gift shop area.

He was about to remove the thicker jacket from under his rain jacket and put it over Willie's shoulders, when he spotted a limp, black leather-look jacket hanging on a hook near the door, its folds gathering dust.

"Here," he said, swinging it down and around her, hardly taking notice that it was a man's large size and that Willie nearly disappeared beneath it.

"Come on. You'll have to run to keep up with Koski and me."

He would insist, when they got to the forward gangplank, that Koski take the girl and go down to the dock. Now he shouldered the door to the hallway, prepared to thank Koski for her uncharacteristic patience.

Chapter 41

When Falk and Willie had entered the projection room, it had taken Koski less than two minutes to grow tired of waiting in the hall. Waiting was not one of her strong subjects. Particularly idle waiting. As a general rule, to make any period of waiting more tolerable, she usually did at least one other thing while she waited.

In a doctor's or dentist's office, she read or knitted. At home she seldom did one thing at any given time. When she watched a video (or on the rare occasion when she caught a show on television), she also read or wrote in her journal or knitted.

Outside the projection room, she quickly grew antsy, pacing the floor. Her stomach growled, reminding her that she was hungry, and she reached into the pocket of the tee beneath her sweater and extracted a power bar.

She had nearly finished it when she heard something that caused her to turn, and saw a door closing at the end of the long corridor. Someone had started to enter the passageway, had seen her and changed course. Without thinking, she bolted in the direction of the suspicious door.

Racing down the long artery, she drew her Beretta. She did not know if the phantom she was pursuing was Bonecutter or Willie's attacker, but she guessed Bonecutter. Wouldn't the man who was after the briefcase have stopped and confronted her? A man strong enough to lift the corner of the heavy musician's platform in the ballroom and drag it over Willie's bound body would not run from Koski. It had to be Bonecutter, running to elude her. Well, she was prepared for whomever. She hefted the automatic.

There was a time when the mere thought of carrying a gun scared Kosksi to death. That changed when she excelled in marksmanship at Quantico, and full knowledge of a pistol fostered confidence in the spectrum of its applications as a deterrent. But it was not at the FBI Academy that she gained true respect for a gun's killing qualities. She had learned that on a dark, isolated stretch of highway in Nevada when she had killed her first man.

"It's okay," Falk had whispered. "It's all right."

But it was months before she could put the killing out of her mind, and she wondered if she would ever be truly okay with it.

Kosksi stood behind the door through which the phantom had disappeared. She was confident but strained. She listened. Hearing nothing, she burst through, leveling her weapon. There was no one. She was in another narrow corridor, nearly one hundred feet in length, and complicated by dozens of intersecting doors, which she took to be individual cabins.

She stood for a long moment, listening. Silence was all, at first, but then a shoe surrendered a slight squeak somewhere ahead, and she heard the muffled but definite sound of movement.

Slowly she made her way down the passage, cautiously opening each door, scanning every cabin, and when she reached the last, saw that it had a second door, which was ajar. Stealthily, she approached the door and pushed it open, and the maze she had gotten herself into deepened. She was looking at yet another, identical corridor. She took a deep breath.

She knew that their phone ear-buds were receiving erratically, but she tried again to reach Falk and heard a steady hissing sound broken with intermittent static. Falk had his hands full. Now he alone was responsible for Willie and the briefcase. She knew he would surmise that his partner did not abandon her post outside the projection room frivolously, that she had probably found Bonecutter.

As she continued her search, always just ahead was the occasional squeak of a leather-soled shoe.

Chapter 42

"That was a stroke of genius, Captain."

Colonel Beard patted a sodden Marshak on the back and pumped his hand as the latter, flanked by two equally drenched officers, entered Com-Cen, coming in from the cold wind and the rain.

"What made you think of it? Letting Drummond simply walk

onto the ship with that sign. Who'd have believed that such a simple strategy would work?" He shook his head incredulously. "Sheer genius."

Marshak nearly went limp with surprise. Beard wasn't homicidal. Pissed even. Beard thought that he, that he...what?

Miller rose from the monitors. "Awesome," he said and gave Marshak a high-five.

Nakamura handed him a large, white handkerchief to dry his bald pate and the narrow band of dark curls that ringed his head just above his ears.

"Way to go, Captain," he said.

What exactly have I done, Marshak asked himself, and turned to Beard. "Sorry I didn't have time to run it by you, Colonel, escorting Drummond to the ship that way. I realize it was not part of the plan."

"Sheer genius," Beard repeated, ignoring Marshak's awkward apology, and returned to the monitors.

Marshak nodded numbly. He didn't know what was going on, but maybe this was a good time, while he seemed to be on an inexplicable roll, to reveal the crucial cross-section that was in his hip pocket and indicated the location of Bonecutter's bombs.

Of course, he'd have to 'fess up' that he'd had it all day, had lost it, and that Drummond found it in the can, and used it to blackmail Marshak into aiding him. This would not be an easy confession, but he had to do it. He cleared his throat and lowered his head slightly. "Colonel Beard, there's something I've got to..."

"Take a look," Beard interrupted, pointing at the bank of screens. He was practically gleeful. "It's working, all right. Your plan is working."

Marshak looked at the monitors. One, a shot of the bow of the ship, evidenced the ferocity of the storm that now raged through the area. Another picked up reporters and cameramen packed into the temporary tent shelters that had been set up for them near the front gate. A third displayed Simon Drummond in the officers' quarters, below the bridge, searching.

They saw Falk and Willie as they raced through rooms and passageways in the direction of Trafalgar Square. Falk showed characteristic grooves deepening between his eyebrows. Willie was nearly buried under a slick black coat. Neither Koski nor the Latin man was visible.

Marshak turned quizzically from the screens.

"Look," Beard persisted, pointing to a particular monitor that intermittently came alive. "Thanks to your brilliant strategy of letting him know by way of the note that there are volatile chemicals on board, the crazy bastard is retrieving his bombs."

Marshak squinted at the screen. "Holy shit!" he whispered.

It was true. There was Bonecutter, a plastic Queen Mary souvenir bag slung over his arm, pulling a mound of explosives from the underside of a bench in Trafalgar Square.

Still stunned and confused, Marshak turned to Beard.

"We can't profess to fathom the deranged mind," Beard said as if he fathomed exactly that, "but your hunch was right on. This chemical factor has thrown him. He doesn't really want to destroy anyone but himself and the ship. He doesn't fancy himself as a murderer. So he's gathering the bombs. Probably devising a new plan. But at least this buys us some time."

He turned to Miller. "Try Falk again. I've got to get this news to him."

"Now that the phones are working," Miller said, "we can call him, sir. Or use the PA system."

Beard ran a finger across his thin upper lip. "No, Miller. At this sensitive time, when he's collecting the bombs, I don't want to take a chance on alerting the bastard to the fact that Falk and Koski are on the ship, in the event he doesn't already know."

Slowly Marshak began to comprehend his luck. He breathed deeply and straightened his shoulders. Maybe, hey, subconsciously, he had this fortunate turn of events in mind all along, as Beard accredited. Maybe, on some subliminal plane, he instinctively knew that Bonecutter would react in this manner.

Yeah, and maybe pigs fly.

In any case, he doubted that this would change Bonecutter's mind about destroying himself and the ship at the prescribed time. He remembered Norman Chaum's words from this morning: "The first bomb that goes off may be in Jack Bonecutter's head. You may get your explosion before you expect it."

If poor, bomb-infested Bonecutter and the briefcase met and ignited at any time, in any part of the ship whatsoever, a huge chunk of humanity would go with them.

Touching Marshak's elbow, Beard steered him to the other side of the room, his voice lowering to a near whisper. Marshak figured he'd had all the accolades he was going to get from the good colonel this day."Captain," Beard lightly squeezed Marshak's biceps as he spoke, "from Bonecutter's reaction to Drummond and the note, it appears that we were, ah, wrong when we tried to delay the Limy's access to the ship earlier."

Beard's eyes narrowed as he looked into Marshak's. "Or, is it possible that I misremember that the Navy SEAL operation we had planned might not be viewed after the fact as a delaying tactic at all? How do you see it, Captain?"

Marshak savored a long moment of sweet comprehension

before he said with obvious magnanimity, "Actually, Colonel, I don't recall any such plan."

Beard released his muscle and slapped his shoulder. "Good man." He immediately turned his attention back to the monitors.

Marshak stood alone for a full minute. So Bonecutter was collecting his bombs from where he originally hid them. Man, it was funny how things sometimes worked out.

He jammed the hopefully-forever-moot cross-section farther down into his hip pocket and wondered if he could talk Drummond into doing the same with his copy. True, his problems were far from over, but maybe not all of the wiry, highly charged energy of the day had worked against him.

Chapter 43

Stealth and cunning, two qualities Quintero had in abundance, were needed to stay ahead of the tenacious young woman with hair the color of a collie he owned as a boy in his abandoned homeland of Venezuela.

At first, Quintero's plan had been to follow the male American agent, who he initially believed would lead him to the briefcase. But the Latino had judged the character of the male and found it to be lacking, evidenced by his release of the child Quintero had waylaid, then by allowing himself to be saddled with two females.

Quintero concluded that he would do better to separate himself from what he saw as an inept trio and search on his own, but then was discovered by the woman in the corridor. More like a pesky bloodhound than a collie, she had been nipping at his heels ever since.

At the same time, Quintero was torn with indecision. What should he do with this woman who would not give up, who followed him down endless hallways, through countless rooms, up and down stairways? He could easily have killed her if he made up his mind to do so. She was surprisingly prepared and acutely alert, quick in her thinking and in her physical dexterity. But Quintero, too, was all of these, and more. Quintero had manpower.

Hidden behind a door, he might have lunged at her, overpowered her, and snapped her neck in one well-executed twist. But that meant explaining that death to the Catholic Padre tomorrow. How could he justify another life-taking this day, especially that of a woman?

Time raced on. Quintero's desperate mind was on the threshold of formulating a motive that he believed to suffice in the confessional, when an alternative plan presented.

Chapter 44

In her dogged pursuit of the man she thought was Bonecutter, Koski had cautiously turned a corner into another hallway, and heard the whirring, metallic sound of an elevator.

She dashed down the long corridor and discovered that there were in fact twin elevators, the arrow on the lighted half-moon panel above one indicating that it was descending.

She jabbed the Down button of the second, fidgeting and cursing at the few seconds it took the doors to open. The other lift continued to descend to the lowest level of the ship, it seemed.

"Down," she demanded as she rushed inside and stabbed the small red button.

Ten decks later the doors opened into a narrow passageway, at the end of which was a door with a red metal sign printed in faded white letters: Boiler Room.

The twin elevator's doors shut. Koski looked up and down the passage but saw no other door.

"Aha!" she whispered. "Now I've got you, Jack Bonecutter."

She approached the boiler room door, Beretta in hand, and it flashed through her mind that, yes, she had him; but since there was only one way out of this passage, he had her, too.

She took a deep breath, turned the doorknob, and burst into the room, swinging her back to the wall and fanning the width of the room with her pistol. Then she dove for the only cover available, a huge chunk of rusted, indistinguishable machinery on the floor.

Two small, amber lights at shoulder height on opposing walls cast dim, dawn-like light and created long, eerie shadows around the room, whose size seemed to swallow her.

Trained to marginalize risk in such situations, she peered through crevices in the antiquated metal she'd chosen as cover. She scanned the area for another exit, keen to any sign of movement and saw a door at the opposite end of the room.

Good.

The air in the room held cool, uncanny silence. It was a dank room, more than twenty feet high, and broad. The boilers had long since been removed; the room had gone to wreck.

Ruined pieces of equipment—a portion of an anchor, rusted chunks of chains and pulleys—littered the gutted expanse. Some resembled sleeping cats, some armored armadillos.

Slowly she rose, convinced that she was alone in the room, and began crossing to what she both hoped and feared would be the final door. Then she halted. She had heard a slight click behind her. A dark moth fluttered in her chest.

No! No!

She whirled around and raced to the door she had entered moments before, grabbed the knob and turned and pulled. And pulled. It was locked!

Oh God!

She kicked furiously and pounded it.

"Bonecutter!" she screamed. "Bonecutter, you bastard, let me out of here!" She kicked again, as if kicking herself. A stupid, rookie mistake. "Bonecutter!"

It was the twin elevator. She should have checked the other out. He must have been hiding in it, waiting, as she exited and, like a lemming going to the sea, entered the boiler room, which was now her prison.

"Damn."

She kicked again. She'd been outsmarted. Another kick, then she stopped and listened. A muffled, grating sound. One of the elevators was ascending

The motherfucker is leaving me here.

She froze, an inhalation lodged in her lungs, and listened again. Slowly the sound faded, and she knew then she was truly alone in the silence.

Perspiration broke out on her face and palms. She swung around to face the room, her tomb. But, wait, she'd forgotten the other door. She darted to the opposite side of the room, unafraid of what was behind that final means of exit.

It was a way out; wherever it led she would follow. When she reached it, she grabbed the knob and turned.

It opened to an empty closet.

Or was it?

She leaned in. The dim light behind her offered little illumination and created a diagonal coal black shadow in the small chamber. She stepped closer. A musty coolness hit her, and a hollow roar assailed her ears. Jabbing a hand into her jeans pocket, she extracted a small cigarette lighter that she never used but carried.

She swiveled her head in and peered up. And up. And up.

The tiny room had no visible ceiling. In fact, it was not a room at all, but a narrow, vertical shaft only slightly wider than a human body. Wooden ladder rungs built into one wall vanished into the ascending blackness.

Lack of proper illumination disclosed only dust and cobwebs on the first dozen rungs and kept Koski from noticing the splinters of wood at her feet, evidence of fresh disturbance of the upper, unseen rungs.

Was it possible that this interior ladder went up to the next deck; or up through many decks? If so, one could avoid all stairs and elevators by utilizing this to climb all the way to the top deck of the ship. She shuddered; but what a climb.

She backed out of the chamber, a hot flash of blood flooding her cheeks as she recalled the long crawl through the conduit with Falk this morning. As bad as it had proven, she had been with Falk. She had not been alone like she was now.

She had one moment of utter, sickening fear. She could not swallow, and her entire body shivered. Then she froze with a profound realization. For her, the ladder was the only way out of this room, and there was no force on earth that could impel her to climb it.

She breathed deeply for several seconds, and then spoke into her ear mic. No use. The entire ship was full of dead spots. "Can-you-hear-me-now?"

Shit.

She pulled out her phone and texted a message, but was certain it wouldn't be received. Sweat broke out anew on the surface of her skin as, painfully, reluctantly, she let her vision drop to her watch. It was seven-fifteen.

Chapter 45

"I hope Susan is okay." Willie breathed heavily as she spoke.

She and Falk had been racing through the interior of the ship, and now they halted beside the bench Bonecutter had been concerned with less than ten minutes before.

"I'm sure she is." Falk, too, needed to catch his breath.

The thought of time running out was as exhausting as physical activity. And, despite his encouraging words to Willie, he was not sure Koski was okay.

He hadn't a clue as to why she left her post in the hallway while he and Willie were in the projection room, but assumed she must have had a good reason. Perhaps the man who imprisoned Willie earlier had come into the hall and found her. No, Falk would have heard the sounds of the fight Koski would have waged against the man. Unless he surprised her from behind, as he had Willie.

"Look," Falk said, as if Willie had protested his attempt to assure her about his partner, "Koski's fine. She's well trained and smart and physically strong. She's fine. Wherever she is, she's just fine."

But instinct screamed the opposite at him.

"Willie," he said, "I have to get to the bridge, at the front of the ship, not far from here."

He looked around for a place to tuck the girl away, where she'd be safe but out of his hair.

"But..." she began.

"No 'buts'. This is serious business."

He turned to the nearest shop. The Press Museum. Inside he saw racks of old newspapers covered in plastic, their headlines depicting historic world and local events.

"Perfect," he said. "A newspaper museum." He tried the door, dug into his pocket for a ring of universal keys he'd been given before boarding and unlocked it. "Great for an intelligent, well-read young lady like you."

"But I want to go with you."

Falk put his arm around her shoulder, steering her toward the door. "No. This is important, national security business."

That should do it.

"But I helped you before, with the computers. I could..."

"Look," he struggled to keep his voice steady, "Willie, remember the man we saw on the monitor before, the one who was here by the gift shop?"

Her brown eyes narrowed, intense and interested. "Yes."

"Well, he's a danger." A sigh. "He's a very sick man who is confused, and I've got to find him and get him off the ship and to a doctor."

An old grandfather clock inside the museum struck, and Falk looked at it. It was seven-fifteen.

"Oh, God."

He put his hands on her shoulders and shoved her into the shop. "Stay here until I get back." He pulled the door shut and ran.

He raced down the long corridor, angry and frustrated, and the one thing he hated most—unsure. He had only questions, no answers. Where was Koski? Had she found Bonecutter? Where was Willie's attacker? Where was the MI6 agent who Beard said would assist in the search?

He tried his ear-bud. Where was the verbal communication they'd been promised? Where was the freakin' briefcase? And, finally, where had his groove gone?

He was always at his best when the challenge was greatest, when all pistons were firing. Instead, the heat of frustration burned his cheeks as he charged forward, past staterooms, the Observation Bar, heading for the exposed staircase leading to the bridge, where he hoped to get some answers.

Chapter 46

Willie looked around the museum, unsure how she wanted to proceed. Beside her was a rack of plastic-wrapped newspapers, and she speculated that if she were going to stay here as instructed, she could pass the time by reading.

The one-word headline of a Los Angeles Times Extra dated Tuesday, June 6, 1944, read: INVASION! Willie leaned toward the rack and silently read the ensuing story: "Allied forces landed in Northern France early today in history's greatest overseas operation, designed to destroy the power of Hitler's Germany."

She moved on to the next, a Connecticut newspaper, The Torrington Register, dated Saturday, September 10, 1960. "Hurricane Donna Rakes Florida Keys" was the headline.

The front page of the Los Angeles Citizen News of Friday, November 22, 1963, had a full-page, black-and-white picture of a handsome man with thick hair, a kind face, and sad eyes under the headline: MARTYRED.

Willie turned away from the rack and looked out of the museum. She didn't want to read old news. She wanted to be where things were happening *now*. And she decided that if the man who attacked her this morning was nearby, she would be safer with Falk than here alone. She ran to the door, threw it open, and took off in Falk's direction.

Chapter 47

Falk was drenched when he reached the bridge. Once open, the heavy door was held in that position by near-hurricane-force gusts of wind that drove through the navigational area, whining at every crevice and hurtling a thick film of rain against the surrounding windows.

His mind screamed he should have brought Willie, taken her down the gangplank, handed her to someone ashore. But he knew that unless he found Bonecutter and stopped him from igniting his bombs, it would make little difference where she was when that terrible occurrence took place. There'd be few left alive to witness the result.

A rope ladder hanging from the crow's nest slapped powerfully against its restraints. It was dark outside, but Mother Nature's aerial display and the army of klieg lights brought in by the Long Beach PD to the dock ten stories below augmented the Queen Mary's usual lighting. The ship was awash in surreal radiance, keeping total darkness at bay in some areas while creating more and deeper shadows in others.

Activity was at a standstill on the port side dock. Except for those armed, slicker-covered sentries at strategic posts, police and security personnel had taken shelter in Com-Cen or one of the temporary shelters that were set up.

Starboard, the crisscrossing searchlights of several Coast Guard vessels made silver beads on the cresting surface of the black water. They patrolled the area outside the rock jetty that separated the Queen Mary's berth from the bay.

Salvage vessels loaded with Coast Guard and National Transportation Safety Board personnel still combed the bay. They were hampered by waves that battled each other and broke on the jetty, sending whorls of water high above the rocks and slamming down, then running off in a smother of writhing foam.

Falk took only a second to shake the collar of his rain jacket to disperse some of the water that had collected and chilled his neck and shoulders. Cautiously, he scanned the bridge for Bonecutter, but there was no sign of him or anyone.

He entered the small chart room, which was deserted, and as he did, his hunch that the briefcase was somewhere in this area grew stronger. Like a bloodhound on the trail, he sniffed into every oblique corner of the room. He flung open any cabinet large enough to hold a briefcase or an incendiary bomb, checking for hidden compartments, feverishly overturning everything that was not nailed down.

One unusual cabinet contained pigeonhole compartments stuffed with old, rolled signal flags; he tapped them lightly, almost absent-mindedly in his haste to locate Bonecutter and the briefcase.

"The briefcase has got to be here somewhere," he said aloud.

The only clue he had was the old scientist's disclosure to the FBI agent, that it was hidden where no one would find it.

A clap of thunder rolled like a heavy wooden barrel across the sky.

Think, his mind whispered. *And remain calm.*

Then he hated that he'd thought that. He was always thinking. He was always calm. He'd find the case, God damn it!

Looking at his watch, he realized its hands had not moved since he last looked. His fine, precision Swiss movement chose precisely the worst moment to stop working. Fate was playing another dirty trick against him.

He sighed deeply and stepped past a bulkhead, surveying the

area as he went. Creaking timbers groaned, warning that something would eventually had to give. Moving to his left, he passed the large, waist-high chart table and began opening and checking cabinets and drawers in the wall facing the bay.

As he moved to the second wall, he noticed a long, low wooden bench. Did it open? He stooped and tried the seat, first pulling, then clawing at the worn, faded oak. But it was just a seat.

He stood and, with a fist, tested the wall behind the bench, searching for a movable panel, anything. But it was solid.

"Damn."

His hands flashed through every cabinet, every cubbyhole, most of which were empty, disused for years.

An instinctive glance at his useless watch exploded his frustration. He'd put his trust, his hopes in instinct—a clear sense that both Bonecutter and the case were on the bridge or this adjoining room. He'd been wrong about Bonecutter. Anxiety heightened in him. Was he wrong about the briefcase, too?

Then something drew him back to the chart table he'd passed moments earlier. On the wall above the right side of the table were framed sepia notices from old cargoes, wind velocity readings, a portion of the tidal atlas of the Solent and the approach to Southampton, England. All were scraps of paper that once were whole and held meaning for captain and crew. He moved to the left side of the table.

The bulkhead above it was battered with nail holes, and several people—no doubt tourists in recent years—had stippled their affection there: "Bob loves Carol." "Don" with a heart next to "Louise."

The shipbuilder's original name and insignia were embossed there: Cunard White Star Line, the outline of a stout, five-point star the symbol. He reached up and let his fingers read the Braille-like outline. If only these walls could speak.

Testing the area of the star, he knocked all about it for some sign of give, but no. He looked down, squatted, and realized for the first time that there was a wooden cupboard built in beneath the table.

He touched the door. It was ajar.

He opened it. The cupboard was empty, the walls solid and firm. He tapped the floorboard. At the hollow sound his tapping produced, excitement quickened his breath.

Could it be? Finding a groove in the wood, he raised one side and pushed the floorboard up against the inner wall, surprised it gave so easily after all the years. Too easily.

Dear God, if someone has been here before me...

He looked down into the black hole, the overhead light insufficient to penetrate its depth. Dropping to his knees, he began to grope gingerly inside the hole, but felt only gauzy webs. Because the section of floor opened up to the right, he had to reach in with his left arm.

He leaned farther into the unknown darkness and swept his hand under the surrounding floor, locating what felt like a ladder and three walls. Where the fourth wall should have been, directly under the portion of the floor on which he knelt, there was only space.

He dropped his body flat on the floor, face down, his left armpit crammed against the lip of the cupboard, attempting to lean farther, but his Beretta in its holster dug into his ribs and restrained his movement.

He carefully removed the weapon with his right hand, balancing his weight carefully so as not to fall into the black abyss, and slid the gun to the floor just outside the cupboard.

He was at last able to stretch in as far as he dared, fingers working, searching, locating a shelf and something else: the curved, glass neck of a bottle. It lay on its side, and he groped to position it so that he could grasp and extract it, but it swiveled, and his hand, trying to catch it, knocked it instead to the lip of the shelf and it fell.

Falk could not see but could hear its dizzying descent as it glanced off one wooden ladder rung, then another, hit the side wall of the shaft, bounced back against another rung, and continued to fall, seemingly forever.

Its motion resounded through the twelve-story chamber, until the echo grew faint and faded, evidence of its final disposition silenced by its distance from the range of Falk's hearing.

Stretching his body as far as he could now, he reached for the shelf again. His fingers touched a flat surface that felt like old, crusted leather. He held his breath as his fingers slowly crept over the perimeters of the object: a handle.

Slowly, for his arms and fingers quivered with muscle tension, he inched the handle toward him. The leather case attached to it was heavy and thick. He remembered Healey saying that the container inside the briefcase was reinforced with steel. If the steel had corroded, the chemicals begun to leak or decay, what would he do?

In desperate, intense concentration, an exaggerated vision crept across his mind, depicting his hand coming away from the shaft as an aberration of dead cells, their hideous withering spreading quickly to his wrist, his arm.

Then the case came off the shelf, its surprising weight swinging it downward, nearly escaping from his grasp. He shoved his other hand into the shaft to steady the burden, nearly toppling in himself, and carefully, in a lifetime of seconds, wormed his body back along the floor and withdrew the briefcase from the cupboard.

Breathing for the first time in minutes, his heart hammering in his chest, he got to his knees, then stood and eased his prize to the chart table.

"Aageeegh!"

The sound quivered gutturally from his throat. Violent jerks and shudders convulsed his body as he tried to fling his right hand away from himself, propelling the black, spindle-legged creature on it across the room. He shuddered several more times before he could dispel the sensation of the harmless yet repellent spider's touch.

Falk blew a layer of dust from the weathered leather and quickly inspected the case for signs of erosion that would signal leakage of the compound. He thanked God there were none. In the lower right-hand corner, burnished gold initials were recognizable: GJM. Gordon James Metcalf.

Staring at the name, he wondered how this man had been able to get into the chart room of the Queen Mary while at sea. Maybe during a shift change. Did he bribe a crew member? However Metcalf managed it, and with whom, would never be known.

Suddenly elation ran through Falk like a shot of adrenaline. He'd found it! Despite many years of action, it was still in good shape.

He remembered with irritation that Koski had in her pocket the chemical wrap in which he was to enclose the case. Well, right now, he just had to get the damned thing, and Willie Dill, off the ship and find Koski, who he hoped had collared Bonecutter.

Then, for no knowable reason, he had a chilling sense of a presence in the room with him. A vision of his Beretta flashed across his mind, and he looked down at the floor where he'd left it and prepared to bend and retrieve it.

It was gone.

Chapter 48

Hampered by pelting rain and the gnarled shape of the plastic bag slung over his forearm, a sodden Bonecutter stumbled up the exposed stairs toward the bridge while Falk was in the chart room, extracting the briefcase from the cupboard. The door of the bridge was flung open, transfixed by the wind. Bonecutter stepped inside, slipping the plastic bag up to his shoulder.

His wandering brain no longer attended conscious, peripheral matters, and he moved mechanically, as if possessed, concentrating on the right wall just inside the bridge and a small, knee-high wooden cabinet. Inside were dozens of signal flags, stuffed into pigeonholes.

He had yanked out handfuls of flags this morning, finally extracting the one that he used to conceal his tenth and final explosive. He then replaced that flag and the others. Now he would...a strange, guttural, shivering cry came from the adjoining room, above the whine of the wind. Bonecutter took two steps forward and managed a narrow, rectangular peek into the chart room. There he saw a tall, brown-haired man in a rain jacket, wiping his hand as if something diseased had walked across it. He was examining a dark parcel on the table above the open cupboard and the shaft.

The shaft. Bonecutter's shaft. The man had discovered Bonecutter's secret place. The place where Bonecutter planned to make his cake and start the celebration.

Bonecutter whirled and flung himself back down the stairs, pinching his eyes shut against a vision that had come to him again and again in the past few hours. But he could not dispel it this time.

It was there, imprinted on the inner wall of his eyelids: a malignant montage of his Bien Hoa buddies.

No!

He forced his eyes open, but now the men were there, too. Outside, standing in the rain, their uniforms in tatters, their bodies slick and bloodied, missing parts, dripping pieces. One raised a shattered finger like the backbone of a fish and beckoned to Bonecutter. The man was grinning, his mouth a gaping hole.

"No!"

Bonecutter's head tightened. His skin shrunk, crushing his skull. In whatever direction his mind turned there was no solace. Just as he put his right hand to his head, he blacked out. He came to, still moving his hand toward his face. It happened in a flash, but for the few seconds it lasted, it was complete and took a measure of his mind with it.

Twisting wildly, slammed by an icy blast of rain and wind, he stumbled blindly toward the bow. Pursued by demons, he was aware only of blood beating in his head with savage energy as he groped along the rail, tripping over an old gun platform left as a memento from World War II when his genteel ocean liner was converted to a troop ship.

Staggering to the V point of the bow, he turned back and stumbled over the windlass; his foot hooked on the mammoth chain which nearly pulled him to the deck.

Water raced down inside his clothes, soaking his skin, but he knew this more than felt it. His fingers clutched at a rail and found something—rope—the ladder leading to the crow's nest. He looked into the blinding rain, staring up at his past, knowing he had no future.

His last moment of sane, pristine clarity, told him he was being fanciful, ridiculously so. Then the vision he carried inside since he was three overcame him and became his only reality. He was, again, in that place to which he was irrevocably linked. One minute, safe in loving arms, the next flailing, a sacrifice to the wind and wild gray wolf pack. He knew only one truth: his life could not end without resolution in the crow's nest. He grabbed the ladder and climbed.

Chapter 49

Falk looked up from the floor and saw the man who he assumed had come into the room only moments ago. He saw the taut, olive skin around an unsmiling mouth that stretched horizontally back on the right side of his face until it seemed the entire lower jawbone would be exposed. The stretch held for several seconds, then the lips quivered and the mouth closed, settling into a grim, tight line.

The man had a thick neck and massive shoulders; his torso was shaped like a sequoia, although this was not a young man. He saw the pricey, hand-finished lambskin jacket, sodden and dark with rain. But what Falk saw most noticeably was not the man himself; it was the gun in his hand. It was Falk's Beretta.

"Ah," Falk said with inherent sarcasm and controlled fury, trying to make himself heard above wind, rain, thunder and creaking, inside and outside the room. "The man who cannot smile. The man who mutilated an old man in Panama after he was already dead, and who attacked a little girl from behind and nearly suffocated her."

"*Si, Senor*," the man said. He beckoned with upturned fingers toward the briefcase. "Give to me," he said in English.

Falk didn't hesitate, his mind quickly ruling out every other possible option. This guy would kill him. He wasn't sure what time it was, but he guessed sometime between seven-thirty and eight.

If Koski failed to locate Bonecutter, it didn't matter who took the briefcase off the ship, so long as someone did. Beard's people would apprehend the man dockside. He set the briefcase on the floor a few feet in front of him and stepped back.

"Look," Falk told him, palms up in apparent surrender so as not to spook him, "it's yours. You can have it."

Did the Latin grasp the true potential of the trophy he'd won? Did he appreciate its killing power?

"Take it," Falk repeated. "Go. Get off the ship, for Christ's sake!"

Slowly, silently, the powerful man bent and picked up the briefcase, never diverting his eyes or his aim from Falk. He backed slowly to the doorway that separated the chart room from the bridge, bent again, and set the case down on the floor.

Then he made what Falk initially thought was a most unexpected move, but which later consideration proved to be evidence that his adversary was indeed wholly aware of the chemical compound's volatile potential. He placed the Beretta on top of the leather case and, in the same instant, drew a knife from inside his jacket.

Falk saw a deadly glint off six inches of cold steel as the man crouched, facing him, in the menacing, preparatory stance of a master cutter.

So, Falk thought, it wasn't only that his enemy knew of the sensitive nature of the enclosed chemicals and was taking no chances with ricocheting bullets; this was a guy who preferred close physical contact and clean, silent strokes of a blade. He had, Falk realized in the moment, predetermined Falk's death.

The man's physique was impressive, backed up by the instincts of a professional killer. Falk would need to employ physical subterfuge to survive. If lucky, he might get one chance, one split-second opening in which to deflect a blow and to lunge and deliver, with his bare hands, a fatal stroke of his own.

Falk heard a groan—his—as the man attacked. He couldn't know that his life had been saved in that moment by a vision. In mid-thrust, an image revisited Quintero: He saw his blade, attached to the beak of *el pico de pez espada*, spinning in air. He saw his own hand stretching to retrieve it. He saw it fall, blade downturned, before the blade buried itself in his face.

The horrendous vision lasted just long enough to distort Quintero's judgment, and allow Falk to sidestep his initial thrust, which opened a gash in Falk's coat, rain jacket, his shirt, tee shirt, and a marginal layer of flesh beneath. Aware that blood had been drawn, the attacker adjusted his stance, and prepared to deliver the final assault.

Ignoring his wound, determined to invest every ounce of physical strength and mental agility into this fight, Falk yanked his rain jacket from his shoulders and whirled it around his forearm, ready for the fight of his life.

Chapter 50

When the fragments of thick glass shattered to the floor of the open shaft, accompanied by the distinct and powerful odor of aged whiskey, it was a shocking but welcome sign of life to Koski.

Someone was up there. She had no idea who or how far up, but someone was there, and had thrown or dropped the bottle into that black hole.

Earlier her innate sense of humor had kept her from total misery.

"Is this, then, the end of Susan Koski?" she'd asked aloud as she stared at the shaft, her claustrophobia gripping her in it's iron claws.

Sitting on an old piece of rusted machinery in this forgotten, high-ceilinged, hollow hell in the bowels of the ship, she fought back tears and gave in to her despair. She was on the verge of completely giving up hope for the first time in her adult life.

More than once, she played out in her mind the stupidity of allowing herself to get outsmarted and locked in this room. Hotly aware that time was running out, she felt pressure in her chest, as if a truck had pulled up and parked there.

Then the bottle had smashed to the floor, and she got up and ran into the shaft.

Now she waited and listened. There was nothing but the constant scream of air. She looked back at the huge, imprisoning room behind her, at the chunks of dead machinery covered with dust, and a vision of her bones being found here, years from now, draped over her. That moment of utter desolation finally sparked an emotion more powerful than her fear of enclosure: Rage.

"Fuck!" she hollered. "No way am I going to die here!"

She took two gulping gasps of air, as if she were about to dive into the deep end of a pool, and started up the ladder at a run, her nostrils filled and flaring with the sting of liquor.

And if I'm really lucky, she thought, *I'll be drunk before I reach the top.*

Chapter 51

With a flourish, Falk's opponent swiftly, deftly brandished the knife. Falk saw it flash like sliver writing in the air. Writing his name or his epitaph? A slight light-headedness passed over him.

His left hand went to his side and came away sticky with warm blood. No matter. It would take more than a flesh cut to inhibit him. He was back in his groove.

Two, three more times, the blade flashed by him; so close that his jacket was slashed to raw threads in several places. Each time his body's quick response to his mind's ability to read and interpret his enemy's movements saved him. But just as he was aware of his own capabilities, so was he mindful of his diminishing energy. How long could he hold out?

Then he heard a voice. A small voice, reaching to the top of its range to be heard above the thunder, and he saw Willie Dill standing in the doorway behind his attacker.

"Drop the knife," she demanded with a ferocity and seriousness beyond her years.

When the man tensed but did not move, not so much as turn toward her, she tightened her steady, two-fisted grip on Falk's Beretta.

"I said, drop the knife, dickoid."

Falk knew in that moment that it was possible for him to love, wholly and unashamedly, a human being he had met only hours before.

Chapter 52

Seconds after she started to climb, instinct developed into full awareness, and Koski realized she had climbed the height of three stories. She was suddenly keenly aware of the walls on all sides and that they were nearly touching her.

She slowed and gripped harder the rungs above her, planting her feet more deliberately on each rung below. She allowed herself to think only that she felt uncomfortable, and ordered her body to keep climbing.

This worked for several more minutes, until she lost awareness of her feet and of how far she had climbed. All that existed was the screaming air above her, the sense of being unnaturally high and of being suspended in a close, smothering space.

She swallowed dryly and paused. What finally pushed her on was the thought of the blackness below, which did not recede but seemed to rise on its own like an unrelenting tide beneath her.

Now every rung was an achievement. She pulled herself painfully upward, hand over hand, foot over foot, fighting desperation, concentrating on the knowledge that there had to be an end, that she would reach the top at any minute.

Recollection of the long conduit she and Falk had traveled this morning pushed its way to the forefront of her mind. She had, for several seconds, lost consciousness then. Or had she?

Was she in fact extremely conscious, too conscious, so that the ebony darkness around her took on form—her form? It was she, her corporeal being, not her consciousness that was lost. She shook her head to clear the fantasies, prepared to shut down all her thinking processes and again ordered her body to move forward but faster.

Then a rung gave way. Then another. She began fighting her way upward to find a rung that would hold.

Every muscle was stressed to its limit. Having at last located two solid rungs, she shivered uncontrollably and clung to the ladder. Tiny slivers had imbedded themselves in her damp palms where they had desperately grasped at decaying wood, and she felt her knees and shins bleeding, scraped by the sharp remains of broken steps she had somehow climbed.

She was perspiring profusely now, and the smell of her own

sweat made her stomach lurch. Bile, bitter and intolerable, convulsed into her throat, her mouth, and spilled out between her lips. Pure fear, irrefutable and paralyzing, struck her. She'd undertaken the impossible.

She could not go on. She needed to go back down, but the broken rungs ensured that she couldn't. But neither could she bring herself to continue up. The panic that was overwhelming her was like a fire, raging out of control. A voice appeared in the flames screaming at her to give up, give up.

Fingers that seemed not her own vised around the rungs. She felt a stream of warm wetness snake along her thighs and down her legs. A shudder overtook her body. Nausea welled, followed by a rush of heat and then exquisite, exhilarating   dizziness. The screaming voice no longer ordered her to give up but to let go, let go.

She could feel the muscles in her fingers obeying, when, next moment a different voice refocused her senses on the looming blackness above her head. Above her, a determined child's voice boomed, "I said drop the knife, dickoid."

Koski knew that voice. It was that not far above her. Oh, God! She pressed her head against the ladder. Fear and the exertion of the long climb had robbed her of most of her strength. She tried but couldn't move.

Oh, God, please. I can do this. I can, she thought, but her body refused to obey.

Chapter 53

Falk closely watched as Quintero, blade in hand, turned quickly, then back, seeming to divide his attention between the agent and the girl. Then he looked into the black orifice of the Beretta as if to gauge the determination of the brassy child behind it.

Falk, although not seriously injured, was in pain from the stab wound Quintero had inflicted. In fact, at the girl's appearance, he sank onto the long low bench against the back wall. But he would be up again soon.

Meanwhile, this little one stood less than ten feet from Quintero and demanded again that he drop his weapon. At this distance she certainly wouldn't need to be a crack shot to kill him. Still, fright or nervousness or inexperience might work to Quintero's advantage.

Falk imagined that Willie knew nothing at all about guns. Probably, she was never allowed to touch one. He remembered only half-listening as she chattered about her father who had once purchased what he called a Saturday Night Special. For the protection of his family, he had told them. In a long monologue Falk had mostly tuned out, Willie described how she watched from the hallway while her parents stood in the kitchen and examined the weapon, her father explaining how to disengage the safety lock.

"Now it's ready to shoot," he had said.

But Willie's mother always tested the depth of the water before going in. She carefully placed her trembling hand over the weapon in his and replied gently but firmly, "George, do you realize that something with killing power is in your hands? It will be in our home, where our daughter lives and plays. And you have just demonstrated to me and her how to render it unsafe."

Willie told Falk that her father had returned the gun that very day.

Falk was sure Willie was afraid of the gun, but he knew she was a loyal friend who wanted to protect him against Quintero, who she likely recognized as her attacker.

Falk followed Quintero's stare at the girl while he weighed his options with the instincts of a fox. He probably saw what Falk noticed: a sudden, delicate dilation of the girl's pupils that might be a sign of indecision sparked by fear. Quintero lunged.

And met a bullet.

He arched backward. His beret flew into the air, and a dark red furrow parted skin and hairs above his left temple. But not for a moment did he lose his vise-like grip on the knife.

Immediately righting himself, he leapt forward, smashing a massive forearm across the side of the girl's head. The Beretta hurtled into the air and clattered to the floor at the agent's feet.

Falk caught his second wind and scooped up the gun just as the Latino bolted towards the door and grabbed the briefcase.

"Hold it, amigo!" Falk shouted. His head was clear again. He gestured toward the chart table. "No more games. Put the knife and the case on the table, now." He watched the slick bastard affect an ingratiating posture.

"*Si, senor*," he said. With his forearm, he swiped at a thin line of blood that veined down his face, but made no move to comply.

A thunderbolt slammed the ship with such force it seemed to Falk that the rivets in her hull would pop. The lights flickered. Rain blurred every window and thrummed on the roof of the bridge. Willie, thrust to the floor by the force of her attacker's blow moments earlier, sat, dazed and gasping for the breath that had been knocked from her. Now she roused herself and rushed to Falk's side.

Falk again gestured to the man, raising his voice above the dissonance of another thunderclap.

"You have to the count of three to put the knife and the case on the table."

"*Si, si.*"

Slowly the man moved to the chart table and placed his blade on the wooden surface.

"The briefcase," Falk demanded.

But what Falk saw in the man's eyes was the realization of an advantage, and slowly, almost imperceptibly, the Latin slid the case up to an angle covering his chest, his neck, his chin and the lower part of his nose.

A flush of rage overtook Falk. He had underestimated his adversary. Frozen in indecision, he felt Willie's eyes turn to him.

"Hul-lo," she said. "What's happening?" When Falk still did not move, he felt her pull at his pants leg. "Joe," she insisted, "shoot him like they do in the movies."

The man reached out, beckoning again toward Falk with his indecent fingers.

"We have one more hand to play, *senor.* The weapon, please."

"No!" Willie shouted, and stamped her feet. She stared at Falk. "Joe. The guy will kill us! Why don't you…?" her voice trailed off, as if she were finally aware of something of greater consequence in the moment. She released Falk's pants leg and moved slightly behind him.

The bastard knew Falk would not take the chance of hitting the briefcase being placed directly in the path of a bullet.

"Look, pal," Falk tried, "Put the case down or I'll shoot your balls off."

Quintero gave a sneering smile, sure that a gringo could never do such a thing.

Willie's voice was small again. "It's a bomb, isn't it?"

Falk sighed and pulled the trigger. Quintero's face tightened in disbelief as the 9 mm slug ripped into his scrotum, thinking in a silent scream, *An Americano would never do such a thing!*

As the briefcase slipped down his body, Falk fired a second shot and Quintero took it between the eyes, removing any doubt what this Americano would do.

Chapter 54

Koski's sweaty, purple-red face rose from the dark space in the compartment beneath the chart table. She pushed farther up, her knees clearing the floor of the cupboard.

"What happened? Joe, you're hurt."

Despite the loss of blood, of which he was acutely aware, Falk sounded the depth of his own strength. "I'm okay, Koski. Look at you!"

"Joe shot the bad guy, Susan! He was going to kill us!" Willie ran to her side. "Where did you come from?"

Koski held the girl tight for a moment. "From way down in the ship."

Without warning, with no attendant sound but the wind and rain that lashed around him as he burst through the doorway from the exterior gangway and into the bridge, Simon Drummond halted at the chart room door, unsure of what he was seeing.

Drummond had spent the last few hours frantically trying to locate Bonecutter's bombs with help from his photocopied schematic. He'd found three of the sticky devices and removed the remote controlled detonators, but there were still seven and time was running out. He'd decided to make one last-ditch effort, hoping that some forgotten corner of the bridge would yield results.

Then, suddenly, the photograph he had taken from Marshak's "Pete Powers' envelope" came into focus in his mind. Drummond had studied the old picture again. He concluded that the man behind Angus Bonecutter in the chart room was not, as Drummond originally surmised, disappearing into the room's focal point, but into the partially constructed floor. He was about to descend into an interior passageway, possibly leading to the lower decks. This he saw as his last hope of finding the briefcase, somewhere between the bridge and the decks below.

Now, however, none of that seemed to matter. The Girl Scout that Beard had mentioned sat on a low bench at the back of the room, next to the female agent Drummond recognized from the blow-up in Beard's office.

The other agent, he knew from a similar photo, was Joseph Falk, known to British Intelligence as the man who cracked the case of the murdered lawyers. He had literally saved the U.S. from total domestic and economic disaster.

In the present instance, however, Falk looked considerably worse for the wear and his clothes were stained with blood. He stood next to the body of a man stretched out on the floor whom Drummond knew to be a terrorist.

Everyone in the room froze in silence at Drummond's unexpected appearance. Then Falk reached down and wrenched the briefcase from Quintero's fingers.

Falk turned to Koski, who seemed numb and was mechanically hugging the child, shielding her eyes from the sight of close-up death. Renewing his grip on the briefcase, Falk shot a glance at the chart room clock: seven-forty-five. If Bonecutter had not been apprehended, they had exactly fifteen minutes to get off the ship before all hell broke loose.

He gently but urgently touched his partner's shoulder. "Koski... Bonecutter?" She lowered her eyes and silently shook her head. He turned to Drummond with the same question in his eyes, but Drummond opened his arms in a futile gesture and shrugged.

"Come on," Falk said. "We've got to get out of here." He nudged Koski's elbow, and she rose from the bench, one arm still around Willie, whose face was partially buried against Koski's sweater.

Falk thought that they, himself included, must look as if they had just returned from a war zone. Although unhurt, Drummond was soaked from rain and disheveled from hours of rummaging into musty corners of the ship.

The Englishman now wore a shell-shocked expression from the scene he'd walked into. The body of a professional murderer who, moments before, was alive and ready to kill them, lay before him. Willie, too, was obviously mentally and physically in tatters. A contusion swelled above her right eye from the force of Quintero's earlier blow.

As Koski passed in front of him, Falk wanted to take her in his arms and hug her and, somehow, erase the pain of this long day.

Her clothes were stained with dirt and dust. Her glorious blonde hair wildly crisscrossed her head and clung with perspiration to her forehead. The odors of urine and liquor hovered around her, replacing, for a time, the scent of Savon Doux Place des Lices Pivoine.

Falk knew how much she must have struggled to overcome her claustrophobia. She might have lost control and tumbled to her death, but she didn't. They were a team, links in a never-ending chain of unsung men and women who affected world events in a positive way. How much he loved her at this very moment.

"Hurry!" Drummond said, awakening from his shock.

Falk pushed the two females into the wheelhouse, still ignoring the knife wound that continued to dampen his side.

Lightning zigzagged into the bridge, a sharp, prolonged series of electrical flashes bolting across the sky. Before the outburst ended, all but a few scattered lights on the ship sizzled out, and most of the vessel was plunged into darkness. A nearby transformer had been knocked out, Falk guessed, as rolls of ear-splitting thunder followed its eternal partner across the sky.

Then Falk heard a familiar, nasal voice in his ear-bud."Falk, Beard here. Do you have the compound?"

"Affirmative. And I have Koski, the Englishman, and the girl with me. The Latin is dead."

"And Bonecutter?"

"We don't know where he is, but he's got the bombs on him. Seven as far as we know. Drummond found three and disarmed them."

"Okay. Get your party off the ship immediately," Beard ordered. Then, in the next breath, "'On him' you say? Are they still armed?"

"We believe he defused them, but if one fuse, or even portion of one, is left in one of those babies…"

Beard cut in. "Well, in any case, he's no longer your responsibility. Get off the ship! Now!"

The reception was clear, no static. As Falk surmised earlier, static and dead spots in parts of the ship were due to steel and iron construction. On deck and in the bridge area the Bluetooth system posed no problem.

He didn't like being told to leave without having found Bonecutter. Yes, the man was dangerous, but the poor bastard was sick and might possibly still blow up the ship. Then a wave of dizziness washed over him and he shoved the briefcase into Drummond's arms.

"Go!" he hollered.

They faced a cold blast of wind and rain as they left the wheelhouse and trooped down the gangway.

"Follow the gangplank escalator," he shouted to Drummond, who led.

Chapter 55

Wind roared through every open portion of the ship, and rain battered every surface, producing an almost musical steel drum sound as water hurtled itself against metal. Except for shore lights trained on her port side, the ship was now in darkness.

While the others raced on ahead, Falk halted at the bottom of the gangway, a lightning flash causing him to look to his right, where a section of the bow was still illuminated. There he saw movement on the foreword mainmast.

Squinting into the storm, he looked up. His breath caught when he saw Jack Bonecutter in the crow's nest high above the deck, his body strobed by lightning, winking like a full moon intermittently obscured by clouds.

"Shit!" Falk whispered.

"It figures," Drummond hissed when the three reached the escalator, and he saw that Falk was not with them. They huddled beneath a huge, blue canopy that covered the gangplank at the top of the unmoving stairs.

"That agent's more than an idiot. Probably found Bonecutter," Drummond said. "It seems to be his nature to be the hero."

Koski's benumbed state following her ascent in the shaft and the horror of the chart room having passed, she was once again Special Agent Koski again.

"Here." She handed Drummond the chemical wrap she had kept in her pocket.

"Take this and Willie and get down to the dock," Koski shouted. "That man's my partner, and I'm going back for him."

Drummond saw a ring of police and army personnel gathering on the dock below. The Haz-Mat unit stood by to deal with the myriad hazardous materials they might encounter.

Drummond recalled the PM's voice from earlier today, telling him not to let the amalgam out of his sight if and when he found it. "Above all else," the PM had told him on the phone, "we have to get our hands on that briefcase, Drummond."

Drummond understood what "above all else" meant. Get off the ship with the highly desired briefcase in possession. He had been fully prepared for that and had came through the ordeal comparatively unscathed, but without the briefcase. Now, here was the briefcase, being offered to him, and his chance for undying glory.

As Koski turned and charged back toward the bow of the ship, Drummond unceremoniously whipped the chemical wrap around the briefcase, tucked it under one arm as if it were an old newspaper, swept Willie into his arms, and started down the large, grooved, metal stairs.

"We've done our good deed for today," he whispered, unsure if Willie heard.

Chapter 56

For Bonecutter, high above the decks, this was the resolution of his experience as a three-year-old, and the reclaiming of his life. It was the completion of a scene, which, too long, had survived behind his eyelids, never wholly having been acted out.

"Whee," he screeched above the sound of wind and thunder. "Whee, little Jack."

Every detail of that long-ago trauma flooded into his mind, as if he had stored up the abuse, waiting for this moment to fully unleash it.

As the wind hurled rain at him, he leaned out over the rim of the crow's nest and slipped the souvenir bag from his shoulder, offering it to the storm.

"Whee. Whe-e-e."

The image of his grandfather took on flesh and impulse. Bonecutter was spirit, playing out the terror again and again. But it was too late for exorcism. There was nothing left but revenge, before his world went totally and violently insane.

Chapter 57

Falk passed the bridge gangway and stumbled across the bow deck. The klieg lights from the dock hardly penetrated the heavy, wind-driven rain. He could see the fore-rigging, jerking and clanking violently this way and that.

When he got to the rope ladder Bonecutter had used to climb to the crow's nest, which Falk thought to use to get to the man, it broke loose at its base due to the pummeling of the wind. It flapped dangerously about in the air, whacking against the mainmast, twisting and turning like a furious snake finally freed from the restraints that bound it.

Frantically, Falk sought another way to save the deranged man. He took a step forward and stopped, feeling something beneath his shoe. Looking down, in the profound darkness he couldn't tell for certain, but it looked like a pager. He bent down and picked it up. A remote control.

Bonecutter's remote.

It must have fallen. That meant Bonecutter couldn't detonate the bombs. A wave of relief washed over Falk. Yet, why did a foreboding sense of time escaping, hissing away like air from a pricked balloon, still press against his heart?

He looked up again, the rain pelting his upturned face, and heard Bonecutter screeching, saw him leaning far out over the rim of the bucket and laughing a lunatic laugh that could be heard above the storm.

It seemed that, any second, he would topple from his precarious perch as he swung a plastic bag in his outstretched arms toward the lightning that, again, lit the sky.

The bag. Falk thought. The plastic bag full of bombs.

Grim foreboding turned to concern and then outright fear. Beard had said that Bonecutter defused the bombs, but if even one fuse remained, even a portion of one, anything could still set them off even without the detonator.

There was a sudden, deafening silence. Then a splintering crack, as if the sky split above them. Falk whirled and saw Koski rushing toward him, ready to help, unaware of what Falk would know in nightmares for the rest of his life.

In that chilling moment of supernatural clarity, Falk lunged headlong through the air, tackling Koski and propelling them both as far as he could from the death he saw coming, while pinning them to the deck behind the thick metal gangway of the bridge.

Thunder and lightning collided in the sky overhead. The sound, like a million crashing thunderbolts, screamed through the air. A long flash of lightning hit the crow's nest, snaking its sizzling tendrils into the bag Bonecutter was holding out and rocketed life into the one partially armed explosive.

In one instant, Bonecutter there, in the next he was a sparkler, a core of white-hot energy of electricity gone mad, spiking incandescent flares into the ebony sky.

The next moment, he and the nest that had nurtured his madness were blown apart, the detonation hurtling rigging, scraps of metal, and shards of human debris in every possible direction.

Before he forced his eyes to shut, Falk saw bulbs of flame, like comets, rip into the bow, splintering the heavy wooden deck planks into shreds. Wet wood went furiously aflame. Chunks of steel, timber, rope and glass torpedoed everywhere, exploding windows and ripping holes in the wood about them.

Chapter 58

Falk swam against the waves of sleep that washed over him threatening to sent him back to a hideous dream of death. Drummond appeared. He ran, racing to get off the ship but couldn't get off soon enough. The vessel exploded around him; the briefcase he carried burst into a million malignant molecules and diseased cells spewed and wriggled in the scorching, burning, debris-filled air. The malevolent pieces buried themselves like leeches in his flesh.

Falk thought he screamed.

Then he slept again, until, at last, knew he was dreaming, as the tide he swam against became a voice.

"Joe? Joe?"

His mouth was sour. He gulped saliva that tasted of rust and kept escaping from lips that felt weighed down. Slowly he opened his eyes.

"You're going to be okay, Joe." It was Koski. She was safe. But her words quivered with tears. "You've got bruises, and lacerations, and you've lost a lot of blood from the knife wound, but you're going to be all right."

He tried to raise his head and look around, but even the slight movement of his eyes made his head hurt. After a few seconds it became clear he was on a gurney, no doubt on his way to an ambulance. His head was bandaged; a mask hissed over his nose and mouth mouth, and the IVs in his arms were attached to bags of fluids held high in the air by a paramedic who walked briskly along his right side.

"Koski," Falk rasped. "You okay?"

She was walking on the other side of the rolling stretcher, which was propelled by another paramedic at Falk's feet. Her warm hand held his, and she bent down toward him as he was jostled along.

"I'm fine," she whispered. "Thanks to you. You saved my life."

"Good," he barely got out. "And Willy?"

"In the ambulance that just left. Her parents are with her. She was banged up some, and has a slight concussion, but she'll be fine. Her Girl Scout troop is already calling her a hero."

She didn't wait for his next three questions.

"The briefcase is intact, safely contained in the chemical wrap and on its way to a secret location. No doubt it will be the subject of years of discussions between the British and American governments and a source of wild speculation on the part of the press."

So it was over, Falk thought. Hopefully, the world would never have to know the weapon's true sinister potential; or that two so-called peace-loving nations had commissioned its creation. He sighed, letting go of the sense of obligation that lifted from his shoulders.

He thought of the scientist in Panama, and what anguish he must have suffered during his years of exile. Maybe the three traditional words invoked at funerals and etched into countless headstones would, in the old man's case, finally be prophetic.

Koski murmured some encouraging remarks, but Falk

momentarily lost her words. His heart was light and his senses seemed to be soaring. Another huge sigh caused his body to seem to float in air.

Finally, "Drummond?" Falk asked.

"Fit as a fiddle, thanks to you."

"Where is he?"

"In Beard's office, being debriefed. I heard him acting Mr. Humble in there, constantly praising you. But the press is making such a fuss over him. Looks like he is going to be an international hero."

Falk squeezed her hand. "So Willie and Drummond are heroes, are they? What does that make you, Koski?"

At first she registered surprise at the question, then a small smile. "I'm enough to be me."

Falk thought that this was probably the most inappropriate time for the words he was about to say, but a fine, warm certainty made him utter them. "Know what I'm going to be?"

"What?"

"A husband. If you'll have me."

Koski bolted straight up and stopped as the gurney continued on and was wheeled to the open doors of the ambulance. She watched in surprise as its wheels folded under and it was pushed into the back of the vehicle. Then she caught up, and they let her hustle in beside him.

She huddled close to his face.

"I guess I need to go to the hospital, too," she whispered with dead seriousness. "To be checked out. I think I'm hearing things that couldn't possibly have been said."

An exquisite tiredness came over Falk, and he slipped back into a much needed sleep.

Epilogue

As the ambulance passed the mobile command post, Marshak was in his small office, packing up his paperwork. He had his wife on the speakerphone.

She said, "Thank God you're safe, Bukka."

"Of course I'm safe, woman."

"The bomber, he's dead?"

"Yes."

During the long hours that constituted this tragic day, Marshak had given more thought to the man and his motives. "You know," he told his wife, "I've been thinking that maybe the guy didn't really care so much about destroying this ship as he seemed to let on."

He looked around the room as if checking to be sure no one else heard him make what he thought was a pseudo-psychological concession.

"Maybe, for some weird reason that we'll never know, that maybe even Bonecutter didn't know, he subconsciously hated the ship. And maybe he had a damned good reason to want to wreck her."

"Maybe," his wife acknowledged, uncomprehending. "Has General Beard gone?"

"Colonel Beard?" Marshak corrected. "No, not yet; he's about to talk to the reporters. I understand that 'we', meaning the United States Army, are taking full credit for the success of this operation."

"Success? But we all watched on television most of the bridge and bow of the ship blown away."

"Well, she didn't sink. And since the damage was confined to the upper decks, she's repairable. But the main thing is, only two lives were lost." He looked around the room again. "And some secret hazardous material, that would have poisoned the entire planet if we hadn't found it, is safely on its way to an undisclosed underground lab. Of course, that's between us."

He paused to drag on a cigarette before concluding, "I knew, first thing when I got up this morning, this day was going to be a doozy."

The Complete Koski & Falk

Book Five

Dedication

To all my readers who enjoy the Koski and Falk stories. Truth is often hidden behind a layer of fiction, as I find in life today in many instances.

Acknowledgements

To Kaethe Kauffman, my editor, who, again, has done a terrific job. She was my compass throughout the journey.

Chapter 1

This wasn't how her week had begun.

Earlier, when Kate had finished researching the background of literary agent, Lev Leventhal, an old and trusted friend of her father, she had looked forward to meeting him. Arriving at his office on South La Cienega in Hollywood, Joanie Malone, Lev's assistant, greeted her and apologized for his absence. He was out of town at Time Was, a small hotel in the Santa Barbara Mountains, helping one of his writers suffering from writer's block, teetering on the brink of a nervous breakdown.

Naturally, Kate was disappointed, although the thought that he had gone to help a client impressed her. Joanie served coffee in the office and filled her in on her own background. Graduated from college with an MA in Information Management, she had become a temporary librarian. Two years later, she moved to Hollywood where she met Lev, who offered her a real job. She and Lev were as different as chalk and cheese. Nonetheless, within a year they had become a dynamic duo. Joanie, smart and good-looking, was superbly organized. Lev, fifty-seven, had, over the years, earned an open door to most of the top producers in town. Although he had a small stable of writers, they were all top notch. Even the young Turks recognized his Hollywood shrewdness. During their first year together, Lev discovered he also had talent as a sleuth when he single-handedly solved the murder of Cy Wald, a Hollywood mogul.

Joanie ran the office whenever Lev was out of town, and over a second cup of coffee, mentioned Lev had said the contract between the Leventhal-Malone agency and Katherine Keenan was, despite his absence, ready to sign if she was.

Kate signed right then. The thought of an agent in Hollywood who would go help a client on the verge of a breakdown cinched the deal.

Two days later, Lev Leventhal met Kate in person. He rose from behind his desk, shook hands, and indicated a well-worn leather armchair. He did not look like a sleuth who could solve a murder. Thin on top, thick around the middle, and height about five foot six, maybe eight if he stood straighter and squared his rounded shoulders.

"Sorry I was unable to be here when you came in to sign the contract; an unexpected problem." His voice was crisp, his green eyes intense. Kate instantly knew this guy could solve more than a murder.

When Lev sat back in his chair with narrowed eyes, Kate could literally feel his high hopes for her.

"Why me?" he asked.

"We met briefly when I was a student at UCLA. You said you were interested in movie technology, and I learned you are well connected in the movie industry. When I came to visit, your assistant, Joanie Malone, told me about your success as a detective, and that's something I need. Besides, my father, Ethan, always said you were someone I could trust if I needed help."

Placing her laptop on his desk, Kate sat down, smoothing the darts of her green Lyell Claire dress that showcased her unruly red hair.

Lev reddened slightly. "Thanks. Well, now that we've gotten all that out of the way, we can discuss the Frank Primo pitch."

Kate explained, "I'm ready to present my work to Mr. Primo, but I want to go over few details with you first."

"Of course, go right ahead," Lev said, his foot tapping a subtle rhythm on the floor, as if in anticipation.

Joanie's voice cut in on the intercom. "A courier is here with a package for Kate."

Perfect timing, thought Kate.

Lev snapped the intercom switch. "Bring it in."

Joanie entered carrying a small flat rectangular package and laid it on the desk. Kate smiled. "Thanks, Joanie."

Joanie left, and Kate quickly opened the package and removed a slim device about the size of an iPod. Kate attached a cable from the laptop to the device and said, "Technology will play a major role in the way this century will unfold. Computing, robotics, and biotechnology will be revolutionized."

Lev looked mystified, and nodded slowly.

Booting up her computer, Kate angled the screen toward him. "Can you see okay?"

Lev nodded.

She tapped the play button and sat back. Lev watched and heard what looked like a movie clip: A man and woman walked beside a mountain lake to soft background music. Stopping at the edge of the water, the man scooped up a flat stone and skimmed it across the lake. The girl laughed, "Not bad, three daps. Bet I can beat it!" She sorted through a few stones on the shore with the toe of her shoe until she found the right one, picked it up and sent it soaring across the lake. The screen faded to black.

"What's this?" Lev asked, his curiosity alive in his eyes.

"A clip from a computer software program I designed. I key in description, just as I would type narration in a book. However, in this case, this little box I've just attached changes what I've written into a visual scene. I describe the characters and they appear. I type dialog and the box changes it into spoken words." Looking at Lev, Kate could see he was not entirely on the same page. "Okay, picture a film script."

"Go on," Lev said, both feet now audibly tapping on the floor.

"When I type, instead of letters of the alphabet, my keystrokes are changed into a moving picture. Watch."

Kate typed: The man, dressed in a blue shirt and brown shorts is reading a book, sitting on a park bench. Then she clicked play and Lev immediately saw what she had typed in full color.

"As with the written word, Mr. Leventhal, when we need more detail we have to show, not tell." Lev nodded, his lips slightly parted, as if subtly panting.

Again, Kate's fingers danced across the keyboard: An elderly man dressed in a beige three-piece suit walks beside a busy highway, dazedly watching cars pass in either direction.

She glanced up at Lev. "I think I should give him a cane."

Kate keyed in: He is carrying a wooden walking stick. The picture on the screen immediately conformed to Kate's typing. Lev's body jolted in his seat.

Kate smiled at his reaction and clicked pause. "Different from anything you have ever seen, right? My software program, housed in this little side box, is unlike anything known. I direct who wears what, how they speak, move, everything. Whatever I write turns into an instant movie. This is, of course, a prototype. Later designs will include a more sophisticated dictionary of specifics to work with." Lev stared, wide-eyed, at the still frame of the old man and his stick.

"Editing, both visual and audio will be the same as polishing a draft of a typewritten script. I find that when people work with my program, they become a part of the movie. They feel it and hear it as they write. They become a part of it."

"You have a patent on this?" Lev gulped, his Adam's apple

sliding up and down several times, reflecting his intense interest and rapid thoughts. "I mean, I was ready to contract with you as your agent just from what you'd said. But seeing it, however, is..."

"Yes, amazing, isn't it. That's why I want to demonstrate it to Mr. Primo. As for the patent, the US Patent and Trademark Division moves slowly. I've filed and expect a reply any day. My program also includes anti-key-login software."

Lev looked puzzled, "Key-logging? That have something to do with security?"

"Do you use a computer, Mr. Leventhal?"

"Don't even own one," he said, then paused. "Joanie has one in her office, and a laptop at home. I never got comfortable with computers; too late for me, I guess."

Kate had guessed as much and bet he did not know a Mac from a PC. "I wouldn't say that, Mr. Leventhal. Given the right introduction, I imagine you'd do fine."

"Call me Lev, Kate," he said warmly. "I didn't even learn to type, never mind a computer. I use a cell phone, though, and I'm thinking of switching to Bluetooth."

Kate nodded, "Great. Now about key-loggin. Hackers have multiple ways at their disposal to secretly record anyone's keystrokes, and in so doing can read passwords and other private information. However, anyone attempting to hack my system will automatically destroy whatever it is they're seeking."

"How does that work?"

"I don't want to overload you with too much of the technical whiz-bang. Let's just say that every time I type anything, it's absolutely safe."

Lev pointed at the slim piece of equipment delivered by the courier and attached to Kate's computer. "What's that?"

"That is the reason I'm able to create what I type into a moving, speaking picture. Technically speaking, it's called an interpreter program. It's what powers the base program on my computer. Both have to be connected to do what I've just demonstrated to you. You might wonder why I didn't bring it with me, but, instead, had it delivered."

"Yeah, I did."

Kate quickly detached the slim pack and pushed it across the desk to Lev. "I need a detective. I'm being watched and followed. I have no idea by whom. I never carry the two pieces together anymore. Tomorrow evening, when we meet Mr. Primo, I want you to carry this in your inside jacket pocket. It's small. No one will know you're carrying it."

Lev began to object, but Kate held up a hand. "I will feel better if you do this. You don't mind do you?"

"Of course not, but have you spoken to the police about being followed?"

"No, I didn't want any publicity. I don't want anyone knowing what I've told and showed you."

"What you have here, Kate, is worth millions, and before our appointment with Primo, I have a lot more questions about your invention." Lev's voice quivered like a tightly strung violin string.

"I'm sure you do. Once Mr. Primo decides to use my system, all my patents are registered, and you and he sign contracts, I believe whoever is trying to steal my invention will have lost their chance."

"Let me get you a bodyguard, Kate," Lev pleaded.

"I won't need one if you just keep Al Jolson here safe. That's all I ask."

"Al Jolson?"

"When Al Jolson sang 'Mammy' in *The Jazz Singer*, he changed Hollywood overnight. My Al Jolson here is going to do the same."

Chapter 2

Lev and Kate circulated through the crowd of partygoers on stage four at Galaxy Studios in Burbank. Music blared, conversation and laughter vied with the clink of glasses. Kate turned to speak to Lev to find he was no longer at her side. As a result, Kate ended up chatting with a group of strangers standing near the band when the music suddenly stopped and producer Frank Primo, tall and elegantly dressed in an impeccable dinner jacket and black tie, stepped on stage and waved to the crowd.

"Thank you. Thank you all, but this is *your* wrap party folks."

A wrap party was a cross between a political convention and a brawl, and held at the completion of a movie. Primo ran a finger around the inside of his shirt collar, licked his lips and continued.

"I couldn't have made this picture without every one of you here, with big special kudos to our stars, Stella and Chaz."

Pushed up close to the stage, Kate saw sweat break out on Primo's temples and his knuckles whiten as he gripped the microphone stand. A spotlight jabbed down from above and enveloped Stella Rae, a young woman in her early twenties in tight, low-slung jeans and a brief top revealing a red rose tattooed on her right shoulder. High cheekbones, blonde hair cut short, spiky, and red pouty lips completed her stylish look. Next to her slouched hunk Chaz Falconer, Stella's highly publicized future husband. Chaz, with a three-day stubble and uncombed dark hair, wearing an Armani tuxedo and an open neck red shirt, smiled graciously and waved to all the little people. Each time either one of them made a movie, Stella and Chaz each made twenty million dollars. Rumor had it that after they were married, they were going to a village in China to adopt a baby girl and name her Olympia in honor of the Beijing Olympic games.

Suddenly, Primo convulsed in a paroxysm of coughing. One hand firmly gripping to the microphone, he clawed frantically at his tie, eyes widening into a terrified stare as his knees buckled and he crashed to the stage dragging the microphone with him.

Utter silence, then cries of dismay rose from the audience.

Someone turned to a security guard and grasped his arm. "Call an ambulance!" The guard pressed the send button on his shoulder-mounted two-way. "Code eight. Stage four."

Paramedics arrived and Primo made his stage exit on a gurney amid rumors that he had suffered a heart attack. Security then began ushering the crowd out of the sound stage; being close to a door, Kate was one of the first pushed out into the night.

Chapter 3

"Hell of way to go, Lev."

Lev turned. Charles Vance stood next to him holding a glass of vodka. "Yeah, what happened?"

"Don't know, could have been anything."

Vance, in his mid-sixties and healthy, was still remembered as a star of the forties and fifties who'd sung his way to a fortune, collecting several glamorous wives along the way. He'd appeared in musicals during the Hollywood Golden Era when Astaire and Kelly danced for MGM. Now he owned a posh supper club on the Strip, Charley Vee's, and would belt out a song at the club on special occasions.

"I'm searching for Kate," Lev muttered.

"I saw her talking to a group of the A-list guests just before the ruckus." He aimed his glass in the direction of the stage.

"Thanks. I'm sure she's here someplace," Lev said

"How long has she been with your agency, Lev?"

"A week. Joanie signed her up when I was up in Santa Barbara. Kate's a great talent and I'm lucky to get her."

Vance took a sip of his vodka and said, "I hear she's a smart cookie."

Lev nodded, "Rich grandparents, too. They educated her in private schools in Switzerland and the US. She's fluent in German and French. Graduated Cum Laude from UCLA film school prior to her twentieth birthday. Her first screenplay, *Mouse Trip*, a murder mystery solved by a teen-aged computer hacker, won the Grand Jury Prize at Sundance. Her second film, *Download*, another mystery that took place in the world of hi-tech computers, and software piracy took second at Cannes."

Vance finished his drink. "Sounds like a winner. Don't worry, she's around here some place. Take care, Lev, Vicky calls." There were still a few guests standing around and talking while security was busy ordering them to leave.

Lev took a quick circuit of the cavernous sound stage but it proved fruitless. Kate was gone. He stepped outside, knowing that Charlie Vance's longevity in Hollywood was partly due to his being a master bullshitter, and the rest due to his latest trophy wife, Vicky Vance, a syndicated newspaper columnist, always ready to crank out the latest celebrity news including inside dirt on Hollywood scandals. Vicky had a weekend TV show that could churn out more gossip in ten minutes than Oprah could in one hour. Vicky carried influence in town.

Lev was almost to his car when he remembered Kate always

carried a cell phone with her. Luckily, he'd entered her number on his phone's list.

Her cell rang ten times; it didn't even switch to call forwarding. Something was wrong. She normally picked up a call on the second ring.

He called her home phone and left a message on her answering machine.

Driving out the studio main gate, he decided to go to her place and check things out. His intuition told him to be extra cautious, especially after what Kate had said about being followed. Turning left onto Barham Boulevard, he headed toward the Hollywood Freeway.

It was after eleven when he pulled into her driveway noting there were no lights on in the single story stucco house. Lev rang the doorbell and heard an "Avon Calling" chime. He waited, then headed down the driveway and checked the back door. It was unlocked. No one left a door unlocked in Hollywood, especially at this time of the night. *Was it left unlocked on purpose or had someone unlocked it and entered?* he wondered.

He should call the cops, but there was no guarantee they'd show up simply because of an open back door.

That shifted Lev's paranoia into overdrive. She could be lying in a pool of blood somewhere in the house. Hurrying back up the driveway to his car, Lev grabbed a flashlight from under the front seat, returned to the kitchen door and slowly pushed it open. He remained motionless for a few seconds, scarcely breathing. There was not a sound in the house.

Snapping on the flashlight, he bounced the beam around the kitchen and cautiously headed toward the front of the two-bedroom, one-bath home. It didn't take long to assure himself that

Kate was not slumped unconscious in the living room. In fact, nothing at all seemed to have been disturbed.

He made his way down the hall to Kate's home office, opened the door and snapped on the light switch. *What a mess!* his mind screamed. Books and papers were scattered all across the floor. A computer desk held no computer. A three-drawer file had all three drawers open; two drawers were empty. Not only was Kate missing, so was a hunk of her home office.

Lev made an anonymous call to the cops, reporting a break in at 933 N. Sweetzer, then, moving fast, returned to his car and headed home.

He should have waited for the police, but he was in no mood to go through the usual Q and A procedure. He was too worn out. He needed time to think and if possible, grab some sleep.

His dash clock showed one fifty a.m. as Lev turned off the ignition, locked the car and entered his place on Lookout Mountain Avenue. His house was located in a tangle of twisting roads and lanes that twined through the hills above West Hollywood.

Lev and his sister had grown up in this very house. She'd married a patent lawyer a year after she completed college, and now lived in Florida with two kids. Their parents had long since passed and he'd inherited the house. The rambling redwood with a huge outdoor deck perched on stilts cantilevered deeply into the side of a ravine overlooked the lights of an ever-growing Hollywood.

The quietness of the hills was always a welcome solace after the intense hustle and bustle of Hollywood. Despite his tiredness, he took time to listen to the silence, something he found himself doing increasingly these days. He opened the fridge, grabbed a Bud, headed out to the deck and slumped into an old Adirondack chair, pulled the tab and took a deep swig as the distant howl of a coyote floated on the night breeze. Given half a chance, life could be sweet.

Chapter 4

Amid the jostling crowd outside the sound stage, Kate suddenly felt a hand grip her arm and heard aman's gruff voice ordering her to go with him. She pulled back, but he already had her in the shadows. "Kate, come with me. Right now. You're in danger." She twisted back and saw it was a security guard, tall and intent, his eyes full of urgency. "Frank Primo was murdered. You could be next. Come with me."

The shock of what he'd said temporarily stopped any further resistance, and Kate was pulled deeper into the darkness. By now, most of the crowd had left the building and were some distance ahead, streaming towards the main gate.

He yanked her to the side towards the blackness of the studio back lot. It was then Kate knew something was wrong. She tried to pull away and took a swing at him, but he moved too fast and kicked her Sergio Rossi's out from under her until she was face down on the asphalt.

"Bitch," he grunted, pulling her arms behind her back and snapping on a pair of cuffs. "Do as I tell you next time."

Kate tried to lift her head and scream. But, sprawled face down, all she could do was suck grit and dust.

She felt him push up the sleeve of her jacket, and twitched at the jab of a needle into her arm. Immediately, she felt a sliding, sinking sensation as if her entire body was slowly soaking into the earth, while a voice, far away, repeatedly told her to relax.

The next she knew, she was on her back on a canvas cot with

the mother of all hangovers. Trying to open her eyes was a chore. Her head thumped like an uneven load in a washing machine. She tried to move her hands and found them still handcuffed beneath her back.

As Kate struggled to focus, the same security guard leaned over her, his breath reeking of stale fast food. Quickly, she snapped her eyes shut.

"Can't fool me, Kate, I know you're awake. You're a missing person and only I know where you are."

Think! her brain screamed. Kate Keenan had written hundreds of scenes like this. She knew about bad guys, from chain saw murderers to clowns who bury their victims under the house. Slowly, she opened an eye."Where the hell am I?" she asked.

"You're a writer, Kate; you know the best villains would never answer that question. And I'm top of the line," he said, smirking at his joke.

"Take off the manacles and I promise to listen up. They're so tight they might have already done permanent damage to these fingers I depend on for my living."

A flicker in his eyes told her that, for some reason, her hands mattered to him. He flipped Kate over like a hamburger and unlocked the cuffs. Her hands were numb and she rubbed them hard to get the circulation moving. Then she sat up, eyes darting around the cell-like cinderblock room with its single light bulb dangling from the ceiling. Where was her laptop? Kate had carried it with her to the wrap party, slung across her shoulders for safety. Her skin tingled with the realization and panic it was nowhere in sight.

"You stole my computer, you son of a bitch!" Kate yelled. The security man leaned against the wall and watched her. "It's safe. It's not going any place. I'm being paid to look after you and your gear."

The last buzz from whatever he'd stuck in her arm was starting to wear off and she was beginning to feel almost normal. "Why the hell did you drug me? And what on earth for?"

"Your own safety," he drawled.

"From what?" Kate asked rubbing her still sore hands. "You're not the safest person I've ever met."

Opening the door of the concrete room, he stepped aside and signaled with an upturned hand. "C'mon, I'll show you your office where you'll be working until your assignment is complete."

Kate crossed to the door and into a larger, rectangular room with the lingering musty smell of an unused cellar. Three parallel metal racks standing over six feet tall ran off into the darkness. A light abruptly clicked on in the distant corner, followed by another immediately above a large wooden desk located ten feet in front of her. On it was her laptop. She noted a bright yellow cable snaking from the darkness plugged into the side of the computer.

"Just like at home, Kate. No one to disturb you," the skinny man purred. "Controlled air temperature year round—a writers, or in your immediate case, a programmer's dream."

Kate turned and looked across at her keeper lolling against row after row of film canisters stacked on the metal shelves, and asked, "What assignment?"

"You'll know soon enough," and asked if she'd ever been in a film vault before. With the realization, Kate felt a tightness grip her chest. She was underground! She began to breathe fast and shallow, the word "vault" conjuring up a place of darkness, doom and death. Seeing her reaction, he again assured her that her safety was his responsibility. No one knew she was here except himself and the person who'd hired him.

Kate slumped into the ergonomically correct office chair in front of the desk and stared vacantly at her silent laptop.

"And if I need something in order to finish this 'assignment'?" Kate asked.

"Anything you require will be provided. By me. You just have to ask." The man pointed to the yellow cable indicating it was her only connection to the outside world.

"Access to the internet?" she asked, already knowing the answer.

"Kate, Kate, Kate," the man replied shaking his head from side to side. "Please don't underestimate me or the man I work for. All possible access to the world, outside of this single cable, have been blocked. As to any further requests, I can only assure you that I will provide you with anything you need to complete your assignment. Anything within reason."

So, she was a prisoner in a film vault. Less than an hour ago, she'd been with her agent at a wrap party, waiting to show Frank Primo her revolutionary program. Everything was going great until the man collapsed. If she'd just been able to find Lev before this creep grabbed her, she wouldn't be in this mess.

Chapter 5

The distant but incessant ringing of the house phone awakened Lev with a start. Night was already shifting to day, the sky tinging with the orange streaks of dawn.

Hauling himself awkwardly from the hard wooden deck chair, he stumbled into the house and snapped on the kitchen light. The phone quit ringing. The microwave clock broadcast six a.m. in light-blue digital numbers.

He didn't usually fall asleep on the deck; he'd been worn out last night. Then he remembered Kate. Damn! That could have been her calling! There was no message, so he dialed her home number. Her answering machine eventually told him to leave a message.

He showered, shaved, and ate a fried banana sandwich and was on his third cup of coffee when the phone rang again. Scooping it up before the second ring, he rasped, "Hello, Kate?"

"No. It's me, Joanie. What's with your voice?" Before he could answer, she continued, "I'm at the office. I came in early to finish some work and I found an envelope stuffed under the door."

Envelopes stuffed beneath doors never bode good news. "Read it to me," he growled.

"Okay. 'Kate will contact you soon'."

"That's it? Nothing else?"

"No, except the letters of each word were cut out of a magazine or a newspaper, you know, like a ransom note."

Lev choked, "Cut out letters? Ransom note?"

"That's why I called at once, Lev."

Chapter 6

"It's on my desk." Joanie Malone handed her boss a mug of Grand Marnier-laced coffee, her standard sedative for his nervous tension attacks.

Lev accepted the cup and took a long draught as he studied the pasted words.

"Holy shit! She's been kidnapped!" he again concluded.

"The note says Kate will contact you soon. It doesn't say she's been kidnapped, Lev."

"A note spelled out in newspaper clippings and pushed under our front door sometime in the night doesn't smack of a social letter, Joanie."

"There's nothing mentioned about a ransom."

He signaled for another ration of brandy. "And yet..."

"You're going to call the cops?"

"Calling the cops could compromise Kate's safety. I need to think. In the meantime, get me the list of the 'A' group at last night's wrap party."

Joanie tipped some more Grand Marnier into his mug and left. She returned with the list and laid it on his desk. "There were nine people on the 'A' list."

Lev scanned the names: Charles and Vicky Vance, Stella Rae, Chaz Falconer, Pattie Primo, Don Ames, Franz Villand, Stacy Hart, and Hank Tolomeo. He knew all of them personally except Franz Villand and Hank Tolomeo. He'd heard Villand's name sometime in the past. Tolomeo's name had been in 'Varity' several times the last few months concerning his hi-tech computer company, TolomeoTechnics.

Lev ordered Joanie to get Charles Vance, the celebrity nightclub owner, on the phone. Three minutes later Lev was listening to his booming voice resounding in his ear.

"Hell of wrap party, don't you think, Lev? Primo went out in style."

"I'm not calling about Primo."

"Vicky's been swamped with calls from around the country trying to find out what happened."

"What do you mean? I thought Primo died of a heart attack."

"Word around town is someone might have arranged for his heart to stop."

"Murder?" Lev whispered.

"Yeah, I thought that's what you were calling about."

"No, I was calling to ask about Kate. I still haven't heard from her, and I recall you with her at the party."

"Yeah, she was talking with me, Stacy Hart and Stella Rae as Primo came on stage."

"Did you see her after Primo keeled over?"

"No, like everyone, my attention was on the stage. You think Kate was involved?"

"Involved? You mean because of what she might have seen? Or something about the way he died?"

Charles hesitated. "Well, from what you're telling me, she seems to have vanished, so. It could be either. Have you called the cops?"

"Spoke to them last night." This wasn't a lie. He'd called about the break-in to Kate's place on Sweetzer.

"Well, that's about all you can do, Lev."

"I'm planning on questioning various people who were at the party. Someone might be able to tell me something."

"I'd leave that to the cops if I were you."

"It's not about it being a possible homicide, Charles. I need to find my missing client. Don't you understand?"

"Of course I do, Lev, and I'll do all I can to help." Clearing his throat, he continued, "You might want to start with Stacy Hart."

"Thanks, Charles, I'll do that. Talk to you later."

Lev tilted back in his chair and stared at the ceiling. What was he getting into? He'd known Stacy Hart for years; she was highly respected in both Hollywood and New York. She owned a press agency which represented many of the top names in publishing and show business. What Charles' or his nosey wife, Vicky, might not know, Stacy would.

He pressed the button on his intercom.

"Joanie, get Stacy Hart on the line, please."

Chapter 7

Joanie's voice came over the intercom: "Stacy Hart on three."

"Thanks, Joanie. Stace, can you make lunch? It's important."

"What's up?"

He brought her quickly up to date about Kate.

"You think she's been abducted?"

Who else but Stace would jump to using a word like that in this town? "I don't know. There's certainly a possibility, but I can't think why."

"Right, you can buy me lunch at the Polo Lounge. Shall we say one?"

"One. See you there."

The Beverly Hills Hotel was an oasis amidst palms and splendid flower gardens that bloomed and blossomed year round. Lev drove up the curving driveway toward the imposing pink building that for so many years has been the cradle of luxury to the rich, famous and notorious.

Stace, already seated, was sipping a tall drink; Lev knew it was not iced tea. She reminded him of a quote he'd once heard: "Taking joy in life is a woman's best cosmetic." Stace was a woman with a brilliant business mind, matched with striking beauty. Not yet forty, her two publicity offices, one in New York City, the other in Beverly Hills, were in constant demand.

"Am I late?" Lev pulled out a chair.

Stacy smiled. "Fashionably so. Now what's all this about Kate vanishing?"

Before he could answer, a waiter appeared at the table to take his order. "Give me one of those," Lev said, indicating Stacy's drink.

"I'll have another and the McCarthy salad," Stacy added.

"Make it two salads." Lev announced as he shook out the pink linen napkin and placed it across his knees. "Charles Vance said you and Stella Rae were talking with Kate when Primo made his grand entrance.

"He's correct. Kate was standing right between us. We all turned toward the stage at the same time."

"Was she still with you after Primo collapsed?"

Stace looked deep into her drink before answering. "When that happened everything went wild. I'm not sure."

"Did you recall seeing her after the medics arrived?"

"No. I remember Stella talking with Chaz." She paused. "To be honest, Lev, I don't know where she went."

What he was hearing was so far not worth the price of lunch at the Lounge.

"Wait a minute!" Stace exclaimed. "I do remember something."

The waiter returned with the drinks and salads. Lev leaned forward eagerly as the waiter left and Stacy continued. "Franz Villand, the actor, and Don Ames, the writer. I recall them standing by an exit talking to Kate. Next time I looked, all three were gone."

Two writers and a latter day Lon Chaney had mysteriously vanished from the scene, he thought. Taking a long sip of his drink, Lev asked, "I've met Don Ames, but I only know of Villand. Villand was the 'Man of a Thousand Faces', right?"

Stace nodded. "Right, but he's not done much work the last few years."

"Ran out of faces?"

"I guess. Today, computer graphics do a better job without having to carry workman's comp."

"I think I may have seen Hank Tolomeo at the party," he ventured.

Stace sighed. "So did a lot of people who wished he'd never been born."

"What do you mean?"

"You're kidding, Lev. TolomeoTecnics has been impacting the entire movie industry with its increasingly sophisticated robots Frank Primo had told Hank Tolomeo he might consider using TolomeoTecnics robots in place of stunt actors in his next production. They were this close to a deal. If the deal went through, many thought the impact on the movie industry would be greater than the introduction of sound." She held her thumb and forefinger almost touching each other.

"What is it exactly about this kind of technology that has the town so rattled?" The incredibly realistic scene of the couple walking besides a lake that Kate had produced for him in the office flashed across his mind.

"Wish I knew for sure. I've heard rumors that the right technology could save producers a ton of money and put a lot of people in the industry out of work. Not even Vicky Vance and her spies have found out what's going on, but whatever it is, it's big."

"We've both seen new production systems impact Hollywood, Stace: Cinemascope, Three-D, Wide-Screen, I-Max. All were similarly hyped, but in the end, they've ended up requiring more people and money."

She patted her lips with a tip of her napkin. "All I know for sure is that TolomeoTechnics was betting all their savings on Primo using their system. It was to be TT's big showcase for the industry worldwide. People like Franz Villand should be happy Primo's gone."

Lev nodded. "Meaning the longer computerized productions and imagery are kept out of film, the better the chance for actors like him, right?"

"Yes, also many special effects companies, production companies, and stunt persons would find themselves out of business." Stace shook her head, "Hollywood without real live actors, videographers, gaffers, makeup artists, scene builders..." Stacy's voice trailed off as she skewered a piece of tomato. "If and when that happens, Lev, *we* could be in the same boat."

The lunch proved a bummer. Bad news. No leads. Talk about doom and gloom. Lev pushed his plate aside. "You really think it'll happen, Stace?"

"Not overnight I don't, but think about it: What if it were possible to make and show movies without the cost of stars, supporting actors, backups, stand-ins, extras, and all the various trades, guilds and unions that go into making a feature. Perhaps I should take on TT as one of my clients."

Lev switched the conversation. "Any idea where I can find Franz Villand? He might have a lead on where Kate went after they left the sound stage."

"No; however, you said Villand, Ames and Kate were together. You know Don Ames well and he's quite approachable. How about trying him?" Stacy asked.

"I turned down one of his scripts once, and he's never forgotten. He bad-mouths me every opportunity he gets. He hates my guts," Lev admitted.

"Then call Vicky Vance. If anyone, she'd knows how to find Villand."

On that positive note, they switched to ice cream, coffee and gossip.

On the way back, traffic on Sunset was, as usual, at a crawl. Lev figured Stace would have called Vicky Vance by now and word would be out that Kate was missing, just as he'd planned. Their tête-à-tête had also helped Lev identify another place to start in his search.

Driving past the UCLA campus, his mind returned to the days when Kate was still a student there in theater arts. He had been asked to address her class and remembered her vocally emphasizing the future importance of having a platform in which one could create moving images constructed digitally to simulate imagined realities. While others continued to talk about it, she had gone ahead and done it. Later, when she approached him as her agent, he didn't have the chance to go into details with her, or for the two of them to present her system to Primo. After talking to Stacy about TolomeoTechnics, could it be possible Kate had been spirited away because of her new technology? Or, was someone attempting to steal Kate's program to sell it to TolomeoTechnics? If he understood what she'd said correctly, her program wouldn't work without the part nicknamed Al Jolson, that he carried in his pocket. If someone abducted Kate or stole her program, how long would it take the thief to figure out her agent had the missing piece of the puzzle?

Chapter 8

The first thing Lev heard as he entered his office was Joanie's animated voice. "You didn't turn on your cell, did you? You left it off, and I couldn't get hold of you."

"What happened?" The way the day was going, he wasn't sure he really wanted to know.

"A friend of Kate's called. He wants to talk to you."

He definitely wanted to know more about this. "Phone lines run all the way to the Polo Lounge, Joanie. What did you tell him?"

"To hoof it over here. He sounded upset."

"Good girl. In the meantime, get Vicky Vance on the line." Lev walked into his office and closed the door. A moment later, he was on the line with Vicious Vicky.

"Lev, darling, how nice of you to call," Vicky drawled. "What juicy morsel you have for me?"

"Actually, Vicky I'm seeking, not giving."

"Oh, you wonderful man. Didn't I see you at last night's catastrophe?"

"I saw you there, but, as usual, you were busy and I didn't want to butt in."

"Silly boy," she cooed. "I would have loved to chat awhile with you. What is it you seek?"

"I need to talk with Franz Villand."

"Franz! What has that recluse done now?"

"Well, nothing as far as I know. I just wanted to ask him a couple of questions."

"Is it about what happened last night to poor Primo?" At least she mentioned the deceased.

"No, not about 'poor Primo'. I wonder if you knew where I could contact Villand." He had no doubt that by now, Stace had told her he was searching for Kate.

"Well, I could put out feelers for you. We have to work together in this town, don't we, Lev?" which was columnist code for, you scratch my back and I'll scratch yours.

"Vicky," Lev replied softly. "Do it and I'll owe you."

"Yes, yes, you will, dear Lev. Give me your cell number. I may have to call you at an odd time. Never know in our business, do we?"

Lev gave her his cellular number. "Call any time, Vicky. I'll be available."

"Call me anytime, too, Lev. Ta-ta."

Lev was glad the fencing match with Vicky Vance, wife of Charles Vance, the owner of Charley Vee's, was over. In one short afternoon, he'd had to come into close contact with a press agent and a gossip columnist deluxe. He squirmed, fully aware he'd have to pay dearly for each later. There were no freebies in Hollywood.

Leaning back, he replayed the dramatic end of the wrap party in his mind. Stace said Kate had been standing next to the exit with Ames and Villand. Until Lev located Villand and listened to his version of what happened, he was stuck on square one. He pulled the 'A' list toward him and put check marks next to Vicky Vance, Stacy Hart, and Charles Vance.

Chapter 9

Joanie announced over the intercom, "Kate's 'friend' is here. Shall I send him in?"

"Yes, of course," replied Lev.

There was a light tap on the door before it opened, revealing a dark haired man in his mid-twenties peeping in.

"I had to come see you, Mr. Leventhal."

"Come in. Sit down." Lev indicated the comfortable client chair. The young man smiled and folded his slim form into the well-worn leather seat. Legs crossed, he leaned back and quickly scanned the cluttered, untidy office, and then stared at Lev with deep brown eyes. "Kate gave me your number," he said, "in case anything happened. My name is Melhi Pashagora. Kate and I went to UCLA together. We were classmates."

Lev felt a surge of adrenalin. "Exactly what do you mean, 'if anything happens'?"

"She told me she had a feeling she was being followed. It was one reason she said she wanted to meet you."

"When was this?"

"Last week. I asked her to call me and check in every day. I called her house and cell phone the last two days with no answer. I'm worried, Mr. Leventhal. I notified the police but was told they don't consider anyone a missing person until seventy-two hours have passed."

"When exactly did you contact them?"

"This morning. Then I called your office."

Here was someone who'd spent four years with Kate at UCLA. The young man could be a big help.

"Did you both study film writing at UCLA?"

"Yes, we used to compete with each other, in a friendly way, of course." He smiled, as if talking about Kate made him feel better.

Lev nodded. "Kate also studied computing in film and the arts, right?"

"We both did. TFT—Theater, Film and Television. They used to call us the Competing Computerites."

"Are you a working writer now, Mr. Pashagora?"

"Not in the literal sense. And please, call me Mel, everyone does." He took a deep breath then continued. "After graduation, Apple recruited me, and now I write software and work closely with the digital environment platform group Apple runs in conjunction with UCLA."

"Sounds like an important position, Mel."

"It is, and like Apple says, 'the importance of having a platform in which one can create moving images that are artificially constructed to simulate imagined realities cannot be overestimated'. Apple firmly believes it will increasingly become the basis for all art forms in the future.'"

"You sound very sincere."

"I am. And it's the reason I'm deeply concerned about Kate's disappearance."

"What do you mean?"

Mel glanced at his hands clenched firmly together on his lap. "It all began two days before we graduated. It was late and we were the only two left in the 'Bull Pen,' a nickname for an area of the lab that students have access to twenty-four/seven. It was two fifty-eight a.m. I recall the exact time, I still have the digital copy I made of a test she had run.

"What sort of test?" Lev asked.

"Kate had designed a radical piece of software and wanted me to see it. We were both jazzed with the results."

"Tell me about it," Lev said. Mel hesitated, but his concern for Kate was stronger than his reticence to share about the program.

"I must first ask you one thing, Mr. Leventhal. What I'm about to reveal could well be tied to her disappearance and be detrimental to her ever being found alive. You must agree not repeat what I'm about to tell you to anyone. Anyone, understand?"

"You have my word, Mel. I also want to find Kate," Lev replied in all earnestness.

"Thank you." Mel chewed his bottom lip for a second. "What would you say if I were to tell you that it is possible to create movie action on the big screen just by typing in dialog and description as one would do when writing any normal script? With her new program, instead of type, the actual movie activity appears on screen." A faint smile crossed the young man's face. "John

Landis, the famous movie director, always said if Hollywood could find a way to make a movie without a director they would. Well, Kate has. Without a director, producer, actors, supporting staff, background, sound, you name it."

Lev leaned forward and said softly, "Kate gave me a demonstration of this program, here in my office." He didn't reveal that Kate had contracted with him to be her agent and had left a crucial part of the equipment with him.

Mel stiffened visibly. "Why would she do that?"

"We were to meet with Frank Primo after the wrap party for his latest film. He had let it be known to the movie community of his interest in doing a technologically innovative film next. Unfortunately, Primo died before we could meet with him and demonstrate Kate's system. Who else knows about this system?"

"No one as far as I know. Kate made me promise to keep it quiet because we knew her discovery would change Hollywood filmmaking forever. She alone knows the actual construction design of the program. I only saw it work, as you apparently did," Mel said.

"Could someone have picked up on her test from the Bull Pen?" Lev asked.

"It's possible, I suppose, although she kept the details strictly to herself," Mel replied.

"What about hackers? There must have been some in the class," Lev inquired.

"Kate and I are good enough programmers to know how to prevent the best hackers from breaking into her computer or program. Towards the end, she announced she had built in several 'safeguards' which she never shared with me. In the end, we were both recruited by top companies. I had to decide between joining the FBI computer fraud division and Apple after graduation." Mel said, unabashed.

"And Kate decided to continue writing screenplays while continuing to advance her computerized movie production system?" Lev offered.

"Not exactly. The National Security Agency approached her and would have taken her in a moment. She told them she'd seriously think about, while she finished a couple of films," Mel said.

"Sundance and Cannes, right?" Lev asked.

"Yes." Mel appeared increasingly uncomfortable with Lev's surprising knowledge of Kate and her program. "She's a very determined woman, Mr. Leventhal. She takes after her father, Ethan."

Lev raised his eyebrows. "Meaning?"

"Ethan Keenan, was a screenwriter here Hollywood some twenty years ago. He suffered a breakdown after his wife's death, took to drinking, and eventually abandoned Kate. She was reared by her grandparents—rich grandparents, who made sure she had the best education possible. She grew up believing her father was dead. It was not until her third year at UCLA that she discovered he was still alive."

For Lev, the disappearance of Kate was taking on a decidedly different tone. He clearly needed to learn more about the relationship between Kate and this young man. Lev wondered about NSA. If they wanted her to work for them, they likely knew about her program and it's implications beyond Hollywood. Now reported missing person, Lev speculated whether NSA might also be attempting locate her. Or were they perhaps involved in her disappearance?

Chapter 10

Her scumbag security guard had been gone for almost two hours leaving Kate plenty of time to scrutinize every inch of her prison. The film vault smelled of acid and aging rubbish. Workbenches lined three of the four walls. The benches, unlike the rows of film canisters stacked neatly on the metal shelves, were heaped with bent film reels, some containing deteriorating celluloid film. Old newspapers and tin cans were scattered about the cement floor.

A dingy bathroom with a rust-stained washbasin and a mirror of flyblown glass was located down a short hallway off the main vault area. Kate pulled a couple of pieces of toilet paper from a half-filled roll and wiped the mirror. Her reflection was not complimentary. Her hair was a tangled mess. Dirt streaked down one side of her face. Her diamond earring had disappeared from her left earlobe. The hot water faucet refused to budge, and when struck repeatedly, groaned and vibrated as she cranked it until a trickle of cold water begrudgingly dribbled into the grimy bowl. Kate removed the other stud, tucked it into her pocket and attempted a wash and brush up.

A second reconnaissance of her prison, revealed that the only exit the film vault to the outside was the solid metal door her captor had gone out of a couple of hours ago. She toyed briefly with the idea of trying to hide and overpower her jailer when he returned with food, but decided brain over brawn was a better plan. She'd wait and see how things went when he got back.

Returning to the desk, Kate slumped wearily into the chair and turned on her computer. It booted up, displaying the expected screen saver of Mount Lee, only now it had the Hollywood sign superimposed on it within a red circle with a black line running diagonally through it. Below that were three new word-buttons: "Welcome," "Notes" and "Menu." Someone had been tampering with her computer, but hadn't attempted to hack into the movie production program. Had they tried the latter, her computer would have been a pool of melted metal and plastic. It was one of several safeguards Kate had added before appealing to Lev for help. Kate clicked on "Welcome."

Her computer screen went blank for a moment, and then some text appeared as if being typed on a distant typewriter: "I will visit you soon. It will be beneficial for us to meet in person."

Kate next opened "Notes." This time the computer responded: "Leave notes, we will go over them tomorrow."

Who is this nut? Kate cursed silently.

"Menu," when clicked, simply resulted in: "To be filled in before eight o'clock in the morning each day."

Clearly, Kate's computer was directly linked to another by way of the yellow cable. That meant that even if there was a way to send a message, her abductor and likely her service guard would immediately know. Kate clicked on Notes and, ignoring the previous response, typed, "I quit playing games in the eighth grade." Then she switched off her computer and glared at the screen, her mind screaming, *Where are Mel and Lev when I need them?*

Chapter 11

Before his next meeting with Mel, Lev had discrete inquiries made into the man's background, and discovered Mel was Kate's fiancé. Furthermore, the two appeared to be keeping the fact a secret from his father, Kumar Pashagora, owner of the largest film production studio in India. Bollywood already out-produced the rest the world and if they got hold of Kate's program, they could easily monopolize the world entertainment market.

As agreed, Mel stopped by Lev's office late the next afternoon and Lev immediately launched into the questions he'd been stewing over.

"Why did you remain in the U.S. after graduation? Surely, your father could have used your expertise," Lev began.

"Yes, of course." Mel's eyebrows arched, making his eyes widen as if he hadn't expected the question. "Kate and I were… well…secretly engaged to be married, and I wanted us to be married *before* returning home. My family, Lev, has many long held traditions. They'd never permit me to be married outside of the family religion."

"So what would happen when you returned to India with an American wife?"

Mel shrugged, "Kate and I agreed we'd cross that bridge when we came to it. For now, all I want to do is to find my fiancé."

Lev swigged the remains of the coffee Joanie had served before leaving for the day. He decided not to ask any further questions, and instead, urge the young man to talk while observing him closely.

Mel, obviously uncomfortable with what he'd just disclosed, asked, "So the next person on your list is Villand, the Man with a Thousand Faces?"

"Yes, I'm waiting for a call as to where I can find him." Lev had no sooner spoken, than his cellphone rang. It was Vicky Vance. Lev tapped it onto speaker and nodded to Mel.

"See, dear boy? I said I'd get back to you. Now, about Villand. I could compose an entire column on his goings on but it wouldn't interest most of today's readers. Not spicy enough. He's just another washed up actor. A nobody."

"He made it to the wrap party, Vicky."

"So did many other nobodies, Lev. He was there in the hope of sniffing out a walk-on in poor Primo's next picture. He and Don Ames..."

"Don Ames? That creep had nothing to do with Primo's next picture. It was going to be Kate's film."

"Ah, so right, dear boy. I'm told that Ames was very unhappy when Primo turned him down. My spies report both he and Villand saying how they hoped something would occur to stop the picture going into production."

"Who heard them?"

"Can't say," Vicky said quickly. "But I trust my sources."

"So where do I find Frank Villand?"

"North Hollywood, an area east of Vineland, houses and commercial buildings mixed together. Fourty-five-thirty-one Sherman Court. He arrived home a short time ago."

"Thanks Vicky, I owe you."

"Of course you do, silly boy. So stay in touch, especially if you find something I should know."

"You'll be the first, Vicky. Ta-Ta."

Lev raised his eyebrows and shrugged. "That, Mel, was Vicious Vicky, the gossip columnist. Now I know where to find Villand."

"I'd like to go with you," Mel stated quickly. "If it's okay." Villand's address was a twenty-minute drive via Laurel Canyon. 4531 Sherman Court turned out to be a scruffy yellow stucco house that had been through too many earthquakes, and had not received enough aid from FEMA. Pulling to the curb, they stared at the forlorn residence.

"Wow. It's hard to believe this guy was once a big name in movies," Mel whispered.

"That's show biz. Let's pay him a visit."

A rusted alternating convex and concave galvanized metal tapestry of neglect that once had been a four-foot cyclone fence sagged around the property. Lev had to push hard to open the gate, causing it to scrape on the cracked concrete pathway. He rang the doorbell, no answer. He rapped on the front door and waited.

"Maybe he's not home," Mel began.

Lev held a finger to his lips. "Wait." Finally, the front door creaked open about half an inch.

"If you're selling, I'm not buying. If you're preaching, I'm not a believer."

"My name is Lev Leventhal, I'm an agent."

The door opened another inch, and one of Frank Villand's thousand faces peered out. This one was pinched, gray and wrinkled.

"What kind of agent?"

"Theatrical." The door swung wide enough for them to see a jockey-sized man in his underwear and carpet slippers.

"Hey! You're the guy who helped solve the murders in Santa Barbara, right?"

This was the last thing Lev expected, but before he could answer, Villand continued. "Read about it in *Varity*. My pal says you're a prick."

"Thanks. I'd like to ask you a couple of questions."

"Don Ames, that's the guy who said it," Villand offered.

An overpowering smell of stale cigarette smoke wafted from within the house. "Well, yeah, he would," Lev said. "We had a falling out. Can we come in?"

"Who's he?" Villand pointed a thin, furrowed finger.

"A friend of mine," Lev said.

"He looks like vice to me."

Mel stepped closer. "I'm not, but I'll wait in the car if it'll make you feel any better."

Villand squinted him up and down. "Okay. You can stay. So, what's this about?"

The interior of the house reflected the outside: complete and total neglect.

"Take a pew." Villand waved around the squalid living room. The carpet, once orange shag, was flattened to an evil reddish color with dark splotches interspersed with bald spots. Lev looked for somewhere to sit that wouldn't contaminate him and noticed Mel doing the same.

"Hey, don't stand on ceremony, sit anywhere."

Lev eased into a green leatherette easy chair with a Gaffer's tape patch on one arm; he didn't lean back. Mel perched on the edge of a wooden chair facing the TV while Villand dropped into a beanbag that barely changed shape under his skinny frame.

"I came to ask a couple of questions about Kate Keenan. She talked to you and Don Ames at the wrap party. I'm trying to locate Kate."

Villand's beady eyes darted to Mel. "So why's he here then?"

"He wants to find Kate, too."

"We weren't the only ones who spoke to her."

"I know. I want to speak with as many people as I can who saw her at the party."

"Yeah, okay. The last I saw her was when we were all told to leave by security. We said goodnight, then Don and me left. Kate was remained inside the building."

"What were you talking about?"

"Computers. Don was thinking of getting a new one and asked Kate what she was using."

"Unusual question to ask someone on the spur of the moment, wasn't it?"

"Dunno, it was just conversation."

"I was told that you and Don had been overheard agreeing you hoped something would happen to stop Primo's next film from being made."

"That's a lie."

"Wasn't Ames pissed-off that Kate was being considered to write Primo's film and not him?"

"Give me a break. You're an agent. It happens all the time. Writers and actors—bitch, bitch, bitch."

"Look, the chance of finding her is lessening by the hour."

"The only people I recall talking to her other than Vicky, Stella and Chaz, were earlier in the evening before Primo came on stage."

"Who were they?"

"One was Hank Tolomeo. He was arguing." Villand lit a cigarette and blew a smoke beam toward the nicotine-stained ceiling.

"Arguing with whom?"

"Jilly Suede, that's all I know."

Jilly was Primo's assistant, Gal Friday and personal confidant. She'd been with Primo for more than twenty years.

Lev rose and walked to the door, Mel following like a pet dog. "Thanks for your time."

Villand remained sprawled on his beanbag. "If you hear of anyone in the business who could use my talents, Leventhal, let me know, okay?"

"Sure. I'll keep my ears open." All three knew Lev was lying.

"He wasn't much help," Mel said as they walked back to the car.

"Hank Tolomeo is one of the people on my list. I'll arrange a meeting with him."

"I know him. When would you like to talk to Hank?"

"Wait! You know Tolomeo?"

"He offered me a job with him when I was still at UCLA."

"And you went to Apple. Bet that didn't go over well."

"He's not that way. He does a lot of business with my father in India."

In the car, heading for the freeway, Lev asked, "What kind of business does your father do with TolomeoTechnics?"

"Dad runs a film studio in Mumbai." Mel smiled thinly. "I think you already knew that. Anyway, to answer your question, my Dad buys digital equipment from Hank."

Lev grunted. "From what I understand there are a few tricks we can learn from India in the area of digital film making."

"Yes, progress is very important to India. TolomeoTechnics advancements in fiber optics, computers and robotics have been amazing the last few years."

They were almost back at the office and Lev wanted to turn the conversation back to Tolomeo. "So when do you think you can get hold of him?"

"I'll call him tonight."

"That would be great."

Lev turned into his parking space behind his office; there were only three cars in the lot. "Which one are you, Mel?"

"Silver Audi," Mel pointed. "There, on the right."

Lev waited as Mel got in, turned on the motor, switched on the headlights, gave a honk and drove out of the lot. Mel turned right on La Cienega.

Lev headed for the back door. He decided to check any messages or notes Joanie might have left for him. He stopped abruptly in the hallway when he heard the cough of a car engine starting. Easing the outside door open a few inches, he was able to make out the silhouette of a car with no lights move out of the driveway and turn in the same direction as Mel.

Chapter 12

"You said this was going to be easy." Villand, hunched on his beanbag chair, had assumed a different one of his thousand faces: a scared-shitless face, a cigarette quivering between his lips, his phone pressed to his ear. "Leventhal was here with some young kid asking questions. Yeah, I let him in. What was I supposed to do?" Villand paused to listen to person on the other end of the phone, then added, "I don't know who the kid was, but he had an accent. Sounded like he was from India. Hindu, maybe." Stubbing out the cigarette, he shook another from a crumpled pack. "Listen, Ames, I don't like this." He tuned in to Ames and listened impatiently for awhile, finally interrupting: "No, I'll come over there. My place might be under surveillance."

Chapter 13

Kate, dozing in her new office chair was startled by the sound of a key grating in the lock. *Scumbag must be back*, she told herself, and spun around to get a direct view of the metal door. It swung only partly open. Kate watched a cloth-covered tray being pushed across the threshold. The door then closed and she heard the lock reengage. Scumbag hadn't even entered.

Kate walked over to the tray, picked it up, and carried it back to her desk, where she removed the cloth. A hamburger and fries. She touched the bun with the back of her hand. Cold. The coffee however was lukewarm, and she noticed three chocolate chip cookies on top of an envelope. Taking a bite of one, she ripped open the envelope and removed a typewritten message: "Leave the computer on at all times."

Taking a second bite, she booted her computer. The "Welcome" button that was there earlier was gone. "Notes" and "Menu" were still there. "Notes" was glowing. Clicking on it, another message appeared: "Get some sleep. Tomorrow will be a busy day."

Having noticed that her built-in camera light was glowing slightly, she assumed that when she was anywhere in front of her computer she was also on closed circuit TV, she gave the camera lens the finger, picked up the coffee and the last two cookies, and headed for her cot.

Chapter 14

Lev dashed to his car, departed the parking lot, and hung a right. Both cars had turned north on La Cienega, heading towards Hollywood. He didn't know Mel's address but kept driving in the hope of catching up with the man's silver Audi. Then Lev called Joanie on his cellular.

"Joanie, it's me. Did you get an address for Mel Pashagora?

"No, why?"

Lev groaned, "Because you are always so efficient."

"Thanks. I did get his phone number."

"Give it to me, Joanie. It's very important."

"You expect me to remember it of the top of my head? It's

nighttime and I'm at home! His numbers are in the daily log on my desk."

Lev pulled over. "Numbers?"

"He left both his home and cell. Where are you?"

"I'm in my car completing a U-turn in the middle of La Cienega." Lev sped back to the office and went straight to Joanie's desk, snapped on the lights and opened the log. Half way down the page, he saw Melhi Pashagora, with two phone numbers precisely written next to his name. Lev tapped in the cell number and waited. Four rings. Five. Something was wrong. He hit redial and heard, "Mel here." A wave of relief swept over him.

"Where are you, Mel?"

"I'm on my way home."

"What's your location?"

"Heading west on Sunset," replied Mel.

"How far from home?"

"Couple of miles. I live on Shoreham Drive."

"Anyone following you?"

"Following me? No."

"Keep an eye on the rearview mirror. What number on Shoreham?"

"Eighty-seven fifty. It's a condo. I'm in unit twelve-oh-eight."

Lev recalled the place: a high-rise overlooking the Strip. Exclusive digs with underground parking.

"Mel, listen to me. You know Vendome Liquor on Sunset?"

"Sure."

"Go in and wait until I get there. Tell the clerk you're being followed and you've called a buddy for backup. Okay?"

"What if he wants to call the police?"

"Fine. Let him. I'm on my way."

Lev screeched to a halt outside of Vendome Liquor, and saw Mel standing inside at the counter talking to the clerk.

Mel turned nervously when Lev entered. "Ah, Lev. Bill here." He pointed to the man behind the counter. "He called the cops, but they said it wasn't enough to order a car directly there. Instead, they ordered a drive-by whenever a nearby cop car has the chance."

"Have they?"

"Not yet. Or if they did, they didn't stop," Mel said.

Lev glanced out the window as a customer pulled up. "Okay. I'll follow you up to your place." Turning to the clerk, Lev said, "Thanks pal."

"No problem, man."

They each drove up Shoreham into the underground parking lot, and then rode the elevator together to the twelfth floor.

A hundred feet west of Vendome Liquors, the man in a car parked on Sunset watched the arrival of Lev, then the departure of Mel's car followed by Lev's. He tagged along at a distance until they turned into an underground parking facility. The car did a U-turn and travelled back down to Sunset.

Mel's apartment was large and tastefully furnished.

"I could use a drink, how about you?" Mel asked.

"Small brandy would be fine, if you have it."

Mel removed his jacket and tossed it across the back of a ten-foot leather couch. "Coming up." He walked to a well-stocked drinks trolley while Lev stood in front of the floor-to-ceiling window and looked out across the twinkling lights of Hollywood below.

"Nice view, Mel."

"Everyone says that." Mel handed Lev a crystal snifter of

brandy. Sipping his own drink, Mel asked, "So a car followed me out of your office parking lot?"

"Yeah," Lev said, swirling his brandy. "Whoever it was had evidently been waiting. When you left my place, he followed you, lights off. By the time I ran outside, the car was out of the driveway, and, dark like that, I couldn't see the license or make. Any idea who might want to follow you?"

"No."

Lev sipped his brandy. The disappearance of Kate, and the mysterious tail on Mel made him wonder about their connection. At this rate, the next to vanish could be Mel.

"Okay. Keep your door locked and bolted, and get a good night's sleep. Call your office tomorrow and say you need a couple of days off. I'll pick you up around nine. We'll work together, checking any further leads."

"I do have personal time due," Mel commented.

"Fine, then that's settled."

"Wait, Lev. Before you go I want to call Tolomeo. I know it's late, but I'd like to make an appointment for us to see him first thing tomorrow."

Lev grinned, toasted Mel, then sank into a comfortable armchair while Mel made the call. Hank Tolomeo answered on the first ring.

"Hank, this is Mel. Hope I'm not calling too late." He glanced at Lev. "Good. Listen, I have a favor to ask. Someone would like to talk to you before you head back to Palo Alto tomorrow. Won't take long. It's about my friend, Kate. I believe you met her once." Mel shook his head in the negative and laughed. "No, Hank, he's her agent." Shaking his head in the positive and smiling at Lev, he continued, "Thanks. See you at ten," and hung up. "Hank wanted to know if you were a cop. He's heading north later in the morning but can see us at ten at his office."

"Perfect. Then you and I will meet as planned at nine and we'll go in my car."

As Lev drove down the hill and turned west on Sunset, he took a deep breath. His mind was running in too many directions.

He toyed with the thought of driving north along the coastal highway to Malibu. The sea air would clear his head and allow him think better; however, a couple of miles down Sunset, amidst the glow of neon signs, he saw a sign that made him change his mind. It was the big red and yellow marquee of Charlie V's. The building stood on the site of the old Ciro's, a celebrity nightclub of the thirties and forties that faded in the late 1950s and eventually disappeared.

He drove into the parking lot and switched off the engine. A parking attendant immediately opened the car door.

Inside the nightclub, a quartet on stage was blasting out a tune Lev had heard before, but couldn't name. A dozen couples were together on a diminutive dance floor. He was ushered to a small table, and while a waiter in black tux awaited his order, a voice he recognized at once wafted from over his left shoulder. The voice was that of Pattie Primo.

"Lev! I haven't seen you in ages, darling. How are you?"

There she was, Primo's grieving widow, dressed in a black low cut evening gown with several thousand dollars-worth of diamonds draped around her neck.

Lev signalled the waiter away, stood, turned and took her hand. "Pattie. I'm so sorry about Frank. It was all so sudden."

"Yes, it was. You will be at the service tomorrow, won't you?"

"Of course I will. He'll be missed. The town won't be the same without him." He had no idea when or where the service was going to be.

"Thank you, Lev. So glad I bumped into you. I'll look for you tomorrow at the service." She turned and swirled away into the darkness.

It was then he decided to see if Charles Vance was in the club. Signaling to the the waiter he'd just dismissed, he asked if the owner was in the club tonight.

Realizing Lev was not going to order, the surly waiter replied, "I'll try to locate him for you."

Lev left the table and sat at the bar sipping soda water for ten long minutes. When the waiter didn't return, he decided to leave and call Charles. As Lev headed for the door, he noticed one of the bartenders who had been eyeing him pull out a cell phone, turn away and begin talking.

He was standing outside with some other patrons waiting for their cars, when he checked his wristwatch. It was after midnight, so he decided the trip to Malibu was out. He had a lot to complete the next day and if he didn't get a lead on Kate soon, she'd officially become a missing person and a police matter.

Chapter 15

Kate slept a fitful couple hours before being jolting awake. There was someone in the vault! She moved her head to hear more clearly, but all was silent. She was certain she'd heard something in the main room. Her heart pounded and she broke into a cold sweat. The door to her "bedroom" was closed but it didn't have a lock—anyone could walk right in.

Easing off the cot, she crept barefoot toward the door, arms outstretched, praying not to trip over anything. The coldness of the concrete floor instantly began creeping into her legs. At the door, she remained motionless, straining to hear the slightest sound. She had no means of defense. Should she open the door and go further, or remain in the cell and wait until whoever it was burst in and overwhelmed her? Making up her mind, she eased the door open a few inches, peered into the main room and saw her computer on the desk, it's screen still brightly lit. There was that sound again! Something or someone was out there. She quickly pulled the door shut.

Now fully awake, she realized she'd heard that kind of thrumming, whirring, jingly sound before. Then she remembered. Robotics! She'd participated in various robot classes at UCLA and had become fascinated with the possibilities for their future use in the making of movies. There was a robot at loose inside the vault!

She tweaked the door open and this time gasped aloud. Standing sentinel-like outside her door was a squat, four-foot-tall Robo-Cop-like piece of complicated electronic equipment. The robot, claw-like pincers hanging at it's side, continued whirring lowly but remained completely motionless.

Pushing the door wider, Kate walked into the room and turned to face it. The previously inert-appearing robot immediately spun its head in her direction, revealing a compact video camera where it's head should have been. A synthesized voice rasped, "I'm sorry. I did not mean to wake you, Kate. Please forgive me."

"Who are you?" Kate hoped her voice didn't reveal her fear.

"Your constant companion and intermediary, when your human guardian isn't here, until you have completed your assignment."

"I was told to communicate through my computer."

"That is correct. I am here as extra precaution against unforeseen problems."

"Meaning what?"

The damn thing ignored her question, offering instead, "There is a change of clothes for you on the bench over there. I thought they might make you feel more comfortable."

No words were exchanged while she crossed to the bench where found a carryon sized soft bag. The robot's video eye, however, followed her to the bench and as she returned to her bedroom cell.

Kate closed the door and checked out the bag. Everything provided fit her perfectly: clean jeans, a turtleneck sweater and a pair of Nikes. Whoever had captured her knew her exact sizes. After changing, Kate headed back to the main room, the robot's video eye following her.

"I am programmed to recognize your presence whenever you are within fifty feet of me."

Kate sat at the desk, selected "Notes," and typed on her computer, "Who the hell is this robot?"

The reply was instantaneous: "You are a light sleeper, Kate. Rob doesn't usually awaken people."

"He did me," she tapped. "So I'm a prisoner in a film vault with a robot jailer. Unless I'm released immediately I'll press charges for holding me against my will."

"Sorry to hear that, Kate," came the reply. "I'm not sure anyone has ever pressed charges like that against a robot. But more importantly, unless you do exactly as you are told, your friend Mel may never see his father in India again, and that would be a real pity."

Kate stared at the screen as more appeared.

"No more talk. You are safe as long as you follow orders. I've programmed Rob to be your constant guardian until the assignment is finished." Kate heard the robot Rob roll forward and stop next to her.

"Stay seated and turn toward me," Rob commanded.

Kate angrily spun her chair until they were eye-to-eye.

"Place the palm of your right hand on the flat pad next to the video camera and stare into the lens."

She did as ordered, and three seconds later the robot said, "Your hand and fingerprints, iris and retinal patterns, heart rate, blood pressure and other pertinent identifying data are now successfully recorded in my memory. As long as I am near you, no harm can come to you."

She growled, "Protected! Prisoner is more like it."

Rob simply turned and rolled back to his post in front of the door to her makeshift bedroom.

Chapter 16

Franz Villand's '96 Chevy was half way down Vineland Avenue when his cell chirped. Driving with one hand, he searched his pockets. "Sonofabitch." The chirping continued and Villand finally clawed the phone from an inside pocket.

"Yeah, who is this? I can hardly hear you. Talk louder." Villand hated cells; he was always either losing or having trouble hearing them. He was, nonetheless, carrying one in the hope that his agent might contact him in a hurry with a job. Fat chance. "I said I was coming over to your place. What do you mean, telling me now that you don't want me to? Why not?" Villand paused to receive Ames reply. "I might be followed and you don't want to be implicated? Ames, are you crazy? *You* involved *me!*" Villand stopped for a red light and the engine quit. "Shit! No, I stopped at a light and the car quit. Something about the carburetor. Gotta' get it fixed." Villand cranked the engine, listening to each groaning revolution get slower and weaker, praying the battery would hold up. The engine finally caught and he moved the car forward. "So where you wanna' meet? Okay. Yeah, yeah, I'll keep checking I'm not being tailed."

Chapter 17

Mel was waiting outside the entrance to the underground garage of Shoreham Towers when Lev drove up the hill, pulled to the curb, leaned over, and opened the passenger side door.

"Morning, Lev." Mel folded into the seat and snapped on the seat belt.

"Sleep well?" Lev asked as he pulled away.

"Better than I thought I would."

"Good. Where do we meet Hank Tolomeo?"

"Marina Del Rey."

"I thought he lived in Palo Alto."

"His plant is in Palo Alto. When he's in Southern California he lives on his boat and does most of his business by video conference from his office in the Marina."

"What kind of man am I going to meet, Mel?" Lev honked the horn as a messenger on a ten-speed, cut between his radiator and the trunk of a Mercedes.

"Hank's a nice guy when you get to know him."

"How long does that take?"

"Depends," muttered Mel.

Lev nodded, "On what?"

"Well, you know." Mel tipped one hand side to side. "He's usually at his best in the mornings. You'll get along fine with him. You seem like a people-person type of guy."

"In my business I have to be."

Mel leaned back, and explained that he'd met Hank while attending classes at UCLA. The moment they met, they struck up a friendship of sorts. He'd have dinner with Hank every few months or so, and they'd talk about Mel's father, Indian movies, and how Hank hoped his dad would travel someday to LA. Hank said he wanted to show the man around his plant. Mel's dad, however, didn't like flying. It made his feet swell, even in first class, Mel's father complained.

"So Hank and your father do business together?"

"To quote Hank," Mel said, "'top secret genius stuff'."

Lev made the transition onto the San Diego Freeway. "Sounds like the kind of guy who doesn't play poker with his back to a mirror."

Mel chuckled. "He doesn't."

The traffic was now up to its usual 75 miles per hour, and traffic was nose to tail despite the speed. Lev completed the transition to the Marina Freeway and approached Lincoln Boulevard, where Mel began giving directions.

"Once on Lincoln, stay in the right lane. The office is about a mile on our left. A three story beige colored building just beyond a small boat yard, you'll see it."

A few minutes later, Lev saw the building and asked about parking. "Around the back, turn into the driveway. That's Hank's car." Mel pointed to a silver 1938 SS Jaguar sitting close to the back entrance.

"A car buff, too," Lev grunted as he pulled into the first available slot.

"Hank has many expensive things, Lev."

The door to Hank's outer office swung open before Mel could

turn the knob.

"Hi, come on in." A smiling young woman held the door open. "He's waiting for you, Mr. Pashagora."

"Thanks, Sue." Mel turned to Lev. "This is Sue Hawkins, Hank's Southern California Rep. Sue, meet Lev Leventhal."

Lev trailed Mel into an inner office. Mel knocked once at the door and entered.

A heavyset man sat behind a refectory table he used as a desk. Piles of books and papers were scattered across the mahogany surface.

"Mel! Come on in! Sit down!" He pushed out of his throne-like chair, waddled around the table and gave Mel a hug and a brisk slap on the back. Hank Tolomeo was an inch shorter than Mel and at least seventy pounds heavier. His dark hair showed flashes of gray at the temples. He wore a pair of Maui Jim sunglasses pushed up on his forehead. Hank scrutinized Lev with his inquiring kelly green eyes. "Glad you called, Mel, it's been too long since I've seen you."

Mel grinned, "Just over a month, Hank."

"Too long. Now sit down, both of you." He waved in the direction of two slate-gray leather armchairs facing the table. "You must be Lev Leventhal, Kate's agent." He offered a beefy hand. A single strong squeeze and he returned to his throne. "So bring me up to date about Kate."

Hank remained silent as Mel and Lev went through their last couple of days searching for Kate.

"You'd like to know when I last saw her, right?"

Mel nodded.

"Primo and I were having a drink before he went on stage. He'd told me he was going to make an innovative movie with a young woman with a big future. He was very excited. Said it would be a closed set production. Already there were rumors surrounding the secrecy. Primo was no fool. He knew the power of gossip in Hollywood. Primo pointed Kate out to me. She was talking to Stella Rae and the actor, what's his name?"

"Chaz Falconer," said Lev.

"Whatever. That was the last time I saw her."

Lev leaned forward. "Frank Primo was hyping his new movie to you just before he went on stage?"

"Yes, he was."

"It was common knowledge in town that you, Primo, and Jilly Suede, not Kate, would be working closely together with him on the production."

Hank's green eyes flashed. "How do you mean?"

"Rumor has it that TolomeoTechnics was going to 'revolutionize the movie industry'."

"Who told you that?"

"Stacy Hart."

"See? Primo knew the right places to drop hints. Well, it's obvious the film won't be made and TT won't be involved, so it's of little consequence. I'll admit my company is working on a system to bring movie making into the twenty-first century." He nodded to Mel. "My company has been working closely with his father's for some time."

Given what he was hearing, Lev decided not to reveal that he understood some of Kate's own revolutionary technology. It was better, he decided, that Hank feel he was in complete control. That way, he might reveal an additional kernel or two of information.

"So no one you've questioned saw Kate after the party, right?" Tolomeo asked.

Lev nodded. "Correct."

"You said when you went to her house her computer was missing and the place had been tossed. What feedback did you get from the cops?"

Lev paused a moment. "Burglary, no prints. No different from a couple a hundred others that happen in LA each day."

Hank switched to Mel. "Any idea what was on the computer that would make it important enough to steal? I mean like anything she would rather not have anyone besides herself see?"

Mel shrugged. "Maybe a treatment of the script she was doing for Primo."

"Primo, would have had a copy, of course."

Lev cut in. "No. She pitched to Primo over the phone and he's agreed to meet her after the party. They'd never met in person. Kate was going to give Primo a demo of her work on her laptop after the wrap party." Lev omitted mention of the device she'd entrusted to him.

Hank frowned. "No else one at the studio was involved in the decision?"

"You know Primo," Lev offered. "He owned the studio, always did whatever he wanted. He often made deals in secret one-on-one. Everyone in town knew that."

"Yes, of course," Hank snorted. "It's still a curious way to do business in this day and age."

"Absolutely, I agree," Mel said. "However, Primo was always different."

"So Kate and her laptop are both missing, and who ever has her, also has a copy of her work, if nothing else from inside her mind."

"Whether they had Kate or the computer or both, they'd still have to open and run the program to see what she'd written," Mel added.

"Shouldn't be a problem. There are plenty of hackers around."

"True. However, I know Kate. Anyone attempting to hack her computer would find nothing if they did succeed. All they'd get would be a pile of sizzling metal and plastic."

Hank's eyebrows arched. "Self-destruct! Then Kate would have no back up."

"Kate backed up everything she wrote. Copied it to a second computer for safety. Every word, every night, she transferred the latest version without fail," Mel said.

"Where is this second computer?" Hank asked.

"Can't help you there. But Kate said her work was completely safe once she made the transfer."

Hank looked dubious. "Weren't you curious? You're her best friend."

"A secret remains a secret only when it's known to but one person."

Hank glanced at his watch. "Well, I have to go, Mel. Hope it wasn't a waste your time, Lev."

"Actually, you've been a big help," Lev replied. "We appreciate your time."

Mel stood. "I'll tell my father we saw each other when I call him this weekend."

"You do that, and let's get together for lunch soon."

Chapter 18

Back in the car, Lev phoned Joanie and instructed her to contact Jilly Suede. He needed personnel and parking permits for entry onto the Megastar movie lot, for a "drive-on" for Mel and himself; they'd be at the studio gate in forty minutes to pick them up. Ten minutes later, Joanie called back. "Okay, the passes will be at the gate. Don't forget: Primo's memorial is at three this afternoon at the Wee Kirk 'O the Heather in Forest Lawn-Glendale. Stacy phoned and said to tell you to get there early. She has something for you." Joanie paused. "You didn't mention anything about a service, Lev."

"I only found out last night. Sorry."

"Thanks, Lev." She replied testily and hung up.

Lev asked Mel, "Does Kate have any ex-boyfriends, anyone who might have a grudge against her?"

"Not that I know of. There was a guy who said he was a Hollywood writer. He'd somehow gotten hold of Kate's phone number and he kept calling her at home."

"Do you know his name?"

"Don Ames. I heard Villand mention the name when we were at Villand's last night.

"What did he want?"

"He'd found out she was a screenwriter and student at UCLA, and wanted to meet her, saying he could maybe help her find a producer for her scripts. We both knew that was bullshit, as Ames hadn't sold anything in years."

"How'd you find that out?"

"Easy. I called a couple of friends. One of them advised me Ames had tried to sue a major studio a while back claiming they'd stolen one of his stories. He's never worked since. From what I can tell, no one would ever want to steal any of his work."

"Did Ames ever try to contact you?"

"No."

Lev thought that odd. If Ames knew Kate had been studying at the UCLA, he must have done some research, and Mel's name would certainly have come up somewhere along the line.

Mel shifted uneasily in his seat. "After we've visited the studio, could you drop me off at Shoreham? Memorials depress me."

"Do you want to go home now? I can drop you off. Sunset Boulevard is coming up ahead."

"That's okay, Megastar movie lot first. I want to help all I can."

The guard handed the passes through the gatehouse window. "Leave them in view on the dash while you're on the lot. Drop them off when you leave, Mr. Leventhal."

Driving onto the lot, they headed toward the Megastar building located midway between the main gate and the first sound stage.

"Where was the wrap party held, Lev?"

"Stage four. Why?"

"Just wondered. Kate invited me to go with her. Said she wanted me to meet her new agent."

"I wish you'd taken her up on it," Lev said. A group of extras dressed as cowboys sauntered past, and a forklift loaded with fake Alpine landscaping rumbled in the opposite direction.

"I can't help thinking that if I'd been there, this might have never happened," Mel said.

"I didn't mean it that way, Mel."

"I know, but that's how I feel. I have ever since I heard she'd gone missing," Mel explained.

Lev pulled into an empty visitor's slot. The time was eleven fifteen. "Let's go meet Jilly Suede. Jilly's been Primo's personal assistant for over twenty years. She knows everything that goes on at Megastar. Maybe we can get her to join us for an early lunch in the commissary."

Lev had gotten to know Jilly over the years when he'd

accompanied his writers to Megastar for various story meetings. Somehow, she always managed to spend at least a few minutes with him at every meeting. Jilly was somewhere in her early forties, single, and all business. When they arrived at her office and he asked to see her, they were told she had taken a couple of days hiatus.

"My secretary just phoned Jilly and got us a couple of passes," Lev said. The receptionist smiled. "Yes, I know. I know who you are, so I called the gate."

"Will Jilly be at the memorial this afternoon?" Lev asked.

"Yes, well, at least I suppose so. I phoned her home and left a message on her machine. The memorial date change was a sudden decision by Mrs. Primo. Originally it was to be next week."

Lev asked, "Any idea why it was fast forwarded?"

"No. We received the memo late yesterday afternoon."

Lev thanked her. Mel suggested they take a walk and check out stage four.

It was not to be.

A red light flashing outside the entrance to the building, indicated that shooting was in progress. While they waited for the green light, Lev checked around the area. There was the usual clutter of scenery and portable arc lamps parked in the street with electric golf carts and trucks flowing past, a typical studio day.

"Did everyone leave the party through this door?" Mel asked.

"As far as I recall, security ordered people to leave and directed them to this door. I don't recall them directing guests to any other exits."

"Then Kate most likely left the party here." Mel sounded as if he were assuring himself that Kate was not still somewhere in the huge building. Lev glanced back toward the main gate, up the street toward the back lot, with Mount Lee rising behind the studio.

"You think she might still be on the lot?" Lev asked.

Mel didn't answer, but he walked slowly along the side of the sound stage pointing toward the back lot, then quickly bent down and scooped something off the ground. He cupped it in his palm as he turned and walked back to Lev.

"This is one of Kate's earrings. It's one of a pair I gave her for her birthday last year. That means that Kate was here, and wherever Kate is, she didn't go willingly."

Chapter 19

Kate was half-asleep in her chair when the "Notes" button on her computer screen began flashing. The robot was on sentry duty, silent as a moorland hillside.

Clicking on the button, a message appeared stating simply: "This is today's assignment: I want you to write the first act of the screenplay you pitched to Primo."

Kate stared at the words, and then typed. "I need a hot shower first."

"First, carry out today's assignment," came the response.

"I need a hot shower, clean underwear and sanitary living conditions."

"You are a prisoner. Obey orders."

Already the musky odor of her body was beginning to mix with the staleness of the air, despite the year round air conditioning mentioned by 'Scumbag' on her arrival. "I don't have my notes. They're in my home office."

"Check the top right hand drawer of the desk. You will find everything you need there."

Two clicks sounded from the drawer that she'd attempted

without success to open earlier. It slid open with ease. There were her outline notes, and a spiral notebook along with the yellow legal pad she used in her home office.

The assignment is to write the first act, but for whom am I writing it? she wondered. She glanced at the screen. It was blank. *At least whoever it is isn't telepathic.*

This is ridiculous, her mind screamed, *bossed around by a computer screen and monitored by a robot. Whoever's holding me thinks Primo was interested in a screenplay. that means that just perhaps, he or she doesn't know about my program!*

Rob whirred and rolled his way over to the desk and rasped, "Begin work, Kate. Begin now."

Chapter 20

Lev stopped the car next to the main gate security office, scooped the passes off the dash and headed inside. Mel remained in the car staring at the diamond earring in his hand.

"You can't park there, Mr. Leventhal." Luckily, it was one of the guards he'd known for years.

"I know, but I need to ask you a quick question, Mike." Lev handed him the passes. "The other night, when Mr. Primo died on stage four, did all the guests return their passes?"

"I assume so. Studio rules, you know, and with security being increased nationwide, I'm pretty certain they all were."

"You know someone went missing that night, yes?"

"I was informed today when the police came asking questions —it was a writer, a young woman."

"She's a client of mine, and we drove on the lot together. After Mr. Primo died, there was a lot of confusion and I couldn't locate her. I searched until the crowds had thinned, and security demanded everyone leave. I concluded she'd met some friends and left with them. When I drove off the lot with all the others, the guard simply waved me through without asking for my pass. I didn't think about it at the time, I was still concerned as to her whereabouts. The passes were still on the dash of my car the next morning."

Mike looked embarrassed. "Given the uproar, it is possible some of the passes weren't collected."

"So my missing client could have just as easily been driven off the lot by someone without showing a pass."

"I'm afraid so, Mr. Leventhal."

"Thanks, Mike. If you hear anything, let me know." He placed one of his business cards on the security guard's desk.

"Sure will, and I'm sorry about the break down in procedure."

Returning to the car, Lev brought Mel up to date.

"If that's the case, Kate's abductor could have been anyone on the lot, not just guests on the A list."

Mel opened his hand and gently bounced the diamond. "And she could equally still be somewhere on the lot."

With those chilling thoughts in mind, Lev headed back into Hollywood to drop Mel off at Shoreham before going to the memorial service. He intended to arrive early enough to have plenty of time to talk with Stacy Hart.

The massive wrought-iron gates of Forrest Lawn-Glendale were wide open, making Lev think of the Pearly Gates of Heaven, although he felt sure that many of the departed who went through the iron gates feet first would never make it through the Pearly ones. Hollywood celebrities used Forrest Lawn for weddings and funerals, the funerals being by far the more lasting of the two.

Over the years, he'd been to several final farewells, and was familiar with the location of the beautiful little church, The Wee Kirk O' the Heather. When he arrived, he noticed a solitary car in the parking lot, and recognized it at once as Stacy Hart's.

On closer examination, the car was locked and she was nowhere in sight. He looked inside the church; empty except for a woman arranging flowers on the altar. Checking the time, he saw it was a little before two, and decided to walk around the outside of the church and think. He'd almost made a complete circuit when he saw Stace sitting on a bench beneath a willow tree, writing in a notebook. She glanced up and waved as he approached. "I didn't expect you quite this early, Lev."

"Joanie told me you had something for me." As he sat next to her, she closed her notebook.

"I do. I discovered Charles Vance was heavily in debt to Primo. In fact, he was close to losing his club."

"Oh, boy," Lev muttered.

"That's why I called. It seems the debt had grown over the last year, with Primo lending good money after bad. There were no actual legal papers signed. It was purely personal friend-to-friend hand written IOU's from Vance to Primo. Well, the last couple of months, the debt grew beyond a handshake and Primo pressed Vance for a conclusion, either in cash or through forfeiture of the club."

"How did you find out?"

"Jilly Suede," Stace said softly.

"She who knows all when it comes to Frank Primo's personal and business life, right?"

"Yes," Stacy agreed.

"How much are we talking about?" Lev asked.

"A million five."

Lev gazed across the green manicured lawns, curving amid trees and gardens, that peacefully containing the souls of those who now had no such problems. "Where does Jilly come in?"

"She notarized the IOU's. Primo, like many executives relied on Jilly to take care of details, even personal ones. Jilly also mentioned that Primo had assured her that she would be remembered in his Will, and would be safe and comfortable after he'd gone."

"Perhaps she feels Primo should receive his loan in full and wants to be sure the million five is paid back."

Stacy sighed, "No doubt. Only natural, I suppose."

They watched in silence as a couple of limos slowly drove up the hill toward the church, no doubt the vanguard of many.

"Did you know Jilly's taken a couple of days off?" Lev asked.

Stace looked toward the church where the cars were parking. "Yes, she phoned me a couple of hours before I left to come here."

"Will she be at the service?"

"Of course she will."

A few more early arrivals were making their way up the hill, and groups of people in the parking lot were chatting with that air of uncomfortable tension that often accompanies such affairs. A couple of young men in dark suits stood in the church vestibule handing out programs to those entering. Lev checked the time. "It's twenty to three."

Stace nodded at the road winding up from the main gates. "It's going to be a big send off for Primo," she said sadly. The line of vehicles had now increased to a slow crawling procession inching up the hill.

They rose from the bench and sauntered toward the church. As they drew closer, they could hear the sound of the church organ playing a medley of tunes from past Broadway hit musicals. At least the theme of the memorial would be what Primo loved best: show business. Stace raised her eyebrows and smiled as they entered the church.

They sat in a row near the back, which give them an excellent position to observe the mourners arrive and take their seats. Lev noticed Vicky Vance and Pattie Primo already seated in the first row along with Stella Rae, Chaz Falconer and Jilly Suede.

The music played quietly on, blending with the hushed murmurs of the congregation, until piped-in music began playing through the faux organ pipes in the choir loft.

The last of the invited had finally taken their seats and the music faded, as the minister, in surplice, walked to the altar and faced the beloved. Pink-faced and white-haired, he looked the perfect clergyman as he laid his heavy leather bound prayer book on the lectern.

He began to eulogize the life and virtues of Francis Primo, his deep droning tones continuing for almost ten minutes. Finally he ended with, "And so, as we are gathered here today to remember Francis, if there are those among us who wish to say a few final words, please step forward."

Lev watched as men and women from the congregation went one-by-one to the lectern to speak. Some of the epitaphs were amusing, others simply said how much he'd be missed. The last speaker had returned to his seat when the organ softly crescendoed to a heart-pulling rendition of "Going Home." Then from the choir loft, a beautiful tenor voice sailed out. People, surprised, turned to see Charles Vance standing alone at the choir rail, singing,

I'm going home, I'm going home

When my life here is o'er, I'm going home
Won't it be so sweet, to rest at Jesus' feet
When my life here is o'er, I'm going home

I'm traveling in the light
And my way is clear and bright
Some glad day I'm going home
Heading for the pearly gates for there my
Savior waits when my life here is o'er, I'm going home.

When the last lyrics soared out across the church and the music faded, there was absolute silence from the congregation. Then a burst of applause quickly grew and filled the place of worship. Everyone present knew Primo would have approved. It had been years since Lev had heard Charles sing and he'd never sounded better.

"That was beautiful," Stacy said quietly. "What a breathtaking end."

People filing out glanced up at the choir loft, but Vance was no longer in sight. Outside, the usual quiet conversations began bubbling up, most surrounding Vance's solo.

"I had no idea Charles was going to sing, I think it was wonderful. Primo would have loved it. They were such good friends, you know."

Stace and Lev glanced at Vicky Vance, making her gushing remarks to the clergyman.

"It was a last minute decision," the minister replied. "Mr. Vance brought a tape recording of the organ music and we just slipped it in at the end."

"I must find Charles and thank him," Pattie Primo simpered to

Vicky Vance. "Where is that wonderful man?"

Many of the cars had already left, going toward the reception at Musso and Franks on Hollywood Boulevard. Lev told Stace he would see her at the reception, and was heading to his car when he heard two horrifying screams. Vicky Vance and Pattie Primo were rushing wildly from the church, their faces ashen, eyes wide with horror. Lev raced toward them and was among the first to arrive at their side. Vicky Vance collapsed in his arms. "Charles is dead! He's been murdered!"

Pattie pointed a trembling finger at the church. "He's up in the choir loft, a knife in his back."

Lev's first reaction was that the murderer must still be in the church. He started for the entrance when he felt a hand grab his shoulder. Turning, he looked into the face of Hank Tolomeo holding a cell phone.

"What's happening?" Hank asked. "I was phoning for a cab when I heard the screams."

"I didn't know you were here, Hank."

"Almost wasn't. I was in a cab on my way to the airport when I got a call on my cell, saying the memorial service had been moved up to today at three. I arrived just as Charles was ending his hymn."

"Charles is dead. Someone stabbed him."

Hank blanched. "Oh, my God!"

Someone brought a couple of chairs from the church, and deposited limp Vicky Vance into one. Pattie Primo plopped down on the other and sipped from a proffered glass of water. Cars stopped. Car doors opened. People spilled out on to the parking lot all talking at once.

"I'm going inside," Lev said.

"Right, I'll come with you," Hank said.

The minister, his voice quivering, stood shaking at the foot of the stairway to the choir loft.

"No one can go up, gentlemen. Police orders. I informed them at once, and was given strict instructions to allow no one into the loft. Our heavenly loft has become a crime scene."

As if on cue, police sirens appeared, quickly winding down and groaning into silence. Two black and whites slowed to a halt and parked at 90-degree angles outside the church blocking access. Seconds later, an unmarked Crown Vic squeezed around them.

Stace grasped Lev's arm. "I think we should leave while we can." As Lev turned to speak, he noticed Hank was gone.

Chapter 21

Kate switched off the computer. No way was she going to type a draft, notes or not.

"You were told not to turn off the computer, Kate," Rob announced.

"Fuck you, Rob."

"You will be punished, Kate." Rob extended a long pincher arm and turned the computer back on.

Kate switched it off and pulled out both the wall plug and the yellow cable.

"Go ahead. Plug them back in, smart ass."

There was no way. Rob had no knees, and he couldn't bend at the waist. The video camera where his head should have been turned, and she heard the hum of the zoom motor as he zeroed in close.

"Kate. Mel will suffer. Plug in the computer and the cable. Hurry."

That was it! Her pent up resentment exploded, and she shoved back her chair, directing the high leather back into Rob's mid-section.

Rob didn't budge. "If you feel the need to communicate, then do it through me," Rob said. "Then write the outline. In the morning you will feel better and have a visitor."

"I have to go to the bathroom."

"No problem, Kate. You will be perfectly safe. I will stand guard and protect you," Rob replied, moving toward the meager washroom and stopping at the side of its doorless arch.

Kate followed into the decrepit washroom and, sitting on the closed toilet seat, began looking for anything she could use to put Rob out of action and escape. The air conditioning duct that ran the length of the main room caught her eye. Mid-room, an industrial-sized air vent dropped down and opened over one of the benches. *There's no air conditioner in the room, so it must be located outside the vault. Could I use that vent as a means of escape?* she asked herself. The answer was, in order to find out, she must first immobilize the tin man.

Flushing the toilet to cover her thought-pause, she returned to the main room and began searching.

A careful examination revealed an old paperback, a book of matches tucked inside the cellophane wrapper of a crumpled cigarette pack, an old can of spray paint and an old rag mop. Shaking the paint can, she pressed the button. A stream of black paint surged out. Her heart beating hard, she collected everything, reviewed her plan in her mind, took a deep breath and returned to the toilet. After a few moments, she called from inside, "I need your help here, Rob."

Clinking and whirring, Rob centered himself in the center of the archway. His synthesized voice rasped. "What is the problem, the plumbing?"

"It's your damn presence!" she yelled, holding the spray paint behind her back while making sure the mop was in a place she could easily reach.

The diminutive four-foot creep moved slightly forward, then stopped. "What is the problem, Kate?"

Stepping forward, Kate aimed the spray can at his video eye and pressed the plunger. A jet of black paint hit the lens and splattered down the front of his metallic chest. Kate grabbed the mop, stuffed the handle underneath him and twisted hard. He went over like a ninepin, hitting the floor flat on his back. In this position, he was as helpless as a turtle on its back. He couldn't see. He couldn't recover upright. His metallic voice screeched as he wildly flailed his pincer arms.

"You're mine now, you little bastard," Kate hissed, "and you can lay there until you blow a fuse." She removed the shaft of the mop and thrust it like a lance, plunging the end directly into Rob's electronic eye. With a hiss of air, the vision unit imploded.

Chapter 22

Lev and Stace never made it out of the parking lot. Another Black and White blocked the backed the gate, its blaring speaker ordering everyone to leave his or her cars and re-enter the church.

"What about those who've left already?" Stace asked.

"The cops will undoubtedly visit them at home. Might as well get it over with now."

Back in the church, the mourners were shepherded to sit in the first few rows. Lev noticed more than half the original congregation had made it out of the parking lot before the discovery of Charles' demise.

Two men in dark suites stood facing them. The taller of the duo, a skinny guy with a dour face took over.

"I'm Agent Harcourt." He moved his gaze towards his shorter partner. "This is Agent Kirkland. We're FBI working with The Office of Homeland Security." Before anyone could question his authority, he explained, "Yes, this is a police crime scene. Nonetheless, we have questions for folks."

The questioning was polite and professional. Held at a small table set up at the side altar, Agent Harcourt asked the questions, and Agent Kirkland took notes. Harcourt began by asking if they had seen anyone leave the choir loft at the end of the service. Lev noticed the two Feds exchange tired glances as each occupant answered no to this and every other question of the rest of the half hour.

Finished, Lev and Stacy drove down the twisty road from the church and through the gate. They had agreed to meet at the Musso and Frank's, a celebrity restaurant in Hollywood after Lev picked up Mel.

"This wake would bring a smile to the lips of the Devil himself," the widow Primo said as she sipped champagne. Vicki was already writing her column in her head.

"You sure you feel up to this, Pattie?" Stella Rae muttered, scanning the crowded room.

"I feel better among friends." Pattie held out her empty glass to a passing waiter who swapped it for a full one. "Everyone who's anyone will end up here tonight. No one misses a free meal at Musso and Frank's."

"Any news on Kate?" Stella asked.

"Not yet." Pattie set her drink on a side table. "To tell you the truth, Stella, I know nothing about the girl and neither do the cops."

"Welcome to a Hollywood wake," Lev said as the two entered the standing room only restaurant. "Do they do things this way in India?"

Mel shook his head in the negative. "Not exactly." It was his first glimpse of raw Hollywood self-indulgence. "Things are a little more subdued, except for the funeral pyre."

"Well put, Mel," Lev replied, grabbing two flutes of champagne and offering one to his friend.

Chapter 23

Don Ames wished he'd never become involved. He'd once been a man about town, making loads of money. Nice clothes, several luxury cars, great apartment and plenty of women. Then four years ago, he began a downward spiral. He blamed his agent, bad mouthed the wrong people in the right places, and that was the end of his career as a writer. Sitting in a red plastic chair in the snack bar of the Hollywood K-Mart he looked in astonishment at the scrawny looking woman wearing too much mascara sitting opposite him.

"You went to Primo's memorial looking like that?"

Villand looked pained. "I'm a pro. No one recognized me."

Ames sucked the last of his Big Gulp. "I bet. It's a wonder the ushers let you in."

"I sat in the back row, slipped away and did what I was told, then returned to the back row without anyone noticing. I was first outta' there before the cops arrived."

"You're lucky your car started."

"Okay, so what's next? Or are we just going to keep meeting in places like this?"

Ames glanced around, "Until further orders."

"I don't know Ames, first Primo then Charles."

"And no more phone calls between us," Ames said. "See that phone on the wall?"

Villand nodded, "Yeah."

"You be next to it every day at ten o'clock in the morning starting tomorrow. She'll phone you."

"The K-Mart North Hollywood would be more convenient for me."

"Fine, *you* tell her that. I'm out of here. Wait five minutes, then you leave."

Villand snapped his purse open, removed a makeup mirror and checked his lipstick.

Chapter 24

Jilly Suede sat curled in the big swivel chair behind Primo's desk wondering how many times over the years she'd sat opposite him taking letters, notes, and attending to so many details of his business. She knew when his Will was read and the news came out that Primo had bequeathed her the studio and home, Pattie Primo would go ballistic and immediately contest the will. Especially the house. Pattie would try to uncover any lever that might keep her from losing the house and its contents to Jilly. It wouldn't work, though, as Primo's Will was clear. In the end, Pattie would end up with a token one dollar a year for the rest of her rotten, backbiting life. Jilly snuggled deeper into the chair. Two days from now, all this and more would be hers.

Tapping a French-manicured fingernail on top of the highly polished mahogany desk, Jilly smiled. She'd be very rich in a couple of days, a lot richer than most of the bitches she'd had to put up with over the years.

She would own Megastar studios due to Primo's kindness and Charlie V's' on the Strip by her own cunning. Pattie Primo and Vicky Vance might scream till they turned blue, but it would be to no avail. Jilly had further plans to ensure that Hollywood became her oyster. She sat up straight as a soft double brrr-brrr issued from one of the deep drawers of the desk. She quickly opened the drawer, removed a state-of-the-art encrypted phone, and unplugged an earring from her right lobe. "Yes?" She toggled a control box on the desk and a one hundred-inch plasma flat screen came to life on the wall.

"Congratulations," a man's voice purred. Jilly's eyes riveted on the screen as flashes of color zigzagged back and forth.

"I understand you have our little lady hard at work. How is she by the way?"

"Fine. She's fine."

"I expect it will take her a little while to understand the worthiness of our endeavor. That's to be expected."

"Right now I've got her thinking all we want is the screenplay. Once she begins cooperating, it'll be a small step to engage her about the program," Jilly replied.

"Yes." The voice hardened. "However, we don't have any time to waste, Jilly. With viewer sensibilities changing, we've got an almost unlimited demand for niche, special effects movies exploring new themes. Business has swelling."

The caller never appeared on screen. He was sensitive about his privacy. The screen continued to display a kaleidoscope of color, scientifically designed to thwart any interception of their conversation.

The bodiless voice continued. "With her program, we will control the future of moviemaking worldwide. Persuade her to do the right thing. You have twenty-four hours. If you fail, I will have her transferred to Mumbai. We've no time to waste."

The picture dissolved and the phone disconnected.

Jilly shivered. Everything depended on her obtaining Kate's program. Frank Primo and the Mumbai film industry had grown steadily close over the last year. Her position with Megastar had made her aware and fully involved in every shift the two men made. Primo's film with Kate's program was to have been Frank's lynch pin in an agreement with Kumar Pashagora that would have made Megastar the largest and most powerful studio in the world. Jilly spun the chair to face the window, and gazed at the Hollywood sign on the side of Mount Lee. She did not intend to see the sign changed to read Bollywood, and she would never let any interfering Hollywood agent searching for Kate to derail her.

Turning back to the desk, she picked up the phone. "Get me Hank Tolomeo. Tell him it's urgent."

Thirty seconds later Hank was on the line. "Jilly, what's up?"

"Pashagora has given me twenty-four hours to get the program, otherwise his people will take Kate back to India."

"Have you talked with her?"

"Not in person, only by computer."

"Then I suggest you get over to the vault soon as it's dark. I'll fly down tonight. If Pashagora gets his hands on her we'll never see her or the program again."

"How could he get her to India, Hank? Getting through airport security—hell, we have to take our shoes off to fly anywhere."

"Don't kid yourself. He could spirit her out of the country any moment hidden in one of his private jets. Trust me. Arrange a

walk-on pass for me at the studio gate. I'll join you at the vault."
He hung up before she could answer.

Chapter 25

Kate knew it was only a matter of time before someone came. Taking Rob down had no doubt triggered alarms. If she was to escape, it had to be now. She stared again at the air-conditioning duct. Surely, it must lead somewhere outside. Clambering onto one of the benches and standing on tiptoe, she could almost grasp the galvanized metal vent. She would need a tad more height to get close enough to pry open the industrial sized outlet vent. Jumping down, she looked for a chair, a box, anything to stack on the bench. She'd also need a tool to pry it off.

"You don't honestly think you can make a break for it through the air vents, do you?"

Kate jumped at the sound of the voice. Jilly was standing in the doorway.

"It might work in one of your scripts, Kate, but not in real life."

Kate didn't recognize her at first. "Who…?"

Jilly sauntered into the room. "Jilly Suede, remember me? I was at the wrap party."

Kate sighed. "You gave me a scare. Thank God you found me."

"I never lost you, Kate. I was the one who put you here."

The room seemed to tilt causing Kate to lose all sense of reality for a moment. *What is this woman saying? Why would Jilly entomb her in a film vault?*

"You did a hell of a job on Rob." Jilly indicated the hapless automaton. "Sit down, Kate. We have a lot to talk about."

Chapter 26

A trumpet-like "Yoo-hoo" from Vicky Vance cut through the din at Musso and Frank's.

Lev grimaced. "Stay close, Mel. If she asks you any questions, act dumb."

"Vicky, dear." Lev air kissed her rouged cheek, inhaling her fragrant, heady perfume.

"So glad to..." Vicky stopped in mid-sentence at the sight of Mel. "Who is this wonderful looking young man, Lev? One of your writers?"

"No. He's with Apple."

Vicky's eyes devoured Mel and she was ready for more. "Do you mean the computer company?"

"Yes, he's a friend of Kate's. They were at UCLA together."

"Does he have a name?"

"Sure. Mel, meet Vicky Vance, ace Hollywood reporter."

Vicky's mouth tightened as she took Mel's hand. "I'm very pleased to meet you, Mister...?"

"Pashagora, Melhi Pashagora"

Mel's looks, accent and last name immediately rang a bell for Vicky. Her eyes lit up.

"Don't tell me. You're the son of Kumar Pashagora, owner of Mumbai International Studios," she purred.

Mel nodded.

"Then you must be here to represent your father. He was a very good friend of Frank Primo. Poor Primo."

"Yes, my father sends by me his sincere condolences to Mrs. Primo." He glanced around the room. "Unfortunately, I haven't met her yet."

"Then you come along with me and I'll introduce you." Reaching out a thin, claw like hand she snagged Mel's sleeve and tugged him toward her. "She will be touched to know your father sent you as his emissary."

Lev snagged a proffered glass of white wine from a passing waiter and tagged along behind the twosome.

"Your father was a close friend and business associate of my husband," Pattie Primo said after introductions. "I had the pleasure of meeting him once when he came to visit Frank on business. I heard he's given up international travel."

"Yes, his age has slowed him."

"What a pity."

"It is. However, he is a keen believer in modern electronics, especially telecommunications. He says he can now travel more rapidly over the radio waves than he ever could before."

"What a wonderful attitude." Pattie turned to Lev. "Is Mel one of your clients?"

"He's a friend of Kate's and has volunteered to help me find her."

"No one's heard from her yet?" Pattie looked alarmed.

"The police are investigating. In the meantime, Mel and I are doing our own search. Rumors fly through Hollywood faster than spam on the internet. As the word gets out that we're searching for Kate, someone will recall something we can use."

Vicky glared. "Are you insinuating that my lines of communication to the inner circle of this town are lacking?"

Lev swirled the remains of his wine. "No, Vicky, not at all." He drained his glass and nodded to Mel. "Shall we go?"

"I think you really pissed Vicious Vicky off back there," Mel said as the two walked away.

"No doubt," Lev grunted. "She'll go all out to get info on Kate now, just to spite me. Besides, how many women do you know who would attend a party hours after her husband was brutally murdered? Then again, Vicky and Charles were never very close."

Chapter 27

A private jet turned from base to final approach above the Santa Monica airport, and Hank Tolomeo tightened his seat belt as the landing gear groaned into position. Unless Jilly got Kate's program before Pashagora's people spirited her ass to India it would be the end of TolomeoTechnics. An image of Jilly perched on the edge of the desk in the vault with Kate, white faced and tense, slumped in the office chair, ready to do whatever he and Jilly asked came to him.

"Frank said your program will transform the industry. We have to gather our forces to keep it here in America. We'll make millions. You *have* to work with us, Kate."

Kate glared, "Us? Kidnapping's not the best way to start a partnership, Jilly."

Easing off the desk, Jilly unfolded a metal chair and sat beside Kate. "You've been through a lot the last couple of days, but that's past now."

"Yeah, right," Kate snorted, "as long as I turn over my computer program. Keep it in America? Why should I share it with anyone?"

Jilly chuckled, "To remain alive, my dear."

Kate tensed. "Who's 'us'?"

"Mel's father and I," Jilly replied. "In two days time, I'll own Megastar. You're either going to be a part of the plan or dead."

Kate sat upright, a look of amazement on her face as she exclaimed, "Mel's father! Does Mel know about this?"

"No. His father insisted he know nothing."

"I don't believe Mel's dad would get involved in such a scheme." Kate pushed out of the chair. "He doesn't need money. He could buy and sell Megastar a dozen times over."

"He needs your program, Kate. There's a lot of competition in India, new companies are popping everywhere with computer expertise in movie technology."

"Then get one of them to sell their idea to you. You'll get nothing from me."

"If you don't deliver, Kate, Pashagora will take you to India and force it out of you. Either way, we'll get the program. The question is whether it will most benefit Hollywood or Bollywood."

Kate snorted. "No one can take another person against their will and transport them to India, for God's sake."

"I've been assured it can and will be done, if you refuse to cooperate."

Kate told herself this wasn't happening—it was all a bad dream. *Wrong,* she assured herself. "My program is safe and you'll never obtain it, here or in India," Kate said softly.

"Kate, Kate, Kate. We've already got you and the computer you brought with you to demonstrate your program to Primo," Jilly said, sweeping an arm toward the computer on the desk. "If we can't get what we need from you, then we can extract it from your computer."

"You can access my computer like you have, but if you try to open the program it will automatically self-destruct. It requires more than just a bio-scan of me to get around the self-destruct mechanism. You can run the program with my help, but you need a password to access the program itself and copy it."

"So, give it."

"I can't. I don't know it."

Jilly's face reddened. "Cut the bullshit!" She leapt from her chair and slapped Kate's smug face. "You want to make it hard on yourself, go ahead. But you'll suffer the consequences!"

"The pre-password is a series of thirty-six numbers and letters. I only know twelve of them," Kate said keeping her head turned to the side where Jilly's slap had pushed it. She needed the moment to regather her composure.

"Who has the rest?"

Kate knew she now had the upper hand. All her precautions were paying off. "Mel has twelve, and my father has the remaining twelve. The entire pre-password must be uploaded to Bezirbien-Uster Bank's mainframe computer in Zurich, Switzerland. A randomly generated password will be issued to me that unlocks all the program's functionality including the ability to copy it for twenty-four hours."

Jilly pushed past Kate, and turned at the iron door, her face livid with anger. "I'll have Mel brought here, then your father." She unlocked the door and left, the clanging sound heralding a new problem. Kate had no idea where her father was. She hadn't heard from him in over a year.

Chapter 28

"No, Jilly, Mel and Lev left ten minutes ago. Where are you? You were supposed be here at the reception." Vicky Vance had one ear covered as she spoke; the noise level was rising in ratio to the amount of alcohol consumed.

"He didn't say. Lev made a sarcastic crack and they left." Vicky saw Pattie waving a "come-over-here-quick" sign. "If I hear where they went, I'll let you know immediately, Jilly."

Vicky pushed her way through the crowd of tipsy grievers and joined Pattie who whispered in her ear, "Over there. Don Ames." Vicky looked in the direction of Pattie's pointing finger.

"What about him?"

"He's drunk."

"So are half the people in this place."

"Ames is very drunk and Chaz Falconer was with him when he blurted out he knew where Kate was. Chaz just told me."

"That guy would say anything to keep an audience. You know that."

"Well, Chaz was kind enough to come over and tell me."

Vicki stood on tiptoe trying to locate Chaz. If this was true, she had a scoop.

"Where did he go?" Vicky rasped. "What did he say about Kate?"

"Chaz went to the men's room. He'll be right back; in fact, here he comes now." Chaz was the typical leading man of the twenty-first century, tall, good-looking and with an attitude that every chick should swoon when he appeared.

"This is off the record, Vicky, okay?" Chaz drawled.

"My lips remain forever sealed."

"I was going to tell Lev, but he'd left before I could get to him, so I told Pattie."

"Fine. Now go ahead tell me."

"Don't forget, he was pretty out of it. Anyway, Ames said that Kate never left the lot. She's still there somewhere, 'hidden away'."

"'Hidden away'," Vicky repeated. "What the hell does that mean?"

Chaz shrugged, "Ames suddenly realized he'd said too much and shut up."

"Did anyone else hear him say that?"

"I don't think so. I'd only been talking to him for a few minutes and wanted to get away when he blurted it out."

"Why would he say something like that?" Vicky asked.

"When Ames has somebody to talk to he likes to impress them. You are going to call the cops, right?"

"No, Chaz. I don't think an off-the-cuff statement of a drunk has-been would count with them, but thanks for the tip."

Chaz smiled, showing off his white teeth. "Remember where you heard it, Vicki."

"Of course I will, you darling man." She air kissed him and moved away. "Must be off. I was just leaving when Pattie called me over. Ta-ta."

Chapter 29

Rob still lay next to the desk, flat on his back, a soft humming coming from somewhere deep inside his electronic circuitry. Kate wanted to remove one of his arms and use its claw to pry off the air vent cover. Grabbing the mop, she prodded Rob like a kid poking a crab. Nothing happened. She shoved harder; his metal body scraped across the concrete. Lifting one of Rob's arms, she peered under the armpit. *There must be a way to get inside this bastard,* she thought. She tried to turn him over but the little sucker was too heavy. Kate loosened her grip on the mop and straightened.

Suddenly, Rob's right arm jerked off the floor and his pincher-shaped right hand snagged the edge of her Nike, ripping the shoe from her left foot. Screaming, she jumped back as his left arm rose in the air, the claw snapping, zigzagging randomly, desperately seeking a target.

Scrambling away from the writhing robot, her foot accidentally kicked against one of the old film canisters. Scooping it up, she ran to one of the side benches and shakily pried open the can. It contained a deteriorating roll of 35-millimeter film, three quarters of it dust. Celluliod, she recalled, was prone to deterioration, but retained its flammability, and the vault was full of film. Air conditioning meant air in/air out. *I could build a fire and the smoke would attract attention,* she thought, realizing as she thought it, that if she was discovered, she'd have died from smoke inhalation. *Shit.*

Staring at the metal entrance door, she noticed a sliver of a gap at the bottom of the door. Crossing to the entrance, she pushed one end of the film under the gape. It slid forward with no problem. If she could push enough film under the door, then light it, someone outside might see the sudden flame and smoke. But how to light it? She was torn between elation and despair when she remembered the book of matches inside the cellophane of the crumpled cigarette package. She'd replaced it in the desk drawer, so it meant having to get past Rob. There was no other way. She had to get the matches. Returning to the cube, she kicked off her remaining Nike.

Chapter 30

Lev had driven less than a mile from Musso and Frank's when his cell buzzed. It was Pattie. "What? And you didn't call the cops? The entire studio has to be searched. Right now, for God's sake!"

When Pattie explained that Vicky Vance had said the police wouldn't take any notice of a drunk's remark, Lev yelled, "Pattie! She wants the story for herself! Call the cops now. I'm on my way to Megastar. Call me back if you find out anything more!"

"What was that about?" Mel asked.

Lev barreled down Hollywood Boulevard. "Stupidity and celebrity. Pattie Primo says Vicky has a clue to Kate's whereabouts and intends to go public with it before notifying the cops."

"Did she say where Kate might be?"

"Yeah. Hidden someplace on the Megastar lot."

Chapter 31

Hank Tolomeo was in a rented car when his cell rang. It was Jilly.

"Hank, we have a problem. Vicky Vance called and said the word was out that Kate could possibly be somewhere on the lot. She wanted a quote from me. She said she was going national with the story and asked if I'd agree to permit the police to search the studio to demonstrate cooperation with the authorities."

"What did you tell her?"

"I said yes, of course, that Megastar Studios had nothing to hide and would assist in any way possible to help find Kate."

"What?"

"Relax. I'm on the lot and I'll have her out of the vault along with the computer before any search can take place. I also told Vicky that studio security and our insurance carrier would insist on a search warrant before allowing anyone to tramp around a complex structure like a movie studio. That should buy us some time."

"Get her out of the vault fast, and be sure no one sees her. When I get there, I want Kate ready to be smuggled off the lot in my car."

"Where are you going to take her?"

"You'll know soon enough. Just get started."

Chapter 32

Two drivers with the same destination headed to Megastar

studios. Lev, already on the Ventura Freeway was nearing the Barham Boulevard off-ramp, while Hank Tolomeo was stuck on surface streets, cursing the evening commuter traffic.

Jilly's mind was whirling with the events of the last few minutes. She hadn't told Hank about the special password, hoping to somehow get Mel in her grasp. All thoughts of that, however, vanished with the phone call to Hank. It was almost dark, and there was also no time to contact the bogus guard, the out of work actor who'd been only too happy to score points with Jilly Suede for doing the dirty work. She'd have to let go of the actor and Mel, and get Kate out of the vault herself.

Reaching into a desk drawer she removed a Ladysmith .44 derringer, a compact two shot weapon, and slipped it into her jacket pocket as her phone rang. She had expected Hank, but when Lev asked for personnel and car permits for himself and Mel to enter the movie lot, she couldn't believe her luck.

Lev braked at the entrance of Megastar and the guard slid open his window. "Go on in, Mr. Leventhal. Ms. Suede said go straight to her office. She's waiting for you."

"Thanks, Mike."

A generator truck parked outside stage one caused Lev to slow down, and bump over a tangle of cables snaking across the street.

"Setting up for night shooting," Lev commented to Med.

Mel nodded, "Busy night." He watched as technicians and gaffers pulled cables while stagehands yelled back and forth, moving scenery.

Jilly's intercom announced their arrival. "Send them in." Jilly indicated a couple of chairs when they entered. "Sit down. Let me bring you up to date." She verified she'd heard from Vicky, that the cops would arrive after they'd obtained a search warrant. She didn't mention her conversation with Hank. "I've ordered studio security to search the lot. It'll make for better publicity for the studio if we locate her rather than the police."

"When we were here the other day, Mel found one of Kate's earrings outside of stage four," Lev said.

Jilly stiffened. "Why didn't you tell me, Lev? I would have started a full search that very moment."

"You'd left the studio. I was told you'd taken a couple of days off."

"You're right. The shock of Frank's death and everything." Her eyes flicked to Mel. "Where exactly did you find the earring, Mel?"

"Alongside stage four."

"If someone forced her to go with them, they'd have most likely taken her toward the back lot," Lev added.

"From that point, they would pass the old film vaults," Jilly said. "You don't think it at all likely..." She delivered her lines like a pro and Lev and Mel seemed to fall for it.

"Still, it would be a good place to start," Lev suggested.

Jilly yanked open desk drawers, saying, "There used to be a set of dupe keys for each vault. Yes, here they are." She held up a bunch of old-fashioned keys. "It must be fifty years since they were last used." She blew imaginary dust from the tangled bunch.

Lev darted a glance at Mel, wide-eyed, perhaps thinking the earring might be the clue to finding Kate.

She jangled the keys. "Let's go."

"Maybe we should have security join us," Lev added.

"No need. We can handle this," Jilly said.

Chapter 33

Rob was once again as still as an empty suit of armor. Kate approached the damaged robot with caution, carrying the empty film can. Eyeing the distance between herself and Rob, she took careful aim and rolled the empty reel like a hoop toward him. The reel spun across the floor without a waver and struck Rob in the side. Rob's arm struck with the swiftness of an aggressive snake and flattened it. It happened so fast, it was almost a blur. The stubby android couldn't see, but its other sensors were as sensitive as ever.

Picking two more reels off one of the racks, she placed them a safe distance from Rob. Carefully snatching her jacket from the office chair, she added it to the reels.

Taking a deep breath she lobbed her loosely balled jacket and watched it arc toward Robs chest. Again Rob's lightning-fast reaction snagged the coat in midair, the claw gripping and waving it like a flag causing the material to crack like a ship's sail in a windstorm. Then she rolled one of the reels towards him. Harsh grinding sounds of tin on concrete assured her the other arm had also gone into action.

While Rob was thus engaged, she reached carefully forward and rummaged through the drawer until she found the matches. Retreating, she glanced at the vent. She was certain that once she got the grill off, she could squirm into the duct and hopefully find her way out.

Walking barefoot around the desk on Rob, she glanced toward the bathroom and saw a mop bucket. Grabbing it, she cranked on the faucet; again, a slow trickle of rusty water. *Not fast enough,* she thought.

Walking back to the desk, she carefully grabbed the metal folding chair Jilly had left. Hefting it, she whispered in her mind,

Heavy duty. Perfect. Grabbing its back, she swung the legs hard against the rusted tap, snapping the faucet off the washbasin and causing water to gush up to the ceiling. Snatching up the mop bucket, she held it under the water bouncing off the ceiling. Within seconds, the bucket was brim full and she dragged back to the desk, where Rob was still waving the jacket and hammering away at the film can.

Focusing on the gaping hole where his video eye had been, she held the bucket handle, and slowly began to swing the bucket back and forth, getting the feel, balancing the weight, eyeing the target —the jagged hole where the eye used to be.

Focusing all her concentration, she took a deep breath and launched the bucket. It flew in a low arc tilting forward as it neared the target. The bucket was upside down as it crashed onto Rob's head, releasing the contents into the hole where the robot's eye had been. Blue flashes shot outward, followed by sparking, sizzling and the smell of burning circuit boards. A second burst of sparks, then silence. In his death agony, the arm holding her coat had become detached and lay beside the blackened metal body. Kate picked up the folding chair and heaved it across the room where it landed squarely across his chest. Nothing. Rob was history.

Kate smiled wickedly, walked over, picked up Rob's arm. She now had the tool she needed to remove the grill.

Chapter 34

The trio passed stage four and continued toward the absolute blackness of the back lot.

"You found the earring around this area?" Jilly asked Mel.

"Yes, over there, next to the wall."

"Stage four's the last main building before the back lot," Jilly said, switching on a large flashlight. "There's nothing much back there except an old western set and some old film vaults."

A flash of light momentarily lit up the night sky, then dimmed and was gone.

"What the hell was that?" Lev asked.

Jilly knew the flash had come from the vicinity of the vaults, and quickly said, "Most likely the security search party."

The vaults, similar to military bunkers, were built underground, and had concrete steps leading down to a metal door entrance. Only the concrete domed tops of the structures were visible above ground. Jilly knew Kate was in the nearest of the vaults where the flash had appeared.

Jilly shone the flashlight beam down the flight of steps. "Be careful," she warned, noting the pile of melted celluloid in front of the door. She had the preselected key in hand. She wanted her visitors inside. Fast.

"What's that odor?" Mel asked.

"Smells like burnt plastic," Lev replied as Jilly unlocked and pushed the metal door open.

"Whew! It smells different in here. Much stronger." Lev stopped when he saw the desk underneath the overhead lamp, smoke emanating from behind it.

Jilly shut the door, her right hand gripping the Ladysmith in her pocket. She registered mock surprise, saying, "What the hell?"

"Hi-tech squatters?" asked Lev, as he approached the work desk. "What do you make of it Mel?"

"That's Kate's computer!"

Mel plugged it and the yellow cable into the laptop and tapped a few keys. "This unit is now a slave, and only able send and receive to one other computer."

Lev leaned in. "You mean, like an intercom?"

"Good analogy, Lev. That's exactly what it does."

Jilly fumed. If Hank had arrived sooner, they'd have had these meddlesome fools tied up and the place locked down permanently. But more important, where was Kate?

"We should lock up and wait for the police, Lev. This is a possible crime scene," Jilly suggested. A quick survey told her Kate was gone. All she wanted to do now was get out of the vault before Hank came on the scene and blew both their covers. "I'll go outside and call security. My cell doesn't work in here. You two stay and see what else you can find." She handed the flashlight to Lev and left. The longer she and Hank could remain innocent bystanders, the better.

Lev watched her leave. "Okay, let's check out the rest of this place, but do it carefully. As Jilly said, this is a possible crime scene."

Jilly hit Hank's number as she hurriedly made her way across the back lot. "Hank! Come straight to my office and stay away from the vaults! I have no idea where the hell Kate is."

Pushing a side door open, Lev entered the cramped sleeping quarters and saw an unmade cot with items of women's clothing tossed across it, and on the floor beside the cot, a single Nike running shoe.

"Mel, get in here!"

"Those are Kate's clothes," Mel confirmed and paled. "She must be here somewhere."

Exiting the sleeping room, they were stopped by a heap of scorched electronic gear.

"Whoa, what's that?" Lev asked, pointing the beam onto the metal heap that had once been Rob.

Mel gave a low whistle. "TolomeoTechnics builds those." Slowly he walked around the broken robot. "I've seen this model at the plant in Palo Alto." He pushed his foot against the remaining arm. "This guy looks as if he was hit with mortar fire."

"Hank Tolomeo's company manufactures those?"

"Sure, among other things. Wonder what happened to his other arm?"

"Hank Tolomeo makes robots."

"He's been into robotics for several years. It's a fast growing industry. They use them, dolled up to look human, in place of stunt men. The government loves them, too."

"I bet." Together, they searched the semidarkness of the vault, Lev swinging the flashlight beam side to side, as they passed rack after rack of the stored film reels.

A mutilated grill cover lay on a bench and next to it Rob's missing arm. Lev gazed up into at the open duct. "I think I know where Kate went."

Chapter 35

"What?" Franz Villand rasped into the phone.

"Kate's escaped from the vault," Ames said.

"You gotta' be kidding!"

"I'm not."

"I sat by that phone at K-Mart three mornings in a row and no one told me." Villand's voice quavered. "I told you I didn't like this."

"First our boss, then Hank Tolomeo called. We're supposed to find her. She's running loose some place on the Megastar back lot. I'll pick you up at your place." A dial tone droned in Villand's ear.

Villand hung up, his lips tightening. He went into the men's room and stared into the mirror. Within seconds, there was no sign of worry or concern on the face reflected back. In fact, his eyes had taken on steely glint as he said aloud, "It's show time."

Chapter 36

Outside the vault, Lev's flashlight beam picked out an industrial air conditioning unit sitting in the shadows. One side of the unit sagged open on a broken hinge. Studio security swarmed around it.

Lev whispered to Mel, "Exit Kate Keenan." In the distance, he could see the moving lights of other search parties. "More studio cops," he added. "By the time the Burbank Police get a search warrant, any clues will be trampled."

In the distance, a police siren warbled its approach and Mel said, "Kate's going to have find a way to make it off the lot."

"She could head for the night shoot," Lev said. "Hide in full view with a clipboard and a smile, and easily merge with the rest of the crew. Wait! Here comes Jilly and Hank."

Jilly and Hank joined the studio security standing outside the vault entrance.

"There was no one in the vault, Ms. Suede," a grizzled captain reported. "We've searched everywhere. There was a pile of burnt electronic gear and the air conditioning grill was knocked off. A small person could have squirmed through."

"Did your people check where the AC entrance and exit points are for that vault?"

The burly old captain bit his tongue. He'd served twenty-five years with the Los Angeles Police Department before serving eight more with the studio. His sour expression betrayed his dislike at having to report to a civilian, especially a bitch like Jilly Suede.

"Yes, Ma'am, we did. The door on one of the surface units was hanging open. She could've made it out. I have a party working the area."

"Keep me informed, Captain." Jilly and Hank remained silent until the captain had moved away.

Hank muttered, "Bloody Keystone Kops!"

Jilly hissed, "Let's get back to my office. If you'd have arrived sooner, we could have had Kate in our hands and Lev tied up and locked away forever."

"Mel and I will stay with security, if it's okay with you Jilly," Lev called out from the group of security men near the vault.

"Appreciate it Lev," Jilly called back. "Let's stay in touch."

Hank crossed to the portable bar in Jilly's office and poured two fingers of single malt.

"I told you what Pashagora said on the phone," Jilly said curtly. "He's going to have his people haul her off to India, and if you mess with Mel, he'll include us. Mumbai doesn't sound like my kind of place."

Hank sipped his drink. "I've alerted Ames and Villand. They're coming on the lot to help in the search."

"Hank, studio security and police are already swarming the place. What good will those two idiots do?"

"Kate knows them and will trust them."

Chapter 37

Villand answered the door with the chain latched; his eyes glittered as he squinted through the gap.

Ames grunted, "Come on, get moving. We don't have all night."

Closing the door behind them, Villand, dressed in blue jeans, a dark gabardine windbreaker and a baseball cap pulled low over his eyes followed Ames to the car.

"What's the moustache for, Villand?" Ames asked as he switched on the ignition. "One of your 'thousand faces'?"

"I feel better in disguise. I don't want anyone on the set to recognize me."

Ames sniggered. "I wouldn't worry, the last time you were on a working set was so long ago, whoever was there will be in the Motion Picture Home for the Aged."

Villand smoothed the moustache, "Thanks a lot."

Chapter 38

Pressing back into the deep shadows cast by a saloon on the western set, Kate heard then saw search party flashlights swing from side to side in the blackness. All she had to do was walk toward them, call out, and it would be over. A chill trickled down her spine. More likely, she would be safe only for as long as it took someone to abduct her again.

The threat from Jilly Suede that she could end up a prisoner in India caused her to linger in the shadows. She needed help, but who could she trust? Was Mel part of the plan? They were engaged to be married. The plan was get married in America, then, in time, go meet his father. Jilly may well have been lying regarding Mel's father being any part of the kidnapping. Her mind spun. Flashlights again pierced the dark air, this time closer. She must get off the lot.

Chapter 39

Jilly and Hank walked onto the sound stage just as John Bizet, the director called cut. The high-powered spots dimmed, and the set lighting brightened as stagehands began preparing for the next set up. The director saw Jilly and waved.

"I'm surprised to see you, Jilly. What's up?"

"I came by to give you a heads up. There's a search on for the woman who went missing at the wrap party the other night. Police are involved. I'll ask them to wait until you finish this shoot. How much longer do you figure?"

Bizet looked surprised. "You mean Kate Keenan, the writer?"

"Yes, but it could be a false alarm."

"No problem, Jilly. We should be through in about a half hour. We've just one more short scene and we're done."

Jilly indicated Hank. "You two have met I take it?"

Hank offered a hand to the director. "Sure, good to see you again, John. It's been awhile."

Jilly scanned the set for signs of Kate while the two men chatted. Finding none, she remarked, "Come on, Hank, we don't want to hold up production."

Bizet turned back to half a dozen antsy assistants waiting to ask questions.

"I saw Ames, but not Villand," Jilly said as they walked carefully through a maze of cables strewn across the sound stage floor.

"He's here," Hank said.

Jilly grabbed Hank's arm. "Damn! Look who's butting in again."

Hank turned in the direction of her gaze and saw Lev and Mel standing inside the entrance.

"No problem," Hank said. "Let's go over and talk with them."

"Are you crazy?"

Hank chuckled. "Your guilty conscience is showing, my dear. They know nothing."

Squaring her shoulders, Jilly walked over to Lev and Mel. "Hank suggested we alert the night shoot to expect an interruption."

Lev gave a terse nod. "Did you expect Kate to be here?"

Hank cut in. "No. John Bizet, the director was at the wrap party and I thought we'd ask if he'd seen Kate."

"Had he?"

"No. But it was worth a try." Hank indicated they should move outside. "I thought you were going to work with security."

"And I thought you'd gone back to Palo Alto. We decided to search on our own. If it was Kate locked in the vault, we know how she escaped," Lev said.

All at once, Mel blurted. "Then she's somewhere on the lot!"

"Likely she's left the studio by now and is contacting the police," Lev added.

Jilly's face blanched at the thought. She clutched Hank's arm. "Her kidnappers will likely hunt her down again. This is terrible. She might make for your place, Mel."

"Possible. Maybe I should get back there," Mel said, glancing at Lev.

"I'll drop you off," Lev muttered.

"I'll stay with Hank," Jilly said quickly. "If we hear anything I'll call you at once."

Chapter 40

Kate was remained inside the saloon, but was standing in the deep shadows, peering through the slats of the batwing saloon doors. She was sure she'd heard something, but could see only blackness. Moving to one side, she bumped against a table and knocked over a chair. She caught the curved back before it clattered to the floor, then she heard the sound again. Gripping the chair, she held it over her head ready to clobber who ever came through the door.

A lone man pushed open the right hand swing door and Kate brought the chair down hard, smashing the top of the door. Splinters flew and Villand leapt to one side. Had he pushed open the left batwing, he'd have had his head split wide open.

Kate's arms tingled from the force of the blow.

"Jesus! Kate! I came to help you. Take it easy."

"Franz, is that you? What's with the mustache?"

"You almost killed me."

"What are you doing creeping around the back lot? I thought you were one of them."

"Them?"

"The scum bags who held me in the film vault."

"Everyone's searching for you," Villand lied. "That's why I'm here."

Kate lowered the remains of the chair. "How did you find me?"

"Lucky guess. I was trailing along behind the security search team. Some of us from the wrap party volunteered to help."

"Thanks."

"You're safe now. No one can hurt you."

"Yeah, right," she said bitterly, thinking, *where have I heard that before?*

"Come with me. I'll take you to Jilly Suede's office"

Kate had decided she didn't care for the Man of a Thousand Faces after meeting him at the wrap party, and now that she was again face-to-face with him, she liked him even less. "I want off the lot, as far away as possible," she replied. No way was she going to trust this quirky cretin and have Jilly get her hands on her again.

Still, her inclination was to play along and follow him until she had an opportunity to dump him and go solo. Creeping along behind his skinny ass, she removed the steel finger she'd broken off of Rob's claw hand from her pocket.

"Okay," Villand said agreeably. "Let's go."

Chapter 41

"Where exactly are we going?" Mel asked, as Lev turned right out of the studio gate onto Barham Boulevard, continued for a block, then made a second right turn.

"Back into the studio through gate three," Lev replied.

"I thought we were going to my place in case Kate showed up there."

"That's what I wanted Jilly and Hank to believe."

"What's going on, Lev?"

"Listen, I have a hunch Jilly and Hank have something to do with Kate's disappearance."

"Jilly and Hank?" Mel exclaimed. "Why do you think that?"

"Remember when we first entered the film vault and found Kate's computer?" Mel nodded. "Well, Jilly suddenly became agitated. She couldn't wait to get out of the vault to call the cops."

"Oh, yes, and we found the robot from Hank's company in the vault along with Kate's clothes," Mel said, his eyes squinting as if thinking it through. "But I've known Hank for some time. Why would he want to kidnap Kate?"

"I don't know. I could be wrong, but in the meantime, we're going back on the lot to continue our search, starting with the night shoot on stage one," Lev said.

A walk-on permit authorized by security was good for all

Megastar's studio gates. He was going to secretly reenter the studio at a side entrance, gate three, a lesser entrance used mainly by trades people and studio transport.

Chapter 42

"Once Kate contacts the police, it'll all be over," Jilly's voice quavered.

"I have no intention of allowing her to contact anyone, Jilly," Hank rasped, removing his cell phone from his pocket. "Where are you?" he ordered and turned away from Jilly to listen to the voice of Ames telling him he was still on stage one. "Well, get out of there. Right now. Go over to Shoreham drive and stake out Mel's place. I think Kate's heading for the Pashagora apartment. She's not on the lot."

"You want me to locate Villand first?"

"No, get over to the apartment now. No time to waste. I'll call him."

Villand's cell vibrated and he stopped, Kate bumping into him in the darkness.

"Yeah?" he whispered, glancing nervously at Kate.

"Get over to Shoreham drive," Hank commanded, "and meet Ames. Kate's off the lot."

"What are you talking about? She's right here beside me, I found her, and I'm bringing her in."

Kate gripped Rob's metal finger tighter, but the angle wasn't right. Her foot rattled against a rock as she sidestepped away from Villand. Instantly, she scooped it up; it was heavy, and fit into her hand as if tailor-made. Without hesitation, she hit him at the base of his skull. He went down without a sound.

She patted the ground, trying to find the cell phone in the

darkness. When she found the phone, she heard Hank's voice calling Villand's name. She disconnected, and tapped Mel's number.

Lev and Mel had passed through gate three without problem, and were driving toward stage one when Mel's cell chirped.

"Kate! Where are you?"

Lev immediately braked to a stop. "Give me the phone." Kate brought him quickly up to date to the moment Villand hit the ground.

"I'm near the western set, and I can see flashlight beams in the distance," she whispered.

"Good. Listen carefully: Stay right where you are. I'll contact security and they'll come and get you."

Kate shot back, "No way Lev. They'll get me and take me to Jilly. She's the person responsible for my kidnapping."

"Good God! In that case, go back to the western set and lay low. Mel and I will be there in less than five minutes to pick you up."

"Lev, there's a search party heading toward me. I told you, I can see their flashlights."

"Then hide! They'll see Villand and take him to security. When they leave, run back to the saloon."

"Yes but…" The phone suddenly went dead.

Parking the car, Lev and Mel hurried in the direction of the western set. The evening was moonless, and the back lot encompassed in absolute darkness.

Kate stuffed the cell phone into her pocket. The moving lights were getting closer, and she could hear voices calling to each other. She had to hide. Glancing to her right, she saw a mass of old scenery silhouetted against the glow from the night shoot. Within seconds, she was amidst the wood and canvas, crouched low as the search party came upon Villand sprawled on the ground. It happened the way Lev said. They picked up Villand and carried him toward the sound stage, leaving the way clear for her to head back to the saloon.

Lev and Mel were standing in the shadows on the wooden sidewalk next to the saloon when Kate slinked by. Lev saw her first. "We're here Kate! Come on," he whispered urgently.

Less than five minutes later, with Kate curled on the floor under a blanket behind the front seat of Lev's car, the three exited the gate.

Lev waved to the guard as he drove off the lot. "Okay, Kate you can come up for air now."

Chapter 43

Studio security called half way through Jilly's second gin and tonic. Her face paled as she asked, "When?"

Hank scooped up an extension, and heard security tell Jilly they'd found Frank Villand unconscious near the western set. He was now in the studio hospital.

Jilly slammed the phone down. "I don't believe this! That little bitch is going to ruin everything."

"Order security to stop all traffic entering or leaving the studio. Also, find out if Leventhal cleared the lot. We need to be sure if he left."

Jilly dialed security.

"Mr. Leventhal left through the main gate at seven fifty-five." There was a pause, and the security guard continued. "Seems he returned to the lot through gate three at eight-oh-two and left again at eight-fifty," she said to Hank.

Jilly hung up. "Lev got her off the lot, Hank. Contact Mumbai and alert Pashagora."

Chapter 44

Lev drove straight to his place on Lookout Mountain. He'd decided they should stay together, keep away from Shoreham and plan their next move. Kate didn't want to go to the cops, fearing the media would become involved and turn everything into a circus.

Sitting at the kitchen table, Kate finished a bowl of Lev's homemade spaghetti.

"Like more?" he asked.

"No, I ate too much already. Good pasta, Lev."

"Leftovers always taste better. I made that two days ago."

"Better than the slop that scumbag in the vault served."

"You two both need a good night's sleep. Come on. I'll show you your rooms." When they stood, Lev continued, "It's so good to have you here," he said, giving Kate a brief, but substantial hug. He shook Mel's hand with a smile, "Sleep well."

Fifteen minutes later, the house was silent. He must decide his next move. He decided to make a list of the players and mark which ones might know his home address.

Chapter 45

Hank Tolomeo returned to his Palo Alto plant and chaired an emergency meeting of his board of directors, bringing them up to date on Kate's program, and his intention that TolomeoTechnics obtain it. His ferret-black eyes flicked across the faces of the men sitting at the long, polished teak conference table.

Hank Tolomeo had come a long way since he'd earned a living repairing television sets in Hollywood back in the late fifties.

Tolomeo had taken out a loan on his modest house in the San Fernando Valley, offered a job to the smartest technician in the company and started a small electronics lab in what later became Silicone Valley. His technician turned out to be a whiz kid with the new craze device called a computer. His two-man operation grew lightening fast and both men made millions.

Mr. Tolomeo held up a boney hand. "We're talking billions here. MGM, Paramount, Warner Brothers, to name a few, would love to know what I know about her program."

Tolomeo turned the pages of a thick ledger on his desk. "And we mustn't forget Bollywood." Hank was a man of power, with an alpha ego, driven by an insatiable inner force to control the film and mass media market. What Kate had written was his taste of honey, and he sought it with an urgency bordering on lunacy.

Tolomeo leaned forward. "This meeting is over, people." A florid faced man wanting more details objected. "Relax, Jonathan, I'm meeting a few friends in LA tomorrow. We'll get the girl and the program, and I'll have everything wrapped up in twenty-four hours."

Chapter 46

"Believe me, Stace, I rarely do this," Lev whispered. He was sitting in the Adirondack chair on the deck, a cell phone pressed to his ear.

A sleepy voice answered. "You know what time it is Lev?"

"That's what I mean. I hardly ever call anyone this late at night."

"It's *morning*, Lev. Very early morning. What's up? And why are you whispering."

"I'm outside on my deck."

"Fine and I'm fully awake with the light on. This better be good."

"Kate is here at my place."

"You found her! Where was she?" Stacy was now wide-awake. "Does anyone else know you have her?"

"Yes, I'm afraid they do."

"What's that mean?" asked Stace slowly.

"Trouble," Lev whispered. "At the least, Kate's life is again in danger. She was held in a film vault on the lot at Megastar."

"Have you've been drinking, Lev?"

"Not since lunch with you. And get this: Hank Tolomeo and Jilly Suede were part of the plot. Can you drive up here right now? I can go over everything with you then. One other thing, don't tell a soul. Kate's life may depend on it."

"Put a pot of coffee on, Lev. I'm on my way."

Lev switched off, patted his pocket to be sure Al Jolson was still okay, and then went inside to make coffee.

A few minutes later, Stacy Hart was squinting at Lev over the rim of a steaming mug of coffee. "You can't keep Kate hidden up here forever."

"I know, and I don't intend to. I'm going to hustle Kate and Mel out of town for a few days."

"Okay, then what?"

Lev sipped his coffee thoughtfully before saying, "That'll be up to you, Stace."

"Me?"

"Okay, maybe I should have asked if you help first"

This was a first for Stacy. In all her years as a publicist, no one had ever asked her to abet in getting anyone *out* of town.

"You hide Kate and Mel and I do what?"

"Pretend you don't know where we are while keeping your ears and eyes open for any reactions among those who were at the wrap party."

"I see. You want me to act dumb and play spy."

"Well, yes, if you want to put it that way."

"Okay," Stace agreed. "And if I see or hear anything, then what?"

"I'll call you at least once a day."

"Lev, despite Kate's concern about turning this into a media circus, it might be best to report this all to the police. A whole lot safer, too."

"Yeah, I know, but she has her mind made up. Besides, she wants to see her father. She says it's important."

Stacy sputtered, "Her father? I didn't know she had one. I thought she was brought up by her grandparents."

"She was, Stace. It's a long story. Will you do it, play the dumb spy?"

Stace brightened, "On one condition, Lev."

"What's that?"

"When it's all over, I get to be Kate's publicist."

"I guarantee it, Stace."

Chapter 47

Stace drove Lev to a car rental agency in Hollywood.

"Call me every day, Lev."

He watched her drive off, rented a car and headed home. The sky was turning from dark to pink when he pulled into his driveway, recalling the old saying, "Red sky in the morning, sailors warning."

His car was in the garage, making anyone interested think he was there. The rental would lessen the chance of anyone recognizing him when they drove away.

Lev roused Kate and Mel; they entered the kitchen complaining about needing fresh clothes. Lev poured them coffee and said they could buy some later in the day.

"Where are we going?" Kate asked.

"Away. You didn't want the cops to help, so it's up to me."

"Do you think it's wise to vanish, Lev?"

"In this case, yes. You saw the way Hank Tolomeo and Jilly Suede acted. They're playing for keeps."

Mel looked tired. "I've known Hank for some time and I never dreamed he'd be a part of a plan to kidnap Kate."

"Yeah, well, it's hard to know people today, Mel. Finish your coffee. I want an early start. Kate, any idea where your dad is right now?"

"When I last spoke to him a year ago, he was in Arizona."

Lev frowned. "Nothing since?"

"No. He was "going hermit" as he called it. He was starting a new book."

"Where in Arizona was he last time you spoke?"

"Flagstaff. But, like I said, he was going hermit." Kate crinkled her forehead. "Wait a minute. He said something about heading to some desolate place called Dolan Springs. He'd chosen it because it had small local library with a couple of public computers with internet access."

"Doesn't your Dad use a computer?"

"Yes, he does, but without internet service?" Kate shrugged her shoulders. "Anyway, I remember he said he was going to rent a trailer." She paused, "Wait, I have an idea."

Kate returned to the kitchen with her laptop.

"I didn't know you had that. I thought you'd left it in the vault."

"The one in the vault was compromised. Just before I left, the self-destruct program did it in. This is yours, silly."

She flipped the lid open, booted up and Googled "Library, Dolan Springs, Arizona."

"Here we go. There's a Skype phone number. It's too early to phone, but it shows we can Fax to this number even when they're closed."

Kate typed, "IMPORTANT! Call me as soon as you receive this. Collect if necessary. It's a matter of life and death." She inserted her name and cell number and hit FAX. Within seconds, it was on its way and they were ready to fly out the door.

"I'll need to stop briefly to pick up my spare computer. It's a duplicate of the one that was destroyed. Is that okay?"

Lev nodded his approval.

"In that case, I'll stay behind to collect and pack some necessities. When you've got the computer, swing by and we can load up and leave.

Thirty minutes later, the three were back at Lev's house. Kate slipped her secret second computer into a carrying case Lev provided and slung it over her shoulder like a tourist in a bad neighborhood. "It's part of me," she explained. "You still have Al Jolson, right Lev?"

"Yeah," Lev answered, "'Never leave home without it'." Lev glanced around and noticed that Mel wasn't in the room. He also noted that Kate hadn't mentioned Al Jolson in front of her fiancé. He frowned.

Chapter 48

Ethan Keenan was sipped his first cup of coffee of the day

when he heard a snuffling sound outside of his trailer. Still in his shorts and tee shirt, he tugged open the warped front door.

A shaggy haired, tongue-lolling mutt sat on a shabby doormat. The word "Welcome" had worn off long before Ethan moved in.

"Morning, Yellow Dog," Ethan growled.

"Ethan, do you have a daughter?" A loud voice rang out from across the trailer park as a large woman appeared from within a large cloud of cigarette smoke and waddled toward him.

"Who wants to know, Judith?"

"The library lady." Judith was almost at the front door and Yellow Dog slunk into the shadow of the trailer.

Judith was short of breath most every day and hefting herself the twenty feet from her battered Airstream had left her gasping. "Well, do you?"

"Yeah, she lives in California."

Judith took a deep suck on her cigarette and rasped, "Urgent message. C'mon."

Ethan followed her across the dusty lot to her trailer where she pointed to a phone—a black rotary job at least thirty years old. "The library lady's on the line."

Ethan picked up and answered, "Yes it is." He looked around for something to write on. Judith, reading his mind, turned over a store receipt and pushed it along with a stub of a pencil across the tabletop. "Okay, give me the number." He jotted the number on the piece of paper, thanked the woman at the library, and hung up.

"Not bad news, I hope."

"Don't know yet. I have to call this number to find out."

Judith had taken over managing the trailer park after her husband died in an accident on the interstate outside of Phoenix. That had been nineteen years ago. She knew everything about everyone in the park with the exception of Ethan. All she knew about him was that he kept to himself and paid his rent on time.

"Use the phone again. I'll wait outside."

"Thanks, Judith." He waited until the screen door had creaked shut, then dialed the number, remembering when phones took this long to crank.

Kate answered on the third ring, "Dad?"

"What's up?" he asked. "You okay?"

"I'm fine, but I have a problem. Mel and I are on the run. Jilly Suede and Hank Tolomeo are after me and my computer program. They want to steal the movie program. Jilly threatened I would be hijacked to India and forced to give the program to them. I told them that even if they did, I couldn't give them the program as I didn't have the password."

"Whoa, whoa, Baby. Slow down. How did you find me?" Ethan asked.

"I remembered you saying you were going to 'hermit away' in a place called Dolan Springs out in the desert. You mentioned there was a library. I left a message with the library and they called me back, telling me a person of your description used one of their computers at least once a week. You didn't have a card, never mentioned your name or where you lived, but the librarian said that if anyone in the area knew you, it would be Judith out at the trailer park."

"So much for being a desert recluse," Ethan muttered. "Jilly Suede and Hank Tolomeo. So they know about our password arrangement?"

"Yes, I told Jilly I didn't have the full thirty-six alpha-numeric combination and I had no idea where you were."

"Did she believe you?"

"I think so, but I bet Tolomeo is arranging to locate you as we speak."

"Great," Ethan said sarcastically.

"Lev suggested we three should meet in Las Vegas and talk over the situation."

"Who's Lev?"

"My new agent. Listen, Dad. Can you meet us in Vegas? You do have a car, don't you?"

"Of course, I do. Where in Vegas and when?"

Kate consulted Lev, then shot back, "Binion's Gambling Hall and Hotel, one-hundred-twenty-eight East Freemont Street."

"Why there? You own stock in the place?" Ethan asked.

"No. Lev just pushed the yellow pages in front of me and tapped their ad. It's downtown. Lots of people. A good place to vanish. Joanie, that's his secretary, will book four rooms in her name. What do you think?"

"I'll pack a bag. What name are we booked under?"

"Malone. Joanie Malone. She's prepaying with her credit card and I'll have it with me. Our names won't be used."

"Okay, Kate, I'll leave in the next half hour. Vegas is seventy-five miles away, so I should be on Freemont Street in less than three hours. Where are you now?"

"Don't rush, Dad. We're still in LA. Meet us at six this evening in the foyer of Binion's. Wear a red carnation."

Ethan hung up. *She still had a sense of humor, my gal*, he thought and smiled.

Ethan told Judith he would be away for a couple of days, and if anyone came asking where he was, to tell them she had no idea.

"That's easy. I really don't know," Judith said.

"Right. Be sure to give Yellow Dog his bacon rind every

morning."

Chapter 49

Jilly Suede was well aware that the murders of Frank Primo and Charles Vance, two men who had been close friends and business associates for many years, would, eventually put her in the circle of suspects. When the reading of his Will revealed Jilly as heir to Frank's fortune, the circle would tighten considerably.

Jilly had made certain that Frank's doctor, a man he'd seen at least once a month, wrote the death certificate showing the cause of death as a heart attack. There was no autopsy and Frank had gone out the way he wanted to—cremation.

Charlie Vance's departure from earth, murdered with a knife between his shoulder blades after singing a hymn in church, was altogether a different story, and Kate being on the run made everything worse. Should she tell the police of her incarceration in the film vault? Or would remain silent, knowing the possibility of she herself being shanghaied to India if she wasn't successful in recapturing Kate. Both Hank and Jilly knew Kate had to be located and temporarily coerced into silence, no matter what it took.

Glancing at her watch, Jilly gauged that Hank would be arriving in the next few minutes. She had grown comfortable sitting behind Frank's large desk, and everyone at the studio took it for granted she'd remain in charge until further notice. Her phone rang.

"Hank, I thought you'd be here by now."

"Running a little late," Hank said, "I want you to meet me at the Mexican Place, say in half an hour. I booked our usual booth in the back. We'll have dinner and I'll bring you up to date."

Jilly hung up. There would come a time, soon she hoped, when

Hank would be out of her life. He was getting too damned bossy.

A half hour later, Jilly slid into the red leather booth she and Hank always used. The server, seeing her, smiled and called her by name. "Evening Ms. Suede, we alone tonight?"

"No Fran, I'm a little early. Mr Tolomeo will be here soon."

Fran nodded, "Two glasses of white wine as usual?"

"Sure Fran. On second thought, bring a carafe. We'll order later." Fran set two leather-covered menus on the table and left.

How long ago was it when she and Hank had first come to the Mexican Place? That's what they called it, never by its correct name, just the Mexican Place. It must have been two years at least. The restaurant was located opposite the main gate of Megastar and served delicious food, good house wine, and, for Hank and Jilly, pleasant times.

Fran returned and set an empty wine glass and a carafe of white on the table, along with a glass of the same for Jilly.

"We were all so sad to hear about Mr Primo. He was a wonderful man."

Jilly sipped, and then smiled sadly saying, "Yes, we all miss him terribly." Fran shook her head, and backed away from the table leaving Jilly with her own thoughts.

"Sorry, I'm late." Hank slid next to Jilly, filled his glass and drank half of it in one gulp. "I needed that. No news on where they went yet. I have a top crew working on it."

"Who are they?" Jilly asked.

"No one you know. Trust me, they're good."

"So is a thirty-six digit password, Hank."

"Yeah, but don't worry. We'll get her, her father and Mel."

"Does Mel's father know they're on the run?"

"Yes, I talked to him today."

Jilly swirled her wine, took a sip and asked, "And?"

"Mr Pashagora is very unhappy. He advised me that unless we found them in the next twenty-four hours he would send some of his own people over from Mumbai."

Jilly checked the time. "Oh boy, let's order before I loose what's left of my appetite."

Chapter 50

Ethan parked his car and approached the main entrance of Binion's. It was two minutes to six. As expected, Freemont Street was ablaze with neon and filled with crowds. Lev had been right, it was a good place to hide in full view.

Suddenly, seemingly from out of nowhere, Kate was beside him, her arms flung around his neck. "Dad, you look too thin."

Ethan felt a surge of joy go through him; he hadn't realized how much he'd missed her. "Wow, baby you look great. Now tell me what this is all about."

Kate linked arms with him and they entered the lobby. She pointed. "First, let's meet Lev, and you know Mel. There they are."

They walked over to meet the two men; she made the introductions.

"Nice to meet you, Lev. Good to see you Mel," Ethan said, and then asked, "Can we find a quiet spot where you can fill me in on what's going on?"

Lev flicked his eyes upward, "My room's as good as any. Come on."

Kate sat in the only chair and the three men sat on the bed facing her. Kate quickly brought her father up to date, ending with, "So, we left town and came here. Lev will check in with Stacy Hart every day. She'll give us a report on what's happening."

Ethan asked Lev, "Is that the same Stacy Hart I'm thinking about?"

"Stace has been in town a long time. You might have known her from your days in Hollywood."

Ethan nodded, "Publicity, right?"

"Yeah, she has her own place now. I can trust her to help us. Like Kate said, we'll be in touch with each other at least once a day."

"What are the chances you were followed here, or someone knew you were coming to meet me?"

"Slim, I'd say. Stacy won't know where we are until I phone her later," Lev said.

Ethan stood up, walked across to the window, and looked down at the activity below. "I suggest you don't call Stacy, Lev."

Lev frowned. "You mean you don't trust her?"

"If you've made it out of town without being tailed, we should leave it at that for now."

Mel tapped his fingers on his knee. "Now that we're all together, we should pool our password numbers and contact the Bezirbien-Uster Bank in Zurich."

"That would be foolish," Ethan rasped. "The program is safe. We don't want them to catch us with the computer and the password, do we?"

"Good point, Dad. When the time comes for us to share the program, we can contact Zurich."

Ethan grinned. "Good girl. Now, this place is famous for a good steak. How about we find a dark corner in the dining room and see how good they really are?"

Lev heaved off the bed and rubbed his lower back. "I agree, however, one stop before the dining room. First, we get a wig for

Kate."

A short time later, a young brunette and three men were eating dessert in the dining room. "Been awhile since I ate so well. And they're right. A great steak," Ethan declared.

"The first thing I said to you, Dad, was that you were too thin. Must be your desert diet."

"You might be right." He almost said "Kate." He'd have to get used to her wig and stop calling her by her name.

"I know it's early," Lev said, "but we'd be safer going to our separate rooms and staying there tonight. The less we move around the better. We have each other's room number. We can stay in touch on the room-to-room phone service."

"If there is anyone here who can finger us, I won't be recognized," Ethan said. "So, if you need anything from the gift shop, like a magazine or a paperback, let me know and I'll get it."

"Good idea, Ethan," Lev said. He glanced at Mel and Kate, and continued. "Under no conditions do I want either of you two wandering out of your respective rooms. It's only for one night, but the risk is too high."

Kate sighed. "Great having dinner with you, Dad. I'll say good night. See you all in the morning."

"I'll phone your rooms and let you know where to meet in the morning," Lev said.

Kate walked with Mel from the restaurant and waved at her Dad, a girlish smile on her face.

Chapter 51

After dinner with Jilly, Hank returned to his boat in the marina. His cell buzzed as he boarded.

"What?" He shouted. "When did you find this out?"

"Breaking news on TV," Jilly said. "Seems one of the security guards at the studio called a local TV station and reported that Kate had been held in a film vault for two days, then broke out and vanished."

"Do you know who it was?"

"No, the reporter said his source was anonymous."

"Yeah, and by morning every reporter working for those supermarket tabloids will be on her trail, along with dozens of paparazzi, their cameras loaded and their photo-fingers itching."

"What are we going to do, Hank?"

"Sit tight and hope my people locate her first. Don't talk to anybody. Understand?"

Jilly hung up and wondered nervously what Frank Primo would have done in a situation like this.

Jilly's problem worsened the next morning when she read the Los Angeles Times and discovered Kate was engaged to Melhi Pashagora, the son of Kumar Pashagora, owner of the largest film studio in India. Mr. Pashagora was offering a reward of one million dollars for the safe return of Kate Keenan to his business associates in Hollywood.

Jilly let the paper slip from her fingers. That son of a bitch Pashagora was going to get Kate, just as he said he would. By now there'd be hundreds of people searching for her.

And she was not the only person reading the same news.

Chapter 52

Ethan was up early and went down to get a newspaper. He glanced at the front page, rushed to his room and called Lev. "Call Kate and Mel to meet us in your room. And hurry."

Mel was the first to comment on the news: "We'll have dozens of people on our trail now. Dad's ransom offer will attract every bounty hunter in California. We should go to the cops now and save ourselves a lot of problems."

"If we do, Mel, the media will learn about Kate's computer program. Reporters can dig up more than you think." Ethan was speaking from experience. He'd had his problems with reporters years back when his agent had screwed his life up for him.

"We can't be on the run forever, Dad."

"We won't, Baby. Just long enough think of a way to solve this problem."

"Thanks to Joanie lending us her credit card, we won't leave an obvious paper trail," Lev said. "Mel, call room service and order breakfast for all of us. Then, I'm turning in the car. We'll rent a new one under Joanie's name."

Kate said, "Using Joanie's card?"

"Yeah, and I want you to wear your brown wig everywhere. It makes you look as ordinary as a mud puddle. Go with your Dad. Ethan can rent the car, showing his driver's license as ID. You'll be Joanie Malone. If they ask for your ID, say you can't drive, and give then the last four digits of your social security number. That sound okay, Ethan?"

"It should work. Dumping the Hollywood rental will slow them down. Tolomeo will have every rental agency in Hollywood checked and will have asked to be notified when and where the car gets turned back in," Lev said.

"Can he do that?" Kate asked.

"Put it this way, Kate: Tolomeo gets things to work by throwing money at whatever obstacles get in his way."

"Yeah, and of course, the Hollywood rumor mill will be in top gear. Vicky Vance, the Wicked Voice of the West will be having a field day," Ethan said.

"Brings back old memories, does it, Ethan?" Lev, asked softly. "That rumor mill is just as powerful now as it ever was." Lev snapped his fingers. "That's it. We'll use it to *our* advantage."

"Miss Information," said Ethan. "She's always a star."

"The town thrives on it, and the population of Hollywood notables and celebrities will eat it up. I learned a couple of hot items when Stacy Hart updated me at Forest Lawn before Primo's service."

Ethan turned at the mention of her name. "What did she tell you?"

Room service delivered breakfast before Lev could answer. Once the waiter had left, Lev said, "Plenty." He grabbed a bagel, spread on some cream cheese and took a bite. "Jilly Suede is heir to Megastar studio, among other things."

Ethan poured himself another cup of coffee. "Toss that piece of info into Pattie Primo's lap and BOOM! The interest in our caper will fall off noticeably."

Lev grunted. "Vicky Vance's lap would make a better landing place."

"You're right, Lev. Pass the bagels."

The rental car return worked out fine. Ethan drove the new rental, followed by Kate driving Ethan's car containing Lev and Mel.

"Where the hell is Bullhead City?" Kate asked.

"About a hundred miles south of Las Vegas, across the Colorado River from Laughlin, Nevada," Lev muttered. "Just follow your dad. He knows the way."

Chapter 53

Vicky Vance received a juicy tidbit from an anonymous caller saying Jilly Suede was heir to Frank Primo's Megastar studios. The caller quickly hung up. Vicky Vance was stunned. This morning's LA Times reported Kate had been a prisoner in a film vault on the Megastar lot before making her escape.

Vicky's forte was reporting rumors and innuendoes skillfully connecting them and dipping them in vats of doubt and fear. She knew her readers and their gluttony for simmered slices of scandal.

Vicky's long red fingernails clicked rapidly over her key board as she prepared her latest scoop.

Ethan pulled over a few miles outside Vegas and swapped cars with Lev. Kate wanted to ride with her father and visit awhile. Lev and Mel waited as Ethan pulled back onto the highway and they followed.

"Lev's thinking of renting a houseboat or something and making our way down river for a couple of days. He says it would be wise to stay off all major roads," Kate said.

Ethan blew out his cheeks. "You have a cell phone?"

"In my purse. Joanie loaned me one," Kate said as she rummaged through her bag to find it.

"Good. Call Lev. I want to update him. By the way, be sure to turn off the GPS locator on the phone."

"Did that yesterday, Dad. But thanks for checking." She dialed and handed the phone over.

"Lev? It's me, Ethan. You flunked geography, right?" Before Lev could answer, Ethan said, "The river ride is out. We wouldn't get far enough downstream. You thought we could float back to California, right?"

Lev sounded unsure, "Yeah, well, close at least. Okay, Ethan, do you know any back roads into California?"

"Sure. How many do you need?"

Lev chuckled. "The quickest way with the least chance of anyone knowing we're back."

"Okay, but first we should grab a bite in Bullhead City. It's a long drive to California on the back roads. And make sure the GPS locator is turned off on your and Mel's phones."

Ethan handed the cell back to Kate; "Tell me more about this Tolomeo guy. He wasn't around when I was last in town."

It took twenty-five miles for Kate to bring her dad up to date.

"He sounds like a definite problem, and him being cozy with Jilly Suede adds another dimension to the trouble dynamic. When we stop to eat, make me a list of everyone involved so far."

They were on the outskirts of Bullhead City when Ethan pulled into the parking lot of a Kentucky Fried Chicken.

Minutes later, Kate was pushing a greasy piece of paper across the plastic tabletop and taking a final bite of a chicken leg.

"There you are, Dad, the list you asked for." Mel and Lev exchanged glances. Kate explained, "A different cast of characters since your days, but I bet not all that different in their methods of wheeling and dealing."

Ethan grunted, "William Shakespeare made the definitive statement in, *All About Nothing*."

Lev said quickly, "When you show up in Hollywood again, you may discover enemies you've forgotten about. Enemies waiting to finish you off."

Ethan wiped his fingers on an already tired napkin, "I never forget, Lev. Trust me. That's why I'm going to say it again. Don't phone Stacy like you promised. If you do, you'll be talking to those who want Kate's program and all us out of the way."

Lev frowned. "Stacy?"

"She's a publicist, and a good one. One of the best, in fact. I remember her from when I was a writer in Hollywood and my work was stolen and given to Don Ames."

"Stacy was part of that?"

"All I'm saying is, everybody in Hollywood is part of something one way or another. The bigger they are, the more enmeshed they become in everything."

Chapter 54

The Burbank PD's search warrant for Megastar included the film vaults. The crime scene investigation was wrapping up when the two Feds who had investigated Vance's murder at Forest Lawn entered. Agent Harcourt looked as peevish as ever as he scanned the empty room. Agent Kirkland, at his side, wisecracked, "'Tales from the Crypt'."

Ignoring the remark, Harcourt turned to the CSI leader and asked, "Anything?"

"She was here, that's for sure. We've just finished doing the HDS."

Harcourt nodded, he knew HDS or high definition surveying involved reflecting a laser light off objects in the room and back to a digital sensor, creating three-dimensional spatial coordinates that are stored. He was thankful to be retiring soon; he was finding it hard to keep up with the new technology.

"Take a look in the back room next to the bathroom. Someone lost an arm." The rest of the CSI team grinned at Harcourt's reaction.

Rob's arm was in a thick plastic bag on the bench. A CSI policewoman was making notes.

"What is that?" Harcourt said pointing at the bag.

"Far as we can tell, Agent Harcourt, it's what's left of a robot." She pointed her pencil towards the desk. "We found the remains of an electro mechanical device, a robot I'd say. From what was left, it looks like it blew up and burned."

"A guy murdered in a choir loft and a robot in a film vault," Harcourt muttered.

"An *exploded* robot," added Kirkland.

"Yeah," said Harcourt. "This gal who escaped from here, she was a client of the guy we interviewed at Forest Lawn."

"Lev Leventhal. The publicist."

"You have his address?" Harcourt asked.

"I have a list of everyone we talked to."

"Good, let's go talk to him again."

Three hours later, Harcourt and Kirkland were re-interviewing Joanie Malone. "This is a murder investigation, Miz Malone. Every person in the church remains a suspect until the case is closed." Joanie had no answer for Harcourt when he asked why Lev hadn't been in for three days. "Everyone was instructed not to leave town without notifying Office of Homeland Security first."

"I never said he left town. I said he hasn't been in for three days."

"Is it usual for him not to show or call in?"

"No, it's not unusual. Sometimes he works from his home office."

"But you phoned and got no answer, right? His client, Miz Keenan has been reported escaping from a film vault, and no one has heard from either of them for three days."

"I'm sure I'll hear from him," Joanie calmly insisted.

Harcourt straightened his skinny shoulders, "If he doesn't contact me in twenty-four hours, I'm putting out an all-points bulletin."

Joanie waited until the agents had left, then called the cell she'd loaned Kate.

Chapter 55

Pattie Primo's morning was shattered when Vicky Vance phoned and brought her up to date on the pending loss of Charley Vee's due to a bad debt between her husband and Frank Primo. As heir to Frank Primo's studio, Jilly Suede was now the holder of the loan, a debt of one million five hundred thousand dollars.

Pattie screamed into her phone, "What are you talking about Vicky? The Will hasn't been read yet. You're a Goddamn rumor monger! I'll sue for deformation of character."

"Calm down, Pattie. I'm your friend. You know that. I'm just giving you a heads up. We have to work together as always."

Pattie knew that was a crock, but settled down to hear more. "I'll talk to my lawyer, anyway. Someone is leaking information meant to harm me."

"Of course, you're right, Pattie. We have to discover who's behind all this, and why."

"We both know who's behind it: Hank Tolomeo! And it's due to that damn program of Kate's. I hope they never find that smart-ass little techy. This town would be far better off without her and that program!"

"She'll be back, mark my words. Kate Keenan is too big a prize for Tolomeo to let go. And when he does find her, he'll get her program and sell it to the highest bidder."

Pattie was sitting up in bed with the speakerphone on; lying beside her was Chaz Falconer, hair tousled, a crooked smile on his thin lips.

"Morning, Vicky dear," he drawled. "You left out the bit about Kumar Pashagora in Bollywood."

Vicky's tone changed. "What about him?"

"Just that his son, Melhi, plans to take Kate back to India and get married. Then Kumar will have legal possession of the program, and can run it and put Hollywood out of business. No one will be able to make movies as inexpensively as he will." Chaz paused, "One other little detail. In India, domicile is the key to matrimonial proceedings. Mumbai's High Court has held that Indian domicile is an essential condition for both the bride and groom. They both must reside in India at the time of their marriage ceremony. Kate will remain in India for the rest of her life."

Vicky was shocked at the news. "Who told you?"

"Kumar, when I signed a contract with him. I've been his American contact for quite a while now. Stella and I will remain here another couple of years or so, then move to India and live the high life."

"You're a jumped up little traitor Chaz. I'll see to it you never work in this town again."

"Cool the rhetoric, Vicky. I read the book: Stella and I both have unbreakable seven-year contracts in Bollywood, so go ahead. We'll be paid whether Hollywood remembers us or not. And remember, you heard it here first."

The line went dead.

Chapter 56

Across town, two stellar citizens of Hollywood were starting their day with coffee and doughnuts at International House of Pancakes. Ames and Villand hunched over a white plastic table discussing their new orders, received last night from Tolomeo.

Ames, haggard of face and suffering a nasty attack of diverticulitis, gazed dully at Villand and gently rubbed his painful left side. "Fuck Tolomeo. I've had it. Go here, do this, do that. I'm getting too old for this shit."

Villand took a third donut, licked his fingers and gulped down half a mug of coffee before saying, "Don, I feel your pain."

"Bullshit," replied Ames, and gave a halfhearted burp.

"I really do. Look. We do what he wants and it will be the last time. Trust me."

"Too bad you aren't a man of a thousand brains, Villand. I say Tolomeo will be the death of us."

"Don't talk like that, Don."

"I mean it. He called last night and told us to wire Leventhal's house for a remote controlled high explosive charge. Neither of us know jack shit about wiring or explosives."

"That's okay. We just go online and find out."

Ames looked even more pained. "That hit on the head has made you even crazier. Ever think perhaps he's setting us up? We agree, he waits until we're halfway through doing whatever you find out on line, he calls the cops and we're hauled off as suspected terrorists."

"I'd cop a plea and make a deal to give information on who stabbed Charles Vance in the choir loft."

"How do you know who killed Vance?"

"I know."

"Okay, Sherlock, who was it?"

"A skinny lady sitting in the back row of the church. She did the deed and was away before anyone had a clue Vance was dead."

"How do you know that?"

"Simple. I used one of my faces, a dab of lipstick and a dress.

Tolomeo paid me ten big ones."

Ames's diverticular pain soared. "I'm not sitting here with a confessed murderer! I could go down for aiding and abetting. Forget about Leventhal's house." He shoved back his chair and rushed from the restaurant. Villand finished his donut, drained his cup and lit a cigarette. The tinsel of tinsel town was beginning to tarnish for many of the locals.

Chapter 57

Hank phoned from his yacht in the marina. "A rental company said the car Leventhal rented in Hollywood was turned in at one of their branches in Las Vegas. He paid the bill and left."

Jilly Suede's face was tight with worry. "Was Kate with him?"

"No."

"They could be anywhere. If she goes to the cops about us holding her prisoner on the lot..."

"She won't. Not yet, at least. I bet she'll contact that bank in Switzerland first, and approach another studio," Hank said.

"What about Mel?"

"Kumar has given him his orders. He's to take Kate to India along with her program and talk her into getting married over there, saying his father had finally given permission and welcomes her into the family."

"That bastard had everyone fooled, Hank. I had no idea he was working for his father."

"Blood's thicker than water, and Kate's program is thicker than blood to Kumar Pashagora."

Jilly fumed. "What about those two has-beens, Ames and Villand? What about us?"

"I've made arrangements. Don't worry about us. But from here on out, we need to stick close together."

Not the most romantic suggestion in the world, Jilly thought, rolling her eyes upward, but Hank was usually right.

Chapter 58

Agents Harcourt and Kirkland saw red and blue flashing lights as they turned on to Lookout Mountain Avenue. An emergency vehicle sat parked at an angle outside Lev's house beside two black and whites.

The Medical Officer glanced up as they approached, and turned his flashlight beam on the body, "These fractures are from blunt force trauma, Agent Harcourt."

Harcourt leaned forward and studied the victim. "ID?"

The MO nodded and a police officer handed Harcourt a driver's license. Harcourt glanced at it, and indicated the house. "Anyone at home?"

The officer shook his head, "No one."

Harcourt didn't know the name on the driver's license, but Donald Ames was either leaving or going to visit someone in the house, and Harcourt guessed that someone was Lev Leventhal.

"We're going in, officer. Bust down the door."

Chapter 59

Stace got a phone call as she entered her office. It was barely eight thirty in the morning, and the caller was Villand, who demanded an appointment with Stace at one. Villand said Tolomeo had insisted, saying it was of utmost importance. Stace begrudgingly agreed, then quickly dialed Vicky Vance.

"Vicky, it's vital that you phone me at exactly five after one. You do this and I'll have a big story for you, I promise. No, I can't tell you right now. Call me at exactly five after one and I'll tell you. Thanks, Vicky." Stacy hung up and stared at the instrument. It was now her lifeline.

She'd become involved with Hank Tolomeo over the last couple of years. The affair grew into a love/hate relationship, whereby Stace had been fool enough to slip information to Tolomeo on the inside workings of a number of Hollywood production companies. The knowledge she passed to him enhanced TolomeoTechnics' bottom line. Finally, she decided to end the affair. Tolomeo, however, threatened to break her by leaking controversial information, making her company seem as if it could not be trusted.

Stace had intentionally arrived early at the Forest Lawn memorial for Charlie Vance on Tolomeo's orders. He was already waiting and suggested she stay until the end of the service. When asked why, he'd laughed, saying she would learn what would happen if she had any ideas about ending their working relationship. He left, returning later as if just arriving at the service.

Stace had almost told the whole story to Lev as they sat on the bench beneath the willow tree, waiting for the mourners to arrive.

Her morning at the office was been ruined by Villand's call. It was five minutes to one and Stace suddenly felt chilled. She reached for a sweater from the back of her chair.

"Your one o'clock is here, Ms. Hart," a voice announced from her desk intercom.

"Thank you, Sally. Send him in."

"It's a she, Ms. Hart, a Mrs. Applebaum."

"Oh," Stace paused. "Very well, Sally, send her in."

When the door opened, a small hunchbacked old woman entered and Stacy knew immediately she'd been right to call Vicky.

"Sit down, Franz. What do you want?"

"How did you recognize me, Stacy?" Franz Villand asked petulantly.

"You're getting too old. You've used up all your faces."

Villand sat down slowly; his eyes held a glint that frightened Stacy.

"I'm here as an emissary for Mr. Tolomeo, bitch. He wants you dead."

Stacy's eyes cut toward the phone wishing it to ring; it was almost five after one.

Villand reached inside his jacked and removed a long, thin-bladed knife. "Mr. Tolomeo wants it done quick and silent." He grasped the knife; his knuckles whitened. He smiled and began to push back the chair. Then the phone rang. Stace snatched it up.

"Vicky, Franz Villand is here in my office and he wants to talk to you." She turned toward Villand but he was already at the door.

He turned before exiting. "Very clever, Stacy. Next time, no appointment. You won't recognize who it is until the very last moment. Then it'll be too late."

Stace became aware of Vicky Vance's trumpeting voice and placed the phone to her ear. "You just saved my life, Vicky. Here's your scoop."

Chapter 60

Ethan returned the rental in Bullhead City; they'd decided to use one car, Ethan's. It was after midnight. Ethan was at the wheel; Kate was half-asleep in the back seat, her head on Mel's shoulder. Bright moonlight reflected off the narrow ribbon of road unwinding ahead of them when her cell jangled.

"Hello."

"Kate?"

"Yes, who is this?"

"Joanie. Where are you?"

"Not sure, somewhere on a back road in California. You're lucky you got a signal. We're in the boonies. What's up?"

"I've been trying for hours. LAPD busted down Lev's front door at the house after finding Don Ames dead on the front porch. There's an All Points Bulletin out on him."

Lev turned from the front passenger seat. "Who is it?"

"It's Joanie. She's got some bad news." She passed the cell to Lev.

"Ames, dead on my front porch?" Lev said dazedly. "The cops kicked in my front door?"

"Agent Harcourt called me at home." Then she informed Lev about his office visit.

"So, I'm a suspect in Ames' death?"

"I'm sure everything will turn out fine, Lev. It's just a misunderstanding. By the way, I called your lawyer."

"Oh, thanks, Joanie. What else can you tell me?"

"Vicky Vance had a scoop about Primo leaving the studio to Jilly Suede and something about Charlie Vance owing a huge amount of money to Primo."

Lev sighed, "And?"

"You can imagine. Vicky and Pattie are at each other's throats."

Lev stared vacantly at the moonlit road and wondered if it was worth returning to Hollywood.

"Are you still there, Lev?"

"I'm afraid so."

"Good, Kate said the reception is spotty out there. When will you be back?"

"I don't know. I might turn myself in at Parker Center. I'll talk it over with Kate and then I'll call you back."

Ethan pulled over to the side of the deserted road and switched on the dome light: It was decision time.

Mel looked tense. His eyebrows drew together, giving his face a fierce look. His fingers tapped more rapidly on his knee.

Ethan leaned over the back of the driver's seat. "I'm not going to sit by and let Hollywood yank your chain like they did mine, Baby. Jilly Suede and Hank Tolomeo are going to answer for sticking you in that film vault and threatening you for your program. And don't give me anything about the media turning everything into a circus. From what I can see, it's already a five-ring circus with media stamped all over it." Ethan came on hard when roused.

"I know Dad, you're right. With what's happing with Lev and the cops, it might be best to turn ourselves in."

Mel cut in, "I prefer to contact the authorities and mediate a meeting where we can clear up any misunderstandings." His scowl, nervous fingers and agreement with the others made him seem overly concerned for their best welfare.

"Okay," said Lev. "Before or after we contact the Swiss bank?"

"Before, while we're all safely together. Who knows what'll happen once the police get involved," Kate said. "We'll need a secure environment to do the whole process."

Mel's face and hands relaxed, as if in relief, and he gave a quick grin.

Ethan started the engine. "Fine, then we have no need for back roads anymore. We just passed Amboy a few miles back. We'll stay on this road until we get to Ludlow, then pick up Highway Forty and head back to LA."

It was almost daylight when they arrived in Los Angeles. Lev recommended they go to his office, the safest place he could think of. Upon arrival, Lev suggested Kate get Mel and Ethan's password numbers and use Joanie's office phone to call the Swiss bank and download the program copying key. He removed Al Jolson from an inner pocket and passed it to Kate, saying he'd get the coffee started and be in his office when they were through.

Mel's eyes widened as if in surprise when he saw Lev had been carrying and hiding Al Jolson the whole time. His eyebrows narrowed once more.

Lev wearily slumped into his chair, dialed his lawyer and left a message that he was back in town, and then told Joanie's home machine that they were at the office. Done with the essential phone calls, he pondered: he'd been searching for Kate, now others were searching for them. Most importantly, they must stay out of Tolomeo's grip.

Kate concentrated on getting through to the Bezirbien-Uster Bank in Zurich. Finally, after a five minute wait on the line she received clearance to enter their combined 36-digit password.

During this time, Ethan nodded off in one of the armchairs in the waiting room. Mel slinked into the washroom, called Hank Tolomeo on his cell and updated him on their location. Tolomeo immediately gave Mel his orders, and then contacted Villand.

Mel returned and sat opposite Kate. "You get through okay?"

"Finally," she said, closing the lid of the laptop, "The program is fully functional for the next twenty-four hours." She began unplugging Al Jolson when suddenly Mel grabbed her arm.

"Leave it connected. I want to be sure everything works. Type in a few lines and create a picture for me."

"I'll need some of Lev's coffee. It smells so good."

"I'll get us both some. Just check everything out, okay?" Mel headed toward the aroma of coffee.

No longer wearing her drab wig, Kate's sumptuous red hair sparkled and she smiled as she typed. "The bride radiated happiness walking down the aisle, holding her father's arm and carrying a bouquet of dark blue violets."

Mel set a mug of steaming coffee beside her and leaned in to the screen. "Show me what you created."

Kate played back the short scene. Mel put his arms around her and whispered, "It will all come true, very soon now, my darling."

Joanie heard Lev's voice on her answering machine and tried to get to the phone before he hung up. She missed him by seconds. When she called back, the line was busy. She quickly dressed and started immediately for the office.

Chapter 61

Kumar Pashagora, tired of the delays in getting Kate and her program to Mumbai, finally contacted associates in Los Angeles and ordered a special extraction team to bring Kate Keenan, Mel Pashagora, Frank Tolomeo and Jilly Suede to his office in Mumbai within 72 hours. Once located and brought together, they would be flown to Mexico and then on to London by private jet. Kate would be forced to marry Mel, and she, Frank and Jilly would remain in India until they died. He then ordered a hit team to assist the extraction team. He wanted no trail left. Once in Mumbai, India would be large enough to hide almost anything.

The hit team knew where their targets were thanks to a call placed by Frank Tolomeo to Kumar Pashagora, telling him that Mel had secretly phoned from Lev's office at 201 South La Cienega Boulevard. Tolomeo said he'd already arranged to send someone to clear up the problem and bring back Kate, the program and Mel. Unfortunately, Tolomeo, as the saying goes, had sent a boy to do a man's job.

Villand drove toward his target, hoping the car wouldn't stall at a light. He'd be able to buy more than just a new car with what Tolomeo was paying for this job. The Pashagora hit team, heading across town on the Hollywood freeway, drove a much nicer car.

Joanie parked in her usual place and switched off the engine. There was a strange car on the lot and she assumed it was the one Lev and the others had driven. She was about to get out, when a battered '96 Chevy limped into the car park. She recognized it at once as Villand's.

What happened next was like a bad dream. Joanie watched Villand get out of his car. Wearing a long drab raincoat, he stood beside the car, reached into an inside jacket pocket and removed a 9 millimeter automatic fitted with a suppressor. After inspecting it, he slid it into the right hand pocket of the raincoat.

Joanie scrunched down in her seat as Villand surveyed the lot. For a second she thought he might have seen her and was going to check her car. Thankfully, he didn't.

Keeping his right hand in his pocket, Villand walked slowly toward the building.

Joanie's hands shook as she punched the numbers into her cell phone: one, two, three anxious rings before Lev answered his cell.

"Lev! Get downstairs and lock the front door! Don't ask any questions, just do it now! Stay on the line, and then speak to me as soon as you have the door locked. Move!"

Lev wasted no time. Kate and Mel looked up as he flashed past. Ethan was still asleep on the waiting room couch.

Lev went down the stairs three at a time and threw the dead

bolt to the locked position.

"Okay, Joanie. The door's locked," he answered in between breaths. "What's going on?"

"Villand. He's outside heading to the entrance with a nine millimeter automatic. Get back upstairs and warn the others. I'm going to call 911. I'm under a blanket on the floor of my car outside the office. Bye."

Chapter 62

Hank Tolomeo and Jilly Suede were sipping coffee in the main salon of Hank's 50-foot Aldon Flying Bridge Express twin diesel yacht.

"Sending that creep Villand to Lev Leventhal's office was a mistake. He's an old fool. Even if he does get in, he'll leave enough evidence behind to nail us."

"Thanks for the vote of confidence, Jilly." Hank got up from the table and looked out across the marina as the early morning fog began to swirl away in the first rays of sunshine. "Villand is going to lose face this morning, my dear. Successful or not, he'll be wiped out by Kumar's hit men."

Jilly looked unconvinced. "What do you mean?"

"When I called Kumar, he told me that his people will be bringing Kate, her program and Mel here to the yacht. We are to sail them to Mexico and rendezvous with a private jet that will fly us all to Chicago. We'll fly by a privately chartered commercial jet from Chicago to Mumbai by way of London."

Inwardly, Jilly was pleasantly surprised at Kumar's ability and cunning. Then again, the bastard had worked his way up from working in a small film studio to owning the largest movie enterprise in India.

"Can we trust him?" she asked.

"No, but for the moment, we'll have to. We've had too much bad publicity in this town. I've taken care of business at TolomeoTechnics. I sold out to a company that's been trying to buy me out for months. The transaction won't become public until long after we arrive in India. Also, my legal department has transferred all monies and other funds to a Mumbai banking concern."

Jilly's face clouded. "What about the possibility of extradition, Hank?"

"With my money and lawyers, it would take forever, if it ever happened at all." Tolomeo deeply regretted not getting Kate and her program out of the country and to Mumbai sooner. He would have if it hadn't been for Leventhal arranging for her to meet with Frank Primo.

Fast thinking and Jilly's organizing ability to outfit the film vault had bought them time to work on Kate. Then, just when success was in sight, the damn techy had escaped after destroying one of his robots.

"I don't like the idea of walking out on Frank's Will. It would have made me a rich woman."

"Listen to me, Jilly. Having one of your own security people call a TV news network and telling all, will not endear you to a jury when Pattie Primo contests the Will, which she will most certainly do. Don't even imagine she won't."

Jilly remained silent and thought fast. She'd been carrying out electronic transactions with her bank for years. What Hank was saying made sense: It was time to vanish. She picked up a phone. "Okay, Hank, what's the name of the bank in Mumbai? I'm going to make a transfer."

Chapter 63

Villand heard someone behind the door and the lock click. For a moment, he was undecided whether to shoot off the lock. Then, with the weapon still gripped in his hand, he sidled around the outside of the building, looking for a back entrance. That was when the hit team saw him.

A dark haired woman in her mid-thirties pointed toward the building. "There he is, the creepy dude in the raincoat."

The driver, a swarthy man with curly hair and close-set eyes, grinned. "Roll down your window. I'll drive closer. Take him down fast." He started the engine and eased forward.

Villand looked back over his shoulder at the sound of the engine starting, and when he saw a car approaching, he panicked. Was it an unmarked police car?

He knew it wasn't the cops when he saw the elongated, silenced barrel of an automatic aimed at him. The soft phut-phut was inaudible as the woman planted two head shots into his final face—one of total astonishment.

"Now we'll take care of the others," the man said, parking the car. "This should be easy."

Chapter 64

Upstairs, Lev assured them Joanie had called 911 and he had locked the front door.

Mel looked tense as Kate snuggled next to him and tightly held his hand.

"What about the back door, Lev?" Ethan asked, awakened by all the commotion.

"Bolted from the inside every night. It's the last thing we do before arming the alarm."

"Don't worry. I'll take care of you, Kate," Mel said softly. "Stay here while I take a peek outside." Mel rose and walked towards the window.

"Stay back from the window!" Lev yelled. "Everyone stay where you are away from the windows and just sit tight."

Mel bristled and shot Lev a vicious look as he slunk back to his seat.

The look was not lost on Lev. He'd noticed signs of a change in Mel in the last few hours. His eagerness to mediate with the authorities when they had returned to the office was one of them. He wondered if Mel had fooled him from day one, and had his own agenda as to why he wanted to find Kate.

Lev felt his cell phone vibrate; he'd switched off the ring tone after speaking to Joanie.

"Villand was just shot dead by two people in a car," Joanie said huskily. "They drove on to the parking lot after I called you. I came up from under the blanket when I heard their car. I thought it was the cops."

"Are you okay?"

"I'm fine, but the police aren't here yet. The couple in the car are trying to find a way into the building."

"Don't let them see you, Joanie."

"Roger that. Should I make a dash and get off the lot?"

"No. Stay put until the police get there."

The two-story building containing Lev's office dated back to the early thirties. Part brick and part stucco, it was originally built for storage. The top floor was later redesigned as office space. The entire ground floor was a satellite book depository for a publishing house back east. The only entrances to the second floor were front and back, and both were secure.

A loud crash and a shower of glass across the floor announced the arrival of a tear gas grenade. Lev moved with amazing agility, grabbing his metal wastebasket, scooping up the smoking canister, and hurling the basket out the window leaving only a trace of acrid, eye-burning odor in the room.

"Ethan!" Lev yelled. "Go into the bathroom and wet down anything you see to put over our mouths and breathe through. Whoever's out there is serious."

Ethan moved fast, but Mel moved faster. It was likely this was the hit team sent to get him, Kate, the computer and now Al Jolson out of the office and down to the marina. It had to be. Time was running out.

While Ethan returned with wet washcloths and towels, Mel took the opportunity to grab a stiletto-like letter opener off Joanie's desk and secrete it up the sleeve of his jacket. Lev, fearing a second tear gas canister, ordered everyone into the small windowless kitchenette.

As Kate got to her feet, she tucked Al Jolson into her computer bag, slung the computer and device around her shoulder and started for the kitchenette. That was the move Mel needed.

"We'll be less susceptible to the tear gas if…" Lev's voice faded when he saw Mel holding Kate in one hand, the other gripping a letter opener, the sharp point pressed against Kate's jugular.

"You two get in the kitchenette. Kate and I are leaving," Mel hissed. Ethan made a move toward him. "Back off, Ethan, you don't want to be responsible for Kate's death, do you? Get in there. I mean it."

"Stay back, Dad," Kate pleaded. "Please. He means what he says."

"She goes with me and no harm will come to her." With his

arm around her shoulders and the letter opener still held against her neck, they backed out of the room and down the stairs. In seconds, he had the door front door unlocked and was out in the parking lot.

The curly haired man saw them first. "There they are! C'mon!" Tossing aside the tear-gas launcher, he and the dark haired killer ran to their car and drove toward Kate and Mel. The woman opened the back passenger door, yelling for them to get in.

Mel pushed Kate in first, followed and slammed the door shut. The car burned rubber heading across the lot and out onto La Cienega Boulevard.

Within seconds of the car leaving, Lev and Ethan were in the parking lot. The car was gone.

A double beep-beep issued from Joanie's car. As they ran toward it, she swung open the doors.

"Get in. I saw them leave. They headed south."

Lev sat next to her, Ethan in the back seat. "I can't believe all this has happened and no one's showed up to help us," Lev gasped. "You called 911, right?"

"I did," Joanie replied as she sped across the lot and turned south. In the distance, police sirens sounded. Lev and Joanie exchanged glances.

"We must catch that car," Lev urged.

Ahead, La Cienega Boulevard was almost empty of traffic, unusual for this early hour of the morning. There was no sign of their quarry.

"They've vanished. Now we have no idea where they are," Joanie wailed.

"Keep driving," Lev muttered. "They're probably ahead somewhere."

Ethan leaned across the front seat, "Sorry I bad-mouthed Stacy

Hart. If I'd let you stay in touch with Stace on a daily basis, this might never have happened."

Lev twisted in his seat. "What do you mean?"

"It's a long story. Let's say it'd be a good idea if you give her a call, and see what she knows. Blame me for not calling each day as you promised."

"Nothing!" Joanie cursed when the car they were seeking never showed up.

"Okay. Joanie, then let's get back to the office. I'll tell the cops what we know, and then call Stace."

Chapter 65

Joanie turned onto the office parking lot. A yellow police tape fluttered across the entrance and an LAPD officer stopped them.

"Now they show up," Lev growled, rolling down his window. "Officer, inform whoever is in charge that we were in the building when it was attacked. My name is Lev Leventhal."

The uniform walked over to a group of suits and pointed toward their car. He returned, lifted the tape and jerked his thumb —drive in.

The skinny figure of Agent Harcourt stood next to a body bag. He looked up said something to a plain-clothed cop and stalked over to them. From his look, it was apparent they were not welcome.

Harcourt leaned through the open car window. "*You*, Mr. Leventhal, were told not to leave town."

"It was a matter of life and death," Lev replied.

"We'll see about that. What's this about being attacked in the building? We got a call someone was shot."

"Right, and someone fired a tear gas canister through the

window. I threw it back out before it overcame us."

"Yeah, we found it," Harcourt growled.

"Plus one of my clients was abducted with a letter opener held to her throat."

Harcourt shook his head in disbelief and jerked his thumb over his shoulder, "Get out of the car; the three of you are going to Westwood."

"Hey, hold it mister. His client," Ethan pointed at Lev, "is my daughter. We lit out after her and the bad guys, but they got away. What are you people going to do about that?" While Ethan offered his challenge, Joanie made a fast call to Lev's lawyer before they were transferred to a black and white.

At the Federal building in Westwood, Lev explained the situation, from the wrap party to the moment when Mel took Kate hostage. Lev's lawyer, now also present, added his assurance that from now on, Lev would not leave town and that they would notify Harcourt of any new developments.

Harcourt silently recorded every word. Finished, he said, "The time is eleven fifteen a.m. and the Leventhal interview is ended." Switching off the machine, he tilted back his chair. "I'm going to give you some information Leventhal, then maybe you'll pay more attention. The Office of Homeland Security was on this case from the moment Frank Primo died at the wrap party." Lev opened his mouth to speak, but Harcourt shook his head and continued. "Burbank, Glendale, and Los Angeles Police Departments have also become involved. Agent Kirkland and I have been tied at the hip to all three."

A plainclothesman leaned in, "OHS, working in concert with The National Security Agency, NSA, intends to resolve what could turn out to be a serious loss to America's future security." The man nodded at Harcourt.

"Thanks, captain." Harcourt continued addressing the trio: "The program Miz Keenan designed is of interest to the NSA. The possibilities of its utilization in military circles are beyond imagination. OHS is fully aware that a Mister Kumar Pashagora in Mumbai has been, and still is supplying aid and information to radical Muslim factions in Pakistan, hoping to destabilize the region."

The hair on the back of Lev's neck rose.

"On the surface, Kumar Pashagora appears to be exactly what he is: a wealthy India film industry magnate, well known and respected in the field of entertainment worldwide. With such credentials, he is able to wield considerable power. OHS can't simply reach into India and arrest him, but we definitely intend to stop him from getting the young girl and her computer program."

"That's what *we've* been doing, Agent Harcourt!" Lev exclaimed.

Harcourt smiled thinly. "Yes, we know, and we want you to continue. They know you're looking for Kate, so any sudden change in tactics might alert them about us."

"Fox and Hounds," Lev's mind raced back to Kate's reference to NSA offering her a position after graduation. Her mention of feeling followed and the car tailing Mel from the parking lot to his apartment suddenly made sense.

"You could say that, Mr. Leventhal, but remember: OHS is the Master of the Hounds. Continue to go about your task. We'll be close by and ready when needed." Harcourt scribbled on a piece of paper and handed it to Lev. "My cell number. Call anytime, day or night."

On the cab ride back to Lev's office, Ethan suggested it was time to call Stace. Lev agreed.

Chapter 66

"Lev, where are you? You were supposed to call every day and keep me posted!" Stacy Hart was pissed.

"It's a long story, Stace. You'll understand when I explain everything."

"Listen to me Lev. Pattie Primo called with Vicky Vance screaming and yelling on her speakerphone. Chaz Falconer was with her and cut in with that nonchalant drawl of his and said Mel was in on everything from the beginning. Mel Pashagora intends to shanghai Kate to India and marry her. Once they are married in the eyes of Indian law, Pashagora will see to it Kate and her program remain in Pashagora possession. That means she'll be a prisoner there the rest of her life.

"Then Falconer boasted that he and Stella Rae had served as the American contacts for Kumar Pashagora, and when the right time came, they'd head off to India, where they planned to live high and continue working with Kumar. If you'd called me every day you would have known this two days ago."

"You're right, Stace. I've just got back from the Federal Building in Westwood and received a similar lecture." Lev made no mention of Harcourt's Fox and Hounds operation. He retold Stacy about their trip from the moment they'd left town after she had dropped him off in Hollywood at the car rental agency, right up to Mel taking Kate by force from the office to a car waiting outside. He added that no one, including the Feds, knew where Kate and Mel were.

"That's a lot of drama, Lev." Stacy said quietly. "When can we meet?

"It's noon now. How about in an hour in your office? I have someone for you to meet."

"Who's that?"

"It's a part of a long story, Stace."

"Okay, one o'clock here at my office." Stace's reluctance to hang up revealed her craving to hear the rest of the story.

At one o'clock precisely, Stace heard a light knock on the door. She glanced up from her desk to see Lev and Ethan enter. She leaned back in her chair and indicated Ethan. "Is he part of the long story?"

Ethan answered, "Guess I am, Stace."

"Sit down both of you. Where did you spring from Ethan? It's been a while since we last met," Stace said.

"Arizona, and I'd still be there if Kate hadn't called me," Ethan said.

"Kate?"

"Yeah, and it's my fault that Lev didn't stay in touch like he promised. After being screwed over by my crooked agent and the breakup with Kate's mom, you were the only person in this town who tried to help me. I ignored your help, became a full time drunk and took off to Arizona. I've been living in a trailer park for almost two years," Ethan admitted. He rubbed his forehead slowly, "A lonely existence: sun, fresh air, and my only friend a dog who loves bacon rinds. I finally got tired of feeling sorry for myself, quit the booze and started to write again. Then I got a message from Kate."

"You should put it all in your book, Ethan," Stace replied.

"Already have, Stace, and you're in it, too."

Lev broke the trance between them by asking if she knew whether Tolomeo was in town.

"I heard he's aboard his yacht, the *Technocrat*, in Marina Del Rey. Jilly's with him." She paused. "You think Mel might take Kate to the yacht?"

"It's a possibility Ethan and I intend to explore. Do you know where he keeps his yacht in the marina? The dock, the slip or whatever they're called?" Lev asked.

"I've been on board the *Technocrat* a couple of times. I don't know the actual address but I'm certain I could lead you to it," Stace offered, inviting herself.

Chapter 67

"What if we didn't sail to Mexico, Hank? What if we leave the boat, hide out somewhere, and keep the program?"

Hank stared at Jilly. "Are you crazy? Do you have a death wish or something, because our deaths are what would result if we tried to thwart Kumar Pashagora."

Jilly pouted. "I suppose you're right."

"Suppose? I can't imagine how Frank Primo could entrust you to help run his studio. You're nuts, Jilly."

"Maybe I don't want to live in India."

"You try a stunt like you just proposed and you won't get to stay alive anywhere. We're going through with his plan and will deliver to him Kate and the program. Once we've done that, he won't care what we do."

"You ever think that by now someone will have figured out where Kumar's thugs will take Kate?" Jilly asked.

"Yeah, and as soon as Mel and Kate get here, we move out."

Jilly brightened, "Where to?"

"I've arranged to have the yacht go into dry dock for its yearly maintenance. It'll be out of the water for a week. After Kumar's people deliver Kate and Mel and we've left my yacht in the dry dock, we'll go board a charter vessel I have waiting, and head for Mexico."

Jilly glanced out the cabin window. A car had stopped and Mel got out, gripping Kate's arm. "They're here."

"Fine, after they come aboard and the car leaves, we move out."

"Kumar's people, that curly haired man and mean-looking woman, will drop them off and leave, just like that?"

"Yes, but they'll never make it back to LA."

Her face tightened, "Meaning?"

Hank watched the car pull away, "Arrangements, Jilly. Kumar leaves nothing to chance."

Kate struggled against Mel as he pulled her aboard. Within minutes, Hank had moved the yacht out of the slip into the channel.

"You'll never get away with this Mel! Kidnapping is a *Federal* offense," Kate grated.

"True, but only if we're caught," Mel shot back.

"You will be, I'm sure of it. Once Lev finds Hank's yacht is missing, the coast guard will find and will haul this yacht back."

"The Coast Guard won't know where we are. If they bother go to the trouble of locating this yacht, they'll find it in a dry dock facility. Hank's arranged for us to switch to a charter Grand Banks Forty-two that'll be waiting to sail us down to Ensenada, Mexico, where we'll be picked up and driven to a private airstrip to begin the next step on our journey to India," Jilly informed her.

Kate slumped in her seat at the galley table, knowing that if no one rescued her, she knew she would harassed until she relinquished her program to the Pashagoras.

Jilly Suede leaned across the galley table and narrowed her eyes. "Listen, girl. Just thank you're lucky stars you weren't killed and your program taken the night your ass was hauled to the film vault. If I'd have had my way, that's what would have happened."

"So, who stopped you?"

Jilly jerked her thumb toward Mel. "He did. He told us that your computer program was useless without the password." Kate flashed back to the unbelievable moment when Mel had dragged her from Lev's office with the tip of a letter opener pressed against her neck.

The curly haired hit man checked his side mirror, successfully making the transition from the Marina to the Santa Monica Freeway. All clear, he stepped up his speed to merge with traffic on the 405. Three seconds later, their car exploded in a ball of flame, slid across three lanes, smashed into the center divider and crumpled into a twisted smoking tangle of metal.

Chapter 68

"I could have sworn this was the right place." Stacy Hart muttered as she walked back and forth on the sidewalk looking down at an empty slip. Already dusk, it was becoming increasingly difficult to distinguish one yacht from another.

"We could knock on hatches and ask someone," Ethan suggested, indicating the other boats in the dock.

"We need a key to get onto the dock," Lev said.

"Wait! I just saw someone on that boat." Stace pointed to a sailboat, sails fluttering in the night breeze. "I'll call and attract their attention."

"I'll call," Ethan countermanded, cupping his hands and bellowed, "Ahoy, sailboat!"

"The name on the stern is Sea Dwarf. Try calling Sea Dwarf." Lev suggested.

Ethan did, and this time a man came up on deck. "We're looking for Hank Tolomeo. This is his slip isn't it?"

"Yeah, but you missed him. His yacht left about ten minutes ago."

"Was Hank onboard?"

"He was earlier. I was busy below, and just caught a glimpse of the hull through a porthole as the yacht moved out. Can't say with certainty that I saw him at the helm."

"Okay, thanks," Ethan shouted. "Well, you had the right slip, Stace. We just didn't get here soon enough."

"Can't we notify the Coast Guard and ask them to pull him over?"

"For what, Stace? We don't know for certain Kate's even on the yacht."

"There must be a way to find out. Call agent Harcourt and tell him we think she's being shanghaied."

Despite the situation, Lev had to smile. "I bet it would be the first time Harcourt ever got a call like that."

Nonetheless, Lev called and brought Harcourt up to date.

"You're on Los Angeles Sheriff's Department turf, so now I'll have to tie in with a fourth law enforcement agency. They're going to love you, Leventhal."

Lev added the information on Chaz and Stella, closed his cell, slipped it into his pocket and stared into the watery darkness. If Kate was on the yacht, she could be miles away already.

Kumar Pashagora had the rich man's ability of eliminating any 'loose strands' that stood in the way of in his international skullduggery, and there were two left to go: Chaz and Stella.

Chapter 69

The thud and clash of drums and cymbals beneath the dissonant wails of electronic guitars shook the drapes causing the amplified sounds to ricochet around Stella Rae's living room.

Stella, slumped on a once exquisite Victorian settee, now stained with red wine, cigarette burns and other unnamed blotches, stared with a glazed look out of the window holding a glass of vodka. It was three in the afternoon.

"Stella," Chaz shouted as he entered. "Hey, come alive, we have an emergency. Kumar called."

"Fuck off," she shouted, taking another deep suck from her glass. "I'm through with Pashagora calling the tune."

"We're to join Hank at the dry dock in Seal Beach, and go with them to Mexico and on to India. He's ordered us out of here, Stella. A million tax free dollars and life in an exotic land."

She nodded but remained silent.

"Put the glass down and listen up, you dumb bitch."

The heavy cut crystal glass barely missed Chaz's left ear before smashing into pieces against the wall.

He sighed, walked across the room and slapped her hard across the face. "Fine, if that's the way you want it, then I'll take care of myself and you can stay here." Chaz reached across and picked up the almost empty vodka bottle from the coffee table. "Here, finish it off. There's more in the kitchen if you can walk that far."

The slap had knocked a little sense into her dulled mind. If he left her, Stella knew she'd be dead in a week, and by her own hand, not Pashagora's. "You can't just walk out and leave me," she slurred.

"Oh, yes, I can. Vicky Vance is about to feature us in her gossip column and we'll be thrown out of town. I'm not about to wait for that to happen."

"You screwed up telling her anything in the first place, Chaz, and you know it." She took a pull from the bottle.

"You're right. It was dumb. But not as stupid as sticking around and letting Vance tie us in with Jilly and Tolomeo."

Stella tipped the bottle upside down and watched the last drops drip onto the thick pile carpet. She started to speak then her eyes rolled back in her head and she crumpled into the couch, out cold.

Chaz kicked the empty bottle aside and left the room. He'd carry out Kumar's orders and leave. Stella'd made her own choice.

Chapter 70

Since 9/11, America had gradually become accustomed to an undercurrent of intrigue in all walks of everyday life and possibly unknowingly, come to accepted it. Thus, the rights of individuals, no matter whom, helped cover the subterfuge of others. By constant manipulation of greedy and fame-crazed personalities, Kumar Pashagora was able to move in on Hollywood's exclusive networking system.

Vicky Vance's gossip irritated Kumar, and such loose strands infuriated him. He told himself repeatedly that the tittle-tattle would, like all other celebrity stories, fade with time. In the end, he would permit her to live, as she would be easy to control now. However, he didn't intend to leave anyone else alive with knowledge of his plans, and Kate, the program and Mel would remain forever in Mumbai.

Chapter 71

The month of March in Southern California can be sunny, dry, wet or cold. This time around, it was wet. Rainwater gushed from broken gutters of a derelict old building that had once been the packinghouse headquarters of Pacific Fruits from the Sea.'

Sitting on four acres of land located between Long and Seal Beaches, the structure, long abandoned, had been crumbling around the edges for decades. Kumar Pashagora had purchased the parcel years ago, and now the acreage alone was worth triple what he'd paid.

A shadowy figure inside a dome-tent erected in a corner of the dilapidated factory watched a video image transmitted from a security camera a thousand feet away.

Several hours would pass before Tolomeo's yacht arrived at the nearby dry dock and Scumbag, Kate's guard from the film vault, would see a clear picture of the yacht when she arrived at dawn's early light.

Chapter 72

When Stella awoke, it was dark outside. Her housekeeper had covered her with a blanket and left. She was alone and scared. Her head thumped and her hands shook as she reached for the phone.

Vicky Vance answered. "Hello, is that you Stella? Are you all right?"

"No, I'm not. I must talk to you."

"Go ahead, dear, I'm all ears."

"No. In person, Vicky. Not on the phone. What I have to tell you is not for phone chat." Stella's voice was shaky.

"Do you want to come over now, Stella?"

"No way, I'm hung over and don't want to drive."

Vicky, smelling a story, replied quickly, "Stay still, be calm, and make coffee. I'm on my way."

Stella showered and drank three cups of coffee, but she remained shaky. Headlights shone up the driveway and Stella went to the front door to greet her as Vicky slammed the car door shut and headed up the steps.

A few days earlier, as Lev and Mel were leaving the Wake at Musso and Frank's, Lev mentioned that Vicky and Charles Vance were not very close as man and wife; he'd been right.

Vicky eye's narrowed with concern as Stella poured out her story of how Chaz had become involved in Kumar Pashagora's intrigues and dragged her reluctantly into the web.

"You did the right thing to call me, Stella. This is awful."

"Chaz has gone to join Hank and the others. I could be charged with aiding and abetting a terrorist."

"Now, just a minute, Stella. I wouldn't go so far as to call Pashagora a terrorist. An overzealous business man, maybe, but not a terrorist."

"Chaz wouldn't agree. He told me that once in India, the program would be adapted for military use. That's why he left in a hurry while he had the chance. What can I do?" she sobbed.

"For now, stay at home. I'll take care of everything. When your housekeeper comes tomorrow, tell her you're not well and stay in the house. Don't make any phone calls and don't answer the phone, okay? I'll come by tomorrow." If her vision hadn't been blurred, Stella might have seen Vicky's smile at her plan to keep Stella isolated and beholden only to Vicky.

"Thank you, Vicky. Thank God, There's someone in this town I can trust."

"It's all right, dear. We ladies have to stick together, I always say. Now turn in, and try to get some sleep."

Stella saw her to the door and walked back to her living room.

Before Vicky had driven out of the driveway, went to kitchen and opened a fresh bottle of vodka.

Chapter 73

Joanie had overseen the window repair at the office and cleaned the place. Several hours later, after making fresh coffee, she sat at her desk and dialed Lev's number.

"Where are you Lev?"

"Joanie, I was just about to call you. We're down at the marina. Ethan and Stace are with me and we're heading to the Sheriff's office. We think Kate's been kidnapped by Hank. Listen, gotta go. I'll call you soon. I promise."

Lev parked in the lot at the Sheriff's office on Fiji Way. "Let's go inside and introduce ourselves before Harcourt arrives."

The desk sergeant informed Lev that Agent Harcourt had already called and talked with the captain on duty, and she was ready to see them.

Captain Patricia Powers, a well-built woman of color around forty with a touch of gray in her hair, looked up from her paper work when the sergeant knocked on her door and entered, saying, "Mr. Leventhal and party, Ma'am."

"Ah, yes," she replied. "Come in, Mr. Leventhal. Sit down." She indicated a couch and chair. Lev took the chair and introduced Stace and Ethan who shared the couch.

"I hear you've been alerted to the problem at hand and will bring us up to date," Lev said.

Captain Powers' face clouded. "Yes, that's correct. And we've alerted the Coast Guard and radio contact has been made with other marinas to be on the lookout for a fifty-foot Aldon Flyingbridge Express, especially marinas and docks with a dry dock facility. Agent Harcourt has gone ahead to the Long Beach area as he feels that could be the yacht's most likely destination." The captain smiled with satisfaction at having all the available information at her fingertips, her eyes twinkling at Lev's surprise. "One of agent Harcourt's men questioned someone in a slip next to where the yacht is normally docked, and was informed the yacht was going in for its annual dry dock service," she explained.

"We also talked to a man on a sail boat. He said the yacht had left, but nothing about a dry dock," Lev informed.

"Perhaps you didn't ask the right questions, or you left too soon," the captain chided.

She, of course, was right. Lev wondered how Harcourt had someone there so quickly, and then remembered Harcourt's remark about Fox and Hounds and OHS being the Master of the Hounds. "Did agent Harcourt say where exactly in the Long Beach area?" Lev asked, leaning forward eagerly.

Powers shook her head, "No."

"Long Beach covers a large area, Captain," Ethan remarked.

"It does. However, as I mentioned, we've alerted the Coast Guard and sent radio alerts to all the marinas to be on the lookout for the yacht just in case they change their minds."

Stace asked, "If the craft heads for a dry dock as everyone suspects, what would Hank use as transport? If he does have Kate, he'll have to keep moving."

"He could have a car or truck waiting," Ethan suggested.

"Yeah," Lev nodded. "Being at the docks, he could also have a boat waiting. Kate said they planned to take her to India. To avoid all OHS contact, a clever man like Tolomeo might switch boats, cruise to Mexico and begin the flight to Mumbai from there."

"If he does that, Lev, no one will have a description of the boat or much of a chance of finding them."

The storm that battered the old warehouse near Seal Beach moved northward, and rain began slanting hard across Marina Del Rey.

"Wherever the yacht is, this weather's going to slow her down some," Captain Powers said, glancing at her office window as a gust of wind rattled the frame, and pressed her intercom button. "Sam, print out a list of all dry docks in and around Long and Seal Beaches and bring them here." She looked directly at Ethan. "I'm sure agent Harcourt has a list, and I've no doubt you intend to go down there and poke around. I would, too, if I had a daughter in the same predicament. I thought this list might be helpful."

"Thank you, Ma'am, we appreciate that," Ethan remarked.

"We all do," added Lev. "Thanks again."

Chapter 74

Joanie was about to leave the office when the phone rang. She returned to her desk and scooped it up. "Hello?"

It was Stella Rae. "Let me talk with Lev, it's very important."

Joanie caught the slur in her voice and told her Lev was not in the office.

"Shit! It's a matter of life and death, and I mean it! Can you give me a number where I can reach him?"

With all that was going on, Joanie didn't hesitate.

Rain falling heavily outside the Sheriff's office. Lev's windshield wipers were slashing on high speed with only minimal effect, when his cell vibrated. "Reach into my right jacket pocket, Stace, and answer my cell."

"Hello, who is this? Yes, he's here. He's driving in a rain storm and wants me to convey your message. Speak louder, I can hardly hear you. Who? Stella Rae? What do you want at this time of the night, Stella?" Laying the phone on the carseat between them, Stacy said, "She'll only talk directly to you."

Lev nodded, "The Western Avenue off ramp is coming up. Tell her I'll pull off there and we can talk."

Lev pulled to a stop on Western. "Go ahead Stella, what is it?"

Stella told him Chaz had walked out on her, and was going to join Hank and the others.

"You mean you know where Hank's taking his boat?"

"Yes, and I have a bad feeling about it. Do you have a map, Lev?"

"Sure, hold on." Rummaging in the glove compartment, he pulled out a battered Southern California map book. "Okay, Stella, tell me." Stace grabbed a notebook and pen from her purse and snapped on the dome light.

Lev repeated aloud each direction Stella gave. "Get back onto the four-oh-five and head east toward Seal Beach. Take the Lakewood off-ramp and stay on Lakewood Boulevard south all the way to Second Street."

Stace wrote each repeated word.

"Turn left onto Second Street. It dead-ends at an old unused warehouse complex. We probably won't see the building in the dark. It's in the middle of about four acres of empty land, located near the turning-basin in the Seal Beach marina."

"Lev," Stella implored. "Hank Tolomeo should arrive there early in the morning. He plans to secretly switch to a waiting charter boat. I was down there with Chaz on an errand for Pashagora about two months ago. It's a rough area. And Lev, be careful. Pashagora has the warehouse and surrounding wasteland covered with concealed high-tech video security cameras. You'll be seen, rain or not."

"Thanks, Stella. You okay?"

"No, Lev, not really. Good luck." Lev's phone clicked off. The driver of a black Ford Explorer parked in the shadows five hundred yards behind Lev watched the dome light go out, headlights come on and the car make a U-turn north heading back to I-405.

"He's moving, sir."

"Fine, keep me updated," Harcourt said. "We're on our way."

Chapter 75

Chaz Falconer had taken his time after leaving Stella at the house. He'd stopped for dinner, then completed the drive to the Seal Beach rendezvous. Now, as he approached the wasteland surrounding the warehouse, he carried a flashlight, aimed it toward the derelict building and pressed the switch three times. Seconds later, three quick winks of light issued from the building. Contact made.

Five minutes before, Lev had stopped at the end Second Street. A lone street lamp shone dimly through a swirling halo of rain.

"What a dismal place," he remarked as he turned off the engine.

"Can you see the warehouse?" Stace asked, wiping the steamy car windows with a Kleenex. "And don't forget what Stella said about the security cameras being able to see us."

"That's why I drove the last quarter mile with the lights off, Stace." He pointed at the distant street light. "That was my beacon. Ethan, reach up and turn off the switch on the dome light before I open a door."

"Okay, it's off."

"Good, stay here until I get back."

"Hold it, Lev," Ethan said quickly. "We go together. Stace can wait here. Either of you have a problem with that?"

Stace unclasped her white-knuckled hands, relieved to stay in the car.

"Lock the doors after we leave," Lev ordered. "The keys are in the ignition. If anything goes wrong, call Harcourt and get the hell out of this area."

"What's a turning basin?" Ethan whispered as they picked their way down the side of the waste ground.

"A place where a boat can turn around at the end of a dead end channel," Lev suddenly reached out and grabbed Ethan's arm. "Hold it. Stay still." They both froze.

"What is it?" Ethan whispered.

"Over there on your right, in the middle distance, a flicker of light." Ethan squinted into the driving rain.

"There! Did you see it?" Lev said.

"Yeah, looked like a flashlight, just a quick glimmer."

"Okay, let's get back to the car. This is a 'No Man's Land' and we're not going to try to cross it."

Stace, alone in the car felt a shiver of fear run through her veins. Her years of intrigue and pressure of running a high-powered publicity office in Hollywood had, over the last few days, began to tell on her. She had become, unknowingly at first, a part of what was unfolding out there in the darkness. She knew Tolomeo and Kumar Pashagora had used her, along with other fools.

Groping their way back to the car had taken almost five minutes. Lev rapped on the driver's side window, "Stace, open up it's us." Nothing happened. Lev cupped his hands and peered through steamy window then rapped hard, "Hey, Stace, open up."

He tugged the door handle; it wouldn't open. Ethan went around to the passenger side and checked the doors. It was no use, Stace didn't answer and all the doors were locked.

Chapter 76

It happened swiftly. The driver's door flew open and Stace was hauled out of the vehicle. Now, slumped next to Harcourt in the back seat of an agency car, she realized who it was beside her.

"Sorry, Miz Hart. We had to move fast. I assure you, your life was in jeopardy."

Stace blurted. "But I had the doors locked!"

"We, like our adversaries, have means of overcoming locked doors."

"What happened to Lev and Ethan?"

"They're okay. Two of my men have them. We'll meet at the Harbormaster's office."

Chapter 77

Scumbag focused a security camera across the acreage through the rain and mist, and held a zoom image on two men exiting a car.

"Take a look, Chaz."

Chaz moved in close. "Damn, that's a hell of a sharp image, despite this shitty weather."

"Yeah, TolomeoTechnics makes cutting edge thermals. The heat from the car's engine acted like a magnet soon as I switched this camera on."

"How come we didn't see them sooner?"

"I can't monitor every camera at once. I've been scoping out the marina and the channel. I just now turned this baby on. Hey! Check this out, there's another couple of guys in the picture."

"They look like cops," Chaz muttered.

Scumbag kept the camera on the men and zoomed in tighter. "You recognize any of the four?"

"Yeah, one of them looks like Lev Leventhal. He's that meddling theatrical agent who thinks he's a detective."

"If it's Leventhal, someone's been mouthing off too much. Tolomeo ain't going to like this."

"What do you mean?"

"The plan is for Tolomeo to sail up the channel, dock in the marina then switch to a waiting charter boat that'll take them Mexico."

"I know that. I'm supposed to join them and go to Mexico, too."

"Man, you're all screwed up," Scumbag sneered. "You and me are here to be certain Jilly Suede never leaves alive."

"Jilly?"

"Yeah, someone wants to get rid of her, and I can't blame them."

"But Hank said I was going with them!" Chaz yelled.

"Hold it down, man, and listen to me: You and me are here to take care of Jilly. To see she never leaves this place after we bring her here from the yacht."

"I'm not going to be part of a murder. No way. I'm getting out of here."

As Chaz turned to leave, Scumbag grabbed him by the collar and yanked him back. "Fine, then I'll have to kill you first and then do Jilly. No problem."

The impact of what Scumbag was saying finally soaked in. Chaz had to run. Now. But Scumbag was armed and he wasn't.

Chapter 78

Halyards snapping against aluminum masts of a forest of sailboats bobbing in their slips beat a steady tattoo as the storm moved north. Only one or two lights dotted the darkness; it would be dawn in a few hours.

Stace, Lev and Ethan sipped strong hot coffee in the warmth of the Harbormaster's office. Harcourt, the Harbormaster and a couple of his agents were also there.

"Okay, now we know the plan is for them to switch to a charter boat," Harcourt said, "As soon as they arrive at the drydock entrance, they'll disembark and head to the charter. And before anyone asks, yes, we've taken over the charter."

"What about the warehouse?" Lev asked.

Harcourt nodded, "Two SWAT teams are moving in as we speak."

"You're aware of the security cameras, I suppose."

"Yes, we're working the problem." Harcourt stretched his thin body and twisted his scrawny neck from side to side. "Tell me, Mr. Leventhal, what do you know about the security cameras?"

"If Tolomeo Technics manufactured them, they're good.

"In that case, for your own good, I'm ordering you three off the dock and out of the area until this situation is over."

Lev pushed back his chair and stood holding his coffee mug. "Agent Harcourt, Ethan and I both recognize your position in all of this. Nonetheless, I'd like to make a suggestion."

Chapter 79

A wall-mounted chronometer clicked its minute hand to vertical. It was four in the morning. Twelve miles off shore from Seal Beach, Hank Tolomeo, his face a mask of determination, was at the controls of *Technocrat*, hands gripping the wheel as the craft rose and fell through the rough sea. New orders from Pashagora had reached him shortly after leaving Marina Del Rey.

Kate and Mel must to be set ashore at first light on State Beach in San Onofre, Orange County. A car would be waiting on Highway 5 to drive them to Ensenada, Mexico, and on to an airport, chosen for its remoteness. Hank held the twin diesels at full throttle.

Hank had heard that Vicky Vance had contacted Pashagora, informing him of the Stella/Chaz argument and break up. Understanding Pashagora's mind, he immediately recognized that such a split would alert too many people. Just how far would Pashagora go to ensure the silence of his American minions? Wouldn't he show some gratitude to them for their help? Hank Tolomeo hadn't gotten where he was today by believing in pipe dreams. He prepared for the worst.

He knew by now the US Coast Guard would be on the lookout along the coast and around Long Beach/Seal Beach. He planned to remain 12 miles offshore until he reached the right coordinates, then make a fast run into San Onofre to put Kate and Mel ashore.

He'd checked the weather and it looked good, one to two foot swells with the wind from the East at five knots. Once he dropped off Mel, Kate and the computer equipment, he and Jilly would make a run for Ensenada, keeping to international waters.

Chapter 80

Lev set his coffee mug on the table. "Has it occurred to anyone that Hank Tolomeo's orders to come here and switch to a charter boat may have been changed since I was brought up to date by Stella Rae?" he asked looking hard at Harcourt. "If they have, we could all be wasting time."

Harcourt's head snapped up. "Clarify that remark."

"If I got the news about the rendezvous, it's possible others did, too, and while we continue waiting for Tolomeo to show and he could be going elsewhere."

"That's a possibility," Harcourt said begrudgingly. "I'll have the Harbormaster contact USCG and get an update on their search."

Before Harcourt could leave the room, a hand-held two-way radio on the table buzzed. He turned back and scooped it up. "Harcourt. Come in, over,"

"There are at least two people inside the building. We're moving in to reconnoiter the situation closer."

"Roger that, SWAT One," Harcourt switched off the radio and glanced questioningly at Lev.

Chapter 81

Chaz Falconer generally played heroic parts in movies, but they used blanks in their automatic weapons. Scumbag was holding a Glock 17 under Chaz's chin and Chaz had no doubt that every one of the rounds in it were real.

Scumbag jerked his head toward the TV screen. "You tipped off the cops, didn't you, you dumb shit. Look."

Chaz moved his eyes to the screen and saw crouched figures moving toward the building. If he could break free, he'd have a chance of escape, but it was risky. Scumbag had been assigned to kill Jilly; he'd have no qualms in killing him, also. He could just make out several sticks of dynamite strapped together, with a taped timer attached, in the musty darkness beneath a crumbling stone stairway running from the main all the way to the top floor of the warehouse. The deadly device had been prepared by Scumbag who had bragged to Chaz that once he had Jilly back at the warehouse, he'd place her bound body beneath the staircase then remotely detonate the bomb, destroying any forensic evidence he might have left behind.

"We can still get away," Chaz wheezed.

"I didn't come here to get away. My job is to eliminate Jilly. If I fail, I'll be a dead man." He ordered Chaz to walk ahead, the barrel of his gun now inches from the back of Chaz's head, while he patted his shirt pocket to reassure himself that the remote detonator was still there.

Chaz forced himself to remember the last time he'd been in the warehouse. It had been daylight. Even then, the inside of the building was dark and gloomy in places. Huge overhead, beams ran from wall to wall. Parts of some of the upper floors had fallen away, rotted by rain and time. If he could break away from his captor, he'd have a slim chance of hiding amidst the rubble of the ruined building. That risk was counterbalanced by his knowledge that he'd never leave the structure alive if he didn't make an attempt. Physically, Chaz was in better shape than Scumbag. He just needed the right moment to make his move.

"Stop right there," Scumbag snarled. They were next to the dome-tent. Scumbag backed toward the tent, clearly wanting something from inside the tent. The Glock held steady in his right hand, he left felt back with his left for the tent opening. Chaz knew his moment had arrived.

"Hey! Someone's inside the tent!" Chaz yelled.

Scumbag reacted without thinking and turned to look. As he did, Chaz flew forward pushing Scumbag into the tent, and ripping one side of the flimsy tent across the entrance. His captor momentary entangled in the tent, Chaz kicked the Scumbag's outline hard in the back. The tent collapsed, entangling Scumbag like a fly in a spider web.

Two bullets ripped through the side of the tent missing Chaz by inches as he fled across the stone floor. Grabbing the bottom rung of an old iron ladder attached to the wall, he heaved himself up and continued climbing. Another shot sent brick splinters past his cheek as Scumbag struggled to get free.

Reaching an iron beam that had once been part of a truss holding the second floor; Chaz straddled it, and, carefully balancing himself, ran across it into the darkness. At the end, he arrived at the remains of the original wooden floor and gingerly rolled on to it, one hand on the iron beam in case the floor gave way. It held. Getting to his feet, he flattened as close to the brick wall as he could and continued shuffling deeper into the darkness.

Scumbag growled, grabbed a triple-X flashlight, and shined the beam upward. The light danced across the old brick walls and vanished in the black void above. "You're a dead man, dickhead! You'll never leave this place alive! I know every nook and cranny of this ancient pile of shit. There's no way you'll get away."

Chaz pressed against the wall and a brick rattled next to his hand. Gripping the loosened brick, he slowly withdrew it from the wall. He could hear Scumbag somewhere below, huffing and puffing in the darkness. Weighing the brick in his hand to get the feel, he tossed it toward the wall opposite from where he'd crossed the iron beam. He heard it hit something and rattle downward. A second later, he saw three flashes from the muzzle of Scumbag's automatic and heard three echoing shots.

"Dead man actor, you're playing your last part."

The stress in Scumbag's voice was apparent, giving Chaz a moment of hope. From the direction of the muzzle flashes, he had a good idea of his hunter's location. All the same, he remained stock-still, hardly breathing in the blackness.

The beam of the flashlight moved away from him and danced on the wall fifty feet in front of him, then flashed, one step at a time up the stone staircase. Scumbag was ascending it. Chaz could see the source of the beam slowly moving upward. It would only be a matter of time before they were on the same level. Chaz had to stop him.

With his back to the wall, Chaz edged along the outer rim of the wooden floor toward the spot where Scumbag would finally arrive at the top of the staircase. Inch by inch, every step a threat to his life if the floor sagged and collapsed, the two men slowly advanced toward a final destiny.

The old stone staircase that Scumbag was climbing had long ago lost its handrail to time and weather, leaving a drop of a hundred and twenty feet to the flagstones below. He continued steadily upward, the flashlight beam flickering across a three-foot length of rotted beam hanging like a broken tooth from the brick outer wall at the top of the stairs. Chaz saw it, too, and decided if he could loosen it and toss it down the stairs, he have a good chance of knocking the crazy bastard off the stairs.

Hearing Scumbag grunting from the climb, Chaz moved fast. At the top of the stairs, Chaz grasped the beam. Pieces of plaster showered around him and the beam loosen almost at once. For the moment, he had to hold it in place to get his footing more secure. Slowly, he lowered the beam toward his shoulder. It was heavier than he thought, and the end tipped forward, pulling Chaz off balance just as Scumbag came into view.

The flashlight beam caught Chaz in a black and white tableau of horror as he and the beam pitched forward. The tip of the timber beam smashed into Scumbag's face with a loud crunch and both men went off the stairs in a rattle of loose bricks. Scumbag hit the ground first. In the shower of debris, a piece of brick pressed the wireless detonator in his shirt pocket, and a thunderous explosion brought down the ancient stone staircase creating a mountain of rubble thirty feet high.

Chapter 82

Harcourt updated Lev and the others that the SWAT teams had heard gunshots from inside the warehouse followed by an explosion and now considered it unsafe to enter. It would be some time before further details became available.

A Coast Guard cutter sailing between Long Beach and Seal Beach received a message from Harcourt updating them on the warehouse explosion, suggesting the possibility that the information about the yacht being in the area was no longer correct.

"So what happens now?" asked Ethan. "Are they going to go home and forget it?"

"No, sir," Harcourt said. "The search will continue north and south along the coast. Rest assured the yacht will be found."

"I'm concerned about my daughter, not the yacht," Ethan grumbled.

"Of course, I understand. The Office of Homeland Security will continue the investigation using every available resource."

"That's fine, and in the meantime, we're supposed to just wait around?" Ethan asked petulantly.

Stace exchanged looks with Lev who suggested the three get some breakfast, then reconsider their part in the unfolding drama.

As Stace buttered her toast, Ethan said, "Why do I get the

feeling we've been played for suckers? That phone call you got from, what's-her-name..."

"Stella Rae," Lev said.

"Yeah, she could have been ordered to give you a false lead allowing the yacht time to head somewhere else."

"That's true, but somehow I believe she was telling the truth. If someone found out she alerted us, then yes, the plan could have been changed."

"So the yacht with Kate aboard could be sailing south as we sit here eating breakfast," Ethan quickly added.

Lev pushed the remains of a fried egg to the side of his plate, cut a piece of toast in half and wondered if Ethan was right.

"If what Stella said was true—and I, too, believe it so—we're at least in the right place to hear if something breaks," Stace said. "It's not even daylight yet. The Coast Guard is doing their job and Harcourt said he'd let us know as soon as he had any information. I say we hang around here awhile and see what develops."

With reluctance, Ethan had to agreed.

Chapter 83

Tolomeo was holding steady on the corrected coordinates. Daybreak was still an hour away. He'd take them ashore in the inflatable at first light. Kate had remained in her bunk throughout the journey, unable to sleep due to the rough seas and seasickness, but he guessed she'd probably overheard the others discussing what to do next.

"Show time in fifteen minutes, Jilly," Hank called.

Jilly went below. "We're almost there, Kate. Get your stuff together. The moment Hank drops anchor, you and Mel must be on your way, so Hank and I can head back into international waters."

Kate followed Jill onto the main deck and sat cradling the computer case in her arms as Mel and Jilly unlashed the inflatable. The yacht was rapidly nearing its drop point and Kate shook with a combination of seasickness and apprehension. Anyone who glanced at her would conclude that she was far too weak to cry out or escape.

Mel carried an outboard motor across the deck, installed it on the transom of the inflatable dingy, and immediately began stowing his and Kate's personal belongings, including the laptop and Al Jolson in a canvas sea bag. Finished, Mel attempted to cheer Kate up. "Kate, look at it this way: We were going to be married and join my family in India. Nothing's really changed."

"You must be out of your mind, Melhi Pashagora! *Everything* has changed," she lashed out. "You and your father were plotting to get my program from the start. I've never meant anything to you!"

Mel stared down at her, shrugged and turned away. "Then look at it another way: You're lucky you're still alive, Kate."

"Make ready to drop anchor, Jilly, when I give the order." Hank watched his gauge until he could confirm the right depth, then switched off the engines and called out, "Weigh anchor!"

Jilly stood in the bow and lowered the Danforth anchor over the side, the thick coil of line unwound then stopped as the anchor bit into the sandy bottom of State Beach. The yacht immediately swung slightly to port and the line tightened. They'd arrived. Hank looked over his shoulder to the East as the first streaks of light broke low on the horizon.

"Okay people, let's move," Hank yelled, handing the helm over to Jilly and going forward to help slide the inflatable over the side. "Keep the line secure, Jilly."

Once in the water, Hank climbed aboard and primed the

outboard motor. Mel brought Kate to the dingy and held her arm as she stepped aboard.

"Sit there," Hank ordered Kate, pointing to the center of the craft, "and don't move about."

Mel lowered the sea bag aboard and followed. Hank yanked the starter cord and the outboard came alive on the first pull. Adjusting the throttle, he headed for the beach. The morning air was cold and he could taste salt on his lips. In the distance, he heard the sound of breakers hitting the shore.

Less than five minutes later, they rode a wave onto the beach. Mel jumped out taking the line and holding the boat for Kate to follow. Hank heaved the sea bag in an arc onto the beach and waved for Mel to let loose of the line. Opening the throttle, Hank urged the dingy forward into the waves.

Mel grabbed the sea bag and Kate's hand and tugged her across the beach to Highway 5. Still too dark to see much, he swiveled his head both ways looking for the pickup vehicle. The highway was empty.

Hank made it back to the yacht under his estimated time limit. He and Jilly pulled the inflatable on deck and, as Jilly tied it down, he had the yacht under power and heading back out to beyond the twelve-mile limit.

"We're on our own now, Jilly," Hank rasped.

"Why didn't you just refuse Pashagora's new orders? We had everything we needed: his son, Kate and the program. He'd have had to let the original plan stand."

"Jilly, we are back to the original plan. Kumar wanted to be certain Kate and the program arrived in Mumbai. That always was the plan. Too many people came to know of it, so things had to be changed, but minimally, subtly, so that he could still take advantage all the arrangements he'd made."

Jilly snorted, "Yeah. And that includes leaving us to run the risk of being captured by the US Coast Guard."

Hank notched up the engines and headed southeast; it was getting lighter by the minute. He told Jilly to make a pot of fresh coffee.

On shore, Mel paced beside the highway as the sound of the outboard faded.

"Seems your friends got lost or have abandoned you," Kate said looking up and down the vacant road.

"I don't think so. My father doesn't hire fools." He removed a cell phone from his pocket snapped it open and saw they were in a no reception zone.

Chapter 84

Achy breaky Heart twanged from the dashboard speaker of the battered '74 Dodge van as it cruised along Highway 5. Jack Alard and Zeek Fell sang along with the music. Jack was driving.

"Well lookie there, Zeek, will ya?" Ahead, two figures stood at the side of the highway, a canvas sea bag between them.

The old Dodge squealed to a halt. "The red head looks good. You can have t'other one, Zeek."

Jack and Zeek were on their way to Mexico with twenty dollars between them; the two strangers beside an empty highway looked like an ATM machine to them.

Zeek rolled down the window and gave a snaggletooth grin. "Morning folks, you need a ride, I reckon."

Even in the half-light of early dawn, Kate knew they were bad news. Her seasickness had abated sufficiently for her to feel her skin prickle with alert tension.

"No problem," Mel said. "We're being picked up. But thanks for the offer."

"'Taint no problem, boy." Zeek pulled out and pointed a Colt Forty-five at them. "Jest open that there side door and climb in." He waved the revolver side to side. "This here's the gun won the West, or so my granddaddy used to say. Show some respect. Get your asses in the truck. Now." Kate knew that if they got in the vehicle, they'd likely never get out.

"Hey! Whoa!" Mel said. "I'll give you some money if you beat it." His eyebrows narrowed and his fingers did a nervous tap-dance against his leg.

"How much you got, boy?"

"A couple of thousand," Mel said.

Zeeks eyes widened, "American dollars?"

"Yes, of course."

"How about the little lady, how much she got?"

"About twenty bucks," Kate replied.

"Okay, tell you what. You, young fella, give me the two thousand dollars and you can stay and wait for your ride. Red Head comes with us. She can make up her two thousand in one way or another." Zeek leered at Kate and grinned.

A car zoomed past, definitely not driven by a Good Samaritan. The van swayed in its backwash.

It was growing lighter and Zeek acted antsy. Billy Ray Cyrus was still singing, "'And if you tell my heart, my achy breaky heart, he might blow up and kill this man'. Oooo."

Kate's eyes glinted for a moment as she imagined Mel spattered across Highway 5 by the gun that won the West. "I think our ride is here," Kate said, pointing back in the direction from where the truck had come. Zeek twisted his scrawny neck to glance back, and Mel was on him with the speed of a striking cobra, wresting the revolver from his grasp.

Mel fired one shot into the side of the van. "Okay, you can drive away or stay and wait for the CHPs and file a complaint. It's up to you." Like father like son.

"Pick up the bag, Mel," Kate hissed. "It's yours if you give me the gun. I'll take their truck. Hurry."

Mel looked up and down the road, wanting to keep the gun and discover their prearranged ride. In the end, he decided the sea bag with its computer equipment was most important. Let Kate take care of herself. He grabbed the bag, trotted back down the road about twenty feet and tossed her the gun. Kate caught it in the air, opened the side door of the van, climbed inside and aimed the gun at Jack, the driver.

"Move out fast and keep looking straight ahead. My granddaddy had one of these Peacemakers, and taught me how to use it when I was ten years old." Jack and Zeek heard the hammer click back and stared straight ahead, the van gathering speed.

Checking his rearview mirror, Jack said, "Hey, that guy you were with is just staring at us. Well, whadduya know? The jerk is smiling. Now he's looking t'other way, prob'ly for that lost car of his."

The country western song, *Refried Beans*, had replaced *Achy Breaky Heart*, and was playing at full blast. "Turn that off. I can't hear myself think," Kate ordered. Zeek leaned forward and obeyed.

"Keep driving till I tell you, then stop. Let me out and you can continue on your way."

"What about my granddaddy's forty-five?" Zeek asked, still staring straight ahead. Kate looked at the untidy mess these two most likely called home. "When I leave, I'll put it under your mattress."

"You sure you wouldn't like to join us, Red Head?" Zeek wheezed. "I kinda like yer style. We could make a U-turn, go back and get the money off your boyfriend there. With his two thousand and your twenty we could live high on the hog in Mexico."

"Don't think so. We'll do this my way." Kate paused. "Do either of you have a cell phone?"

"Nope," Jack said. "Neither of us knows anyone to call, and besides, Zeek is hard of hearing." Zeek laughed nervously at Jack's joke.

As the sun rose higher in the East, the highway 5 became easier to see. Kate peered ahead hoping to see a public rest stop or mobile border checkpoint; they could appear anywhere, or for sure, at the USMC base at Camp Pendelton, two miles away according to the most recent sign.

"Unless I tell you otherwise, take the Camp Pendelton turnoff. Same drill. I'll say you gave me a lift, and then you guys can move on."

"Marines don't care for our sort," Zeek growled.

"Yeah, well, don't worry about it, fellas. The Marines won't care about you two." Kate prayed she'd get to Pendelton safely. That way she could get word to Lev and agent Harcourt.

Chapter 85

Standing with the sea bag at his side, Mel tried hitching a ride. Someone was going to pay for this fuck-up. Several cars passed before a black BMW came to a stop. The passenger door opened and a tall thin man got out, his eyes reflecting concern. "Mr. Pashagora?"

Mel felt like punching the man in the face. "Where the hell

have you been?"

"It couldn't be helped, sir. We had a flat. I tried but couldn't raise you on your cell."

"Put that in the trunk, we've lost valuable time," Mel ordered. The tall man hurriedly stowed the sea bag, opened the back passenger door for Mel, then returned to his seat next to the driver.

"Step on it!" Mel yelled. "We have to catch up with an old Dodge van. They have a fifteen minute lead, so move it!"

Kate saw the Camp Pendleton turnoff sign, and said, "There! Hang a left." She ordered, jabbing the nozzle of the .45 in the direction of the turnoff. The van slowed, turning and following in the direction the gun was pointed.

"When we get to the gate, do like I said. I'll tell them you gave me a lift. You turn around and leave. End of story."

When the van came to a stop, Kate was out the side door faster than the Marine guard walking toward them.

"They gave me a lift," she jerked her thumb over her shoulder. "I must speak to the camp commander. It's a matter of life and death."

Jack immediately backed up the truck, made a three point turn and whisked away, the radio blaring out a new country and western song.

Chapter 86

Harcourt received a call from the Camp Pendelton Commandant's office inquiring about a Miz Kate Keenan. Harcourt brought Pendelton up to date explaining she was an important part of an ongoing joint OHS/NSA investigation and requested clearance for a helicopter to land at Pendelton and fly her to the Federal building in Westwood for questioning.

Kate was safe. Harcourt contacted the Coast Guard and updated them, assuring them that although they had Kate in possession, the search for the yacht and its occupants should continue.

Within minutes of the helicopter landing on the pad atop the Federal building, Kate was hustled to a secure debriefing room where Harcourt and several other personal from the FBI and the NSA awaited

"Please sit down Ms. Keenan." Harcourt indicated an empty chair at one end of a highly polished oval conference table. Two men and a middle-aged woman were already seated.

Kate, exhausted from her ordeal, dropped into the chair, brushing her fingers through her tangled red hair. She looked up as a cup of coffee was set beside her.

"That will be all," Harcourt said, dismissing the woman who had brought in the coffee. "Now, Miz Keenan, I'd like to introduce you to everyone at the table. My name is Agent Harcourt, FBI, working with the OHS, the Office of Homeland Security. The lady on your right is Agent Pritchard, FBI." Kate glanced at her and nodded. Harcourt continued, "Facing her, Agents Richardson and Falk, National Security Agency." Agent Falk, lean, with chestnut hair falling towards his eyebrows, rustled his notes and Kate studied at him. For some reason, Harcourt noticed, Kate's gaze sharpened at Falk's presence. Harcourt cleared his throat. Kate looked back at him and nodded.

"As you are aware, NSA, the National Security Agency, indicated an interest in your computer program when you attended a job interview some time ago." Kate remained silent.

"Now, Miz Keenan, the government is more than just interested. Your program has been reclassified top secret. As you well know, your life is in jeopardy. Those responsible for the actions taken against you over the last few days are being pursued and, when apprehended, will be brought to justice."

Kate took a sip of her coffee, holding the saucer in her left hand beneath the cup, like a Duchess at afternoon tea. Setting the cup and saucer on the table, she glanced again at Falk, then addressed Harcourt.

"I see. The government will of course, pay for the honor of keeping my program out of circulation?"

Harcourt was at a loss for words. Agent Falk sat straighter in his chair. NSA Agent Richardson's ruddy face got redder as he spluttered, "Miz Keenan. We're talking national security here."

"I understand," Kate acknowledged. "However, you must understand that more than my physical security—my fiscal security is also at risk. I designed the program for civilian use in the entertainment sector. That alone would make me financially independent. If the government wants to use my program for military purposes, then they will have to pay for it."

Agent Richardson narrowed his eyes. "Then we will have to take this to a higher level, Miz Keenan."

"Yes. As high as it takes." She pushed back her chair and stood, fingertips spread lightly on the edge of the table. "Am I free to go then, Agent Harcourt? If so, I would like to make a phone call to have someone pick me up."

"I must warn you Miz Keenan, you will be in mortal danger the moment you leave the building."

"Yes, but then, I was in danger before you brought me here. Remember, *I* called *you*. Your organizations together have been unable to find me for over a week. I'll take my chances, at least until we can come to a reasonable agreement. Oh, and if you're worried about the computer, don't. The password was only good for twenty-four hours. "

Chapter 87

Lev decided they would wait until daylight, and if they heard nothing from Harcourt, they'd return to Hollywood. Daylight had arrived, and the trio headed for home in a somber mood.

Lev's cell chimed as he approached downtown Los Angeles on the Santa Anna Freeway. "Yes, this is he."

Stace saw his face brighten and asked, "Who is it?"

Lev ignored her, concentrating on the call. "You're with Harcourt at the Federal Building? That's great news!" His smile faded as he continued to listen. "Well, I'm sure everything will work out. Yes, I can there within the hour." He flipped the phone shut. "Kate's safe and sound at the Federal Building in Westwood. We're to pick her up."

"Thank God!" Ethan exclaimed. "How did Harcourt find them?"

"He didn't. Kate called him from Camp Pendelton." Lev made the transition onto the Hollywood Freeway and headed west.

"What happened to her abductors?" Ethan asked.

"We'll find out when we see her." Lev's voice had a lilt of relief in it, and the atmosphere in the car lightened considerably.

Lev, Ethan and Stace cleared security at the Federal Building, were issued plastic visitor ID tags to place around their necks and told to continue to the fourteenth floor. Harcourt was waiting beside the door of the elevator when it slid open.

"Where is she?" were the first words out of Ethan's mouth when he saw Harcourt.

"Follow me," Harcourt growled and led them to the debriefing room. Kate was alone at the table. The others had left.

Ethan rushed across the room and hugged her. "You all right, Baby? How did you get away?"

"I'm fine, Dad." She looked over his shoulder at Lev and Stace. "I'm glad you're here. It's a long story. I'll fill you in when we get home."

Harcourt cut in. "Miz Keenan, again I must warn you that you will be in mortal danger without government protection. We are well aware of Kumar Pashagora, a man of seemingly unlimited wealth and power with the ability to give orders in Mumbai and, within hours, have them carried out here in the United States."

"Then why wasn't government protection given to her earlier?" Ethan rasped.

"Her kidnapping at the studio happened before we were aware of the extent of the Pashagora organization," Harcourt snapped.

Lev and Ethan exchanged glances. "Are you suggesting the government offer my daughter some sort of 'bodyguard service'?" Ethan asked.

Harcourt shook his head. "Not exactly, sir. It is absolutely important that Miz Keenan be kept in a safe location until we have secured all of Pashagora's players."

"What happened to her computer, Harcourt?" Lev asked. Harcourt glanced at Kate before answering.

"Miz Keenan stated that Kumar's son has it, along with Al Jolson. Oh, yes, we've know about Al for some time, Mr. Leventhal."

"And the government wants to keep my client in a safe house until they've captured all of Pashagora's men and have the computer in their care?"

"That is our—my—suggestion."

"Well, when I last checked, we were living in a free country. Let's ask Kate what she would like to do."

"Get me out of here, Lev. Dad and I will be fine. Pashagora's men can't use the computer. The password has expired. If they try to force it, it'll disintegrate before their eyes."

Harcourt shrugged, his thin body rigid with anger. "Very well, Miz Keenan, so be it." Despite Harcourt's acquiescence, Lev knew they hadn't heard the end of it by any means.

Lev drove along Wilshire Boulevard, heading towards Kate's house in West Hollywood. "Maybe you should have taken the government's offer more seriously, Kate," Stace offered.

Kate shook her head. "Not right now. First I want to check my mail, get a few things together, then Ethan and I will find a good hotel for a couple of days."

"You can both stay with me. I have plenty of room," Stace urged.

"She's right, Kate," Lev said quickly. "There's safety in numbers. He parked in the driveway, recalling the last time he'd been there. It seemed an age ago.

Kate stared at the house. "I'm glad to be home. Come on in. We'll make some coffee and I'll tell you what happened."

Twenty minutes later, after Kate finished her story, Lev was the first to ask a question. "So Mel has the computer and Al Jolson. What happens now?"

"Correction, Lev. Mel *thinks* he has everything. He and his dad are in for a shock when they try to make use of it." Kate had a sudden thought. "Hey! I didn't check my snail mail."

Kate walked to the hall and picked up a pile of mail scattered on the floor. "There it is." She pulled a slim package from the letters and held it for all to see.

"You mean..." Lev began,

"Yeah, Lev, I mailed the real Al Jolson home for safety and substituted a fake one just in case."

"But I carried it with me all the time we were in Nevada, until returning to my office," Lev said.

"You left your jacket draped over the back of a chair in your room at Binion's. I made the switch while you, Mel and Dad were in deep conversation about the Hollywood rumor mill while we waited for room service."

"Wait! Where did you find a fake Al Jolson?"

"I took the real one out of your jacket and replaced it with my iPod wrapped in toilet paper. It fit perfectly into the envelope you were carrying it in. Before we left the hotel, I took the real Al Jolson to the front desk and had them box and mail it first class to my house. Here it is, safe and sound."

Lev was dumbfounded. "You took a big gamble, Kate."

"Hey, we went to Vegas and never even dropped a quarter in a slot machine. I did what most people do when they go to Las Vegas. I took a chance."

"So Mel has a computer set to destroy itself if anyone tries to mess with it, an iPod, and an expired password," Ethan said quietly. "When Kumar Pashagora finds out, it might be wise to be under government protection, Baby."

Stacy suddenly said, "Looks like the government has sent you some mail already, Kate."

Lev saw what she was referring to, reached down, and retrieved a buff colored official looking envelope. "It's from the United States Patent office, Kate," he said with a smile.

Chapter 88

The BMW zoomed past Camp Pendelton a minute before the Dodge van returned onto Highway 5.

Mel squinted into the sun, trying to spot the decrepit Dodge van in the thickening morning traffic as they approached Oceanside. The BMW steadily widened the gap as the Dodge trundled behind them.

Chapter 89

The pushing currents rushed Hank Tolomeo and Jilly Suede closer to their Mexican destination, Ensenada. Suddenly, the jangling sound of the satellite phone sounded. Hank's ear was immediately assailed by the angry voice of Kumar Pashagora, informing him of Kate's escape and the need for yet another change in plans.

"You understand, Tolomeo, that had it not been for quick work on the part of my son, we would have lost everything again. Follow my new orders to the letter." The phone went dead.

Jilly had seen the anger rise on Hank's face as he listened to the call. "What was that about?"

"Damn Pashagora's altering plans again."

"Why? What happened?"

Hank pulled a chart toward him, his eyes flickering across the instrument panel then back to the chart. "That little shit Kate escaped. She's gone. Mel has the complete computer system. Pashagora's wants us to rendezvous with a Mexican trawler out of Ensenada. We're to transfer aboard. A couple of the crew will sail my yacht further down the coast to a remote fishing village."

"If we rendezvous, what's to stop them from killing us, Hank? Pashagora has everything he needs. We're a liability now."

"Tell me about it, Jilly."

"What are we going to do?"

Hank throttled back on the engines, checked the amount of fuel remaining in the tanks and made a fast decision. "We're going to Marina Costa Baja. The La Paz region of Mexico. I can sell the yacht for cash there, then we can decide where to go. In the meantime, while we're still in the Satellite footprint, we're going to retransfer our money from the bank in Mumbai to an offshore investment corporation I know in Jersey. Get the papers. We need to do it now."

Time differences, normally a problem for domestic banks, were no problem for the international banking community, especially offshore banks acting as tax havens. Jilly handled the phone and paper work while Hank plotted a new course. Less than an hour later, they were sailing in an area where the Mexican fishing boat would never locate them; and their bank accounts now had new homes in the Channel Islands.

Chapter 90

The US government had ears all over the world. Several people, high in Mumbai business circles, had received coded messages alerting them of the US govenrment's need to know a great deal more about Kumar Pashagora's activities.

One of those who received a message was Pradeep Kurade, a short, soft-spoken, middle-aged man with an office in Cuffe Parade, an important business district of Mumbai.

Pradeep worked as an analyst for the Indian government documenting the growth and progress of the Indian Film Industry, a perfect cover in a city such as Mumbai where life was fast, growth unparalleled, action unconstrained. In short, a dream hoards of young Indians wanting to become instant millionaires.

Of course, few ever did. Most eventually ended up in the gutters of Calcutta, or worse, dead. In Kurade's case, that was not so. He had a direct line to NSA.

Rick Richardson, the ruddy faced NSA agent replaced his secure phone to its cradle. "The word is out in Mumbai. One man in particular will, I'm sure, be able to get us the background information we need."

Harcourt grunted. "But will he be able to get hold of the computer?"

"Put it this way, Harcourt. I've already got people in place who working on that problem. Time will tell."

"Yes, however, in the meantime, we have to be sure we have Keenan covered. If Pashagora's people get her, that'll be the end of it."

"She's covered," replied Richardson.

Chapter 91

Kate scooped up the rest of the mail, quickly checked through it, then set it aside and announced, "I've thought of something, Lev. I have a key to Mel's apartment on Shoreham. Let's check it out now that we know what he really wanted."

"Good idea, Kate, and you know what? Maybe you should stay at his place. They have top security there."

"The apartment is large—three bedrooms with an office—and, yes, security is excellent. But how do we let management know I'll be staying there without tipping of the Pashagoras?"

"I'll make a couple of discrete calls," Lev said. "It's possible no one here is aware that Mel's left town."

A few "discrete" calls later, Lev announced, "Looks like things are finally going our way. Everyone I contacted thinks Mel is still here in Hollywood."

"Do you remember his apartment number, Kate?"

"Sure, twelve-oh-eight," Kate shot back. "I've been there enough times over the last couple of years."

"Even better. You won't seem a stranger to the doorman." Lev checked the yellow pages and phoned the desk at the Shoreham Towers. The phone rang twice before it was picked up.

"Yes. Good evening. My name is Lev Leventhal," Lev said nonchalantly. "I was just speaking to Mr Pashagora, and he asked me to call and convey a message to his fiancé, Ms. Kate Keenan. Would you connect me please?"

"Mr. Pashagora is away at the moment, and Ms. Keenan isn't here."

"Yes, I know he's away. That's why he asked me to speak to his fiancé. She'll be staying there until he returns sometime next week."

"Oh, yes. But I'm afraid she's not arrived yet. However, I can give her your message when she arrives."

"No, that's all right, she's probably getting together a few things to take with her to the apartment. A couple of her friends are picking her up and driving her over. No doubt there's a lot of luggage. You know the way women are."

"Yes, sir. I'll be here at the desk when she arrives. My name is David."

"Thank you, David." Lev grinned impishly at Kate and closed his cell. "Well, it doesn't seem Mel or his father has canceled the lease. Let's hide you in the lion's den. Okay with you, Stace?"

Stace nodded, "Sure, as long as I get a bedroom of my own."

"Fine, Ethan and I will notify Harcourt, although, I'll bet he'll know where Kate is within five minutes of when you arrive at the apartment."

David greeted them with a smile and a good word, and several minutes later they were in apartment 1208.

Ethan surveyed the view. "Wow, Mel really lives big. This is a lot better than my place in Arizona."

Stace paced the living room looking at the furnishings with a practiced eye. "There's several glasses that have been used recently. Where did he keep his papers and things like that, I wonder?"

"Come, Stace. I'll show you. He has an office."

Kate opened a door at the end of the hall to reveal chrome and leather office furniture, track lighting, a bank of computer screens and two telephones, the red one, a satellite phone. Stace was about to speak when Kate grabbed her arm and walked her out of the office.

"What's wrong, Kate?" Stace asked. Kate shook her head, held a finger to her lips, and whispered, "He's installed a video camera since I was last here. I saw the glint of a lens in the crown molding."

"So we're on tape and maybe also on someone's silver screen somewhere, too." Stace looked worried. "What do we do now?"

We'll walk back in and act as if we're looking for some papers. If I know Mel, he'll have everything recorded and transmitted every fifteen minutes. We find it and disable it. Get Lev and Ethan in here. We have to be fast."

Methodically, the four checked out the office and five minutes into the search, Ethan whispered, "I've found it." The small recorder was hidden inside a sliding panel in the closet.

"Neat installation," Ethan muttered, "a built-in cubbyhole. And the recorder is connected to a satellite cable. Here's a transmission schedule tapped next to it. We've got ten minutes before the next transmission."

"Very professional," Lev agreed as he switched the unit off, removed the disk, and asked, "Anyone find anything else of interest?

"These." Kate slapped a collection of head shots onto the desktop. Five had a red slash drawn diagonally across. "The ones with a red slash means they're dead," Kate said slowly. "Look, these others are of us. I don't recognize a number of the others, do you?"

Lev studied the photographs, then abruptly said, "We're leaving. Bring the pictures, Kate. We're going to the Federal Building right now. Harcourt will be interested in this rogues' gallery. Besides, it means Mel might have given his apartment keys to his father's goons."

Chapter 92

It was midmorning when the BMW dropped Mel off at Mexico City's Benito Juárez International Airport. He purchased a decent piece of carryon luggage, a new shirt, a jacket, a pair of Italian leather loafers and a pair of slacks. In the men's room, he transferred the computer to the carryon, stuffed his old clothes into the sea bag, and dumped the bag into a trash bin.

After cleaning up, he checked the new Indian passport and first class ticket on British Airways to Mumbai, with stops in Chicago O'Hare and London Heathrow, that his contact in the BMW had supplied him.

Thirty crisp new one hundred-dollar bills tucked neatly in the back of the ticket holder completed his accoutrements. His flight was due to leave after noon, 12:44 to be precise. He had two days of peaceful flying ahead of him.

Chapter 93

As Harcourt entered the room, Richardson hung up the phone. "One of our people called from Mexico City International Airport. Mel Pashagora is due to leave on a British Airways/AeroMexicana flight at twelve forty-four hours in the afternoon, arriving at Chicago O'Hare at fourteen fifty-five hours Eastern Standard Time.

"Good work. We'll be waiting. He'll never clear customs. We'll take him on home ground and have the US Marshals haul his sorry ass back here to LA."

Richardson's intercom announced a Ms. Keenan and party had just arrived carrying important information.

Harcourt reached across and pressed a button,."Send them up."

The four visitors were directed to main conference room in the Federal Building. Harcourt was standing; Richardson speaking. "These photographs," NSA Agent Richardson spread them across the table and aligned the pictures of Frank Primo, Charles Vance, Don Ames, Franz Villand and Chaz Falconer into a single row, creating second row of unrecognized faces beneath the first, "are very helpful. Three with red slashes were murdered by unknown assailants, one in an explosion and Villand shot dead by a hit squad outside of your office, Mr. Leventhal. Is that right?"

Lev nodded. "That's correct."

Richardson arched his eyebrows and tapped Ames' red slashed photo.

"This man was found dead on your doorstep, I believe."

"Yes, he was. I wasn't at home at the time."

"I know. You, Ms. Keenan and her father were wandering around Nevada after having been instructed by Agent Harcourt not to leave town."

"We've been through all that, Agent Richardson. We came here to help, not to rehash past events."

Richardson ignored the remark, and rearranged the pictures into two rows, one of the men, the other of the women. "Well, Miz Kate Keenan and Miz Stacy Hart, I know where you are at the moment. What about the others here, any idea?"

"At home, I would imagine," Stacy said quietly.

"You're all acquainted with the women?" Richardson waved a beefy hand over the collection.

"Yes, but my Dad never actually met Stella Rae. She came to LA after he left town several years ago."

Harcourt cut in. "You found nothing else in Pashagora's apartment that might be of use to us?"

"No," Kate slid a key across the table. "Here check the apartment for yourselves. You won't even have to use a lock pick this time. We brought you the pictures and the tape. That's all we found. It looked like some people had possibly been visiting, and, what with the photos and active video surveillance equipment, Lev thought it wise for us to leave as quickly as possible."

Harcourt bristled for a moment, and then gave a thin smile, remembering his bosses had ordered that he maintain a "good working relationship" with Ms. Kate Keenan.

"We'll get in touch with these ladies, and work on identifying the rest of the men."

Lev pushed back from the table and asked Harcourt, "Any news on the yacht or where Mel Pashagora might be?"

"Nothing yet. However, we're following a couple of leads. I'll let you know when we something more definite."

Richardson glanced at Harcourt, then asked Kate, "What made

you decide to go to Pashagora's apartment anyway?"

"You did, actually," she replied.

"Me?" Richardson grated.

"What exactly are you saying, Miz Keenan?" asked Harcourt.

"Both of you advised us to be careful. That we could be watched. That our lives would be in danger."

"Yes, and we suggested you accept our offer of governmental protection and you walked out on the idea."

"I feel you two have been making more of an effort to get my computer program than to provide for my safety, Agent Richardson." She paused before turning to Harcourt. "You had your people check out the apartment before we got there, didn't you?"

"Of course," Harcourt replied.

"Why didn't you take the photos and tape?"

"You know, Ms. Keenan, it's we who usually ask the questions. Nevertheless, we made copies of the photos and left the originals. As for the hidden recorder, we weren't looking for it."

"We wanted to see what you would do when you found the pictures," added Richardson.

"You didn't know the office was being monitored?" asked Ethan.

"I didn't say that. You're welcome to return to the apartment. It's been thoroughly gone over. As for its security, NSA added substantially to it."

Harcourt opened the door. "We'll keep in touch."

"Could you drop me off at a car rental agency, Lev?" Ethan asked as the four filed out, stunned by what they'd heard. "Your car is known to too many. Leave your car in the driveway. I'll rent a car, park it down the hill, and call you. Then send Stace down. I'll have her rent a second car and, from then on, one can watch the other's tail."

Chapter 94

Hank slept a couple of hours with the yacht on autopilot. Jilly remained close to the helm; she was no sailor, but she could awaken Hank if an emergency arose. Sitting in complete blackness except for the soft green glow of the instrument panel, she checked the chronometer: 3:30 a.m.

The soft thud-thud of the engines and the splash of the sea against the hull were the only sounds. Jilly wondered if she had made the right decision to go on this crazy escapade. Hank drove her nuts at times, but at least he always had a plan for their next move.

Hank's voice jolted her out of her revere, "Everything okay?" He quickly scanned the instrument panel.

"Damn it, Hank! You scared the hell out of me, creeping up like that."

"Who were you expecting? There's only the two of us on board."

"I was miles away," Jilly grumbled.

"Yeah, well, we need a few more between us and the Coast Guard before I'll have time for daydreams of my own."

"I was thinking of our future, Hank. What are we going to do?"

"Did you ever hear of Lord Lucan?"

"The name sounds vaguely familiar, why?"

"He killed a woman in London back in 1974. He escaped capture and has never been found."

"What has that to do with us, Hank?"

"It proves to me that if high profile people like Lord Lucan can vanish and never to be heard of again, so can we."

"So we're going to commit ourselves to a life on the run, forever having to look back over our shoulders? Remember, one of the guys who did the great train robbery and escaped from prison in England? He hid out in Rio for years. They eventually found him."

"They did, and couldn't extradite him back to the UK. He returned forty years later on his own accord. He was promptly sent back to prison."

"You seem to know a lot about people who run, Hank."

"I work in Hollywood, where movies of hideous horrors and astounding escapes are commonplace. Anyway don't you worry, no one will find us. We have money and brains."

"Make that cunning and ruthlessness, Hank, and I'll believe you."

Hank chuckled, and pushed the throttles forward and the yacht came to life, its bow rising as he set the speed at a steady twenty-five knots.

Chapter 95

Ethan rented a low profile car, phoned Lev, and told him to put Stace on. "Hi, Stace. Now listen carefully: Meet me at Oakstone Way and Lookout Mountain. I'm driving a green Echo. Oakstone's about a quarter mile down from Lev's place."

"An Echo?" Stace repeated.

"Folksy," Ethan muttered.

"Sure is. I know where Oakstone is." She closed the cell and turned to Lev. "He's in a green Echo."

Lev grinned, "Better than a blue funk. Call me from the car rental office, okay?"

"Yes, and don't tell me what to rent." She waved to Kate and left.

Stace signed for a steel gray Toyota Corolla, called Lev and drove off the lot followed by Ethan's green Echo.

Twenty minutes later, Stace was raising her voice to be heard over the noise and constant clatter of dishes. She and Ethan were sitting at a table for two in Denny's Hollywood.

"Lev lives at one of the most difficult addresses to find in all of Hollywood. Narrow winding roads. Make one wrong turn and you end up driving a mile before you discover it's a dead end and have to drive back again." She sighed. "Why doesn't he sell the place?"

"That's why he's been able to last so long in Hollywood. Every night he comes home to quiet and solitude."

"Yeah, so did Harry Bosch and look what it got him."

Ethan smiled at her reference to one of Mike Connelly's character heroes. "Perhaps the narrow winding roads will help Kate and him to get away from the house without being seen."

Stace nodded, "If they are being watched."

"I'm sure NSA will have tabs on them and maybe Pashagora's people, too."

"But why would his people bother now they have the computer?"

Ethan hesitated to answer, then, choosing discretion, shrugged. "I'll be on the watch, until I know that answer."

"You should have been a cop, Ethan."

"Yeah, and if I had, I'd be retired and not in this mess."

"Then maybe we wouldn't have met up again, Ethan." She reached across the table and touched his hand. He encircled her hand with his, and gave it a loving squeeze.

"You're right there, Stace," he said, his hand lingering over hers.

Chapter 96

Mel shuffled toward O'Hare Customs doing his best to appear bored. He mentally checked everything as the line inched forward. Passport. He knew it looked perfect, but would it pass the high tech scrutiny of today's technology? Three thousand in cash should be no problem. They only investigated people carrying over ten thousand. The computer was an ordinary laptop; it would pass with no problem. Inside the extra box would be what appear to be specially designed iPad or such.

A voice behind him murmured, "Would you come with us, sir? This way, please."

Two suited men led him out of line toward a special room. Mel's blood felt like it was draining from his brain and he experienced a feeling of lightheadedness. He sagged and his stride faltered. The two men supported him and continued walking. He didn't attempt to resist.

The special room was claustrophobic and smelled of collected fear and tension. Lev was made to sit at in a chair at a table, both bolted to the floor. He was informed that they knew who he was, and told him he was being sent back to Los Angeles for interrogation. Mel rehearsed in his mind several explanations, but they asked no questions. In LA, on familiar ground, he would demand a lawyer and let the Pashagora machine grind into action.

Later the next day, red and green lights twinkled on the helipad atop the Federal Building in Westwood as a Blackhawk lowered to the pad. It was still dark; dawn was a couple of hours away. Richardson and Harcourt turned aside from the downdraft of thrashed air. Within seconds, the blades began their wind-down, the door opened and three men exited, hunched in the usual manner of those running beneath whirling helicopter blades.

"We've got him at last," Richardson said to Harcourt, his words scattering away amidst the noise and clatter.

Mel's escorts handed him over to Harcourt and Robertson and returned to the waiting helicopter.

"Why were you returning to India with Ms. Keenan's computer, Mr. Pashagora?"

Mel took a deep breath. "We were to both go to Mumbai, but became separated."

"Separated? Whatever do you mean?" Harcourt asked, facing Mel, Richardson at his side, across the conference table that earlier sported Kate Keenan and crew.

"We were held up by two men in a truck. I managed to take away the man's gun, but they grabbed her into the vehicle and drove away," Mel said warily. "I would like to call my lawyer, if you don't mind."

"Where did this happen? Didn't she struggle? Didn't you try to save her?" continued Harcourt, ignoring the man's request.

"On Highway Five," Mel answered brusquely, "And I want my lawyer. I have a right to…"

"You didn't think to call the police?" Richardson asked.

"*I want to speak with my lawyer!*"

The agents exchanged glances. The government had the computer, and technically their work was complete. Someone else could take over if he was to going to lawyer up.

Chapter 97

Vicky Vance had not spoken to Kumar Pashagora in years, and when she heard his voice on the phone, it turned her blood cold.

Kumar was quick, simple and direct. He'd arranged his son's bail. He wanted his son back in India at once, and he ordered her to make it happen. Now.

Vicky Vance was used to deadlines, but also knew if Kumar's orders were not carried out, she'd likely be found dead. The queen of gossip and dark secrets weighed her chances and promptly decided it was time to retire. The internet was beating the hell out of her profession anyway.

"Lev, this is Vicky. Thank God you're at home."

"I was just leaving, Vicky. What's up?"

"It's about Mel."

Vicky hastily told him about the call from Pashagora.

"Where are you, Vicky?"

"At home. Can you come over?"

"Listen, Vicky, this is what I want you to do."

Lev turned to Kate, "You're not going to believe this. Vicky Vance is going to pick us up. An elderly woman driving alone and stopping momentarily to consult a road map won't be suspect. We'll be out the door and into her car in seconds."

"Why did she phone you?"

Lev told her and watched Kate's eyes widen by the second.

Normally, there was no way the notorious Vicky Vance would do another's bidding. Nevertheless, she was happy to drive over to Lev's house and pick him up as long as it included the possibility of saving her ass from the wrath of Kumar.

She drove from her home in Beverly Hills and headed up Laurel Canyon toward Lookout Mountain Avenue. It was already dark, and she had a hard time reading the names of the myriad streets that branched off Laurel Canyon. The further she drove up the winding gorge, the harder it became.

Finally, she pulled over, and not at Lev's house. She'd made a wrong turn somewhere. She cussed and muttered to herself as she rummaged for her cell phone.

"Lev, I can't find the way to your dammed house! I'm on a narrow road, trees all around me, not a street lamp in sight."

"What's the name of the street, Vicky?"

"I can't remember. I've been up and down so many damn twists and turns."

"Okay, Vicky. Calm down. Turn around and go back until you reach Laurel and find a street sign you can read. Then stop and call me again. I'll direct you from there."

Vicky was about launch into a tirade, when she remembered Kumar's orders. She needed Lev. "Right," she said and snapped her phone closed.

It took five minutes and about an inch of paint off the left fender to get her car turned around on the narrow road. Finally, back on Laurel Canyon, she got a bright idea. No way was she going to be driving those bloody footpaths these canyon dwellers called streets. She dialed Beverly Hills Cab.

Five minutes later, a cab pulled up behind her. Vicky got out of her car, locked it, walked to the cab and got in. "Two-one-three-three Lookout Mountain Avenue and step on it."

"A cab just pulled up outside, Lev," Kate said.

"Who in the devil?"

"It's Vicky," Kate exclaimed.

Lev opened the door as Vicky marched up the path.

"What are you doing? Lev, you and Kate follow me back to the cab and make it snappy. The meter's running."

Very little in the way of conversation was exchanged on the ride back to Vicky's car. Lev cast many an anxious glance through the cab's back window but there were no signs of a tail. Vicky paid the cab and the three of them quickly climbed into Vicky's car.

"Are you sure none of Kumar's people are trailing us, Lev?" There was a nervous edge to Vicky's voice.

"Not that I can see, Vicky." Lev was, however, certain that the NSA were following somehow. Fox and Hounds. "Did Kumar say where Mel was, Vicky?"

"Yes, at Stella Rae's house."

Chapter 98

The two government technicians examining Kate's computer leapt back from their workbench. The screen suddenly went blank, the computer began hissing, and a pale greenish smoke with an acrid odor issued from within.

"What the hell?" a young man in a white lab coat cried.

The other tech, a young woman, stood petrified, fully aware of the consequences that would arise from the mishap. "It happened the moment you tried to extract the program."

Richardson got the news in his office and slammed down the phone. Fuming, he took the elevator to the basement of the Federal building. Two steel reinforced glass doors whooshed open as he entered. The two techs stood nervously beside the growing heap of melted metal and plastic that moments before was Kate Keenan's computer. Richardson waved a hand in front of his face, trying to rid the terrible smell of burning printed circuitry. One of the techs handed him a wetted paper towel to place over his nose and mouth.

"What happened? How long is this going to take to repair?"

"Sir, there's no possibility of repair. This computer is totaled."

"No chance of repair? Totaled?" Richardson roared. "There has to be a way! This piece of equipment has national security preferential treatment clearance, do you understand?" What was left of the laptop lid suddenly fell backwards and dropped off.

At the moment the smoking lid toppled, Kate, Lev and Vicky were entering Stella Rae's home. Lev had contacted Ethan and Stacy, given them his location, brought them up to date, told them to park on the street, a car facing each way, and instructed them to call if anything suspicious, like an unmarked vehicle with government plates, showed up.

Stella was sober. However, she had a drink in one hand as she led Kate, Lev and Vicky into the living room.

"Where's that Sonofabitch?" Lev growled, scouring the room with a glare that would have melted iron. He wanted to wring Mel's neck. No one hauled a client out of his office with a letter opener pointed at the jugular. No one!

Stella pointed upward, "In the master bedroom. He's armed and has locked himself inside. He won't come out until Vicky presents him with an acceptable plan to move him out of the country."

"I can get him back to India. I'll have the swine deported!" Kate fumed.

"Stop! Everyone!" Vicky's trumpet voice took over. "Remember, I'm the hostage here. If I don't get that bastard back to India, Kumar will…"

"Vicky's right," Lev soothed. "Mel is waiting to be escorted out of this house for a safe trip to India, and he's expecting you to make it happen."

"Why did Kumar choose you, Vicky? What connection does he have with you?" Kate asked.

Vicky slumped into an easy chair, her face, usually perfect, was in need of repair. "Blackmail." Her voice cracked with emotion as she spoke the word. "I became part of Kumar's world several years ago. I've been passing him inside information on anything to do with Hollywood for years."

Stella drained her drink. "'Spy' would be a better word, Vicky. That's what we've all been at one time or another. Mel, myself and God knows how many others. We were all tools."

"I need a drink," Vicky said.

Stella refilled her own glass and then poured vodka for Vicky. "Start drinking and thinking, old lady."

The image of Vicky Vance disheveled and tired, clutching a glass of vodka in a shaky hand, acutely aware of the errors of her past caused Kate to pause. Her program to change the face of Hollywood had a darker side that could possibility bite her, too, one day.

Lev broke the silence. "Well, Vicky, what's it going to be?"

"I don't know what to do, Lev." Her chin dropped to her chest and the glass fell from her fingers. Sobbing uncontrollably, she said, "For the first time in years, I don't know what to do."

Kate stared at the glass. It hadn't broken. It lay on the thick carpet, its contents soaking into the pile. Crouching in front of Vicky, Kate took the woman's scrawny hand in hers and looked up at Lev. "I think it's time we called Harcourt."

The tableau presented a tragic spectacle to Lev. He watched as Vicky Vance, the Sovereign of Scandal, whose words, even in these times of 'anything goes' could ruin those who dared not to bend a knee at her every whim, crumpled, her sovereignty ended.

Kate picked up the glass and placed it on a side table. "Lev, call Stace and Dad here. We should be together when Harcourt and the others arrive."

"Okay, I'll phone them, and Harcourt immediately afterwards."

Stella refreshed her drink and sipped twice before asking,

"What about Mel?"

"He stays in the bedroom for now, Stella," Lev replied.

Mel had listened intently to every word spoken in the living room from the moment Vicky, Lev and Kate entered. It had taken all his money and savoir-faire, but he'd eventually persuaded Stella to leave on the wireless intercom between the bedroom and living room.

Chapter 99

Richardson phone-contacted Harcourt about the self-destruction of Kate's computer, moving Kate immediately back in Harcourt's cross hairs.

"That little witch bugged the computer to blow, Richardson concluded.

"Where is she now?"

"Leventhal's place. I have two men parked up the street on Lookout Mountain Avenue—no cars have been in or out. A cab dropped someone at the entrance and drove away, that's it."

"Fine, I'll pick her up and bring her here." Harcourt hung up.

Harcourt's phone trilled immediately. It was Lev.

"Where are you, Leventhal?"

Lev told him that he, Kate and several others were at Stella Rae's with Mel locked in the bedroom.

As he listened, Harcourt's jaw torqued. After the explanation, he brusquely ordered Lev and the others to remain where they were until he arrived. *So much for being Master of the Hounds,* he thought ironically.

"Harcourt's on the way," Lev said lowering into a leather easy chair. Ethan and Stace beat Harcourt to Stella Rae's house by five minutes.

Mel reacted to Lev's words at once. He had no intention of falling into the hands of the Feds again.

The master bedroom, in the back part of the large house, overlooked a garden of trees and bushes. Switching off the bedroom lights, Mel went to the window, slid it open and stuck his head out. Ten feet below, the edge of the patio roof jutted out into the yard. Stuffing the 9-millimeter Beretta his 'Pashagora owned' lawyer had left him into his waist band, Mel eased out of the window and nimbly lowered himself to the top of the patio.

Within seconds, he was across the back lawn, over a redwood fence, and into a neighbor's yard. Thankfully, there were no barking dogs with which to contend.

Vicky slopped vodka into her empty glass with a shaky hand. "Lev, I'm going to tell all I know about Pashagora's criminal intrusion into the workings of Hollywood and seek protection under the government's Witness Protection Program."

Lev and Stace murmured approval.

"What are you going to tell them, Kate?" Ethan asked.

"Well, Dad, assuming they've gotten hold of my computer and have unsuccessfully tried to copy the program off of it, they're most likely going to want to haul my ass back to the Federal building."

"If they've lost the computer, you're all that's left, Kate," Lev said.

"Okay, you're my agent. What do you think I should say, Lev?"

"Why not cut a deal?" Ethan cut in softly. "Sell the Feds the program. You own the patents; you could negotiate for millions. Think about it, Baby. If the program fell into movie industry hands, Hollywood could end up the same as the steel mills did in Pennsylvania with thousands out of work. The mills never made it back and neither would Hollywood."

"Yeah, Dad, you're right. I've been thinking about that. Director John Landis was right about Corporate Hollywood searching relentlessly for a way to make movies without the cost and headaches of stars, crews and directors, but I don't think it's ready for my program."

"They're here," Stella whispered, peeking through parted curtains as the doorbell chimed.

"I'll get it." Kate went into the hall and opened the front door. "Good evening, Agent Harcourt. Do come in. You're in luck. Two of the ladies you said you were interested in interviewing are here."

Harcourt and two agents followed Kate into the living room. He took in the occupants with a sweeping glance. A drowsy-eyed young woman with a red rose tattooed on her shoulder was draped in a chair. A blotchy faced old woman stared up at him over the top of her tilting cocktail glass. The others in the room, he knew already.

Kate indicated Vicky. "Ms. Vicky Vance," Then Stella. "Ms. Stella Rae."

"Good evening, ladies. I have a few questions before Miz Keenan and I return to the Federal building," Harcourt announced.

"I know everything about the Pashagora cartel," Vicky blurted out, rising half out of her chair. "You have to put me into a protection program! They're going to kill me!"

Chapter 100

Vicky Vance and her lawyer sat in the conference room at the Federal building. Vicky was talking. Harcourt, Richardson, the tight-faced middle-aged woman and Falk were silent, listening.

A change had come over Vicky. She sat relaxed; the knowledge she was safe inside the Federal building had eased her fears.

"Getting involved with criminals was a damn silly thing to do. Becoming involved with Pashagora and his gang was beyond stupidity. Nonetheless, I did. At first, it was easy. They made me feel important, saying I was the best reporter in Hollywood and that I could be useful to Bollywood." She smiled, adding as postscript, "It's a common ailment in Hollywood, believing your own publicity." Vicky turned to her lawyer; they spoke briefly, and at his nod she continued. "Does the name Abul Abu Gulshan mean anything to you?" she asked.

The trio looked at each other. Falk sat straight up, but remained in the role of an observer. He watched Kate closely. The middle-aged woman said the name was familiar, but to continue with her story.

"Run his name through your computers and see what pops up. It could save me a lot of talking," Vicky shot back.

The woman gave a 'do it' nod to Richardson, who pushed away from the table and left the room. The middle-aged woman taking the deposition leaned forward, recorded the time of Richardson's exit and announced a short intermission. Fifteen minutes later, Richardson was sitting in his office behind his desk, stern faced, hands clasped together, elbows on a leather edged blotter. Kate sat across from him. Harcourt stood behind Richardson. Falk was sitting quietly in a corner.

"Miz Keenan. Listen to me carefully." Richardson nodded to Harcourt who switched on the tape recorder and announced time, place and occupants. Kate surveyed the room's occupants and stared at Falk, her eyes sharpening.

Looking down at a piece of paper as if reading it aloud, the continued: "Vicky Vance has given us some startling facts and a name of interest, which, in conjunction with the recent attempts to kidnap you and steal your computer program have our government even more deeply concerned. Abul Abu Gulshan is one of Interpol's most wanted. A central figure in organized crime in India and Asia, he's also a prime suspect in the ninteen-thirty-three Mumbai serial explosion case that ripped through the city killing two hundred and fifty-seven innocent people, injuring over seven hundred more. Kumar Pashagora is the nominal head of the India cartel overseen by Abul Abu Gulshan."

Richardson glanced up from the paper and glanced at Falk, who nodded, as if already familiar with everything Richardson had said. "The cartel is operated out of Europe. Gulshan's *forte* is extortion, and with Pashagora's assistance, it is rife throughout the Indian film industry. Most producers and directors have had to interact indirectly with this man, who ultimately demands the overseas rights of their films in return for 'protection' during production and 'insurance' during post-production. Gulshan, we believe, was involved in the murder of business Tycoon Rajesh Rocha, the killing of actor Manisha Koirala's secretary, and the attempted murder of film producer Pradeep Jain."

Richardson paused, glancing up again. "These names meant little to us here in California. Nonetheless, given what we now know, as Agent Harcourt suggested earlier, you would be well advised to consider our offer of protection."

"Where does Mel fit into all this?" Kate asked, staring at Falk, recognizing at last where the real power was within the room.

"At this point we have no idea. When we have him in custody, he'll be interrogated, then most likely deported back to India."

Richardson pushed aside his fact sheet, glanced again at Falk, and leaned forward. "I've been authorized by our government to make you part of our Secure National Twenty-one Black Ops computer network at NSA—top security clearance, a generous fee for the 'purchase' of your system, plus a well-paying government job."

"And if I accepted this offer, you could use my program any way the government saw fit and I'd have no way to stop you. Correct?"

Before Richardson could nod his agreement, Kate held up a hand and spoke directly to Falk. "The offer is enticing, and working for NSA could indeed prove interesting. Still, I must make a decision, and knowing my program has potential for military use, as a good citizen, I have no wish to stop the program getting to the DOD as soon as possible."

Harcourt and Robinson brightened somewhat. Falk remained neutral, his eyes, like a laser, boring into her.

Kate reclined in her chair and stared at the ceiling. "My Dad and I have decided my program could be more of a hindrance than help to Hollywood. Too many people would lose their jobs, and the economy being what it is right now, well, I'd hate to be responsible for turning Hollywood into a ghost town."

Harcourt and Richardson bent forward, eager to hear her decision. Falk remained relaxed and focused on Kate.

"However, I would prefer to continue my work in private with an organization within the government that might allow me more autonomy," Kate said to Falk, who gave a small smile.

Richardson jumped to his feet. "You can't do that!"

"I'm sure there's some agency within the government other than NSA that would be interested in my work and could meet all the terms of your offer, Agent Richardson," Kate said, staring into

Agent Richardson's eyes, but speaking as if talking to Falk.

Kate continued to stare at a dumbfounded Richardson and Harcourt.

Satisfied she'd correctly voiced her counteroffer, Kate redirected everyone's attention to a second issue that was of personal concern. "Is my friend Vicky Vance going to be safe? You will be arranging something for her along with her new identity, say in communication, I'm sure, won't you?" Without waiting for an answer, Kate rose to her feet and smiled wryly. "Vicky will be sorely missed in Hollywood."

Chapter 101

The next few days were hectic.

"Your experiences since the wrap party, Kate, lead me to believe you'd be a gift to the NSA," Lev said quietly. Joanie and Stacy were sitting on a plump settee in Kate's living room, Ethan comfortably between them.

Lev and Kate relaxed in twin beige easy chairs facing Joanie, Ethan and Stacy.

Stacy took a sip of her wine. "Are you nuts, Lev? They'd take her program and have Kate sitting behind a desk eight hours a day doing some humdrum office job."

"Sitting in an office all day, at best, managing other people" said Joanie. "It's out of character and would be a terrible waste of your scientific, programming and writing talents."

Ethan exchanged a grin with Lev. "Lev's not crazy, Stace. He and I felt it might be a good idea if Kate worked for NSA, or, better yet, the Defense Advanced Research Program Agency, DARPA, or maybe the Defense Intelligence Agency, DIA."

"Dad, we've already discussed this at length. I've already

assured you that I'd run my decision past you guys before committing to it. And I've come up with one I think would work for me."

Everyone perked up.

Stace nodded. "Tell us more, Kate."

"Well, NSA offered to 'buy' my program. I've already advised them that I will talk with my patent and business attornys and get back to them."

"I meant about DARPA. Or the DIA. I don't see you in either an office," Stace said.

"NSA offered to introduce me to them as well as several other agencies within the government. If one suits me, then they'll train me. After that, I'd be back here in Hollywood, doing what I've wanted to do before all this blew up: writing. Given all I've experienced, I've a particularly good thriller screenplay in my head that, with some adjustments for national security, I'd like to see brought to the silver screen. Megastar studios, at NSA's encouragement, has already agreed to option them and pay me an advance even before I put it on paper. After my 'agency' training, I'd be consulted on a 'need to help' basis."

"By 'agency' you mean DARPA or DIA?" Stace asked.

Kate smiled. "Not exactly. I'm not really at liberty to say." Kate had figured out that Agent Falk worked for a 'special' agency, as the head of the agency had put it "in association with various government agencies." The biggest attraction, however, was Falk. She wanted to see more of him. She felt his authority, his piercing intelligence and a connection with him that she was hoping was reciprocated.

"Of course, we understand. Well, it all sounds very intriguing," Stacy said, disappointed not to hear the details.

"As I said, whatever agency she finally chooses to work with, it'll be Kate's decision. Either way, I'll still have my star client."

"Anything new on Mel's whereabouts?" Stacy asked, attempting to change the subject away from what seemed to her like Kate's possible excursion into the dark world of cloaks and daggers.

"Not a word," Lev said. "I'll give Harcourt a call in the morning, but I don't expect he'll tell us even if he knows. He was glad to see the end of us."

Chapter 102

Pradeep Kurade, the government asset with an office on Cuffe Parade, Mumbai, placed a coded call by satellite phone to his contact in Washington, reporting that Melhi Pashagora had definitely arrived back at his home in Mumbai. Since then, no one had seen or heard from him.

Chapter 103

Hank and Jilly sailed into Marina Costa Baja shortly before darkness and tied up at an overnight courtesy mooring. Hank checked in with the dock master, booked a three-day mooring and inquired about the best yacht broker in the area.

Back on board, Hank related to Jilly the results of his inquiries as she fried eggs on the galley stove. "I go see a man named José Gutierrez in the morning. He's supposed to be the best ship broker around."

Jilly grunted, flipped the eggs over easy and slid them onto a plate. "I hope they have a decent store. God, I'm tired of fry-ups."

Hank dipped a crust of bread into a yoke and agreed. "The dock master said this José guy he is trustworthy and has rich clients, as well as a seaworthy inventory to choose from, should we decide to do an exchange."

"They all say that, Hank. I vote we sell the boat, get off the ocean, fly away someplace safe and drop out of sight."

Hank finished his eggs and leaned back. "Maybe you're right. I'll definitely see what I can get for the yacht. Remember when I told you about the sale of the company and the bank transactions?"

Jilly nodded, "Yes, of course."

"Well, I got a call from a man who has a business not dissimilar to TolomeoTechnics. He'd heard I was selling my business, and, hearing it had already sold, asked if I'd be interested in buying in with him. I said I'd get back to him."

"You told me the transaction wouldn't be known until after we arrived in India."

"I said it wouldn't become *public*. There's always a few who hear of things before they become public."

"You'd leave a trail a mile wide if you went back into business now, Hank."

"I don't think so. His plant is in Wales."

Jilly looked surprised, "Wales as in Welsh?"

"Lovely country, Jilly. We could have a house there and another place in London. Make up a legend. No one would know or care who we were. I'd be the silent partner. It's mostly my contacts he needs."

Jilly, always one to make up her mind quickly, leaned across the galley table and kissed Hank on the forehead.

"Sell the yacht, call your friend, and let's go to Wales."

Chapter 104

It was early June when Kate returned to Hollywood. Lev and

Ethan met her at LAX and updated each other as Lev drove her to her home on North Switzer Avenue.

"It's good to be back in my own place," Kate said tossing her carryon onto the couch and slumping into one of the easy chairs.

"It's good to have you home, Baby," Ethan said. "Stace would have come with us to pick you up, but was busy at the office."

"Your few emails sounded like you were enjoying your training," Lev chimed.

"They kept us very busy."

"Will you have to go back, or are you assigned to a local office?"

"Just like they said, Dad, I'm free to do as I please until they call me on a 'consultation' or give me a permanent assignment. Could be a day or a year. Who knows." She grinned. "For now, I'll be working from home, later from wherever they send me. And that's all I can tell you."

"Sounds like a dream job," Ethan said. "Now I have some news for you, Baby: Stace and I are getting married. We haven't set a date yet, but it'll be before the end of the year."

Kate jumped up and flung her arms around Ethan's neck. "Oh, I'm so happy for you, Dad! You'll make a great couple."

"Lev will be best man and we'd like you and Joanie to be maids of honor."

"A church wedding!" Kate exclaimed. "Who's giving the bride away?"

"Stace has an uncle who lives in Denver. He's all the family she has now."

"I can't believe this. It's such a surprise."

"Stace and your Dad knew each other years ago," Lev said. "They lost touch after he left town. Things rekindled since they met up again after our trip to Nevada."

"We should celebrate. Any wine in the house? I want to make a toast." Kate, suddenly in wedding mode, was bubbling over with excitement.

Ethan, who had been house sitting while Kate was away, answered. "There's a bottle of Chablis cooling in the refrigerator. Will that do?"

The bottle was half-empty when Kate asked, "Which church did you two pick?"

Lev and Ethan exchanged glances before Ethan answered, "The Wee Kirk O' The Heather in Forest Lawn, Glendale."

Lev saw Kate's eyes widen with surprise. "They match and dispatch at Forest Lawn, Kate," he explained with a smile.

"Yes, well, I know. It's just that…"

Ethan reached out and grasped Kate's hand. "Stace loves that little church. Her mother and father were married there. She used to visit it often, and sit and enjoy the peace and quiet. She wants something beautiful to happen there again, to erase the horrible memory of what occurred there a few months ago.

Chapter 105

Toward the end of August, Kate had finished outlining her screenplay, tentatively called, "Charlotte's Webpage," a story of a woman and a man who vanished while sailing their yacht in the Pacific.

The chime of an incoming email made her pause. Clicking to her incoming box, she read the message: "Contact us by agreed method. We have need to know concerning a major breakthrough in robotics. You will be working from the London Office. Details to follow."

Kate, as she learned during her training, permanently erased the message and sat quietly at her desk knowing that Hank Tolomeo and Jilly Suede were no longer missing at sea as the "major breakthrough in robotics" had the former TolomeoTechnics written all over it.

The assignment would require a rewrite of "Charlotte's Webpage." But first the assignment, then the rewrite.

Book Six

Dedication

To those who believe in in freedom, justice, democracy, and Koski and Falk.

Acknowledgements

I want to thank Raymond Gaynor for his brilliant ideas and all the hard work that went into QUANTUM DEATH. Thank's Ray, it's a joy working with you! Special thanks to Patricia Holmberg for pre-proofing the manuscript and helping seamlessly stitch together my and Ray's contributions.

- A. G. Hayes

I was surprised when several ideas we each were discussing for a new political thriller suddenly came together in QUANTUM DEATH. Collaborating has been sheer delight. Another special thanks to Patricia Holmberg for her assistance helping smooth transitions between A. G. and my contributions.

- Raymond Gaynor

Chapter 1

Susan Koski eased out of bed without making a sound. Joseph Falk never moved, the top of his head showing from beneath the covers assuring her he was fast asleep. Slowly she crept to the bedroom door, turned the knob...and the bedside phone rang.

"Damn it!" Her birthday surprise breakfast for Falk was ruined. She waited while Falk growled and snatched up the phone.

"Falk." Within seconds he was sitting on the edge of the bed wide awake, listening intently and waving for Koski to pick up the extension on the dressing table on the other side of the bed.

Koski immediately recognized the voice of their boss, Tom Stewart, head of Cerberus, America's ultra-secret "off the board" information and action agency.

"You on the line, Koski?" Stewart asked, continuing a moment later, "Good. Now both of you listen up."

There was a soft click and the tone on the line changed. Both Koski and Falk knew what was coming was top secret. "We have a problem."

Koski looked across the bed, raised her eyebrows and mouthed the words...Happy Birthday.

Chapter 2 - Earlier

"Something happened?"

"Yes. Tonight at oh-two-oh-sixteen hours, sir."

"Okay. What?" asked Tom Stewart, trying to shake off his grogginess, having been awakened from a deep sleep at four in the morning.

"That we don't exactly know, sir."

"What the hell does that mean: You don't 'exactly' know? What, then, do you know 'inexactly'?"

"We don't exactly know that either, sir."

"Then why are you waking me at this God-awful hour? It better be a significant 'something'!"

"That we do know."

"Go on..."

"At least we know it's *probably* significant, and..."

Stewart slid an arm into the sleeve of yesterday's rumpled shirt, while trying to hold onto the receiver of the conventional phone he kept beside his bed, in the process becoming hopelessly entangled. "For God's sake! Cut to the chase, soldier!" he growled into the shirt-covered receiver.

"Sir! Tonight at oh-two-oh-sixteen hours, there was a pointed fluctuation in the internet, Sir!" The voice on the other end paused to allow Stewart time to absorb the importance of the message. Whatever significance it had, however, was totally lost on Stewart, who was busy untangling himself, repeatedly brushing away the offending phone cord while attempting to button the front of his shirt. "A 'fluctuation'...an *intentional* 'fluctuation'?" asked Stewart, his irritation growing by the second.

"Ah, well, Sir, no one actually detected the fluctuation, only its echo. A majority of our cyber-security guys, however, are certain it was intentional. The remainder aren't even sure it happened. It was the intensity of their debate that caught the Night Ops Officer's attention, and apparently caused him to 'push the button' so to speak, which requires me to call you."

"An echo? An *echo* of a *possible* fluctuation in the internet? You woke me for something that might not even be real?"

"Who's to say what's real with the internet, Sir. But you see the dilemma, I hope. Given these times, if it is real, it's unique and quite likely intentional. And it's something we've never before seen with which we presumably have no experience. Our counterparts, the senior cyber-analysts at NSA, are already calling it a 'singularity,' and the implications of that, well…"

"Alright, alright. So you called me as required. What else can you tell me about this 'echo of an intentional fluctuation'?" Stewart asked shaking his lower body into last night's pants while attempting to grasp the tab of the fly and hold the phone in the crook of his neck at the same time. The visual impression, if anyone had been watching, would have been that of a failing contortionist.

"Our cyber experts have shifted from talking their recognizable, but normally indecipherable 'computerese' to what the Night Ops Officer is calling 'real quantum gibberish'. Physics stuff. Like, some are calling this unobserved event a digital 'big bang,' you know, like the big Big Bang. The beginning of the cosmos. Except this one wasn't really that big or that bangish from what I could catch."

"'Bang'?" repeated Stewart, slipping on his favorite London Fog coat and one of his many fedora hats while searching about for his car keys. "You say something went 'bang'?"

"Well, 'bangish' as far as anyone can say regarding a digital event, reserving a real 'Bang' for the Big Cosmic One. The unsettling part is hearing them use the two increasingly interchangeably. I overheard one of the more understandable experts call it a 'multi-dimensional quantum ripple in space-time fabric'. That's when Mister Rellin, the Night Ops Officer, ordered me to call you, Sir. To be honest, it's total chaos over here."

"I can hear the shouting in the background over the phone. But why call me? Why not first call..."

"Mister Relin told me to tell you that one theory—he stressed the word 'theory'—is that while no one observed the actual event, 'echo-ripples' from it appear to be expanding out in every direction from a specific geographic point, and, while most of them don't appear to be doing anything in particular, a few have been reported to have caused byte-changes in nearby computers. For example, a few minutes ago, a 'ripple-edge' passed over and apparently interacted with a supposedly secure nuclear-missile launch site. The Launch Officer said it didn't initiate a launch sequence, or shut down the facility, or cause any permanent damage that they could ascertain, but the targeting sequences for two of the missiles were scrambled, making them temporarily inactive. Mister Rellin said to stress to you that, so far, these are the only two intercontinental ballistic missile targeting sequences we know of that were changed, and the targeting code, in each case, automatically reverted back after the 'echo-ripple' passed and their internal computers rebooted. He also said to stress that the change, if it had happened during an actual launch crisis, would, at best, have made the missiles miss their assigned targets, and at worst caused them to detonate in their silos."

"Okay. That's more than serious enough to justify waking me. Tell Mister Rellin I'm on my way," Stewart yelled into the phone while heading for the door of his Washington DC apartment. The phone line abruptly snapped taut, issuing a vibratory warning.

"Ah, that's not all, Sir," the voice from the receiver end continued.

Stewart stopped dead, took two steps back and returned the landline receiver to his ear. "Yes...?"

"Well, again there's disagreement about this, but there's some, like I said, who think that the 'event' itself, although not observed, may be significant. It appears to have lasted less than a hundredth of a millisecond, but *while* it happened, it looks like for the briefest moment an unusual transmission link of some kind was established with, of all places, Laplacia, Vermont—that's a very small town outside Battleboro on the way to Marlboro, which is..."

"I know where Battleboro, Vermont, is! Finish what you were saying about the transmission link, man. What more can you tell me about this?"

"Yes, well, it appears that for an instant—we're talking less than the duration of the event—something in Laplacia self-actuated, then, immediately after, disappeared."

"What?"

"Just a moment, Sir. Mister Rellin's conveying more information he wants me to pass on. It is possible—no, Mister Rellin says it's now 'likely', Sir—that some kind of separate internet 'transaction' also occurred *immediately after* that. We've no idea what kind of transaction, but preliminary information suggest that someone—or 'someones'—were sending bids ostensibly for the purchase of the Eastern seaboard of the US. This could represent a second type of 'event', Sir."

"What the hell? Is this for real?"

"None of it makes sense to me, Mister Stewart. I'm only the

messenger, and Mister Rellin's trying his best to summarize what the geniuses here are guessing based on multiple ongoing inter-agency analyses of the originally undetected event. Mister Rellin says now that there's little question among the group that this event —they're all officially calling it an 'event' rather than a 'bang' now —is undoubtedly more significant than our current interpretation. The event, he says, is similar to...no, now they're saying it *is*...a 'quantum event'. Sir, you've got to get here. Some think this may be the beginning of a new kind of cyber-attack against the United States, and whoever's behind it is screwing with the very fabric of space-time. Our analysts are talking things like 'targets' and 'side-effects', like creating parallel worlds, with further effects and outcomes that could threaten our very physical existence. One expert is claiming it has already changed our future 'timeline'. I mean, Jesus, Sir...!"

Stewart checked the clock on the wall. It was already oh-six-hundred hours. He tossed the land phone, fished his cell phone out of his pants pocket, and speed-dialed his two best field agents.

"Falk," a sleepy voice on the other end said.

"This is 'Father'. You on the line, Koski? Good, now both of you listen up: We have a problem. Get your asses down to the Cerebrus situation room. Now!"

Chapter 3

Susan Koski and Joseph Falk joined Stewart just outside the Cerebrus situation room inside one of a row of nondescript greystone buildings lining a nondescript street in the Washington DC suburbs. The unobtrusive brown door looked exactly like that of all the other houses, belying no indication of the frenetic activity inside.

During the time it took the three to arrive, it had become irritatingly clearer to the night shift denizens that some kind of event and bidding had indeed occurred—a bidding, as the liaison officer had indicated over the phone, resulting in what appeared to be purchase, and, by implication, possession and control by "persons unknown" of the United States Eastern Seaboard. Whether the 'event' and 'auction' were separate, or two aspects of an integrated, more sinister action, no one was yet willing to volunteer.

Koski and Falk followed Stewart up five rows of steps, and, after providing the required identification to the audiovisual box beside the door, slipped in, passed a couple of armed military hallway guards, and through one of many unlabelled doors. Inside the room, everything was, as the liaison officer had indicated, total chaos.

The huge room, usually outfitted in largesse "boardroom" style, and sporting all the latest in digital information communication technology on one wall, had been organically subdivided along it's perimeter into fifty or more makeshift, working command and control centers, each with a Cerebrus representative, military liaison, security officer and several to many technicians. The room buzzed like a disturbed beehive. Several dozen or more uniformed runners carrying Post-It notes, manilla folders and briefcases, some chained and locked to the runner's wrists, dashed from one temporary command center to another, as well as and in and out of various doors located strategically throughout the room. The subdued lighting and somber atmosphere offered the only hint of control. A small dias at the far end of the room surrounded by a half-circle bank of monitors being watched by frowning senior Cerebrus and military staff members, separated the raised platform from the rest of the room and at least made the chaos look purposeful.

What it all meant remained unclear, but the key to it all, Stewart surmised, must lie in Laplacia where he immediately dispatched Falk. After ordering one of the agency's Gulfstreams at the nearest airport to be on alert for Falk, Koski, on Stewart's orders, settled in at Cerebrus headquarters to act as field liaison between Stewart and Falk. Her immediate job would be to make sense of everything that was going on and instantly relay that information to Falk.

Koski made no effort to hide her displeasure at being physically separated from Falk. They had become a highly skilled, two-person field team. Stewart, sensing Koski's barely hidden anger, tried unsuccessfully to explain the necessity, in his mind, of having her constantly informed and ready to travel elsewhere, should another event occur. His unquestionable logic, however, did little to diminish her concern at being separated from Falk, the seemingly all encompassing chaos going on all about her only heightening her concern.

Chapter 4

In Laplacia, Falk booked a room at the town's one and only motel, a run-down derelict from the 50's done in faux Hawaiian decor, then walked to its one and only cafe to grab some breakfast after his early morning flight arrival. In the cafe, he took a pedestal stool in the center of the long 'bar' and began chatting up the locals. Each of the men he politely interrogated proved, as expected, to be completely "small town" odd in character, manner, interests and voice. Each seemed wary, leading Falk to wonder whether, they might be culturally xenophobic. If so, good. That would mean they would be aware of anything at all out of the ordinary. The other possibility, of course, was that they were collectively hiding something. In the end, Falk ended up calling Koski and reporting that nothing at all related to the event appeared to have happened or be happening in the little town of two hundred.

Chapter 5

Stewart listened with one ear to Koski's near continuous grumbling at being separated from Falk, and with the other to her recount of Falk's uneventful phone report. Both jumped when a klaxon suddenly blared, a indication that an official cyber-attack alert had been issued.

Over the last few hours, reports of more and more small but potentially damaging computer "glitches" had begun streaming into Cerebrus' various command centers, as echo-ripples from the "non-event event" continued to spread out from Laplacia. Most worrisome, was a report that four American Air Force F-15E Strike Eagle interceptors passing through the widening, outermost echo-ripple's circumference simultaneously experienced a five-second loss of power before automatically re-powering.

A few minutes later, two Canadian CF-18 Hornets, flying wing-to-wing on a training mission out of Canadian Forces Base at North Bay, Ontario, as they passed through the northern edge of the same echo-ripple, similarly lost power for several seconds and, momentarily helpless, crashed into each other, killing the both airplanes' pilots and weapons systems officers.

Moments after that, a report came in from NSA that Internet browser giant UpOn reported ten seconds of simultaneous unexplained blackout in a thousand distributed servers located in a small town several miles southwest of where the F-15E Strike

Eagles momentarily lost power, again just when the edge of the ripple passed over their location. The moment the wave passed, all the servers began rebooting at the same time, causing an electrical drain that triggered an area-wide electrical power network failure, further delaying return of the servers to normal operation.

Later, as the perimeter of the echo-ripple continued to spread outward, two trains on the Chicago to Washington DC route experienced a momentary loss of power, the one, twenty minutes ahead of the the other unable to restart, the one behind abruptly returning to power and colliding into the backend of its stalled sister, derailing both trains. Some of the passengers, including several congressmen, several high-ranking military officers and a high-profile industrialist, were reported dead. Injuries were being reported in the hundreds. It would have been the news story of the day had it been the only major catastrophe. Instead, it ended up as an aside in that hour's television news report, lost in an ever-expanding number of accident reports from throughout the Northeast.

As the ripple expanded into Canada, Cerebrus began receiving reports of momentary computer shutdowns from domestic, government and Canadian military sites. One shutdown caused electronic stock prices in the Canadian Stock Exchange to flicker, and, in an attempt to auto-reboot and self-correct, display stock values at random lower or higher values. Ten minutes later, the values inexplicably returned to their pre-glitch prices but only after the error had triggered a full-scale "adjustment," initiated by millions of preprogrammed "buy" and "sell" orders. No one at this point had any idea how to actually correct the market, now in total chaos.

In Northeastern USA, city and state police were reporting an sudden rise in automobile accidents, most the result of momentary failures of electronic components within the cars. As a result, major TV news syndicates, at the request of Homeland Security, had begun advising people in the northeastern states not to drive unless it was an absolute emergency. The announcement caused further confusion as growing numbers of viewers and investigative journalists began calling in to ask if the sudden spates of accidents didn't themselves constitute an emergency.

The most serious automotive failures were those occurring in cars on multi-lane highways equidistant in any direction from Laplacia, as the echo-ripple's edge continued to expand outwards. A report came in of a two thousand car pile up on the first major interstate freeway encountering the ripple. Hundreds were being reported dead or injured on news flashes across the country. The ever-expanding "Circle of Death" as it was coming to be known, was not only causing cars and trucks to experience some seconds of complete loss of control—just enough to wreak havoc—but also causing those that were not permanently disabled to suddenly roar back to life to wreak further destruction and carnage.

The increasing numbers of auto accident reports were already causing the insurance industry and auto giants to begin seriously considering the financial and litigious consequences should the Circle of Death continue.

Chapter 6

Back in Laplacia, Falk was notified by Koski that the NSA cyber-geniuses now "mostly agreed" among themselves that the instigating event had indeed begun in Laplacia, as evidenced by the fact that the echo-ripples were continuing to spread out equally in every direction from there. Furthermore, the bizarre bidding for the Eastern American Seaboard had been, according to the latest reports by US cybersecurity and internet specialists, followed almost immediately by a massive exchange of electronic BitCoins. With BitCoins, the newest introduced form of world currency, the identity of sellers and buyers was electronically opaque even to NSA, fueling further concern of a coordinated cyber-attack of a manner and magnitude never before experienced.

The effect of the unprecedented exchange of BitCoins was now causing collateral damage of its own in participating American financial institutions, raising the specter of regional financial systems collapse. Anything that involved BitCoins, including online consumer purchases, gaming, bill payments, real estate transactions, even bank-to-bank currency exchanges, appeared endangered. The question on everyone's mind, including Stewart's, was what it all meant.

It was difficult to determine, NSA cybercrime technicians were assuring Cerebrus and thereby Koski, Falk, but still highly *likely,* that while the initial bids appeared to have come from a number of sources, a "final purchase" was completed between seller and buyer, the actual payment coming from a variety of different sources, located both within and outside the USA. The total purchase of the auction was currently estimated in excess of one hundred *million* bitcoins, which, at current US dollar exchange rates, translated loosely to a hundred *trillion* American dollars purchasing power, an amount sufficient to instigate, inflate, deflate or even destroy the various world currencies depending on timing, collateral damage, and investor reactions. Homeland Security and the Department of the Treasury were questioning whether the unprecedented exchange of BitCoins represented an attempt to launder stashes of heretofore hidden "dark" money accumulated by international criminal organizations, possibly under the aegis of a newly organized cartel of criminal or terrorist organizations. Their questioning, unfortunately, remained speculative, in the end adding to the general confusion rather than mitigating it.

Two important pieces of information, however, had come to light, Koski informed Falk. First, the Circle of Death, as it continued to expand outward, was now slowly diminishing in strength, causing less damage to fewer digital electronic devices. Second, NSA and Cerebrus cyber-jockeys had confirmed that an unusual transmission had indeed been momentarily centered at a farmhouse registered to a Mister Aaron Hempsted, an elderly, retired man who lived alone on the outskirts of Laplacia.

Falk sighed, wished Koski well, signed off, and left the cafe to visit what he felt would likely prove to be one very dangerous old man.

Chapter 7

As Koski signed off, Stewart announced loudly in the background that a second event had occurred, again lasting only a fraction of a millisecond, and that, according to initial electronic failure reports, the epicenter this time was in Fulton, Ohio, another isolated country town with fewer than a couple hundred residents. Located due north of Columbus, it was a town like Laplacia that one had to work hard to locate on any map.

As with the first, the initial second event passed undetected, its initial echo-ripples causing little damage other than a rash of irritating, momentary home computer failures at various nearby farms. Within several hours, however, Cerebrus situation room monitors were flashing reports of destruction and loss of life associated with the sudden collapse of the Central United States

Power Interconnect and a regional power network in southern Canada, interestingly both networks having power nodes located where the echo-ripples from this new event converged with those from the first event. It quickly became clear that while damage from the first event echoes was diminishing, wherever those from the two events intersected, damage was compounded.

Stewart was already beginning to wonder aloud if, even without corroborating evidence, the underlying purpose of the events was to produce specific event-echo intersections at key locations, and whether that reflected a highly sophisticated underlying strategic attack plan. If so, additional events would surely follow, and the number of intersections would increase exponentially, quickly overwhelming America's resources and ability to respond.

Even without proof, Stewart felt justified sending Koski to Fulton, while the various departments of the United States government, working together, continued to attempt to determine if the two incidents were actually connected, and, if so, if they were indeed harbingers of what Stewart suspected represented a massive cyberattack. No more stealing names, addresses, social security numbers, credit card numbers and government personnel files. If what he feared was true, this predicated all out cyber-warfare like the world had never seen before.

Chapter 8

Koski's drive to the airport left her feeling even more concerned and irritated at being apart from Falk. During their last assignment, code-named The Chemical Factor, each came frighteningly close to dying, and yet, in a surprise turn, each had snatched the other from certain death and the process had brought them closer together than ever before. Initially, she had had to focus all her efforts on being a superior agent for her unquestionably superior partner. Recently, however, occasional tugs of affection had begun popping out of nowhere, especially when they were in close physical proximity, more so when in danger. Falk had as much acknowledged the same. It seemed that danger was tempering their affection into something more akin to…what? Were they falling for each other? No! Neither could. Each carried too much past emotional baggage. Besides, they were professionals! Yet her awakening feelings were even now morphing from concern into an aching—or, was it longing—deep in the center of her being.

Speeding along the freeway, musing over the new way she was coming to regard Falk, Koski missed the moment when her car engine suddenly died, and, shaken abruptly out of her reverie, panicked.

To her alarm, the engine, power steering and power brakes had all gone out. The only working device left was the manual hand brake, which she began pumping aggressively to slow the car and keep it from spinning out of control.

Koski had to marshal all her emotional reserves to tease the fishtailing car to a stop. It was only when the car was resting silently on the shoulder of the freeway that she breathed a sigh of relief, then noticed the many other cars on the freeway knocking into each other like bumper cars, tearing at each other's plastic and metal exterior like angry dinosaurs fighting over their territories. As if that weren't enough, fifteen seconds later all undamaged car engines, including Koski's, abruptly roared back to life, hers lunging forward like a lioness springing for the kill, hitting the safety railing and bouncing the car back onto the active freeway.

Wrestling for control of the car while dodging vehicles flying at her from the left, right, ahead and behind, it was only a matter of time before one smashed smartly into the passenger side of her car and another immediately afterwards into the driver's side, causing her rental car's multiple airbags to deploy. No longer able to see, Koski fought both car and mounting claustrophobia, her stomach lurching, her initial panic quickly superseded by outright terror. Fighting the desperate feeling that she needed to exit what otherwise might become her tomb, but aware of the mortal danger of getting out with so many cars zooming and spinning out of control all about her, Koski plunged her hand under the gel-like folds of the now deflating front air bag until she could feel the ignition key in her fingers and turn off the engine. Drivers about her, seemingly on cue, began turning off their cars, or, reacquiring control, eventually braking them to a stop. The freeway soon looked like a spent battlefield, littered with damaged cars, smoking debris scattered everywhere, the continued brunt of the attack shooting like an arrow ahead up the freeway.

After checking carefully in every direction, Koski climbed out of her car and joined one of several lines of dazed drivers and passengers walking zombie-like in single file along the cluttered freeway.

Koski couldn't help but wonder if the sudden, eerie silence now closing about her, punctuated by the piercing cries of frightened children, was a premonition of more to come.

Chapter 9

Back in Washington DC, computer experts at Cerebrus headquarters huddled over one of the many super-computer displays to debate the validity and implications of a hastily prepared computer simulation of the effects of the so far two events. The terminal displayed the two event-location-points in pulsing red, each with ever-expanding, ever-intersecting, florescent-green, curved echo-ripple lines emanating outwards, overlaid on a hazy grey topological map of America. But the focus of the experts' concern wasn't so much on what the terminal was displaying, as it was on their speculation about the nature of the actual events, which seemed to appear out of nowhere and the next instant, disappear entirely. Unable to pursue their concern further, they turned their attentions to various interpretations of what appeared to be another auction. A huge monetary transaction had occurred fractions of a second after what looked like a frenetic burst of "bidding," ostensibly for possession of what they surmised to be the Eastern Central Region of the USA. As a result, the experts were falling into two groups: one focused on the events, the other on the auctions.

The first group continued discussing how it was that an event phenomenon of this magnitude could appear, then disappear without any indication at the source of having ever occurred. Initially branded a "freak anomaly," then "a non-real occurrence," the event recurrence had advanced it to being an actual, real, if momentary and incredibly puzzling, event.

"They seem to materialize from nowhere and instantly revert back to whatever they were before," a white-haired, sallow-faced physicist offered, awe apparent in every word.

"Fiddlesticks, Bert! Nothing can come from nothing!" a flame-red-haired, middle-aged mathematician, standing elbow-to-elbow with the physicist countered sharply as the two watched the resulting, now familiar echo rings continue to expand and intersect.

"But how, Francis? How? How do you explain...?" Bert asked.

"I can't! At least not yet," replied the mathematician. "But I'm certain an explanation will present itself. One more event and my group should have enough data to prove what we both know: The laws of physics require that nothing can come from nothing!"

"A couple of peculiar 'singular singularities', then? Some new kind of 'Little Big Bangs'?" offered Francis jokingly in challenge.

"A 'singular singularity'? What the heck does that mean, Bert? And while they may *look* like similar 'Little Big Bangs', mathematically, they can't be. The mathematics are all wrong. Their Circles of Death don't act like the result of *any* kind of bang or bump. The events are momentary, pin-point, time-space continuum disturbances. Like what would result from tossing a massively powerful but subatomic sized 'stone' into our particular time-space 'pond'. Or, given the presence of two events, maybe skipping a stone into it. I don't know, but in each case, I suspect a sudden, short-lived, though *very* powerful rent in time-space, though not in the electromagnetic sense as everything at the moment leads us to believe. Allowed to speculate, I'd say the two events are 'quantum explosions'. It's those damn enhancing waves where the ripples from each meet that make them…"

"More like quantum *im*plosions?" offered the first.

"Yes. Tiny quantum implosions! And incredibly powerful ones. As if an infinitesimal speck of space-time just suddenly vanished. Or collapsed. Then reappeared, or reorganized, or disappeared. I've asked my group to focus on looking, if you will, for a resulting 'fingerprint' that might tell us if what reappears after the event is exactly the same or slightly different from what disappeared at its beginning, and…"

The second group of specialists were busy speculating about the flow of BitCoins that had once again occurred, some saying just before, some just after, and others saying simultaneous with but not quite *completely* simultaneous with the events. Above the general din, it would sound to anyone listening from outside, that, despite the awesome assemblage of experts, their respective agencies' massive, shared resources, and the group's best collective effort, no one yet really had a clue as to the source or destination of the BitCoins.

"It's like a damn Sujiko puzzle of the tenth or eleventh order..." began an economic analyst, shoving his hands in frustration into the back pockets of his frayed jeans, his branded heavy-metal-rocker t-shirt looking decidedly pre-adolescent despite the fuzzy stubble on his cheeks and chin.

"And you, Martin, how would you know a Sujiko from a Suduko puzzle?" teased a female colleague several years his younger, wearing an expensive, designer work jacket over a permanently-pressed white blouse and perfectly-matched black slacks and shoes.

"Eh?" the man replied, looking as if he actually didn't know the difference. "I mean, hey, it's all just another puzzle. A game. A complex one, admittedly, but rationally solvable. All games are. Look, Jeebs: Assume n-sellers and m-buyers, each with an unknown amount of untraceable BitCoins, but each with a unique bid and purchase style. It's like someone's trying to hack their way with brute force into..."

"The key is the BitCoins, not the persons behind them," the young woman interjected with authority. "What we're seeing isn't anything like the n-dimensional construct you're proposing. As I see it, these are careful, cleverly constructed, business exchanges with a common, practical, underlying financial purpose. This isn't a puzzle, game or new kind of hack. It's a sophisticated crime, and everything resulting is part of a crime scene investigation. A mostly digital crime, perhaps, but a physical crime nonetheless. And, by the way, my name is Mary. Dr. Mary Johnson, not..."

"Oh, for Christ's sake, Jeebs! Take off your Sherlock Holmes' hat and leave that kind of mundane thinking behind. Climb into the rocket seat next to me and jet into the future, girl. Today's future! This isn't Hawaii-Five-O or NCSI.

Dr. Johnson looked floored.

"Everything said, Jeebs, I believe you're both right and wrong. You're right that, technically, it really *isn't* a new kind of puzzle, game or hack. I just said that to stimulate your intellectual hormones. In fact, there's no hacking involved at all. And the pre-event didn't *start* with anything digital or even internet-based, yet it's being *propagated* as if it were. In my mind, the event and the auction are, as you mentioned, clever, purposeful, and designed with a singular purpose in mind. But what we're facing is still a puzzle or game, a highly complex one with a hidden agenda, as I said before I was so rudely..." Jeans and T-Shirt replied.

In the end, neither agreed on anything except that, given the appearance of the second event and auction, something had *recurred* and, like the first auction, was associated with a major global financial exchange, the two taken together big enough to bring down countries.

Frowning, arms folded across his chest, Colonel Rellin stood resolute next to Stewart, the two a distance behind the mass of experts. Each encouraged his constituents to continue their work, Stewart, for the moment emphasizing the importance of developing testable hypotheses regarding the actual nature of the events, Rellin stressing documenting the flow of BitCoins. They concluded, reminding everyone of the importance of using any and all information to predict the location, timing, and expected results of a third such event and auction. In fact, no one was listening. Each was totally absorbed in solving his or her small part of the seemingly incomprehensible overall problem.

Stewart turned to Rellin and noticed the man's slumped shoulders. Walking out of the command center alongside each other and down the long hallway, Stewart *felt* the man's exhaustion. As they went, Stewart overheard some Cerebrus aides huddled together in front of a closed door, discussing the absurdity of "buying" regions of the USA, and decided, like them, that the whole "sale of property" scenario was simply too outrageous. Like Jeans-And-T-Shirt had said, there had to be more to it than the auctioning off of the United States of America. There had to be an *endgame*, and it was his job to uncover it. For the moment, he might not be able to explain the who, what, when, where or even how, but knowing the why was what his work was all about, and knowing it was what typically gave Cerebrus the edge it needed to successfully resolve even the most opaque threats. His strength had always been to play to the "why," and with that solidly in mind, he rethought recent events.

The best "why" he could figure right now, was that the *events* had been carefully located so that their "echoes" would intersect at specific locations that would invoke maximum disruption. There had to be a greater purpose to the events than what was so far visible. The part that kept nagging at him was whether they were a prelude to a larger plan to bring the USA to its knees. But if so, why only brief failures? Why temporary disruption rather than permanent destruction? The only explanation he could come up with was that someone wanted to paralyze, but not permanently damage the nation.

As for the *auctions*, this *had* to be a diversion—a huge red herring—designed to engage and deflect America's intelligence resources away from the less well defined events.

That took him full circle back to the events: There *had* to be something more behind them than the temporary power disruptions. Perhaps they were meant to humiliate the United States? To scare its citizenry into frenetic mis-action? Or perhaps these first two events were merely tests of something more sinister, like Hitler testing his newest weapons of war on unsuspecting populations during the Spanish Civil War.

Stewart's best plan was to continue personally directing Cerebrus' two finest resources, Koski and Falk, to scour the two event locations for any clues as to what might actually be going on. He needed more information in order to proceed with identifying the *why*. The rest would follow: *who* might be causing the events, *when* more events might occur, and exactly *how* "they," whoever they were, were causing the events to happen, as currently held, "out of the blue." Frustrated, heels clicking on the polished tiles, he broadcast a challenging scowl to anyone unlucky enough to glance at him—which, given the situation, meant no one.

Stewart squared his shoulders. For now, he needed to trust in the abilities of his two finest, and wait for something useful from them, or for a third event to occur. Either way, he needed a greater pattern to emerge.

Chapter 10

In Laplacia, Falk rolled his rental car to a stop in front of the Hempsted residence. Sliding his legs out, he stopped on impulse and reached inside the glove compartment. Removing his automatic, he placed it in his well-worn shoulder holster.

Standing before the dilapidated old house with it's cracked, boarded, dirt-opaque windows, he removed the gun, released the safety, chambered a round, and held the weapon at ready behind his thigh.

The moment he rapped on the door, it cracked open, and through the slit a single eye fixed warily on him. Falk took a step back, searching unsuccessfully for the rest of the answerer's face. What little he could see fit how the townsfolk had described Aaron Hempsted: A rheumy eye floated in a drawn, bloodless vertical slit of elongated face, topped by a wisp of uncombed white hair. The crack opened slightly more to reveal a pair of thin, tightly closed lips above a stubbly chin.

"Wha'd'ya want?" growled the lips, barely moving.

"Mr. Hempstead? Mr. Aaron Hempsted?" Falk asked, his sixth sense warning him not to relax for even a second.

As the two talked, Hempsted slowly cracked the door further, enough for Falk to make out the man's shoddy, disheveled clothes.

Falk's grip on his weapon tightened.

Over the next few moments, Hempsted carefully avoided answering every one of Falk's questions, essentially giving out no information beyond his name. During their talk, the door opened slightly wider and clunked against a fully extended door chain.

It didn't take long for Falk to discern that Hempsted was elderly and unclear in thought, which would make the man, at best, computer-challenged. Concluding the old man couldn't possibly be behind the event, Falk inquired if anyone else lived in the dusty-smelling, unkempt house he could see above the hunched man's white-haired head.

Hempsted paused, then hesitantly related that he was renting an upstairs room to two girls in their late teens. When Falk asked their names, the old man's white eyebrows crinkled, merging in the center of his forehead, and he became obstinately defensive, saying only that they weren't home.

When Falk asked if it would be possible to see their room, Hempsted become agitated and ordered him coarsely off the porch and property.

Odd way for a person to act, even a recluse, thought Falk on his way back to the car. As he climbed in, he noticed out of the corner of his eye a flash of light off an odd-looking, rooftop satellite dish, its antenna wire winding its way into the upstairs bedroom window.

Chapter 11

At the airport, Koski negotiated the next available flight to Columbus, reflecting uneasily on the anxiety that being cooped up in a confined space like a small commuter aircraft always caused her. It was a "gift" from her traumatic childhood.

These days, the resulting anxiety attacks had a habit of occurring out of the blue, much like the present "events," ending just as abruptly as they began, leaving her with an uncomfortable, stunned feeling. The most distressing thing about them, however, was knowing that they would return again and again, typically when she least expected it, until she exited the tightly enclosure that had brought them on.

Barely twenty minutes into the flight, acutely missing Falk's reassuring presence, her nerves frayed, she fell into an exhausted sleep.

Moments later, the mesmerizing hiss of the air conditioners and whine of the engines abruptly cut out.

For a while the plane continued knifing silently forward

through the air. Sensing her body floating above the seat, she felt rather than saw the planes nose begin to decline ever-so-slowly until the aircraft entered a steep dive. A series of pops, and a rain of oxygen masks deployed. Mothers, too stunned to reach for a mask, clutched their children. Some whimpered with fear. Others screamed. It was at precisely that moment the full-fledged anxiety attack she'd been awaiting gripped her.

The plane, nose down forty-five degrees, continued to fall soundlessly through the air through one after another thick layer of clouds for perhaps ten thousand stomach-wrenching feet by Koski's panicked mind's auto-calculation before the cabin lights and engines suddenly came back on.

The plane shuddered.

Outside, a metallic scream arose as the wings and fuselage tried to respond to the air crew's frantic attempt to halt the plane's descent. Kiosk's body weight abruptly quadrupled and passengers throughout the plane began taking up the children's screams.

The next ten seconds seemed like an hour. The plane was now at so low an altitude she could make out through her window the different colored clothes people in a large parking lot below were wearing, and see the whites of their eyes, wide in horror, staring up at the falling airplane.

Hands shaking, she tried to call Falk only to drop the phone, and upon retrieving it, find that it was irreparably damaged.

Bracing for what could only be a fatal impact, Koski jerked awake when the flight attendant tapped her shoulder saying, "Fasten your seat belt, please. We're coming into Columbus." Clutching her seat arm rests in a vise-like grip, her knuckles white and bloodless, she looking frantically out her window to see that the plane was, indeed, gently descending for landing.

Her confidence thoroughly shaken, she couldn't help but wonder if the 'daymare' she had just experienced was yet another premonition of what was to come.

Chapter 12

In Columbus, Koski rented a car only to have to fight her way to Fulton on packed roads. It reminded her of a mission with Falk in which they'd become entangled in a similar traffic snarl. In her mind she could hear Falk's voice saying he felt like a spawning salmon trying to fight its way upstream. Koski couldn't help but grin at the thought. The ethereal sound of his voice lingering in her head helped calm her.

Just before her exit, the rental car shuddered, stopped running, and plowed, *sans* brakes and steering, off the highway, slowing to a near stop as it rolled onto the shoulder. As it approached the safety railing, it abruptly roared back to life, slamming through the railing and surging on towards a massive Fulton city signpost.

Koski wrestled the rental car to a stop inches from the signpost. Her GPS locator on the passenger seat was on the floor in pieces. Noting a Fulton police SUV parked behind the signpost, she got out, flashed her federal agent identification and requested assistance in locating the geographic epicenter of the second event using their police GPS and the coordinates Stewart had provided.

Though wary, the male officer and his more sympathetic female compatriot put away their radar gun and entered the coordinates into their GPS locator, determining it to be those of "Old Man Thorsdan's farm" located on the outskirts of the city. At their invitation, Koski parked her rental car and jumped in the police SUV. The next thing she knew, she and the two officers were cruising down a side road. The policewoman pointed out the window at an infinite line of heavily weathered fenceposts whipping by the passenger side of the SUV, explaining that they marked the border of what used to be a large commercial ranch and farm. The greying wood fenceposts contrasted sharply in the late, almost florescent afternoon sun against a distant, growing darkness.

By the time they arrived at the entrance gate, turned right and continued down a bumpy, weed-overgrown dirt roadway, dusk had fallen, requiring the driver to turn on the vehicle's headlamps. Between their present location and the farmhouse was a single, intervening hill.

Proceeding, the policeman pulled the SUV to a stop atop the rise. In the distance, at the end of the straight-line dirt road, the three could just make out a lightless, matchbox-sized house and barn located atop a lightly wooded hill.

Resuming their approach, the house and barn resolved into a more weathered, dark and abandoned couple of dwellings than Koski had at first imagined. Black clouds, pregnant with rain, were gathering immediately above the two buildings, creating a suffocating blanket of silence about the car so profound that Koski could hear the breathing of the driver and the heartbeat of his assistant.

Koski unrolled her window to get a better look. The air outside had had become so heavy that when she stuck out her hand, tiny raindrops began forming, tracing a path through the otherwise still air.

After rattling over an old livestock grating, the SUV began climbing the final hill. As they went, Koski could make out numerous large pens, each devoid of animals. At the top of the hill, between what looked like an abandoned house and barn was an old, gray-primer-coated Ford truck with several bundles of hay piled in its bed. As they approached the farm house, the hairs on the back of Koski's neck reflexively stood.

The SUV pulled to a stop and Koski started to climb out, then, on impulse, removed her automatic from its shoulder holster. The two police officers remained in the SUV, staring at the black, foreboding house and the armed agent slipping and sliding her way through the wet mud and up the wooden porch steps.

At the top of the steps, Koski paused, hand in mid-air, about to knock on the rickety screen door, when she sensed movement inside and, having second thoughts, released the safety, chambered a round, and held the readied weapon down at her side. Flattening her back against the wall, she rapped loudly on the edge of the screen door. The weather-warped door clacked noisily with each strike.

A few moments later, an old man cracked open the inside door, and eyed Koski warily. "Wha' d'ya want?"

"Good evening, Mister..." Koski began.

"Thorsdan. Name's Thorsdan. An' why in God's name would the likes of you be a-comin' to a place like this, in this kind a weather and at such an hour?" he asked breathlessly.

"Mr. Thorsdan," Koski began again. "I've been asked to come here to investigate..."

"Nothin' here t'vestigate, young lady. Nothin' a'tall. I suggest you mind yur business an' leave." After the briefest pause, he re-summarized: "In case you didn't catch what I jus' said, it means 'git the hell off my land'. Now!"

The female officer in the SUV watched Koski and Old Man Thorsdan talk. After a few minutes, she nudged her partner with an elbow and reached unobtrusively for her weapon.

Koski attempted to continue engaging the crotchety old man, but try as she might, she couldn't. Furthermore, she imagine him being any part of the highly sophisticated technological "event" the two police had assured her had definitely originated on his farm. Recalling the truck, she inquired politely if there were any farmhands present.

The old man half-mumbled, half-complained about "a couple a' no-good rascal girls" who had contacted him during a trip into town to pick up supplies.

"They tol' me they waz farm hands, tho' I doubted 'em right away from th' look of their pristine hands." Nonetheless, he'd signed them on about a month ago, he said. They'd agreed to help him fix up the house and barn in return for free room and board. The problem was, the old man continued, typical of young folks today, they didn't ever get around to doing any fixing. Instead, they spent most of their time "holed up in the barn, playin' video games."

When Koski asked if she could meet them, the gruff old man became agitated, and told her he'd "said enough for one night," ending once again demanding she leave. Now.

On her way back to the SUV, a slapping noise directed her attention to the barn where a wire from a new-looking satellite dish on the roof was flapping in the wind and repeatedly striking the side of the barn. The cable disappeared through a crack in the first floor siding.

It wasn't so much the presence of the satellite dish or the cable that bothered her as it was that the line was directed into the least likely place she could imagine. Not the farmhouse, but the old, dilapidated animal barn where the two girls, according to Thorsdan, liked to "hole up." Strange.

Chapter 13

Back in the Cerebrus Situation Room in Washington DC, a gaggle of computer technicians were noisily discussing the displayed echo-waves on the big board emanating outwards from the first and second point-sources for the umpteenth time. While each set of echo-waves was clearly diminishing in strength as it spread, particular mayhem occurred everywhere echo-waves from the two Circles of Death intersected. Furthermore, whenever an intersection occurred immediately outside a high-rise urban center, some of the waves deflected off the larger buildings, effectively creating a new point-source to appear and, from it, a spate of new waves emanated, creating a new Circle of Death and a spate of new intersections with their attendant electrical shutdowns.

It was clear now that the intersections were causing the greatest damage to everything electrical or electronic. All available computational resources were being called upon to help predict the exponentially increasing number of point-sources and intersections in order to provide citizens a few minutes warning before the havoc. Reports continued coming in from regional, even national —most often military—centers of command and control located throughout the Americas, and none were encouraging. After recovering from a temporary shutdown, security at one after another installation was switching to high, meaning deadly force, alert.

How many more of these events, each propagating yet more echo-waves, back-echoes, point-sources and intersections can we survive? Stewart pondered. *What good is 'purchasing' a crippled region for billions, even trillions of dollars when it's damaged and not legally possessable?*

His thoughts were interrupted by a call from Koski that had been patched into the local DC police network and forwarded to him. The two were immediately joined in conference call by Falk on his cellular. Both agents conveyed their sites as lacking anything unusual on inspection, other than the presence at both sites of a single, elderly person (not really all that unusual), renting out a room to two youths (an interesting congruity), both sites having new TV satellite antennas (probably not all that unusual for an isolated country locale). As for the barn cable that concerned Koski, perhaps, as the two local police officers had jokingly suggested, Thorsdan was a progressive farmer, providing entertainment for his animals.

Is it possible, Stewart found himself considering while he listened, *that the computed event epicenters might not be the actual source epicenters?*

Ridiculous, he chided mentally, while grabbing the first passing computer geek for a quick hallway consult regarding the idea. The geek listened, only to shake his head dismissively at having been subjected to so incredibly stupid an idea before moving on.

Stewart conveyed the result of his hallway consultation to Falk and Koski.

For Falk, the emerging question was *how* the events were actually being brought about; for Koski, it was whether the abruptness of each of the farmer's requests for her and Falk to leave *might indicate something much bigger and darker.*

"Add cleverer and inherently evil," added Falk, "and I'll have to agree."

While Stewart quickly reassessed his agents' observations, hypotheses and suggestions, a voice on the building's public address system interrupted, announcing that a third event had just occurred, this time in Red River, Montana. Voice activity in the command center where Stewart was standing abruptly ceased, then resumed at a rapidly increasing level until it drowned out any hope of further conversation with his two field agents. Stewart yelled into his phone for Koski and Falk to stay where they were, and continue nosing about their respective epicenters, deciding in that moment to return, albeit briefly, from management to field work, to look into the newest event himself.

Chapter 14

At the Laplacia Diner, Falk returned his cell phone to his pocket and his attention to his now stone-cold plate dinner and to *how* exactly the now *three* events might have been created. A single event could have been the result of some kind of unusual 'natural' event. Two events could still be a 'natural' coincidence, though it would be unlikely. But three, regularly spaced events, all causing similar effects, suggested decidedly human intervention.

How are these events being created? Falk mulled.

Individually, the events seemed to him to most resemble an electromagnetic pulse, or EMP. EMP's, however, were typically associated with a nuclear blast. Given his and Koski's sites were physically intact, an EMP clearly couldn't have started there. It was, of course, possible that these were some new kind of EMP. On the other hand, non-nuclear EMPs, or NNEMP's, were still on the drawing board, and, even so, weren't predicted to result in waves that, upon intersecting, *multiplied* in strength.

A sudden electrostatic discharge or ESD, much like a lightning strike, could interrupt and damage nearby electronic devices, but, again, hadn't ever been known to cause echo-ripples or new reflective point-sources to occur. In addition, an ESD would directly effect living things as well.

No, the events could be *likened* to EMPs or ESDs, and they probably were being so likened in civilian and military centers throughout North America. But in deference to his partner, Koski, he had to admit, these events had the feel of something more. Something, as she said, dark, sinister and directed. As if behind everything lurked a malevolent intelligence—clever and ruthless—testing and flexing its muscles.

So far, his and Koski's sites had yielded few relevant clues as to the *how* of the events, other than the implication that they were, indeed, unique in nature. Something never before experienced. As he sat, he reviewed yet again everything that was currently known about the first two events:

In each case, the initializing event occurred suddenly and unexpectedly.

In each case, the event seemed centered in an isolated backcountry location.

In each case, an old man was housing two "difficult" youngsters. *That was interesting.*

In each case, there was no sign on cursory examination of any technology other than a TV satellite dish.

Finishing his cold dinner and washing it down with an equally cold, viscous cuppa, Falk decided to focus on the satellite dish. It could be nothing more than an improved, television antenna made specifically for use in the backcountry, but it could also be a specially designed satellite up- or down-link. If so, it would likely be attached to an equally specialized receiving device.

Trying without success to recall in exactly which direction the satellite dish had been pointed, he grabbed his cold-weather coat, pulled a twenty out of his wallet and tucked it under the saucer of the empty coffee cup. Returning to his car, he commiserated that, despite the hour, he needed to determine in exactly which direction the antenna was pointed and somehow get a look inside the room the cable entered.

Chapter 15

At the Regent Hotel Cafe in Fulton, Ohio, Koski, like Falk, ended her call. While reiterating her experience at the Thorsdan farmhouse to Stewart and Falk, the feeling of evilness again prickled her spine. To Koski, it was more than just a hunch. The old man was off-putting, but, on careful reconsideration, he seemed not as much off-putting as...scared. Yes, that was it. Fearful. There had to be a connection of some kind between the event, the isolated farmhouse, the reticent owner, and the two boarders she had yet to meet and interview, and, with deference to her partner, the satellite dish with its wire going, at her site, into an animal barn of all places.

Koski raised her hand to call for the bill for her late night dinner.

Her waiter responded immediately. The young, lanky, sallow-complexioned boy of perhaps seventeen stopped in front of her table, shifted his weight onto one leg, and rested a hand jauntily on his lower hip. "You're new to Fulton," he stated, his inquisitiveness enhanced by his deep, post-adolescent voice. "Haven't seen you hereabouts before."

Koski nodded in the affirmative. "I dropped in to Fulton to visit...a relative. 'Old Man Thorsdan' people call him around here. He lives on a large farm-ranch on the outskirts of town. He's getting old and I heard he had had to hire a couple of young girls to..."

"Yeah. Know him. He's my sort of honorary uncle. Doesn't much come to town, and when he does, everyone mostly avoids him. It's like even though he's there, he's never really there, if you know what I mean. Those two girls on the other hand, when they come to town, they stick out like a sore thumb. Strange. Uncle Thorsdan never mentioned you."

"What do you mean by 'stick out...?'" Koski began her inquiry, only to be interrupted a second time in mid-sentence.

"I mean that, like you, they aren't from these parts. Oh, they're both pretty enough. One's a classic Oriental beauty. She never talks to anyone but her fairy-partner, and then they talk in some language that's definitely not English. Foreign. Sounds Japanese or Chinese."

Feeling irritated at being repeatedly interrupted, Koski tried again. "Can you describe..."

"Sorry. Can't. Well, won't, really," he said, removing his hand from his hip. Placing both elbows on the table and leaning forward, he whispered conspiratorially, "I *like* my job here, see, and that means 'no gossiping'. I just thought...well, you being alone, and..."

It was Koski's turn to interrupt. The young man's attempt at a pickup was lame. It sounded as if he'd taken it from of an old 1940's movie. "I'm not 'alone', and while I appreciate your concern, I'm more interested in what you can tell me about your 'uncle's' boarders. Especially the Oriental. What...'"

"It's like I said, " he interrupted a fourth time. Looking over his shoulder to the left, then right, and, satisfied no one was watching or listening, he sat down beside her. "I don't want to start any rumors, see, but there was something definitely...*weird*...about them. Both of them. They were like, more than friends, but clearly not sisters or family, if you take my meaning. That reminds me, how exactly are you related?" The waiter paused, clearly expecting an answer.

"What did the Oriental look like?" Koski asked, carefully directing the conversation away from her factitious relationship to his "honorary" uncle back to her interest at hand. "Describe her. How tall is she? How old is she? How much do you think she weighs? Is she tall and thin? Short and stocky? What color are her hair and eyes?"

"Well, like I said, they don't much come to town, and, to be honest, I only really saw them once. Don't know much about the height and weight of the pretty Oriental, but she was shorter than her partner. Maybe a little older, too. I think her hair was black. Yeah. Come to think of it, it was jet black. And combed straight. Don't recall the color of her eyes, but they were suspicious looking. Like those Oriental spies you see in the movies. You know, 'spy-eyes'. Not at all like yours..."

"Yes, well, how about her partner? Can you describe her?" Koski introjected, trying again to keep the focus of the discussion on the two girls.

"Hmm. Well, she wasn't as interesting as the other. Taller. Thinner. Younger. Kinda clingy. She kept watching her partner, as if she needed permission to talk. To me, they looked and sounded like mismatched lovers. But why so much interest in these two? Name's Josh, by the way. People hereabouts say I'm pretty handsome and much more interesting..." Josh extended a hand and, without asking, latched onto Koski's, covering their momentarily joined hands with his other. After nervously looking about, he released her hand, leaving a small piece of paper in it. When Koski looked startled, Josh nodded, ahem'ed and said simply, "Your bill," then stood and walked away.

Examining the actual bill that Josh had earlier placed on the table, Koski reached in her wallet for a fifty and slipped it under the foot of her empty wine glass, clutching the piece of paper her waiter had palmed into her other hand after their brief and marginally helpful conversation.

Outside the restaurant and back in her car, she turned on the overhead car light and opened her hand to examine the tightly-folded piece of paper. When unfolded to eight times it's former size, it boasted a handwritten telephone number and two words: "Call me."

Chapter 16

Stewart was driven to a small private airport to board one of Ceberus' small, private, charter jets. Mister Rellin had called ahead to Cerebrus' chief mechanic, Max, a lanky ex-marine combat officer and aircraft engineer who, once inside an engine space, seemed to sprout two additional hands. Max had jerry-rigged Farraday cages around the engine's computer, radar, GPS and radio to hopefully avert any loss of electricity should the plane pass through an event-wave or an intersection not predicted by computer models. Whether they would work or not was anyone's guess. In fact, predictions about the paths of waves and moment-to-moment number of intersections were growing super-exponentially, and were already taxing the capacity of the Cerebrus' most advanced computational resources.

Stewart's flight to the airport nearest Red River, Montana, was uneventful. Upon arriving in Red River proper, Stewart had barely settled in at the only local motel, when an intersection hit, plunging his room into total darkness. Power, surprisingly, was restored in less than ten seconds. Apparently people in Red River, including the motel, had emergency power generators. And emergency food, emergency water, emergency clothing, as well as emergency guns and ammunition. The parking lot outside the motel restaurant was apparently the *de facto* emergency meeting place, and it suddenly bristled with what looked like a rapidly forming military commando squad composed of rough-hewn survivalists, gathered about several four-wheel drive "monster" trucks.

"What the hell's going on?" asked a man wearing camouflaged body armor, cradling a fully automatic assault rifle in his arms. Stewart watched the man nervously flick the safety on and off, as if suffering from a neurological tick.

"Someone's jerked our power supply. Radios, cell phones, appliances, cars, hell, even our ham radio operators all went temporarily dead."

"Most are up and running again," offered another "commando," apparently their default commander.

"Damn Ruskies!" called out a woman, all in black, brandishing a modified AK-47 in the air. A black head scarf hid her face, revealing only two, red, and to Stewart's trained power of observation, scared eyes. "God-damn..."

"It ain't the Ruskies, Helen," returned the commander, speaking as much to her as to the other twenty or so armed men and women in varying degrees of combat dress. "More likely the Chinese. 'Been waiting for 'em to make a move on the good ol' USA for several decades. If it is them, they're in for one hell-uv-a-surprise if they get this far!"

The crowd shouted back a single loud "Huzzah!" in perfect commando unison.

"An' who the hell are you?" asked the commander, noting

Stewart on the sidelines holding a government-issue pistol at his side, looking like a bewildered child who'd stumbled into a covert military field operation.

"Stewart," he replied curtly. "I'm from Washington." Stewart flashed his wallet identification, then snapped the wallet shut and replaced it in his hip pocket. "I'm here to investigate a power pulse that is said to have originated some time ago in the Red River area. There's no need for weapons..."

"Right," said the commander, smiling laconically while he and the rest of the Red River's self-made soldiers stared at Stewart's gun. "Right..."

"Right," echoed Stewart, replacing the weapon into it's shoulder holster and very slowly pulling out a map, hoping by the action to de-escalate the situation.

The crowd murmured, then began approaching in an ever-closing circle.

Stewart made a show of laying out the government topographic map on the hood of the nearest huge, black, jacked-up, off-road mega-truck. The ninja woman pulled out a military-issue flashlight and shined its beam on the map. "Right here, in fact," he continued, pointing at a spot some distance from where they were gathered.

"That's the Jersey place," a voice volunteered anonymously from within the crowd.

"The Jerseys," the commander repeated, his deprecatory tone revealing that they were not valued members of the elite force surrounding Stewart. "Old Man Jersey and his wife. Their homestead's located right beneath your finger. Those two might as well not exist at all, as they refuse to be part of our militia 'ready force'. Hardly see 'em in town anymore since they took on boarders. One of 'em's a foreigner."

Stewart looked up at a chorus of bobbing heads and yeah's. "What kind of foreigner?" asked Stewart, his interest piqued.

"Oriental. 'The Boss' we call her. Chinese, Japanese, Korean, hell, all 'em Orientals look the same. In this town, we don't like foreigners, period."

"How about the other?" inquired Stewart.

"Nice country girl. American, though not from here. Maybe from Nebraska. She seems to look up to The Boss. Ought to be the other way around, if you ask me," the commander offered. Once again heads bobbed, followed by a chorus of yeah's.

"Could you take me there?" asked Stewart, unsure whether to broach either event or auction details with these people. Stewart's request proved a balm to the mob's frayed nerves. Trigger fingers relaxed. Everyone suddenly seemed interested in helping the "government man."

"Sure," acknowledged their commander. "Frey! Smart! Lexington! Come with me," he barked, signaling them with his hand. "The rest of you go into the restaurant and wait. We'll take my 'horse'," he continued, indicating with his thumb the monster crew-cab truck on the hood of which Stewart's map was positioned.

Quietly refolding the map and replacing it in the inside pocket of his coat, Stewart climbed up into the cab and assumed the passenger seat. Peering behind him, he watched two men slide into the back seat followed by the jihadist-looking woman swathed in black. Each sat stiffly, weapon at ready on his or her lap.

"Name's Greyside," the commander said, offering a large ham of a left hand, it's back covered with wiry black hair, while inserting the truck key into the ignition slot with his right. The behemoth's instant awakening growl, followed by several diesel knocks and another louder growl reminded Stewart of an Abrams tank engine being cold-started. "I'm the leader of the Red River Militiamen..." he chatted, adding quickly after glancing in his rearview mirror, "...and Militia women, of course."

On the way to the farm, Stewart attempted to question the group about the Jerseys but to no avail. To the group, the Jerseys were little more than ignorant homesteaders, and the two girls unwanted foreigners.

Chapter 17

Falk inched his rental car quietly up the driveway of the Hempsted residence. The dilapidated old house with it's boarded up windows somehow looked colder and even more uninviting than before. At first he couldn't put his finger on it, but walking up the rickety steps, it hit him: The front door that Aaron Hempsted had reluctantly cracked open and kept chain-locked throughout their talk on the last visit was now ajar, the door's rusted hinges squeaking ominously with each change in the night breeze. Shoulder against the side of the building to provide the least possible target, Falk called out several times without receiving any response. Carefully removing his automatic from his shoulder holster and slipping off the safety, he grasped the door's edge and called directly inside. Again, no answer except for another hinge squeak, this time caused by Falk's further opening the door.

After his eyes adjusted to the darkness, he noticed a shock of white hair above the back of an easy chair facing away from him.

"Mr. Hempsted. It's Agent Falk," he said working his way through the door and cautiously around to the front of the chair. "I visited you earlier, and was wondering if we might..."

Aaron Hempsted was sitting, head erect, rheumy bloodshot eyes staring fixedly at Falk, his mouth limply agape, his unshaven face even whiter than before. A bloodless hand gripped each of the threadbare chair arms, making it appear as if he were pushing himself back into the seat. A small rivulet of dark, coagulated blood had worked its way alongside his nose and down one cheek from a small, round entry hole in the middle of his forehead. The man's shocked expression was accentuated by a halo of red splattered behind the man's resting head onto a white embroidered doily draped over the back of the easy chair.

Falk squatted, raised his weapon and held it with both hands as he swept the room. Recalling the old man saying that he was renting an upstairs room to two girls, he located a curved stairway and worked his way silently up. As he reached the top, he was startled by a girl's scream followed by a the report of a small-caliber pistol. Crouching on the floor and surveying the dark hallway for where they might have come, he was about to press forward when another report sounded, this time coming without a doubt from behind the first closed door on his left.

Reacting with the trained agility of a professional agent, he sprang forward and assumed a low position, his back flat against the side of the wooden door jamb, gun braced at the ready. As he shifted his weight to smash his way in, the door abruptly flew open. A short body in a billowy chiffon dress exited backwards, bumped into him and bounced back into the room falling on the floor with a loud clump. A cloud of whitish-grey smoke hung shoulder height about the room. The smoke had the familiar, acrid smell of gunpowder.

Sprinting though the now open door and into the room, Falk noticed directly in front of him a young Caucasian girl lying limp on her back in a rapidly enlarging pool of blood, her eyes staring fixedly upward, her forehead pierced with the same telltale hole he'd seen moments ago on Aaron Hempsted's forehead. To his right a slightly older Asian girl was scrambling for a small handgun on the floor. Falk raised his gun and shouted, but the girl was so agile she recovered the weapon before he finished, turned it in her hands to point, not at him but at herself, and pulled the trigger. The girl's body shuddered, then slammed against the right wall, the weapon, a Chinese-made Type 77, dropping to the ground in front of her lifeless body.

Chapter 18

In her car outside the Regent Hotel Cafe in Fulton, Ohio, Koski considered calling the handwritten telephone number she'd been palmed by her nervous waiter, Josh.

The young man was assumedly privy to some information, or, at least, he'd made it sound as if he were, but (and "but" was the operative word here), she had a bad feeling about him. "Call me," the note said, followed by a local phone number. That was all. Reading the words again, it felt to her like an invitation to danger. The lingering sense of danger, and her need to know more about Thorsdan paired with the earlier feeling of frank evilness while at the farm, all shouted caution. Both Josh and the old man had appeared...scared. In her mind she didn't doubt there was a link between the event, the dark farmhouse, the reticent owner, the two boarders, the odd-looking satellite dish, and, call it as she now saw it, Josh's fear.

Nervously fingering her cell phone, Koski reviewed in her mind what she'd learned thus far from Josh: There were two "weird" girls. The first was a black-haired Asian, shorter and older than the second, who was less well described, other than being taller, thinner and "clingy." Maybe frightened. What was it he'd said exactly? "She kept watching the other, as if she needed her permission to talk?" Something like that. The second girl was, then, likely being controlled and could very well be nearly frightened to death. That made both of them especially dangerous.

Koski placed her cell phone on the passenger seat beside her. It would be awhile before Josh finished his shift, and Koski was feeling pressured to find out something—anything—about this second event. Exchanging the cell phone for her rental car keys, she tucked away the phone and inserted the master key into the car's ignition slot. Cautiously turning it recalled the recalcitrant but responsive car to life.

The drive to the Thorsdan farm proved even creepier than her first visit.The long line of weathered fenceposts reminded her of the owner's edginess which had morphed into a definite warning when she'd asked about his boarders.

After clawing up the muddied dirt road to the old farmhouse, the car rattled loudly over the livestock grating, and, as it did, Koski once again experienced that sense of profound silence that had so unnerved her the first time. The animal pens were still empty. The Ford truck she'd noted before, however, was gone.

As she prepared to climb out, she removed her automatic from its shoulder holster, holding it to her side and behind so as not to seem threatening. The farmhouse looked exactly like it did before but darker and more deserted, if that was possible.

Walking sideways up the creaky, wooden porch steps, Koski paused, recalling Old Man Thorsdan's brusque, intimidating manner. Stepping up to the door, she rapped on the screen door. There was no answer, but across the yard, she caught a movement inside the barn out of the corner of an eye.

That might be one of the two female "farm hands" Thorsdan had taken in to help restore the farm in return for free room and board. She wanted to meet and question both, but even more, she wanted to continue her interrogation of the old man. Anything she could get him to reveal would prove helpful when confronting the two girls.

Returning her gaze to the old house against which her shoulder was resting, she did a quick resurvey of the outside, the animal pens, then the barn, noting as before that none showed the slightest sign of restoration. In fact, the farm as a whole looked like it was about to fall apart. Peeking through an open crack in a broken, dirty window, it looked to her like no one was home.

It was then the movement that had caught her eye before repeated itself, this time directing her attention to a long black cable from the roof antenna, thudding loudly against the side of the barn. The wire snaked down the barn and disappeared into a crack in the siding where Koski assumed the two boarders kept the video game equipment about which Old Man Thorsdan had so vociferously complained.

Noting that, she returned her attention to where the old pickup truck had been parked. The bales of hay that had been in its bed were sitting haphazardly to the right and left of a set of bald tire marks which stretched on down to the approach road. Whoever drove the truck must have left very recently, she thought, given the clarity of the tire impressions, either carrying something else in its bed or having emptied it in anticipation of picking up something. Given the state of the house, she assumed the driver was Thorsdan. If indeed the old man had left, there would be no further advantage in waiting to talk with the girls.

The wind picked up, ruffling her hair and cracking the cable smartly against the side of the distant barn.

Abandoning the house, Koski crept cautiously to the front of the barn, where she located a chin-high open window and peered in, searching for where the cable entered.

It was difficult to make out anything in the darkness except the slightly blacker silhouettes of a large table with what looked like a pile of boxes on it. A moment later, her eyes adjusted enough for her to see that the boxes covered only half of the table and were, in fact, individual electronic devices dotted with scales, knobs and switches. *An odd collection and arrangement of video game boxes*, she thought. None appeared to be turned on. Scanning the room, she saw no signs of movement, so she slipped in.

What she saw as she cautiously approached the table piqued her immediate interest: The labels on the electronic devices were mostly handwritten in what looked like Chinese characters. What she saw next sent chills down her spine: Each "box" had two bullet holes in it. Walking closer, she tripped over something that chilled her even more: a wooden chair lying on its back in the dirt cradling the limp body of a young girl. The girl's face was turned away to the side, but there was little question about her state. She, like each of the electronic boxes, had been the recipient of two slugs. Koski checked for a neck pulse, and feeling none, did a cursory survey of the body, realizing in the process she was standing in a pool of bloody mud.

Her senses heightened and her mind now on high alert, Koski crouched low and swept the room. Seeing no movement, she slipped quickly from the body to the side of the table and, gun braced in both hands, once again swept the interior of the barn for any sign of the second boarder.

There was no indication of life anywhere. The only sound was the continued slap, slap, slap of the cable line outside, the end of which Koski quickly ascertained was lying loose on the table, no longer hooked up to any of the deceased electronic devices.

Leaving the barn, she backtracked to enter the farmhouse. On entering the kitchen, it hit her: Crotchety Old Mr. Thorsdan was sitting in a kitchen chair on the other side of a square kitchen table, head thrown back, hands hanging down limply on either side of the chair. Behind him, the sink, cabinets and stove door were splattered with darkening blood and tissue. The man's face was staring wide-eyed directly towards heaven, having one, small, round, entry hole in the middle of his forehead. Koski did a quick search of the kitchen, but found nothing in there or in the adjacent living room that could shed any further light on what had happened. A careful examination of the rest of the house revealed nothing extraordinary.

Piecing together what she could, it seemed to her that whoever had shot the girl in the barn must have first shot Thorsdan. There being no signs of struggle on either body and the shots being delivered at very close range, it was likely that the shooter was known to each. That the barn table was only half loaded with "murdered" equipment suggested to Koski that some of the equipment had left the scene probably with the second houseguest, not long ago in the bay of the old, grey-primer-coated Ford. Her principal worry at the moment was if and when the shooter would return to pick up the rest of the equipment.

Satisfied she had extracted everything she could for the moment, Koski placed a call to the local police, and described the scene to the female policewoman who had earlier accompanied her to the Thorsdan farm, promising at the policewoman's insistence to return to her car and stay alert until help arrived. The officer assured her she would put out an All Points Bulletin for a Ford pickup driven by a young Oriental female.

Koski, however, did not return to her car as promised. Instead, she returned to the barn to examine more closely the equipment and the satellite dish.

The equipment was definitely exotic in nature. It all appeared custom made, some labels looking like they had been created with a Chinese-character label-maker and hastily stuck on. It would take an expert to figure out what each of the units was designed to do, and that would require alerting Cerebrus as soon as she checked out the antenna. She needed to give them as accurate and comprehensive a field description as possible.

Climbing a ladder into the loft, she opened the loft window to gain entrance to the roof and examine the antenna dish. In doing so, Koski noticed in the distance a set of headlights bobbing along the approach road. Given that it was was not flashing red lights, she surmised it was the old Ford truck with the Oriental.

The antenna would have to wait. It was too late to hide her parked rental car. For now, the best she could do was to locate a secure place from which she could observe and, if necessary, defend herself against what was, by all accounts, an exceptionally dangerous, professional killer.

Chapter 19

The black, half-bed, crew-cab truck, it's six over-cab floodlights ripping through the darkness, jostled along the dirt side-road that led to the Jersey's. Stewart's teeth chattered as the truck barreled down the washboard road. Hitting a pothole, he and the Red River Militia flew into the air. Greyside, the driver and militia commander quickly ground the monster machine into low four-wheel drive to avoid losing further control and they plowed through the deeply muddied ruts that on the surface looked like long, narrow lakes of brackish black water.

"Hold on!" the commander yelled.

The next moment, Stewart, Frey, Smart and Lexington were again airborne, the latter three a mixture of flying limbs and weapons. Frey and Lexington seemed to be enjoying the moment. Smart, sitting between the two muscle-bound men, swore quietly to herself that she'd never travel with the Keystone Cops again.

Stewart, despite the jostling, maintained his focus and concentration on his mission to investigate the isolated homestead from which the most recent event was calculated to have emanated.

"The Jersey place," a gritty male voice volunteered from behind Stewart, laying a hand on Stewart's left shoulder and pointing with the other to the right of the road where, outside of the cone of light from the headlights and over-cab floodlights, everything looked opaque black.

An instant later, Greyside snapped off all the lights, and brought the truck to a stop in front of what looked like two log cabins in the middle of a forest clearing.

"The Jerseys," the commander repeated, pointing at the closer of the two lightless cabins swallowed whole by the moonless night. "Macintosh Jersey, his wife, Elaine, an' those two foreign girls I told you about." Climbing out of the cab, he barked, "Frey! Lexington! You're with me. Smart! You're wing and point man, er, woman, for our government man here! I'm counting on you to make sure nothing bad happens to him!"

Wrapped entirely in black, the woman looked like a pair of

floating, disembodied, demonic eyes against the background of darkness. Shifting on her seat, she snapped a clip into what Stewart had earlier identified as a frankly illegal, fully automatic, Russian-made assault rifle, then grunted.

In seconds, the three men had deployed soundlessly about the nearer cabin, weapons at ready. Stewart slid out of the truck with Smart, his "point-and-wing-woman" following several steps behind him. Crouching against a large tree trunk twenty-feet from the first cabin, Stewart paused to assess the situation.

The cabin's far windows were shuttered, but the ones to either side of the log door weren't, being only curtain-closed from the inside. There were no signs of life, but it was late at night and Stewart felt certain from the cabins' rustic appearance that the Jersey's didn't do much socializing after sunset.

As his eyes adjusted to the darkness, individual pinpoint of stars began to appear above him, then more and more, until the sky-dome above looked like it was splattered with bags of crushed diamonds, some running together into a swath of what truly looked like spilled milk. Living in Washington DC for over twenty years, he'd forgotten what the night sky looked like behind the constant hazy illumination produced by the nation's energetic capital. Following the outer rim of the Big Dipper constellation that pointed without fail to the North Star, he noticed below the pole star the dark nondescript outline of the smaller second cabin.

The presence of the smaller cabin emphasized the size of the larger, nearer one, it's expected silhouette broken by an exotic looking satellite dish pointing low to the horizon. *Interesting*, he was thinking, when a flash appeared in the corner of the window to the right of the first cabin's door. He heard a thup behind him, then a deafening report that echoed into every corner of the night.

Looking behind, Stewart watched his point-and-wing-woman fall hard and lifeless onto the forest floor.

Before Stewart could call out to Greyside, all hell broke loose. Flashes, thumps and reports erupted from seemingly everywhere, a whiz of bullets surrounding him. Falling flat on the ground, he retrieved his automatic from his shoulder holster and was about to brace and fire when the flashes, whizzes, thumps and bangs all abruptly stopped.

Stewart waited, expecting to see the outline of Greyside, Frey or Lexington approach the cabin doors or creep back to the truck.

Neither occurred.

Instead, absolute darkness and quiet once again prevailed. Crawling backwards to where Smart had fallen, the head of Cerebrus felt her unmoving neck for a pulse. Finding none, he lay beside her and thought hard about what to do next.

There was no movement he could see inside or outside either cabin. The silence that had re-engulfed him was heightened by the heightening sigh of the night wind working its way through the tops of nearby pines, including the one behind which he had crouched and then judiciously abandoned.

After what seemed hours but what was likely only be minutes, Stewart began inching his way further behind the dead woman, hoping to use her body as a shield between himself and the cabins. Having accomplished the task, he called out, "Mr. and Mrs. Jersey —Macintosh! Elaine!—I don't know what just happened, but I'm a...a scientist with the...Montana State Department of Natural Resources," Stewart fabricated as he talked. "I was sent here to find out about a...freak electrical disturbance...reported to have occurred in this area."

Waiting patiently, hearing no answer and seeing no signs of

movement, he allowed himself to shiver from the cold that was already penetrating his clothing, and continued with his *ad hoc* "explanation," hoping it would make just enough sense to whoever heard it to say something. Anything.

"I've been sent to make sure you and your boarders are okay."

Again, no reply. No sound or movement anywhere other than the now continuous sigh of cold night air working its way from the tops of the trees to where he was lying. Unable to think of anything further to say, Stewart decided to change tack. "Greyside! Frey! Lexington! Anybody!"

Again, no reply. Stewart slipped his cell phone out of his pocket and speed-dialed Cerebrus headquarters. Immediately after the first buzz, a reassuring female voice answered: "The James' residence."

"Code five-four," Stewart answered, repeating it again a moment later as protocol required.

After a click and a brief pause, a male voice replied, "Is this an emergency, Sir?"

"I really don't know. There's been a firefight at Thunderbolt. I repeat, a firefight at Thunderbolt."

"Are you in need of assistance or extraction, Sir?"

"What I need is for you to direct an infrared eye over the area where I am and tell me what you see."

"Yes, Sir," came the immediate reply, and several minutes later, "We see one 'hot' life-form on the ground lying prone next to a 'cold' one…"

"The hot one would be me, the other, Smart, a militia woman who accompanied me here and was shot dead," Stewart interrupted.

"…with three more 'cold' lifeforms outside either end of two small wooden structures. Inside the structure nearest you there appear to be four more 'cold' lifeforms. Wait, one is only borderline 'cold'. It's hard to tell for sure when looking through a roof. There are none, 'hot' or 'cold', inside the structure furthest from you. Behind you is what looks to be an empty SUV..."

"Thanks," Stewart interrupted. "That's all I needed. I'm going to inspect the first structure. I'll get back to you after that. Code five-four out."

Moments later, shoulder against the door of the first cabin, his body aligned to project the least possible target, Stewart called out several more times, each time receiving no response. Having sufficiently announced his presence in the most benevolent manner he could come up with, he gripped his automatic in his right hand and pressed his other hand hard against the door. The door swung open, and he called out a final time. Yet again, no answer.

He didn't enter, however.

Instead, after allowing his eyes to adjust to the even darker cabin interior, he peeked carefully from the lower corner of the doorway. "Mr. Jersey? Mrs, Jersey? My name is Stewart. I'm a representative of the Montana State Department of Natural Resources. I was asked to investigate an unusual electrical outage. I'm just checking to make sure you and your boarders are okay." It remained a flimsy explanation at best, but, as field protocol dictated, he would continue with it. "Mr. Jersey? Mrs. Jersey," he repeated, working his body slowly sidewise through the narrow doorway opening into the cabin.

The two now open-curtained windows on either side of the door offered no light, but his eyes, having already become accustomed to darkness, he could vaguely make out a log cabin interior with sparse wood furnishings: a rough picnic table with attached benches on the far side of the cabin, a smoldering wood stove, a tin sink with a hand water pump. There were two open doorways on the far wall, each presumably leading to a bedroom. He could just make out two adult-sized bodies sitting at the picnic-table, each slumped awkwardly forward. On the floor between the wood stove and sink, next to an orderly stack of wood was a smaller unmoving body. Stewart couldn't make out any chest rise or fall. These would be the three "cold" bodies. So where was the...

A shadow moved out from the right bedroom doorway and disappeared behind the far side of the picnic table. Stewart crouched and braced his weapon, pointing it at the place where the shadow disappeared. "I didn't come here to hurt anyone. I'm here to check and make sure everyone is okay. If you'll just..."

Three flashes from behind the table were followed by the zing of three bullets passing immediately to his left. Stewart fell flat on the floor, re-braced his weapon and squeezed off two shots into the darkness just above where he suspected one of the two boarders to be hiding.

"Those were warning shots!" he yelled loudly. "Put down your weapon and let's talk..." He was interrupted by three more flashes in quick succession from behind the table, followed by three dull thuds in the wall where he'd been crouching a moment ago. Whoever it was had a small caliber semi-automatic pistol, assumedly the same Type 77 that the other Oriental agents had. Assuming it hadn't been reloaded, that left, at most, one bullet, in the chamber.

Stewart rolled silently to the side, re-braced and was about to speak again when, hearing the click of an ammunition clip being replaced, he sprang forward, gun leveled directly at the barely perceptible shadow-form in front of him. A quick sweep with his weapon-hand knocked the gun and two clips from his assailant's hands across the floor. Pointing his automatic between the whites of two youthful but scared Oriental looking eyes, he said, "It's over. I told you, I'm just here to help. Now stand. Slowly. I don't want to shoot, but I will if you make me."

The shaking figure slowly unraveled itself and stood before him revealing a very frightened Oriental youth in her early 20's, her narrow ferret-like eyes darting from Stewart to every object and corner of the room. Moving slowly to his left, Stewart picked up the impotent weapon and balanced it in his hand inspecting it with two quick glances. "Chinese made Type 77," he confirmed. As he spoke, the girl sprang towards the door, only to trip over Stewart's suddenly outstretched leg, and fall smartly face down onto the floor.

"We really need to talk," Stewart said, indicating with the barrel of his gun a lone wooden chair sitting against the far wall between the two open bedroom doors.

Chapter 20

"Talk," Stewart repeated firmly, but before she could begin, his cell phone interrupted.

The girl stared at Stewart, squirming uncomfortably, a desperate wildness in her eyes while he listened to the voice on the other end of his phone and watched her closely.

When Stewart signed off, he returned his full attention to his captive, beginning his field interrogation with a test of her English. "There's been...an electrical problem reported. I was sent here to make sure everyone was okay. I'm here to protect you. Do you understand? I'm here to protect..."

His question was cut short when her squirming abruptly stopped. Her body became rigid, and she pointed her chin haughtily up towards the rough-hewn ceiling.

"So you *do* understand me?" Stewart half-asked, half-stated. "Okay, let's start with a name. As I said, my name's Stewart. I'm here to protect you, but I need to know who you are and from what exactly I am protecting you. Can you tell me? Do you have a name?"

"Dah Choo-Tow," the girl replied icily.

"Is that your name?" Stewart asked.

"Dah Choo-Tow," the girl repeated.

"Okay, Dah Choo-Tow, I need to know what happened here."

"American mother, father, wake us. 'Soldiers outside,' they say. Mother and Father say, 'Go into bedroom.' We sit quiet on bed. We hear noise outside. Father Jersey, he get gun and shoot out window. Kill all soldiers but one, I think." The corners of Dah Choo-Tow's mouth thinned and her eyes widened as if reliving the event. "Soldier...he shoot Father, then Mother, then Mary. Try shoot me. I shoot him first." Tears began flowing.

Stewart was certain Dah Choo-Tow, if that was, in fact, her real name, was doing exactly what he had been doing a few moments ago while lying outside in the dirt using Smart's lifeless body as cover: constructing a cover story on-the-fly.

"I think not," Stewart replied, offering the girl a second chance.

"I...I...scared. Maybe happen different. Can't think. I guess..."

"I'm guessing that you're making this all up," Stewart interrupted, waving the handgun she had pointed at him only moments ago. "Let's start over and try again, beginning with this weapon."

The girl abruptly stopped crying. Her eyes narrowed and in the next instant she exploded from her seat, spinning and directing a heel, like lightening, at the center of Stewart's chest. The thud of the impact should have filled the room. Instead, Stewart reflexively thrust his gun arm forward, barely deflecting the foot-thrust, and, dropping both weapons, locked his fingers about the base of her wrist. With a twist, he knocked her off balance. The girl screamed in pain and fury.

"Let's start again," Stewart said, shaken, calmly picking his gun up from the floor while continuing to hold her wrist in the paralyzing one-handed Aikido hold.

The girl tried to struggle, but, realizing that even the smallest movement elicited incredible pain, immediately stopped. Acknowledging defeat, she relaxed. Stewart guided her back onto the chair. "So, once again, Dah Choo-Tow, I need to know what really was going on here."

A gust of wind rustled the leaves outside and rattled a window. The girl startled in her seat, a look of unbridled fear flushing her face. "I can not tell you that," she replied in perfect international English. "If I did, I would soon be as dead as they are," she said, inclining her head towards the bodies in the cabin. Continuing, in the same breath she said, "You can not protect me. Not now. No one can."

Stewart listened with growing interest. And concern.

"No one can!" she repeated more forcefully with a sob. Then after a pause, "Can you?"

"I don't know. I can't until I know what is going on, Dah Choo-Tow."

The girl paused as if thinking. "Dah Choo-Tow' means 'Die, Pig!" and, in another sudden burst of energy, she threw herself directly at Stewart. To his horror, he felt his gun ripped from his hand. The next moment, she placed its point in her mouth, and, before he could react, pulled the trigger.

The explosion was deafening. Her young body flew against the back of the chair.

"Damn!" he shouted to himself, realizing that the person he had been attempting to interrogate had been a highly-trained and utterly dedicated professional. Laying the limp form aside, he wiped the blood splatters from his hands onto his pants, searched for and located a lantern, lit it and began inspecting her and the other bodies in the room. All, it appeared, had met their death at the hands of an expert using the weapon he'd obtained from her, and she used on herself.

It was, then, she who killed everyone in the room, he mentally summarized.

Searching the room, he found two thirty-aught-six caliber hunting rifles with military grade sniper scopes, one beneath each of the two open windows. Both had been recently fired based on the sharp smell emanating from their breaches. This was confirmed by the presence of twelve, large, empty casings littered about on the floor. Mr. Jersey's trigger finger and the right side of his face showed faint powder marks, presumably from firing one of the rifles. The same was true of the other girl, "Mary." Mr. and Mrs. Jersey, he surmised, had, in the end, in the process of "defending" themselves, somehow gotten in the way of whatever the two girls were up to.

From a cursory examination of the room, Stewart guessed that the Jersey's were indeed rural survivalists. They'd probably heard the SUV approach, and, for some reason, both Mr. Jersey and Mary, if that was indeed her real name, had donned rifles and began expertly picking off the militia and very nearly him. That strongly suggested that Mary was more than just a "farm girl from Nebraska." The incidents, in light of Mr. Jersey and the girls' behavior, elevated the events in Stewart's mind to acts of terrorism, and given that the Chinese girl had been the sole initial survivor, quite probably a carefully planned act perpetrated by China. Either way, he had to get in contact with the Joint Chiefs, Falk, Koski and Rellin, and return to Cerebrus headquarters as quickly as possible with the odd electrical equipment he'd noticed shoved haphazardly under one of the beds, and he needed to do it quickly. In that order. And now!

Chapter 21

Back in Washington DC, Cerebrus and NSA computer experts were working around-the-clock, nervously anticipating a fourth event, predicting that if the current pattern held, it would occur somewhere in western or central Washington state.

The large, multi-screen situation board displayed the three current event epicenters. About them were thousands of red dots. The dots ranged in diameter from pinpoints to half-inch, most individual but some amalgamated, the whole forming rings of concentric red circles about the event epicenters. The boldness of the dots and the lines reflected the number of deaths and injuries. Millions of softer grey points, representing unconfirmed reports of incidents created a disturbing surreal background. The current focus of this shift of analysts, computer specialists and electrical engineers wasn't so much on the three epicenters, however, or the rapidly growing and coalescing dots, as it was the points where the expanding rings intersected. Wherever event echo rings from separate events intersected, the resulting damage was far in excess of what each's diminishing power would predict.

While hotly arguing and re-arguing the physics of what they were observing and its implications regarding the nature of the originating events, the eastern portion of Washington state began pulsing a pale yellow, and a date-and-time stamp appeared in its upper right corner, indicating, based on accumulated information, the broad area-location of the anticipated fourth epicenter. The fact that they could predict and sound an area alert at all offered some small reassurance, and allowed area authorities to prepare. To everyone's consternation, Spokane was located in the exact center of the area alert. A vibrant city of 250,000, a major United States Air Force Strategic Air Command base was located less than twelve miles away.

As this realization sunk in, debate stopped. No one was willing to offer an opinion about what this might portend, but it was clear from the resulting murmurs that everyone was concerned that if the actual epicenter occurred in or anywhere near a large urban center like Spokane, the new event would likely demand application of all available city, state and federal resources. That would leave few available for the next event, which, if the pattern held, was already being predicted to occur in or around Seattle, Washington (unlikely, given the relatively short distance between Seattle and Spokane); San Francisco, Los Angeles, San Diego or Anchorage (again unlikely, as they would represent a significant North/South shift in direction); leaving Honolulu, Hawaii the most likely fifth epicenter.

Seconds later, a new flashing dot appeared, as feared, ten miles outside of Spokane, Washington. At the same time, reports began coming in regarding the presence of the anticipated auction, this time for possession of the Western non-coastal states. Though things were looking bleak, a cheer arose in the room when Colonel

Rellin announced they'd finally narrowed down the auction source and some of the BitCoin bid locations and the albeit circuitous internet pathway being used. Both the previous and current auction were relayed through multiple complex networks of TOR-related Internet Service Providers, ISPs, scattered all over the world. The initial sell offer, it was back-calculated, had most likely originated from somewhere near the Russian/Chinese/North Korean border. Bids had originated from hundreds of different areas around the world, the exact points of origin of all of the bids still being determined. With this information in hand, Rellin's experts could now state with certainty that three times a major financial exchange had indeed taken place, and with the anticipated fourth transaction, the absurdity of "buying" regions of the USA had reluctantly congealed into a still formless but overarching fear of, when all the transactions were completed, what would be the result and its additive effect.

It was at this point Colonel Rellin excused himself to take two urgent phone calls first, from the Chairman of the Joint Chiefs of Staff, and then, on hold, from Cerebrus field agent Joseph Falk.

Chapter 22

Stewart's first call had been to General Richard Cavors, the tall, aloof, acerbic Chairman of the Joint Chiefs of Staff. General Cavors received Stewart's information politely and respectfully, but with audible disbelief. There wasn't time for Stewart to ask why, but it seemed likely it involved the General being privy to information he was reticent to share at this time.

Disappointed but nonplussed, Stewart, like all players in an ascending "need to know" organization, accepted the situation for what it was, trusting General Cavors would share what he, Stewart, had provided with the other chiefs of staff, and would, when appropriate, share back with Cerebrus the apparently restricted information to which Cavors alone was apparently privy.

Next he called Falk, Falk's site being the first, and Falk having had the most time to investigate. What Stewart heard was troubling.

"Falk," his number one Cerebrus agent answered.

"Report, Joe," Stewart ordered.

"Not good, sir. When I returned to the Hempsted farm, I found Aaron Hempsted in the living room, a bullet through his head. It was a professional job. I searched upstairs for the two female boarders, and heard a scream followed by gunshots. A young Caucasian girl had been killed, or rather, executed, in the same way as Aaron Hempsted. The second, a young Asian girl, supposedly the murderer, shot herself before I could stop her."

"God Almighty!" Stewart exclaimed, shocked at how similar their investigative field experiences had been. "Any suggestion of what they were up to? Any idea how this might relate to the events and auctions? And any idea if the satellite dish you mentioned might be involved?"

"I'm going on the assumption my two girls worked as a team," Falk replied. "The Asian's weapon was an older Chinese-made, 7.62 millimeter Type 77 semi-automatic, the preferred weapon some years ago of the Chinese intelligence community. I'm again assuming she murdered Hempsted, then her partner, then, being the leader and surprised by me, shot herself to avoid being taken and interrogated. What she would have done had I not surprised her, and where she would have gone afterwards are, at this point, pure conjecture; however, I'm going to guess her next action would have been to destroy what looks like a number of very unusual custom-made receivers that I found in their room. All are physically inter-connected, the whole being attached by a wire to the outside satellite dish.

"There were no commercial marks on the equipment or the dish, although there are some labels written in what appears to be Chinese" he continued. "As I said, both equipment and antenna appear custom-made. Looking over the equipment, my best guess is that it represents some kind of advanced EMF generator. Except, of course, that wouldn't fit what we're seeing in terms of the 'echoes'. No, not an EMF generator. Something different. Something incredibly more sophisticated. The receivers, if that's what they are and antenna look quite complex, and I'm guessing that the core electronics are distributed between the units and antenna. That is, they are integral parts of a single device, making it difficult for someone acquiring any one part to ascertain the actual manner in which the event was generated. It all smacks of a very sophisticated job by the Chinese, or by someone using Chinese-made or, at the least, Chinese acquired resources. Alternatively, they could be meant to *implicate* the Chinese..."

"Make arrangements to ship everything to Cerebrus," Stewart said, "and I'll call in our best electronic geniuses. By the way, how do you think the Chinese or whoever else is behind this, got hold of this kind of technology when we don't have it? Or do we?" Stewart continued, thinking out loud about General Cavors' reluctance to share, and, after a pause, adding, "Koski is investigating at the second event epicenter..."

"The Asian was a professional. Tell Koski..."

"I'll notify her immediately," Stewart interrupted. "In the meantime, as I said, package up the equipment, including the unusual antenna, and have it all sent to Cerebrus Ops Central and notify Colonel Rellin when it's on its way. By the time the equipment gets here, General Cavors of the Joint Chiefs of Staff will have advised him of what we've collectively found and ordered Rellin and our staff to figure out some way to defend against this technology."

Stewart clicked off and speed-dialed Koski. What he heard was even more disturbing.

"Koski," came the familiar female voice on the other end of the connection.

"Stewart here. I've just talked with Falk. I need your report."

"Is he..."

"Yes," Stewart responded with audible compassion. "He's fine." In the momentary pause, Stewart heard Koski let out a soft sigh. "But I need to know everything you've found out, Susan. Now!"

"On a tip from an anxious hotel waiter, I revisited the Thorsdan farm. I knew there was something wrong when I saw bales of hay I had noticed before in the back of an old pickup truck dropped haphazardly into the mud, and no truck. No farmer would leave stockfeed laying in the mud like that.

"I decided to check out the barn's satellite antenna like Falk indicated he was planning to do in Laplacia. Walking alongside what appeared to be a deserted barn, I located the cable running through a crack in siding. Inside the barn was a table covered with a number of interconnected electronic boxes. The equipment looked handmade and the labels appeared to be in Chinese. On closer inspection, each unit was heavily damaged, shot through several times. It also appeared from a number of clean 'squares' on the tabletop that half of the equipment was gone. In the center of the floor was a tall, thin, Caucasian girl. She'd been shot once in the forehead and a second time from behind. All very professional."

Koski paused a moment to regain her composure and force the image of the girl's devastated head and face from her mind.

"I left the barn and checked out the farm house. There I found Thorsdan tied to a chair, killed in a similar manner. The second girl wasn't there. Assuming the frightened hotel waiter's description correct, she's a short, black-haired Oriental. I'm guessing she's using the truck to dispose of the equipment. I called the local police, then climbed up onto the barn roof to check out the antenna as I'd originally intended. While doing so, the truck returned, presumably to pick up the rest of damaged equipment."

Again Koski paused.

"And?" Stewart asked impatiently.

"I tried to capture her, but the moment she saw me running towards the truck, she shot herself."

Chapter 23

"Sir?" asked Colonel Rellin, holding the receiver of the "red" landline phone stiffly to his ear as if listening and saluting the voice on the other end of the line. General Richard Cavors, the Chairman of the United States' Joint Chiefs of Staff "humpfed" in confirmation. Cavors had just finished updating him on the information he'd received from Stewart, and informed the NSA liaison officer in no uncertain terms that it was absolutely necessary to expedite things or there'd soon be no reason left to do so.

"Our military and civilian resources are being rapidly exhausted," Cavors warned. "Civil unrest is on the rise, to the point of anarchy in some regions. An hour from now, the President will announce nation-wide martial law. Our most immediate problem, however, is we still haven't come up with an effective military response. Basically, no one has yet claimed responsibility for the situation. In short, there's no one for us to defend against or fight except our own citizens!"

"Sir. Are you saying the President is about to declare a state of 'war' against an unidentified enemy?" Colonel Mike Rellin asked, eyes widening, lines of worry cutting into his usually boyish face.

"Immediately after the first event," Cavors continued in a strained voice, "the President tasked my group with determining the endgame behind these 'events' and 'auctions'. Unfortunately, my colleagues and I still can't agree whether what's going on constitutes an 'untoward technical phenomena', a 'new kind of hack,' a 'malicious, coordinated terrorist attack' a prelude to war or an actual act of war, and, if the latter, by whom, how and why. The older, more persuasive members are certain our long time 'enemy', Russia, is somehow behind it all and are talking of advising the President to consider a tactical pre-emptive nuclear strike against Russia before our nuclear arsenal becomes inoperative."

"Russia?" echoed Rellin hollowly, stunned that the Joint Chiefs would perseverate on Russia, and that they were considering a "nuclear solution" with all that would likely encompass not just the two warring countries, but the entire world. "Has everyone gone crazy?" Rellin asked.

"Careful, Colonel. That kind of remark might be taken by someone other than me as insubordination or even outright treason. Most of the joint chiefs see today's world as an extension of the cold war turned hot. You've got to remember, they're from the 1960s through the 1990s and have seen Russia repeatedly act the master puppeteer. An hour ago they were arguing whether a tactical nuclear response even *could* stop the events, and whether we would be remembered by the world as defenders or aggressors. I don't share their opinion about Russia, and the longer I listen, the more I fear that if I can't identify who's really behind it and fast, Russia will by default become the enemy. It doesn't help that we've had no word—no word at all—from the Russians. One chief suggests they're trying to force America into the same kind of *perestroika/glasnost* situation the former Soviet Union faced before breaking up. It seems like nothing would please their current President, the ruling party, military and regional moguls more than to see the United States of America dissolve into pieces like the former Soviet Union did."

"An American 'restructuring'," murmured Rellin, stunned even further. "It does make an odd sort of sense. Our nation has been torn these past years by one after another reactionary splinter group attempting to foist their way of thinking on the public as a whole. Whether one calls it the a Conservative revival, the re-emergence of the 'Old Southern Confederacy', 'White Supremacy,' 'Fascism' or a 'Second American Revolution', it's a reflection of a nation being forced to redefine itself. Are the Joint Chiefs thinking that a consortium of disaffected American splinter groups with or without the assistance of organized crime might be behind these phenomena, with Russia behind them?"

The line fell silent in Rellin's hand. General Cavors, obviously not wanting to go there, replied instead, "Unless your group can clarify the source of the threat, or at least come up with an effective defense against these 'events', Russia, I'm afraid, will very soon cease to exist, and, in its wake, possibly the entire civilized world."

"That's a heavy responsibility to place on my people, Sir. We've been working around the clock in a co-ordinated, inter-agency effort to do just that."

"And...?"

"The shared thinking here *at the moment*," he ventured cautiously, "is that it might actually be China rather than Russia."

"China?" asked Cavors in a flat voice. "A nation of workers led by a business-suited Communist bureaucracy? A nation so out of touch with its people, it no longer knows what's going on within its nation and its people? No, The Joint Chiefs wouldn't buy that China has sufficient interest at this time in covertly planning and launching such a dangerous operation, or having at its disposal the advanced technology that's being employed here. Hell, in their mind, China's leaders are on the verge of becoming rich, just like ours. You might better invoke the 'Big Conspiracy Theory' that everyone, inside and outside the USA, who, for one reason or another, hates us or what we stand for, is secretly colluding to bring us down. Listen, Rellin, if there's one task the United States has been consistently good at over the years, it's intelligence gathering, and there's been nothing on the 'whisper network' indicative of any kind of Chinese conspiracy real or shadow. No, the Joint Chiefs think it's got to be Russia. As far as the observation that most of the equipment you've gathered has labels in Chinese, and the *agents provocateur* are of Oriental extraction, the Joint Chiefs think it's all just too obvious. It's so obvious, they think it's more likely Russia framing China. Our current thinking is that Russia would benefit both directly and indirectly from a war between us and China, irrespective of who 'wins."

"So...?" Colonel Rellin asked.

"So, I need you to ramp up your efforts and *prove* it is or isn't Russia, so we will have someone concrete to fight. If you don't, and I mean soon, my group will certainly lay the blame on Russia and recommend initiating plans to..."

"I understand," Rellin replied with determined finality. "Every agency here will do what's necessary to work the problem and get you the answer you need."

Chapter 24

Stewart's dead captive hadn't provided her real name. Or her mission. Or for whom she was working. He had obviously interrupted her while she was trying to clean up after the event that had occurred in the cabin in the woods just before the militia and he arrived. Even so, despite the briefness of the interrogation, he'd noted the Chinese weapon she was carrying, and, was certain, despite her perfect Chinese, from the inflection of her voice, she was not really Chinese. From what little she'd said, she sounded to him more Korean than Chinese. Invoking his linguistic skills, he would say North Korean, if he had to hazard a guess.

As much as he wanted to, he knew he couldn't safely conclude anything just yet. A Chinese weapon, while suspicious, didn't *guarantee* that the Chinese were behind any of what was going on. The Type-77 was an old issue and while still in use by some Chinese foreign agents, was no longer standard issue, having been replaced by the larger magazine, 9 millimeter QSZ-92 Type 92 semi-automatic. The gun could be a plant. And international spy agencies today typically recruited potential agents to fit specific requirements for a specific action. Even if she was Chinese or North Korean, that wasn't sufficient to implicate either. Worse yet, her North Korean roots could be a ploy by China to misdirect attention *away* from it and towards North Korea. No, he couldn't directly implicate anyone. Not yet.

On the other hand, in the bigger scheme of things, unlike the heated *military* encounters that were recurring between the United States and Russia throughout the world, *tensions* between China and the United States were always smoldering despite one after another "goodwill" gesture or cooperative agreement. And as for North Korea, it seemed be forever verbally provoking the United States and its partners, trying to goad them into action, and recently, this had become increasingly so. With the announcement of new and ever stricter United States initiated and supported sanctions, North Korea's usual hyperbole had escalated to venomous threats of mass destruction.

Still, the public was constantly being reminded on the hourly news of the increasing number and severity of Russian 'interventions' throughout the world. Was it any wonder then that top level military strategists were inclined to conclude that Russia was secretly attempting to resurrect a new USSR, or worse, in retribution, attempting to force the USA into a *perestroika/glasnost* of it's own? Such constant, high-visibility altercations could also serve as perfect cover distractions for China, or North Korea for that matter, to advance their own secret agendas. Also, since the United States had became more and more embroiled in containing Russian-supported insurgencies throughout the world, US and NATO alert levels had successively increased, with Russia following suit, most likely with China secretly laughing while North Korea egged all three nations on from behind.

Irrespective of who or what was behind the events and auctions and why, it was evident to Stewart that the three dead "Oriental" girls and their three American assistants or girlfriends were part of a larger cohesive plan. That the Oriental's role was significant could be deduced from the fact that their American "helpers" were, from the beginning, expendable. The Oriental he'd encountered knew something important, or she wouldn't have been so frightened of his offer of protection. What had she said? "You can not protect me. No one can." That suggested that they had handlers or supervisors probably located not far away. The capture of a handler, supervisor or even a live Oriental agent if possible had to become Stewart's new priority.

General profiles describing two female "students," one Oriental, the other Caucasian, boarding with an elderly American whose house had a new or "unusual" satellite antenna, were sent to all agency representatives converging on the predicted next event site along with a warning that the girls were to be assumed armed, dangerous and quite willing to kill. That said, it was of highest priority to capture rather than kill them and anyone in any way associated with them for further interrogation.

"What news?" asked an exhausted looking Stewart of Cerebrus' current shift Information Control Officer, after having returned from Montana.

"So far, nothing more," the equally exhausted Information Officer replied. "You're aware that the equipment you sent went down with the plane?"

"Wha...?" began Stewart.

"The Faraday cages didn't work. Apparently you were lucky to get there and back alive. Still, we have the equipment sent to us by your two agents, and, despite the equipment being custom-designed, and some of it being missing and some of it having been shot through several times, we're slowly piecing them together an aggregate whole."

"We don't have much time," Stewart half-thought, half-replied, sifting in his mind every bit of information he'd thus far gleaned. His best efforts unfortunately continued to refuse to yield anything actionable.

What he did know at this point was that it wasn't the events, but the fluid intersections of event-echoes that were doing the most damage, and that their number continued increasing. Every added event carried with it the promise of a massive number of new potential intersections. The more intersections, the more damage, with no upper limit in sight.

Two events created a predictable intersection pattern, three, within hours, required the best supercomputers the United States to predict intersections and issue warning to the citizenry. Add the fourth event and there were so many possible intersections that there was neither time nor sufficient computer resources to fully analyze the data. Within hours of the fourth event, even the most powerful, multiplexed, military/civilian computing resources would be exceeded. The bottom line was that the events had now assumed the character of an all-out cyber and quite possibly physical attack. One like no other. And after a fifth event? Who knew?

That the primary target was United States was now also blatantly clear. There was no question either as to whether the intersections would eventually involve other countries. They were already affecting Canada *and* Mexico, though, of course, it wasn't yet clear if they represented collateral damage. Whether the events or intersections would spread to South America, Europe and Africa wasn't yet known. If Stewart's worse-case scenario were correct, in the end, not just the United States, but the entire Americas and perhaps even the majority of the world's nations would be brought to their knees. And who would be exempt? Who would benefit from global chaos and be willing to risk a global retaliatory attack? Who? And why?

There also remained the unsettling question of who was buying up the different geographic regions of the USA, and more importantly, who was selling, and why.

That the seller would amass a fortune was evident. Then there was the unthinkable question if whether the escalating events and intersections might not themselves be a distraction, a red herring, a rehearsal or means to "soften" the nation, predicating something even more deadly. The rapidly spreading sense of helplessness and panic that was sweeping the United States was proving an effective form of psychological warfare, if that's what it was meant to be. Add to that the specter of losing one's political identity to unknown aggressors, and the Blitzkreig of World War II, and nuclear threats of the 1960s and 70s paled in comparison. If the situation wasn't addressed soon, there'd be, as Rellin quoted General Richard Cavors, "nothing left to address."

One promising lead was that the events seemed connected to the equipment and satellite antennas that he, Falk and Koski had each noted at their respective sites. Sufficient equipment had reached Cerebrus' and NSA's joint technical expert teams to quickly determine that they weren't, in fact, of purely Chinese design and manufacture. Various components had come from a variety of countries, some even from the USA. More important, however, was what continued to elude the best minds Cerebrus had at its command, namely, the manner in which the equipment generated the events. The equipment was complex and immensely sophisticated, with its components distributed over many boxes. The two sets of equipment, while similar proved slightly different. Being hand-made, each set was probably designed for one use, and seemed more and more likely to be dedicated to the establishment of a unique two-way link for only a fraction of a second before shutting down entirely. To make things worse, electronic "red herrings" had been cleverly distributed throughout the system alongside auto-meltdown sections, the whole being designed to prevent anyone from extracting the technology involved. And it didn't help that neither of the groups of surviving equipment were complete, and that much of what they did have was partial, piecemeal or had been severely damaged.

Experts were frenetically trying to piece together parts from the two different systems to create a single functional system in hopes of gleaning what, if anything, could be done to stop, counteract or at least mitigate the events and their echo-effects.

The key, Stewart's Cerebrus' experts confided, was understanding the physics. While the purpose of the events and auctions, the critical "why" remained elusive and, at best, speculative, after sifting through the debris, all agreed that the event and echoes were indeed the result of a quantum effect, exploiting a quirk of quantum physics. That the quirk, whatever it was, caused destruction and death added to their increasingly popular attribution of the instruments being harbingers of "quantum death," which the overall operation had come to be labeled.

Separately extrapolating from Koski, Falk's and now the Washington equipment, it was possible for Cerebrus to extrapolate, based on the direction each of the antennas had been oriented, a single point above Earth from which the incoming "start" signal would likely have originated. The problem was, they hadn't been all directed at a single point in space, and extrapolating, there was nothing located at the most likely point. Nothing! The assumption had been they would find a small, previously unnoticed geosynchronous satellite located at that point and would need only identify its owner to figure out who was at least behind the events. That assumption, however, had been proven incorrect. There was nothing anywhere near the predicted point except empty space.

Stewart left the Operations Room to attend a multi-agency update. After the lengthy briefing that disclosed nothing more than the current estimates as to the time and location of the next event, Stewart called Falk again.

"Falk," the voice on the other end answered.

"Stewart," he replied. "Have you got anything more for me?"

"Negative," Falk replied. "I've questioned everyone in town, but no one knows how the two girls ended up at old man Hempsted's. Their choice of hosts, however, couldn't have been better: He was an irascible old recluse, and pretty much avoided everyone."

"Any indication at all," Stewart asked, "if someone might have been waiting to spirit the Oriental girl away? It seems likely she would have had valuable field information to bring back to her controllers after the event. If nothing else, she would have had names, descriptions or locations of her controllers. Clearly the lead field agent was important, given that not one hesitated to take her life after eliminating everyone else associated with the event. I guessed there must be one or more nearby collaborators when I offered protection and the agent I was interrogating replied, 'You can not protect me. No one can.' It's a far shot, but..."

"Sorry to interrupt," Falk said, "but I've already 'been there, done that'. There's no indication whatsoever at this site that there were any other new or unusual additions to the area other than the two girls, or that they had consistent contact with anyone other than their host."

"Then I want you on the next available flight to Honolulu.

Everything points to Honolulu being the next event site. I want you to oversee the various agencies while you do some snooping on your own. If there is one place where an agent provocateur could be most easily smuggled out, it would be Hawaii with it's distinctly 'rainbow' population. See if you can come up with something. Report anything suspicious. Anything at all."

"Right," Falk acknowledged, adding, "Civilian air travel's a mess. Is the military still able to predict intersections enough to give a military pilot enough warning to avoid them? Most of the intersections, anyway. Can you ask Rellin to divert something military to Laplacia airport?"

"'Been there, done that'," Stewart replied. "Drive to the Laplacia airport and be waiting on the tarmac in half an hour."

After contacting Colonel Rellin and arranging for Falk's flight, Stewart turned his attention to Koski.

"Koski here."

"Stewart, here," he replied. "Anything new?"

"Nothing," Koski replied, tiredness and frustration permeating her voice. "I've passed on everything like you ordered to Colonel Rellin. I interviewed Josh, the waiter I told you about who slipped me the note. For a seventeen-year-old, he was an excellent observer and quite the talker." Koski cleared her throat, thinking about the young waiter hitting on her. "Thorsdan was, like he said, his *honorary* not his real uncle."

The two paused for a moment, taking in the implications.

"Anything else?" Stewart finally asked.

"Aside from Josh's assessment that the two girls were possibly lovers, neither having responded to his advances…"

"Anything *pertinent*?" Stewart snapped.

"Sorry. Not really," Koski replied, angered by men constantly interrupting her. "The two girls kept pretty much to themselves and the townsfolk didn't go out of their way to inquire about them, which, now that I think of it, in itself seems unusual. People in small towns are usually quite interested in outsiders. Come to think of it, Josh, while talkative, has always seemed cautious, even fearful, as if concerned someone might overhear him. I need to go make some additional inquires."

"Be careful, Koski. According to our newest scenario, the agents might have one or more local handlers—someone watching them to make certain they carry out their assignments, and after completion, perhaps extracting, even eliminating the principal field agent. There's also the possibility of the handler being under the thumb of a near-site operations controller. If my hunch is correct, the two would likely be inconspicuous. People who had been there 'forever'. Persons I'd expect who would quietly disappear soon after the event was completed, with or without the principal agent."

"So you're calling them 'agents', now?" Koski mentioned. "Agents of…?"

"Everything ostensibly points to China, but I'm beginning to think that this may represent an ruse to put us off the trail of the real culprits. The 'Chinese' agent I tried to salvage and interrogate was actually of North Korean extraction."

"North Korean?" Koski reiterated, a distinct note of question in her voice. "Stewart! Wait a moment!"

Stewart overheard hurried but muffled talk on the other end of the line. "Our young Josh has disappeared! I've just ordered an areawide search for him."

"Consider him armed and *very* dangerous…"

"What about Falk?" Koski interrupted. "Anything new? Has he identified a handler or controller? How…how is he?" The concern in her voice was palpable.

"He's fine. Nothing new in Laplacia. I'm sending him to Honolulu to see if there's a way to somehow nip in the bud what otherwise promises be the next event."

"By air?" Koski asked plaintively. Hearing no reply, she asked again, "By air, Stewart? I barely escaped death when an intersection passed over my *car*. The highway was left in chaos. While flying here, I had a...premonition...I mean, our air transportation system is unraveling...isn't there any way of protecting...?"

"Well, we tried Faraday cages, but have since learned they don't work against this...whatever it is. My plane was rigged with Faraday cages, and though my flight to Montana was uneventful, the plane carrying the site equipment never made it back. However, I'm informed that the military still have the capacity to compute, predict and avoid intersections. I sent him a military plane, like I'm sending you..."

"Wait! Me? But I've got Josh to locate and..."

"By now, I suspect your Josh, whether he was a handler, controller or either attempting to turn informer will already be dead or long gone. I've issued an order to deploy another agent to Fulton to pick up where you leave off. I'll inform him regarding the young man. I want you at the Fulton airport, on the tarmac, ready to leave in twenty minutes. Go!"

Colonel Rellin was less affable when he received another military air transportation request. Stewart, in the meantime, decided to turn his attention to the enigmatic BitCoin auction and why, in light of the latest information, it was associated so closely with the events. One thing was clear: If China or North Korea was involved, it wouldn't be anything pleasant.

Chapter 25

Stewart grabbed the nearest Cerebrus officer. "Drop what you're doing and come with me. I'm calling a Tiger Team! Assemble our best in the conference room. Now! The meeting begins in ten minutes."

Exactly ten minutes later, nine harried looking men and women were choosing a seat around a large conference table.

"'Rocket fuel', anyone?" offered Stewart, holding up a glass pot filled with steaming, black, viscous coffee in one hand and a stack of styrofoam cups in the other. After accommodating the few takers, he replaced the pot on its heating pad and began.

"Thank you, ladies and gentlemen. I've called this Tiger Team to come to a consensus regarding the current situation. Whatever is happening is admittedly still in evolution, and while a pattern is emerging, the endgame is as yet not apparent. In the meantime, the world as we know it is spinning out of control. General Cavors, Chairman of the Joint Chiefs of Staff have conveyed to us an ultimatum: Identify the perpetrators *now* while our military resources are intact and we still can still mount a response."

Cerebrus' lanky Programs Manager, Franklin Gaston, second in command behind Stewart, shifted uneasily in his seat. "I fear there are at least as many theories floating about as to what's going on and who's behind it, Stewart, as there are persons around this table. How can you expect a consensus where there isn't any? Given what little we as yet individually and collectively know, I don't even see how a relevant consensus is possible."

"Good point, Franklin," replied Stewart. "Even so, as I said, it's soon going to become impossible for our nation to respond at all. According to General Cavors, we're losing this 'war,' if that's what it is, even as we talk. To defend our nation, we need to come to a common understanding regarding who is..."

"Isn't th...that your job, chief?" interrupted Dr. Jerry Falmouth, Cerebrus' Chief of Information Analysis.

"It would be, Jerry, if I had an understanding I could trust," replied Stewart. "As it happens, I have a guess, but it's as yet little more than that. Everything's happening so fast my 'guess' is hampered by our shared inability to keep up with all the incoming information. I might as well be wearing blinders. The situation continues to unfold too furiously to trust what any one person can construct in terms of a reliable or even reasonable overview. Everyone here's been concentrating on the evolving situation from his or her unique perspective. I assume we each have information we haven't yet had time to share, and a perspective that everyone else doesn't. If we pool what we know and what we suspect, I believe we might be able to come to a working consensus..."

"C...Consensus?" repeated Falmouth. "Is that r...really enough for the Joint Ch...Chiefs to concoct an effective response?"

"Another good point, Jerry," Stewart acknowledged. "In the mid-1960s, the United States was faced with a not dissimilar problem: It was impossible to know the former Soviet Union's tactical nuclear response to various situations with any certainty, so the government contracted a then deep-cover 'think-tank' to invent a method to force consensus. What resulted was the 'Delphi Technique'. It didn't result in a complete or perfectly valid understanding of the former USSR's most likely tactical nuclear responses, but it was good enough to allow us to create a response plan that later proved sufficiently effective. I propose applying this technique here, now, so we will come to a consensus that we can offer the Joint Chiefs to help them decide what to do.

"Like each of you, I've been sifting through everything I know again and again, attempting to assemble it into something cohesive and meaningful with which to work. Everyone here, I know, has been doing the same. I believe it's time to share with each other all we know as of this moment, and our best guesses as to what is going on. Applying the Delphi Technique should help bring us all to a consensus."

"How much time will this take? Things are evolving pretty rapidly and each of us needs to stay on top of his or her respective areas," inquired David Hallard, Cerebrus' normally dashing but currently harried-looking Head of Field Operations. "I'm responsible for directing unfolding operations in multiple locations which are continuing to emerge as we speak."

"Then let's limit ourselves to five minutes each to summarize what we've each uncovered and have concluded thus far from our respective points of view," Stewart recommended. "I'm familiar with Delphi. I'll lead us through it."

"Interruptions?" inquired Hallard, clearly concerned about diverting *any* of his attention away from field operations.

"Permitted, as the situation continues to unfold," answered Stewart. "We have, unfortunately, little time before the next event. Shall we begin?"

"I'll start," offered Kate Keenan, Cerebrus' new Chief Scientist and Technical Advisor, an acknowledged physics genius and computer wizard. "I've been investigating the details of the events, and who in the world would have the technical knowledge and resources to pull them off."

"Good," interrupted Stewart. "So...?"

"These days, practically any nation, multi-national corporation, rogue state or criminal organization could scrape together the necessary logistical *resources*. Few, however, would have the knowledge to understand, apply and manage the whole. The effects of the *events* seem straightforward, so I've had my group focus on the 'auctions', the effects of which are anything but. Specifically, I've been attempting to trace the path of the BitCoin transactions.

"I've come to the conclusion that it's more beneficial to determine who would have the *desire* or, restated, *be desperate enough* to try an auction like this. The key, I think, is identifying which of the many groups would stand to gain the most from such a gamble, and a big gamble it is.

"That the 'events' and 'auctions' are related seems incontrovertible. And, while the *who* and *how* are both necessary, our immediate need remains to ascertain the *why*.

"From this," Keenan concluded, "should come the who and how."

Stewart nodded in agreement. Several other participants around the table shook their heads, some in agreement, others in disagreement. It was clearly hard for anyone at the table to imagine a single entity in this intricately interconnected world of global economic and military *detante* that would have the audacity to risk total financial excommunication or physical obliteration for *any* end. Yet, if Kate was right, and it appeared to Stewart and many about the table that Cerebrus' technical genius was at the least on the right track, and that that was exactly what whoever was behind it was doing.

"Okay. Any ideas as to...?" Stewart began.

"Nothing certain," piped up David Hallard, Cerebrus' Head of Field Operations, stimulated by Kate Keenan's analysis and the freedom they were being given to express themselves. "If it were a nation, my money would have to be on North Korea. They, more than any other nation, have the need, desire, and, given their current state of affairs, the most to gain if successful as well as the least to lose should it prove, in the end, unsuccessful.

"A multi-national corporation? Name practically any global corporation, and it's *possible*. It's not that big a step from manipulating national economies using financial derivatives to fielding these auctions. Add to that, today's business ethics have, for years, been on a fast slippery slope. If it were a multi-national corporation, and I had to bet on one today, it would be SysGen. Tomorrow, who knows?

"As for a rogue state, any number of emerging, hyper-religious, xenophobic, terrorist 'states' would fit the bill. However, none have stepped forward to claim responsibility, so this situation, in my opinion, doesn't have the usual 'terrorist' ring to it. What we're experiencing seems darker, more organized and secular. If this were the brainchild of a rogue terrorist state, my bet, and it would be a poor one, would have to be the Islamic State of Iraq and the Levant—ISIS.

"There are currently several global *criminal* organizations that might have the interest and desire, but I imagine them to be the buyers rather than the seller or organizer."

"A...Agreed," interjected Falmouth. As the attention of everyone sitting around the conference table shifted back to Falmouth, Stewart, Keenan and Hallard relaxed back in their seats. "As K...Kate said, the key is *p...purpose*. Nonetheless, my group's work has been t...tightly focused not on p...purpose, but who was b...buying."

"And...?" Stewart asked.

"The buying seems highly c...competitive. That makes me th... think the bidders represent d...different groups. They could conceivably represent a c...consortium of anti-American nations and organizations, bidding one against the other for various 't... territories'. Spheres of influence. If so, each would have it's own r...reason and m...motive. Their principal commonalities would be, first, a long-standing d...desire to 'open up' the United States to global organized c...crime; second, their having sufficient monetary r...resources to 'compete' in an auction of this scope; th...third, there being an interest in obtaining wh...what amounts to the 'rights' to control a particular r...region of the United States."

"What about China, Jerry?" Stewart asked, reflecting on the Chinese labels on some of the recovered equipment.

"Ch...China?" Falmouth asked. "The equipment c...collected from each event site so far has 'Ch...China' written all over it. But, no, I can't see China b...behind these auctions. It would be easier for them to simply 'b...buy' the United States outright than to engage in a s...secret cyber-war with all-out, nuclear war a likely result. Any war between the US and Ch...China, would have an uncertain outcome, at best. Also, a global holocaust would destroy the very r...resources that China so c...covets. Besides Ch...China is heavily invested in the USA. Hell, they p...practically own America's debt. If China *were* behind this, it would be like attacking itself. If for that reason alone, China, in my opinion, w... wouldn't likely be the organizer, despite the obvious s...signs. A covert 'helper' perhaps, or the dupe, but the p...principal instigator? I don't think so."

"If I catch your drift, Jerry," Stewart replied, "China, in effect, already controls our resources and market simply by virtue of holding the mass of our national debt. Calling in the debt and publicly lording it over us in front of the would be easier and more 'Chinese-style' than this.

"Y...Yes," Falmouth agreed excitedly. "Any organized, combined cyber-phyiscal-economic attack against the USA, wh... which this is quickly becoming, w...would also, by d...definition, seriously effect China. Already the events and echo-intersections, though so far restricted to the USA, southern C...Canada and northern M...Mexico, are sending shock waves not just through our nation but th...through our allies as well as our adversaries, b...because we're all so economically dependent on each other. Irrespective of the instigator, the events seem to be p...pointing towards a f...final coordinated strike. Even if Ch...China *had* the means—and I'm not saying it d...does—if what I know is correct, it has no m...motive. And as to p...purpose, why make their participation so obvious by leaving Ch...Chinese labels on the field equipment? Ineptitude? No, the labels have the distinctive feel of a r...red herring..."

"If not China, then who?" asked Stewart.

"W...why not North Korea?" Falmouth half-asked, half-replied.

"How about you, Bob? What have you eked out from your group's global strategic analyses? What's your idea about who's behind the events and auctions?" Stewart asked, shifting the group's attention to Robert Small, the diminutive but brilliant Head of Cerebrus' Gobal Strategic Analysis Division, who, for an outspoken man, had thus far remained unusually silent.

"Huh?" Robert asked as if startled back to reality. "Sorry, I was considering whether the event epicenters and auction items would remain in the continental USA, or, if the next one did indeed occur in Honolulu, what the impact would be on the Pacific Rim nations. It seems like it would, in effect, bring them all down with us. Both events and auctions have thus far been confined to the continental

USA." Robert Small, having shared, appeared to retreat back into his thoughts.

"I'm having serious reservations about the whole China-North Korea-Hawaii thing," stated Lou Richards, Cerebrus' Head of External Security, the youngest of the individuals around the table.

"Perhaps you'd share your concerns, Lou, and shed some light on who you think might be pulling the strings," suggested Stewart.

"Okay," began Lou Richards in a calm voice despite his visible excitement. "North Korea keeps announcing to the world that they're a global power. And they're constantly publicly reiterating that their global objective is to rid Asia, the Pacific, and eventually the world, of what they perceive as 'The Great American Threat'. They've always been given to hyperbole, but recently their threats have hit an all-time high, threatening the USA most recently with outright destruction.

"Even so, it seems inconceivable, given their limited economic, financial and natural resources, their social backwardness and their excessive military spending, not to mention their silence regarding the recent 'events' and 'auctions', that they're really a major player in this. Most here, I think, would agree that if North Korea *were* a major player, they'd be bragging about it all over the airwaves. No, it's much more likely, as Kate suggested, that they're playing a supportive or co-enabling role..."

"You really think so?" Kate interrupted.

"Well, I think, like you, they're probably involved in some aspects, from imagining the events to directing the auctions, and maybe, providing the field agents. These all play to their particular strengths.

"With those thoughts in mind, let's revisit these auctions a minute: My group has, for years now, been been following North

Korea's burgeoning interest in cyber-warfare. Consider, for instance, the existence of their ultra-secret 'Bureau 121'. And it's certainly not news that they've been attempting to slip sleeper agents into the USA for the last twenty years. As for directing the 'auctions', they would, I assume, receive a hefty 'commission' and thereby garner the wealth they so desperately need. A single "sale" would not only provide the massive amounts of money needed to finance the rebuilding of their social infrastructure, essential to prevent an internal 'revolution-against-the-revolution', but to also fund their propaganda machine, provision their military with yet more weaponry, including nuclear weapons, and finance their secret police's efforts to continue their control of the people. All this while supporting their leaders' foibles. Don't discount their experience in cyber-warfare! North Korea may be one of the most experienced nations in regard to cyber-warfare. How many successful 'hacks' have they pulled off in the past year? One? Five? Ten?" Richards asked searching the faces around the table. "Our branch contends it's more in the neighborhood of *hundreds of thousands*, most of them successful and not reported to the public."

A sober hush spread through the room.

Chapter 26

Engines whining, the odd-shaped plane lurched forward, pressing Falk deep back into the form-fitting copilots seat of the B2 "Spirit" fighter-bomber. His hastily written orders and field notes, taped against his skin beneath his flight suit already itching. The runway, barely visible through his helmet on his side of the cockpit fell quickly away and out of sight. What in a commercial airplane constantly zigzagging to avoid expanding and intersecting event echos would have taken eight to twelve hours to reach

Hickam Air Base, Hawaii, would take less than four hours in the long-range military fighter-bomber, flying a path updated moment-to-moment by the Department of Defense's Advanced Hazard Warning Assistance System. Of course, no one knew how long the system would remain functional. The required computational power necessary to track and forecast the exact locations of the ever-changing intersections in relation to a fast-flying military jet increased super-exponentially each minute. At some point, even the most advanced computer systems would suffer information overload and shut down. If that happened, there would be little the pilot could do to avoid an event-echo or echo-intersection. They would simply have to slam through, lose power momentarily, and trust the plane's auto-restart functions would kick in before they crashed.

Uncomfortable in the tight, all-enclosing flight suit, Falk watched the land below melt away and flow behind him like oozing liquid butter. It was a cloudless day. Directly ahead, he could see a steady distant horizon, the top half a light powder blue, the bottom half a hazy mixture of greens and browns. The greens and browns soon morphed to deep blue, and his thoughts turned to his mission.

His first and overriding concern was whether he would arrive in Oahu early enough before the next event occurred, assuming, of course, the next event didn't show up in Anchorage, Alaska, a far less probable alternative. *Actually*, he thought, *it would be better if the next event* did *occurred there:* At the least, it would afford him additional information that might be useful to his mission in Honolulu. Better yet, the authorities there might capture an agent provocateur or her controller, making his work in Hawaii easier.

Directing his thoughts to Hawaii, he realized he would need to be at the event epicenter well before the event happened in order to observe the event process first-hand. Given his, Koski and Stewart's experiences with on-site agents, he was no longer considering trying to capture one alive. Instead he decided to direct his attention on how to try to capture and interrogate a handler or, better yet, a controller, someone who might know more about the ultimate endgame.

Falk tried to imagine himself a North Korean handler in Hawaii. He would position himself in a heavily populated area, perhaps near a university or North Korean expat community, if there was such a thing. There would likely be something like that somewhere in or near Honolulu. In time his thoughts loosened and the boredom of the flight began to take hold.

Air hissed hypnotically around the cockpit, interrupted only by occasional, hard-to-understand radio communications between the pilot and ground control. The result acted as a strong soporific, and Falk soon found himself nodding, his mind wandering from one daydream to another.

It was in just such a state that his agent's mind typically took over, and he imagined the two girls, one Oriental, the other, Caucasian or at least "American," posing as students rooming together in a nondescript house with a new, state-of-the-art outdoor satellite antenna. The Oriental girl's room would be cluttered with electronic equipment, especially this late in the event preparation process. They would be working feverishly to connect the equipment, making certain it was ready to go. Ready for what might very well prove the capstone event. The *coup de grace*. The event that would bring America to its knees.

Falk startled and shifted his weight to get a better look below, but the body straps fought against him. In the end, despite his best efforts, the harness won.

Peering out of the corner of an eye, he could see scattered, white, cotton-puff clouds projecting discrete shadows onto the surface of a vast, sparkling, deep blue ocean. Flying in the same direction as the earth's rotation made it seem forever afternoon. The feeling was one of relative peace in an otherwise crazy world.

Three hours out, his helmet crackled and the pilot's metalic voice intruded. "Susan Koski, a colleague of yours, is just off our right wingtip."

Struggling once again against the straps, twisting hard right, he saw a flash of sunlight reflect off the fuselage of a sleek-looking jet. Within it, he assumed, would be Koski, his trusted colleague and, more recently, the singular woman who had somehow found her way into his heart. Whatever lingering feelings of doubt he had about the success of his mission lifted. Raising a hand to his helmet visor, he sent her a salute, hoping she could somehow see the gesture.

"Regulations require we keep a set distance between aircraft; however, the other pilot and I thought you and your partner might enjoy seeing each other a little bit better, at least for a moment." The distant silver jet nudged cautiously closer, until Falk could just make out its helmeted pilot and passenger. The passenger waved, and the aircraft immediately began drifting away and behind.

Ever since the first event, he and Koski had been working separately, leaving Falk feeling surprisingly awkward and incomplete. Despite his finely honed agent skills and extensive field experience, ever since he'd stepped off the plane in Laplacia, Vermont, his normally analytic mind had felt slightly off. Distracted. It was as if he were harboring an itch he couldn't locate, and for that reason, scratch. Falk made a mental note to thank the pilot for the grand gesture, and Stewart for bringing them back together on what promised to be their most challenging mission yet.

His jet abruptly lurched, sending a shiver through the plane and his tightly constrained body.

What the hell? Falk thought as the helmet earphones went dead. Glancing forward and to his left, he could see several instrument lights on the pilot's panel flashing red. It was then he realized the engines had cut off. The next moment, the floor felt like it was dropping from underneath.

What the hell? he barely had time to think a second time before the plane rolled abruptly to the right, the nose pointing down towards a rapidly spiraling, ever expanding ocean. White caps, invisible less than a second ago suddenly appeared as pinpoint dots and a moment later took recognizable shape. The plane, he realized, was spinning downward in what airmen from the earliest days of winged flight called a "dead man's stall." It meant they were dropping like a lead weight.

Before he could think further, the plane once again shuddered, then lurched violently forward. His head filled with the scream of reawakening engines strained to their limit. *That will be the engines restarting. The pilot will be trying to break our stall*, he thought. The spinning quickly subsided, but the plane continued to accelerate nose down.

Falk felt his body press harder into his seat, as though an elephant were leaning against his chest, making it difficult to take a much needed breath. A second, more violent shudder rippled through the fuselage, as the pilot tried to pull out of the dive, causing Falk's helmet to strike the cockpit plexiglass with a loud crack, delivering a vicious blow to his left temple. Dazed, unable to focus his tearing eyes, it was all he do to filter out the nerve-wracking whine of the engines, the buzz of the multiple cockpit alarms, and contain the nausea welling up from the pit of his stomach.

His peripheral vision began to blur. He shook his head from side-to-side, and felt a sharp pain shoot down both arms that brought more tears to his eyes. Carefully returning his head to a neutral position, he looked forward only to see dark-blue filling the entire cockpit window. He could feel the blood draining from his head, and his peripheral vision begin blackening like a closing iris. His situation was further compromised by the copious amount of sweat streaming down from his cold, clammy brow, mixing at the edges of his eyes with the tears from the pounding in his head.

Falk had barely enough time to think, *Shit! We're going to crash!* before the floor abruptly rose from underneath him and finished draining all the remaining blood from his head.

He directed a shaking hand to the outside front of his helmet in a useless attempt to brush away the copious combination of blood, sweat and tears. Unable to do so, the flow began to fill the space between his chin and the constricting neck folds of his flight suit.

"Shit, shit, shit!" he voiced, this time aloud in his helmet to himself, his voice sounding increasingly distant. Everything began to whirl and he threw up just before passing out.

A sudden chirrup pierced the air and a strong, calm, but concerned voice sounded in his ears in the now blood-sweat-and-vomit-pooled helmet. "Sorry, sir. We hit an unexpected event-echo that came at us from the side. To be honest, we're lucky the engines auto-restarted when they did. A fraction of a second later and we'd have become part of the Pacific Ocean. I was barely able to pull us out of the dive. I had to aggressively coax her nose back up without, I hope, causing you too much discomfort."

"Event-echo," Falk mumbled, then, "Discomfort," he muttered with difficulty to let the pilot know he was still alive.

"Yes, sir. The Hazard Warning System failed," the pilot continued, "just before the event-echo hit us. My instructions are to take you to your destination in the least amount of time, so we'll continue on our heading directly for Hickam Air Field." Not receiving an immediate reply, the pilot looked over at Falk and continued anxiously, "You okay, sir?"

Falk carefully stretched his neck, and not experiencing the sharp pain he'd felt earlier, flexed his fingers, arms, legs and toes to make certain he was intact and to allow the blood and vomit to pass from his helmet down into the body of his flight suit. Looking up and to his left, he could make out the near reclining silhouette of the pilot behind a reflected image of his own face in his helmet. The face staring at him looked white as chalk, except for a vivid red line running down from his left temple to his cheek. The blood was already thickening and darkening. His face felt cold and clammy, his mouth pasty and dry. He could taste the acridness of bile and the smell was...indescribably affronting. He swallowed with difficulty. "Shit," he said, clearer, calmer and firmer than the last time.

"Sir, are you all right?" the pilot's voice crackled again in his helmet, reverberating from side to side, causing Falk's head to resume pounding.

"Yeah, well...I think so," Falk replied glad to hear his own voice sound calmly rational and not so distant. "I'm afraid, however, that I'm a horrible mess..."

"Ahhh," the crewman murmured, loosening his straps to better look over his right shoulder at his passenger. "Looks like you've a nasty cut there, sir, but the bleeding has stopped. I'll turn the oxygen up a bit. You should feel better momentarily."

Falk, hurting and still somewhat dazed, sighed. He could already hear the extra oxygen hissing into his flight helmet. "That's much better, thanks," he replied more cohesively and with as much assurance as he could muster.

"My pleasure, sir," the pilot finished, returning his attention forward and mumbling in his helmet microphone something that sounded to Falk like a distress call.

"Please make certain you're completely strapped in, sir," the pilot said. "At this speed and altitude, without Hazard Warning System support, there'll be no advanced warning should we encounter another..."

The vibration from the engines abruptly stopped, leaving the plane slicing silently forward through the air like a thrown knife. This time instead of falling, Falk heard a single loud click followed by an explosion, and the cockpit above and the plane below him disappeared in a cloud of smoke. A moment later, still strapped to his chair, he was falling from the sky at the end of a large, orange-and-white-striped parachute. The plane's fuselage, far ahead, smashed into the ocean in a massive splash and explosion.

The next thing he knew, he was bobbing from side-to-side, the orange-and-white-striped parachute floating behind him in the water like a full skirt, creating a noticeable if temporary visual call for help.

Falk released his harness, unfastened his helmet, and bowed his filthy head to whisper a brief thanks to the God of the skies, in the same breath asking Him to protect Koski, hoping she'd survived the two event-echoes and fared better. What several hours ago had started as yet another challenging assignment was proving nothing less than a one-way ticket to hell.

Freeing himself from the constraints of the chair that had just saved his life, Falk began enumerating the pros and cons of abandoning it. Scanning the ocean about him and not seeing any sign of human life, his rattled brain began anxiously asking over and over, *Where the hell is Koski?* before he passed out.

Chapter 27

"I have to agree with Bob," said the man sitting at the far end of the Cerebrus conference table. Looking like a Sigmund Freud doppleganger, the white-bearded, middle-aged man in a dark tweed jacket raised his hand like a high school student, then, looking at his own raised hand, lowered it and shifted uncomfortably in his chair. Doctor Professor Albert Halsey, Cerebrus' Director of Political Analysis waited patiently to be acknowledged.

"Albert," Stewart called. "We'd all like to hear your take on the situation."

Halsey cleared his throat, looked anxiously at his watch then from person to person as if awaiting their individual permissions to speak, swallowed hard and began: "Despite how much effort the North Koreans put into making themselves *appear* to the world as Lou just said, we've no *proof* that they're anywhere close to having the ability to administer as complex and coordinated an operation as this. Recall the former USSR prior to *perestroika*: The Soviets' had literally hundreds of thousands of the fastest, most powerful tanks in the world, many equipped with nuclear-tipped artillery shells, all lined up several rows deep just behind the Iron Curtain. Highly visible. Attack ready. A constant reminder to NATO and the West that half of Europe could be overrun in one Blitzkrieg-like action before anyone knew it was happening.

"What they purposefully didn't share was that each tank had only five shells, one box of ammunition, and not a single replacement track link. Five shots from its cannon, a couple minutes of automatic fire exchange, and the world's foremost tanks would become little more than useless pieces of junk. Break a tread, and they would became a sitting duck, or worse, an obstacle to their own forces.

"It was the same with the Soviet Air Force at that time. It sported the fastest fighters in the world. Nothing we had could catch up with the MIG 27; hell, it could outrun our air-to-air missiles! What the Soviet propaganda machine carefully avoided disclosing, however, was was that the fighters were fuel-guzzlers. They carried only enough gas for a single 'one-way' flight in support of a major land offensive. There wasn't enough gas to return to base and refuel!"

Halsey looked at his watch, as if calculating the time he had left to speak, then continued.

"Then there was the whole facade regarding the status of their Navy, and, again, of their nuclear missile arsenal. I could go on and on.

"Despite their military *braggadocio*, it was clear to Premier Gorbachev that if the Soviet Union had to actually flex its muscle in a theater-wide conflict, they would quickly lose.

"North Korea, I believe, is in a similar situation, so to speak 'holding a propaganda tiger by the tail', pushing North Korea into taking dangerously overstated positions just like the Soviet Union did. In this case, however, North Korea isn't entirely a 'paper tiger' like we often like to think. It's more like a total destruction machine without any particular focus in regard to what it will destroy. It's simply waiting for someone—anyone—to intentionally or accidentally call them out. To me, it makes a perverse sense that they would be the organizers of the both the 'events' and 'auctions'. If successful, it would become possible for them to purchase the necessary military capacity about which they're propagandizing. Take their perspective for a moment, and I think you can easily imagine them internally justifying the risk of such a gamble in order to bring reality back in line with rhetoric. And that's my five minutes," Halsey said checking his watch and clearing his throat a second time. With that, he slumped back into his chair as if the effort of speaking had completely drained him.

"That does make sense, Albert, though I'm not certain the North Koreans have the will or the propensity to actually take on risk at that level, at least from a political perspective," the final member of the Tiger Team, Helen Schrivener, Cerebrus' Head of Liaison for Middle and Far Eastern Divisions interjected. An attractive woman in her late thirties, and considered a "heavy-weight" among Director Chiefs, she was immediately interrupted by a rejuvenated and surprisingly animated Halsey.

"From a 'political perspective'? A 'purely political perspective'?" Halsey questioned. Standing, he swept his hands to his left and right in an all-inclusive gesture, and continued. "You all must admit that the North Koreans have purpose, motive and, at least, the administrative ability. And their current situation makes them desperate enough to actually take on such risk—at least that's how I imagine their leader would view it. That they're behind it, I'm almost certain...but they could only do it with the assistance of their only close partner, China."

"Then you think China's equally involved?" Stewart asked, nodding subtly at Helen to indicate that her opportunity to speak would be neither forgotten nor lessened.

Bracing both hands on the table, Halsey explained, "Most likely, though perhaps indirectly, *possibly* unwittingly, and always with 'plausible deniability', just in case the venture doesn't work or backfires."

"An increasingly interesting theory, but really, Albert, North Korea?" interjected Helen Scrivener. "North Korea may be an avowed enemy of the USA, and an unpredictable bastard colleague of China, but there's plenty of organizations with sufficient means and motive elsewhere throughout the world. Take the Middle East, for example: Virtually every radical faction in the Middle East is stepping up its threats against the USA in number, breadth and vehemency. These threats are sophisticated, coordinated, multi-national and have resulted in highly successful field operations. While North Korea's threats are many, and vitriolic, aside from cyber-ops, they remain mostly rhetoric and have, to the best of our knowledge, been accompanied by only a few obscure, awkward, and mostly unsuccessful field ops. Think North Korean abductions of Japanese citizens, for instance. What has that really gained them?

"The Middle East, on the other hand, is a quagmire of well-trained, well-equipped, political-religious extremists, both leaders and followers. Each faction is continuously consolidating and reconsolidating its position amongst other factions, most recently under the guise of 'radical Islam'. The result is a slowly organizing network of independent but integrated super-national criminal organizations."

Looking around the table, everyone appeared engrossed in the picture of the world Scrivener was successfully painting.

"And that's what they are in the end: organized criminal organizations," Scrivener reiterated. "Every major Middle Eastern nation—Iran, Syria, Palestine, Yemen, the list is long and growing—like China, has sufficient monetary and intellectual resources to be behind the recent events and auctions. Every Middle Eastern player has sufficient military, intelligence, criminal and often piratical resources to acquire the most advanced technology without impunity. Just look at Iran and it's 'uranium enrichment program'! Do you really think it will stop producing weapons-grade uranium because of an international *agreement*? Every Middle Eastern player has the necessary field experience to implement the events and auctions, or, at the least, participate in them.

"For decades, the American, Chinese and Russian governments as well as their attendant military-industrial complexes have been more than willing to sell sophisticated weaponry and armaments to the highest bidder, basically eliminating the need for errant organizations to fund the expensive basic research necessary to create and produce the new kinds of equipment they desire. Most weaponry advances tend to occur in small, increasingly expensive increments over a long period of time in a decidedly linear fashion. Outright purchase, on the other hand, allows the buyer to take a giant step forward. It's the same with computer technology and people's understanding of it—what the famous Russian scientist, Vladimir Vernadsky called the 'technosphere' and collectively the 'noosphere'.

"As for having physics and computer capability, Iran is long known to have it's own, covert, highly up-to-date and vastly understated but increasingly powerful physics and computational capability as a consequence of and in anticipation its ongoing 'secret' war with Israel.

"Have I missed anything? Organizational ability? Think

Islamic State or Pakistan. Think ISIS—Daesh—and ask yourself if they have the determination and finances to *acquire* rather than develop the organizational, computational and military resources necessary for these events and auctions, and accomplish it all in relative secrecy. They can and do!

"Finally, while it's true that the materials and field agents associated with the 'events' belie the Chinese, it would be in the best interest of any Middle East nation to divert attention elsewhere, for example to China, while implementing a cyberwar like this one. How hard is it to label products in Chinese, and procure some Chinese or North Korean-appearing agents and weapons? During World War II, the US and its allies successfully accomplished such a ruse on an international scale in Operation Fortitude, presenting the German's sufficiently plausible misinformation to hide the entire scope of preparations for D-Day.

"No, I think we would be amiss if we didn't seriously consider that a Middle East nation or coalition could be the organizer, implementer and seller, seeking to strengthen and extend it's global reach all the while appealing to the masses by way of its religious goal of destroying the 'Western Satan'. Behind it, indirectly, probably knowingly, but with assured 'plausible deniability' could very well be the 'new' Russia and possibly China with North Korea following."

As Scrivener sat, Jerry Falmouth rose.

"G...good points, all, Helen. I'll accede that N...North Korea and the growing Middle East C...Coalition are both capable of mounting a well-coordinated cyberwar, like our p...present situation. Our various f...field operations, during the past five years have yielded d...documents indicating that both have been actively engaged in cyberattack after cyberattack against the USA, r...reminiscent, if you will, of H...Hitler's attacks on Spain immediately preceding World War II. The Nazis used Spain as a t...testing platform for their advanced weaponry, and to test th... theater level command and control. It was the Allies' r...reticence to r...recognize it for what it was that kept it from being acknowledged as such. The line between t...terroristic cyber-warfare and out-and-out w...war is increasingly b...blurry. Still, I imagine the current s...situation as one where either, or God f... forbid, both together in some k...kind of unholy alliance, might be t...testing their cyber weaponry and th...theater command and control capabilities."

"Both?" asked Stewart to the suddenly silent circle of experts, each pondering the implications of what had been shared. "Personally, I wish we knew more about these auctions. I feel as though we're missing something, something crucial, something vital," Stewart added, tossing the gauntlet back before the group.

"If I may, Stewart," Kate replied.

All eyes shifted to Kate Keenan.

"There's more than I was able to share in my five minutes."

Stewart surveyed the group and detecting agreement from all, replied, "Alright, the floor's yours once again," and sat.

"For the moment, let's focus on these auctions. We know the key is the use of BitCoins and BitCoin technology," she began.

"Before you go on, could you explain to those of us who are ignorant of everything 'BitCoin' exactly what it is?" interrupted Halsey.

"Yes, of course," Kate answered. "The idea behind BitCoins is tightly linked to the increasingly sophisticated internet. A BitCoin is a digital token that can be used to make decentralized, internet-based, global transactions."

Surveying the table, Kate Keenan could see she was commanding everyone's attention.

"By 'decentralized'," she continued, "I mean there's no 'bank' involved. Furthermore, the transactions, while public, are anonymous, their anonymity coming mainly from the use of an internet-within-the-internet, the massively encrypted 'The Onion Router' network, commonly called TOR. BitCoins are issued and handled by specially dedicated TOR servers according to a fixed set of mathematical rules.

"One of them, for instance, is that the maximum number of BitCoins is fixed forever at 21 million. The system began with less than a million BitCoins in electronic circulation. One can buy existing BitCoins using any world currency from any person on the internet who has some, the 'sell price' fluctuating based on supply and demand. BitCoins back then represented 'potential currency', as there were few buyers, and a very limited number of merchants who would accept them for real goods. One could also accumulate BitCoins electronically by verifying, recording and tracking BitCoin transactions in what is called a public 'blockchain'. In this manner, participants around the world are "paid" in BitCoins for doing the accounting necessary to maintain the system. This process is called 'mining' and it's how BitCoins are 'created'."

"So the value of a BitCoin varies?" asked Halsey.

"Yes, just like stock on the stock market, except that the total number of BitCoins is permanently capped at 21 million, and the system is defined by a mathematical algorithm rather than by governments, bankers and brokers. When it started, the BitCoin was valued at one thousand three hundred and nine BitCoins to a US dollar, or about eight-hundredths of a cent."

"How long have they been around?" asked Halsey, intrigued.

"The concept was introduced on an internet discussion board in October of 2008 by a Mr. Satashi Nakamoto in a referenced 'white paper'. It was further developed and eventually implemented by a band of Nakamoto-supporters who allegedly conversed directly with Mr. Nakamoto via the internet. It wasn't until November of 2010 that the first *physical* 'exchange,' Mt.Gox, was created and the first goods transaction, supposedly two pizzas for the sum of roughly twenty-five thousand BitCoins, took place. By February 2011, there were four million BitCoins, valued roughly at parity with the US dollar, that is, one BitCoin per US dollar. That represents an enormous return for initial investment, and, remember, BitCoins were still largely unknown and unused back then.

"Several defining events helped bring BitCoins before the public: First, as a result of Wikileaks, Wikipedia lost most of it's funding. At around the same time, banks in Cyprus were failing. In each case, BitCoins retained their value and were the main currency used for securing local goods and money. Soon afterwards, there appeared a number of exchanges and internet merchants accepting BitCoins, including the notorious Silk Road. Silk Road was a market not only for domestic products, but virtually anything, legal or illegal."

"I r...remember hearing that f...federal agents shut down the S...Silk Road, but could never identify and p...prosecute the literally hundreds of criminal sellers," offered Jerry Falmouth.

"Correct," replied Kate. "While blockchains publicly list every transaction, they don't reveal the *identities* of the buyers or sellers. Since then, a second, singularly important event occurred: The 'system,' or more accurately the miners and exchanges, were hacked. Not the blockchains, however. They remained unhacked.

Remember, BitCoins are like dollar bills without serial numbers. Whoever *possesses* digital BitCoins can use them as currency for any purpose anywhere in the world.

"Despite the Silk Road and numerous other 'dark' exchanges being shut down, BitCoins *continued to increase in value* to what they were just prior to these events and auctions. At that time, a BitCoin was worth roughly one thousand US dollars. The United States Financial Crimes Enforcement Center, FCEC, had independently begun investigating the 'system' wondering what was continuing to drive up BitCoin values when, in fact, its usage was foundering.

"I promised you some new and important information that might shed light on the auctions, and here it is: Ten days prior to the first event, ten million BitCoins suddenly vanished from circulation. During this time, the individual BitCoin value exploded to well over fifty thousand dollars. FCEC knew about this, but was unable to account for the anomaly, given the anonymous nature of BitCoins and the TOR net. What they *suspected* was that a person or group of persons was attempting to 'corner the market' and artificially drive up BitCoin values using some as yet undiscovered variant of the Silk Road. That, apparently, turned out to be these auctions.

"While we still haven't identified who is selling, bidding or buying, the auctions are, in fact, taking place using BitCoins on the dark TOR net. Given what we've seen so far, my group has taken to calling this new variant the 'Iron Road', and, I believe there is every indication that it is a North Korean effort."

"Why not get hold of Mr. Nakamura?" Helen Schrivener asked. "Surely he would know how to 'mine' his own creation for the information."

"Mr. Nakamura disappeared when things began to heat up, well before the events and auctions. All we really know about him is that the person, group, nation or multi-national consortium behind the creation of BitCoins exercised unparalleled cryptographic skills. As I said, no one has yet been able to break the encrypted public 'buy/sell' blockchains."

Several minutes of profound silence followed in the wake of Kate's revelation. It was Stewart who finally said, "Sounds to me like it's time for a first vote: So, who or what is behind this? North Korea? China? Russia? Organized Crime? A Middle East Consortium? Or some even more obscure, nefarious conglomeration? Albert, please pass everyone a piece of paper. Each of us will write down *one* of these choices. Kate will tally the votes—thank you, Kate—and, when she's done will read the results aloud. If there's any disagreement, we'll continue to follow Delphi protocol, that is, we'll have another discussion round and revote until we reach consensus regarding the most likely culprit on which to focus our and the nation's attention.

Chapter 28

"Tally's done," Kate Keenan announced. "We're split: North Korea with or without China's help is the 'winner' with a Middle East Coalition with or without Sino-Russian involvement a close second. Both seem plausible given what has been presented so far."

"Okay, lack of consensus during the first round is to be expected," Stewart responded. "At least we've narrowed things down to two most likely scenarios. That's where Delphi comes into play. It's time for us to assemble into two groups based on our vote. North Korea in the corner over there, the Middle East Coalition in the other corner over there. Take a few minutes to discuss the reasons why you believe your choice is true, correct or best, and be prepared to argue for five minutes for and defend it."

The participants did as instructed, taking a little less than ten minutes to reaffirm consensus within their groups and prepare.

When the ten minutes was over, David Hallard was clearly chaffing at the bit.

"What say we ask David to go first?" asked Stewart with a smile.

"Thank you. Well," began David Hallard, Cerebrus' Head of Field Operations, leaning forward and placing both hands flat on the conference table. "There's been no indication from any of our or any other agency's field agents we know of, of any increased chatter between North Korea, China, Russia and any Middle Eastern 'coalitions', criminal organizations or known terrorist groups. While our field agents have been reporting isolated instances of information sharing between dark forces, the closest thing we've come to of any major significance was the rogue action dubbed "Operation Imminent Danger" in which Cerebrus agents Koski and Falk were involved. But that was more of a localized 'terrorist' plot involving a radicalized pop star, planning to use a biological weapon to eradicate the world's assembled religious leaders last Easter at the Hollywood Bowl. His only 'outside' associate was a loosely pieced together anarchist group which he himself organized. Now, Stewart mentioned noting a North Korean linguistic pattern in our otherwise singularly uninformative 'Chinese' captive before she so inconveniently shot herself.

"The CIA has several deep agents in North Korea, who have reported that with North Korea sinking further and further into economic mire, it's assets continuing to be seized as a consequence of worldwide trading sanctions, and its efforts at 'running the blockade' being increasingly stymied, unless they do something—something drastic and soon—the nation will implode on its own and its leaders will find themselves in fear of their lives either at the hands of their own people, or facing the World Court for crimes against humanity.

"I agree with Jerry and Albert that North Korea has motive and purpose. Given the gravity of their situation, you could even call it 'need'. They're even experts at cyberwarfare. The real question then is whether they have the kind of *advanced* cyber-technology necessary to pull off the auctions, and possibly also the events.

"Many envision North Korea as an uneducated, backwards country of obligate followers. While much of its *population* fits this picture, its chosen few are quite the opposite: Their techno-elite are highly educated youth, tasked specifically with thinking 'out of the box'." David Hallard straightened, lifted his hands from the table and conceded the floor to the next in his group, Kate Keenan.

Kate and Stewart had been whispering together while David spoke. Breaking from each other, Kate Keenan, Cerebrus' Chief Technical Advisor, stood, looked Stewart in the eyes, and, after receiving an affirmative nod, began. "What I'm about to share with you comes from a sensitive project I've been working within Cerebrus.

"In the late 1990's, we became aware that the North Korean military, frustrated with competing in the world of big-time conventional and NBC—Nuclear-Biological-Chemical—warfare, committed ten, later twenty, and currently as much as thirty percent of their budget to cyber-warfare. This was an arena in which they *could* compete. Beefing up their universities, the military began recruiting the best of their best computer graduates to a secret 'bureau' called simply by the numeric acronym, 'twenty-one', later, 'one-twenty-one'. Headquartered in in the Moonshin-dong area of Pyongyang, the bureau quickly outgrew the limited internet access available from within North Korea.

"In 2005, we traced their activities to Shenyang in China's nearby Liaoning Province. Operating under the guise of a 'North Korean Cultural Unit', the 'hacker hut', as the basement of the North Korean tourist hotel and restaurant came to be called, began testing their cyber-warfare skills using China's more open access to the internet. China continues to deny that it is in collusion with what now became called 'Bureau 121' and that the bureau even exists; however, our agents have documented North Korean and Chinese officials, including key high-ranking military figures, frequenting the restaurant and subsequently the 'basement'.

"By 2009, Bureau 121 had grown from twenty hackers to over five thousand 'specialists', responsible, we believe, for a growing number of aggressive cyber-attacks against South Korea and later the USA and EU. It's my opinion that their level of coordination, sophistication, and more importantly, success at penetrating US cyber-defenses, make them quite capable of instigating and supporting, with China's help, much of what we're seeing now." Kate paused, waiting for Stewart to confirm permission to continue.

He did.

"In 2010, the United States' National Security Agency—NSA —our more public sister organization, tasked Cerebrus with 'back-hacking' into North Korea's computer network. It took some time, but we were eventually able to secretly insert some specially-constructed Sysnet-like code similar to what was used to obfuscate Iran's uranium enrichment efforts. The code has allowed us to track

Bureau 121's cyber operations. NSA has used and continues to use this 'trap door' in the Bamboo Curtain to United States' advantage.

"Having access to their computer systems, and knowing their particular 'fingerprint', we have been able to attribute various hacking efforts to them or not. Gentlemen and ladies, I can now state without reservation that the auction internet code has 'North Korea' written all over it. Of course, it's impossible to prove, given their careful use of the super-encrypted TOR internet.

"The catch to all this is that however coordinated and sophisticated North Korea's Bureau 121's attacks have become, they've never crossed the line from cyber-hacking to what we seem to be experiencing with these events and auctions. I don't believe they have the resources to move from hacking to tactical military cyber-intrusion. However, North Korea could have easily *obtained* it by secret agreement from its big brother and only technologically-significant benefactor, China. In return, the situation would allow the Chinese to use the North Koreans to field test new weapons of war including cyberwar, while at the same time maintaining plausible deniability."

"I have to agree with Kate," Albert Halsey, Director of Political Analysis and a strong member of the 'North Korea' scenario group stated. "North Korea is at the least the mostly likely instigator. Up to now, China, succumbing to global political pressures, has always jerked North Korea's leash whenever it stepped a little too close for, so in this instance, I suspect the Chinese didn't know the extent to which North Korea was applying this technology, purchased, shared, transferred or stolen, against the USA.

"I'd like to present an alternative scenario: What if North Korea, through these efforts, saw the opportunity of maneuvering it's leash-master, China, and United States into a centerstage confrontation? North Korea could stand on the sidelines and watch the two duke it out, waiting until both nations were too engaged to stop and redirect any final efforts at North Korea, before directing their own final effort at their stated enemy, the USA, or both. North Korea could end up the 'savior' of China, or the uncontested victor against both nations. A very clever scenario, you must agree. Were it true."

"F...Furthermore," Jerry Falmouth, Chief of Information Analysis, added while staring at a scowling Helen Schrivener, Cerebrus' vocal Far Eastern Liaison, "N...North Korea is well p... positioned in the worldwide terrorist network to accomplish just such a f...feat. Agreed, five years ago, that title would have been reserved for acknowledged t...terrorist organizations throughout the M...Middle East. But these d...days, that label has expanded to include r...rogue nations and even organized c...criminal organizations perpetrating multi-national crime as a 'b...business'. Add to these the more nefarious multi-national c...corporations, which have no allegiance to any nation or creed other than p... profit. 'If it makes m...money or increases power, it's right,' seems to be their new ethic, w...whether that means working temporarily with extreme r...religious, nationalistic, c...criminal or other corporate organizations. Up to now, these 'soft t...terrorists' have operated pretty much independent of each other, but what if N... North Korea proposed an economic venture in everyone's s... shared best interest? Wh...what if that's what these auctions are about?" Scanning the faces at the table, Falmouth watched many nodding in agreement.

Chapter 29

Koski waited patiently in the driver's seat of her damaged,

rented SUV, watching a small single-prop-engine Cessna float down from the sky, wings fluttering, its nose pointed slightly to the side to compensate for the slightly oblique headwind. It was barely ten minutes since Stewart had called her and ordered her to the Fulton airport to await transportation to, of all places, Honolulu, Hawaii. Visiting the fiftieth state had always been a dream of hers, her work never before taking her to "paradise." It was a dream she had been saving to share with Falk, now that their relationship had advanced from collegial to romantic. She had never imagined when first assigned as an interagency videographer on Operation Who's Killing All the Lawyers that her association with the irascible man would progress to this. Actually, "could" would be more truthful than "would" as they both carried so much baggage from their earlier lives.

Their work together on The Judas List caper brought them closer, but it was during the multiple life-threatening incidents in Operation Imminent Danger that they discovered each harbored more concern for the other than him- or herself. That particular "aha" moment opened a deeply hidden, mutual desire. Since then their relationship had taken on a life of its own, progressing at every opportunity. If there was such a thing as destiny or fate, then it was strongly insinuating itself into her life. A long neglected part of her heart was still finding it difficult to believe in this second chance, while the rest pushed her relentlessly forward.

This was the first time since they'd begun working together that they'd had to split up. Now, if only that same destiny or fate that brought them together would just...

Koski startled at what sounded like a loud, distant rumble of thunder, noticing the next instant what appeared to be a fighter jet appear from within a bank of clouds, scream down to a point just above the end of the short runway to hover in mid-air. Moving sideways like a metallic crab, the plane slowly finished descending, stopping on the tarmac close to the control tower next to where she was parked. It took a moment for her to realize that this awkward monstrosity was the "military transport" which Stewart had arranged. A good thing, too, as, given a choice, she would have balked and declined. As it was, she was quite simply too surprised to object.

The plane's whining engines shut down and the cockpit cover slid back, revealing a pilot encased in a flight suit wearing a white helmet. The man, assuming it was a man, immediately began waving and pointing, indicating she was to take the navigator/ passenger seat behind him. Stunned, Koski gathered together the papers scattered across the passenger seat of her car, unshouldered her weapon, and removed the chamber round and clip, stuffing it all roughly into the standard Cerebrus-issue brown leather briefcase she had with her. Taking a deep breath, she returned her attention to the waiting pilot and plane.

The pilot, still in the front seat, was waving her towards the plane, if anything more ardently than at first. Tossing the keys onto the driver's seat, she exited the car and began jogging towards the plane. It was at this point the pilot climbed out of the cockpit and onto the back of the wing. Taking off his helmet, he knelt and extended a hand in greeting towards her. Stopping just before the back of the wing, she offered her hand to him in return greeting.

Grasping her hand, he pulled her up onto the small yellow-outlined area of the fuselage where he was standing. The area was small, forcing them uncomfortably face-to-face.

"Flight Lieutenant Roger Styles at your service, ma'am," the tall, young man offered, attempting a salute while trying not to touch his passenger. Given the limited space, the salute ended up a feeble and embarrassing one.

Immediately reaching back into the cockpit, he pulled out a bulky flight suit, boots and helmet like his own. "I need you to slip into these as quickly as possible, ma'am." Glancing at his watch, he continued, businesslike, "We'll need to leave in less than three minutes in order to avoid the next echo-intersection."

Koski scanned the man from his midnight black hair, bright grey eyes, square clean-shaven chin and lean physique to his standard-issue flight boots. Taking the flight suit and boots in hand, she answered, "Koski. Cerberus field agent. And where exactly am I to accomplish a less-than-three-minute change of clothes, captain? It is, captain, is it not?"

"Lieutenant, ma'am. Flight Lieutenant Roger..."

"Where am I to change, lieutenant?" Koski asked again, raising her briefcase. "There's a weapon inside with the clip and chamber round removed," adding as she stared at the tiny back seat, "and I'm claustrophobic."

Lieutenant Styles nodded his understanding and looked at what appeared to her like a very cramped back seat. "Thank you for telling me, ma'am. I suggest you change under the wing. Place your clothes in the briefcase, and, I'm sorry, but you've now less than two minutes."

With the lieutenant's assistance, Koski climbed off the wing, changed clothes and packed her 'civies' into the briefcase as fast as humanly possible. As she climbed awkwardly back onto the wing, the lieutenant checked his watch and pointed to the second seat. "If you don't mind, ma'am, we need to leave. Now. Please take your seat. I'll attach the helmet and strap you in. We've only moments to spare."

As soon as she was strapped into the narrow passenger seat, her pilot slipped the briefcase inside the cockpit alongside her seat and, talking calmly, placed the solid-white helmet, which had no way she could see to look out, over her head and locked it in place. Her flight suit instantly began hissing and adjusting to her figure. Ten seconds later, the plane shuddered, lurched, and Koski felt the fighter rise vertically. Looking out of the helmet's surprisingly translucent faceplate, her claustrophobia disappearing as she turned her head from side to side to watch the ground disappear. After rising about fifty feet, the plane hovered, rotated one hundred eighty degrees and abruptly thundered off into the same clouds from which it had appeared.

As the engines settled to a low constant growl, a rich masculine voice sounded in her helmet coming from every direction: "Welcome aboard, Agent Koski. I will be your pilot and flight crew for your trip to Honolulu, Hawaii, where it is currently a balmy 78 degrees. You're flying in the newest modification of a Marine Corps Vertical Short Take-Off and Landing F35B, nicknamed "Lightning III," the most prominent modifications being two seats instead of one and an extended fuel capacity. I noticed your concern when I locked on what appeared to be an opaque flight helmet, which you can see is anything but."

Koski took in the surprisingly wide view afforded by the unusual helmet, nodding to no one in particular, listening carefully while Lieutenant Styles droned on about the wonders of the cramped 'VSTOL' jet. In the end, what should have been a less than four-hour fighter jet flight to Honolulu ended up taking all of six plus hours due to a mid-air refueling, and a number of sudden, last moment zigzags to avoid event-echoes and echo intersections working their way westward.

Sitting in the cramped cabin, encased in the strange, continuously self-adjusting flight suit, she looked forward over the pilot's shoulder at the horizon and settled in for the flight. Eventually, the never-darkening corn-blue sky above abruptly extended below the plane to indicate they had began their flight over open ocean.

Traveling west, the day remained a forever afternoon, and the combination of the bright sun, the constant growl of the engines, the dull hiss of the aircraft slipping through the air, and the occasional chatter of the pilot to various ground controllers as they passed from one control area to the next, conspired to make her drift off to sleep, dreaming of warm sand and swaying palm trees.

A loud crackle, and the pilot's intrusive voice yanked her out of her slumber. "Ma'am, there's a colleague of yours just forward of the left wingtip."

Squirming in her seat to see, she could just make out an all-black, wedge-shaped triangle, and a helmeted passenger saluting at her. Knowing that she and Falk were at last back together made her blush. Thankfully, wrapped in her flight suit and helmet, flying in a military airplane at an unimaginable speed in the sparse upper atmosphere, no one would ever notice.

Her plane drifted nearer his and she returned his salute with a wave. After their brief reunion, Falk's aircraft drifted away and ahead. Whatever awaited them at their destination, Koski felt a wave of gratitude that they would at least be facing it together.

Just as she was ready to resettle in, her jet lurched, the engines stopped, and she felt blood rush to her upper body and flood her face, as if she were blushing again, but this time more extremely and without reason. The plane abruptly shook as the engines auto-restarted and she felt her body pressed hard into her seat. Any panic attacks were overridden as she watched, wide-eyed, Falk's plane begin spiraling nose down towards the ocean below. A moment later, the headphones inside her helmet crackled with chatter between her pilot and Falks', and her plane began a controlled nose dive, following Falk's plane but slower and from a distance.

The hazy corn-blue that had surrounded the plane was suddenly replaced by a blanket of endless, tiny, white dots against a dark blue background. Koski's mind shouted, *Waves! Whitecaps!* in frightened recognition, as Falks' plane shuddered and discharging a belch of flame and smoke, it's engines at last reigniting.

Falk's jet immediately leveled and began shakily climbing, while her plane shot upwards, as if to garner a better view. She felt her stomach sink and saw sparkles appear and dance before her eyes. The next moment, her flight suit hissed and tightened about her lower body, and the sinking feeling in her stomach stopped and the delicate sparkles returned to wherever it was they had previously been. Her jet resumed smooth and level flight, some distance above and behind Falk's.

Koski's helmet suddenly filled with Lieutenant Style's calm voice: "Sorry ma'am. We hit an unexpected event-echo, and, while our plane responded admirably, your friend's encountered some significant problems. They *almost...*"

Before he could finish, Koski's earphones died, and she felt herself tossed forward into her restraining straps, her helmet whipping forward, barely missing the back of the Lieutenant's seat. It seemed like Style, for some reason, had suddenly cut all power to the engines, and the plane had stopped in midair. The next moment the nose pointed down, where, over the pilot's shoulder, ahead and below, she saw two brilliant flashes, and watched in slow motion, two seats eject from the black moth of a plane that tumbled into ocean in an huge spray immediately engulfed in an explosion of flame, smoke, and pieces. One moment the flash was visible, the next, her own aircraft's engines had restarted, her pilot had regained control and her plane had streaked past. It all happened so fast, Koski didn't have time to see if Falk or the pilot had landed safely in the water below.

The plane slowed and made a sharp turn. Lieutenant Style's calm voice immediately cut in: "Sorry, ma'am. Our companion plane is down. I'm circling to try to locate survivors." There was something in his tone when he said "try to locate survivors" that sent a chill down her spine.

Completing a full circle, the VSTOL came to a helicopter-like pause above and to the side of the area where the plane had hit the ocean. At Lieutenant Style's command, they began a search of the area, the pilot concentrating on left side, Koski the right.

There was no sign of wreckage, ejection seats or parachutes. Nothing. Nothing at all but endless choppy, white-capped waves. From where they hovered, the ocean looked an huge blanket of ominous black dappled by small white polka dots.

"It's not unusual not to find anything on first glance, ma'am," the pilot assured her, turning the plane in a slow 360-degree circle, but his assurance did little to quiet her heart. *It's when you think you've lost someone that you learn how much they really mean to you*, she thought, her heart feeling as if it were tearing apart. She realized in that moment how much she had come to love the incorrigible man always ready to put his life on the line for her and his country.

"We're running low on fuel, ma'am, and, given the collapse of the ground-based Hazard Warning Assistance System, our own situation is highly volatile. From here on, we'll be flying by the seat of our pants, meaning we will have no more advance warning regarding echo-intersections. I've radioed the impact area coordinates to Honolulu area military air traffic control as well as input a report into our in-flight recorder. I've also issued a general SOS in addition to your colleague's Mayday. I would like to to stay and search a few more minutes, but we need to continue on our flight plan in order to get you to Honolulu before fuel runs out."

Koski felt sick. Was this how her "second chance" at a relationship was to end? Before it even had the opportunity to formally begin? Shaking her head to clear her mind, she asked the pilot to do one more sweep, a little lower this time. Just one more, she begged, until the lieutenant reluctantly complied. Taking the plane lower was risky. It could be easily flipped by an errant updraft, and would be unable to recover if another intersection hit them.

It was in the last quarter of this second sweep that Koski spotted an ejection seat bobbing up and down with what looked to her like a rapidly sinking orange and white tail. "There!" she shouted, trying inanely to point and, realizing the impracticality of her action in the tight cockpit quarters, added, "To your right. Low. About two o'clock."

"I see it, ma'am!" Style answered, nudging the plane forward while banking to get a better view and hopefully identify the occupant.

"I can't tell..." Koski began to say, when the water about the seat changed in color from inky blue to white and began to boil.

"What the...?" the pilot began, as the water lightened and frothed in a long, wide, whale-like swath, the ejection seat directly forward of it's middle. Seconds later, the top of a submarine sail parted the surface.

Lieutenant Style began backing the VSTOL away, even as he broadcast, "Yankee-alpha-romeo-three-six-niner reporting the surfacing of a submarine..." followed, when the the full sail was in view and it's cyrillic marks accompanied by a set of numbers and a large red star became apparent, "...of a Russian Yassen-class submarine..." The deck hatch opened below them and several armed Russian sailors ran to the ejection seat now fully separated from its parachute and resting next on the submarine's deck.

"Identifying marks, kilo-three-niner-two 'Severodvinsk'. Submarine is attempting recovery of one of the ejected crew from our downed companion..."

Koski watched the Russian sailors lift a limp flight-suited body from the ejection seat and carry the body on their shoulders to the open hatch.

"Falk?" she whispered, unable to make out the captured man's identity as it slipped down the hatch.

"Joe?" she asked again, as if by asking again and using his first name, she could somehow assure that it *was* him and that he was still alive.

The hatch closed and the submarine immediately began descending back into the swirling waters.

In the aircraft, a buzzer sounded. "Ma'am, we need to get the hell out of here. That submarine is state-of-the-art and has the ability to take us down anytime their captain wants.

"Our navy already has this location from the Mayday and SOS, and I've conveyed the name of the specific submarine. America and Russia will most likely soon be working on what to do about their captive, but like I said, we've got to get the hell out of here."

Before the lieutenant had finished his monologue, the plane

was pointing 180 degrees away from where the incident had taken place, its engines screaming, its fuselage straining to get far away from the submarine as possible.

Chapter 30

"It's time for someone to play Devil's advocate," answered Helen Schrivener. "Does anyone at this table really think North Korea capable of leading a multifarious, dark, international consortium? One of *global* extent? Does anyone here other than Kate, David, Jerry and our leader *really* believe North Korea cares one whit about what's going on in the 'outside' world other than to take propaganda advantage of world events for its own purposes?"

Kate, hearing Helen Schrivener's challenge, hesitated, looking to Stewart for permission to speak. Stewart surveyed the room, paused, checked his watch, then nodded his approval for her to speak yet again.

"First," Kate Keenan stated, "my section has narrowed down the location of the likely auctioneer to an area in the Far Eastern portion of Asia where Russia, China and North Korea all converge. Unfortunately the exact location, which might give us more information on the actual perpetrator, hasn't yet been resolved.

"But given this information, while Bureau 121's hackers have been stepping up the number and scope of their cyber-attacks, we've noticed a new and very disconcerting trend in BitCoin usage.

"As I mentioned earlier, it was discovery of The Silk Road that prompted us to reconsider its possible tactical and strategic uses. People were selling not just merchandise, but also drugs, human slaves, and exotic and illegal armaments like former USSR tanks, missiles, uranium, even weapons of mass destruction. From there it would be a small step to selling 'contracts' to remove individuals for control of oil, water, food, cities, regions, even nations. What better way to broker and 'consolidate' wealth and power until the Silk Road was shut down? And remember: there can never be more than 21 million BitCoins in circulation. That means as the number approaches this limit, the relative value of any one BitCoin will vastly increase, and, from everything my section has seen, that's exactly what's happening.

"By participating in the BitCoin world, my section has been able to document an extraordinary increase in BitCoin values during the past four events to a current value of *several million dollars US per BitCoin*. This goes way beyond supply and demand. What it means is that BitCoins are likely being used and manipulated in these auctions to launder money. BitCoins, given their anonymous nature, are perfect for that.

"In the last three weeks we watched twelve million BitCoins disappear from circulation and then suddenly re-appear. At this moment, the current exchange value is *twenty million dollars US per BitCoin*. That provides a laundering capacity of four hundred trillion dollars worth of currency, and the bidding war has yet to reach it's peak. Given the trend, by the time of the next event all twenty-one million BitCoins will likely be in circulation at an estimated value of *five-hundred to a thousand-million dollars US per BitCoin*, for a total laundering and purchasing capacity of roughly *twenty-one quadrillion dollars*. One can only imagine the auctioneer's fee."

Kate's disclosure animated Jerry Falmouth, who accepted the right to speak from Kate and Helen and immediately launched into his own passionate argument. "F...Freed from financial and economic constraints, N...North Korea would be able to pursue its stated primary interests without c...constraint. And how could they b...best accomplish this? One assumes that, simply by hosting the auctions, th...they would amass financial resources well beyond that of any other n...nation, including their stated arch enemy, the USA. N...North Korea has watched Ch...China attempt to accomplish the defeat of the USA by temporarily letting go of 't... true' Communism and substituting profit-motive c...capitalism, but, of course, its leaders can't publicly acknowledge that, not without losing d...dictatorial control over their g...government.

"That m...means to me that N...North Korea has to be the s... seller, at least until it has accumulated enough f...fees from brokering to allow *it* to p...play in the 'big sandbox', too. Given what I've h...heard so far, it will reach that p...point just in time for the auctioning off of Hawaii and, one assumes, the W...West Coast and Pacific Trust Islands. And, we all have to acknowledge the p...possibility, that his next auction might actually include Pacific Rim *countries* as well. That could include Indonesia, Australia, and J...Japan, territories N...North Korea has at one time or another greatly c...coveted. And should N...North Korea's ambitions increase in p...proportion to its increasing w...wealth and p...power, the next auction or subsequent auctions might also include Eastern R...Russia, Alaska, Western Canada, Central America, C...Coastal South America, even Ch...China.

"Initially, North Korea needed sufficient b...buyers, either competing or working in c...concert, to amass the immense initial monetary assets it n...needed simply to survive. That requires dark money. Lots and lots of laundered d...dark money. And since the initial auctions have th...thus far been strictly for United States p...property, the participants would likely be ones that, for one reason or another, harbor a gr...grudge against the USA or its allies. Maybe even a gr...grudge against *all* the n...nations of the world that have participated in any way in restraining N...North Korea. Or their focus may instead b...be against 'United States Imperialism', d...democracy or c...capitalism. Such an idea isn't n...new. But it would represent a d...dangerous, re-envisioning of a *new* New W...World Order like so many talk of and fear these d...days." With that, Jerry Falmouth sighed and fell back into his chair.

Stewart noted the eyes of everyone sitting around the table wide with concern. Slowly attention turned to a tense looking Franklin Gaston, Cerebrus' Programs Manager. Frank was sitting in the midst of the Middle East Coalition group with Helen Schrivener, who was visibly encouraging him to speak.

"Whether or not that's truly valid," Gaston began, "remains to be seen. I must admit, however, based on what I've just heard, it seems that North Korea by itself *would* be capable, through subterfuge and with a bit of assistance, of devising, organizing and implementing the kind of attack we're experiencing. While I still advocate a Middle Eastern Consortium, here's an afterthought on the North Korean scenario: The bidders won't likely fear that North Korea will cheat them and try to 'take over the world', not with the successful buyers possessing in hand what they consider to be agreements of regional purchase or control. That, of course, assumes that America's ability to mount a cohesive defense ultimately collapses, as it appears to be doing right now. Actually, I am suddenly reminded that during the last decade, the USA experienced near *financial* collapse *several* times. These events and auctions, however, represent something else. I think of it as a tipping point. If North Korea's truly behind them, then it should, even now, be near rich enough to break entirely free of sanctions and achieve it's wildest dreams, cementing in its current regime while at the same time eliminating its perceived worst enemy."

"Anyone have more to add?" Stewart asked as soon as Gaston had finished.

The tense silence suggested not, but before Stewart could call for a second round of voting, a muted alert sounded and a red colored dot appeared in the center of the situation screen behind him immediately next to where Spokane, Washington, was located. Everyone's cell phones began ringing. Stewart turned his face away from the table and the myriad conversations that were taking place to take a call from Colonel Rellin.

"Well, Stewart, this is exactly as we feared," Rellin confimed, "but with a small yet significant twist: This time the event epicenter is located in the center of urban Spokane, and the echo-waves are disrupting things on a much bigger scale than before. Looks like your idea that the three previous events were preludes to something bigger and more aggressive were true after all.

"Reports are coming in of cars, buses, trains and airplanes, all momentarily stalling wherever an event-echo passes over them. Worse, echoes from the other events have already begun reaching Eastern Washington, and will soon begin intersecting with those from this new event. The situation is already heavily stressing the Western power grid. Train stations, airports, hospitals, radio and television stations, military bases, the national guard, everything, after going out, is being switched to emergency power, or, where there is no emergency power available, they're simply working as best they can. Our NSA analysts project an imminent general blackout in the Northwest that will spread across the United States, taking down every regional power grid in its path. This one is lethal. And it should hit Seattle, its port and the nearby Naval, Air and Army facilities very soon."

"Was there an auction?" asked Stewart.

"Yes. Same as the other events, but this time, we had all available military and governmental resources poised and ready to watch, observe and analyze. We may not yet know how to stop it, but we're getting pretty darn close to being able to predict where the next event and auction will occur and what it's effects will be. Everything points to the next epicenter being in urban Honolulu, Hawaii.

"Although we still don't know the identities of the bidders, the ultimate buyer or the seller, this time we were more successful tracking the flow of BitCoins through the dark TOR system. I can now say with reasonable assurance that this auction was the biggest yet, it's total value close to three hundred *trillion* U.S. dollars, depending on when and how the BitCoins exchanged were actually purchased, and how the base currency, whatever it was, was laundered. In today's market, we're estimating the seller's commission at roughly *one hundred trillion U.S. dollars...*"

"God almighty! That's..." began Stewart.

"Yeah," replied Rellin. "Multiply that by the number of auctions so far and it's going to be more than the USA's gross national product and debt combined. Looks like we're approaching the endgame, and it looks like it's going to happen in Honolulu."

"I've just sent Koski and Falk there..." Stewart replied, the tone of his voice betraying equal amounts of satisfaction, determination and concern.

Chapter 31

Stewart removed his cellular from his ear and held it at his side, his hand hanging limply. Turning back to the assembled group, he said with finality, "We must complete this exercise."

"I've one more thing to add," interrupted Kate. "It occurs to me that, in spite of the insights we've gained and our closeness to consensus, we've still not come up with a way to stop the events and auctions from happening. We're closer than ever to a possible *why*—and attendant who, what, when and where—but we're just as helpless now as we were before at stopping the nation's fall into chaos. We may have ferreted out the purpose, and even the most probable instigator, but we still don't know *how* the *events* are propagated."

Everyone quieted and took a seat around the table while Kate assumed a command position next to the situation screen. Pointing with a finger at Laplacia, Vermont, and tapping the monitor screen at each subsequent event epicenter, she said, "I initially envisioned what we're seeing as a row of falling dominoes, ending in the collapse of our government, but now I'm wondering, given the change from country to urban epicenter, if the present event might represent the first in a *new* line of dominoes.

"With whatever we can glean from Spokane, and with Koski and Falk in place in Hawaii well before the next event, we might, this time, be able to capture the agents, their handlers or controllers for questioning. Given what Mr. Stewart shared regarding the nature of the Oriental agent he attempted to interrogate, I say let Koski and Falk do what they're best at doing: dealing with the agents, handlers and controllers. In short, I now believe it really doesn't matter so much what we come to consensus about at this moment, but more that we're finally able to *focus our efforts* in the most productive direction. What we need is another field team working alongside Koski and Falk to identify the *how* and possibly prevent the next event in Hawaii from happening. What we really need is…"

"You, Kate," completed Stewart for those sitting anxiously around the table. "We need *you*, working the technological aspect *in the field*, focused entirely on *how* the events are propagated and might be stopped, in parallel with Koski and Falk."

Stewart returned his cellphone to his ear, and issued the beleaguered Colonel Rellin yet another priority request for air transportation, this time for Kate Keenan to join Koski and Falk in Hawaii as soon as possible. This time, however, Colonel Rellin balked, military planes being subject to rapidly increasing priorities, and acknowledging that he would make the arrangements if Stewart would provide a Cerebrus plane. Steward reluctantly agreed.

Pocketing his phone, he nodded to Kate to acknowledge that preparations were underway, then, he made a sweeping gesture that encompassed everyone sitting about the table. "I agree with everything Kate's just said. It's absolutely clear to me that we need her in the field more than we do here. But I still think a true consensus opinion from this group will still be useful to the Joint Chiefs as well as our three agents. So, I reiterate: It's time for a second vote. Let's finish this Delphi session and arm our nation and field agents with the best intelligence advice possible at this time. Any objections?'"

Everyone around the table looked to their left and right, and seeing no dissenters, retook up paper pen and scribbled a vote. Moments later, Kate, having collected the sheets and counted them, announced simply, "North Korea. Unanimous."

As each member rose and prepared to leave the room to apply what they had as a group decided to his or her particular area of expertise, Kate slid to Stewart's side. "You know, Tom, except for Operation Finding Kate after which you recruited me, I've never actually 'been in the field'. I've always been..."

The phone in Stewart's hand buzzed.

"Stewart here," he announced, signaling for everyone to remain in place for the moment while turning his face aside. "Yes. Yes." The moment he signed off, the phone buzzed again. "Stewart here. Yes. No. Yes. I'm sending Kate."

Closing his cell phone, Stewart turned to address his audience. "The first call was about Falk. He was in a stealth B2 bomber-jet about two hundred miles out of Oahu when the plane's engines shut down..."

The collective intake of breath could be heard throughout the room.

"The second was about Koski. She was in a military fighter immediately behind Falk. They experienced a similar shutdown, but their engines restarted in time. They had just enough fuel to follow Falk's plane down, mark it's position, and continue on to Hickam Airfield on Oahu."

Fixing his eyes on Kate, Stewart continued: "I've informed Koski you're coming. Looks like our Honolulu field operation's going to depend entirely on you and her."

"Yes, sir," answered Kate seriously, turning and walking towards the door. Stopping just before exiting, she turned to face the group, offer a jaunty military-like salute and a decisive, "Yes, Sirs!" before leaving.

One by one, the members of the Tiger Team left the room. When at last it was empty, Stewart slumped into a chair to steal a moment and think.

A North Korean venture made sense.

He imagined the various dark elements of the world negotiating, forming and reforming alliances in preparation for each auction, each alliance intent on winning the next bid and "rights" to a region of what was rapidly becoming the "former USA." Would these players come together in the end? Who would eventually "own" the former United States of America? What would the consequences be? Would there be anyone left to jump in and protect the world from destroying itself as the world's policeman, the "good ol' USA", had done so many times in the past? If the criminal element took precedence, it would likely result in organized crime at a level never before imagined. And until the "new" New World Order, or whatever it finally called itself came into being, what would happen to the balance of power that had served to protect the world and humanity from utter destruction?

The world would, he decided, most likely be engulfed in a power struggle of epic proportions that would bring out and sadly legitimize the worst of anarchy, crime, militarism, capitalism, and, if, as the Tiger Team suspected, North Korean despotism. At the least, the newly purchased, "autonomous regions" of the former USA could be expected to immediately begin negotiating between each other to form new political, economic or ideological consortiums. The number of permutations were as staggering as Stewart's wildest imaginings, and, unfortunately, none bode well.

Chapter 32

Kate's transport arrangements happened so fast she barely had time to exit the building before she was met in front of Cerebrus' headquarters by a sleek, black government limousine. A "man in black" escorted her into the car. Once inside, Kate chose the front-facing couch seat at the back. "No point in getting too comfortable, ma'am. We'll be arriving at the airport very soon," the man said, driving skillfully into traffic. Having said what was apparently required, the man returned his attention to driving, providing Kate a short, but welcome modicum of privacy.

Relaxing on the smooth leather, she did a quick inventory of her travel resources. She hadn't had time to pack clothes or even piece together a travel bag. All she had was what she wore to work that day and whatever makeup she had in her purse.

She was interrupted in her task by the driver.

"This is for you, ma'am, compliments of Mr. Stewart," her driver said, holding a shoulder bag at length towards her without turning around. Kate scuttled forward, grasped it from the man's hands and returned to her seat. Opening it, she was delighted to see a variety of amenities including a pack of washlets, a fold-out hair brush, several sandwiches, a bottle of water and a blow-up neck pillow.

Before she could sort through the remainder of the much-appreciated provisions, the limousine slowed and passed through a gate into a nondescript private airfield where a single sleek, white commercial jet with upturned wingtips and a pregnant bump slightly amidships lay poised and ready, engines whining. The limousine proceeded to the foot of the passenger ramp and stopped.

"Your plane, ma'am," the man who had handed her the flight bag said, opening the car door for her.

The plane was impressive. It bore no commercial markings, only the minimum required identification numbers. Noting its eight passenger windows, Kate wondered with whom she would be flying. Climbing up the ramp, she was greeted by a uniformed flight attendant, who ushered her into the main cabin.

The interior was decorated in calm, pastel earth tones. The

attendant offered her seating in one of two, facing, plush leather, executive-style chairs, one in front, the other behind a sizable work table. On the other side of the plane was a long leather sofa, extending the length of the interior. Sitting in the further executive chair, the flight attendant buckled her in, walked silently forward and closed the pressure hatch. Scanning the interior disbelievingly, Kate became aware that she would be the only passenger aboard this flight.

As the plane rolled down the runway, the flight attendant returned to advise Kate of the safety features of the Gulfstream G650ER, which blessedly included a shower and a closet full of clothes, all in exactly her size chosen by fashion-conscious preflight attendants on contract to Cerebrus. *They've gone all out for me,* she thought. *Or, this is all that happened to be left at the time,* her unconscious mind mulled, adding, *or this is an elegant goodbye for a mission from which I am not likely to return.* Her first thought was her first choice, she told herself. Irrespective of the situation awaiting her at the other end, this portended to be a most pleasant flight, and she would at least arrive fresh and well dressed.

Chapter 33

The two o'clock Hawaiian sun pressed heavily on the red-haired CIA officer's exposed lily-white face and arms. The burning sunlight was made even hotter and more intense by his standing, unshaded and restless, on the hot black asphalt tarmac at Hickham Air Force Base, located not far from Pearl Harbor Naval Base. Agent Ben Azaga, a fit, clean-shaven man in his early 40s, wearing an aloha shirt opened at the neck, white linen pants and a white linen tropical jacket with the sleeves rolled up, raised a bare forearm to wipe off the sweat that was beading on his forehead. New beads immediately replaced them, coalescing and flowing in small rivulets down his face. *Sweat is supposed to make you feel cooler not hotter,* he thought.

He'd never experienced anything like this in his natal Ireland or on the Continent where he'd recently been loaned by British MI5 to the US CIA. *Only the American CIA,* he mused, *would have the gall to transfer a man with such fair skin, acclimatized to cold, clouds and rain, to a location with such intensely unremitting sunlight.*

Azaga shrugged to readjust the uncomfortable shoulder holster sticking like strapping tape against his thoroughly soaked chest. A gentle, flower-scented breeze mercifully rustled his red, wavy hair, providing a moment of relief. But only a moment. It was one of those days in paradise when the trade-winds were absent, replaced by a southeast "Kona" wind blowing off of Kilauea volcano on Big Island. The effect was like that of standing in front of a giant hot hair dryer. Kona winds further portended heavy evening humidity and unremittingly uncomfortable nights.

Where the hell is the military plane carrying that hot-shot Cerebrus agent whom I'm supposed to meet? he thought looking at his wrist watch for the umpteenth time over the last hour. True, they supposedly had another twenty-four hours before the next predicted "event," hopefully the final one, unfortunately, the one that was predicted to be the last the United States of America would experience as an intact nation. After that, who knew? Would the events stop in Hawaii or continue marching west? Obtaining an answer to that question was why he had been loaned to the CIA. On the other hand, maybe the predicted Hawaii event would prove a dud. Maybe it was too close to the Communist axis: Russia,

China and North Korea. Too much collateral damage. Enough damage had already been wreaked on the USA, leaving it ripe for whatever nefarious endgame was supposedly about to come into play.

In the far distance, a dot appeared, growing steadily in size in the shimmering heat. Azaga squinted and wiped his eyes to see better. It didn't look like the B2 he was impatiently awaiting. It looked more like one of the new fighters recently deployed at Marine Base Kaneohe, an F35 "Lightening" VSTOL. Kaneohe, however, was on the other side of the island, and the Marines rarely used Hickham. His interest increased further when the fighter slowed its approach and began hovering over a spot a hundred feet in front of him.

The moment the plane touched down, the cockpit slid back revealing two helmeted individuals instead of one like the F35s he'd seen. Even more unusual, when the second person climbed out onto the wing with a large brown briefcase and the flight helmet was removed, the expected man turned into a woman.

Curious, Azaga thought as the male pilot and his female passenger climbed off the plane's wing and walked directly towards him. On the way, the woman paused, awkwardly opening the briefcase and removing an automatic and a loaded clip, which she held up in one hand, showing them to the sun-reddened man standing wide-eyed in front of them.

Curiouser and curiouser, Azaga thought, reaching his right hand instinctively towards his own weapon.

The pilot offered a hand. "Flight Lieutenant Roger Style, Sir, delivering…"

Koski slipped the weapon and clip back into the briefcase, shifted the helmet and briefcase to her left hand, and thrust an open right hand towards the man in front of Lieutenant Style. "Cerebrus Agent Susan Koski," she interrupted.

The man sweating profusely before her looked puzzled.

Who the hell are these two? Azaga wondered, hesitating to shake either's hand. The pilot hadn't identified himself as Falk and didn't look at all like the photo he'd been shown at briefing, and he had been led to believe that Falk was a man not a woman. It was never a good sign when pre-arrangements didn't work out.

Must be Falk's CIA liaison, Koski concluded, scanning the discomforted man. Observing him closer, she concluded, *Looks like a mummified roast chicken.*

"Wha...?" the white clothed, sunburned chicken asked, glancing from one to the other of the two wrong people greeting him while grasping the handle of his weapon firmer.

"What news of Falk?" Koski blurted. The mention of Falk's name afforded Azaga instant though limited relief.

"None," replied Azaga cautiously, even more perplexed. "I was supposed to meet him here. He was *supposed* to arrive an hour ago in a commandeered B2..."

"We were escorting his plane," interrupted the pilot. "It experienced an echo-intersection and went down in the ocean about 200 miles off Oahu..."

"...where he or his pilot, we couldn't tell which, was picked up by a Russian submarine," concluded Koski. "I take it you haven't heard..."

Jesus! What kind of circus is this? Azaga thought. Satisfied nonetheless that the two were genuine, he released his grip on his weapon.

"Ben Azaga, MI5 on loan to the CIA. You're right Agent Koski, I haven't heard any of this. Things here have been...well...

complex...what with all the interagency preparations for the next event. Like I said, I was sent to meet Agent Falk and act as his international interagency resource liaison while he was here. It was my understanding that he was to head up a special field operation to locate a couple of foreign agents and hopefully a handler or controller here on the island. The ocean? A Russian submarine?"

Koski's voice broke when she continued, unable as she was to hide her personal concern. "We don't know if it was Falk who was taken. I...we...don't even know if he's alive..."

"I radioed the information ahead about twenty minutes ago," the lieutenant added, as if trying to mollify Azaga and afford the man some justification for his confusion. "I'm sorry, but I must get back in the air. I have urgent continuing orders..."

"Yes, of course you do," Azaga replied, picking up Koski's briefcase and slipping a free arm under her slumped shoulders. She looked distressed and exhausted. "I can take things from here, Agent."

Lieutenant Styles offered the MI5/CIA agent the briefest of salutes. It had been hard on his passenger to witness her companion's jet explode in the ocean in a ball of flame, and worse, to watch helplessly while they backed away from the Russian submarine that had captured one or the other of the plane's inhabitants. There was no indication of the second inhabitant's condition or whereabouts, and the one aggressively taken aboard Russian submarine, for all anyone knew, might already be dead.

Chapter 34

Captain Alexander Konstantine Korovich stared at the limp, wet form tied onto a metal folding chair in the middle of the briefing room. The form was surrounded on three sides by armed

Russian "marines"—military-political Spatznatz forces specifically detailed to this newest of fast attack submarines—and wondered what he'd "caught."

It was always risky, on several levels, to surface. Most dangerous was that it revealed one's existence and position. In waters like these, so close to Hawaii, that was never a good thing to do. Besides, his ostensible assignment was to silently gather intelligence, and neither be seen nor engage. Hawaii was the westernmost home to a forward branch of America's Pacific military forces, and that included a fleet of modern, efficient submarine hunter-killers.

His secondary, more secret mission, the one that took him to this dangerous location and forced him to briefly reveal himself, was to find a way of opening a communication back-channel with America.

America's forces were at full alert, and the situation in the USA had become so tense his military superiors felt that any direct communication from Mother Russia right now might cause America's military to reflexively squeeze the hair-trigger. At best, anything coming from Russia at this time would likely be construed a prelude to an overt act of Russian aggression. Another Pearl Harbor. All that being said, he couldn't pass up the opportunity to "save" what seemed to be the pilot of the downed American B2 they'd spotted and been tracking with interest.

The mere presence of a solitary B2 in this part of the Pacific reflected the level of desperation the United States of America had to be feeling, given its state of affairs. For some reason that entirely eluded Korovich and his military superiors, Eurasia and Africa were being spared the crippling incidents that were bringing down the most powerful nation in the world, and, if Russian computer experts were right, after that, Canada, Mexico, and possibly then Central and South America. In summary, the whole of the Americas. In short, he knew he'd not only caught a big one, he'd caught the right one.

It was nonetheless difficult to tell exactly how big or right, given that the man—he assumed it was a man from what he could make out of its general physique enclosed as it was in a wet, bulky, pressurized flight suit and opaque black helmet. The figure hadn't struggled while they hurried it through the hatch into the bowels of the submarine. It didn't struggle now, while the ship's doctor and medic worked to carefully detach the helmet.

"He's breathing, Cap' Korov, Sir," the doctor announced in Russian, inspecting, then laying aside the intriguing helmet. "Cap' Korov," as his crew fondly called him, watched the doctor and his assistant begin cutting off the flight suit of their surprise guest.

Cap' Korov, a squat man with a head of ultra-short, white fuzz instead of hair—rubbed his wiry white chin stubble with a ham of a hand. His rumpled, short-sleeved working uniform looked as if he had worn it constantly throughout the week. He was joined by a tall, thin, officious-looking man in a smartly creased uniform, whose military insignia identified him as the submarine's political intelligence officer. The pair stood next to each other, observing the slowly emerging figure. The two officers' divergent physiques made them look like a cartoon caricature of Mutt and Jeff.

"And what is this you've brought aboard, Korov?" the tall one asked in crisp Muscovite Russian, shaking his head from side-to-side in mock disgust. "We're supposed to be running reconnaissance, not stopping to shop at every American garage sale we happen by."

"I'm not sure, Comrade Grigorov," the captain replied in his signature St. Petersburg accent, scratching his chin and smiling. "But this is what's left of an American B2..."

Grigorov's thin eyebrows joined together and rose in a surprise salute. "An American B2?"

"Of that much I am certain. While following it on radar, we intercepted a 'mayday' and a few moments later an ejection seat appeared on our sonar on surface..."

"The plane, Korov? What of the plane?" interrupted Grigorov greedily.

"Nothing but tiny pieces scattered over a kilometer-wide area, none of which, aside from this man's ejection seat, were large enough show up on our sensors. Of course, we couldn't stay to inspect. We had barely enough time to capture him and hide. An American military VSTOL plane was hovering nearby. I pinged it with our attack radar and we each took off in opposite directions."

"So we are compromised?"

"One can never be certain of the outcome of such an encounter," Korov replied carefully. "But we can surmise from the VSTOL pilot's unwillingness to engage, the quickness with which the plane turned to run, and the direction in which it fled, that it had an agenda even more urgent than recovering one of their own. What, Grigorov, could be that urgent? There's been no sign of military air or surface activity beyond the usual high-readiness preparations. Now why is that, do you suppose, Comrade Grigorov?"

Grigorov shrugged his shoulders conveying his lack of interest in military tactics, instead carefully eyeing the man being stripped to his non-military skivvies.

The man's head lolled forward chin to chest, revealing a small stack of papers taped to one side of his chest. Barely able to restrain himself from grabbing the papers and interrogating the captured pilot, Grigorov offered a controlled nod to the medical officer to remove the papers and hand them to him.

The medical officer did as ordered and Grigorov immediately began rifling them. "*Der'mo*, these smell awful! I know sufficient English to recognize that they are not military, Korov," Grigorov announced. "In fact, they seem to make little sense, which suggests to me they're somehow encrypted, which further suggests this man is more than a pilot. I must assume they are intelligence documents, and need to send copies to Moscow immediately for further analysis." Finished perusing the horrid-smelling papers, Grigorov thrust them into the hands of a reluctant seaman waiting at stiff attention on Grigorov's right. The man, who sported radio operator's insignia, turned smartly and left for the radio room clutching the sheaf of papers in two fingers at the end of an outstretched hand.

Grigorov returned his attention to the intriguing and still unconscious man seated before him.

In the absence of any counter-orders from his political intelligence officer, Korov continued, "As I said, the other aircraft flew away in the opposite direction, towards, I presume, one of the many American military bases located in the Hawaiian Islands. I also presume the pilot issued a report stating that we have one of their pilots. By all expectations, the United States military should be scouring the area as we speak, unless, for examle, this man and his 'papers' are a decoy meant to distract us from what was on the VSTOL."

His counterpart nodded but continued staring at the man in the chair.

"On the other hand," Korov continued, "it seems more likely to me that the American military are too preoccupied at this moment to divert resources to search for him. They must be heavily engaged in preparing for the next odd occurrence, and trying figure out how to defend themselves from what everyone expects to be the final blow. As command has pointed out, these strange occurrences seem purposefully designed to individually be too small to be labeled as overt acts of war, yet collectively too complex and damaging to be mere acts of terrorism. It is in their cumulative effects that they are so destructive to a highly integrated digital/electronic society as the USA. As a whole, they are insidiously stripping that nation of its ability to function, while leaving all its natural and industrial resources intact for the taking. In that sense this series of occurrences presents an incredibly powerful opportunity—powerful enough tempt any enemy wait to acquire its people, land and resources without having to fight. An ingenious alternative to our present *detente*, is it not?

Grigorov continued to stare at the figure in the chair, as if trying to interrogate it telepathically.

"Is it then, Comrade Grigorov, presumptive to assume that their military authorities are simply too engaged at the moment to attempt the rescue of a man who has their ear and whose likely intent was to convey some crucial information? Surely even you couldn't have anticipated coming across a downed *intelligence agent* at just this moment. I'm guessing this man's mission somehow has everything to do with the next occurrence." *And what better backchannel conduit than such a man?* Cap' Korov stated emphatically in his mind.

The doctor cautiously lifted the figure's right eyelid, then the left, checking each eye's response with a pocket flashlight.

The figure in the chair groaned.

"He's coming around," the doctor said, stating the obvious.

"Good," said Korov. The two line officers took a step back to resurvey the man in the chair, then each other, as if testing each's mettle.

"What exactly do you have in mind?" asked Grigorov, resuming his role as submarine intelligence officer, only marginally subordinate to the captain. "If the Americans are, indeed, 'momentarily distracted', that leaves us little time to extract…"

"He's a 'guest', Comrade Grigorov. A 'guest'. As soon as he recovers his senses, I will notify United States Pacific Fleet to advise them of his 'rescue'…"

"What…?" Grigorov interrupted, astounded.

"…and gladly arrange to release him back to his own kind," Korov completed calmly.

The figure in the chair moved. His dazed eyes rolled, focused, then darted warily from one to another of the men around him. The medic opened an emergency first aid kit, and began wiping clotted blood from their 'guest's' face and mixed blood and vomitus from the rest of his body, while the doctor opened a suture kit.

"Amerikan…Agent," Korov addressed the man in broken-English, while slowly approaching the heavily bruised man sitting tensely and testing his restraints. "We…save…from…ocean. "

"The plane? The pilot?" asked Joseph Falk, parsing the room, and noting his flight suit on the floor to the side, little more than a cut pile of strips with the highly advanced flight helmet resting intact on top of the pile.

Noting their 'guest's' concern, Korov continued, "Plane…gone. Pilot…" he shrugged his shoulders while indicating by his facial expression that he shared his guest's pain. "I have…message…for

Amerika," he concluded while Grigorov stared at his comrade, dumbfounded.

Chapter 35

It took some time for Falk's head to clear, for Korov to convince Grigorov of the authenticity and primacy of his heretofore secret secondary orders, and to obtain the political-intelligence officer's reluctant cooperation, then, through Grigorov, who spoke much better English than the captain, to better convey his "message" to Falk and the USA.

What Korov had shared regarding his secret secondary objective was true, however, he carefully omitted his tertiary agenda: not only to establish a communications back-conduit between the US and Russia, but to inform the United States that Russia was as surprised by the occurrences as everyone else, and that she had no part in them. In short, Russia didn't want war. There was already shared worry in the Russian government and military command that the occurrences would be attributed to Russian, but equally, that they might not stop at the westernmost border of North America but continue to march across the Pacific and wreak havoc in their nation. To bolster their claim, the Russian government had ordered the military to share everything they knew about the occurrences, which Korov through an astonished Grigorov, assured Falk was substantive. They would do this, Korov qualified, if Falk could assure Russia's President and head of military command that the United States would, in return, stop regarding Russia as the immediate "enemy," and step down the alert level. In addition, in return for sharing information on the event occurrences. Russia wanted the USA to share everything known so far about the especially perplexing *pradazha* or sales accompanying the occurrences.

At Falk's nod of assent, Korov, through an increasingly astounded Grigorov, offered as proof of Russia's goodwill, that prior to the start of the occurrences, Russia had been secretly working on weaponizing a quantum physics phenomenon called 'entanglement'. In the process, they had shared the their work with China in order to enlist the Chinese military's assistance in producing an operational field prototype. The prototype, thought to still be in China, could not, however, be loosed without the necessary 'initiator' which Russian scientists had cautiously withheld from their Chinese colleagues.

Falk's exhausted body reawakened more with each revelation. By the end of the explanation, he wanted to offer Korov a triply heart-felt thanks, first for rescuing him, second for sharing the information he'd just received, and finally for the offer to work together to resolve the situation for the benefit of the USA, Russia, and, hopefully, the world.

Priority-wise, the most important thing now was for him to report what he'd learned to Stewart. It was likely that the hard-liners in the Pentagon were even now finalizing what actions they were planning to take against Russia, America's proverbial "enemy." Falk desperately needed to pass on what he'd heard to Stewart, so Stewart could vet it and pass it up the chain to the Joint Chiefs of Staff.

That was, of course, assuming that what he was being told was true. Korov's demeanor suggested to Falk that the man *believed* everything he was saying, though not necessarily so, the translating officer. The cold, careful manner in which Grigorov translated what Korov was saying, shouted caution and distrust. On Russian submarines, the political officer, which Grigorov's uniform and brusque manner clearly identified him as, often had secret orders or withheld key information until a critical moment, and was the only crew member who could directly countermand the captain's orders. And it looked to Falk's tired, but activated mind that Korov's sincerity was not shared by his political officer. That spelled trouble.

Falk listened carefully, probing wherever possible, and at the end was still waffling as to whether the pair's declared intent was genuine. In the end, he believed the captain, but couldn't fully convince himself that Korov was not a pawn in a political ruse to defuse or neutralize the threat of a pre-emptive strike by the USA against Russia, leaving Russia to deliver the final blow. It could also be meant to buy time for the fifth occurrence to happen, thereby denying the USA any ability at all to retaliate. Falk *wanted* to believe that, as Korov said, Russia, having been involved in the theory, design and development of the *kvantovaya mashina smerti*, referred to by Russian military scientists by the acronym "KMS," and translated literally, "Quantum Death Machine," was willing to share details about the technology. If true, it would be his, Cerebrus and the USA's first major break.

When questioned further about the weapon's status, Korov, through Grigorov, claimed that Russia had be unable to advanced the prototype, Russia's computing power being insufficient, Russian military research and development having taken a hit in the latest of a succession of increasingly austere budgets, national military priority having sifted from exotic weaponry to rejuvenating Russia's disorganized army and navy.

Questioned about how the device actually worked, Korov replied with difficultly through Grigorov, that it was a 'delivery system' like no other, as the USA could well see. In fact, though "weaponized," it wasn't technically a weapon at all. It was a system capable of instantaneous teleportation, the idea having been gleaned from watching the old American television series, "Star Trek" and its "transporter." It wasn't technically electronic at all, applying instead a unique property of "quantum strangeness."

The field equipment at the starting and ending locations, Grigorov explained, translating Korov's monologue, had to be *exactly* the same in overall mass, structure and function, in order to "synchronize" the two places in their respective "time-spaces."

Hence the 'custom design' look, thought Falk.

The synchronized sites took advantage of a *kvantovoye yavleniye*, a "quantum phenomenon," explained Korov through Grigorov, though the two were beginning to apologize for their lack of ability to fully explain the physics and effect a meaningful translation. Instead, at this point, Korov switched to reassuring Falk that if Falk provided a knowledgeable American scientist, their Russian scientists could better directly convey the details.

When queried about the satellite antennas, Korov, again through Grigorov, explained they were only necessary to synchronize the two spaces, allowing an object placed in either location to momentarily simultaneously appear in both. The object would then equally instantaneously revert back to one object in one of the two spaces. The simultaneous "transfer" as well as the execution of any actions the object was programmed to perform would appear to an observer to happen without taking up any time whatsoever. It didn't matter where the antennae were pointed, only that they were a perfectly functioning part of the equipment. For nationalistic reasons, they had all been positioned to point towards Sirius, the "dog," or "Red" star.

Hence their pointing to nothing located in near earth orbit, thought Falk.

Despite the seeming truthfulness of what had been shared, Falk still harbored the fear that he might be being used to blindside things in Honolulu and, by doing so, strip the USA of it's last opportunity for defense. What he desperately needed was the "knowledgeable American scientist," one who could be trusted with what could very well prove to the most dangerous technology ever created. It would have to be someone who was not just a world-class scientist, but who could be entrusted with such power. It would need, he concluded, to be someone in Cerebrus.

"I need to communicate what you've shared to my superiors in Washington," Falk urged Grigorov.

"With whom exactly do you propose to communicate?" asked the political officer warily.

Falk thought a moment. To reveal the identity of any agent in any clandestine organization was anathema; to give out the identity of the head of Cerebrus, was strictly taboo. Thinking fast, Falk eliminated Stewart, then Koski, assuming that if she hadn't gone down like him, she would be busy searching for the foreign agents and their handlers or controllers—his original task—in anticipation of the next event. Contacting her would also mean revealing the identity of not just another colleague, but, yes, his lover. But he needn't make that decision. While he had frequently trusted her with his life and the fate of the world, she wasn't the "knowledgeable American scientist" he needed.

In his head, Falk quickly ran through the names of the various chiefs of departments and divisions within Cerebrus and came up with only one person who fit the bill: Kate Keenan. She was a department head. She would have direct access to Stewart without Falk having to reveal him. Cerebrus' Chief Technical Advisor was an acknowledged scientist and, from his past dealings with her, one who was completely trustworthy. Revealing her identity would be a serious breach of protocol that would place her in imminent danger, but he was certain that she could handle it.

"Keenan. Kate Keenan. She's a 'knowledgeable American scientist' with access to civilian, military and governmental officials, as well as our best scientists and researchers."

The radio operator, having finished forwarding the images of the papers found taped to Falk's body, had returned after placing the papers in the security safe.

"Take our guest to the communications room," the Political Commissar told the stunned man, "and assist him in making contact with his colleague. And give him back his papers." When the radio operator hesitated, Grigorov added, "Comrade radioman: That is an order!"

The radio operator, mouth open, obliged after receiving Cap' Korov's grave and unexpected nod of assent.

Chapter 36

The private Gulfstream G650ER carrying Kate Keenan was less than two hundred miles out of Honolulu by the time she'd showered, made up, and donned an off-white, silk, two-piece tropical business suit from the closet. *Commanding,* she thought looking at her reflection in the closet's full length mirror. Something inside told her she would need that look to pull off her assignment. When she returned, she would have to thank Stewart.

This was, in fact, her first official Cerebrus field assignment, and given its gravity, Kate hadn't been surprised when she began receiving in flight situation reports—"sit reps"—from Cerebrus' Head of Field Operations, David Hallard, followed by Directors

Halsey and Small on the ever-changing international, national and regional political situations. Keenan was awaiting a call from Lou Richards, Cerebrus' Head of External Security, about any security changes, when she was interrupted by the flight attendant.

"Ma'am, I've a call for you," the she announced softly. "It's a radio-communication from the Pacific Ocean not far from where we are now. The instigator is Russian and speaks broken English. He keeps mentioning the name 'Falk'. For security reasons..."

"...I'll take it. Patch it over to me now, and secure this communication as best you can."

"That will mean revealing our position and that you are on board. There is a chance, ma'am, that it's a ruse to gather intelligence information and, if so, to possibly compromise this mission. I can't be responsible for your safety if you..."

"I accept full responsibility. Please make the connection now!"

A moment later, her cell phone rang. Kate held the phone to her ear with both hands, shaking with what would appear to any onlookers as anxiety or fear. But that would be because they didn't know of Kate's strong personal affection for Falk, he having swept her off her feet during their very first encounter. She never knew if her feelings were mutual, Koski having joined Falk as his partner shortly afterwards, and the two of them having been out on one after another assignment since. This situation presented her an opportunity to find out.

"Yes," Kate answered, her throat dry, her hands visibly shaking.

"Falk, here," replied a constantly distorting voice shrouded in static.

"We've been able to establish an emergency encryption protocol, so the line is now secure, ma'am," the co-pilot broke in.

"Falk, is it really you? I was advised that your plane went down and no survivors had been found. I…we…thought…"

"I'm okay. I'm a 'guest' aboard a Russian submarine. The captain assures me that Russia has nothing to do with the events or auctions. He says if I can identify a 'knowledgeable American scientist,' he will put that person in communication with Russian military scientists who have apparently been working on a device that could account for the events. I've been able to loosely corroborate some of what he's said, but I don't know enough quantum physics to be certain this isn't an elaborate counter-intelligence ploy. I need you to…" Falk's voice—Kate felt *certain* it was his—was slowly becoming re-engulfed in static. She *felt* certain, but was she certain enough to trust her life, that of her Cerebrus colleagues and the fate of the USA and possibly the entire world?

"Falk? Falk? Listen! I need you to tell me something so I can confirm your identity. Think. Something only the two of us…"

Falk's voice reasserted itself above the noisy background. "Operation Finding Kate. It's where we first met. We were quite attracted to each other. You asked about the faint white circle around my left ring finger where one expects a wedding ring. I…"

"Enough! Joe, what do you need? How can I help?" Kate replied, letting out an audible sigh. It had surprised her when he chose to reveal intensely personal details rather than a shared identity code or phrase. Then it occurred to her: Falk doesn't entirely trust his source. He's being careful not to compromise Cerebrus any further than is absolutely necessary. Okay, she would do whatever she could to help, but keep up her guard.

"I need you to stay on the phone, so the folks here can patch you to Russia and the military research team. Then I need you to conclude whether or not what they're saying is valid. When you come to that conclusion, I need you affirm or deny the validity and then contact your superiors and convey *everything you've found out*. If the info is true, I'll then need you to try to convince your superiors to contact the Joint Chiefs and assure them Russia is an ally, not an enemy. Can you do all this?"

"Yes," Kate answered without hesitating. "I'll wait for the patch and, if the information is valid, will convey my assessment to you, and then your message and what I've learned to my superiors. But what about you...?"

"I'm being treated well. As soon as the Russians are convinced we're playing honestly, they said they'll begin working out an 'exit' strategy for me. Kate, the radio-operator is running a finger across his throat meaning..." Falk's voice once again began distorting only to be engulfed completely in static.

"We've lost contact, ma'am," the co-pilot announced.

How am I supposed to validate technical information if we've lost contact? she thought. *All I know is that he's aboard a Russian submarine somewhere 'not too far away'.* Kate was about to call Stewart, when the co-pilot announced over the cabin speaker, "Another call, ma'am, from one of your colleagues. I'll route it, like the other, to your cellular using secure encryption.

"Falk?" Kate answered the moment the call went through.

"Falk?" came a puzzled, too-clear response. "Kate, this is Lou Richards. What? Have you heard from Falk?"

Kate explained as quickly as she could to Cerebrus' Head of External Security about what Falk—she was now convinced it was indeed Falk she'd talked with—had conveyed, and that the communication had broken before the link to the Russian military researchers had been established. She carefully avoided any mention of her feelings for Falk, or that they were one of the

1352

reasons she had been quick to accept the dangerous field assignment when Stewart suggested it. True, she wanted her own field mission, but she had to admit that she didn't want to lose the opportunity of meeting Falk and clarifying the attraction to her he'd just insinuated was real. She had been extremely careful to separate her feelings for him after Operation Finding Kate.

She was interrupted in thought and explanation yet again. "Ma'am. I've received another radio signal, this time via a Russian military satellite link. They're waiting."

Lou Richards had heard enough. "You have to follow up on this, but, Kate, be discrete and debrief with Stewart or me as soon as your talk with the Russian military scientists is over. Good luck, and welcome to the field."

Chapter 37

"Seventy-eight degrees, clear and sunny with constant fifteen mile per hour northeast trade winds. Light showers in the mountains in the early mornings and late evenings. Surf on the leeward side of the island is two to three feet with occasional swells to four. Another perfect day in paradise," the television weatherman droned. Koski had just awakened from a quick cat-nap in the quiet of her temporary billet at the Transient Officer's Facility at Pearl Harbor Naval Base. *Must have fallen asleep with the television on,* she mused. It felt good to hear something in this crazy would was "normal" for a change.

If fact, as far as the average Oahu resident was concerned, the events and auctions on the "mainland" might as well be happening on another planet. People in Hawaii seemed to her very insular in their thinking. Right now, they were busy preparing for work, a quick after lunch surf, and, for dinner maybe a picnic at the beach, all as if nothing had or was about to happen. *The joys of children and fools*, she thought enviously.

Having brought only what she'd stuffed into her briefcase, she'd dozed off in yesterday's clothing. Looking forward to taking a quick shower and ironing her rumpled clothes before grabbing a cup of coffee on her way to the multi-agent command post a few blocks away, Koski stretched and yawned. She sorely missed her usual five plus mile morning jog, but then, things had been anything but usual for her during the last few days.

The US Navy had taken the lead in assembling the special Joint Civilian/Military Command Center that was being brought up to speed even before she'd left Fulton, Ohio. Yesterday, upon arriving, Koski had successfully situated herself within the various military, federal, state and county agencies and could at least compliment herself on that. Now would come the harder and more important part for her work: attempting to locate the expected two agents and their handlers or controllers, assuming Honolulu was indeed the next target and that the event process proved the similar to Spokane.

The latter assumption particularly worried her. The Spokane event had occurred in the middle of a high-density urban area, not at an isolated country farmhouse like the others. Word had reached her that the two agents had been located several hours after the Spokane event, both dead, the "American" one having been shot by the "Oriental" who then ended her own life. There was no evidence that might suggest any extraction plan, but then, government officials had burst in on the remaining agent, and from what had been reported, the Oriental's suicide seemed more impulsive than planned.

Posing as a Chinese student interested in learning English and her American friend, they had been assigned by an English Second Language school to a matron who routinely offered a two-student "homestay" experience.

The remainder of the event and auction had been in the *modus operandi* of the prior events: There had been another auction near simultaneous with the event. This time the whole weight of the government's collective computer intelligence groups was brought to bear towards identifying the auction's place of origination, the locations from which various "bids" had come, and the trail of the winner's BitCoins. As yet, all the information hadn't yet been processed, leaving more rather than fewer hypotheses, and no really solid information.

Except for a few things: All the Oriental girls it had been discovered had entered the USA between one and two years prior, and records indicated they'd entered using what had proved to be a fake Chinese passport and visitor visa. They had immediately "disappeared" into the population at large. Also, each Oriental agent had entered the USA close to her final destination. A fast analysis by Homeland Security in Hawaii identified roughly twenty thousand Oriental girls with Chinese passports who had entered the USA via Honolulu during the past twenty-four months, two hundred of whom had not exited after their visas had expired. That narrowed the field considerably.

Furthermore, assuming the process would be the same as Spokane, Koski's first priority would be to identify Chinese *homestay* visitors with expired visas. In addition, the homestay placement should include an American girl who appeared to be a close pal. Finally, the home where they were staying should have a recently installed, new satellite antenna. Unfortunately, all the previous antenna installations had proven untraceable. To Koski, that meant the installation had been done non-commercially, which gave further credence to the idea that the two girls at the least had a local handler, most likely the person who installed the antenna. All that was unique enough to work with. It was too bad that, as Stewart had predicted, her replacement had found no further sign of Josh, the boy who had made contact with her then disappeared. The same appeared true of the Spokane girls suspected handler. If one had been present, he or she had disappeared and was dead or gone.

There was still a half day before the next event was expected to occur. Every moment of Koski's time for the next few hours would be focused on directing inter-agency field teams to check out each and every situation that fit the foreign agent's standing criteria.

After showering and running a conveniently supplied steam iron quickly over her clothes, she exited her room for the small cafeteria located near the building entrance. Pouring a cup of syrupy black military coffee into a styrofoam cup and selecting a small croissant that seemed to be calling to her, she was about to sit at one of the few empty tables when a very military looking Naval officer grasped her by the elbow. "Agent Koski? My apologies. I've been sent by Commander of Naval Intelligence at Pearl Harbor. Something's come up. Something you will definitely want to hear."

Chapter 38

Stewart was interrupted while nervously pacing his office in Washington DC by a ring on his cellular. It was out of his pocket and against his ear so quickly he fumbled and almost dropped it.

"Stewart here!"

"WHAT THE HELL ARE YOU DOING GIVING A RUSSIAN

SUBMARINE LOADED WITH MISSILES PERMISSION TO DOCK AT THE CIVILIAN PORT OF HONOLULU? What were you thinking...?"

"Whoa, General Cavors. I didn't 'give permission.' I asked Naval Command to grant permission for the submarine to dock at Pearl Harbor and they denied it. The only other place available was the civilian port of..."

"God damn it, Stewart! Didn't I tell you that the President and Joint Chiefs are one step away from a pre-emptive strike against Russia? Didn't I ask you...*beg* you...to identify and inform me of *any* other possible source for this mess we're in? I appreciate receiving the results of your Delphi, but the joint chiefs didn't by into it. Not yet, anyway. In the meantime, how could you direct an *enemy* submarine to dock in exactly the place where it can wreak maximum havoc all around the Pacific Rim, not to mention setting them up in the best possible place to assess for themselves exactly how vulnerable we actually are...?"

"I thought word had gotten to you that agent Falk, whose plane disintegrated over the Pacific, had been rescued and taken to Hawaii aboard that very submarine. Furthermore..."

"Furthermore, you and your whole Cerebrus organization are one step from being deactivated and having your 'assets' chewed out and handed over to NSA!"

"That may be, Sir; however, Falk reports that the captain of the submarine has information that may be crucial in discovering how the events are created and propagated. Another of my agents is, at this very moment, communicating with Russian military researchers who, I've been told, created and developed the theoretical physics necessary to create..."

"Jeeze, Stewart. Things here are about to explode and you pass this on to me as a consequence of *my* calling *you?* But okay, okay. So we've now got a fully functional Russian submarine docked at the civilian port of Honolulu. Tell me the rest! Now!"

"The captain insists that the Russian military were involved in the creation and development of an event generation machine, but Russia never deployed it and isn't behind the events. They, like us, are mystified about the auctions, and are concerned the events and auctions may not stop with Hawaii..."

"That's interesting," General Richard Cavors, Head of the Joint Chiefs of Staff replied in a calmer more controlled manner. "But has it occurred to you that this whole thing might be a ruse to place Russia in the perfect position to take over the USA and all our resources, natural, civilian and military, *without firing a shot?* Even if Russia isn't behind it all, what if they're one of the 'buyers'? What if they're behind *all* the buyers? This is quite a gamble you're taking, I must say, 'on behalf of America, the President and the Joint Chiefs..."

"Admittedly, I should have kept you better informed, and, yes, it is a gamble..."

"You're damn well right! Are you aware that in the last hour, rumors have surfaced of dissident citizens assassinating government leaders?" demanded Cavors.

"No, I didn't..." began Stewart somewhat mollified.

"Perhaps your friend, Colonel Rellin, has too wrapped up in matters to keep *you* up to date? Our civilian counterparts are totally engrossed in simply stemming the chaos. In fact, city, state and federal governments are no closer maintaining law and order than you are to apprehending these 'foreign agents' and their handlers!"

"The endgame," offered Stewart.

"The endgame?" repeated Cavors. "The endgame? Hell, we

still don't even know who started it!"

"General. Falk is one of my best. If he says the Russian submarine captain is genuine, then I believe him. I have a report coming in from a second agent momentarily. She's talking directly with the Russian military researchers who claim to have created the event generator. I'm also expecting a report from a third agent, who's already on the ground in Honolulu. As soon as I know *anything* more, I'll call you personally. For now, please do what you can to assist Falk in setting up what the Russian captain is calling "a back channel" of communication between you and their country's military leaders, and ultimately directly between the two Presidents. This is our only solid lead just now."

"Okay, Stewart. Consider it done; however, no matter how this plays out, I'm holding you *personally responsible…*!"

"I understand, General, and I take full responsibility for my, my agency's and my agent's actions," confirmed Stewart.

Chapter 39

As her plane began to descend from cruising altitude on approach to Honolulu, Kate Keenan listened, aghast at what she was being told by the Russian military scientists through the Russian interpreter. There would be a flurry of Russian, only a little of which she could understand, then a crusty pause followed by the slow, almost mechanical voice of the military linguistic interpreter.

"Maybe ten years ago…yes, ten years…the Russian military… tasked a secret…'think tank' I think you would call it…to theorize a weapon that could…destroy a nation's infrastructure…without harming it's basic resources, including its people. Over."

"A 'weapon'? Over." asked Kate of the disembodied voice on the other end of the crackling but secure line.

"I'm sorry. Exact translation is difficult. Perhaps 'a solution' or 'an approach'...the idea was to theorize a weapon or solution or approach...that could take the place of nuclear weapons. Mutually Assured Destruction—MAD—was never a solution acceptable to our military leaders. Over."

"And they came up with...?" Kate probed.

"They came up with...the *kvantovaya mashina smerti*...the KMS...the 'Quantum Death Machine'...which our researchers here believe is being deployed against the United States of America. Over."

"How exactly does it work? Over," Kate demanded.

"Assembled perfectly...it must be *twice*-perfect...I will explain that later...it becomes a...specialized quantum...ah...teleportation device. When...awakened...even for the shortest time...less even than a formal 'jiffy'—the amount of time light takes to travel one fermi, about the size of a nucleon, in a vacuum...an object from one place will appear simultaneously in another predetermined, linked location. Distance doesn't matter. Only the...fixing...of the two points in absolute time-space. It was based on...no, inspired by...the thought-experiments of the Austrian physicist Erwin Schrödinger in 1935. He proposed a thought experiment...later called 'Schrödinger's cat'...in which, given the 'rules' of quantum mechanics...a cat inside a box could, for the briefest of moments, be...both alive and dead at the same time. Over."

"You mean *actual teleportation?* Over," asked Kate.

"Everyone here is shaking their heads 'no'...not *real* teleportation. For just an instant the object...it appears in two places simultaneously. For just instant. Then...depending on how equipment and object are...manipulated...'programmed' would be a better word one researcher says...another says to remind you that no programming is actually necessary at all...at least within the system itself. The two perfectly matched sites are...completely passive in the electronic sense...as would be an unprogrammed object. And the device...remember, there must be two of them...a duality, you see...one at at each site...they must be as I said, *perfect* copies. The device must be *twice* perfect. In order for a twice perfect system to work...the two devices must be precisely located in absolute space-time...for that particular instant. This requires considerable...computational skill and power. Over."

"Indeed," Kate agreed. "The world we experience every day *seems* fixed to us, but, in fact, everything in the universe, including our world and us upon it, even our universe itself, is constantly moving, in one or another direction, at one or another speed while time marches on. Fixing two points in space-time would be *extremely* challenging. I don't know that its ever actually been done. Over."

"Yes, this proved the most challenging part...of moving theory to physical prototype. We...that is, this group of scientists here... needed more computing power than was available at that time in Russia...so we...they...turned to the Chinese, with their...Tianhe super-massive computer. 'Tainhe' means 'Heaven River' or 'Milky Way.' The world knows the 'Tianhe-1A' as the fastest computer that has ever existed, but our...Chinese military comrades...had in their possession another...already ten or more generations more advanced. Our leaders agreed to share the workings of the KMS, the *kvantovaya mashina smerti* or Quantum Death Machine in return for use of their advanced Tianhe, their...top secret super-massive military computer...to calculate the simultaneous space-time coordinates necessary to perform an actual...ah...'proof of concept' you would say. Over."

"A working Quantum Death Machine actually exists in China? Over."

"Well, yes...and no. We built the prototype...they provided the necessary coordinates for a test...but we never completely trusted our Chinese comrades...more so the North Korean military scientists who were there working side-by-side with the Chinese... so we provided the prototype machine, but withheld the....'initiator'. Over."

"Were the 'tests' successful? Over," asked Kate.

"Again, yes and no. We were able to make a molecular sized object...simultaneously appear in another place...but had difficulty making it stay at the desired location. Most often the...object of interest...simply vanished after momentarily appearing in the place where we directed it. This made it of...less interest...to our military leaders, since consistent 'delivery' of a larger payload could not be assured. Over."

"What happened to the prototype? Did the Chinese advance it further? Are they behind this, do you think? Over," requested Kate.

"The prototype and initiator were destroyed...by the very scientists standing about me...of this, they are certain. However, having further considered their time there, they now think the Chinese may have successfully built a *copy* of the *kvantovaya mashina smerti*—less, of course, our initiator which we never revealed. This copy, our scientists believe, would likely be a system of interconnected modular elements...a dual copy, hand-crafted to correct for the...deficiencies...in the prototype...in order to continue their investigations. It would likely consist of numerous interconnected boxes..."

"So you think the Chinese are behind this? Over."

"You Americans are always...so direct. No, we, that is, the

scientists standing around me, don't think so. According to Russian intelligence, the Chinese never...figured out...how to recreate the initiator. Besides, what exactly would they 'deliver' with this device? Aside from being...an instantaneous way of delivering a small...currently less than three centimeter object—it can not be larger due to the inherent 'rules' of Quantum Simultaneity—how could they be certain what they delivered would remain at the delivery point...and not end up remaining at—you may also think of it as 'returning to' if you like—the source point. Were it even possible to create, say, a microminiture nuclear weapon...how could they be assured they wouldn't obliterate everything at the point source and leave instead in their their enemy's hands one of the required dual systems to take apart and learn from? Over."

"Then what exactly are you saying? Over."

"We believe North Korea to be responsible for these...events. North Korean scientific and military observers worked next to Russian and Chinese military scientists. They saw and examined the original prototype...our intelligence service believes they remained on the project for several years helping the Chinese devise the Chinese prototype. We believe that...the Chinese, unsuccessful at creating a working initiator...abandoned the project and the North Koreans returned to their country...to, we believe, create their own version. The problem still remains that... one, they still didn't have an initiator...and, two, they had no idea at the time what to 'deliver'. Over."

"At the time?" Kate inquired. "At *what* time? Over."

"Yes, but now we believe...they have solved both problems and...identified a 'use' for the KMS. Over."

"And?" demanded Kate.

"We believe their military researchers...have devised a way to create an occurrence...an 'event', as you call them...by tearing a rent in space-time at the target location...with assurance. That is, they deliver not an object, but the occurrence or event. The scientists here believe what you are experiencing is the result of the momentary creation of a...'special singularity'. Over."

"A *tiny* 'Big Bang'?" asked Kate, quickly coming to believe what she was hearing, and now more interested than ever.

There was a pause on the other end, during which the researchers there engaged in an audible debate.

"I'm sorry. There is considerable disagreement here about that. Some say, yes, it is an artificial 'Big Bang'...but one that is... tightly 'contained'. The detractors point out that...the technology for containing even a *nuclear* explosion...still doesn't yet exist... and, anyway, why, they argue, would North Korea care if the 'Big Bang' were...contained...or not? To this, another group here replied...that containing it would resolve the problem of the event happening only where it's directed...instead of possibly at the source. To which an opposing group is arguing that under any circumstances...anything present within a small...'location zone' would simultaneously appear at both...and remain at one or the other. Whether contained or not, it's a fifty percent phenomenon...'quantum mechanics'...they are all yelling at each other here, so perhaps I am translating this incorrectly and it doesn't work exactly that way. Still, the North Koreans must have figured out how to make the occurrence non-statistical...not unprovable...sorry, I should have said 'no longer unpredictable'. So there you have it. Over."

There I have it, thought Kate. Instigator, method, and purpose. "Our scientists have been experimenting with artificially-created 'Big Bangs'..." she offered in return.

"Yes. Everyone is. According to...M-Superstring Theory...if one can...posit...the right circumstances in all eleven-dimensions of space-time, one can create using the *kvantovaya mashina smertia*...and teleport a 'Big Bang'."

Indeed, thought Kate. The 'bang' would be instantaneous. Before it would be noticed, the rent in space-time would collapse, instantaneously disappearing from our world, leaving a "new" universe pinched off from ours to grow side-by-side, forever unnoticed. M-Supersting Theory, in fact, predicted this. However, before the new universe pinched off, it would create an event-echo of it in our space-time exactly as was being observed. Nothing would be left pointing to its ever having happened. Just the hand-made, modularized machinery and perhaps a special antenna to all synchronization of the two points in time-space, allowing the translocation of the 'bang' from the first location to the second.

"But why the auctions? Over," asked Kate aloud, as much to herself as to the scientists on the other end of the line.

The person on the other end translated this to the scientists. After some discussion, he replied, "All of this...the scientists here...it's impossible to translate exactly what they are saying... they 'speculate with certainty' that...the 'auctions', as you call them, would be a purely North Korean phenomenon. Relying as they do so heavily on an extensively developed cyber-warfare expertise...I'm sorry, but the political officer standing next to me... is warning me that...such a statement as I have just made...is outside the bounds of our discussion. The group has shared with you everything they can."

Any more, Kate thought, *would actually be superfluous.* She had enough to certify the veracity of the information she'd received and assure everyone technical it was genuine. While doing so, her thoughts began racing ahead, thinking of possible ways to thwart the upcoming event, and a concept of exactly how to do it was already forming in her brilliant, fertile mind.

Chapter 40

Stewart received Kate's summary of her discussion with the Russian military scientists with a sigh of relief. If he was to believe Falk, the Russian submarine captain and Kate Keenan, Cerebrus' New Technology Advisor and all-round science and computer genius, then this was the breakthrough he'd been so nervously awaiting. It would mean that the "enemy" was no longer invisible. It meant that he had both the why *and* the how behind the events, and a first glimpse into North Korea's endgame. As for the auctions, Stewart had already been near certain that North Korea was behind them, though he still needed actual proof in order to present the information to his long-time friends and colleagues, Colonel Jack Rellin, Cerebrus' liaison to NSA, and General Richard Cavors, Chairman of the Joint Chiefs, the "brains" and the "brawn" respectively of America. Still, the information he now possessed was significant. And, he had Kate's assurance that she already had the makings of a countermeasure in mind, one, she had assured him, that was already well tested and, given some quick work regarding the particulars necessary to apply it in this specific situation, was available for deployment.

What he still desperately needed was *proof* that North Korea was behind both events and auctions—hard, explicit proof—and for this, he needed his Honolulu field team, namely Falk, Koski, and Kate to capture an agent, handler or controller alive.

Chapter 41

Koski took a quick sip of the potent military coffee, and left it and her pastry to make her way to the *ad hoc* Ops Center. Her plan was to get updated—that's what the Commander of Naval Intelligence's aide had been sent to call her in for—and then immediately begin deploying the field investigation teams. Time was of the essence, and without Falk, she was on her own. Not that being in charge bothered her that much; she and Falk had always shared equally in devising field plans, and she felt no less adept now than before.

What was bothering her like a stone in her shoe was Falk's absence. She knew he was alive—she'd celebrated his "rescue" alone in her room with a flood of tears that she couldn't hold back. He was, she reassured herself, in "enemy," albeit "friendly" enemy hands, and, having successfully established a back channel of communication between Russia and the USA, he would, she assumed, be soon released. The news of the Russian submarine docking at the Aloha Tower pier in Honolulu had spread like wild-fire, totally eclipsing public concern over what locals were celebratorily calling the impending "non-event." The populace had, in the last year survived three non-hurricanes, two non-tsunamis and a non-volcanic eruption. In each case, the public had been "prepared to da max," only to experience two usual tropical depressions with the usual moments of blinding, pounding rain; two tsunamis, the largest one only six inches above mid-tide; and yet another unfelt eruption of Kilauea that, in the end, barely received mention the next day. *Thank God the populace here doesn't understand that much about what's happening, especially the intensely critical nature of the coming event.* Koski thought. *The endgame. That's what both Falk and Stewart had deemed this one. Thank God it's happening in Hawaii, where most citizens this morning were more concerned about the surf and whether to take a drive to Aloha Tower to see the submarine.*

And thank God that Falk is alive. Now if only he were here...

Falk, she was no longer reluctant to admit, had become more than her "other half" in more ways than she could recount. When he was with her, she *felt* his presence, his calm, his deep sense of duty, his focus, his concern...and admittedly, his protective love, for that was what it was: love. Pure and simple. Standing on the steps leading up to the Ops Center, she paused, took a deep breath, envisioned him, and let her breath out slowly. He might not be here in the flesh, but she could vividly imagine him walking up the stairs at her side, the two of them planning out the day's work together.

Passing through the glass doors, she glanced behind her as if to say goodbye to the all-too-quickly fading mental image of her lover, and bumped into someone. Hoping it wasn't some high-ranking military officer, she was surprised to see Kate Keenan, kneeling, picking up the papers that had dropped from her hands as a consequence of their encounter. "Kate! What are you doing here?" Koski asked incredulously.

"Picking up what you so ignominiously knocked from my hands. It was my morning briefing. I don't know if I can get them all back in order before..."

Kate Keenan looked bright, confident, smelled like a freshly picked flower and was dressed to the hilt, causing Koski to look down and survey herself. Her clothes still looked rumpled and she was sure they smelled of having been previously worn and, last night, slept in. She felt anything but confident and could only imagine the puffiness about her eyes after her night's cry and how bloodshot they probably looked after only a few hours of real sleep. For some reason it disturbed her more than it should have.

"Glad to see you," Koski said, consciously softening her voice. "With Falk almost dying and still gone, I'm in charge of the entire field operation including pre-pinpointing the event's epicenter and, if possible, capturing the two agents."

"Which is why *I'm* here," replied Kate with command and authority. "I've been talking with the Russian military scientists who created the prototype device that causes the transmigration of a spatial-temporal rift from one location to another via quantum entanglement..."

"Have you talked to Falk?" Koski asked, interrupting, not wanting to have to ask Kate what exactly she was talking about.

"Yes," Kate answered, aggravated at having her rehearsal cut off.

"Did he sound okay? I mean..."

"Yes. In fact, he sounded fine. What's...?"

"I'm sorry. Your talk with Russian scientists," Koski offered, "does this mean that you know how the events are created?"

"Yes, I do," stated Kate haughtily, the question, *Why don't I like this person?* running reflexively through and around her mind. "And I may have a way to stop this one from happening, but I need to be at the event epicenter *before* it happens."

"So you'll be working with me, then?" asked Koski, gathering her wits and, as Falk would do, refocusing on the problem, thinking, *Why don't I like this person?* but saying, "I don't think we've formally met since..." The inanity of her comment took a moment to strike the two women, causing each to involuntarily cringe.

"That's probably because we haven't *formally* met, though I know about you, and you have most likely heard about me from

Falk." Kate offered a hand. Koski didn't return the gesture. People were coming in and going out of the center, flowing around the two as if the women were a couple of rocks in a the center of a rushing stream.

"Falk?" repeated Koski with suspicion. "No, he never mentioned you." He had, of course, but long after Koski and Falk had met and become a team. "But I know of you from reading the summary of Operation Finding Kate. I assume then that they 'found' you…?"

Kate laughed and extended her hand once again. "The 'affair' was given that name *ex post facto*, and, yes, I was 'found'. And later recruited by Cerebrus. And don't let my clothes deceive you. I've been field trained." It wasn't a complete lie. She *had* completed field agent training, but her technical and administrative skills kept taking precedence over any actual field work, so, in fact, she'd not yet taken part in a field operation. "In case you're wondering, I'm the head of Cerebrus' Advanced Technology Division. It's so advanced and secret, I'm supposed to kill you having mentioned it. Perhaps that's why our paths haven't crossed until now."

The satire wasn't lost on Koski. This time, she took Kate's hand and shook it, though she felt strongly off-put at Kate's use of the word "affair" to describe Operation Finding Kate and the inherent threat in the use of the word "kill." Initially, Kate's grip felt overly strong, like she was trying to establish dominance. But then the woman's grip lessened, leaving Koski without a reason to adjust the strength of her grip accordingly.

"Who 'found' you exactly?" asked Koski, wanting to put Kate back in her place.

"Actually, I found myself. That is, I figured the way out of my dilemma. To be completely honest, Joe 'rescued' me, though it was afterwards. Ever since, I've had stars in my eyes and a place in my heart for that man, but that's a different story altogether."

Now I know why I don't like her, thought Koski. That would mean Falk 'knew' Kate, whatever that meant, well before he 'knew' her in the way that usually meant. The thought toughened her, and Koski extended to her full height, her mind questioning, *Why am I doing this? So Falk had a prior relationship; most people did. Wasn't that to be expected?*

It's because the woman standing across from me oozes confidence and is being overbearing, her mind replied.

Having sparred and established a mutual wariness and dislike for each other, the two women smiled and walked together from the stream of people into the briefing room.

"The briefing I'm supposed to give is actually more for you than anyone else. Stewart asked me to work in parallel with or as part of your field team. As soon as you locate the upcoming event epicenter, I can begin my 'counterstrike'."

The briefing was short and to the point.

Kate disclosed only enough to establish that she had significantly advanced the technology that had gotten her into trouble in Operation Finding Kate, such that instead of "passively receiving the event," she felt reasonably certain she could counter it with "exactly what the perpetrators are wishing for." The "something," she assured, was being weaponized in her division laboratory in Washington DC even as she spoke.

Towards the end of the short joint agency briefing, a commotion arose in the back of the conference room. Koski peeled her angry gaze from Kate and looked to discover Falk standing there dressed in a Russian seamen's garb. Falk, catching Koski's eye, smiled, shrugged his shoulders and raised his hands, as if apologizing for the plane crash, his unannounced arrival and unusual attire.

Koski's jaw dropped and she stared open mouthed at Falk. She couldn't help but think the man standing at the other end of the room was *the* most appealing man she had ever laid eyes on, and wanted to rush to him, throw her arms about him and show him just how much she cared.

Instead, she laughed circumspectly at his appearance. In his Russian sailor clothes, he really did look silly. Then, out of the corner of her eye, she noticed Kate also staring at Falk with an obvious, dreamy, longing in the woman's eyes. *She's not at all surprised at seeing him*, Koski observed, concluding, *so she must have known he was coming to the briefing but withheld that during our short tête-à-tête.* If Koski disliked Kate before, the resentment she had been feeling upped her dislike to outright disdain.

It was Falk who, extricating himself from the clamor of well-wishers, walked up to and stood comfortably beside Koski rather than Kate. "It's good to see you, Koski," he ventured, turning a lock of her hair in his fingers.

"It's good to see you, too, Falk," she responded quietly, in an attempt to keep their conversation between the two of them. "It's *so* good to see you. It looks like the Russians treated you well."

"The fact is, they saved my life. I hadn't fared well during the flight, and when the plane experienced an unanticipated intersection, I damn near died. The pilot still hasn't been found. If it hadn't been for Captain Korov being in the right place at the right time with the right orders, I wouldn't be here beside you."

"But you *are* here," Koski affirmed, taking his hand in hers and squeezing it. "And you look downright sexy in that Russian naval uniform."

"Uh...yes," replied Falk, suddenly looking the awkward boy. "We barely begin a life together and this happens. It's exactly what I've been concerned about from the beginning: Our work, Koski, is so dangerous, and it will always be getting between us. Either one of us may end up dead anytime. That was my second to the last thought before I blacked out in the water. My last was simply of you."

Falk smiled warmly and Koski returned the same.

"But right now, I've got to talk with Kate," he continued, his smile fading. "I need to know what she was able to make of what the Russian scientists shared. She needs to quickly locate..."

"...the epicenter of this next event, assuming it is indeed in Honolulu and not Alaska," Koski finished for him. "She told me she has a possible countermeasure, but that it requires her to be at the epicenter before the event occurs. She'll therefore be working 'closely' with us in the field, traveling with us wherever we go."

Falk thought for a moment, weighing the implication as much as the content of what Koski had just said. Koski, he ventured, had been acting strangely from the moment he saw her. He was certain it had something to do with whatever it was she *wasn't* saying, but whatever it was, it was totally eluding him. Taking a chance, he added, "No problem. Kate's a trained field agent as well as a talented scientist and a genius with applied physics and things computational. It'll be good to have her with us. We might..."

"There was more than simple 'comradery' in Kate's eyes when you appeared. Do you two have a history?"

"Well, yes, in a way," Falk explained, suddenly cognizant of what was likely going on based on where their conversation had suddenly digressed. "I met her immediately after Operation

Finding Kate and based on what I'd leaned of her, recommended her to Stewart. But no, we have no history as lovers."

Koski palpably relaxed.

So Koski, his "partner" was feeling jealous? It wasn't uncommon for paired agents, especially those "with a history" to react overly emotionally immediately before or after a life-threatening situation, and this one was life-threatening for everyone American. "Really, I must talk with Kate. Would you like to accompany me?" Falk asked in all honesty.

Koski affirmed her desire to accompany Falk with a slight nod, and walked hand-in-hand with him over to Kate.

As he'd stated, he and Kate exchanged information. In the end, all three shook hands in acknowledgement of their forced trio-ship, Koski noting with concern Kate's attempt during the handshakes to hold Falk's hand distinctly longer than propriety required. Of more concern to Koski, however, was that Falk didn't make any visible attempt to break the longer-than-needed physical contact with Kate. *They may not, as Falk assured, 'have a history'* thought Koski, *but they damn well have something!*

Chapter 42

The new field team of Koski, Keenan and Falk spent the next hour pouring over and collating everything that had been gathered about visitors from China, English-Second-Language schools and students in homestay. Using a composite description of the previous girls and another of the antennas, calls for public assistance were issued by participating agencies to be carried on radio, television and social media sites in Hawaii.

Their next task was more difficult: prioritizing the list of names and addresses that resulted from their effort, and working out a schedule for each of the twenty or so inter-agency field teams, Koski, Keenan and Falk reserving the most likely sites to visit themselves. While Koski and Falk worked out the final details of the schedules, Kate called her laboratory in Washington DC to confirm that the countermeasure device was on its way directly to her to Honolulu.

It was a warm, cloudless morning, promising temperatures in the high 80s with a heavy UV exposure for the unprotected, and as yet it was only ten o'clock. It would be a scorcher by three, the computer-predicted time of the upcoming event. That left the team less than five hours to locate a Chinese-Asian agent from among the many Chinese in the "Rainbow State." Sadly, residents and visitors alike typically appeared to "mainland" eyes as all Oriental, so the presence of an Oriental girl, even one holding hands with an American female companion would be quite commonplace. Strike one.

The forty ESL schools on Oahu had been fully cooperative. Unfortunately sixty to seventy percent of their students were Oriental, about thirty percent of whom identified themselves as Chinese. Most of the schools maintained files on their students, especially the Chinese for visa reasons, and many maintained a homestay registry. Some, however, did not. Collating all the information together narrowed their search to slightly less than two hundred potential homestay sites with some omissions due to missing data. With less four hours to go, it would be difficult to impossible to visit and carefully interview each. Strike two.

Further, not all students would homestay through an ESL-affiliated school, and non-school-affiliated homestays would prove much more difficult to identify. In fact, of visitors who chose homestay *without registering at an ESL school*, by far most were

"Oriental," albeit "Chinese females." "If they aren't accepted at premiere schools in their own country, oriental boys," it was explained, "irrespective of their academic prowess, are often second-choice shipped off to the USA to bolster their English and attend an American college or university. Academically-gifted girls, on the other hand, are generally given a non-school-affiliated English language homestay in Hawaii as a 'consolation prize'." Placement of the foreign agents in out-of-the-way country locations had reflected the general need for secrecy. In a more urban setting like Honolulu, a non-school-affiliated homestay seemed quite likely.

The list of "consolation" homestay sites had proved surprisingly extensive. Adding these to their list of ESL-school-affiliated homestays resulted in two *thousand* possible sites, with an increased number of omissions. Strike three.

By two thirty, the team had cross-indexed the two hundred Chinese girls who had not returned to China after their visas had expired with the various homestay permutations and whittled the number of site visits to less than a hundred. With twenty teams that meant five site visits each with Koski, Kate and Falk reserving the mostly likely for themselves. It was during this time that Kate received the package she'd ordered from her laboratory. It proved a surprisingly compact, nondescript "black box" that fit comfortably in the palm of her hand. Base hit.

Their break came when a Makiki neighborhood area resident living not far from the University of Hawaii at Manoa responded to one of the public service announcements. He called in to report the appearance of a new satellite antenna in a neighboring house, at which two good-looking girls, one Oriental and one "*haole*"— meaning Caucasian in local pidgin—were staying.

Minutes later, the threesome were sitting in a car a block from a nondescript blue and white split level house sandwiched between two similarly constructed but differently colored houses.

From the public sidewalk to the main door of the house was a short twenty feet; the spaces between the sides of the houses appeared, at most, fifteen. Each house looked to have a small backyard, this particular one surrounded by a four-foot-high chain-link fence with a fence gate conveniently dangling open.

The house and yard in question appeared maintained. There was a single "island car," a dented Toyota station wagon with a surfboard rack, parked on the street immediately in front of the house. The house's roof featured a satellite dish antenna that was relatively new in appearance and not dissimilar from the ones Koski and Falk had encountered at their sites.

"This might or might not be the epicenter," Kate, examining the blasé house with obvious disinterest, ventured.

"We should pay them a visit, nonetheless," reminded Koski. "We're near the university. Its a good place for our two girls to blend in. Even if it's not the right place, perhaps whoever lives there has seen or knows something..."

"You're right, of course, Koski," Falk agreed, a little too quickly and assuredly for her. "We're nearing three o'clock, and none of the other teams have turned up anything better. The governor has just issued a call for residents to remain in their workplaces and home, to turn off and disconnect all electrical devices, and not drive. Emergency Services are on highest alert. The National Guard is poised to quell any resulting civil disturbances. Our combined military forces are ready to respond to any identifiable threat." As he talked, all of Honolulu, normally a boisterous city, abruptly fell silent.

Kate slipped the black box into her pocket, and the three prepared to leave the car to interrogate the house's inhabitants when the sound of a single gunshot broke the silence and echoed loudly down the street.

All three huddled reflexively behind respective car doors.

Gunshots, thought Falk, pulling out his weapon, clicking off the safety and chambering a round.

Definitely a handgun, thought Koski, pulling out her weapon, clicking off the safety and chambering a round. *Just like at the Thorsdan ranch in Fulton.*

Good God! We may have actually stumbled onto the epicenter! thought Kate, pulling the diminutive black box back out of her pocket and shifting it to her left hand while grasping her weapon tightly in her right. She was surprised to notice that the palm of her gun hand was suddenly damp.

The three agreed to approach the house from different directions, Falk reminding everyone that their priority was to take the agents alive if at all possible. Capturing their handlers or controllers would come later, assuming they could take at least one of the two girls alive.

On Falk's signal, slinking out from behind the car's front passenger side door, Koski ran in a crouch behind and to the back of the residents' old parked car. Kate, at the same moment, ran from behind the back passenger side of their car in an arc to the right to the chain link fence. Falk ran from behind the driver's door, around Koski and up to the front door of the house, where he flattened his body against the paneling to the side of the door, his gun ready. While knocking and announcing himself, two more shots rang out. *Small caliber Type 77 handgun*, he mused, *like the one at the Hempsted farm.*

The two shots, like the first one, all came from inside the house and apparently weren't directed at him or his companions. Given what he'd seen in Vermont, the shots probably meant at least two persons had just met their death, the first, most likely the homestay parent with one shot. The question was, whether the remaining two were directed at the Oriental's companion, or one at her leaving the second one to be self-directed by the shooter.

Falk signaled for Koski to approach the other side of the front door. As she ran, Koski signaled for Kate to slip through the fence gate, and cover the back entrance.

The moment Koski joined Falk, he swung around to face the door, kicked it open and swept the room, his weapon braced in both hands.

The living room was appointed "island-style" with worn, rattan furniture that had probably been purchased from a second-hand hotel outlet. It looked unoccupied. The sofa was situated to look out two windows onto the small front lawn. A modest entertainment center, a well-used, overstuffed, leather low-boy chair and the open front door occupied the rest of the space between either of the windows. An old surfboard stood upright in a corner of the room.

A rustle sounded upstairs.

Falk signaled for Koski to search the adjoining kitchen while he crept stealthily up the worn, carpeted stairs.

What Koski discovered in the kitchen was what she expected, given her experience in Fulton: A middle-aged man with lightly greying temples was sitting in a kitchen chair, arms, legs and head splayed limply out. He was wearing a white airbrushed t-shirt and blue shorts. His shoes, a pair of island flip-flops, had fallen off his feet when he was thrown backwards. Blood was pooling about the chair's two back legs. The kitchen table and appliances behind him were polka-dotted with bright red.

At the top of the stairs, Falk paused, facing the length of a hallway, noting an open door on his left, waiting for release from the *deja vu* that was haunting him of having been in this same situation before.

Premonition?

Falk pointed his weapon at the open door and proceeded cautiously forward.

Lying in the center of the bedroom floor was the body of a young American girl, blood streaming from a high left neck wound and and another on her left thigh. Crouching lower, scanning the room and not seeing the expected Asian counterpart or any equipment or antenna wire, he knelt beside the limp figure and pressed two fingers against her neck artery. Locating a definite pulse, he thought, *She's still alive, though not for long without emergency care,* noting next, how odd it was that her partner, undoubtedly a highly trained professional like all the other Oriental agents, had botched the killing.

A noise from the hallway bought his survival senses into high gear, and he turned, swung up his weapon, braced and pointed it at the doorway. Two dark silhouettes flew from right to left outside the doorway, from what little he saw, both females, both crouching, each holding before her a weapon that in outline looked remarkably like a standard Cerebrus-issue automatic.

Falk sighed, thinking it had to be Koski and Keenan attempting to back him up, then he abruptly sucked in his breath when he heard three loud concussions, one immediately after the other, ostensibly from the hallway and saw one silhouetted figure fly this time from left to right and out of his sight. The remaining dark figure jumped into the room in which he was crouching and, pointing her weapon at the doorway, turned a pale face towards Falk.

"Oh, God, Falk! I think I just shot another human being!" replied Kate breathlessly, her face and knuckles turning whiter by the moment. Clutching the black box in her left hand and her smoking weapon in her right, she moaned, "Oh, God! Oh God! Oh..."

"Kate! Stop!" demanded Falk. "Are you hit? What about Koski?"

Kate looked dazedly at Falk, then at the barely breathing girl lying beside him in an ever-increasing pool of blood. "Oh, God! Oh, Falk!" she exclaimed reaching out for him, pausing in mid-reach to declare, "I think I'm going to faint."

"Not now!" Falk commanded. "Focus! What about Koski?"

"Koski?" Kate repeated distantly, eyes already glazing.

"Damn it woman! Shake it off! Remember your training! Put down your weapon and the box, and press one hand on this girl's neck wound and the other on her thigh wound. If she stops breathing, give her CPR. We need her alive!"

Kate, despite her unfocused eyes, dropped her weapon onto the floor and placed the black box delicately next to it.

"The event, Falk!" she exclaimed as she reached for the girl's body, her color slowly returning as she refocused her attention onto the wounded girl. "Falk! It's about to happen! The box! We've got to locate the event equipment!" she exclaimed. Pointing to the box beside her gun with her nose, she continued, "That box needs to be inside the room when the event happens. Do you hear? It's got to be inside the..."

Falk scooped up the box in his blood-stained free hand. "What do I do with it?"

"Nothing," Kate replied, recapturing some semblance of calm at last. "Just make certain it's in the room when the event happens."

Falk was out the door and into the hallway before Kate finished. Facing the end of the hallway, gun in one hand, the small black box in the other, he now faced one of the most difficult decisions of his life: whether to backtrack down the stairs to check on Koski—he couldn't see or hear her—or to plunge ahead and make certain the black box was in the room at the right moment. His choice, however, was opted by a an even more urgent mental question. *Which room?* There were three closed doors, one on his left near the end of the hallway, and two on his right. While staring forward, searching heart and soul, he heard a familiar voice behind him and felt Koski's familiar hand on his right shoulder.

"Koski, are you alright?" he whispered, not daring to take his eyes off the hallway.

"Good enough…to back you up," she whispered. Her words were clear, but she seemed breathless and was gripping onto his shoulder tightly as if something were wrong. The hand gave a little squeeze, then let go.

"Damn it, Koski! You're hurt!" Falk exclaimed, rescanning the hallway in front of him, in the process noting a spattering of red on the left side of the far wall and what looked like a trail of red dots leading to the single closed door on the left. Kate's shot must have indeed connected with its target.

"I just said, 'I'm good enough to back you up'. Now go, Falk! I'll cover you."

Falk dropped low, and half-crawled his way to the closed door on his left. Squatting, he looked momentarily back down the hallway from where he'd come. Where he'd just been, he could make out the top of Koski's head, her body flattened against the carpet, both arms extended forward grasping her automatic, a gash of red where her left temple hair should have been. Hearing a noise, he returned his attention back to the door.

There movement inside the room. It sounded like someone shuffling about carrying something. If so, then this would be the time to enter. Hopefully the Oriental agent would be pre-occupied with whatever final actions were needed before the event happened. He stood and violently kicked in the door.

Inside, below the far window, he could see a table with several rows of inter-connected metal boxes much like the ones he had seen in Laplacia. The window was open. A long cable snaked through it onto the table. A short, thin girl with long, jet black hair had her back to him. Startled by the noise, she dropped the box she was carrying onto the table, and without looking back, shoved the end of the cable into a receptacle of the box she had dropped on the table, and the connector of the wire from another box into the one she'd just dropped onto the table. The right side of her brightly patterned dress, Falk observed, was soaked with what was unquestionably blood.

He was about to shout, when she flipped a switch, spun about, and pointed her weapon at him. Three shots shook the room, the first from just behind Falk, the second from the girl's weapon, and the third from his.

Falk heard the whizz of a bullet pass over his shoulder and watched it strike the surprised girl in the center of her chest, throwing her backwards against the table, jarring the table's contents. The boxes were humming, responding to the jolt with countdown beeps, the light next to the switch the girl had thrown changing from flashing yellow to constant red.

The same instant, Falk felt a hard slap, as if he'd been punched in the upper left side of his chest by a bareknuckled prizefighter. Momentarily stunned, he watched the girl jerk a second time, and scream with mixed pain, fear and rage, her left arm twisting and flailing backwards out of control.

Falk didn't wait for her to fire again. He tossed the small black box into the room and, with all his strength, heaved himself out of the room.

To both Falk's surprise, the impending event occurred without flash or bang. The constant red light on what seemed to be the master control box simply went out, the humming ceased, and the black box he'd tossed lay inert on the ground.

From the hallway, Falk could see the girl holding onto the edge of the table behind with her right hand without letting go of the gun, while she gasped, eyes wide, lips twisting into a sudden snarl. Letting go of the table, she began falling to the floor, her dress creating the illusion of a leaf falling in the wind. As she fell, she swept her right arm forward and pointed her gun between Falk's startled eyes.

Falk, normally wary of a wounded antagonist, should have immediately flattened on the floor, but the excruciating pain in his chest refused to allow him. Instead, he continued staring helplessly down the distant muzzle of the foreign agent's gun, while clasping his left chest. In slow motion and with the hyper-acuity that typically accompanies imminent death, he watched the girl's index finger tighten about the trigger of her weapon, even while her body continued its loose fall to the floor.

Behind him, he heard Koski whisper, "Good enough to back you up," and was startled by two more loud reports from behind his left ear, followed by the familiar whizz of two bullets, each passing barely an inch away from the side of his head. A puff of smoke stung his eyes, briefly obscured his field of vision, and he felt his nose involuntarily wrinkle from the acrid smell of spent gunpowder. He knew there were loud sounds all about him, but the strength of the two reports had by now temporarily robbed him of his hearing on his left, leaving in its place an irritating buzz. Suddenly lightheaded, his vision, still focused tightly on the muzzle of the weapon pointed at him from the far side of the room, began narrowing. *All the cardinal signs of shock*, he thought before his head began to swirl and darkness overtake him.

From Falk's diminishing perspective, the two bullets fired from behind him sped, one immediately after the other in slow motion across the room, leaving what he saw or imagined were spiral wakes trailing behind.

The event was his last cohesive thought. Just before passing out, he thought he saw a momentary bright white light. Assuming he wasn't dying, at least not yet, that meant either the event had just occurred, or a bullet with his name on it was even now speeding on its way towards him. The terrifying thoughts, however, never completely formed. Falk was out cold.

Chapter 43

Falk woke in the arms of a woman.

He tried desperately to focus his blurry eyes, but lying on his back, staring up, all he could make out was a white-flocked popcorn ceiling, its tiny bright peaks and valley-shadows playing games with his mind, creating images of random objects, animals, places and faces from his past.

Faces.

His first cohesive thought was a question. *Where is Koski?* As his field of vision slowly expanded he noticed the face of the woman looking down at him. She was holding and rocking him. It was Kate Keenan, tears streaming down her cheeks, the tears splashing on his face. It was her tears, he realized, that had awakened him.

Kate was sitting cross-legged on the floor, cradling Falk's head, rocking and sobbing. Slowly he realized four other persons were peering down at him. Two were surprised-looking fluorescent-orange-and-yellow-clothed EMS technicians. The other two were worried looking policemen.

The two EMS technicians dropped to their knees. "It's a miracle," voiced one to no one in particular. Kate paused in her rocking to look into Falk's eyes. He attempted a smile, but ended up cringing, an electric pain coursing from his left shoulder throughout his body.

"Oh my God! Oh my God, Falk! You're alive!" Kate voiced from above.

"Koski?" asked Falk, his voice weak and trembling from the searing pain. "Is she alright?"

"Koski?" replied Kate. "Yes. I think so. She asked about you repeatedly while they were taking her away."

One of the EMS technicians attempted without success to loosen Falk from Kate's embrace. "Ma'am. We need to look at his wound and get him to a hospital. Please..." The second technician slowly worked an arm between Kate's shoulder and the man she was so desperately clenching.

"Ma'am. Please let go," the first technician ordered, while his partner gently tugged the two apart.

"Falk?" Kate asked, the single word pregnant with meaning.

"Koski?" Falk replied, and fell back into unconsciousness.

When he next awoke, he was lying once again on his back but this time on a moving stretcher, a plastic prong in each nostril hissing lightly, a bag of IV fluid swaying precariously above his right shoulder.

He felt better. The pain in his left shoulder was still there and, surprisingly, just as intense, but it seemed distant and unimportant. He felt as if he were floating rather than being whisked along on a litter. One of the two technicians was trotting beside him.

"Koski?" asked Falk, his mouth fighting him, feeling like it was filled with dry cotton. The technician bent over and gently probed his patient's neck and shoulder while they continued moving.

"Do…you…need…more…pain…medication?" he asked, as if talking to a recalcitrant child.

"Koski?" Falk asked again.

"The woman holding you when we arrived? She's okay. She left with some black-suited men. As far as we know, she sustained no injuries."

"Koski?" asked Falk again, more emphatically.

"The other woman? The one on the stairs? She's being treated at a nearby hospital. The same one where you're going."

"How…is…she?" Falk asked shakily, trying to keep away the blissful curtain of mist that seemed to want to close over him.

"She was…wounded. She's in surgery. Where you'll be going next."

"The…other…ones? The…girls?" he asked with increasing difficulty.

"The one we found in the room next to the table with the equipment was dead. The American in the bedroom was still alive when we arrived, and is also on her way to the hospital. She actually looked better than you..."

"I...I..." Falk stuttered, unable to formulate his next question, giving in at last to the medication.

Chapter 44

At Falk's next reawakening, he found himself tucked between crisp, white sheets, in what was clearly a hospital room. A uniformed guard was standing at attention at the inside door of what he assumed was a private room. Looking to his right, he was disappointed at not being able see outside through the expected window. Instead, a white curtain blocked his view.

Falk began moving fingers, toes, then hands, feet, arms and legs, noting the IV in the back of his right hand. *Okay,* he thought, *everything's still there,* until he attempted to move his chest. The resulting pain almost knocked him back out. *I must be better,* he thought acerbically, *they've stopped the morphine,* wincing again as he slowly moved his left shoulder.

While he was exploring the room and his body, a nurse entered with a tray of unappetizing liquid hospital food and several medications, each of which he was ordered to take.

Encouraging him to use his right arm and hand to drink, the nurse silently surveyed her patient. The man in the bed facing her was handsome, in a rough and attractive way. Despite the extent of his injury, he appeared alert, cooperative and...well-muscled... again, in a rough and attractive way.

"Nurse?" he asked, breaking the silence, finishing what liquid he could after taking his medications. "I was told that I was brought to the hospital immediately after a woman-colleague of mine. Her name is Susan Koski. Can you tell me how she's doing?" Sensing the nurse's interest in him, he flashed a winning smile while giving his best impression of a lost puppy.

"I...well, we're not supposed to talk to patients about other patients, Mr. Falk, but I can say she survived surgery and, following discharge from the ICU, is recovering in the bed next to you. We don't usually accommodate two persons in a private room, but it was your superior's specific order. She's resting at the moment."

"Thank you," Falk offered with genuine joy. Koski was alright! He could wait to talk with her, as long as he knew she was alright!

The medications quickly made him feel sleepy, and the next time he awoke it was late afternoon. He knew this because the curtain separating him from Koski had been drawn back, and yellow-orange sunlight was streaming in obliquely through the window.

Koski was sitting up in bed, a turban bandage about her head.

"At last, our heroes awaken!" said Stewart gruffly from the foot of their beds. Beside him stood two uniformed officers. "This is Colonel Jack Rellin and this is General Richard Cavors," Stewart said pointing from one to the other. "Friends of mine. They're here to thank you."

Falk hardly heard what his boss was saying. He was trying to position himself to get a better look at Koski, who only had eyes for him.

"Ahem. You two can 'catch up' later. You'll have plenty of time recovering as you are, next to each other."

"How...how did you manage a room like this for...us? We're not formally married. I didn't know anyone knew of our affection for each other."

"Feelings for another are not easy to conceal," Stewart replied obliquely.

Koski smiled, rolling what she had just heard around in her mind: not *formally* married. "I'm glad to hear your voice again, Falk. I thought...I thought you were..." she began.

"Like I said," Stewart interrupted, "you two will have plenty of time to catch up on everything over the next few days while you're here recovering. Right now, General Cavors and Colonel Rellin have something they want to share with you."

The general immediately stepped forward and cleared his throat. "I've been instructed by the Joint Chiefs of Staff on behalf of the President, the combined military forces and people of the United States of America, to formally thank you, Joseph Falk, and you, Susan Koski, as well as your partner, Kate Keenan, for stopping what appeared to be collapse of the United States of America, and doing so at great personal risk."

Falk, lacking the details, could do little more than nod.

Koski glanced from Falk to the two officers then back at Falk, looking momentarily flattered, and offered the same simple nod.

General Cavors, at a loss for further words, cleared his throat again and stepped back.

"You also have the thanks of the National Security Agency and the combined security services of the United States of America and her allies. On all our behalves, I offer you our collective, and my personal thanks," Colonel Rellin added.

Koski and Falk acknowledged the thanks with a simple "Your welcome" and confused, guilty-looking smiles.

"There are many others wanting to thank you three. From individual Americans to heads of state. It's been difficult maintaining your and our organization's anonymity given the magnitude of what you three accomplished," Stewart added, looking anxiously at his watch. "But more of that later. Colonel

Rellin and General Cavors are on strict schedules. I'll remain for a few more minutes to answer any pressing questions. The hospital is very strict about visiting hours."

The two military men saluted Koski and Falk, then turned on heel and exited, striking up a conversation on their way out of the room. The guard at the door clicked his heels and stood stiffly, opening the door and offering a salute as they passed.

"What exactly happened?" asked Falk, after the door closed behind the two men.

"A few minutes isn't time enough to go into the details, but suffice it to say that your mission to Hawaii to capture an agent and handler was successful."

"Really?" asked Falk sincerely. "I thought the Oriental girl died."

"Yes, well, that's an interesting story in and of itself. She did, but the American, you see, survived, and provided us with enough information to locate and capture their handler. We're currently interrogating each separately, but on threat of returning him to North Korea, the handler gladly offered us everything he knew, and we have the girl to corroborate it."

"The other girl was a professional's professional," said Falk in a hushed voice. "Why didn't she dispose of her American partner like she did their American homestay parent?"

"Like I said," Stewart replied. "'Feelings are not easy to conceal'. Apparently the two had formed a more than collegial bond, and when it came time for the North Korean agent to kill her American friend, she wavered, her first shot wounding her in the neck, her second more hurried shot striking her girlfriend in the thigh. With all the blood from the two hits, it's easy to imagine the killer assuming that her partner was mortally wounded. As you said, she was a professional's professional, but for just a moment, it looks like she let her feelings for her American girlfriend get in the way."

"And the event?" Koski and Falk asked together, exchanging a look and smile at the unusual synchronicity of their questions.

"Ah, yes. The 'endgame event', for that's what it was. It never happened. It *should* have, but the black box you tossed into the room did its job. Kate was *mostly* certain it would, but I have to admit that, at the time, the rest of us didn't share her confidence.

"According to her, the laws of quantum mechanics do not allow two of exactly the same objects to continue existing. Kate's black box—I'll let her explain the technical details surrounding it—was designed to react to two situations: First, if it were present during the moment of quantum entanglement, it would assume precedence, appear simultaneously at both locations, and remain after the entanglement ended at the second site. Second, as soon as the entanglement resolved, it delivered what Kate is calling her 'gift that couldn't be refused'. Again, I'll let her fill in the technical details. She'll be coming by later when she can wrangle some time away from the NSA folks, who are falling over her to find out how exactly her device works."

"What of the auctions?" Kate, sitting up straighter, asked.

"Some thought they were a red herring, but I always suspected they were more," Stewart replied. "As it turns out, they were a key part of the overall endgame, but I'll let David, Lou and Kate fill you in on that. They would feel sorely affronted if I stole their thunder. They'll have an opportunity later to congratulate you in person and recount their part in ending the auctions.

"Kate, by the way, played no small part in it all," continued Stewart. "While she was busy concocting her 'gift' to send back to the folks at Pyongyang, she was also acting as devil's advocate to the NSA computer geeks. Her foil, in addition to what we obtained from our mole in Bureau 121, was exactly what was needed to allow David, Lou and the NSA to track the fifth auction through the dark TOR internet and definitively locate both seller and buyers. It was also Kate's genius that gave the NSA folks a way to end the auctions in our favor. But, again, my time is limited, and those are stories I'm certain David, Lou and Kate would rather tell you themselves."

Falk shifted his weight slightly in his bed, wincing uncomfortably, and nodded his agreement. In the next bed, Koski's smile turned to the semblance of a frown. It wasn't that she couldn't bear to see her lover in pain. She'd seen that before and would undoubtedly see it again. No, it was that the showdown for the world had ended, and it was now time for her more difficult woman-to-woman showdown with Kate.

Chapter 45

As promised, David Hallard, Cerebrus Head of Field Operations, and Lou Richards, Head of External Security, dropped by just before evening.

"We tried to get here sooner, but things at Cerebrus are pretty crazy right now. How are the two of you doing?" asked David.

"Okay," Koski and Falk replied together and laughed.

"Okay," Falk repeated. "We're both okay. So tell us what happened with the auction," he urged.

Hallard and Richards looked at each other. Richards nodded to Hallard, so Hallard began.

"First, I've got to say that the 'Tiger Team' exercise proved... prophetic. You know about it, right? Stewart told you about it?"

"No," Koski and Falk answered again together.

"Well, that isn't really surprising. A lot was going on just then," Hallard reported. "Stewart heard from his contacts that the Joint Chiefs were seriously considering a pre-emptive strike against Russia, assuming that Russia was attempting to humiliate and destroy the USA in a manner similar to that which they experienced during *perestroika* and *glasnost*.

"Stewart called a 'Tiger Team' and used the Delphi Technique to force consensus among us where, truthfully, none existed. The result was unanimous agreement that Russia couldn't be directly behind either the events or the auctions. Given the evidence, it had to be North Korea. We found out later, through you and Kate, that Russia had been developing a prototype device which they were field testing with the help of the Chinese. The Russians called it a *kvantovaya mashina smerti*—a 'Quantum Death Machine'."

Hallard paused to take a breath and Richards took over. "So, you see, in essence, both were right in regard to the events, but each only partially so. The auction, on the other hand, while clearly a correlated phenomenon, had a different 'feel' to it. Our 'Tiger Team' came to consensus that the auctions must be almost entirely North Korean, primarily, we surmised for economic reasons. In short, the money received from the 'sale' of regions of the USA was used to, first, have the USA fund its own demise—more about that later—and second, to secure North Korea economically. Clever way to get around all the sanctions, if I do say so. With enough money, they could solve their 'quality-of life' problems, impress the citizenry with their ability to rule, and obtain the weaponry needed for full-scale theater warfare. They could buy anything they needed. Rags to riches in one swoop."

"They had the means and desire," continued Hallard. "The only thing they lacked was the mechanism, and that proved to be the BitCoin auctions. BitCoins were the perfect medium: Untraceable, they could be used directly or exchanged into any currency, their value only increasing with time and demand, and the mechanism was already in place worldwide. It remained only for them to locate and convince potential 'bidders' that what they were 'selling' was 'real'. That's where the events and auctions operated symbiotically. The challenge for us was to figure out a way to stop the combined processes before it was too late."

"And it almost proved so," Richards picked up excitedly. The two were obviously enjoying relating their stories Tweedle Dee and Tweedle Dum style to their captive audience. "By the second auction, we had already begun participating in bidding for our own regions. It was Kate Keenan's idea to tag some 'return receipt' code packets onto our 'bid'. It required two more auctions 'return receipts', and final confirmation by our mole in Bureau 121 to feel confident that we'd identified the electronic pathway. Once we confirmed it was North Korea and knew the bid pathway, we set about identifying the bidders. In the end, we needed the Hawaii auction to conclusively track and identify all of them, but, of course, by that time, it could have ended up an academic exercise as the USA should have functionally ceased to exist. Just before the Hawaii event, NSA convinced the electronic security forces of our allies to join us in aggressively seizing control of the entire dark TOR network and all BitCoin exchanges. Stewart came up with the idea that after the successful bidder had sent his money, we would flood the market with our own secret stash of BitCoins, effectively driving their value down to near nothing, leaving all the auction participants holding massive debts, in many cases larger than their net worth."

"It was a big gamble," Hallard said, taking over again from Richards. "In fact, we went dangerously beyond 'breaking the bank' in order to participate in the auctions. Luckily we 'owned' the value of the BitCoins, having begun aggressively mining them immediately after the first auction, in an ultimately failed attempt to break the block encryption and identify the participants that way."

"This has got to be one of the most complex terrorist attacks yet," Falk interjected.

"Seems more like a brutal act of war," summed up Koski.

"Ah, but technically, it wasn't either," said Richards. "That's the beauty of it upon looking back. 'Terrorist attacks' are defined as non-state attacks, and 'acts of war' as involving the use of physical force. Neither technically occurred, though the Joint Chiefs were ready to characterize what was happening as an 'act of cyberwar' and actually instigate a global military response. It doesn't even fit the definition of 'cyber espionage', as, if you think about it, nothing was ever actually stolen. The closest anyone came to naming what we have just experienced is 'organized hacking' and even that's flimsy at best given the extent of it."

"So we're entering a new age of conflict," Falk ventured. "One more insidious than ever before. Just when the United Nations was making inroads against war by agreeing to hold leaders of the attacking nations personally responsible for the suffering and loss of life, and the aggressor nation for not only the direct expenses of the war, but for the cost of both aggressor and defender population's physical and mental 'recovery' to pre-war levels. Just then, along comes this incident to blur everything."

"So North Korea starts a world war and gets off Scot-free?" inquired Koski.

"Not entirely so, but that's Kate's story to tell," Hallard added cryptically. "She's been in debriefings all day, but she told us to tell you that she would be visiting as soon as she could break away, perhaps later tonight or tomorrow."

"Brilliant woman, that Kate," concluded Rogers, gathering up his coat and hat, and preparing to leave.

'*A truly brilliant woman*', thought Koski with a mixture of awe and antipathy.

Chapter 46

"Bandage changes before dinner!" the physician's assistant announced with a cheerfulness that neither Falk nor Koski shared. "Think of it as an appetizer." he added with a smirk.

For Koski, the bandage change was quick and mostly painless: Unwrap the old head bandage, remove the gauze pad, check the ten or so wicked-looking scalp sutures that would one day be hidden beneath her hair, place on a new gauze pad, and rewrap. She would need to remain in the hospital, the physician's assistant advised, at least for another day of observation before being free to leave.

For Falk, it was a different matter entirely. After his left arm sling was carefully removed, the shoulder bandages needed to be unwrapped. During this time, even the slightest arm movement, actively or passively, resulted in a flurry of gut-wrenching pain, reminding him of how he felt just after being shot. Tossing the black box into the room had proven almost unbearable. It was pure luck that he was able to toss it at all.

In actuality, Falk was more than lucky. The bullet had struck and bounced off his left collarbone, leaving it shattered. A higher caliber bullet would have penetrated through and likely punctured his lung. Half an inch lower and major arteries, veins and nerves would have been shredded. The surgeons had repositioned the two broken ends, inserted a temporary rod and packed in bone chips from elsewhere in his body then sewn him back up leaving a nasty-looking, four-inch long, gross looking, black-sutured gash. Looking at the heavily bruised wound in the mirror during the dressing change, it left him feeling like he was part Frankenstein monster. It would be at least a week before they would issue a final prognosis and, then, a carefully planned, rigorous, only slightly less painful physical therapy regime awaited him in order to keep his muscles from weakening during his anticipated three-to-four-month convalescence.

As the physician's assistant with the help of the private duty nurse wetted and removed the gauze pad, Falk held his breath and gritted his teeth. The PA picked and prodded, finally declaring the wound to be, "Looking good."

Falk tried to turn his head left to see directly for himself, but the pain was too much, and he ended up easing his body carefully back in the bed.

"It is," a familiar voice offered from the bed next to his. Falk turned carefully to his right towards the two alluring eyes peering at him from beneath what looked like an Arabian turban.

It thankfully proved much less painful to turn his head toward Koski. "Thanks, Koski. I needed to hear that. With medical people, 'looking good' can mean almost anything."

The alluring eyes blinked and Falk imagined them looking warmly and lovingly at him while the two made passionate love. *It will be awhile before that fantasy becomes...* he began thinking, sadly interrupting the thought. But at least they were both alive, intact, and, with time, would resume their work and relationship.

When the gauze pad over his stitches had been replaced with an "ouch-less" non-stick pad, the area re-bandaged, and the arm returned to its protective sling, Falk let out a long sigh and relaxed. The physician's assistant and nurse were quickly replaced by a passable hospital meal.

Late the next night, a frazzled Kate Keenan knocked at Koski and Falk's hospital door. Their twenty-four-hour guard cracked open the door, and after some discussion admitted her. Kate walked soberly, hands behind her back, to halfway between the foots of their beds, looked long at Falk, briefly at Koski and back at Falk.

"I...I..." she began as if unsure what to say, swinging her right hand forward and presenting a bright flower bouquet to both and neither. Falk smiled. Koski stiffened. Kate continued to direct the bouquet between Falk and Koski's beds, drifting slowly towards Falk's.

An awkward silence ensued, which, Falk noted quizzically, was quite unlike Kate. Once again, he sensed something happening onto which he couldn't quite put his finger. He was about to voice a perfunctory "Thank you" when Koski spoke.

"Thank you, Kate," she said. "They're lovely. You can put them on my tray-table if you like. I'll call the nurse to place them in a vase." Koski nodded towards her hospital bed tray located between her and Falk.

Falk watched Kate closely. To him, she looked tired, haggard, and...what? Contrite? Kate's posture softened and her initially enigmatic Mona-Lisa-like smile was replaced with one of genuine caring. Something was being communicated between the two women, that was obvious, but exactly what continued to escaped him.

A moment later the nurse entered, and, at Koski's request,

selected a plastic water jug in which she gathered and arranged the flowers. Finished, she held flowers out to Koski as if for approval.

"Please put them on the cabinet between us," Koski said, indicating with her finger the metal cabinet located against the wall equal-distance between her and Falk's bed. To Falk, her voice seemed more determined than usual. The nurse complied and, looking quickly from one woman to the other, quietly took her leave. As the nurse left, Falk thought he saw both women relax.

"Susan, I think I owe you an…"

"No, Kate. It's *you* to whom *I* owe the apology," Koski cut in, the tone of her voice firm but contrite and acquiescent.

"No, Susan, I…"

"What the hell's going on?" Falk interrupted, truly puzzled by what he was hearing and seeing. "Is this some kind of new field code?"

Both women stared at Falk, then at each other as if gauging the other's mettle, then both broke out in laughter.

"Girl stuff," replied Kate Keenan, wiping her eyes and resuming her bearing, having been appointed in reward for her actions a department rather than a division and with it a massive new set of "toys," as well as an entirely new perspective on Cerebrus' mission.

"'Girl stuff'," repeated Koski, looking over at Falk and extending a hand towards him.

Falk stretched awkwardly and, in the end, painfully, to touch her fingertips, before wincing and pulling his hand back.

Kate watched the two, her face belying no further feeling or emotion. "I came here to thank you both: Joe for supporting me in the field during a time of…well…personal crisis, and you, Susan, for saving my and later Joe's on the stairway. I realize now that I'm not meant to be a field agent. That's for you and Joe...together...as the incredible team you've always been. I am indebted to you both."

"Thanks, Kate. I appreciate you telling me that," Koski replied. "But in the field, we don't carry debts. Covering each other is our job. You owe us nothing but your continued friendship."

"What Susan just said is true," Falk added, feeling more of an intruder than a participant in the conversation, but wanting greatly to be included, though why, exactly, he wasn't sure.

"I'm here to answer any questions you might have about what happened after you tossed the box into the room just before the event."

"I have several questions," replied Falk. "But first, I think both Susan and I owe you our thanks for not just apparently saving the United States of America, but also saving...us. Exactly how you did it, I'm still not clear, but you ended up playing the principle role in this whole operation, and playing it with an undeniably level head and cool expertise. To you go my personal congratulations, though I would guess they'll be lost in those from every American from the President on down."

Kate blushed. "Thank you, Joe," she said, rather coolly he thought. Turning to Koski, Kate continued, "That's some man you have there."

"I know," replied Koski emphatically, directing another smile at Falk.

Despite all his effort, Falk again felt the outsider in the conversation. There was clearly a purpose behind what the two women were indirectly saying to each other. About one thing, however, he felt certain: Something unsettling was going on right in front of him. When earlier, Kate had blushed, he had felt...

what?…warmness? A protectiveness that he hadn't truly felt before? The feeling, however, disappeared during their discussion as rapidly as it had appeared.

"I'm sure you're wondering about the little 'gift' to the North Koreans," Kate continued in business-like voice. "If you recall, Joe, in Operation Finding Kate, I developed a process where screenwriters could dictate a screenplay, and instead of it resulting in a computer-generated script, it recreated actual audio-visual characters. Robotic characters so realistic that viewers would mistake them for live human actors. Taken together, one could 'dictate' a believable movie. Not entirely, but enough so that the techies could, with say, an hour's additional labor, edit and polish it to the point that it was ready for viewing in theaters. That was what got me into the situation in which you found me and from which afterwards you 'rescued' me.

"At your recommendation, Joe, I was offered and accepted an ultra-secret job within Cerebrus. Initially, no division or department, just me, an amazing laboratory, and unlimited funding to continue developing the technology I'd invented. What we sent back to the Koreans was the result of years of research and development. The scary part for me was that it was also my lab's first full-scale *weaponized* field deployment. I was *pretty* certain it would work, having tested and retested all its various components. We had to put them together into a less than a few centimeter sized "black box" which we tested as best we could in the field under carefully controlled conditions, but never in an actual situation like this. "

"All that must have weighed heavily on you when you joined me in the room with the wounded girl and relinquished the box to save her life," Falk said, choosing his words carefully and watching the two women for their reaction.

Koski said nothing. Her look of respectful said it for her.

"Yes," Kate replied simply. "At that moment, I felt…well, I felt mostly…confused. A lot *was* weighing heavily on my…mind." Falk noticed Kate's face flush momentarily. "Yes, well, the little black box: What we conjured up was an inductive pulse device that, instead of exploding or creating a 'big bang' in *their* room, created a much bigger bang in their minds. Basically, a number of selected, integrated-wave-pulses were produced that stimulate portions of the brain that cause the recipients to see whatever they want to see. Not just 'want', but need, wish or desire to see. And not just 'see' but actually *believe*. It's different from the 'events', in that the pulses from my device diminish slower as they travel outwards.

"The initial effect on those closest would be confusion. You see, those slightly further away would be momentarily *unaffected*, leaving them trying to make sense out of what the effected were saying and doing, the effect slowly rippling it's way outward."

Koski and Falk looked puzzled.

"For example," Kate clarified, "if a North Korean working on the project desperately wanted the event to be successful, maybe for fear of his, her or a family member's life, that person would immediately interpret all sensory information—sight, sound, smell, taste, touch—into the seemingly 'real' experience that the event actually *had* been successful. For that person, in fact, their effort would have been *wildly* successful, while at the same time equally frightening in that they would feel that they would likely never be able to be this successful on any subsequent project. To the affected individual, the combination of relief and new-found fear would be absolutely real. Likewise, any as yet unaffected nearby observer would be thrown into a sense of profound disorientation, knowing the project had failed, despite the opposite behavior of those affected, even more so, knowing that their effort had backfired in some very strange way they weren't able to comprehend."

Kate paused to let the two agents take in what she'd shared.

"My God!" Falk exclaimed.

Koski's expression slowly turned to one of compassion. She was only now beginning to appreciate the immense pressure that Kate must have been working under. Preparing to deploy a singular device, the results of which she was uncertain, in the field, weapon in hand, she would have desperately needed someone to share her burden with. Someone like Falk.

"Yes. 'My God!' That's exactly what kept running through my mind, even as I handed you the device to deploy for me. 'My God, what am I doing? What am I unleashing?' I felt like Oppenheimer, when in a flash, his work was transformed from the greatest gift that humankind had ever been given into the most destructive device ever known. A device far beyond the moral capacity of anyone to understand and, more so, control."

"Wouldn't the effects be limited to those in the room?" Koski asked.

"And why, in the end, didn't we experience the fifth event?" Falk added.

"Both good questions," replied Kate. "I said I had my research group busy preparing the device, but in actuality, they were modifying it in three key ways: According to the laws of quantum mechanics, an object and its 'clone' can only co-exist while quantum-entangled, a state that is so short and ephemeral, we have yet to be able to measure it with any real precision. Call it the 'present' if you wish. The entanglement exists only in the 'present moment', sandwiched between past and future. Once the present moment is over, the quantum entanglement ceases and the paradox of two of the same thing co-existing at the same time in two different places has to resolve. Either it remains at the site of origin, or it remains at the target site. That being said, what ended up in North Korea, wasn't the little black box."

"Huh?" replied Falk. "Then what was sent?"

"The *result* of the device being activated in a quantum-entanglement condition. What was transmitted back to the North Koreans was the *result* of the activated device: a plasma wave packet that experientially altered their minds. Nothing more, nothing less. And, the second trait I asked my scientists to incorporate into our little gift used the same physics that caused the North Korean events to echo and expand. In our case, the 'event' the North Koreans experienced will slowly spread, affecting the same change in anyone through whom the echo passes. Everyone, we think, within several hundred miles of the epicenter. The third trait proved most difficult to engineer but is also the most interesting: Anyone on the other end of any electrical or electronic connection to the epicenter, say, talking on a telephone line, radiotelephone or cell phone..."

"That means the North Korean leadership..." began Koski, astounded at what she was hearing.

"Yes. At this moment they are all suddenly 'seeing' the world as they need, want or desire it to be. Franklin, David, Albert, and Lou have been busy these past hours manipulating world news so that the combination of the news and the perceptions of the affected will slowly chisel out a new 'reality' for them, one where the attitudes and behavior of current North Korean leaders will be altered, hopefully for the better. Remember, we didn't have time to fully test the results of the completed weapon.

"As for our not experiencing *their* 'endgame event', the answer is really quite simple: Mathematically speaking, two entanglements can't co-exist at the same moment in the same space-time. One or the other entangled pair must *never have existed*. My technicians made certain our gift would have a slightly more powerful 'kick' during quantum entanglement than their space-time tear. In short, their endgame event not only didn't happen, *it never existed at all*. If that still seems paradoxical, remember that entanglements can only exist in the true present moment. Whatever ceases to exist in the present moment cannot become past. And because of this, there will be no trace of who or what caused it, or that it ever happened."

"And you accomplished all this between the fourth and fifth events?" asked Falk, overawed in turn.

"Not really. I developed the theoretical foundations during my time with Cerebrus. I had to trust my dedicated crew of Cerebrus research scientists to bring everything quickly to fruition. I imagine the full impact of what we've accomplished hasn't yet begun to sink in. The old Einstein-Oppenheimer effect: By unleashing this new 'weapon', the world as we knew it before has been replaced by one in which quantum entanglement will now play a major role. There's no going back. And the ethical considerations, I suspect, will prove even more challenging than the advent of the atomic age. I don't know whether to smile or cry." Indeed, Kate's eyes were misting as she spoke.

"So, in the end, all our our efforts to capture the two agents and their handler made no real difference after all," observed Falk glumly.

"Oh, quite the contrary," replied Kate with what could only be called a look of love. "The Oriental agent's former 'friend', and to an even greater extent, her handler were quite willing to share everything they knew about the workings of the interconnected receivers, which gave our side something to compare my effort to. Half of any battle is always in the understanding. Hearing what they shared made my seemingly unbelievable explanation all the more believable. Your sacrifices were hardly in vain. Without you two, our future would have been totally different. Instead, there's a world outside this room waiting to thank you. True, the thanks will be filtered through Cerebrus in order to preserve your anonymity and allow you to continue your work. My 'thanks' are my promotion, and with it, even more secrecy and anonymity. Aside from Stewart and you two, I doubt anyone will soon know I did anything or ever existed."

A long silence hung heavily in the air between Kate and the two agents.

"Thank you, Kate," Koski replied softly on both her and Falk's behalf but on two quite different levels,. "Thank you from the bottom of both our hearts."

Epilogue

Koski and Falk walked together, his better right hand grasping Koski's left, along the tree-lined south side of the Reflection Pool of the Washington Mall. By all rights, the night should have been pitch black given the blanket of low-lying clouds above, but a soft side light, emanating as if by magic from the illuminated trees, coupled with the blaze of the Washington Monument behind them and the Lincoln Memorial ahead imparted a truly romantic glow.

Koski hadn't noticed. She was busy studying the face of the man she loved. It was a different face from the one she remembered prior to this mission. Beneath its weathered exterior had always existed a boy's rakish smile; a Peter Pan to her Wendy. Tonight, however, Falk's face looked tense. Faint lines showed in the corners of his eyes and mouth, a residual, she assumed, from the constant pain he'd suffered during the last four months. Getting back in shape after the collarbone fracture had proven more difficult than either had thought. Just when he was starting to feel better, the surgeons brought him back into the hospital to remove the pin, sending him back to where he'd been the night he woke in the hospital after...

It was clear to Koski that Falk was lost in his thoughts. Painful ones. She placed an arm around his waist as they walked together, leaned her head against his good shoulder and smiled up at him.

Falk cringed momentarily, a reflex he'd acquired during the four months of "torture," as he sometimes called it. As an agent, he'd been trained to steel himself against such, but his recovery, stretching out as long as it had, had taken its toll, leaving him physically and mentally exhausted.

"'A penny for your thoughts'," Koski, stretching to her full height, whispered in his ear.

Falk stopped and turned to face the water, Koski positioned between, looking hopefully at him. "I was thinking back to the hallway of that house," Falk replied. "Twice, I didn't know if you were alive or dead. For a while, I didn't know if *I* was dead. I didn't know if we would ever be together again. In truth, I was forced to face our deaths, individually and together. It was't a pleasant...

"Everything happened so fast. For a moment, I didn't know if *you* and I were dead or alive, but here we are, together, walking our favorite walk, with all that behind us and a whole new world ahead.

"For a moment, I found myself mourning your passing," Falk whispered in anguish.

"Oh, Joe! I can't begin to imagine what you were feeling back there, and frankly I don't want to remember how I felt, but we're here. Now. Together."

"Yes," replied Falk, shaking off the agony the incident and his slow recovery for the umpteenth time. "It was the first time I truly felt my mortality. I don't want to lose you, Susan. The doctor's say I'm fit for duty, and I'm ready to serve, but I don't ever again want to lose you."

"You needn't worry about that," Susan Koski replied. "Oh, and by the way, I have a belated birthday gift for you," she added, and touched her lips to his.

Joseph Falk slipped both his hands around her waist, and held her tightly against him in a lover's embrace.

No, each thought. *I needn't worry about that ever again. At least, not for tonight.*

Book Seven:

Dedication
To Lea

Forward

The story you're about to read never happened. However, it could have, and may yet. A. G. Hayes, Multi-Award-winning Author of the both the Koski and Falk Series and the Kate Keenan Special Assignment Series.

Prologue

The lessons of history indicate a real weather-modification capability will eventually exist despite the risk.

History teaches that we cannot afford to be without a weather-modification capability once the technology is developed and used by others.

According to General Gordon Sullivan, former Army Chief of Staff, "As we leap technology into the 21st century, we will be able to see the enemy day or night, in any weather, and go after him relentlessly. In the United States, weather-modification will likely become a part of national security policy including development of weather-weaponry unthinkable now. Such weapons will deter and counter potential adversaries.

"The number of specific intervention methodologies is limited only by the imagination, but with few exceptions they involve infusing either energy or chemicals into the meteorological process in the right way, at the right place and time. The intervention could be designed to modify the weather, so as to influence clouds and precipitation, storm intensity, climate, space, or fog."

Chapter 1

Waves smashed against the one square mile of jagged black rock that comprised the home of Flangenan Lighthouse. The lighthouse had clung tenaciously to the rocky outcroppings three miles west of the Isle of Tiree for over two hundred years.

Flangenan Lighthouse, to a sea-going navigator, was a mere speck in the Atlantic. A place of solitude where even the screech of sea gulls no longer sounded, as if they too had been switched off with the beacons that had once flashed their warning across the turbulent sea.

"We chose it for its neutrality. The Brits opted for its inaccessibility and the Israelis chose it for its impregnability." Agent Joe Falk's low voice crackled into the earphones of Agent Susan Koski, seated beside him, blond and petite, but alert as she swept her binoculars across the vastness of the dark green sea below. Falk brushed a hank of chestnut hair out of his eyes as he swung the helicopter in a tight circle above the craggy island. "The Allies used the island in World War II as a lookout for German shipping movements. It's been abandoned ever since. The lighthouse was decommissioned in the fifties, and, as we know today, ships plying the rigors of the North Atlantic use GPS satellite," Falk explained.

Flangenan Lighthouse was soon to be inhabited once again, this time, by those who knew little of life in a cylindrical tower amidst a sea of many moods. Koski's ponytail bobbed as she turned her head and focused her binoculars on the lighthouse. Once crisp and white, now in the wintry morning sun, its conical structure embedded into the northernmost tip of the land was weather-worn to a splotchy grey. She scrutinized a concrete bunker added to the west curve of the lighthouse and another built into the east face of the rock cliff.

The helicopter circled one more time around the lighthouse and then set course back to Tiree. Although the weather was bright and clear for November, nonetheless it could change in a moment. Falk leaned forward, watching the cliffs of Tiree flash beneath them. The three-mile distance seemed to take no time since they had left the lighthouse.

The copter approached a grass landing strip marked with a red and white radial, then, with a classic nose-up angle, lowered gently to earth. Falk shut down the engine and unsnapped his seat belt. The slowing whoosh of the blades cut through the cold Scottish air, wound down and stopped while Falk and Koski eased out of the machine. A brightly painted logo on the side of the aircraft depicting two sea birds in flight against a yellow and orange sun reflected a splash of color as a shaft of watery sunlight momentarily peeped from behind a low bank of fast moving storm clouds being swept in from the sea.

"Made it back just in time," Falk grunted, scanning the sky. "They warned me how quick weather changes up here at this time of the year." He referred to the contacts he had met in the coastal town of Oban, on the Scottish mainland two days before.

"Scotland in November—this could be a wet and windy assignment, Joe." Koski tugged up the collar of her thick down jacket as she shrugged her shoulders and thrust her hands deep into the large patch pockets. A seasoned agent, she had worked in far worse conditions than this.

This was their fifth assignment together. They'd first met in Nevada when Falk was assigned to lead a task force to solve the mysterious serial killings of lawyers in California and Nevada.

Falk remembered that first meeting. They'd both suffered personal losses. Koski had a husband who was accused of selling drugs while a member of the Las Vegas police department; he was now an ex-husband serving time in the Nevada State Prison in Carson City.

Falk's wife had died in a freak accident several months

earlier. The loss affected him more than he realized. Sadness mixed with the gnawing guilt of not being able to get to her to help her before she died had haunted him with a frustrated sense of helplessness.

Over the years, the situation between Koski and Falk had changed. Now, they were more than just a team.

Falk nodded to a man in a faded orange boiler suit that trotted over to tie down the helicopter. To him, Falk and Koski probably seemed like two members of yet another group of do-gooders. Stopping besides the copter, the mechanic looked at the logo and read, *"The foxes have holes and the birds of the air have nests."*

"Takes all kinds," he muttered to himself as he went about the job of securing the aircraft. "As long as they pay, whatever they do is fine with me. I'll sell them all the fuel they want. This time of the year, there's hardly any helicopters around."

Switching on the ignition of a rented SUV, Falk put it in drive and bumped across the grass field toward a five-barred gate that served as an entrance to the small airstrip. He headed out onto a narrow two lane road.

The four-mile return journey to the hotel had been uneventful. Now, cleaned up and rested, Koski and Falk relaxed on a well-worn leather couch in the lounge of the old Glenn Morgan Hotel on the Hebridean Isle of Tiree, staring unblinkingly at a cold, blustery day that rattled the window frames and dashed icy rain into rivulets across the panes of glass. It was their second day at the Glenn Morgan.

Koski sighed. "What a place; twelve miles long and six miles at its widest point, covering an area of thirty square miles of total boredom. Why would Stewart want to base us here?"

"This time of the year, there's not many visitors and little chance of the media getting curious. As far as any of the locals know, we're part of an ornithologists' team researching sea birds of the North Atlantic."

"How are the others getting here?" Koski asked.

"Jack Tanner and Doctor Kevin Clayton are flying in on Highlands and Islands Airport group," Falk said. "They'll land at the strip and take a car to the hotel. Commander Harris and Professor Victor Teesdale will be crossing over from Oban on the ferry. Doctor Jacob Jenner and Ms. Courtney Spencer will arrive by private plane."

Koski grunted. "A small plane in this weather."

"Courtney Spencer is piloting the private plane in from Glasgow. I hear she's good."

"She better be." A gust of wind again rattled the hotel windows.

"I suppose this is the last place anyone would expect to find three world class scientists specializing in Renewable Energy and Solar Chemistry." Leaning back, he laced his fingers behind his head, ruffling his rich dark brown hair.

Koski nodded.

"The security at the lighthouse must be awesome," Falk chuckled. "Especially when you realize the security on this entire island is in the hands of one Constable."

"You have to be kidding."

"Nope."

"And out at the lighthouse?"

"The scientists will have their own security people."

Koski was silent. The name Tanner rang a bell, but she could not remember why. "Do we know this guy, Jack Tanner?"

"No. But maybe you read about him a couple of years ago. He was in charge of an abortive attempt to flush out a commune, a home-style militia in Idaho. A couple of kids were killed. He got the blame and the bad press."

Koski nodded. "I remember something about that. Now he's in charge of this operation? That's just great," Koski said, rolling her blue-gray eyes upward.

"There's an old saying, Koski. Politics makes for strange bedfellows."

Chapter 2

The fierce Negev desert sun blazed down on a bleached concrete runway in the hot, barren waste. Flat, white buildings decayed in the distance and two Israeli soldiers stood beside Jacob Jenner, a brooding man in his late forties, his eyes magnified and obscured behind thick lenses. He glanced at his watch to remind himself of the date: November 9, 2009, 1440 hours. The plane was precisely on time. Flies buzzed around the three men in the silent, acrid heat.

Jacob Jenner shaded his eyes and, hearing the drone of a small aircraft, looked up and watched as the private plane circled over the buildings and made its final approach to the runway, setting down with a squeak of tires and a puff of dust.

Jenner nodded to the two soldiers, picked up his suitcase, and headed to the plane that had taxied in close to them.

The cockpit door opened and the pilot eased out and stood on the wing. She was Courtney Spencer, tall and slender.

Jenner could not see her face, as the sun blinded him. Standing with feet apart and hands on hips, she appeared like a modern day Sun God, a golden phoenix.

Then Courtney spoke, "Hello again, Doctor Jenner."

Jenner stopped and looked up, shading his eyes. "I didn't know we'd met."

"Two years ago at the Weizmann Institute." Courtney moved slightly and now he could see her face, pale and beautiful.

"Can't imagine how I'd forget."

Courtney reached down and shook his hand. "Your wife, she was still alive then. Welcome aboard. I'm from the Knesset."

Jenner nodded, handed up his suitcase, then went around to the passenger door and scrambled up onto the wing and into the cockpit. There was no further conversation as Courtney took the controls and throttled the plane down the runway into a smooth take off.

Glancing back, Jenner saw the two Israeli soldiers lift their heads as if watching until the plane was out of sight and silence returned to the desert. He imagined they slowly sauntered back to their jeep.

Chapter 3

At the same time, Jack Tanner sat at his desk in Washington, D.C. listening to a voice from his intercom. "He'll cooperate. Just see he watches his manners and keeps his mind on the job. We all know how easily distracted he can get."

The lines of disillusion had finally set into a face no longer young. Tanner flicked a speck from his razor-cut Madison Avenue suit. "Yes, sir, I know."

"Jack, this is essentially an American operation so that puts you right up front where it shows. I know you need this one. Hold off for the best deal and you're back on top. That I guarantee."

Tanner cleared his throat softly. "Thank you, sir." He flicked the switch, lost in thought for a moment. Then he rose and crossed over to a wall mirror. He took a long, hard look at himself. His expression darkened. Then, twisting away, he crossed to a window and stared at the dome of the Capitol Building in the distance. "This time...whatever it takes. That I guarantee." Turning back into the room, he picked up a suitcase and exited.

Chapter 4

From atop Nelson's column in Trafalgar Square, the half-blind Admiral's panoramic view of London below was gray under a driving and unceasing rain. From a narrow avenue housing a row of small, elite hotels, a middle-aged man emerged from one called The Nelson; he paused to look at the rain with disdain. The hotel canopy above his head rapped and thrashed in the wind. The man, squat and barrel chested, shifted uncomfortably inside his thick tweeds and smoothed down the creases in his perfectly rolled umbrella. He was Commander Harold Harris, Royal Navy, Order of the British Empire, and now of the British Foreign Office.

A hotel door attendant hastened to the commander's side and covered him with an oversized umbrella, escorting him to a waiting Rolls Royce. The commander entered the rear of the Rolls. The door closed and the doorman leaned forward with a salute. "Have a good trip, Commander."

The Rolls moved off through the rain. Seated next to the commander was a tired looking aristocrat.

"We've packed you some warm clothes, Commander. Shocking weather where you're going." The Rolls continued its journey through torrential rain as a thunderstorm moved in overhead, blackening and streaking the sky.

Later that day, somewhere in rural England, the Rolls

splashed along a country lane and came to a stop outside a whitewashed cottage. The chauffeur got out and dashed through the downpour to the front door of the small home.

In the rear of the Rolls, the commander and the aristocrat sat in silence, listening to the rain.

A few minutes later the chauffeur returned with a suitcase, loaded it in the trunk, and announced. "His wife sez 'e won't be a minute."

The commander bridled. "Damn it, man! Where the devil is he? We mustn't let the Americans get there first."

The chauffeur jerked his head toward a high privet hedge in front of the garden and grinned. The commander and the aristocrat leaned forward, curious.

From the other side of the hedge a head popped up, the face ancient and crinkled, the high forehead covered by the turn of the century Sou'wester style of hat. Professor Vincent Teesdale held up a seedling. "Early cropper. The dwarf variety with excellent flavor. But needs protection from the rain, you see. Just have to be sure they're covered. Be right with you."

Commander Harris turned to the aristocrat. "Are you sure he's our best?"

Chapter 5

"The guy in the tweed suit," Koski nodded toward the bar. "I heard one of the staff call him 'Commander.' He arrived today with the eccentric looking man with the huge forehead next to him."

Falk saw the person Koski referred to as the commander, a blustery sort, obviously used to giving orders. He and the man she described as eccentric were deep in conversation, sipping from large glasses of what was, no doubt, scotch. A full briefing for the scientist and security agents would be forthcoming upon the arrival of Jack Tanner, from the U.S. State department.

"I also talked to one of the housemaids this morning and she mentioned that last week this place was almost empty." Koski stopped as a shapely blonde and a serious, studious-looking man wearing thick glasses entered. They paused in the doorway, scanned the room, then headed to a table next to a window overlooking the small harbor and sat down.

"The housemaid also mentioned I was the only woman guest." She nodded toward the blonde. "If she's a guest, the housemaid's wrong."

Falk checked his watch. "And I'm sure you reinforced the fact that we were a couple of bird watchers."

Koski smiled and nodded. "Of course."

Chapter 6

In Fort Lauderdale, Doctor Kevin Clayton stood at the airline counter as a computer traced out a VIP's reservation, routing from Ft. Lauderdale to London/Gatwick, and on to Glasgow, Scotland. Clayton, a faint smile edging his bright, intelligent face, nodded to the ticketing clerk. His clothes were casual grays with a dapper splash of color.

"Have a good flight, Dr. Clayton."

Clayton flashed a warm smile and turned from the counter. Two powerfully built no-nonsense men in dark suits were watching Clayton. Their very presence seemed to form a barrier between him and the nearby departure area, but he acted as if he didn't notice them. He walked past the two men toward ticket taker at the door to the plane. The men fell in behind him. Arriving at the entry way, he looked back once, then sauntered down the umbilical cord walkway and onto the aircraft. As the door to the plane closed and the walkway concertinaed inward, Clayton knew one of the men would remove his cell phone, tap a number, and say, "He's on his way."

In Glasgow airport, Kevin Clayton walked through the security gate from the plane and the two large black-suited men who escorted him through the terminal created stares from passing travellers. One man indicated the exit they were to take. Clayton smiled and allowed a glance at their faces, then quickly corrected his expression to match the gravity of theirs. They left the terminal by a side entrance marked *Authorized Personnel Only.*

Jack Tanner sat in the back seat of a car parked alongside the rear of the terminal.

Clayton and his escorts exited the building and went forward to the car. The rear door opened and Clayton got in. One of the men nodded to Tanner as the car moved off and along a private road beside the airport.

Clayton leaned back in his seat. "You part of this outfit?"

Tanner nodded. "I'm running it."

"Then perhaps you'll tell me where we're going."

"Private plane to the Isle of Tiree, a hotel, dinner, a good night's sleep, then to the middle of nowhere."

Chapter 7

Koski and Falk met with Commander Harris and introduced themselves as federal agents assigned to see the scientific contingent got safely to the lighthouse.

"Yes, I was advised you were to join us. London filled me in rather well." Harris took a long look at Koski before continuing. "Where's Tanner? I thought he was to be the one to liaise everything. The meeting, accommodation, schedule, the lot."

"He is, Commander," Falk replied. "He'll be arriving with Doctor Clayton later today."

"I don't understand why it needs two of you to take care of seeing we get off safely. We're not a group of school children, Falk. Everyone in London seems to think security is in order."

"Those are our orders, Commander."

Harris snorted and rudely turned away. They watched him cross the lounge, stopping to chat with others on his way.

"What does he do, anyway?" Koski asked.

"He's one of the coordinators, doing administration and logistics. You know how it is when you get three different governments sending their top scientists to exchange ideas on how best to utilize solar power and weather control to benefit mankind."

Koski raised her eyes toward the ceiling. "Yeah, sure. The rest of the world would wonder what they are really up to."

"Exactly. That's the reason they're having this meeting in a remote location where it will be nigh impossible for the media, or anyone else for that matter, to bother them. Up to now, two of the three brains have made it this far without being noticed. If they'd been stars, the media vans would be out there now with their dishes pointing high in the sky." From where Falk was sitting, he could watch the blonde and the serious-faced man at the front desk.

Chapter 8

Courtney Spencer and Dr. Jenner sat at a table in the window, Courtney twirling the stem of her empty wine glass between her slender fingers. "You haven't actually met this Dr. Clayton, have you?" she asked with twinkling eyes.

"Not yet. Have you?" Jenner asked as he peered around the

room.

"No. But I've heard all about him, and I can't wait to meet him."

"Why?"

"Kevin Clayton has a reputation in both solar energy and energy of a different kind."

"And energy interests you?"

"Reputations interest me." She lit a cigarette and blew a long seductive smoke beam.

Falk glanced at Koski and nodded his head toward the front desk, indicating the commander rapping on the mahogany counter. "Stay here. I'm going to stretch my legs. I won't be long."

Commander Harris, red faced and angered by the lateness in the arrival of the American scientist and Jack Tanner, demanded the desk recheck the arrival of Doctor Clayton's plane. He was informed the aircraft had arrived on time, and that Doctor Clayton had left with Mr. Tanner. Perhaps there had been a breakdown.

"Breakdown be damned. Get me the American Embassy in London." The desk clerk turned toward the phone as Clayton and Tanner entered the front door and walked toward the desk. Something about the two men made the clerk wait until they were at the counter.

"May I help you, gentlemen?"

Falk sauntered to a rack of brochures and pamphlets describing the beauty spots around the area. He was well within earshot of the desk.

"We have reservations. My name is Tanner, Jack Tanner. And this is Doctor Kevin Clayton."

Harris glared at the two men and blurted, "We've been waiting for you. We were worried. You're late."

With the sudden outburst from an unknown, red-faced little man, Clayton and Tanner took half a step back. Then Tanner stepped forward toward the offensive man.

"Who the hell are you?" Tanner said, thrusting his jaw and moving in close to Harris.

Harris backed up a couple of paces and bumped into a potted palm. "I'm Commander Harold Harris. I..."

Clayton stuck his hand out to the flustered commander. "Clayton. Pleased to meet you, sir. Heard a lot about you. Sorry we're late. Airports...you know the way they are."

Harris nodded to Clayton, but cut his eyes to Tanner, indicating quite clearly he'd made an enemy.

Tanner ignored him and continued to converse with the man at the desk. "Are our rooms ready? We're very tired and would like to get cleaned up before dinner."

"Yes, sir. I'll have your luggage sent up right away." He pushed two keys across the counter and rang a bell for a porter.

Clayton glanced at Tanner, standing next to him in the elevator. "Bit hard on the old man weren't you?"

"Bombastic, pompous limey. Have to keep guys like him in their place otherwise they take over." The elevator arrived at their floor and the door slid open. "Here's your key, Doctor."

"Room two-thirty. We're adjoining." Tanner checked his watch. "See you in the bar in twenty minutes, okay?"

Clayton took the key. "Fine with me."

Chapter 9

Part of the hotel dining room had been closed off with a folding room divider to ensure privacy for the international contingent. One long table had been set for nine and now members of the group began to straggle in. The first two to take their places were Commander Harris and Professor Teesdale. The professor, reminiscent of a small child, looked around the room, eyes bright.

"I wonder if they have any Marmite," Teesdale said softly. "I always enjoy a Marmite sandwich and a cup of cocoa before bed."

"First, we have dinner, Professor," the commander ordered. "I'll ask later."

"Ah, yes. Very well. Thank you."

Harris had brought his drink in with him and took a long pull of the single malt.

Courtney and Jenner entered, followed a few seconds later by Clayton and Tanner. Courtney looked up as Clayton took his seat opposite her. Their eyes met across the table. Although no words were exchanged, a certain chemistry crackled in the air and ignited between them.

Jenner leaned toward Courtney and whispered in her ear. "I get the definite feeling energy is flowing," he said, a sparkle in his eye. "Stay tuned for reputation."

Courtney smiled, reached for a glass of water, and sipped slowly.

Kevin Clayton had never been a shy person; he gave her a dazzling smile. "Ms. Spencer, logistics, I believe."

Courtney nodded. "I'm impressed a busy man like you would know my name, Doctor."

"Let's say your reputation as a negotiator and logistician has been brought to my attention."

Jenner muffled a snort of laughter into his napkin and followed it with a sip of water as Koski, Falk, and an Israeli security agent took their places at the table.

Commander Harris took the opportunity to play the speaker

by tapping the side of his water glass with a spoon.

"I see we are all here." He paused to be sure he had their attention. "After dinner we will begin the preliminaries, a short meeting to discuss the next few days and break the ice, so to speak. Then tomorrow we will travel to our secure meeting place where we shall remain in total secrecy and security until the completion of our scientific caucus. But first, allow me to introduce everybody."

"I'll start on my right and circle the table in an anti-clockwise direction." He smiled for effect. "Next to me, Professor Victor Teesdale, Imperial College and Jodel Bank Research, United Kingdom." Teesdale nodded shyly and said nothing. "On the right of the professor, we have Ms. Courtney Spencer, Logistics and Administration, with the Israeli Knesset." Courtney smoothed her tongue across her teeth and smiled icily. Harris continued quickly, "Also from Israel, Doctor Jacob Jenner, the Weizmann Institute of Science." Jenner blinked owlishly and remained silent. "On Doctor Jenner's right, Special Agent Joe Falk. And facing him across the table, his partner, Susan Koski, Special Agent, USA. They will be responsible for our security here at the hotel. Once we arrive at our final destination, internal security will be taken care of by three elite security personnel.

"Agent Mordici Berne is with us here tonight from the Mossad's Special Section. Timothy Swale of MI-6 is already at the secure location with Agent Marshall, CIA. Doctor Kevin Clayton, next to Agent Berne is, as we all know, the inventor of the High Powered Solar Pumped Laser, known to the world media as the 'Engine of Fire'." Harris' eyes flicked the table and finally focused on a glowering Tanner. "I have purposely left Mr. Jack Tanner until the last." Harris indicated Tanner, at the opposite end of the table with a quick jerk of his head. "Mr. Tanner, Washington D.C., is my opposite number in the care and welfare of this confidential assembly." He caught himself and turned toward Courtney. "And, with Ms. Spencer's able assistance, of course, we'll do everything possible to encourage the exchange of ideas on Solar/Laser and the High Frequency Active Auroral project and keep them flowing so as to expedite a satisfactory conclusion to the agreement of our three governments. Now I will turn you over to Mr. Jack Tanner. After he's through, we'll all enjoy a grand Scottish meal."

"Thank you, Commander." Tanner smoothed his tie and continued. "First, I would like to introduce Commander Harold Harris, O.B.E. Whitehall, London. Commander Harris has vast experience serving his government in various and important capacities around the world. I'm sure we will all work well together over the next few days. Remember, we are here to see everything flows smoothly for you three learned men. We are here to help."

The commander listened to his introduction and then Tanner's voice faded to a drone as he thought back over the years, from a young man fresh out of Cambridge, to his first assignment at the Foreign Office, then serving in the Royal Navy during the war. A patriot, dedicated to his country and a man of honor. And then, after the war, returning to government service and the tenuous climb up the ladder of bureaucracy. His father died leaving him the family estate, "Blaydon Hall," in Sussex, a rambling pile that had been in the family for over three hundred years. Death taxes, followed by more taxes, had finally taken their toll. Harris had been forced to sell and take a small flat in London. He had never married, always too busy taking care of affairs of the Crown. He had been honored with the Order of The British Empire, and in two years his retirement pension would be due. Harris' mind returned to the present. But not before recalling the family motto chiselled into the mantle of the great stone fireplace, "*Virtutis Fortuna*"—now in the possession of a wealthy Asian. Tanner's voice droned as the commander mentally translated the Latin. "*Fortune is the companion of valour.*"

There was a spattering of applause for Tanner.

"When do we get to that middle of nowhere?" Courtney asked.

As Tanner was about to answer, the doors to the dining room opened and a lone piper entered with a strident skirl and whine of sounds as he paced slowly around the long table, followed by a stream of waiters carrying trays of steaming food. Kevin looked across at Courtney, raised his eyebrows, and grinned like a schoolboy.

Chapter 10

The dinner appeared to be a success. By the time dessert was served, even the bagpipes sounded pleasant. The three scientists along with Harris, Tanner, and Courtney retired into another room. Falk, Koski, and Berne remained at the table.

"Go ahead, Berne," Falk said. "Turn in, get some sleep. Koski and I will make sure they get to bed safe and sound."

Berne nodded, pushing back his chair. "It's good. See you tomorrow."

Falk turned to Koski. "I checked with the Harbor Master. The morning tide turns at six. That'll be the best time for Harris and Tanner to arrange for the trip to the lighthouse."

"And have they?"

"No idea."

"You sound bitter, Joe. What's up?"

"Maybe it's because there's something odd about this whole thing. I just don't know what it is yet."

"Odd?"

"Yeah. These three guys are super special security risks, right? They're tops in their field of solar, laser, and God knows what other whiz-bang arts of hi-tech, including weather control."

"Go on."

"Well, think about it. It's been arranged for these three to be stuck on a remote island in an old decrepit lighthouse so they can discuss methods of beaming solar energy from space to a yet unknown power grid on earth. They could have done that anywhere. For instance, the Weizmann Institute of Science in Rehovot, Israel. The Israelis have some of the finest security in the world around places like that. Why go to the trouble and risk of sending one of their top men out into the middle of the Atlantic off the west coast of Scotland?"

"They have plenty of security problems at home too," Koski said. "Maybe the UK and the States didn't want their man in Israel."

Falk nodded. "You could be right. But I think meeting on an island makes very little sense."

"*Cerberus* wouldn't have sent us along if it didn't."

"Ever think that could be the exact reason they did send us? To find out what is really going on?"

Chapter 11

The following day dawned bright and clear. The only thing to mar the morning was when the body of Mordici Berne was found on the grounds of the hotel by one of the gardeners. Berne was sitting in a gazebo on a grassy knoll overlooking the harbor. His throat had been slit.

It had taken all the Logistic and Administrative expertise of Harris and Tanner, plus a direct order from London to the lone constable on the Isle of Tiree, that no word of the murder be mentioned until given clearance by Washington, London, and Tel Aviv. In the meantime, the body would be kept, literally, on ice at the hotel.

Commander Harris' usually florid face was noticeably wan that morning as he addressed the scientific and security group at breakfast. "The death of Agent Berne is a great shock to all of us. There is a possibility the meetings will be scrubbed."

Falk and Koski were seated at the back of the room as Harris continued. "I've been in touch with London and, through Mr. Tanner, Washington. As of yet, no decisions have been forthcoming." Indicating Courtney, Harris continued. "Ms. Spencer has been in contact with the Knesset and was informed she will be advised on the future of the talks as soon as possible. In the meantime, we'll remain here at the hotel. Fortunately, this time of the year, the hotel is sparsely populated. This is an advantage which will enable us to keep the matter of Agent Berne's death out of the news.

"Myself and Agent Koski are trained investigators. No sense letting the scene of the crime grow cold," Falk suggested.

"Orders are to wait for instructions," Tanner snapped.

Shortly before lunch, a British naval officer reported to Commander Harris in his room.

"Lieutenant Garvey, British Naval intelligence. I have a message, sir." He handed a brown envelope to Harris, who slit it open and removed a single sheet of paper. The commander unfolded the official document and scanned it quickly. Glancing up at the officer, Harris read it a second time.

British Naval Intelligence—Holy Loch—Dunoon, Scotland. Due to lack of telephone security on the island of Tiree, this message is being hand delivered by Lt. W. C. Garvey, R.N. He will show Naval Intelligence ID. You will hereby notify your party to prepare to return to the mainland and disperse to their homelands. Further information will be supplied by Lt. Garvey.

Signed, Admiral Lawrence Kenilworth, DSO, MBA.

Harris sighed. "Right, Lieutenant. The rest of the story."

"Washington, Tel Aviv, and London have decided that, due to the fragile condition of the scientific exchange as it stands at the moment, the three scientists will remain under tight security. But first, the following evasive action is to take place. Your team will set sail for the mainland early this afternoon. Halfway, you will be met by a Royal Navy pinnace and transferred aboard. Others, dressed to resemble your party, will take their places in your craft and continue to the mainland where they will be met and taken to the airport. Anyone watching will observe eight people, who they will take for your group." The lieutenant paused and asked, "Any questions, sir?"

"Quite a few, actually. Although at this point I can't expect many answers, right?"

"Afraid so, Commander. You and your party will continue to the lighthouse in the pinnace. Darkness will have fallen by this time and no one will observe the completion of the journey. A replacement for Agent Berne will be flown in from the Israel. The Weizmann Institute insists on having one of the Mossad's special security in constant attendance with Dr. Jenner when the meetings begin. Also, Agent Koski will proceed to the lighthouse as security to Dr. Clayton, as we received word that Agent Marshall fell and broke his leg early this morning and is being airlifted to a hospital on the mainland. Agent Falk will follow with the replacement Israeli security agent as soon as he arrives. Falk will assume command of security at the lighthouse."

"And we in the lighthouse, could, to all intents and purpose, be bait. Am I correct?" the commander asked.

The young naval officer looked embarrassed. "The navy has intensified their sea patrols."

After the officer had left, Harris tapped his fingers on the desktop and stared into space. The murder of a security agent had put a totally different slant on the state of affairs.

Chapter 12

Falk was given his new orders and he passed the information on to Koski. "I remain here until the Israeli investigation team arrives and Berne's body is shipped out. Then I wait until Berne's replacement arrives and the preliminary investigations are completed. After that, we'll join you at the lighthouse. Washington and London feel if suspicion falls on any of our group, they'll know where we are."

"That's nice of them." Koski's voice carried an edge.

"They'll continue with the meetings, and when the investigators have done their thing and allowed you and the new agent to join us on the rock, we'll reassemble. 'And then there were ten'."

"Agatha Christie?"

"Right. Ten people on an island and they get bumped off one by one."

Falk didn't add anything because he suddenly remembered a

man named Eiker. A British Soldier of Fortune that had almost killed Koski and Falk during their investigations of Nevada and Californian lawyers being shot dead with hi-tech arrows. Eiker had been hired by the Nevada gambling underworld.

Then, a little over a year later, when assigned to a case in Vienna, Austria, Falk was horrified to learn that not only had Eiker escaped back to England, but he had been offered immunity against all charges for the terrorist actions he and his gang had carried out in the United States in return for his services in a covert action for *Cerberus*. Falk had thought hard and long before deciding to continue to work for *Cerberus*, Falk's ideal agency. A group dedicated to do whatever necessary to rid America of the scum who were slowly, from within, tuning the country into a weak third world mentality ruled by power mad political egotists with their own private agendas, including selling the birth right of every true American to the highest corporate or billionaire bidder.

When informed that Eiker would be part of his team, backing Koski and himself on their assignment in Vienna, Falk's faith and dedication to *Cerberus* was severely shaken. Tom Stewart, head of the agency, urged Falk to trust him saying, "Not everything you see or hear is the truth."

Eiker had died during the course of the assignment, but not before saving the lives of many, including Falk and Koski. Yet later, upon returning back to the States, the act of *Cerberus* using the skills of such a man caused him deep concern and he wondered whether or not to remain with the agency. Koski and Stewart had assured him he would be making a mistake to leave *Cerberus*. Stewart had to utilize the best people he could obtain to bring justice to their cause. There was no such group that could carry out the actions needed to save the country and, at the same time, play by the rules of fair play.

Were they once again in a situation where the information he'd received from Stewart was not all it seemed to be?

Chapter 13

A newly constructed pier jutted from the rocky shores of Flangenan Island, enabling the Royal Navy pinnace to tie up and unload its passengers and luggage. Everyone was ashore in a matter of minutes. Then the Navy craft slipped its moorings and, with the White Ensign flapping, headed away from the island.

Each of the disembarked passengers carried hand luggage. Commander Harris hefted his and pointed to the lighthouse.

"We'll soon have everyone settled. Your luggage will be delivered to your rooms. Follow me."

It was growing dark and squares of yellow light illuminated several of the small windows in the cylindrical tower.

Agent Swale of MI-6 has a light in the window for us, Koski mused. The interior of the lighthouse had been completely renovated. The main entrance room had been painted a soft yellow tone, adding warmth to the previous gray stone walls. The floor was covered in a thick layer of beige indoor-outdoor carpeting. A large round wooden table with several chairs placed around it held center stage.

Harris stood with his back to the table and called for everyone's attention. "I want to take a moment to introduce you to Agent Swale, who I mentioned at dinner last night. He's been here on the island during the preparations for our stay. We were all sorry to hear of the misfortune that befell Agent Marshall."

"Thank you, Commander." Swale indicated the table. "You'll each find a personalized envelope containing information and a floor plan of the lighthouse. The larger of the two World War Two bunkers you may have noticed as you approached the lighthouse have been converted into sleeping quarters. Your assigned room location is in the information package. The smaller bunker is for supplies and also doubles as the kitchen. This area we are in at the moment will act as a common room/dining room. The scientific meetings will be held on the second level. The third level has been set up as a communications center and the old lantern room remains empty. A member of the security team will be on duty at all times, in constant communication with the Royal Navy who will be patrolling the area. The patrols will continue until the meetings have been completed and everyone returned to the mainland."

"Thank you, Agent Swale," Harris said. "Pick up your envelope. Familiarize yourselves with your rooms and we'll meet back here in one hour."

Tanner had remained silent throughout the brief introduction. Now he walked to the table and collected his envelope. Harris exchanged a glance with him, but said nothing.

Koski and Courtney discovered they were roommates. Two single beds, two dressers, and two chairs made up the quarters.

The smell of newly sawn wood and fresh paint hung in the air.

"The construction crews have done a great job. From what I heard from Tanner, this place was a wreck a few days ago," Koski said, tossing her tote bag onto one of the beds.

"Reminds me of the first kibbutz I ever lived in," Courtney replied. "This type of accommodation will ensure the meetings move along and enable everyone to return to the comforts of home."

The quarters inside the bunker had been partitioned into twenty by twenty foot private areas, resembling a cross between a jail cell and a cut-price cabin. A kerosene lamp was the only means of illumination and heat. A porcelain hand basin and a jug of water substituted for running water. Three chemical toilets, as used on construction sites, had been set up along the wall outside. Inside, at the rear of the structure, a "M*A*S*H" type shower had been installed. The information packet informed everyone that hot water would be available between six and eight each morning.

Chapter 14

Pictures of Berne's body had been taken from all angles. Falk had answered questions.

Medical examiners had done their work and the area in and around the gazebo had been measured, photographed, and dusted for prints.

London had sent an inspector from the Yard. Scotland had a man from Glasgow. And two men from Washington had worked closely with the Israeli team. The only fact agreed on was that Berne had died by having his throat cut. The body was to be returned to Israel and the Scottish police would continue working in secrecy at a local level. Falk knew, as far as any of the investigators were concerned, this was simply a case waiting to go into the files of unsolved mysteries. The questions Falk had fielded reflected his and Koski's cover story. A tri-national government team of scientists and ornithologists were on Flangenan Island carrying out a study of sea birds nesting in northern Atlantic tide pools. To Falk's surprise, the investigation team members had written their notes, nodded knowingly, and thanked him for his cooperation. It was obvious the police had been briefed that this was a matter of national security for each country involved.

Falk also had little doubt that Berne's killer fully intended to obtain the final draft of the plans for outer space-controlled solar transmission. Killing the three scientists and everyone in the lighthouse would be no problem.

Berne's replacement arrived at dusk. Aldo Zaslavsky was a man of medium build who spoke perfect English and projected a disarming charm. Falk estimated his age as early to mid- thirties, alert, keen-eyed, and ready to get started.

"It's too late for us to head out to the lighthouse tonight, Mr. Zaslavsky. We'll leave first thing in the morning," Falk told the Israeli.

"Please, call me Zas. It's easier."

"Fine, Zas. We can still have dinner if we hurry. Come on."

They were the last to leave the dining room. Zas discussed his background with Falk and both men had exchanged information on their experiences in their respective agencies. None the less, they were both acutely aware neither one had disclosed too much.

"I'll make arrangements to leave early. We'll take a Zodiac. It's not a bad trip as long as the weather holds."

Chapter 15

Koski and Swale sat facing a console of hi-tech equipment in the communications center on the third level. "There will be one of us here at all times, night and day, until the meetings are over." Swale rose from his chair and crossed to the array of equipment. "This two-way radio is pre-locked to a Royal Navy frequency dedicated to us alone. Once every two hours we'll send a coded message. I'll go over the details when Falk and the new guy arrive.

I'll be on duty here until they do," Swale said. He tapped a computer monitor. "Immediate and direct contact to London, Washington, and Tel Aviv. And, here." Swale picked up a bright yellow cordless telephone. "Incoming and outgoing communication by satellite to any place on earth." He gave a broad grin. "And I mean anywhere on the planet. We could be contacted from a Siberian salt mine if the need arose."

"That's some phone, Swale. Who makes it?" Koski asked.

He shook his head. "No idea. All I know is, it works. No doubt from one of those top secret labs. James Bond stuff." Swale went to the end of the console, turned, and propped himself on the edge of the desk. His face became serious as he reached down, slid open a drawer, and removed a metal container the size of a cigar box, which he placed on the table next to the computer. "Inside is an envelope. See?" Swale held the envelope up like a magician displaying a card for all to see. "The communications equipment here in this room is, as you would expect, top secret. The frequencies and the information that will be exchanged over the next few hours are highly classified. Now, in the rare possibility that anything unforeseen should occur and we have to abort our meeting for any reason..." Swale shook the package. "This little fella would be inserted into here." He walked back to the two-way radio and opened a side panel, revealing a printed circuit motherboard and indicated an empty space, saying how the small PC board in the envelope could be quickly and easily slid into position. "Once in place and a signal transmitted from the radio, the entire system would self-destruct, wiping out all traces of our communications and rendering the equipment useless by an electrical impulse that would make it impossible for anyone to reconstruct or discover any of its secrets."

"That's pretty drastic."

"Indeed it is. But no one would be able to collect any information on the designs and systems used in all this." He swept his arm toward the assembled equipment. Too bad there wasn't one on the US military spy plane that had to be ditched in China in 2001."

"I've had my computer crash and it didn't evaporate," Koski exclaimed.

"I don't suppose it did. Let me finish. In this case, everything electronic anywhere in and around the lighthouse, for half a mile, would not only crash...it would burn. The last act of the transmitter would be to broadcast a signal literally incinerating any electronic circuit board into a melted heap."

Koski grimaced. "Even my cell phone?"

Swale nodded. "That too."

"Ye gods, Swale, who are we expecting?"

"Just plain hardball security. How about a cup of tea?"

Chapter 16

From the window of a small commercial hotel overlooking a poorer section of Glasgow, a Middle Eastern man stared at a rain-sodden vista: rows and rows of brick terrace houses, gray slate roofs slick with rain. A bedraggled old man and a dog were the only pedestrians. The man turned from the window and spoke softly to his companion. "I sometimes wonder what makes the Occidentals feel superior to other races."

"There are quite a few Occidentals who do not know what the word Occidental means."

"I suppose you are right." The Arab turned from the window. "This place depresses me." He glanced around the small room.

"I'm not in the habit of having to meet in such places and wouldn't be here if it hadn't been for that damn fool killing the Israeli security man."

"From what I've been able to put together, there was no other way. The Israeli accidentally overheard our man making his update call on his cell phone from the hotel garden. He had to be killed."

The light-skinned Arab nodded. What he was hearing was not good. "No one was aware that we were able to replace Zaslavsky. Correct?"

"None whatsoever. For all intents and purposes, he is Zaslavsky. Not even our operative in the lighthouse will know he is anything but an Israeli security guard sent to replace the one killed."

"Our operative, as you so nicely put it, will be eliminated by our 'Zaslavsky' along with the rest of them at the conclusion of their operation." He pushed back the sleeve of his jacket and checked his gold Rolex. "Remain here until contacted. I will be at the Tarbot hotel, Loch Lomond. Do not try and contact me there. Your instructions will be hand delivered." He crossed the room and opened the door. "Remember, the Chairman expects the results of all information discussed at the scientists' meeting on Solar and Ionospheric Physics to be on their way to Iran as soon as they are resolved at the meeting. Be sure your team is ready when I send the word."

Ian McLean locked the door after the Arab left. He had been briefed on the importance of his mission and remembered word for word what the haughty man had told him.

Active ionospheric research facilities like HAARP—the High-frequency Active Auroral Research Program—attempt to produce small temporary changes in a limited region directly over the facility which, in no way, compares to the worldwide events frequently caused by the sun. But the extraordinary suite of sensitive observational instruments installed at observatories like HAARP permit a detailed and comprehensive correlation with the induced effects, resulting in new insights into the ways the ionosphere responds to a much wider variety of natural conditions.

McLean knew it meant worldwide weather control and, if he were successful, he and his team would be well paid. If not, they'd be dead men.

Chapter 17

At the Weizmann Institute of Science, Rehovet, Israel, the Director of the Renewable Energy Program at the institute, paced anxiously. "Already we have lost one of our security men." With his arms behind his back, he leaned slightly forward, giving him the appearance of an agitated stork. He stopped, then returned to his desk, sat down, and slowly rubbed his temples, elbows splayed on the desktop.

A dark haired woman lowered herself into a chair opposite.

"You must try to relax," she said softly. "The decision was not ours. We both agree it would have been far wiser to hold the meetings here at the institute, rather than in an old lighthouse off the coast of Scotland."

The woman, a Doctor of Solar Chemistry, had worked with the professor for six years. She, like the director, believed no one involved with their research should be allowed to be at large in a world where they could be held hostage or worse.

"We've been assured that security will be the best, the tightest possible, and the lighthouse an impregnable fortress protected by British Navy patrols 24/7."

"Yes, I know," the director said wearily. "We were over-ruled by the three governments. Forty years ago, similar meetings would have ended on an optimistic note because a universal solution seemed close at hand. Now, with the weapons proliferation between so many nations, we add the fact that solar energy in all its forms has now become, not only the major renewable energy alternative, but also a weapon of terrifying proportions.

"The reason for this situation was inherent in our political system with its intrinsic difficulty of handling short planning horizons and the resulting skidding from one crisis to another."

Snapping open a silver cigarette case, a third person, a thin man of undetermined age, removed a non-filter Camel and lit up. "Because by the time the problems and their possible solutions become apparent, it's too late to address them with any hope of control, a common ailment among politicians. Today, even scientists are not free from this effect, depending as we do on government funding."

"And so our government sends off Jacob Jenner, our top solar scientist, to exchange plans with an American and an Englishman in a remote lighthouse in the Atlantic." The director's voice grew loud and he pounded a fist on the desktop. "The meeting has not yet begun and there is already a murder. No. I stand by my argument with the government. We should have never let Jenner go."

"Too late to do anything now," the thin man said. "At least, when Jenner returns, we will have the means to complete our plan for solar power transference from space to earth by controlled and exact methods." He blew a long stream of tobacco smoke skyward and continued. "Also, the backing of three governments for the continuation of the project."

Chapter 18

Falk turned off the outboard motor and the Zodiac coasted to the dock. "Grab a line, Zas. I'll tie the stern." Both men soon secured the water craft and within five minutes had their gear unloaded. It was shortly after dawn; the sky streaked with a reddish tinge in the winter light that allowed a view of heavy cloud cover. "Another nice day beside the seaside," Falk muttered as he hefted his kit. "Let's hope they have the coffee on." Both men headed toward the lighthouse; Falk noted that the communication room near the top of the building glowed with light.

"I don't think much of the Royal Navy's patrol," Zas said. "We just sailed three miles across open water and no one bothered us. We could be invading the place right now."

Falk smiled. "That's because the Navy knew when we were starting out, how long it would take, and how many were on board. Now they know we're tied up and walking up the front door for a cup of coffee."

"If they're that good, why do they need us?"

"You know the way the services are, Zas, filled with inter-departmental distrust. We can't let the British Navy have all the credit."

They were at the front door and Falk gave it a good pounding. "Come on. Open the door. Anyone up yet?"

"Morning, Joe, I've had a bead on both of you since you stood on the dock." Koski came around the side of the cylindrical building holding an AK47 across her chest. Zas stared at her, eyebrows slightly arched.

"Zas, meet my partner, Susan Koski." Koski slung her weapon onto her shoulder and shook his hand.

"I see she didn't leave everything to the Navy. Glad to meet you, Koski."

She smiled and turned to Falk. "Good morning." They embraced and exchanged a lingering kiss.

Breaking away, Koski turned to Zas with a grin. "It's okay. It's not against the rules. We're going to be married one day."

Zas laughed. "That's fine with me."

The lighthouse door creaked open and Swale peered around the edge. "We don't want any, go away." He grinned and opened the door wide. "Come in and don't let all the cold morning air in. This is a damn hard place to keep warm."

Swale led the way up to the communications room and, after being introduced by Koski, he explained the radio computer drill to Falk and Zas. Then Koski advised Falk that the first meeting of the three scientists was scheduled that morning at nine and that Tanner and Harris were already at each other's throats.

"What's the problem?" Falk asked.

"Tanner thinks Harris is a pompous ass and insists on trying the old man's patience."

Great, just what we need, Falk thought. "Zas and I will take a look around and meet you for breakfast."

Swale said, "I have some good news. Courtney volunteered to be the breakfast cook. Wait 'til you taste her blintzes."

"What about the other meals?" Falk asked.

"Ah, well, I do lunch if I'm not assigned to other duties. And dinner…well, no one's volunteered yet."

Falk grunted and pointed up the spiral staircase. "Come on, Zas. Let's take the fifty cent tour." Swale began to explain the working of the communication center when three abrupt beeps emitted from the speaker array caused Zas to jump.

Swale turned to the transceiver, sat down, and flicked on a microphone. "Sea shell receiving. Code blue."

A voice from the speaker answered. "Respond after blue."

Swale ran his finger down a list of words on a card on the desk. "Response code green."

"Roger that. Sea shell out." Swale leaned back in his chair. "It's a straight forward question and answer code exchange." He pushed the card across the table. "It's all there. I give blue and next to it is green. See?" Falk and Zas leaned in and took a look. "Koski and I went over it yesterday," Swale said. "Nothing to it as long as we give the right color answer." He stretched and yawned. "We exchange codes every two hours as long as all is normal. We can, of course, transmit signals at will. The Navy is covering our frequency 24/7."

Koski eased the AK47 on her shoulder. "Okay, Swale, I'll grab some breakfast and be back to let you get some sleep." She turned to Falk. "He's been up here all night."

Falk tapped Swale's shoulder. "I appreciate that. I'll get a schedule made up and we'll share the load."

Chapter 19

The American and the Israeli scientists sat at the conference table with Tanner as Commander Harris and the professor entered and took their seats.

"Right, now we can begin. As you know, we are back to full strength with our security personnel, and I want to take a moment to introduce you to Aldo Zaslavsky." Tanner indicated Zas standing inside the entrance with his back to the wall. "He informed me it's easier to remember his name by simply calling him, Zas." Zas nodded.

"Okay, ground rules." Tanner continued. "In thirty minutes, a meeting between Ms. Spencer, Commander Harris, and myself will begin, dealing with organization and the obvious economic and political ramifications of this project. If we can agree in principle, then the first scientific exchanges will take place." Tanner checked his papers. "I have no doubt that you, the principles of this scientific exchange, may be wondering why all details were not ironed out prior to your arrival. I'm sure you understand the secrecy and logistics needed to get us all here. Any meetings or discussions in regard to our intentions would have, without a doubt, been leaked to the news media. Not even the Royal Navy knows who or why we're here. Our governments fabricated two cover stories. One for the local population and the hotel personnel who were advised we were an international scientific team studying shore birds of the North Atlantic. The second piece of disinformation was given to the Royal Navy, saying we are part of an Anglo-American-Israeli unit, testing radio, computer, and laser communications with scientific experimentation in timed responses for possible wartime or international emergencies."

Harris put in his two cents worth. "Yes, quite correct. As far as my office is concerned, I'm supposed to be on holiday in the Highlands, studying edged weaponry of the ancient clans." He glanced across at Tanner. "Tanner here is bird watching. But between you and me, he doesn't know the difference between a blue tit and a red breast, right, old chap?"

Tanner didn't actually grind his teeth, but he was damn close. He ignored the commander's remark. "After the details I've mentioned are complete, the scientific caucus will start." He checked his notes. "Professor Teesdale will open with his design and function of his optical communicator, emphasizing the temporal shaping of his non-linear laser beam." Teesdale, relaxed and serene, gazed off into space. "Doctor Jenner will be second, introducing us to his 7.5 MW solar concentrator and his development of a master oscillator power amplifier (MOPA). Thirdly, Doctor Clayton will lecture on 'Metals Producing Hydrogen via Hydrolysis' and the thermal reduction of metal oxides at super high temperature with highly endothermic reactions. When these subjects have been discussed, Doctor Clayton will outline his plan to combine the three subjects into the possibility of becoming one discipline, therefore making his dream of controlled solar energy able to be beamed to one or more earth-located bases, to be prepared and distributed worldwide."

Courtney's voice was low and clear when she spoke. "Or to any target on the face of the earth or satellites in space that we deem necessary to annihilate."

Chapter 20

The lone constable on Tiree had been ordered not to mention anything about the murder at the hotel. Being a career man he'd nodded stoically and gone about his business of seeing the island remained a law-abiding place.

Outside the locked door of the meeting room, Zas was seated on a wooden chair, a mini Uzi resting on his knees. A bare fourteen inches overall, it maintained the larger version's firepower of 950 rounds per minute. Once again, Swale was in the communications room. Falk had arranged for there to always be two on outside patrol within sight of each other at all times. Zas tipped his chair back against the wall. Except for the soft murmur of voices from inside the room, the interior of the lighthouse was silent. Falk and Koski had checked on both of the security guards before they began their outside patrol.

A cold salt-laden wind cut across the island as Falk and Koski trudged over the rocky ground toward where the land jutted out to sea. Koski blinked in discomfort as an extra strong gust of wind threw grit and sand toward them. She would be glad when they circled away from the wind toward the leeward side of a rocky outcropping that Falk had pointed out as their turning point. Falk signalled her to wait and, walking closer to the edge of the bluff, looked down at the breakers crashing over the rocks twenty feet below. He was about to turn away when a sea bird flew up in front of him, banked to the left, caught an upward draft, and soared high overhead, all in a matter of seconds. Curious as to why a bird should suddenly appear out of nowhere, he moved closer to the edge and leaned over, thinking perhaps he would see a nest in the cliff face. Koski, noticing his curiosity, began to approach, but Falk waved her back. After a couple of minutes he backed away from the edge and re-joined her.

"Did you see that bird just then? It came up from below us. I can't see a nest, and I don't know of any birds that nest on the beach."

"Let me take a look." Koski started for the edge.

"Wait," Falk warned. "I don't need to lose another agent. We'll both go, but as we near the brink, we'll crawl to the edge then lay flat. That way we can take our time and not get blown off the bluff."

They lay side by side, craning their necks in all directions, when Falk saw it: the tip of what seemed to be a metal pipe jutting from the cliff face. The pipe was almost at water level amid the large rocks at the base of the cliff. "Over there to the right," Falk said, as he jabbed his gloved forefinger toward his find.

"What are we looking for? I can't see anything except rocks and the sea."

"Three feet to my right and straight down; it looks like the tip of a water pipe. It's almost the same color as the rocks. See it?"

After a few more minutes of scrutinizing the rocks below her, she noticed it. "I see it now. What is it?"

"I don't know, but I'll soon find out. You wait here. Once I'm down you can join me. And be careful."

"It might be safer if we both went the long way around. The land dips toward the beach about a quarter mile back and it won't be so far to climb," Koski said.

Falk knew she was right. One slip and they'd be short one more member of the security force. He got to his feet, looked around, and found a stout stick, then with a rock, pounded it into the ground at the edge of the cliff. "That'll make it easier for us to locate the pipe. Okay, let's go."

Ten minutes later they lined up on the marker, moved in among the rocks, and located the pipe. It was larger than it had looked from up above. Falk estimated it was six feet wide and about five feet high. In the pipe he saw a bird's nest. "That answers the question about the bird," Koski said. "Wonder what the pipe is for?"

Falk had approached and leaned into the pipe. "I don't know. Must have been part of the lighthouse sewer system. It's dry now. No sign of water flow."

Koski moved up beside him. "It's big enough for us to walk upright in there and find out where it goes." She thought back to the assignment when she and Falk had squirmed and crawled on their bellies, deep beneath the streets of Vienna, through old brickwork tunnels of the city sewer system. The memory triggered a shudder as, once again, she relived the moment. The roof at times had been mere inches above them, almost touching their heads. Her fear of close quarters had almost driven her to panic, but she'd persevered and they'd made it. Now, this pipe seemed to pose no problem.

He'd told Koski about his conversation with Stewart and the importance for any intelligence to be fed back to *Cerberus* ASAP. He glanced at his watch. "We can't check further right now. We have to keep to our schedule. I'll return while everyone's preparing for dinner. Let's go."

Chapter 21

The meeting wound down, remains of a working lunch pushed to one side. The scientists had been working over six hours and currently Clayton spoke. "If they allow us to develop along certain lines, the public would be able to run a car for a year on a pair of our hydrogen power cells."

"It will never happen, Doctor," Jenner said. "We both know that. Not until the last drop of fossil fuel has been pumped from the earth and sold by the oil companies would they permit wide use of our systems. Whatever we develop will be used by the military or our own countries."

He stretched his arms above his head before continuing. "Oh, sure, there'll be electric cars, but they'll remain high in cost and low in performance until such times the oil companies are ready to make the switch; then it will be announced what a wonderful discovery solar power is and, even if it costs the consumer a little more than gasoline, it will be well worth the price because of the environmental advantage to mankind." His face darkened. "No matter what we do, solar power for the masses—be it heating homes and business, or powering vehicles—is a long way away."

Teesdale gazed dreamily off into space, drumming his fingers on the table top. "Perhaps there is a way to stop the oil cartels from taking out a franchise on the sun."

Harris and Tanner exchanged glances as Courtney said, "I'm sure what you gentlemen are doing here, exchanging years of research and talking openly with each other, will result in a solution to our solar problems far sooner than we might think."

Despite Courtney's pep talk, an air of thoughtful depression hung in the air.

Tanner quickly took over. "I think we're all tired. You have covered a large amount of technical details, so I think a break is in order." He checked his watch. "It's now just past five. We can rest, get ready for dinner, and then spend a couple of hours after dinner in further discussion. We have allowed ourselves three days of meetings here on the island. We're making good time. Any questions?"

Jenner raised his arm. Tanner nodded. "Yes, Doctor?"

"Has there been any radio communications in reference to the murder of agent Berne?"

Tanner shook his head. "Afraid not. I'm sure the investigation is ongoing, but due to the secrecy of our mission, I doubt if we'll learn much while we're here." Jenner gave a terse nod in return. Tanner scooped up his notes, indicating the meeting was over.

Swale guarded outside the door when it opened and the six occupants filed out. He kept silence as they left the lighthouse and headed for the bunker. They looked as if they'd been playing poker for six hours and who ever had won must have taken the lot and was still wearing a poker face.

Falk entered a moment after the group had left. "Not a

fruitful meeting by the looks of them."

"I was thinking the same thing," Swale said. He looked out of the open door and added, "Heavy weather coming up tonight." The sky was almost black and seemed to touch the ground. In the distance a rumble of thunder could be heard.

"If Koski would like to stay indoors tonight, I'll be happy to swap duties and go with you on the outside patrol."

"I'm sure she'd appreciate it, but I know she'd turn it down."

Swale said, "One of the boys, eh?"

"No. Koski has no need to prove she can do the job. We've been a team for some time, and I've never seen her take the easy way out."

Swale nodded.

"That's okay. We'll stick with the schedule." Falk pointed to a notice attached to the wall outside the meeting room showing that Falk and Koski had the outside patrol starting at eight tonight, Swale would be on radio duty, and Zas would be back in the chair. "Is Zas in his room?" Falk asked.

"If he's not, he'll be walking around the island. I think he's an exercise freak."

Falk frowned. What a man did on his time off between shifts was his choice. He'd better get back soon otherwise he'd miss dinner. No one had volunteered to be the dinner cook and last night's meal had been a make-do affair of canned soup, slices of bread, and what Swale called 'Bubble and Squeak,' an English concoction of leftover potatoes and vegetables, fried in a pan.

Koski sat on her bed cleaning her 9 MM Beretta when Courtney returned from the meeting. Koski looked up. "How'd it go?"

Courtney sighed, threw her notes on to the shared table,

pulled out a chair, and sat down. "I've just spent six hours sitting on my ass, listening to three solar scientist rattle on, using technical terms that mean nothing to me." She rubbed her temples. "I should be outside taking a walk, getting a little fresh air."

"Better take a jacket if you do. It's cold out there and there's a storm moving in." Koski squinted down the barrel of her weapon and continued. "I've got a roast in the kitchen's oven, with baked potatoes and carrots, and an apple pie for dessert."

"Koski, you're an angel. Another one of Swale's English dinners and I think I'd quit and swim back to the hotel."

"Swale relieved me in the communications room early." Koski wiped the automatic with a lightly oiled rag and slipped it into her shoulder holster.

"Do you clean that thing every day?" Koski nodded. "You asked how the meeting went. Well, in one word—tiresome."

"No progress?"

"Oh, yes, I suppose there was progress. It's hard to say. We only have two more days to get everything together and the agreements made. One thing for sure, all three of the scientists have no respect for the oil cartels."

Koski saw it was almost dark outside. She didn't want the dinner to burn at the last minute. She stood up. "Duty calls. Dinner in half an hour."

"Need any help?" Courtney asked as Koski threw a sweater across her shoulders.

"Thanks. I can manage. Take a little time to yourself. I suppose there'll be a continuation of the meeting later?"

Courtney scowled. "Yes, nine tonight, sorry to say."

Chapter 22

Falk walked out from the lighthouse about half a mile after finding Zas' room empty. Why would Zas be out walking alone in the cold? Falk recalled Stewart's conversation when he'd contacted him at the hotel while waiting for Zas' arrival. "He's back on duty after losing a couple of toes on his right foot in action in the Golan Heights three months ago."

Now, with darkness drooping over the island, Falk headed for the pipe, this time carrying a powerful flashlight. He glanced back toward the glow shining from the windows of the lighthouse and carefully moved toward the beach. Maybe Zas walked to exercise his damaged foot. He'd known guys like that. They had to prove they were still a complete person and in charge of their actions.

Chapter 23

Less than a quarter mile to Falk's right, Zas attentively picked his way over the rocks. He was quietly satisfied with his reconnaissance to the northern end of the island. No one had seen or followed him. At the same time, he remained keenly aware he'd have to watch Falk's every move. The north end of the island had a cove and sloping beach with few jagged rocks. A Zodiac, skilfully piloted, would be able to get in and out without too much trouble. He'd made a quick attempt to make contact with the mainland, but the reception had been poor. He hoped his message had been received. He'd try again tomorrow.

Chapter 24

If the pipe had been a few feet lower, it would be regularly deluged by high tides. Luckily, when the pipe had been installed, the builders had allowed for the rise and fall of the tide. Now, it was only a few feet above the sea, but, even so, spumes from the waves crashed and poured in a torrent over the old iron structure. Falk, stepping with exaggerated care, eased his way into the gaping maw, flashlight beam weaving as he struggled the last few feet to the entrance.

Pausing a moment to check his equipment, he moved slowly into the darkness. The bird's nest was now empty and he wondered if his disturbance earlier had made the birds head for a safer haven. With his flashlight beam illuminating the interior of the salty smelling tube, Falk walked deeper into the unknown. A draft of air swept around him, carrying a faint odor of whisky. Falk turned off the flashlight and leaned forward, his ears alert, listening for the slightest sound. Taking a deep breath, he continued further into the darkness, one hand lightly touching the iron tube.

Chapter 25

Zas was almost at the lighthouse when he saw a vague form flit across his vision and vanish into the deeper shadows at the base of the tower. Remaining still, he watched as the dark figure moved to the exterior staircase and began to ascend. Was it Falk? Slowly moving from shadow to shadow, Zas eased forward, his eyes locked on the person climbing silently up the outside stairway of the lighthouse. Sliding the safety of his Uzi to off, he proceeded toward the base of the lighthouse.

Chapter 26

Professor Teesdale and Clayton were already in the dining area, sipping coffee at the table. Except for them, Koski had the place to herself. She had checked the food; it would be ready to serve as soon as everyone was present. Koski poured herself a cup of coffee and, staying clear of the two at the table, found a place to sit alone. Outside, it was almost dark, and the wind began to rise and moan around the edges of the old concrete bunker.

Even with the warmth from the stove and the presence of Clayton and Teesdale, she felt cold and alone. There was something about this assignment that didn't feel right. It was more like a stage play with a cast of actors playing their roles and none of them sure of their lines. Koski watched the two men over the rim of her cup. Teesdale, distracted, seemingly almost senile, a gentle smile on his lips, his thin, delicate hands folded on the table. Yet she knew those hands had designed scientific devices that were desired by governments willing to pay millions for the plans. Or, without a qualm, kill for.

Falk's orders to collect intelligence to be sent back to Stewart seemed odd to Koski. Her previous assignments with Falk had been clear cut. Now they were working in reverse. *Cerberus* was seeking information rather than supplying it.

Chapter 27

It had started to rain and Zas' anorak was soaked in a matter of minutes as he silently climbed the outside steps of the lighthouse. He knew the person he'd seen was ahead of him, and he stopped, flattening himself against the side of the tower, squinting into the slanting rain, trying to see upward. It was no use. He had to keep climbing. Zas knew there was a door leading into the lantern room and it opened inward. Was it locked? Did the person ahead of him have a key? Why would anyone want to climb the outside ladder in the rain when it was so much easier and dryer to use the inside stairs? He knew the answer. Whoever it was wanted no one inside the lighthouse to see him or her. His head was now almost level with the catwalk that surrounded the lantern room.

Slowly, an inch at a time, he raised his head. He could see nothing but the rain-smeared windows and the green iron door leading into the lantern room. The door was closed; the interior of the glass-enclosed room dark. There was no one in sight. Wise in various means of ambush, Zas came up to the catwalk and slithered onto it, flat on his belly, and across to the door. Whoever had been ahead of him could have entered the lantern room. Or, knowing they were followed, moved around the other side of the catwalk and slowly crept up behind him. Quickly, he got into a sitting position outside of the iron door. He could wait a minute or two.

Five minutes passed. He had to make a move. Rising slowly to his feet, he walked the entire circular catwalk and found nothing. Cursing at the waste of time, he returned to iron door and found it unlocked. He had a choice. He could go back down the outer stairway and up the inside stairs to the lantern room. If there was someone in the room, and he took the time to go down the outer stairs, it would allow whoever it was an opportunity to get away. He turned the knob and slowly pushed the door open. He hadn't carried a flashlight, intending to be back at the lighthouse before dark. Now he regretted the careless oversight.

Chapter 28

"Hey! Zas is supposed to be on radio duty. Have you seen him?" Swale said as he walked into the dining area. Before Koski could answer, Swale sniffed the air. "Mmm... something smells good and it's not 'Bubble and Squeak'." Koski turned.

"You can't find Zas?"

"I looked in his room. He's not there. Falk was asking for him before he went out."

Koski frowned and asked, "How long ago?"

"About a half an hour. I said he might be out walking around the island. But I doubt it in this weather."

"Maybe he and Falk are together." There was a tinge of doubt in her voice. "Cover the radio room while I check the lighthouse. We'll be receiving the call-in codes soon." Swale turned and left before Koski could reply. She was worried. It wasn't like Falk to go off without telling her. Quickly, she removed the meat from the oven, checked the pans, and called over to Clayton. "Everything's ready. Tell everyone to help themselves. I'll be back."

Clayton turned from his conversation with the professor.

"Right, I'll tell..." He was talking to an empty room. "Come on, Professor, let's serve ourselves while everything's hot. Smells too good to let get cold."

Chapter 29

Falk checked his watch; it was almost time for the shifts to change. He must get back to the lighthouse. He'd return in the morning and continue his exploration of the pipe.

The faint aroma of whisky hanging in the air caused him to wonder if, at some time in the past, the pipe had been a hiding place for smuggled contraband. He turned and made his way carefully back to the entrance. He knew one thing for sure; Zas had not gone into the pipe.

Chapter 30

Inside the lantern room, a dark figure slid a knife from its sheath, the blade glinting in what little light there was from outside. Zas slowly opened the door and entered, crouching low, his Uzi cocked and ready. Then, without the slightest warning, a dark figure sprang forward, the knife outstretched and thrusting.

Zas turned to defend himself. It too was late; the knife plunged deep into his chest, close to his heart. Zas stared in shock as he recognized his attacker. Then he sank to the floor.

The killer dragged the mortally wounded man out onto the parapet and attempted to push Zas over the rail, down to the rocks and sea below. But, in a final and agonizing struggle, Zas pulled his handcuffs from his belt, tossed the key over the side, and attached one wrist to the railings. The monumental effort completed, he died.

The attacker hesitated, then swiftly pulled the knife from the dead man's chest. He sliced through a layer of skin, about to sever the handcuffed wrist, when a light from below beamed up through the trapdoor into the lantern room. The assassin quickly used the outside staircase and disappeared into the swirling rain.

Swale squirmed up through the trap door and into the lantern room where his flashlight beam swept across the rain-smeared windows and into every section of the room. He found the light switch and suddenly the room brightly shone, turning the windows ebon black with not a sign of light outside. Swale quickly checked the room to be sure it was empty. Then he noticed wet foot prints near the door. He moved closer and saw drops of blood. Someone could be outside and he was in a brightly lit room, a perfect target. He doused the lights and removed his automatic in one fast movement.

Chapter 31

Falk, half way back to the lighthouse, suddenly saw the lights go on in the lantern room. Then, seconds later, go out.

What the hell was going on? No one was supposed to be up there. Increasing his pace, yet, at the same time, keenly aware of the danger of slipping on the wet rocks, he arrived at the lighthouse, entered, and took the stairs two at a time. He was almost at the top rung of the ladder leading to the lantern room when the lights came on again. Climbing into the room he found Swale standing beside the light switch, wet through, his hair plastered to his head and his face the pallor of a dead man.

"I've found Zas."

Falk glanced quickly around the room then back to Swale. "Where is he?" Falk knew to expect bad news.

"Outside. Dead. Handcuffed to the railings."

By the beam of Swale's flashlight, Falk tried to unlock the handcuffs from Zas' wrist. Neither Swale's key nor his did any good on the Israeli-made cuffs. "Damn," Falk muttered as the rain poured down. "Why the hell does everything in the world have to be non-compatible?"

Swale said, "Whoever killed him was about to cut off his hand and toss him over the side when he must have heard me coming."

Swale was right. And the killer had escaped down the spiral stair case, taking the murder weapon with him.

"There's nothing we can do for him now," Falk said. "Check in the communications room to see if there's anything we can use to get him free of the cuffs." Swale turned back into the lantern room and headed for the trap door.

Moving quickly, Falk slipped off Zas' right boot and sock. In the beam of his flashlight he could see all five toes, none missing. He was not the replacement security agent from Israel. Putting the sock and boot back on, Falk now knew for certain that Zas had been a plant. The meeting had to be scrubbed and everyone taken off the island as fast as possible. Swale returned with a file, but any attempt to cut off the handcuffs made little difference to hardened steel. "Forget it," Falk grunted. "We'll need bolt cutters to get these off." They returned inside to the lantern room.

"There are a couple of boxes of tools in the kitchen bunker," Swale offered.

"Fine. We're going to have to close this entire operation down. I'll inform the commander and Tanner of the bad news. See if you can find anything among the tools then get back up here and cut off the cuffs and drag him inside. Lock that door to the outside. Let's go."

Tanner refused outright to cancel the meeting when Falk gave him the facts. "The meeting has started. We must continue."

Commander Harris looked concerned, but at the same time concurred with Tanner.

"My orders, Mr. Tanner," Falk said grimly, "were to abort this conclave if anything detrimental to the safety of the scientists should occur. A second murder is, in my opinion, reason to do so."

Tanner's face reddened. "Then I will assume the responsibility for breaking those rules. This is a three nation summit meeting concerning national security. Your job, Mr Falk, is to see we remain secure until the meeting is concluded." Tanner turned to the commander. "I suggest we get Ms. Spencer in here and make it unanimous so as to assure Mr. Falk will have no problems from his superiors." Tanner was making it perfectly clear that Falk's control didn't extend into the rarefied atmosphere of international decision making.

The commander hesitated for a moment, as if he too should show his authority, but then changed his mind and left to locate Courtney.

Chapter 32

Courtney Spencer knew the importance of the exchange of information between the three solar scientists. Tel-Aviv had instilled into Courtney the need for speed in obtaining the intelligence from the other two scientists. Warned by the Mossad, the Knesset knew that if there was a threat to kidnap Jenner, it would be at such a meeting. Not even the assurance of the British Navy patrolling the lonely island and the internal security at the lighthouse could ever remove the sense of apprehension felt by the leaders of Israel. But when advised of Tanner's decision, she agreed to complete the meeting, even with a murderer in their midst.

Falk was up against a stubborn, determined group of policy makers. Nonetheless, he made one more attempt.

"Ms. Spencer, we've had two people killed in as many days." For a moment he toyed with the idea of revealing that Zas must have had a false identity. "Why don't we take a few moments."

Courtney turned on Falk at once. "I wonder how relaxed you'd be if your country lay downwind from the Lion of Judah. All it has to do is raise its head and sniff."

Falk fumed internally. "I'll advise the Navy of your decision and have them beef up the patrol."

"We'll continue as if nothing has happened," Tanner's voice rasped. "You will exchange codes as usual. If, as you say, we are in danger of being attacked, we do not wish to broadcast the fact another person has been killed. The less we tell, the less there is to be known by any real or imagined attacker. No matter how cutting edge our communications are, there is always someone who can monitor and hack our electronics." Tanner turned to the commander. "We should be finished by this time tomorrow, be off this damn island, and on our way."

"What do we tell the others when they notice the absence of Zas?" the commander asked.

"Stomach flu. Something like that. It'll only be for a day. Now, let's get them in here and get started."

Commander Harris had seemed unusually subservient to Tanner throughout the discussion. Falk wondered if the two men had made a pact.

Returning to the lantern room, Falk covered Zas with a blanket while wondering just who the man had been.

Chapter 33

The Constable of Tiree, Alec Slat, occupied the remotest policing post in Scotland, possibly the entire British Isles. Since the murder up at the hotel, he'd had a strange feeling that all was not what he was supposed to believe. It seemed the orders, so furtively given to him, with words like, "Top Secret," "Important to National Security," flowed with such false authority, he felt out of place being among the big guns from London and Glasgow. The almost theatrically shallow investigation was a joke. The tall, dark haired American was the only person who seemed genuine. He wished he could have had a few words with him off the record.

Constable Slat's beat was comprised of two small islands. Tiree, the larger of the two, was his headquarters. Coll, the smaller, was located a few miles northeast.

The resident population on Tiree was 750 islanders, most of whom relied on the traditional industries of crofting and fishing for their livelihood.

Luckily for the economy, a seasonal influx of tourists travelled to the island to enjoy the many amenities. Idyllic beaches created some of the best windsurfing conditions in the UK.

The isle of Coll offered a more rugged landscape. Coll, almost identical in size to its neighbor, had a population of only 150.

Now a solitary position of law enforcement, at one time Tiree boasted a sergeant and several constables. Constable Slat often read through a series of handwritten incident books stored away in a corner of the Tiree's Police Office. The books went back to the 1960s and painted a picture of a thriving community with all the problems that entails: assault, disorders, ships in distress, rowdiness, and even missing persons. Over the years, a decline in the islands' populations had caused the police presence to dwindle to its present complement of one officer.

Slat had made up his mind to chat with a mechanic who had been talking in the local pub about a helicopter he was taking care of for a couple of ornithologists from America. Deep in his heart, Slat yearned to see some action before he retired and grew roses. He knew his wife would have called him a fool. Perhaps he was. However, there was something wrong; secret or not, he intended to discover what it was.

It was almost noon and the pub had a few early customers at the bar. As soon as Slat entered, he saw the mechanic from the airfield seated at the bar with his nose in a pint of beer. "I nay have seen much of you lately," Slat said, "Things must be busy at the airfield."

The man stopped halfway through his pint, wiped his mouth with the back of a grease stained hand, and contemplated the liquid in his tankard before answering. "Aye, I'm in charge of tending to a helicopter for a couple of Americans. We dinna get too many of them nowadays, you know." He resumed drinking and finished his beer in two long gulps.

Slat caught the eye of the barmaid. "Coffee, meat pie, and chips, Molly." He settled in at the bar, removing his helmet and placing it beside the beer taps. It was his sign that he was off duty for lunch. "So tell me, where do the Americans fly their helicopter to? I haven't seen it much around here."

Molly slid a plate containing a cheese and beef sandwich in front of the mechanic. He nodded at the empty tankard indicating the need for second pint. Then, taking a large bite out of the whole wheat bread, he chewed slowly, saying, "I dinna know. They have nay used the thing for a few days." He scooped up a pile of potato chips and stuffed them his mouth, as if to signal it was all he knew.

Slat didn't want to sound as if his questions were in an official capacity. "Well, I suppose Americans do things like flying out here to fish off the rocks. Seems odd they choose this time of the year."

The mechanic smiled slyly as if he knew something the constable didn't. It probably gave him a warm feeling to be one up on the law. "They dinna come to fish. They're studying shore birds and their mating habits. Fucking waste of time if you ask me."

Molly arrived with the meat pie and chips and topped off Slat's coffee. What the man had just told him made Slat even more interested. Studying shore birds and their mating habits sounded like a damn fool story to him. Taking his knife and fork he sliced open his pie, savoring the aroma of its contents. He ate silently for a while, mashing the potatoes into the rich, thick gravy and loading in a mouthful.

The mechanic said, "Stop by and I'll let you take a look at the helicopter. It has a company logo on its side—most likely some environmental group. They have money to burn." The mechanic sounded as if he had little use for do-gooders poking around the island, as if they would likely cause more problems than good.

Slat agreed he'd like to see the copter up close; he'd stop at the strip later in the day.

"Dinna come too late. I go home at four-thirty." He finished the remainder of his second pint, pushed back from the bar, and left.

Chapter 34

Swale had been able to remove the handcuffs from Zas by the use of a pair of bolt cutters left in the kitchen bunker by one of the construction workers. Zas was in the lantern room, covered by a tarp. Falk told Swale and Koski about the orders given by Tanner. "If we go against his verdict, we're the ones who'll catch all the flack. We're here as security. Nothing else. We have no command decision in any of this operation."

Koski, sitting next to Falk at the table in the kitchen, was fully aware of the frustration seething inside of Falk's gut and she shared it, itching for action. "Okay, Joe. The scientists are back in the meeting. "What are your plans? I know you're not going to just sit here and fume. And what about the pipe? When you came back, you rushed upstairs like a bat out of hell looking for Zas."

Falk sipped his third cup of coffee and reported on his trip down the inside of the pipe; how he'd run out of time and headed back to the lighthouse. He pushed his coffee mug to one side. "There was something I found odd. This place has supposedly been deserted for years until the construction crew came in to clean up and build the rooms in the bunkers." Swale and Koski nodded. "Well, either I was imagining it or the construction guys built a still down there because I got a definite whiff of whisky."

Swale asked, "Scotch or Irish?"

Falk continued. "I didn't have long enough to investigate further. I had to get back here for my shift. Now we'll have to rearrange a new schedule with Zas out of the picture."

Swale said, "I'll do permanent radio room duty if you like. I can keep an eye on the meeting between transmissions. Give you and Koski more flexibility. It's up to you, of course."

Falk nodded. "Thanks, I'll head back to the pipe. I'll take my cell phone, although I don't know if it'll work from inside the pipe."

"Take the yellow one from the radio room," Koski said. "Swale says it'll work from inside a Siberian salt mine." She turned to Swale. "Right?"

"Absolutely. I'll go get it and, at the same time, transmit our code exchanges." He pushed back from the table and left the bunker.

Falk watched him leave. "When I go back to the pipe, I want you to stay close to the meeting. I don't trust any of those people."

With the two deaths, Koski felt the same uneasiness, but she knew Falk's patterns and casting suspicion on the scientists and the governmental minders was not the usual method of investigation for Falk. "What about Swale?"

"Somehow, I feel he's clean. But I'm certain of nothing at the moment. It's just a hunch. We have to have someone on our side."

"And if you're wrong?"

"We'll be in one big hell of a mess." Falk looked into his empty cup.

Koski scooped it from the table and crossed to the stove, poured two mugs of steaming coffee, and carried them back to the table. "We have to abort, Joe." Falk looked as if the truth stung.

Koski wondered if he was showing indecision because they had no real power or control over the situation with Tanner and the commander running the show.

"I know. I'm going back to finish checking the pipe. It's all I can do right now," he said, slamming his coffee cup so hard on the table its contents slopped around.

Chapter 35

The tide had ebbed and Falk found it easier to clamber over the rocks and up inside the pipe. Immediately the musky odor of whisky again assailed his nostrils. Was it his imagination or was the aroma even stronger this time? Creeping softly, deeper into the pipe, he became aware the pipe had a sharp upward slant for about twenty feet and then levelled out. The walls of the pipe were wet to the touch and cold as ice. He tapped his jacket pocket and felt the reassuring bulge of the cell phone Swale had brought down from the radio room.

His flashlight beam stabbing the darkness, he wondered how the advance party that had checked the island for security could have missed the pipe. A feeling of uneasiness swept over him as he thought back over the last few hours. The assignment seemed cursed. Then the flashlight beam shone on a brick wall at what appeared to be the end of the pipe. Moving closer, he ran his fingers across the old brickwork looking for a possible hidden entrance or a concealed lock. Side to side, top to bottom, he ran his fingertips across the rough surface. Dropping to his knees he examined the row of bricks at floor level. Yes. There was a hair-like space between the bricks and the floor, running from the left side of the pipe to the center of the wall. Tracing the space Falk saw, there were marks in the dust and dirt as if part of the wall had swung inward to allow entrance. Lying flat on the ground, he began looking for a means to open the barrier. He felt a soft draft of air on his cheek and, at the same time, a stronger whiff of whisky. If he did find an entrance, he would no doubt find the source of the whisky.

Pushing and probing until his fingers were almost raw, Falk was at the point of giving up when, without any warning, there was a grating sound and a portion of the wall moved inward a few inches. Falk leaned back in surprise; he had no idea what he'd touched to cause the wall to shift. Moving closer to the wall he saw the door was about two feet wide and four feet high. Getting to his feet he dusted himself off, bent forward, and squeezed through the tiny entrance into a small square room with rock walls and a stone-flagged floor. The smell of whisky was now very strong. In the center of the room, a stout wood table and two wooden chairs seemed to be the only furnishings. Then, in one of the walls, he saw a door made out of hand-shaved planks.

His hand on his automatic in its holster, he started toward the door when, without warning, the door flew open and a screaming gibberish cry pierced his ears, exploding into a nightmare of yells and howls as a face, inhuman and rabid, loomed atop a large shaggy body and hurtled toward him. Falk attempted to sidestep something black bearing down on him. He crashed, then fell into nothingness as he crumpled to the floor, unconscious.

Chapter 36

The last meeting of the day in the lighthouse had ended and Koski walked back to the bunker with Courtney. "How's everything going?" she asked, an edge in her voice.

"As well as can be expected, I suppose. None of the scientists are at ease with what's happened in the last few hours. There's an air of tension between them."

Koski wasn't surprised. Discussing high tech secrets in an atmosphere of uncertainty, after having two security men killed within hours of each other, would agitate anyone, herself included.

"Have any of them suggested calling it quits and heading back home?"

Courtney's face hardened for a second. "It's not up to them to decide. This meeting has taken years to arrange and we don't intend to see it go down the tubes."

"Couldn't it be rearranged for them to meet in London or someplace?" They were almost at the bunker, and the cold air after the stuffiness of the meeting room seemed to sweep away some of Courtney's tension.

"Koski, I've no doubt you're good at what you do. But, believe me, rearranging a meeting for those three guys would take another couple of years at least. Besides, we don't have time to waste. If we don't complete our agenda, someone else will and we'll be in deep trouble."

They entered the bunker together and Koski collected a few items from a dresser drawer and turned to Courtney. "You'd better get some sleep. You look beat."

"Where are you going?" Courtney asked.

"Radio room. I'll try not to wake you when I get back." As Koski retraced her steps back to the lighthouse she worried about Falk. He'd been gone longer than she'd expected. Entering the lighthouse, she stood silently in the round chamber listening to the sound of the wind moan across the iron window frames. She wondered what it must have been like to live here for weeks on end. She started up the stairs, telling herself maybe it wouldn't have been much different than some of the places she had lived in as a kid. She'd had her share of run-down housing and drafty rooms with not enough heat in a Chicago winter. That was before her folks had died when she was still in high school. An aunt in Los Angeles had taken her in. Her house had been warm, but the aunt had been a cold, unfeeling martinet. Constantly on her back. Nag, nag, nag, until finally, when Koski was old enough, she took the entrance examination for the Bureau of Land Management, passing with high marks. It was then, during her period of training, she discovered she was a self-contained woman.

She had reassured herself that Falk had the yellow cell phone, and would have called if there had been any problems. Nonetheless, as she neared the top of the spiral staircase she felt a tiny tug of worry, an omen swirling and niggling in her brain as if preparing her for further calamities.

Swale swung around in his chair at the console as Koski entered. He glanced at the clock and exclaimed, "Perfect timing, my girl. That's what I like, punctuality."

Koski smiled and sat in a chair next to him, trying to cover her worries but not doing a very good job.

He grinned and jerked his thumb in the direction of the coffee maker. "How about a cup of Radio Room Rot Gut?"

"No, thanks, I'm fine. I've just seen Courtney to our room. The rest of the scientific party, along with Tanner and the commander, should be in their beds by now."

"But no one can be sure what happens next, right?"

"Joe's out checking that damn pipe. We're a team. I should have never let him go alone." Koski frowned.

"I've no doubt he can take care of himself."

She nodded, but knew her black belts and kick-boxing

prowess could get him out of a tight spot. "He's the best," she said, more to assure Swale then herself.

"That's more like it. I swapped codes just before you came in. Everything's on track."

"Thanks," Koski said, while privately still musing about her teamwork with Falk. He had taken care of himself numerous times before she had been teamed with him. But with their skills doubled, they had more far more security than when they operated alone.

Chapter 37

Falk's eyes flickered open and he tried to focus on a shadowy form sitting across the room from him. A single oil lamp cast a weak light in an otherwise totally black room. He blinked a couple of times and finally focused on an old man. A hunk of an old man, wild eyed; his hoary face hideous in the pallid lantern light. When the man saw that Falk was awake, he left his chair and approached, roaring "AAARRRRGGGHHHH!"

Falk pressed back against the wall. "God almighty…"

The man took a swipe at Falk. "Blasphemous heathen!"

Falk pushed himself against the wall, desperately seeking the slightest chance he could find to get out of the madman's way.

The old man continued ranting, but made no further attempt to strike. "Dweller in yon dungeon dark, hangman of creation mark. Who in mourning weeds appears, laden with unhonored years."

"Hey, wait." Falk, now somewhat more cogent than when he first opened his eyes, tried to reason with the hulk and inched forward.

"Back," the man growled.

"Okay, okay."

"And be still or I'll blow ye heathen head off."

Falk could now see the man was holding a large revolver. "I'm not moving. I'm not doing anything."

"Aye, ye've done enough, I'm thinking." Keeping the revolver trained on Falk, the man moved back and lit a second lantern which added enough light for Falk to see a small table and two wooden chairs and a filthy unmade bunk attached to the wall. Against the far wall he saw a stack of whisky crates, cans of food, and sacks of what could be flour or sugar. Whoever this guy was, he seemed to be planning to stay a while.

The old man closed one eye in suspicion, leaned down, took an open can of beans off the table, and then began to stuff handfuls of beans into his mouth.

Falk shuddered as the man continued feeding, the beans attaching themselves to his large hairy beard as he did so.

Falk decided to try again. "My friends know I'm here."

"Liar!"

Flinching, Falk continued. "They'll come looking any time now."

The man flung the empty bean can across the room in rage, reached down beside the bunk, and came up with a half bottle of Scotch and gulped directly from the bottle. "Tongue of Satan." He'd stuck the revolver down inside his waistband when he began to cram the beans into his mouth, but now he removed the weapon and waved it in the air and staggered toward Falk. "And the guilty shall be punished, and their kin, and all the..." He was looming over Falk, getting closer and closer.

Falk suddenly shot his feet out, toppling the old man, and the gun spun across the floor. Falk quickly realized the old man was strong as they rolled on the floor grappling for the gun. He was also taller and had a longer reach. Despite Falk's efforts, the old guy scooped the revolver off the floor and at the same time pulled the trigger repeatedly. Five shots crashed against the walls. The bullets ricocheted in an insane cacophony of explosions and stabs of orange light. Falk knew there was one round left in the chamber as the smell of freshly fired rounds mixed with the odor of the Scotch, hanging in the air like a fetid blanket of doom. The crazy man stood above him, silent except for his labored breathing after the sudden exertion. Falk wondered if he might die in a room beneath an old lighthouse, killed by a madman drunk out of his mind.

Swale and Koski were crossing through the round chamber inside the main entrance on their way out to the kitchen-bunker when they heard the muffled sounds of gunfire. They stopped, heads twisting from side to side as they tried to locate the sounds.

"That's coming from beneath us, Swale. What the hell's going on?"

Swale dropped to his knees and pounded on the floor. "Solid. I've never heard of a basement in a lighthouse. Have you?"

Koski joined him, she too testing the floor. "Don't ask me. This is my first lighthouse. We'll have to look under this carpet. We'll need something to cut with. Do you have a knife?"

Swale shook his head. "No. I watched the guys put the carpet down. It's a stone flagged floor."

"Did you get a close look? I mean, did you notice anything about it other than it being stone?"

Swale sat back on his haunches. "Like what?"

"Was there anything that looked like a trapdoor, you know, a slab with iron rings to lift it up?"

"Nope, just a stone floor. I didn't take much notice at the time."

Koski got to her feet and rubbed the backs of her legs. "Right. We're going to pull back the carpet and take a closer look. Those shots definitely came from beneath the floor. And there's no other way I know to get down there. There has to be a means of getting under the slabs."

Swale kicked the carpet with a heel of his boot. "This stuff is indoor-outdoor carpet; they stuck it to the floor with an industrial strength adhesive, and it's not going to be easy."

"We'll get one edge up, then pull and rip it back until we find a trap door. Come on, in the kitchen there are plenty of knives. Let's move."

Koski sensed that the gunfire could have something to do with the length of time Falk had been away. He needed help, and fast.

Minutes later, they headed back into the lighthouse armed with assorted knives and anything else that could be used to pry up carpet.

Chapter 38

Dr. Kevin Clayton couldn't sleep. He lay looking at the ceiling and then made up his mind. Silently, he slipped out of bed, dressed quickly in warm clothes, left the room, and quietly made his way to the room shared by Koski and Courtney. He hesitated outside the door trying to decide to knock or not. He knew Koski was going to join Swale in the radio room. She might have returned by now and be in the room. He shrugged and tapped lightly on the door.

Courtney was awake at once, and saw Koski's bed was empty

and still made up. Again she heard the light tapping at the door. "Who is it?" she asked, at the same time reaching for a Walther PPK.380 automatic from beneath her pillow. It was cocked and locked with a clip of Glaser blue tip rounds.

"It's me. Kevin."

"What's wrong?"

"Nothing. I couldn't sleep and wondered if you were still awake. Sorry, I guess I woke you up."

Courtney wondered how she would look answering the door in a pair of flannel pajamas at one thirty in the morning. She went across the cold floor and opened the door. Her feet were freezing.

"It's a beautiful night. I wondered if you'd like to take a walk."

Despite her cold feet and the hour of the night, the lanky American with a lopsided grin looked a welcome sight after hours in a stuffy room filled with tension. "Sure. Let me get something warm on and I'll be right with you."

Kevin smiled as she closed the door, but not before noticing the automatic that was partially hidden behind her back as she turned into the room. This lady got more interesting by the hour.

Courtney and Kevin left the bunker and gazed up at the night sky. Kevin had been right. A rain storm had passed, pushing the clouds out toward the mainland; a sky studded with stars hung overhead, seemingly almost low enough to touch.

Courtney stared at the sky, saying nothing. The breeze from the sea was gentle, but still icy cold. The blustery gust that only a few hours before had rattled the window frames of the lighthouse now barely moved the ends of her hair peeking below the woollen watch cap she was wearing.

"You're right, Kevin, beautiful night." It was the first time she'd used his Christian name and was surprised with the ease she had uttered it.

The moon was large and bright. Kevin glanced up. "A Bomber's moon," he said softly.

"Why do they call it a Bomber's moon?"

Kevin moved in closer to her. "Goes back to the wartime bombing raids. A full moon made it easy for the bombers to find their target. During the Blitz, London did everything they could to try and cover the Thames River during a full moon. The moonlight made a perfect path for the Luftwaffe to follow. The city, totally blacked out, and the moon reflecting from the surface of the river, was like a beacon. The Germans knew every bend of the river and exactly where to drop their ordnance."

"Were the British ever successful in camouflaging the river?"

"No." They walked in silence, following a worn path down toward the small pier until Kevin said, "Tough sledding at the last meeting, wasn't it? If we don't get loosened up, no one is going to exchange anything. You were kind of hard on Tanner when he tried to get Jenner to be more forthright."

"He misplaced his priorities. Right now Dr. Jenner seems to be all Israel has to offer."

"It's got you."

She gave a short laugh. "I'll take that as a compliment. However, I'm nothing."

"Who told you that?"

They stopped at the pier and looked across the water as Courtney continued. "I mean compared with Dr. Jenner."

Kevin's eyes twinkled mischievously as he put his arm around her waist. "I'd never compare you to Dr. Jenner. I'd compare you to Diana." He nodded to the silvery orb overhead.

"The Moon Goddess."

"When are you ever serious, Kevin?" Slowly, they walked the length of the pier and Kevin indicated a couple of coils of rope atop a crate. They sat together, huddled close in the moonlight. It was bitterly cold. Courtney bravely carried on. "When I think of nuclear risks, pollution, and political blackmail compared to underselling the benefits of solar power to the public and its endless supply of energy, I get serious when no one will listen."

"Some of us are listening now. We're here on the island." He turned his face from the moon and looked at her. In the moonshine, with the wind ruffling her hair, she was breath-taking. "Creature of the desert. You're beautiful."

He kissed her, warmly and slowly. "What are you like, Courtney Spencer?"

"Like you, Kevin Clayton. I do as I please. I get what I want. Only I have to work for it."

Kevin was taken back at the answer. "Want to run that past me again?"

"It cost me one hundred percent of myself to be here on this island. I didn't get it handed to me on a silver platter."

"And I did?"

"You're of the Clayton family. Money, yachts, political privileges…"

"No credit for hard work?"

"Of course. You're brilliant."

"Oh, thanks."

"But from a bright family."

"I had it made."

"Right."

"And you didn't."

"Don't get me wrong. Yours is an enviable background, but I prefer mine."

"Then tell me… Israel is your adopted country, right? You were born in America."

"What's wrong with being an Israeli Jew?"

"Dunno. What was wrong with being an American Jew?"

Courtney's face hardened and she inched away from his side. "Never mind."

She saw a soft smile cross his face as he whispered. "Wasn't tough enough for you?"

Her eyes flashed in anger. "It wasn't enough." She held her resentment in defiance of his smile and then suddenly melted at this tall American. She moved closer. "That's always been my problem. I'm never satisfied."

"Can I help?"

Courtney searched his eyes. "I bet you could." They kissed again. This time it was longer and more passionate. Then she broke away. "I have a mission to accomplish, Doctor, and you're turning me on." As she got to her feet, the rope coil moved aside, and Kevin slipped on the planking. "Does this mean it's all over?"

She reached down and offered her hand. "I believe it means it's just begun."

Together, hand in hand, they walked back to the lighthouse, following the silvery path of a Bomber's Moon.

Chapter 39

Falk stared up at the wild man above him. He knew he had to say the right words or he'd be dead when the man fired the remaining round at close range from his revolver.

"You look like the sort of man who savors his solitude and

freedom. Am I correct?"

The shaggy heap of a man remained silent, swaying slightly, his breathing ragged and wheezy. The old .38 Webley was less than a foot from Falk's head.

"You kill me and you can kiss goodbye to your freedom. You'll still have your solitude, but it'll be a cell with iron walls for the rest of your life, without the Scotch whisky." Falk watched the drunken man lower the revolver to his side. Was he getting through? Falk continued, his voice now in the mode of a hostage negotiator, soft and non-threatening. "I understand your feelings. Someone intruding into my space would have caused me to react the same way. No one wants to hurt you. Believe me." Falk was amazed at what happened next.

The man straightened, pulling himself to attention, chin up, eyes front, and in a powerful voice that filled the room, commanded, "Guid save King George and Scotland."

Falk took a chance and groggily got to his feet, keeping an eye on the revolver and the old man's finger curled around the trigger. Standing to attention, Falk saluted.

A change came over the Scot. His eyes brightened and a faint smile curled his lips. "Aye, that's more like it." Sticking the Webley into his belt, he went to the table, sat down, and took a swig from the bottle.

"Why are you hiding down here?" Falk asked softly.

"I was'na hiding until ye all came. Ye sealed me in like a wild animal in a trap." He stabbed a finger to the ceiling. "Sealed ma way in and oot."

Falk looked at the ceiling. Then noticed a wooden ladder attached to the wall seemingly going up through the ceiling. He'd not seen it before due to the lack of light in the room and the sudden attack by the madman. Falk asked softly, "What were you doing here?"

"This was ma home a long, long time ago."

"You lived here?"

"I did. Not in this wee room mind you. I was born and suckled here in the lighthouse. It was ma home. It was here I learned my trade as a Keeper. It was here I learned ma duty. Always lots to do. The light must never gae oot. The oil for the lamps had to be clean. Most men could'na stand the loneliness, but to me and Angus...to us...the lighthouse was our home. Some of the world's finest ships depended on Angus and me ta guide them. Nothing passes anymore. Nothing comes near, now. Angus and me...sent off we were ta graze in the heather."

"Angus?" Falk asked.

"Angus. Ay. He was ma wee brother."

"But you came back." Falk saw that the man was settling down, seemingly more calm now as he continued to answer his questions.

"They sealed the trap door closed."

"Who?"

"I dinna know. They came and changed everything... cleaned and painted, built things in the bunkers. They were here for days. I had to stay hidden down here in this place." He swept his arm around the small room. "This was a fresh water cistern once when I was a boy, a storage place for our drinking water. Every year now, I cross over ta old Lars Vanheut's and he brings me out in his boat for ma two weeks holiday, though they still have me grazing in the Highlands.

"When will Lars Vanheut come back for you?"

"Ach! I've barely arrived, laddie."

Falk expelled his breath slowly. "Well, if what you say is true, you've picked a hell of a time to take your vacation."

The old man shook his shaggy head and a bean loosened from his beard, falling to the floor. He held his bottle to the light for a moment then put it to his lips and drained the remains. At the same moment there was a rasping of stone, and a shaft of light beamed down into the room. Falk moved fast and grabbed the revolver from the old man's waistband as he turned and looked up at the light.

Swale and Koski were down the ladder into the room in a moment, both holding their weapons in the ready position. But this time the man simply sat at the table and didn't move.

"You okay?" Koski asked as she rushed to Falk's side.

"I'm fine." He put his arm around her shoulders and addressed Swale. "Anyone else know about this?"

"No one," said Swale. "We were crossing the floor upstairs when we heard the gunfire. We ripped up the carpet, found a trap door, and here we are."

"Good. Let's keep it that way." Falk went to the table and sat opposite the man. "Look. Tell me your name; I have to call you something."

"Call me, Jock."

"Fine. Listen, Jock, I'm going to have to keep you down here a little longer. I don't have time to go through a long explanation at the moment. Let me say that what you saw going on up above is of vital importance to the country. You have to trust me. I trust you to be a God-fearing man and a patriot. Am I correct?"

Jock jumped to his feet and once again stood to attention and roared. "Guid bless King George and Scotland." Swale and Koski stared at the scene in amazement.

"Just a couple of days, Jock, and then you can have the run of the place, including all the new additions. How's that sound? I'll have to cover the trap door; I don't want any of those up there to know you are here." Falk indicated Koski and Swale. "It'll be between us alone."

"Ye trust me na to escape through the pipe?"

"I do, Jock, if you give me your word on it."

Jock remained silent, studying his work worn hands as they rested on the table. "And ye say I'd be doing a duty for ma country?"

"Yes, Jock, you will."

"And it will help keep the lighthouse from becoming a ruin?"

"Let me say I'll do all I can to see the lighthouse is cared for."

Jock thumped his fist on the table. "Then ye have a deal. I'll remain quiet down here until ye give me the all clear." He held out his hand and Falk shook it, feeling the surprisingly strong grip of the old Scot.

Falk, Koski, and Swale sat in the radio room sipping stale coffee. It was after two in the morning and Falk wound down his account of how he'd entered the pipe and found his way to the hidden room. "Now if Jock can have his pal bring him out to the lighthouse and drop him off and no one knows anything about it, it's time to blow the whistle. Abort the meeting no matter what the three government bureaucrats think."

"We could get in touch with Stewart. He should be able to pull some strings," Koski suggested.

Falk shook his head. "I don't want to chance using the phone. I've no doubt our communications have been compromised. Whatever messages we exchange by phone could be intercepted."

"By whom?" Koski asked.

"Good question. I have to think of a way of getting back to the mainland without causing any suspicion by Tanner and Co."

"This mission called for four security personnel," Swale said, pulling his chair in closer to the desk in readiness for the next code exchange. "We're down to three and you're talking of making it two. I doubt Tanner or any of them are going to go for you buzzing off to the mainland, leaving only two of us to take care of things."

"Then I have to make a quick trip without any else knowing I'm gone." Falk checked his watch. "It's after two thirty and if I leave now, I can be over on Tiree before five. It'll be dark, and I can get ashore and to the constable's house before daylight. I only met the man once, but I got the feeling he wasn't buying the BS he was given by the brass from Glasgow. Once I get his confidence, I'll contact Stewart on the constable's landline. Then, as soon as I'm confident it's secure, I'll request Stewart to authorize a Fast Deploy Team to be sent to the lighthouse, close down the meeting, and evacuate everyone."

Koski nodded. "You can count on me one hundred percent to handle this end and disguise your absence. And if in the meantime, while you're away, the question is asked where you are, what do you prefer we say?"

"Special assignment. Say that due to the mysterious deaths of the two security agents, as the agent in charge, I have been ordered to a top secret radio watch and must remain in the radio room night and day. I'll return tomorrow evening and come ashore after darkness. Any questions?"

"Plenty," Koski said. "I doubt it'll do any good to ask. Just be sure you wear a life jacket." She moved close beside him. "Be careful, Joe. I wish I could be with you. But I have this end covered."

"Yeah, I know. Take good care of Swale." Looking at her face, he could see her eagerness to take on the mission. "And remember, we have Jock down there in his cubby hole."

"As if anyone could forget him," she quipped.

Chapter 40

It was pre-dawn when Falk steered the Kodiak into a still, dark harbor. He'd made better time than he'd figured completing the crossing. The sea had been calm, with a stiff onshore wind. Throttling back the outboard to a low throb, he eased into a tie-down along the harbor wall, close to a built-in iron ladder set into the rough stonewall leading up onto the quayside.

Once ashore, he walked through the darkness, passing a small food market, a bank, and the post office. He knew the constable lived with his wife in small living quarters located above the police station. Falk had walked back to the police station from the hotel with the constable the evening he'd met Zas. Falk glanced up at a lantern-style lamp over the doorway with the words *Police* on the blue-painted front door. Falk reached for the large iron doorknocker and rapped three times, wondering if there were any such police stations left in the United States. A few seconds later, an upstairs window opened and a flashlight beam shone down on Falk. "What's going on? What do you want?" a male voice demanded.

"I have to see you, Constable, it's very important." Falk didn't yell his name in the off chance anyone else in the village might hear him.

Falk heard muffled grumbles and the window slammed shut. When the door opened, and a shaft of bright light from inside the police station fell across Falk, the constable recognized him at once. He pulled the door open wide. "Come in, come in."

Falk entered and the door was closed quickly behind him. "You're the American from up at the hotel. I remember you from the murder investigation; we were never introduced formally. My name is Constable Slat, Harry Slat." He offered a large hand and secured the belt of his bathrobe around his ample waist with his left hand. "Here, sit down." Slat indicated a chair beside a battered wooden desk. "You look frozen, man. I'll put the kettle on."

Falk didn't argue; he needed something to warm his insides after the trip. "Thanks, that'll be great. My name is Joe Falk."

"Ah, yes, the bird man from America." Slat looked over his shoulder with a knowing look as he plugged in an electric kettle on a shelf near his desk. "I'm afraid I can't talk about the murder up at the hotel. It's out of my jurisdiction. Glasgow police took over."

"I'm not here about that murder. I need your help with a different problem, something possibly far more important than that murder."

Slat's eyes widened. In his mind, there was nothing more urgent to investigate than a murder, and he'd been robbed of his only chance by orders from Glasgow. Now here was a Yank indicating there was something bigger to investigate. He placed two mugs on the shelf, took the top off a Brown-Betty teapot, spooned in three heaping teaspoons of loose black tea, and, just as the kettle boiled, expertly tipped the boiling water into the teapot and replaced the lid. "We'll let it steep for a bit. Sugar and milk?"

"Just as it comes from the pot, thanks."

Slat sat behind his desk, looking more like a retired schoolteacher than a policeman. "Now then, tell me what's up."

Falk informed him about the death of Zas and the discovery

of Jock. They had both drunk the last of their tea by the time he'd finished.

Slat leaned forward, elbows resting on the desk top. "I felt certain there was more to this whole thing. The way I was pushed aside, ordered to leave everything to Glasgow. That's not the usual way we operate, Mr. Falk. I hope you realize that."

"I guessed as much. Now I'm asking you to help me get in touch with my agency by using your phone."

Slat looked at Falk for a long moment. "You could have made a call from the public phone on the dock and left me out of it. What's the real reason you came to see me?"

"I need someone I can rely on. Someone who is aware of the importance of getting the scientists away from the lighthouse and back to the mainland before anything else happens out there."

Falk pushed his mug aside. "Also, you didn't seem surprised when I told you about the old man, Jock, being on the island."

"Jock goes out to the lighthouse every year and stays a few days. He does no harm. It used to be his home before the light was closed down."

"He told me. What bothers me is the fact he could get onto the island despite our so-called security. He sails out in a friend's boat, goes ashore, and lives in the damn place while it was being made ready for the meeting."

"He went out there before the clean-up crew, Mr. Falk."

"Then you knew about the lighthouse being prepared?"

"Most everyone on the island knew. Not much goes on in a place like this that isn't noticed."

"Was it common knowledge that there was going to be a meeting out there?"

"Yes, but we thought it was a meeting of ornit…"

"Ornithologists," Falk prompted.

"Right. We had no idea it was an international meeting of solar scientists."

"Good. Let it remain that way."

"Jock's harmless."

"He damned near shot me. He was drunk as a skunk."

Slat's face changed. "That's not like him. He lives a very quiet life in a crofter's cottage on the isle of Cobb, just north of us here. He used to live with his brother after the lighthouse closed."

"Well, he wasn't living a quiet life when I came across him. Who is this friend that took him out to the lighthouse?"

"You must mean Lars Vanheut. He's a fisherman who lives over on Cobb also."

"Odd name for a Scotsman," Falk said.

"He's Norwegian. Got married to a local girl on Cobb, but she didn't want to live in Norway, so Lars stayed. That was thirty years ago."

Falk blew out his cheeks and expelled air. "For what started out as a secret meeting at a lonely location in the North Atlantic, there are far too many people in the know."

Slat asked, "The mechanic looking after the helicopter. Know much about him?" He refilled both mugs.

"Not really, why?"

"I've been doing some sleuthing myself. I've not felt comfortable since that guy had his throat cut, and I was told in no uncertain terms to forget it. The mechanic has been on the island only about a month. No one knows him very well, keeps to himself. He has a place to sleep at the airport, comes into town for lunch each day. He invited me up to check out the helicopter any time." The constable glanced at an old clock on the wall. It was almost six in the morning. "The wife will be down, then we'll have breakfast. I'll get dressed, but meanwhile, you can use that phone." Slat indicated a battered black rotary phone on his desk. "It's not fancy, but it's not bugged."

Falk made contact with Stewart, and quickly informed him of the situation at the lighthouse. The instructions he received from Stewart re-enforced the fact that he'd made the right decision in getting to the mainland before attempting to contact *Cerberus*, due to the almost certainty that communications had been compromised. Stewart's voice came in loud and clear.

"There will be a rapid deployment team on the island within hours—a HAHO drop. That's all I can say over the phone. They'll take up positions around the lighthouse and remain hidden until ordered into any needed action."

"Fine. Advise them of a pipe on the northeast corner of the island; it's almost hidden and juts out over the rocks into the sea. It's large enough to walk inside and leads to a brick wall that can be opened which leads into a small room under the lighthouse."

"That's affirmative." Falk could sense the excitement in Stewart's voice as he continued. "Our contacts in Oban report that several men boarded the ferry to Tiree and should arrive there on the eight o'clock boat. They are known mercenaries. Also, an Arab businessman of dubious legitimacy, who is known to have masterminded several terrorist actions in Europe in the last two years, has been seen in Glasgow and is reportedly staying at a hotel named, The Tarbot. It's located close to Loch Lomond."

There was a pause, and Falk thought they had lost their connection.

"Still there, Falk?"

"Yes, sir."

"Good. I know you can't be in two places at once, nonetheless, I want the men who are arriving on the morning boat watched and followed. Also, we need to find the Arab businessman at the Tarbot Hotel. I don't want local police involved, especially with the possibility of the media getting hold of the story."

Falk didn't discuss Constable Slat over the phone or tell Stewart that he had an ally who would happily work with him with no chance of leaks, otherwise Slat would have his ass in a sling with Glasgow.

"I understand, sir. Do we have any of the Oban detachment following the group on the ferry?"

"No. Those bastards are too smart. They'd know they were being tailed. I'll have worked out the problem by the time they arrive. And, Falk, when you call next time, use your satellite cell phone as soon as you are far away from Tiree. The phone you're using is almost as old as me." The line clicked to a dial tone. Stewart, in his usual brusque manner, had hung up, but he had also indicated that Falk would be receiving orders to proceed to the Tarbot Hotel and find the Arab businessman.

Falk cradled the phone and headed back to the police station. A High Altitude/High Opening jump was an extremely difficult form of insertion which required a tremendous amount of team training. Falk knew a typical HAHO profile has a squad jumping from either commercial or military aircraft with a commercial IFF signature in the normal air traffic lanes so as not to raise suspicion. The jumpers would exit at high altitude—30,000 feet, and deploy their parachutes within fifteen seconds at around 27,000 feet. The team would then form a stack in the air, the low jumper setting a course and acting as the pathfinder. The team would fly upwards of thirty miles in formation, using compass and points of terrain landmarks to navigate to their target.

He had seen the U.S. Navy SEALS carry out such an operation. And he had been in awe of their precision and bravery.

Slat and his wife were standing in the doorway as Falk approached. "I'd like you to meet my wife, Fiona."

Fiona was a buxom lady with red hair tied in a ponytail, about the same age as Slat, solid, but not fat. She also had a smile that an angel would envy.

"Good morning, Mrs. Slat. Forgive my early, unannounced intrusion into your day." They shook hands, Mrs. Slat saying coyly that Falk sounded more like a blarney Irishman than a Yank.

"I make porridge every day for breakfast. Would you care for anything different?"

"Porridge sounds great."

Chapter 41

Tanner shook with fury. Koski was adamant, in her full power now that Falk was gone. "Sorry, Mr. Tanner, the radio room is off limits to anyone but those authorized to handle the codes."

"I don't want anything to do with the codes. I want to see Falk. If he's been given a special assignment to remain at the controls of the radio room, he can spend a few minutes with me."

"Wrong. You know the rules. The chain of command has to be followed." Koski glared at him. "Or perhaps once you break them, it doesn't count anymore."

It was clear she was right; she referred to his actions in the abortive mess he'd created when he broke a chain of command in the hills of Tennessee that had resulted in the deaths of innocent children.

"Then advise him I want to see him the moment he leaves the radio room. Is that clear?"

Koski's eyes spat bullets. "Loud and clear, Mr Tanner." She turned and walked away and saw that the scientists were entering the conference room. The commander and Teesdale were the last to go in.

Swale closed the door behind them and seated himself outside. "Well done, Koski. Don't forget, code exchange in ten minutes."

She nodded and continued down to the kitchen to make a quick cup of tea. She was glad to have a moment of quiet time, but felt exhilarated inside. With Falk gone, she was in command and in her natural element, ready to take on all comers. She knew he'd been right in making the decision to contact Stewart outside the range of an unknown electronic eavesdropper. Her eyes bright with excitement, she sipped her drink, not even tasting the brew.

She'd always been a person to play "what if" games, and she had a nagging what-iffer going around in her head at that moment. What if there was someone inside the lighthouse that could send out information? A call could easily be made while on a stroll around the island. If it was one of the members of the scientific group…who and why? The more she thought about her hypothesis, the stronger the possibility grew; the two murders could well have been carried out by an insider. She ran each person through her mind. Any of them could be suspect, including Swale. She had only herself to rely on. She'd been in many situations like this in the past and was ready to kick some ass.

Chapter 42

The wall clock in the police station showed ten minutes to

eight as the old black phone on Slat's desk rang.

"Constable Slat."

Falk walked away from the desk and studied a group of framed photographs on the wall, past constables and groups of uniformed men that went back over the years. Slat's voice was loud enough for Falk to hear.

"Yes, I understand." He glanced out of the window and down to the harbor. "They should be arriving anytime, then." Slat pushed back his chair and stood at the desk, leaning forward, ready to hang up the phone. "I'll proceed to the dock at once, sir."

Falk heard the phone clatter back onto the cradle.

Slat indicated the phone. "That was the Chief Constable of Oban. There's a Coast Guard helicopter on the way with an armed team who will detain a group of five men disembarking from the morning ferry. They'll be taken into custody as they pass through the passenger check point in the ferry terminal."

Slat and Falk headed to the dock as a helicopter fitted with pontoons came into view, circled the ferry building, and descended to a landing pad at the side of the pier, setting down softly amid flying detritus.

"What are you supposed to do with five hard-nosed villains, Slat? You don't have the space to hold that many." The two of them descended steep stone steps, winding past whitewashed cottages as they headed to the dock.

"The Coast Guard will take care of them. There's a boat coming from Coll. They'll be taken there and kept out of sight for a few days." Slat's eyes were lit with excitement and there was a spring to his step he'd not felt in many a year. "Whatever is going on, it's big, and I'm a part of it. I thought I was going to retire without ever having anything to tell my grandchildren about other than writing parking tickets and keeping order among sometimes rowdy day trippers from the mainland."

It was a three man team that climbed from the Coast Guard helicopter, and Slat pointed them out to Falk. "Our Coast Guard Service is an integral part of our coastal security as well as search and rescue working in concert with RNLI." Slat was referring to the Royal National Lifeboat Institution. "We'll find out who the three man team is as soon as we meet them inside the terminal."

Stewart had worked with his usual fast efficiency, coordinating a combined operations mission to be carried out between British and American forces. The American Navy Seals would supply three men, and a six man team from Britain's Special Air Service would be utilized. Three of the SAS would join the SEAL HAHO team. The other three SAS would be deployed and transferred by Her Majesty's Coast Guard to detain a group of suspected terrorists upon their arrival at the Isle of Tiree. Stewart had also arranged that Falk be flown back to Oban for briefing on the latest information of the Arab man at the Hotel Tarbot. When *Cerberus* made connections with the right people, no time was wasted.

Chapter 43

The ferry boat, the MV Clansman, was almost at the end of its four hour journey from Oban as Ian McLean leaned on the rail of the top deck and watched the Coast Guard helicopter settle on its landing pad. He was alert at once. Something was wrong.

He turned to the man standing next to him. "Are the others still in the cafe?"

"Yeah, why?"

"Follow me." Quickly they raced back to the large cafeteria-style restaurant that served various foods, sandwiches, and drinks during the trip. McLean went to the table where three men were drinking tea and finishing a light breakfast.

"I saw a Coast Guard copter land at the dock. It might be routine, but I'm taking no chances. We're going to break up before we disembark. Once ashore, get up to the airstrip, keep out of sight until dark, then move in and we'll meet in the old unused hangar at the far end of the runway. Everyone know it?" They nodded, finished their drinks, and moved out from the table.

McLean had trained them well and had gone over, in detail, any possible problems that might arise on their arrival. They would become independent of each other until they regrouped at the hangar in the darkness. McLean had planned his back up exit by finding a truck down in the car and truck area of the ship, one that he could slip into without being seen by the driver. He'd checked it out during the crossing. Each man had an escape plan known only to himself in case of capture and interrogation. That way no one could give the others away.

Chapter 44

Falk and Constable Slat met with a wiry compact man, the leader of the SAS team who informed them of their plan to quickly, and without any undue fuss, abduct the men, and then transfer them to Coll by a Coast Guard cutter that was already on its way. Also, Falk was informed he was to be flown immediately to the Coast Guard office in Oban where he would be given further orders.

Falk looked out to where the ship was making its final approach to the dock, people already crowding the rails, wanting to be the first off. "Looks like this is where I leave you, Constable.

Thanks for the hospitality. We'll go up to the airstrip when I get back so you can look my helicopter over."

They shook hands as the three SAS men walked into the ferry terminal. The Coast Guard helicopter had already started its rotors as Falk headed toward the aircraft.

Falk walked into the Oban office of Her Majesty's Coast Guard at a little after ten, escorted by the helicopter pilot. They entered a room marked Operations.

"Good morning, Mr. Falk." A pale, plump civilian, obviously out of shape, was seated behind a plain wooden desk. "Please take a seat." He indicated a chair opposite his desk. "Tea or coffee?"

Falk sat down saying, "Coffee, black." The helicopter pilot nodded to the pale man and left the room.

"Jonah, when you have a moment, we'd like two coffees; one black." He leaned back from the intercom and folded his hands across his well-tailored paunch. "For your information, Mr. Falk, the five men who were to be taken from the ferry by the SAS detachment didn't show up. Or perhaps I should say, were not apprehended. We know they went on board but evidently not how they disembarked. For the time being, we'll have to leave the matter of five terrorists wandering free on Tiree to the SAS while you proceed to the Tarbot Hotel on Loch Lomond." He unfolded his hands and leaned back to allow his assistant to place two mugs of coffee on his desk. "Thank you, Jonah." He indicated Falk get his. "Mr. Stewart also said he would appreciate a call from you upon your arrival here at HMCG. He also suggested you use your cell phone."

Falk sipped his coffee. "Is there an office I can use?"

"Please, be my guest." The pale man rose from his desk and waved to the empty chair. "Take your time; I'll be next door when you're through."

Falk walked around and sat at the desk, took out his cell, and called Stewart.

"Joe. I suppose you heard that the five men eluded us at Tiree?"

"Yes."

"It'll be up to the SAS to find them, and I'm sending backup. If five men can walk off the ship and not be apprehended that indicates they're pros and will be difficult to find."

"Do we know who they are?"

"Not yet. From the intelligence we've gathered in the last few hours, it's possibly a newly formed group known only as 'Opaque,' a soldier-for-hire outfit. We believe a Syrian man by the name of Abu Scha has hired them to steal the solar plans from the meeting." Falk heard muffled voices for a few seconds on the other end of the line, and then Stewart came back on. "Sorry about that. Just had a name handed to me. Ian McLean. He used to be hard liner for the Irish Republican Army. Now he's believed to be heading up 'Opaque'."

"Then we know the name of at least one of the men who evaded the SAS at the ferry."

"Yes. I've also been informed that the HAHO team will be on the island just after dusk and will remain in place until needed."

Falk grunted. "So, Koski has no idea about the drop."

"'Fraid so, Joe. We couldn't risk sending information through a communication link that is possibly monitored."

Falk didn't answer. He was thinking of Koski and the danger she and the rest of them were in. "I know what you are thinking, Joe. You want us to go in and take everyone off the island now, before there is any chance of an attack. I wish we could. You realize how long it's taken for the three countries to agree to let each one look into the others' research. We break it up now and God knows how long it would be before we get back together. Plus, there is always the chance one of the countries might decide at a later date to throw in with one we don't want. It has to be now. Once we have the three pieces of the puzzle, we, as a nation, can rest a little easier in our beds. If the three scientists walk at this point, it would be like breaking up the team at Los Alamos. Think about it, Joe. Would we have gotten the A Bomb first? Or would it have been Germany or Japan?"

Falk remained silent. Stewart was right. They had to wait. It would be up to him to see everything possible was done to stop the threatened attack from becoming a reality.

"Joe? You still there?"

"Yeah, Tom, I'm here."

"Fine, I need you there on the mainland. Listen carefully."

Chapter 45

Mr. Abu Scha, the man who had given Ian McLean his orders in Glasgow, sat at a small table in the window of his hotel room overlooking Loch Lomond. He had chosen the Hotel Tarbot, not for its rustic isolation amid the beauty of the Scottish Highlands, but for the ease it would afford him in leaving the country without the constricting security of x-rays and pat downs of officialdom; it's too bothersome when making a departure through a busy city airport.

Upon final agreements between the three scientists, McLean's men, upon receiving the signal from the "operative" in the lighthouse, would complete their raid. Afterwards, McLean would be picked up along with the solar secrets and flown by helicopter to a pre-arranged landing strip where Abu Scha would rendezvous with him. Together, they would be flown to a private airport where Abu Scha would transfer to a waiting Learjet and fly to Denmark. Abu Scha smiled as he mulled over the plan. He cared little that McLean's men would be stranded to fend for themselves. McLean had readily agreed to abandon his team in return for a ten million dollar payment promised by the Syrian. Sipping his single malt, he savoured the taste. At least the Scots knew how to produce the best whisky in the world.

Chapter 46

Falk drove a rental car out of Oban, heading north. He adjusted the heater in an attempt to warm the interior; everything was so damned cold in Scotland. He was thinking over the instructions Stewart had given him. This time, Falk didn't have the usual feeling of exhilaration he normally experienced when starting a new assignment for *Cerberus*. Jabbing the tuning buttons, he tried to find a radio station with music that would help settle his edginess. Stewart had stressed the urgency in locating Abu Scha. *If we lose him, there might never be another chance. He must be taken without anyone knowing. We can't involve the police and risk a leak to the media. He must not get away. You must keep him at the hotel. Our man is on the way.*

Chapter 47

Constable Slat drove through the narrow country lanes toward the windswept airstrip. He had decided it was time to make a visit to the mechanic on his home ground. Slat had spent time with the SAS team after the fiasco at the ferry, before they had taken off to search the wild and rocky coast around the island, leaving the constable to his duties.

It was almost three-thirty in the afternoon, and he remembered that the mechanic went off duty at four. Shifting into low, he gunned the four wheel drive Land Rover around a sharp bend and up an alarmingly steep hill for the last quarter mile to the airport. Five minutes later, he pushed open a five-barred gate leading to a huddle of small buildings that made up Tiree airport. It had been several years since he had been up there. He took a moment to get a lay of the land.

The huddle of buildings had suffered the toll of disregard over the years, and an old Quonset hut circa WWII, was rusting slowly away. A wooden aircraft hangar, its doors shut, and hanging on sagging hinges with windows boarded up, reflected the neglect of the entire operation. A small building with a sign over the door indicated the office. To his right, Slat saw a gray metal building huddled beneath a row of wind twisted pines. The paint seemed fairly new, and it looked big enough to house a small plane or helicopter. Slat climbed back into the Land Rover and headed toward the office, pulled up outside, and honked the horn. It was no wonder the mechanic was glad to have the American helicopter to care for. There was not much of anything else around that looked as if it might earn revenue for the airstrip. The office door creaked open, and the mechanic stood in the entrance. He didn't look pleased to have a visitor.

"Decided I'd come up and take a look at the helicopter we talked about." Slat slid out of the Rover, slammed the door, and sauntered toward the office; it was obvious the man was not expecting to see him.

"I just finished washing it down," the mechanic said. "It's in there." He pointed in the direction of the metal shed beneath the pines. "The Yank said to keep it washed and clean and always ready to fly. So that's what I do."

Slat stopped at the office door and looked in the direction of the shed. "You said you quit working at four-thirty. Do we have time?"

The mechanic made no move to ask the constable inside. "I suppose so," he grunted begrudgingly. "Come on."

Together they walked across the grass toward the stand of trees as Slat said, "Must be a lonely existence up here."

"I don't like crowds. This job suits me fine."

Slat noticed a large padlock on the door, and the mechanic pulled a bunch of keys from his oil-stained overalls, selected a key, and opened the padlock. The door swung open on well-oiled hinges, and they went inside.

Slat was impressed at the cleanliness. The interior walls were painted white, not a spot of oil on the polished concrete floor. Along one wall a workbench, tools snapped into position in a well-organized array. The mechanic flicked on a couple of wall switches and a bank of overhead lights shone down onto the small helicopter in the center of the building. The mechanic nodded. "There she is, ready to go whenever needed."

Slat walked closer. He knew very little about helicopters other than they were an ideal aircraft to get in and out of tight places. The logo on the side looked colorful, almost theatrical in the bright lights. He read the words aloud. "'The foxes have holes and the birds of the air have nests.' Nice logo."

"Green Peace do-gooders if you ask me. I ha no time for 'em. Seen enough have ye?"

Slat didn't answer as he slowly walked around the inside of the building. Then, stopping, turned to the mechanic who was still standing beside the helicopter.

"I was wondering if you'd seen anyone around the airfield in the last few hours."

"There's been neither hair nor hide around here for days. Why?"

Slat walked back toward the mechanic, watching him carefully for any sign of nervousness. "You hear about the men who came in on the morning ferry and made a run for it after the authorities made an attempt to stop them for questioning?"

"I heard nothing aboot it. I didna go to lunch at the pub. I was here all day."

"I see. Well, if you do see any strangers lurking around, give me a call."

They crossed to the door, and the mechanic turned off the overhead lights, signalling the end of the visit. "Aye, I will."

Slat kept up the conversation. "You said you have quarters here at the air strip."

"Aye, I do; a wee room in the back of the office."

"And when the Americans come back for their 'copter, what do you do after they're gone?"

"I'll close up and return to the mainland. The owner only calls me when he needs me."

Slat indicated the old hangar. "What's that used for?"

"Nothing now. The owner was going to use it for storage, but it needed too much work to be worthwhile."

"Mind if I take a look inside? One never knows if the men I'm looking for could have sneaked in when you were busy."

The mechanic was about to answer when Slat's mobile beeped. Reaching into his pocket he removed the phone and snapped it open. "Slat." The wind was getting stronger now, and as

Slat listened, he noticed several of the wooden planks on the old hangar had broken loose over time and now swung in the wind. The place must leak like a sieve in the rain. Not an ideal place to pick as a hideout. "I'll be right back," Slat said softly. "I'm leaving now." He closed his phone and returned it to his jacket pocket. "Have to get back to the station. The search crew is back and they want to go over notes." Slat jerked his thumb toward the hangar. "I'll have the SAS team come up and check the hangar and the other buildings in the morning." He turned and walked back to the Rover, calling back over his shoulder, "Although, if I were on the run I wouldn't pick a wreck of a place like this."

The mechanic didn't answer as he watched constable Slat drive off, but his left eye developed severe, repeated twitches, and he quickly turned his head aside.

Chapter 48

When Ian McLean had been a young schoolboy, he'd visited an aunt, the Mother Superior of a girls' convent in Belfast. His aunt had informed the priest that Ian wanted to be a priest when he grew up. It was the first Ian had heard about such a wish. The priest beamed, and to his aunt's delight, announced he would bestow a special blessing there and then in the convent hallway. The smell of freshly polished parquet floors filled the small lad's lungs. He was told to kneel, and the special blessing was invoked. Evidently the blessing was a dud because Ian went on to join the Irish Republican Army instead. His aunt died happy, long before Ian joined the movement. Now, as he lay in the tall grass at the small airstrip on Tiree, carefully focusing a pair of binoculars and scrutinizing the police Land Rover as it drove away leaving the mechanic standing at the door of the office, he gave a sigh of relief.

He had watched the arrival of Slat and noted his walk around the premises. He had seen the constable wave in the direction of the hangar, answer his phone, then leave. He remained where he was, bedraggled and unmoving in the grass. McLean was far removed from the picture his aunt had once so lovingly dreamed for him in his adulthood.

After their dispersal at the ferryboat, the five men had melted into Tiree, and within minutes of leaving the ship, each one vanished. McLean trained them well, and they knew where to go and went about it with practiced ease.

It was dark when McLean finally made his way to the side door of the hangar. He didn't have to knock as the door opened a few inches, and a voice bade him enter. They were all there, present and correct. None of them had been challenged in any way.

"Everything arrive as promised?" McLean asked. A flickering oil lamp set on an old wooden crate dimly lit the darkness. Long shadows danced on the faces of the assembled men.

"Yes," a man named Shaun answered. "The mechanic has done a fine job."

McLean knew the guns, ammunition, and three rocket launchers had made their journey safely via private planes. Thanks to the open borders of the European Union, flying in and out of one another's landing strips was no problem.

"Where is he?" McLean asked.

"In his quarters," Shaun replied. "He's sticking to his regular routine as you ordered. He also said the constable is contacting the SAS team to check out this hangar."

"Good. We'll be gone long before daylight. Now get the rocket launchers; I want everyone to be able to strip them down and put them back together blindfolded. We'll go over them inch by inch."

Two men went into the darkness of the hangar and returned with three long wooden boxes. McLean watched as the lids were pried from the boxes, revealing Russian made B40 RPGs. Rocket Propelled Grenades, proven around the world in various wars and skirmishes as a reliable, comparatively easy tool of war to use. The RPG was extremely portable and lightweight with a range of 800+ yards, able to hurl a shaped charge with deadly accuracy. McLean knew that, used against the lighthouse, they would be able to hit and destroy the lantern room as his group rushed the cylindrical tower. His plan hinged on the speed of his attack, and the action of the informer inside the building. For a moment, his mind flashed to the unknown person who had betrayed their country for money, and whose life he would have to snuff out. Ironically, both having committed the same treacherous act, one would die while the other lived.

Chapter 49

At 30,000 feet, six men dropped from an unmarked jet and plummeted to 27,000 feet, through the freezing cold air, before deploying their parasails into a military stack formation, then, turning west by north west, began a thirty mile descent toward Flangenan Lighthouse. Their timing was perfect as they silently descended to land on the island as day turned to night.

Koski was unaware of the landings as she finished sending the reply to the latest code exchange. Glancing at the clock, she knew that the meeting, unless it ran overtime, would be breaking for the evening meal. Quickly, she left the radio room, being sure to lock the door behind her. She didn't want Tanner poking around looking for Falk. She headed for the kitchen and thought about

Jock; she'd check on him later.

Koski smelt potatoes and cabbage before she even got to the kitchen. Swale had prepared the dinner. Bubble and Squeak again.

She sliced bread and made herself a cheese sandwich and poured a cup of coffee.

Fifteen minutes later, the rest of them came into the kitchen and a wail of protest arose from Tanner, Courtney, and Jenner. The professor and the commander had no complaints and helped themselves to a heaping plate, along with Swale.

"I don't know how they can eat the stuff," Courtney exclaimed as she rummaged in a cupboard and found a box of eggs. "Scrambled eggs anyone?"

"Fine," Kevin said. "I'll make some toast."

"We could take a little walk afterwards," Courtney said, breaking eggs into a bowl. "Good for the digestion." Kevin grunted as Jenner edged in to look through the cupboard, trying to find anything that would serve him for his dinner. Tanner sat at the table, nursing a mug of coffee, saying nothing.

After eating, Kevin stood in the doorway of the bunker, staring into the darkness.

"Must have been the scrumptious meal you ate."

Kevin turned at the sound of Courtney's voice. "Oh, right."

"Perhaps I should have said you looked sexy framed in the doorway, staring off toward the sea. I have a great idea. Let's elope to the other side of the island, hmmm?" Courtney said.

Kevin smiled and turned toward the sound of the ocean. "It would never last."

"We don't have to rush into things. Say tomorrow, after the last meeting?" She moved in closer to Kevin, her eyes on his lips. She leaned in to kiss him, and the Professor squeezed in between them.

"Doctor Clayton, I must talk to you."

"We're busy, Professor," Courtney complained.

Kevin looked at the Professor. "That's okay. What is it?"

Courtney bridled at the Professor's timing and marched away to a calculated distance, waiting to get back to the business at hand.

The Professor whispered, "Mr. Swale would like to see you soon as possible, but not when Tanner is around."

"Sure. Tell him to meet me in my room in five minutes. Tanner is still in the kitchen, fixing himself a meal."

The Professor nodded and moved toward the sleeping quarters.

Courtney strolled back to Kevin. "Get a better offer?"

Kevin slipped his arms around her. "Sure. A warm, peaceful deserted cove you fly into by helicopter. A small hut, champagne chilling in the sea, and you can get to suntan all over for about a month. Wanna?"

"You take your wife there?"

"No wife. I figure you like to sunbathe a lot."

"I like to burn."

"Relax for a while. I'll get back soon as I've seen Swale, okay?" They brushed lips. She nodded and headed for the bunker.

At the north end of the island six paratroopers deployed in the darkness to individual positions closer to the lighthouse and dug in.

Swale tapped on Kevin's door.

"It's open. Come in."

"Thanks. I had to talk to you privately."

"What's up?" asked Kevin as he pulled out a chair and pushed it toward Swale.

"Not another murder, I hope?"

"Oh, no. As you might already know, Joe Falk is on special radio room duty for the next twenty-four hours. Security has been heightened since the murders. Agent Koski and I are on double duty, which in itself is no problem. It was decided you should be advised, however, of the possible danger of an attack on this location by persons unknown. The decision is for two reasons. One you are young and physically fit, and, if the need arises, you would be able to assist in the defense of this location."

Kevin sighed and leaned forward.

"How long has Falk been gone?"

Swale attempted to cover his surprise but failed. "What do you mean, Doctor?"

"Give me a break, Swale. If he were here, he'd be telling me, not you. This bullshit excuse about him covering the radio room is really bad. Anyone could sit up there waiting to answer the radio or whatever it is you do."

Swale sighed. He had to tell the truth. "Okay. He left before dawn. We can't trust our communications here at the lighthouse. It's possible we've been tapped; Falk's going to contact authorities from the police station on Tiree."

"You believe there's someone here on the island that's part of a plot to steal the results of our meetings, right?"

"We do. They are here in the lighthouse."

Kevin nodded, looking serious. "Do you have a suspect?"

"I can't answer that."

"Meaning you have no idea."

"Doctor, I have given you more information already than I should have. I'm taking a risk. Let it be enough to say, I would appreciate it if you keep our little talk to yourself. And be ready if I have to call on you in an emergency."

"I'll be ready." Pushing back his chair, Kevin gave a two-finger salute. "Thanks for the warning."

Courtney sat alone in the kitchen, nursing a cup of coffee. She looked up as Kevin entered. "What was that all about?"

He sat opposite her, elbows on the table, hands together, his knuckles forming a resting place for his chin. "Wanted to assure me everything was under control even though Falk has to remain in the radio room and monitor all incoming and outgoing communications."

"He's supposed to be charge, I thought," Courtney said.

"He is. That's why he has to be responsible for all the communications."

Courtney snorted. "Sounds fishy to me. I'll be glad when you guys are all through with the information swap. There's another meeting in ten minutes. Let's hope it makes some progress."

"I'll do all I can. I feel in need of some sun. Scotland in November is no place to linger."

"We both need the sun, Kevin." She slid her hand across the table, and he took it gently, raising her fingertips to his lips.

Jenner and Teesdale came in carrying heavy folders beneath their arms.

Jenner asked, "Ready, Doctor? I think we'll all make progress tonight,"

Courtney grinned. "Progress is our most important product."
Tanner was already in the meeting room when the others entered. He had been very quiet since his outburst with Falk.

"Has anybody seen the commander lately?"

Swale poked his head through the door. "He'll be right along, Mr. Tanner. He's been, err…indisposed."

Tanner glared. "No doubt by that dammed Squeaky Bubble, or whatever the vile concoction is called."

"That's Bubble and Squeak, Mr. Tanner. I don't think that's the problem. I've been eating B&S all my life. It's supposed to be good for you." Tanner said nothing and pushed his papers around and scowled. A minute later the commander entered, looking somewhat white around the gills.

"Are you going to be all right, Commander?" Courtney asked.

"Yes, yes, of course, I'll be fine. Must have been something I ate."

Tanner cut his glance to Swale standing in the doorway. "That will be all, Swale. Close the door."

Swale raised his eyebrows and slowly shut the door behind him.

Chapter 50

Falk drove through the tiny village of Luss as darkness fell across the Lowlands. A few more miles and he would be at the Tarbot. Glancing to his right, he saw the waters of the Loch glinting through the trees, and wished he had the time to explore the wonderful countryside and the fantastic salmon fishing there was to be had. It was not to be. His job was to hunt, not fish. The quarry was wily, a man who had always taken the precaution to assure he was safe at all times. Men like Abu Scha rarely took chances.

Gravel crunched beneath the tires as Falk drove up the hotel driveway toward the front entrance. He could see lights glowing from inside the building as he turned the last bend and pulled up at the bottom of the steps leading to the main entrance.

A doorman appeared. "Good evening, sir. Luggage?"

Falk scooped his case from the floor, handed the keys to a parking attendant, and took his stub. "No, just a carry on." He quickly entered the hotel. On entering, he was immersed in an atmosphere of comfort and ease. Rich wood panelling, thick carpets, glowing brass, and the faint aroma of pipe and cigar smoke.

"Good evening, sir," a cheerful desk clerk said. "Do you have reservations?"

"No. Is that a problem?"

"Not at all, sir. This time of the year, at least until Christmas and Hogmanay, we have plenty of room."

"Hogmanay?" Falk asked.

The clerk grinned. "New Year, sir."

"Of course." Falk signed in, took his key, and headed for the elevator. Scanning the foyer for any sign of a Middle Eastern man, he noticed two beautiful Middle Eastern women sitting together at a table in the bar, facing out into the main entrance. At once, some sense deep within him raised an alarm. They were part of Abu Scha's entourage. Falk could almost feel their eyes following him as he crossed the thick carpet to the wrought iron elevator. He waited as the cage slowly descended to the ground floor. Denying himself the urge to look back, he entered the antique elevator, pushed the third floor button, and stared upward through the iron latticework of the cage as the pulleys and cables smoothly hauled him upward.

Upon entering his room, Falk carried out a drill he always did when checking into a hotel for the first time. There were several points he considered vital to his safety. The windows were the old-style sash opening. Checking them, he discovered they opened and moved with ease, no warped jamb to impair the movement. He moved to the bed. Off came the sheets and bedcover; everything down to the bare mattress. He had learned years ago that some cases of a person falling asleep while smoking in bed had been written off as a death by misadventure—sometimes far from the truth, especially in the world of espionage. Either a transmitter or timer could easily activate an ignition device hidden in the bed. This kind of attack was intricate but foolproof. The victim was given an opiate, either by drink, food, or a barely discernible prick through the skin. The opiate would circulate through the body, having no effect until the person was in bed in a resting and still position for fifteen minutes. At that time, the drug would then settle in the lower brain cortex and, in effect, black the person out. The ignition device would be activated either by transmitter or a pre-set timer and the bed would be alight in seconds. By the time the fire was discovered, the occupant was ash and the device was ash mixed with ashes.

Falk, satisfied he was not destined to die in bed, checked the door and found it sturdy and secure with two locks and a chain. Nonetheless, he slid one of the chairs over to the door and eased the back beneath the door knob to be sure it fit snug, making one of the oldest and yet perfect defenses against a silent entry. Confident that his Scottish hotel room would give him security, he decided to go down to the bar, get a sandwich and a drink and wait to see what developed. He needed to observe the Syrian in an atmosphere of relaxation, and also to see if he could pick out the man Stewart had commanded him to remove from the solar equation.

Falk ordered a ham sandwich and a Glencoe. No ice.

The wall clock behind the bar, half hidden by the head of a

huge Highland Stag, showed a few minutes before seven in the evening.

Chapter 51

Abu Scha was fully aware that he had been followed for the last two days since returning from the meeting with McLean in Glasgow. He also knew that no attempt to arrest him would take place. He was marked to die and his body to vanish. He understood perfectly. He had used the same tactics for years. He had surrounded himself with the best bodyguards that Syria could supply. He had no intention of being killed by some simpleminded Westerner and having his body dumped into a bottomless Scottish loch.

Abu Scha stared at the person sitting in an easy chair facing him. They were seated beside a blazing fire burning in the stone hearth in his suite. "Have we seen this man before?"

"No."

"Then he could be a hotel guest, and nothing else."

"That is possible, but I think not. He matches the description of one of the men McLean phoned to me after he had seen the men waiting for them at the dock at Tiree."

Abu Scha nodded and slowly swirled a glass of brandy, watching the reflections of the flames from the fire dance in the dark gold liquid. "Your intuitions have been right in the past. I want you to bring him here to me."

Falk finished a light meal in the hotel dining room at nine o'clock. The waiter had informed him that many of the guests had gone down to the Loch due to the full moon. The view of Loch Lomond, he boasted, was magnificent. He also assured Falk that the hotel pathway to the Loch was well maintained and lighted.

Falk decided to check it out. There was always the possibility that Abu Scha could be among the onlookers. First he'd return to his room and put on a warm jacket.

The hallway was empty when he left the elevator and started toward his room which was situated about half way down the long carpeted corridor. Deep in thought, Falk wondered how Koski and the others were faring at the lighthouse when around the corner came the two beautiful Middle Eastern women he'd seen in the bar when he'd first arrived, modestly garbed with head scarves. They were laughing and talking and Falk noticed one of them was wearing a knee-length skirt and had a great pair of legs. Before he could wonder why one was wearing a shorter skirt and the other woman a long dress, which was more in style for the time of the evening, Short-Skirt made a kung fu move too fast to comprehend and Falk found himself flat on the floor with the woman sitting on his face. She wore no underwear. The shock of having a gorgeous woman sitting naked on his face was more effective than any karate blow he had been taught to fend off at Quantico. The second woman knelt beside him and slipped a hypodermic needle into his neck.

Getting Falk to Abu Scha's room was no problem for the two women. Supporting him between them as if he'd had too much to drink, they simply walked down the hall to the elevator. No one saw them.

The two ladies of the East, now dressed in matching silken pajamas and head scarves, lounged comfortably on the couch in Abu Scha's suite.

It was an hour later when Falk opened his eyes and stared at the ceiling of Abu Scha's bedroom. He had a dull hangover-type headache, and he gingerly touched a sore spot on the side of his neck. Where was he? Slowly his memory of the occurrence in the hallway came flooding back, and he sat up quickly, causing his head to swim. He told himself it had never happened. It was a dream, some kind of hallucination. Who had ever heard of a woman leaping on a man and bringing him down in such a fashion? He rubbed his head. He hadn't, for one.

"Good evening, Mr. Falk. I hope you are feeling much better."

Turning his head toward the sound of the woman's voice, he saw her framed in the doorway, the red and black pajama suit dramatic against her pale skin. *Was she the one?*

"Mr. Abu Scha would like to speak with you. Take your time." She pointed a slender finger across the room. "There is a bathroom. Perhaps you would like to refresh yourself a little?"

"Who are you? Where am I? How do you know my name?"

"Too many questions, Mr. Falk. As soon as you are ready, please join us in the sitting room." She smiled and slowly closed the door, leaving Falk even more dazed than when he'd awakened.

Fumbling through his pockets, he found he had been cleaned out: wallet and weapon gone. He was supposed to look out for the person sent to get Abu Scha, and now he was Scha's prisoner. Fully aware of the hardball games played by the Middle Easterner, he knew unless he got out of the situation fast, he would be killed and never found. Getting to his feet, he groggily crossed to the bathroom, turned on the cold tap, and splashed the icy water on his face.

Chapter 52

Swale relinquished his chair outside the meeting to Koski saying, "After I've completed the signal, I'll be right down. Then you nip off to bed and get some sleep. Falk won't get back for hours."

"I have to check on Jock and take him some hot food. That guy's been living on whisky and baked beans."

"That's his normal diet by the looks of him," Swale replied as he headed up the stairs.

Koski sat in the chair and tilted back against the wall with her Uzi across her lap. Swale was right. It would be at least several hours before Falk returned.

Two murders, a crazy drunken Scotsman, a group of single-minded scientists being coached by three bureaucrats in a lonely lighthouse, added up to the worst assignment she had ever been on. What had Stewart been thinking to send them on this mission? Had Falk been correct when he thought there was a possibility they'd been sent to discover something *Cerberus* didn't know? *Cerberus* was a well-informed agency, and its information had to come from somewhere. Suddenly the door to the meeting room was flung open, and the commander came rushing out holding his stomach. He continued his headlong dash out the front door without a word. Koski turned and looked into the room. Tanner waved his hand in an "It's okay" sign. She closed the door wondering if the meeting would continue without him, or if this was something else that would slow down the laggard schedule.

Ten minutes later, Swale came back down from the radio room, and Koski informed him about the sudden exit of the commander.

"I'll go and check on him. It must have been something he ate. Be right back."

Swale found the commander in his room with the bedclothes pulled up under his chin. "Don't bother me now, Swale, I feel awful. Go away. Let me try and get some sleep." Swale backed out of the room and softly closed the door.

"He's in bed," Swale said to Koski. "He told me to buzz off."

"It's a wonder Tanner didn't call a break in the meeting." She paused. "Maybe not. They're getting too far behind with everything. It'll soon be time to return to the mainland."

"I doubt if they'll quit before they get everything sorted out. They're past the point of no return now. They'll complete everything, even if they have to go into overtime."

"Fine with me." Koski sighed, checking her watch. "I wish they'd get a move on. I want to check on Jock before I get some sleep."

"Stay where you are. I'll check him out. He's most likely passed out by this time of the night. Be sure to cover the trap door after I go down. I should have made a peep hole so I could check when the coast is clear before I come back up."

Koski suggested, "It might be better if you went out through the pipe and came back across the island. If anyone asks for you, I'll say you're patrolling the perimeter."

"Sounds good. I'll do that." Swale and Koski quickly went to the trap door and in seconds he was gone. She pulled the carpet back into position and returned to her chair. She could hear a steady murmur of voices from inside the meeting room. Things seemed to be moving along fine without the commander.

Chapter 53

As soon as the trap door was closed, Swale knew Jock was gone. The room smelled strongly of whisky, and only one of the oil lamps burned, although the flame flickered, indicating the fuel was getting low. Swale carried a flashlight with him at all times since the murder of Zas in the lantern room. Now, sweeping the beam around the squalid room, he assured himself that Jock was indeed gone, and the door to the pipe was still partly open. Then he noticed a splash of blood on the table and on the floor beside the chair. Lowering the beam, he traced several more drops across the room to the open door. He knew at once that Jock had been taken by force. Whoever had entered the room evidently had the drop on the old Scot. Other than the blood spots, there was nothing to show in the way of a fight. Crossing the room, he turned off the lamp. He had no idea how long Jock had been gone or who possibly could have taken him. Later, when he knew more, he could return and bang on the trap door to get Koski's attention. He decided to follow the trail. They couldn't keep getting picked off one by one.

Quickly, he checked his weapon, eased off the safety, and slipped the flashlight through his belt. Stopping beside the door, he took off his shoes, tied the laces together, and then hung them around his neck. No one was going to hear him walking through the pipe. Within seconds his socks were soaked, and before he'd crept a hundred feet, his legs were cold up to his knees. He stopped, straining to hear the slightest sound. But except for the occasional splash of dripping water, all was silent. Falk had mentioned the distance between the entrance of the pipe to Jock's door, and he knew he must be getting close. He had hoped to see a starlit sky, but at the moment he was still too deep inside the conduit. Step by step, he moved forward. He touched the walls now and then, more for comfort than direction. He remembered Falk had told him the pipe jutted out over the sea. Depending on the tide, it was either close to the surface or fifteen feet or so above the waves.

The sharp tang of salt-laden air suddenly swirled around him.

He was close to the entrance. It was still pitch black as he went step by step, using his feet as sensors, seeking out each inch of footing. Faintly, he could hear the wind gusting around the mouth of the pipe. He wanted to snap on his flashlight but knew he must proceed in the darkness. He had no idea what was out there. He felt his toes reach the rim of the pipe, and he stopped stock still, then lowered to his knees. His eyes had accustomed themselves to the darkness during the long, slow journey to the sea and now he could see the waves foam white as they smashed onto the rocks below. Taking a deep breath, he estimated the water to be about ten feet below him. Falk had climbed up the rocks to enter; now he had to clamber down in almost total blackness.

Swale put on his shoes; he knew the danger of cutting his feet on the rocks. Facing into the pipe, he slid out of the tube, his feet searching for a foothold until he established a firm section of rock and gingerly lowered his weight onto the ledge, at the same time keeping a firm grip on the lip of the duct. The ledge held. Then slowly, a few inches at a time, he made it to the beach and attempted to find his bearings. He could have saved his time because a solid beam of light, almost white in its intensity, hit him full in the face.

"Stay where you are and don't move." The glare of the light removed what little night vision he'd had, and also informed him he was up against someone who knew his business. The light shining in his face was industrial strength, not something you buy at the local hardware store.

The voice had a definite American accent. "Hands on the top of your head. Slowly." Without warning, an arm went around his neck, holding him in a terrible grip. A second person had somehow made it across the rocks in total silence.

This time the voice was in his ear and very English. "Make a wrong move, chum, and I'll break your bloody neck."

Chapter 54

"Well, Mr. Falk, please sit down." Abu Scha indicated an armchair facing his and watched as Falk, with his hands cuffed behind his back, lowered into the comfortable wingback. "I'm very interested in your profession. I too have enjoyed bird watching, although not on a professional scale." Falk remained silent. "You must have very little to do as an American federal agent to take up bird watching, Mr. Falk. Of course, we both know that is not what you really are."

Abu Scha beckoned to one of the two women, and she immediately came to his side. She bent forward to allow the man to whisper in her ear. She straightened, nodded, and left the room. The second woman remained. "We both know the importance of the meetings going on at the lighthouse and what it will mean when the three scientists exchange their ideas and formulate an agreement to work as a single team. My reason for being here is to see that the formula and final plans do not remain the sole right of the three countries involved."

Falk could no longer stay silent. "What do you want from me?"

"Nothing; but then perhaps there is one thing." He leaned forward, the light from the table lamp next to him reflecting in his jet-black eyes. "I want to be sure you die the same as the rest of your people at the lighthouse. There must be no one left to tell what happened."

"If you know who I am, then you must also be aware there are others involved, not just myself, in seeing the meeting is not in interfered with."

"Yet, you have suffered the loss of two security agents already. I would consider that interference, Mr. Falk."

"It was, and the security has been increased."

Abu Scha leaned back in his chair. "You started out with four security personal, including yourself. Two are dead, and you are here, leaving only two trained security agents at the lighthouse." Abu Scha smiled. "I'm counting the replacement that was also killed."

Falk churned inwardly at the man's smooth confidence. It irritated the hell out of him.

"I hardly consider you being here, and only two people left to take care of the scientists, an increase in security." As if an afterthought, Abu Scha waved his hand nonchalantly. "I understand one of the agents is a woman."

Falk knew he'd been correct in surmising there was a traitor in the lighthouse. There was no other way that Abu Scha could know such details. "I would advise your informer in the lighthouse to forget whatever it is you have planned as I can assure you whatever it is will not work out," Falk said. "Do you believe a meeting of such importance would not have contingency back up arrangements?"

"Nice try, Mr. Falk. We will get what we came for and nothing you have in place will stop us." Abu Scha looked up as the woman came back into the room. "All set?" he asked.

"Yes. Mr. Falk's car is waiting. I gave the ticket to the valet parking attendant. There were no questions."

"Very good. You have everything packed?"

"Yes."

Falk cursed softly. They'd taken the parking stub when they'd cleaned him out. Now he was going for a ride in his own car.

"Hope you don't mind. My car is parked in the hotel garage, and I think it would be safer to leave it there. There is a good possibility it is being watched, and I don't want to find out the hard way. It is a small price to pay to assure I make it back to Aleppo without any official interruptions. As for your rental car, you will have no use for it after I arrive at my next destination. So, sit back and enjoy the ride."

Chapter 55

Koski heard the scraping of chairs in the meeting room and then voices as everyone seemed to be speaking at once. Glancing at her watch, she saw it was after three in the morning. She had to leave the door and make the code exchange at three. Swale had not returned and there was nothing else she could do. Now, with the meeting over, she could search for him. As they filed out of the room, still talking, she saw that there was a different, more cheerful attitude between them. She prayed it meant things were almost wrapped up. Tanner and Courtney were the last out. The commander had never returned after his sudden departure at the start of the meeting. Swale's report on his having gone to bed made her feel a little better. She would ask Professor Teesdale to let her know that he was still safe in bed.

"Koski, don't you ever sleep?" Courtney asked as she stood beside Tanner in the doorway.

"I'm fine. I sleep when you guys are working."

"But not tonight, I see," Tanner intoned looking down at her with tired eyes. "I'm going up to the radio room and demand that Falk get down here. The meeting is as good as over. All we need is the commander's signature and it's all done, finished."

Courtney smiled. "I never thought we'd do it. I was getting worried toward the end. Then the commander got sick and had to go to bed."

"Might have been a blessing," Tanner grunted. "We got more done with him out of the way than with his constant nit-picking."

"I don't think going up to the radio room will do any good, Mr. Tanner. He has his orders," Koski said with venom in her voice.

"We'll see about that." Without another word he turned and went up the stairs.

"Let him go, Koski," Courtney said. "He has to get it out of his system. He'll yell and carry on through the door, that's all."

Koski was about to spit out an answer when she suddenly realized she'd left the key in the door. In her haste to return to her post at the meeting she'd forgotten it completely. "Damn," she said as she pushed past Courtney, who stepped back in alarm. "I have to stop him." Koski went up the stairs two at a time. To her relief, she saw Tanner still at the door and yelling for Falk to let him in. Suddenly, Tanner saw the key and, without a second's hesitation, turned it and pushed the door open, finding the room empty.

He turned as Koski entered, a fierce frown on her face.

"What's going on here? Where is Falk? I thought…"

"Sit down, Mr. Tanner," she ordered. She pointed to one of the chairs. "We have a lot to discuss."

Tanner's face was gray when she'd finished talking. "You mean Falk is on the mainland? There's just you and Swale for security?"

"Yeah, and I don't know where Swale is."

Tanner stared at her in disbelief. He opened and closed his mouth as she continued. Koski looked edgy as she said, "That was the reason Falk wanted to call in the Navy. You countermanded the orders and he had do something. He couldn't use any means of communication from the lighthouse since we're sure we've been bugged."

"When will he be back and what are his orders?"

"All I know is he said he'd be back sometime tomorrow evening." She glanced at her watch. "Make that this evening."

Tanner stared at the radio equipment as if willing it to send out a message for help.

"I can transmit a mayday signal," she said softly.

"No, not yet. I need the commander's signature first."

"Then I think we'd better go down and get it at once."

Tanner nodded and went out of the radio room, followed by Koski who made sure she locked the door and kept the key.

Chapter 56

Swale was relieved of his weapon and flashlight, then roughly pulled over the rocks to the sandy beach where he was thoroughly searched. With his hands lashed behind his back by plastic cuffs, he was tossed against a grassy hillock and ordered to remain silent. He watched as his papers were scrutinized, illuminated by the beam of a flashlight.

"Blimey! This bloke's from MI-6." A muffled conversation followed as Swale strained to hear. Finally, someone squatted beside him. "What are you doing here?"

Swale squirmed to get a rock from the middle of his back. "It's a long story. How long do you have?"

The SAS man leaned in close. "As long as it takes for you to tell me and for me to believe what you say. Start talking."

Swale revealed most of the truth about his mission, leaving

out some salient facts. The man grunted, reached into an inside pocket of his jump suit, and removed a card showing his name, rank, and serial number—stamped and dated by British Second Parachute Regiment and nothing else. "If we were captured, that is the only information we would give to the enemy." He indicated the man beside him. "His card is an American version of this one."

"I understand," Swale said softly.

"And the bit about the regiment isn't always true." Swale caught a flash of white teeth as the man grinned.

"Do you have the old Scotsman as a prisoner?" Swale asked.

"We do. What is he to you?"

The rock still pressed in his back, Swale grunted and said, "Hard to say. I think we spoiled his vacation. Where is he?"

"Out of the way for now," the man replied.

"What are you going to do with me?"

"You stay with us. Our job is to watch the outside of the lighthouse until we're told otherwise."

"I can show you a way in."

"Mr. Swale. We know the way in. And if we needed to, we could go through the front door even if it were locked and bolted. We do as ordered. We wait."

Chapter 57

Tanner thrust a document beneath the commander's nose and brought the poor man to a startled awareness. After some complaining, the commander finally signed, saying he was being forced under duress. No one cared what he said as long as he complied. Once signed, it meant they could call for the Navy to take them off the island. It also meant that each of the three mediators, Tanner, Courtney, and the commander would each get a third of the finished agreement, along with the written details laid down by the scientists showing their piece of the final plan for the Engine of Fire. It was like a jigsaw; each piece had to be interspersed with the other.

Tanner, looking flushed and triumphant, turned to Koski. "Okay, Agent Koski, send the message. Tell the Navy to come and get us."

Koski headed to the radio room, unlocked the door, and went to the transmitter where she flipped the on switch and prepared to make her call. A soon as the switch was activated, there was a puff of smoke and an acrid odor came from the transmitter. Then, every piece of equipment in the room sizzled and arced, adding more smoke to the air. Horrified, she pulled open the drawer that Swale had shown her when he first introduced her to the radio room. The small tin box was still there, but the printed circuit was gone. Someone had installed the PC in the motherboard of the transmitter, knowing it would self-destruct every piece of electrical equipment in the lighthouse and surrounding area. She pulled her cell phone from her pocket and switched it on. Nothing happened. It was exactly as Swale had said; there was no way they could send or receive a message. Glancing at the wall clock, she saw it would be almost an hour and a quarter before the Navy transmitted their code exchange. How long would it be before they realized there were problems and send help? Koski remained in the chair; she was the last remaining security agent. Falk would not be back for hours. It was all up to her, and she jumped to her feet, ready for the challenge. She had to discover who had sabotaged the transmitter.

Chapter 58

McLean had spoken briefly with Abu Scha by cell phone

before he had left the hotel with Falk. Now, as the first streaks of dawn clawed through the wintry sky, he called his men together. It was time to move out. McLean's team was ready; they moved quickly and silently out of the hangar, carrying their packed equipment to an old, but superbly maintained three-ton army truck. The engine kicked over at once when the driver turned the key. McLean nodded in satisfaction. This was the way he intended the operation to proceed—efficiently.

The mechanic, in his small room at the back of the office, heard the truck's engine and was immediately aware the team was leaving. He, too, would abandon the airstrip, but he had one more important job to carry out. When it was completed, he would close the five-barred gate, drive to the dock, and take the ferry back to Oban.

The truck was loaded with two deflated Zodiacs, an air pump generating system, ammunition, hard tack rations, water, and a two-way radio communications system that would enable McLean to keep in contact with Abu Scha. The truck drove three miles from the airstrip to a point on a lonely cliff-side road forty feet above the sea. Quickly, the Zodiacs were inflated and lowered down the cliff face to a small, sandy cove. The team followed, rappelling down and quickly loading the boats with ammunition, guns, and supplies. It was still dark enough to make it almost impossible for anyone to see them push off the beach, ride the waves out to the open sea, and head for the Flangenan lighthouse.

Chapter 59

Falk sat between the two demure-looking Middle Eastern women in the back seat as Abu Scha drove through the pre-dawn darkness. Falk could see the dash clock glowing green, showing five fifty-five in the morning. They had been driving for over three hours. Falk wondered if the person Stewart had sent to get Abu Scha would be aware of what had happened.

Falk caught sight of a highway sign indicating they were travelling on the A82, the main route between Glasgow and Fort William, a town in the southern Highlands.

Abu Scha glanced at Falk in the rear view mirror. "Enjoying the ride, Mr. Falk? We're nearing the small town of Glencoe. Historic place, I understand—the infamous battleground of the McDonald and Campbell clans. I study history because it fascinates, and at the same time, teaches me so much about humankind. The Scots were barbaric in their fighting prowess, yet at the same time they were poets. Take the name Glencoe, which, translated means: 'The Vale of Weeping'."

The clock showed it was now almost seven.

Glencoe, in the early morning hours, drenched by rain at all seasons of the year, made the countryside look dramatic and menacing.

"Yeah, thanks for the guided tour, but how about a little relief from these damn handcuffs?"

Abu Scha chuckled. "Don't worry, Mr. Falk, we don't have too far to go now. You'll soon be out of your misery."

One of the women said something in Arabic, and Abu Scha nodded but said nothing. They drove in silence for fifteen minutes and then turned off the highway on to a small, narrow road surrounded by trees and hedges. The sides of the car brushed against the thick foliage in places as it followed the bends and curves, all the time climbing higher into the hills. Abu Scha stopped the car at a branch in the narrow lane; it was no longer wide enough to be called a road. An old wooden signpost leaned drunkenly at the Y, one finger pointing to Ballachulish, the words almost obliterated from years of rain and wind howling down from the highlands. The other finger pointed westward indicating two miles to Clatch. Abu Scha swung the car in the direction of Clatch and drove for less than a mile until they arrived at a wooden gate and what had once been a driveway, now an overgrown slash of gravel through the dense green grass. The woman on the nearside of the car opened her door, climbed out, and went to the gate. She started tugging hard to get it open, pulling and lifting to allow clearance over the uneven ground. Abu Scha drove through and waited until the gate was shut behind him before continuing up the driveway. Falk had felt the rush of icy cold air when the woman opened the door. He knew if the temperature fell another couple of degrees it would begin to snow.

"Once we arrive at the house, I'll see you get the cuffs off, Mr. Falk. You will not be going anywhere. We could all use something warm to drink after our journey. I want to be sure you are well and in good health right up to the moment of my departure. You see, you are my insurance, my hostage. I have no doubt we have been, or will be, followed. I never underestimate my enemy. If you were foolish enough to try an attempt to escape from this place, you would discover you had made a very serious mistake. If you step off this path in either direction, you'll find it is all swampland. You would sink in a matter of minutes. A dreadful way to die, I understand."

Falk digested the threat. The area outside seemed to fit the description. Marshland, bog, swamp, quicksand, call it whatever he wanted, Falk was well aware that there were certain areas in the southern Highlands that, for hundreds of years, had swallowed man and beast, leaving no trace. He had no intention of becoming a victim by running headlong into such an unfriendly environment.

Finally, Abu Scha pulled up in front of a rundown farm house, one window boarded up, and the front porch sagged alarmingly. One of the three wooden steps leading up to the entrance had no cross member. As Abu Scha switched off the engine, the front door was pulled open, and a bearded face stared through the opening. On seeing the Syrian man, the door was opened wider and a shaggy, bent-shouldered man emerged. He looked to be in his eighties and dressed in what had once been a blue serge suit, twenty-five years earlier. A woollen muffler was wrapped around his neck and stuffed down the front of his pants, covering the fact he wore no shirt. On his feet were a pair of muddy green Wellington boots with his pant legs stuffed into them. Topping his natty attire, he sported a filthy, stained Glengarry cap, tilted at a rakish angle with one of the usual two black ribbon streamers missing. Stringy reddish-gray hair shot out at all angles from beneath the cap.

Abu Scha opened his door and called up to the Scot. "Good morning, everything under control?"

"Aye, it is," the man replied, giving the evil eye to Falk.

"We have to take care of him," Abu Scha announced. "He's my insurance policy until the plane arrives."

With the two women on either side, Falk was escorted into the farmhouse behind Abu Scha and the suited Scot.

Inside, the farmhouse was in better shape than it looked from outside. Falk decided it was being used for a safe house and remembered Swale mentioning the Irish Republican Army had discovered it was far easier to move around in Scotland without being hounded by British troops than it was at home. The farmhouse was likely a favorite of the IRA. Abu Scha was probably one of many who used the lonely place.

Falk quickly assessed the hideout. To a casual passer by the place would look deserted, if they even noticed the place from the lane. He saw a portable oil heater in the hallway and another in the kitchen; heat without smoke from a fireplace. Three table lamps in the room were oil fired. No electrical appliances equalled no power to the house, therefore, no utility company to answer to. He had no doubt the same went for natural gas. As far as outside communication, they would use cell phones.

One of the women walked Falk to a chair at a kitchen table and indicated he sit. The other woman, on Abu Scha's orders, went out to bring the car around to the back of the house. The suited Scot went over to a butane-powered stove and removed a brown teapot, brought it over to the table, and set it down. He jerked his thumb toward a cupboard. "Cups are in there." The women crossed the room and collected five cups and placed them on the table as the Scot removed a bottle of milk and a bag of sugar from another cupboard. Abu Scha sat silently at the table, watching the procedure. "As you can see, we are self-sufficient here." He smiled sardonically. "All the comforts of home." A cup of steaming tea was slid in front of Falk, who, with his hands still cuffed behind his back, was unable to reach it.

Abu Scha said a few words and Falk's right hand was released from the handcuffs, and the empty cuff snapped to the back of the chair.

"You said I'd be released from these when we arrived," Falk complained.

"And you will, however, for now, just one hand. Enjoy your tea."

It was obvious Falk would not be given a chance to make any

moves detrimental to Abu Scha's departure. Falk sipped his tea as the Arabs engaged in a conversation in their native tongue. The Scot had left the room, leaving the four of them at the kitchen table. Where would Abu Scha's plane be able to land if what he had said about marshland and swamps were true? Was he trying to make him believe that any attempt to escape would be hopeless? With his free hand, Falk slicked back a strand of chestnut hair that had fallen forward as the thoughts ran through his mind.

The back door of the kitchen opened, and a cold blast of air rushed into the room ahead of a huge, brindle-colored mastiff, held at the end of a chain by the Scotsman. The animal lunged toward the group at the table with a lusty growl. The chain brought the dog up short, although it still tugged forward as if wanting to sink its fangs into the closest throat.

"Down ye bloody heathen, get down." The man thrust one of his green rubber boots into the beast's ribs. The dog slowly obeyed, but its eyes glared at the newcomers with obvious hostility. "It'll nay harm ye as long as I have hold of him." Falk silently hoped the man had a good grip. Abu Scha remained calm throughout the entire entrance of man and beast.

"I am sure you will take good care of the animal, but there is no need for concern." He indicated toward one of the women. "She can speak to animals, they understand her." The dog turned its head toward Abu Scha and growled a rumbling, thunder-in-the-distance sound that would make anyone think twice about talking to it.

Nonetheless, the woman pushed back her chair and pointed at the dog and, at the same time, began making strange guttural sounds as she walked toward the animal. At once the dog sat up straight, ears twitching, its eyes staring straight as the sounds, now a tone deeper, undulated like the sound made by wind through a bamboo stem. Reaching forward, she rested her hand on the dog's head. The animal never tried to move as the sounds grew higher in pitch, and Falk was amazed to see the dog's eyes begin to lower until it was sitting motionless, its eyes closed; slowly it sank from a sitting position and lay on its side as if asleep. Kneeling, the woman leaned over and murmured into the dog's left ear, slowly rubbing and stroking its head. It was as if the dog was in a deep sleep. The old man stood with his mouth open, still holding the chain that was now slack.

"Witchcraft! Bloody witchcraft. I've owned that dog for eight years, since it were born, and never have I seen anything like this. He's na dead, is he?"

"No," the woman replied. "He will sleep until I allow him to awaken. And when he does, he and I will be the best of friends."

Falk had never heard of an animal being hypnotized before, yet that is what had happened as far as he could tell. Unless it was some ancient Arabic trick.

"Witchcraft, woman. I dinna care for such things," the Scot growled. "Wake up my dog."

"The dog will remain asleep until after I leave," Abu Scha hissed. "Why did you bring the beast in here in the first place?"

"I was going to feed it."

"Then it can wait until after we leave." As Abu Scha sipped his tea, Falk saw his watch. It was already nine in the morning. Unless Stewart's man could locate him, he was going to have to find a way to escape. The odds, however, didn't look good.

Chapter 60

Koski opened the trap door and quickly climbed up out of the radio room into the lantern room and opened the door to the outside. The acrid smoke from below quickly dissipated and, for a moment, she was tempted to go back down the outside stairs. Deciding against it, she returned down the ladder to the radio room, took a quick look around, and left, locking the door behind her. She would remain silent about the equipment. There were only two people who knew what had occurred; she and the person who had sabotaged the electronics. She knew she would have to be very careful. Whoever it was, intended to leave no clues when they left the lighthouse.

"Agent Koski." She jumped at the sound of her name. She was almost halfway down the stairs when she saw Doctor Jenner standing at the bottom waiting for her. "I have to talk with you." He looked tired, eyes red rimmed as if he'd not slept in days. For a moment, she had the awful feeling that the smell from the smoke was still clinging to her clothing and he would know what had happened.

"Yes, Doctor, what is it?"

"Now that the meeting is over and plans exchanged, I am very concerned about the safety of the documents. As far as I can see, you are the only security agent I can find. What happened to Falk and Swale?"

She stood up straighter and flashed her eyes at him with confidence, knowing she would have to be very careful about her next words.

"Swale is on outside perimeter patrol, and Agent Falk is in the radio room on special assignment. I can assure you there is no need for alarm."

"If I didn't know better, I would have believed you. You're good at your job."

Koski said nothing, her body at attention, although her mind was racing. What did he mean?

Jenner continued. "I went up to the radio room a few minutes ago, and I saw you going up the steps to the lantern room. Agent Falk was not in the room. I also recognize the fumes of an electrical fire when I smell one. What happened?"

It was very clear to Koski it was time to come clean: Tanner knew and perhaps Doctor Jenner should learn the reality of their situation. Was he covering up for his actions, or was he really trying to find out the truth?

Again, Koski didn't flinch as she revealed the facts of their dilemma and the importance of remaining silent, stressing that he not pass the information on to the others.

"I understand the gravity of our danger, but I do not agree with remaining silent. It would be to our benefit to advise everyone where we stand. We should prepare for the worst and hope for the best."

Koski squared her shoulders and faced the truth. He was right. Although she wondered what Falk might do under the same conditions, Falk had abandoned her. As hard as the decisions were, she relished her power to make the right decisions herself.

It was as if Jenner read her mind as he said, "It seems to me we should take a stand here in the lighthouse until the authorities come to collect us. You do realize that under the conditions we're in, and with the accumulated knowledge we have exchanged between us, we would be a priceless prize for whatever country with the brains and ability to move in and take what they want before we can be evacuated off of this godforsaken place."

"Of course, I know. That's why I was assigned here in the first place." Koski flashed back. But privately, her thinking had evolved to the new circumstances. She believed now that everyone would have to be told. There was nothing to lose. The traitor or traitors would remain silent. It would be up to her to watch for the slightest sign that would give him or her away. To Jenner, she decreed, "I'll inform the group of our current condition."

Chapter 61

"What's wrong with Tanner?" Clayton asked as he sat in the kitchen with Courtney. Tanner and the commander were at a second table across the room.

Courtney studied Tanner over the rim of her cup. "Wrong?"

"I thought he'd be over the moon now that the meetings have been resolved. All we have to do now is wait for the Navy to haul us back to the mainland. He seems to be in a worse mood than usual," Clayton complained.

Tanner glanced across toward them, said a few words to the commander, pushed back his chair and headed in their direction.

"Perhaps he's going to tell us," Courtney said.

Before Tanner could say anything, Courtney spoke. "I see the commander is up and around. Feeling better, is he?"

"Improving, not fully recovered, I can assure you." Without waiting for a response, he continued. "Agent Koski is going to brief us on our situation here at the lighthouse. We'll gather in the meeting room in the morning at nine," Tanner said.

Clayton looked at his watch. "Situation? What does that mean?"

"I think it would be better if we let her inform us, Doctor. I have to tell the others. Excuse me," Tanner said.

He strode across the kitchen, said a couple of words to the commander, and left the room.

"Do you know anything about a 'situation,' Courtney?"

Clayton asked.

"I'm no wiser than you. I'll go and find Doctor Jenner. Excuse me. See you in the meeting room in ten minutes."

Kevin Clayton had sat in on many meetings over the years. The last few days at the lighthouse had been among the most difficult. Not only had the actual scientific procedure been harrowing in its technical aspects, but the constant presence of bureaucratic minutiae, combined with the sometimes abrasive relations between the commander and Tanner, plus the murder of two security agents by a yet unknown assassin, had made it a minor miracle the three scientists had completed their task. He had not mentioned the conversation he'd had with Swale to anyone. He had a feeling he was going to hear more from Agent Koski about a situation that had gone from bad to worse.

Chapter 62

Swale and Jock were being kept together in a freshly dug slit trench cunningly camouflaged in the rocky hillsides within sight of the lighthouse. Two SAS men were their guards. Swale watched as one of the soldiers spun the dials on his compact radio communicator. Something was wrong. The radio operator slapped the side of the radio. "Damn thing's not working. It's dead."

The second soldier, studying the lighthouse through a pair of high-powered binoculars, continued his vigil and said, "Check the circuit breaker; those radios never quit."

"First thing I did. It's fine. I'm telling you, we're off the air."

"Here, let me check it. You keep an eye on the lighthouse." The two men quickly swapped positions.

The second soldier got the same results. Swale saw that the man was puzzled. He apparently wasn't used to equipment failure.

"It's the first time I've seen this model go on the fritz. I'll try my personal." The soldier removed a cell-like phone from his pack and spoke rapidly.

Again, it was apparent to Swale, it too was off the air. There could only be one explanation: someone had installed a self-destruct module and taken out the communications in the lighthouse along with any other electronic transmitting-receiving devices within a mile of the lighthouse.

"One of you guys go get the NCO in charge," Swale said softly. "I have some bad news for him."

The soldier shot him a fast look. "Just keep quiet, mate. You might be a big shot MI-6 agent, but until we've done our job, you are about as important as that old guy next to you."

Jock, who seemed to have been asleep, opened one eye and glared at the soldier. "Ye young heathen, ye should respect ye elders. And if this man has something to say, I'd make sure someone hear him oot."

The man with the binoculars looked back over his shoulder.

"I suppose we'd better tell the boss. We can't stay out of communication." He'd no sooner finished talking when, seemingly out of nowhere, a wiry figure slid into the trench. It was the boss; the sergeant in charge of the six-man team.

"We're off the air," he muttered.

"I know. One of us was getting ready to get over to you. What happened?"

"Dunno yet. We'll stay in our positions, watch the lighthouse. If anything happens, I'll give the signal—three blasts on my whistle. We move out and take them."

"If I may say something, Sergeant, I might be able to save you a lot of trouble. If your mission is to look after the occupants of the lighthouse, our friend here used to be the keeper, lived in the place most of his life. We can take you inside with no problem."

"If you mean the pipe, we know about that," the sergeant answered. "Our job is two-fold. If any attack is made on the place, it's our job to take them out and nab at least a couple alive so we can hand them over to the correct authorities for a full debriefing. As long as there is no actual entry into the lighthouse, the occupants will be safe. The Royal Navy will be notified by those inside the lighthouse."

"Not any more, Sergeant. Like your team, there is no communication into or out of the radio room at the lighthouse."

The sergeant's face darkened, and Swale waved his hand.

"Here's what happened."

When Swale finished, the wiry NCO rubbed his chin thoughtfully. "And this old guy knows all about running a lighthouse, right? I mean the old fashioned way."

Again, Jock leaned forward. "Of course I know how to run a light the auld fashioned way. A mon never forgets."

"Good, you might get a chance to prove it, Grandpa."

Jock glared at the Sergeant. "And I hope I get to show ye how."

Chapter 63

McLean's plan worked perfectly. The two Zodiacs were at sea, two miles behind the fishing boats that had sailed from Tiree before dawn. McLean was fully aware the fishing boats would show up on the Navy's radar. The Zodiacs, small and hidden amidst the reflected signals from the fishing fleet, would be invisible. They would remain inside the radar cone, being sure to stay out of any possible sighting by the fishermen who would be too busy preparing their nets and equipment anyway. As the fishing fleet proceeded past Flangenan Island, the Zodiacs would drop back and sail along the south eastern shore and make a landing in a small, sandy cove. The location had been chosen for its remoteness from their objective and, at the same time, affording ideal natural cover that would allow McLean's men to approach from a direction that made it almost impossible for anyone guarding the lighthouse to observe.

Now, as the boats wallowed slowly through the waves, McLean felt the excitement rise within him. The sea was running just under two feet high, an ideal height to lessen the chance of anyone catching sight of them as they made their move toward the island. McLean throttled the outboard down, causing the craft to slow until he could feel the current pulling him closer to the island. He and his team, some of them men who had sailed these waters for years, had studied seasonal charts and tide reports until they could recite facts in their sleep. They knew the importance of making their landing and attack successful. Each man would be rich for the rest of his life.

Fifteen minutes later, McLean increased the throttle a couple of notches, and the boat surged ahead. Swinging his arm high over his head, he pointed to port, giving the signal to the following vessel, which immediately complied by following the graceful arc of the wake ahead of him.

Chapter 64

"Ma dog's been asleep for almost two hours, missus. He's never slept that long during the day before. If he dies..."

"Your animal is in a deep sleep. He will not die," the Middle Eastern woman replied, adjusting her head scarf.

The ancient Scot was stiff with anger as he turned to Abu Scha. "Ma job was to see you safe until you were collected at the agreed spot, not have her," he pointed an accusing finger at the woman, "cast a spell on ma dog."

Abu Scha had no time to waste on the caretaker of the farm. "You're being paid. The dog is fine. Don't bother me with such things." Scha's words didn't seem to calm the man.

"This is Scotland and I dinna care how much you're paying me. We take care of our animals here. We don't eat our dogs."

Scha's face reddened. No one spoke to him this way. He needed the man to get him to the rendezvous point for his flight to Norway. Swallowing his pride, Abu Scha turned to the woman who had put the dog to sleep. "Wake the brute. Show this fool his dog is fine."

Quickly, the woman crossed the room and knelt beside the hound. Pressing behind the animal's left ear, she again made the deep throaty sound and the mastiff's hind left leg twitched rapidly. Then the dog gave a deep sigh, sat up, and shook itself as if it had just come in from a heavy rain shower. The woman straightened, smiled at the Scot, and returned to her chair in the kitchen.

The old man approached the dog, but the animal bared its teeth and growled as if the Scot were a stranger. Then it turned away, went across the room and sat at the woman's feet.

Falk had watched the performance in awe. He had never seen a dog hypnotized before.

"I see you are impressed, Mr. Falk. There are many things in my country that are not widely known in the Western world."

"I'm sure there are, Mr. Abu Scha. Perhaps there are also things here in Scotland that even you are not aware of."

Ignoring Falk's remark, Abu Scha watched the Scotsman who

was glaring across the room at his dog. The man was quivering with charged emotion; it was almost as if he were possessed by some supernatural force. Suddenly, he turned and went out of the house, slamming the door shut behind him. Falk knew that Abu Scha and the Arabic woman had created a dangerous enemy.

Evidently, Abu Scha was of the same opinion as he gave a quick nod to the woman with the dog at her feet. With a glance toward the door, he indicated she should go after the Scot. The mastiff jumped to its feet and followed her as if it had been her friend forever. The kitchen door clattered shut behind them.

For a moment after she left, silence filled the small kitchen. Then the unmistakable roar of a shotgun came from outside, followed almost immediately by a second blast. The remaining woman was on her feet and out the door with startling suddenness. Abu Scha ran to the window and pulled back a sacking-like curtain. What he saw caused him to back away fast and remove a 9mm Sig Sauer from a shoulder holster.

A woman's scream and the braying of the mastiff came together in a cacophony of fear and rage.

Falk knew something had gone very wrong. Abu Scha's face was contorted with fear as he backed across the room, the automatic levelled toward the door. Then the unforgettable, ugly signature of a shotgun being cocked sounded in the frosty air. Abu Scha rushed to the kitchen door and began to move the iron bolt into place, but it was too late. Again, the shotgun roared, and the wooden door splintered apart in a gush of orange flame as Abu Scha was flung back amid a hail of shattering lead shot whose force spun and turned him before he hit the propane stove and slithered in a bloody mass to the floor.

Falk, still attached by one hand to the back of his chair, stared unbelievingly as the blood-spattered Scot stood swaying in the broken entrance. He could see one of the women on the ground beside the dog. Both were dead. The old man turned as if to leave the building, and it was then Falk saw the bone handle of a knife sticking from between his shoulder blades. The Scot never uttered a word as he fell forward, his mission completed. Falk remembered the old man's words when he'd threatened the woman about anyone harming his animal. "If he dies..."

Standing, Falk lifted the chair, and smashed it against the edge of the table until he could free the handcuff, then, with the plastic manacle dangling from his wrist, walked outside and viewed the carnage. The dog-controlling woman, who had gone outside when Abu Scha indicated she check the Scot, was crumpled at the side of the car, shattered by the first blast from the shotgun. Not only had she been killed, but the shot had also wiped out the front end of the car, blowing the tire to shreds. The dog was dead, lying beside the broken body of the talented and beautiful Middle Eastern woman. The second woman was without a face, head scarf still covering her hair, but flat on her back, only a few feet from the old man. In a matter of minutes, four people had been killed by blind rage. No premeditation. Abu Scha had been killed over a dog.

The car was useless. He had to make it on foot to the nearest town, contact Stewart, and tell him what had happened. It was midmorning, and the sky was filling with heavy clouds that foretold of snow.

Returning back into the farmhouse, Falk searched through a small carry-on type bag that Abu Scha had carried with him from the hotel. A large amount of cash in sterling, traveller's checks, three different passports, and a Beretta 3R, a 9mm weapon with a

15-round magazine in place and another spare in the bottom of the bag. Falk hefted the weapon, feeling the balance of its 2.47-pound weight, and stuck it into his jacket pocket along with the spare clip. He remembered the signpost pointing to a town with an odd name. What was it? He knew it was along the road they had turned off to get to the farm. Clatch. That was the name. At least now he knew where he was going. The sign had read two miles, and they drove half a mile before they turned onto the gravel driveway. He could make the walk with no problem.

But first he had to do something with the damned handcuff.

Quickly, he went through a set of drawers in a kitchen sideboard and came across a hefty kitchen knife. Shoving back the sleeve of his jacket, he quickly worked the knife back and forth under the thick plastic and eventually, it gave way. He was free.

He left the scene of carnage without a backward glance. Stewart would send in a clean-up crew and no one would ever be any the wiser.

Chapter 65

Koski, standing at the head of the table in the meeting room, watched the various reactions to her announcement. Jenner was the first to speak.

"You are telling us that we may have to defend ourselves against a possible terrorist attack. Am I correct?"

"Yes, Doctor."

"When the Navy gets no response from the code exchange, they will proceed here at once," Tanner insisted. "When is the next exchange due?"

"One and a half hours from now," Koski replied. "And I advise we prepare to secure the lighthouse in the meantime."

"I agree with Agent Koski," Kevin said. "It's possible we could be attacked at any moment. And by the time the Navy gets organized and realizes something is wrong, they could be too late." He took the warning seriously, remembering what Swale had told him earlier.

Koski stood with her arms braced against the table and looked at the faces around her, wondering which one was the traitor. Would he or she make a false move? Attempt something that would enable Koski to take him out? She knew there would be no mercy shown if and when they were attacked. She had to be ready, no matter what it took to stop further information from leaking out of the lighthouse. Swale had not returned. Falk was not due back for several hours. The thought that she might never see Falk again sent a shiver of fear down her spine, but at the same time reinforced her determination to defend the lighthouse and its occupants at all costs.

"Agent Koski is correct. We must prepare for the worst." The commander snapped back into his usual bombastic form. "Having served with The Royal Navy with years of leadership in various skirmishes around the world, I will be happy to take command until such time as the Navy arrives."

The commander's words were like a red flag to Tanner.

"Who made you the leader? There are others here who have the ability to lead also."

"I would be happy to donate any military advice I could," the professor quavered. "I served with the LDV during the war. The Local Defence Volunteers, you know. We trained once a week and marched and patrolled around the village in case of an invasion. I remember we were going to be issued rifles, but they never did arrive, so we used to drill with broomsticks. We were rather smart actually."

Kevin and Courtney exchanged smiles at the old man's enthusiastic offer.

"Thank you, Professor. I'm sure if the time comes, you will be a most useful member of the team." Teesdale's face lit up with joy at the positive words from Koski.

"I'm sorry, gentlemen, but as the remaining security agent, in a time of an emergency, you will have to take orders from me. Those were the instructions set up by our governments, and I'm afraid that is the way it's going to be," Koski said. She didn't wait for any arguments. "There are one or two things I want you to see. Follow me." She strode from the room and the others followed. She stopped over the spot where the trap door led to the room and pipe exit. "Beneath the carpet here is a small room. From that room, a large pipe extends out to the sea. It is possible to walk through the pipe to the outside without any trouble." She looked hard at her group. "It is also possible that whoever might be attempting to attack the lighthouse is also aware of the conduit. They may decide to use it as a means of entry. It must remain guarded until the threat of invasion has passed." Dropping to her knees, she pulled back the carpet, grasped the recessed handles, and lifted the trap door. They gathered around the hole as she shone her flashlight beam down into the room. Looking up, she pushed back onto her haunches. "The rest of the story is that we discovered a man living in that room and took him into custody."

"My God!" Tanner exploded. "Who was it? Where is he?" Slowly, Koski straightened to a standing position. She knew what she was about to disclose would not go over well. "We will have to await the return of Agent Swale. You see, he was checking on the man prior to his patrol around the island."

"You mean you had an unknown person living down there all the time we were holding our meeting?" The commander's voice was almost an alto as he uttered the words.

"The meeting was at no time in any danger from the man. He's an old Scotsman who had come onto the island before the meetings started. The lighthouse was once his home, and each year he comes back to spend a few days. This time, however, he found it being prepared for the meeting, and he went to ground in that room."

"Why didn't he leave when he saw the preparations going on? Surely he knew he would be in trouble if caught."

"He had been dropped off by a friend, a fisherman who left him, saying he would return in a few days. It was a ritual they had been doing for years."

"Did you ever think that the man could have killed Swale and be loose out there waiting to lead whoever it is in through the pipe?" Courtney asked the question, and Koski could detect a different feeling between them. She was no longer on woman-to-woman terms.

"Look, Agent Falk made it quite clear to Mr. Tanner that, in his opinion, the meetings should've been scrubbed and rescheduled at a later date. He was turned down in no uncertain terms." She glared at the group. "It was then he took it upon himself to go to the mainland in the hope of saving this entire operation. Now, as it stands, we may have lost both Falk and Swale due to the stubborn refusal to cancel the meetings. All we can do at this point is work together and get this place into some sort of defensive posture. To start with, we should work in pairs for safety. Commander and Professor Teesdale, Mr. Tanner and Doctor Clayton, Courtney and Doctor Jenner. At least this way you will be united nationally as a team. Remember, there can only be one of us in charge. This is no time for bruised egos. Do I make myself clear?" Koski asked.

A half-hearted murmur was the only reply.

"Look at it his way, folks, it'll be far better to be prepared than to argue about who's going to be in charge and then find ourselves in the middle of an invasion of this place. Here's what I have in mind to do," Koski emphatically stated.

Chapter 66

As they grouped around Koski, Jenner's mind drifted back to an experience he'd had as a small boy in Palestine, to the days of the struggle to create Israel. He had been eight years old.

His mother and father had made the journey with their two children: Rachel, aged three, and himself, aged six at the time of their arrival in Jaffa after a long and arduous trek from the crowded transit camps in Villach, Austria. Upon arrival in the new land, his father, once a noted scientist in Poland, had only been able to find work as a part-time photographer for a small local newspaper. They lived in a small apartment eking out a living with other displaced persons.

Then one day his father was given an assignment to cover the discovery of three British soldiers who were found hanging by the neck in an orange grove on the outskirts of Jaffa. Jenner begged his father to let him accompany him, carry some of the heavy equipment that photographers were burdened with in those days. Finally, his father agreed, justifying doing so by explaining to his wife that it was time the boy learned how difficult life in the new country could be. Upon their arrival at the grove, they found the place already filled with news people, British troops, even Movie Tone News was there to record to the world the horrors of terrorist activities being waged in the small country. Arab against Jew, the British trying to mediate a situation to find a peace that was still being sought sixty-five years later. Jenner's father had told him the soldiers had been captured and hanged and they were there, along with others of the news media, to record the atrocity.

Jenner watched as the press moved in closer to the trees with the men hanging from the branches. It was hot, and the sun was directly overhead as ladders were placed against the trees and three British soldiers climbed up, prepared to cut the ropes and take the bodies down. He complained to his father that it was very hot, and he was feeling sick. His father told him to go back and sit beneath some large trees at the edge of the orange grove and wait there for him. His father would collect him after he'd taken his pictures of the men being lowered to the ground. Jenner had followed his father's orders and sat in the cool shade, watching the activity about one hundred feet away.

The soldiers used knives to cut through the ropes as the media went in closer. The soldier on the right was the first one to sever a rope. What happened next would be forever imprinted on Jenner's mind. A bright orange flash! Then the entire area around the trees erupted in gushes of flame. Chunks of earth and pieces of bodies were flung into the bright blue sky. Stones and clumps of flaming grass fluttered down, and the screams of the injured were mixed with the dreadful odor of burning flesh and gunpowder. An area surrounding the three trees had been booby-trapped, and when the rope was cut, it had set off pre-wired landmines hidden in the earth beneath the feet of the onlookers and officials who had come to show the world the horrors of terrorism.

Jenner's father had died that day. One second he had been trying to earn a living, the next he was vaporized. Jenner had never forgotten or forgiven the Jewish terrorist group that had carried out such an atrocious act against mankind. There had been other Jews among the assembled; it had made no difference. As Jenner grew to manhood and proceeded to become a renowned solar scientist, he carried with him a dreadful feeling of shame of what happened that day so long ago. His family had sought a new life in a new country, and it had taken the life of his father. Jenner had never forgiven Israel. He had become withdrawn unto himself and trusted no one. Now he was being asked to team up with Courtney Spencer from the Mossad and put his trust in an American agent.

A loud complaint from the commander brought him back to the real world.

"I don't consider it wise to lock ourselves inside the lighthouse. If we are attacked, we'll be sitting ducks. I suggest we disperse on the outside, hide among the rocks until the Royal Navy arrives. That way we'll have mobility and be harder to find."

"Commander, if you wish to remain outside, please leave right away. I intend to seal and fortify this building against possible attack," Koski ordered. She checked her watch. "In the next five minutes, the Navy will know we have a problem when they get no response from their code check. But until they actually have a rescue party outside the lighthouse, the main door and all windows will remain closed. We have enough water and a few supplies to last until they arrive." It was still early afternoon, and Jenner knew a look of determination when he saw one; Koski was determined to deliver them into the care of the Royal Navy, no matter what it took.

Chapter 67

"Well, looks as if our cushy duty is over, Bob," a young navy radio operator said as he leaned back in his chair and folded his hands behind his head. "I was getting tired of sailing in circles anyway. Can't wait to get back to Holy Loch. There's a girl..."

"Yeah, I know, and she can't live without you, right? We won't get a soft number like this ever again, I bet. I thought we were going to be out here for four days."

"We were until 'Flag's' message changed everything. The lieutenant said the program has been completed faster than they expected."

"I'm not surprised. How long does it take to prepare for communications in time of war? If they're not in place and ready to go when the war starts, it'll be too late anyway."

"Our tax dollars at work, chum. Hey! We're sailing in a straight line for the first time in days. Holy Loch, here we come."

The message from 'Flag' at the Admiralty, London, to the Royal Navy vessels on watch off the coast of Flangenan had been: *Return to base. Operation Watchful is complete.*

The same message was received by high-ranking officials in London, Tel-Aviv, and Washington, D.C.

Chapter 68

A collective sigh of relief must have been given by those who had waited to hear that their scientist was ready to return safely home. Perhaps the happiest of all was the director of the Renewable Energy Program at the Weitzman Institute of Science in Rehovet, Israel.

Doctor Harry Levin was alone in his office when he received word that Dr. Jenner would soon be on his way home; the Royal Navy had completed its task of guarding the meeting and was streaming back to base in Scotland. Levin had slept very little since

Jenner left Israel for the three-nation meeting. He had been against the conference from the very start and when the Israeli security man, Mordici Bern, had been discovered with his throat cut even before the meeting had started, he had complained to the Prime Minister and accused him of endangering the future of Israel by allowing Dr. Jenner to leave the country.

Within hours, Doctor Levin was visited by two members of the Mossad and sworn to secrecy under the threat of death, and then informed why the government had permitted Dr. Jenner to take part in the three-nation meeting. Jenner had been the most valuable human bait ever to be used by Israel. What he would learn and bring back from the meeting could free Israel forever from a constant bloody fight for its existence. His contribution to the weapon was purposely flawed, but in such a discrete manner it would be months, perhaps years before the other two nations would discover the problem. Israel in the meantime would have gone ahead, perfected the Engine of Fire, and would have the ability to wipe out any city on earth in a matter of seconds. *Shadrach, Meshach, and Abednego fell down bound into the midst of the burning fiery furnace.* Doctor Levin felt a great sadness within him. Had it come to pass that Israel would create such a furnace to kill millions? But what the Mossad had not mentioned was the fact that at that same meeting there was also someone else who intended to do the exact same thing. Israeli intelligence had collected background information on each person present at the meeting, some of it sketchy, some in depth. Levin was privy to none of it.

Chapter 69

But halfway around the world, Tom Stewart now had a copy

of the Mossad dossiers on his desk. He found the reading most enlightening. He had arranged them on his desk top, one beside the other. Using a black felt-tipped pen, he had written the names of each person across the cover of their report.

COMMANDER HAROLD HARRIS. JACK TANNER. COURTNEY SPENCER. DOCTOR KEVIN CLAYTON. PROFESSOR VICTOR TEESDALE. AGENT TIMOTHY SWALE.

Stewart had read the reports on Commander Harris and Jack Tanner. Now he reached for COURTNEY SPENCER, glancing at his watch as he opened to the first page.

Fifty-five minutes later, he closed the dossier, leaned back in his chair, entwined his fingers and made a steeple out of both index fingers, placing them beneath his chin and nodded thoughtfully. *Cerberus* was, as usual, amassing vital information. Stewart had been correct in assigning Falk and Koski to the scientific conference. If all went well, America could collect far more than just two-thirds of a solar enigma that would, without a doubt, be the most important addition to its arsenal of weapons since the conception of the atomic bomb.

America would strike a blow against an organized terrorist group dedicated to wreak havoc on the continental United States.

Leaning forward, he once more opened the COURTNEY SPENCER file, turned to page thirty-two, and reread the second paragraph from the top.

Spencer arrived in Israel at the age of twenty-four, having left her home in Boston after an argument with her parents, both Orthodox Jews. The reason for leaving has never been known, although it could have been due to an argument over a non-Jewish boyfriend she had wanted to marry. Her administrative skills were soon discovered, and she was able to rise quickly in various departments of the Knesset, where she finally became the assistant to the deputy minister for Foreign Affairs. It is believed at that time she became a member of the Mossad's 'Black' section, although as expected, there is no actual evidence or hard copy files to prove or disprove this suggestion, despite the report being created by the internal division of the Mossad.

Tom Stewart was delighted with the information. He would be even more pleased if he could get some feedback on the whereabouts of Falk. There had been no word from the man he'd sent to the Tarbot Hotel at Loch Lomond. He reached for a phone and put a call through on the *Cerberus* satellite to his contact in Oban.

Chapter 70

It started to snow as Falk made his way down the narrow overgrown gravel road toward the lane they had turned off a few hours earlier. He'd checked the outbuildings in the hope of finding some kind of transportation: nothing. He had no doubt that the house was deserted in case the police ever checked the place, so there would be nothing to find.

Already, the top rail of the gate had gathered a half an inch of snow. He pried it open and squeezed through. Glancing back up the driveway, he saw that his footprints were already vanishing beneath the fresh snowfall. Turning up the collar of his jacket, he started walking toward Clatch. Once there, he'd contact a number in Oban to arrange a pickup. Fast.

Falk had been walking twenty minutes when he heard the sound of an engine and looked back over his shoulder. Maybe he could hitch a ride. Then he saw a red tractor, moving about ten miles per hour, its huge tires splaying snow aside as it almost filled the narrow lane. The driver, sitting high above the road, must have seen Falk giving the universally recognized thumb-up hitchhiking sign as he stood looking hopefully at the driver. The snow was falling faster now, and the driver had to squint against swirling flakes. He stopped and called down to Falk. "Where are ye going in this weather, man?"

"Clatch," Falk replied. "Car broke down."

"Climb up and hold on," the driver called. "I canna go fast, but I'm faster than walking. Not far to go now." He engaged the gears and moved off toward Clatch. The roar of the engine removed any chance of conversation or questions, which was fine with Falk. He hoped there was a store in town that sold warm jackets.

Arriving in Clatch, the driver slowed his tractor and stopped. "Here ye go. They have a public phone in the pub." He pointed to a group of buildings, one with a swinging sign proclaiming, "The Bonnie Prince."

Falk climbed down and thanked the man, who waved back and set off in a cloud of snow, soon vanishing from sight.

The warmth hit him as soon as he walked through the door of "The Bonnie Prince." A roaring coal fire filled the grate in the fireplace of the public room. There were two others in the room, seated at a small round table near the fire. Both men were old and stopped talking as Falk entered. They gave him a nod as he walked to the bar. The publican behind the polished redwood bar was drying a glass, which he set aside. "You look like ye could use a dram, sir."

"Make it a double," Falk replied. The barman nodded and quickly had the drink on the bar. Falk took a drink and sighed. "Is there a phone I can use?"

"Over there, just around the corner on the wall." Falk took another sip, started for the phone, then stopped in mid-stride. They'd cleaned him out back at the hotel. Moreover, he'd not taken any of the cash from Scha's tote bag. Stewart needed to account for every penny in his reports and through long habit, Falk knew to never touch contraband money.

The barman asked, "Something wrong, sir?"

Falk walked back to the bar. "Yeah, there is. I don't have any money with me." Both men stared at each other. Then Falk continued. "I wonder if you would make a phone call for me. I'm sure that the person on the other end will be able to vouch for me."

"And who would that be?"

"Someone in the government," Falk replied. The bartender leaned forward and took a hard look at Falk. "Whose government would that be, then?"

"The American government."

"I see. You walk in here after riding into town on the top of tractor, in a snowstorm. Without a coat, hat, or any means of keeping warm, order a double whisky and then tell me the American government is going to pay for it."

"How did you know I came on a tractor?"

The man nodded to the window which had a clear view of the spot where he'd dismounted. "We don't miss much in a small town."

"If I tell you I was robbed by three Middle Easterners, would that help?"

"I doubt it, but go on."

"First, make the call to Oban. Then if you trust my government to pay for my drink, and they come and get me, I'll tell you the entire story."

"Oban is it? Well, I'll do that. But I would na put a long distance call through to Washington."

"Fine, I appreciate it."

The publican reached under the counter and placed a battered black phone on the bar. "Who do I ask for and what's the number?"

Falk gave him the number from memory. "Tell who ever answers that my name is Joe Falk, and I'm working with Tom Stewart."

The publican was satisfied that Falk was good for his drink after a few words with the people in Oban. Falk was assured that a British Coast Guard helicopter was on its way. To those guys a mere snowstorm was no problem. They would land in a space at the edge of town next to the historical marker within twenty minutes.

"Have a drink on the house, Mr. Falk, and you can tell me about the three Arabs who robbed you."

Falk took the drink saying, "Two women and a man actually." Koski had been holding the heavy end of the problem long enough. He took a sip and began his story. Twenty minutes later the thwacking rotor blades of a low flying helicopter thundered overhead, and the publican called to his wife. "Lorna, take over, I'm going to drop off Mr. Falk at the monument."

The Land Rover had him there in three minutes, and the copter lowered amid a flying swirl of snow to settle gently on the turf. A door opened, and a man jumped to the ground, bundled in a green flying suit. He hurried over to them carrying another flying suit over his arm and yelled over the roar of the engines. "Thought you might need this." He handed it to Falk, along with an envelope to the landlord. "Thank you, sir, appreciate your help. This is for payment of one double whisky and the phone call."

Falk shrugged into the suit and turned to the landlord. "Thanks for the hospitality."

"Thanks for the story, it was a pip."

Falk and the man ran to the aircraft, climbed aboard, and lifted off. Falk looked down at the landlord waving. Had he believed the story about being robbed by three Arabs in an Indian restaurant in Glasgow, then being hijacked in his own car and dropped off in the Highlands? He hoped so. He hadn't mentioned the exact house in the bog or the old Scot with the mastiff; Steward would clean up that mess in a hurry, so no local buzz could start and alert the media.

The co-pilot indicated a pair of earphones and pointed to his head. Falk nodded and slipped them on. "Here's the drill, Mr. Falk. We are going to fly you to Tiree and put you down at the airstrip. Constable Slat will meet you." The helicopter dipped and rolled through wind and snow. "We'll be in clear air soon as we near the coast." Falk kept a firm grip as he stared out the window at the swirling mass of snow. Being taken to the airstrip would allow him to fly his copter out to the lighthouse, hopefully, before dark.

Chapter 71

Feverish activity prevailed inside the lighthouse. The main door had been secured shut and the table from the bunker pushed against it. Commander Harris and Tanner had taken the scientific documents and sealed them in a cylindrical metal tube, having agreed that the tube would remain in their charge at all times. Neither trusted the other out of his sight.

Koski had secured the cellar room with Kevin and had made sure the movable section of the wall had been closed. Kevin had suggested they make sure the door could be opened quickly in case they had to use the tunnel as a means of an emergency exit.

The time had come and gone for the code exchange, and by now the Navy should have been alerted to check out the occupants. Tanner was being even more acerbic than usual. "This would never have happened if we'd had the United States Navy on patrol, I can assure you."

"I suppose they would have been as well prepared as they were in Yemen when two Arabs in a rubber boat blew up a US Navy vessel in port." Commander Harris' voice dripped with sarcasm as he stuffed a blanket onto the windowsill of one of the staircase windows, well aware it would soon be dark. Winter, in the north of Scotland had no twilight. He stopped and looked down the stairs at Tanner.

"I asked for weapons to be stored in the lighthouse, and I was assured that there would be no need. Security agents would take care of us. Well, to date we've had two killed that we know of. One returned to the mainland, and one lost with some old Scotsman who sneaked ashore and lived beneath our feet without our knowledge."

Koski interrupted before the two of them got into a yelling match. She had no time for arguments. "Okay, listen up. The Navy should have been here by now. We didn't answer the code exchange and they must come looking." She paused. "Unless they were given a definite order to stand down."

"You said the communications were burnt out," Jenner said.

"They are."

"Someone could have sent a message before they were burnt up," Courtney said as she sat down on the bottom step of the staircase.

"The radio room has been guarded night and day ever since we moved in. No unauthorized person entered," Koski growled.

"I wouldn't be too sure," Teesdale said. "There have been some odd things happening since we began this meeting." The professor glanced at the others as if seeking reassurance of his statement.

"Then, if no one was able to get into the radio room and send a false message, why has the Navy not shown up?" Tanner asked.

"I don't know, Mr. Tanner," Koski replied. "However, I do know that when the code was agreed on, the only communication between the navy and us was the coded exchange. I couldn't simply yell help. It was a little more sophisticated." Glancing out of a window, she saw it was almost dark.

Kevin said, "Somebody must have given the order to return to base."

"That would have had to originate in the Admiralty itself," the commander huffed.

"Suppositions are useless at this point. We proceed with what we know," Koski said with finality. "The Navy isn't coming. We're on our own."

Chapter 72

When the Coast Guard helicopter broke through the clouds, Falk could see they were passing over Oban. The skies were clear, the storm they had flown through was now pushing northeast across the Highlands. Fifteen minutes later, the pilot swung his aircraft into position over the small airstrip and lowered softly down. Falk could see Constable Slat holding on to his helmet amidst the down draft, his black raincoat flapping like the wings of a raven.

In a few moments, standing beside Slat, Falk watched the Coast Guard helicopter lift off. "If it wasn't for those guys, I'd still be in a snow storm telling stories to a pub owner in Clatch."

"Clatch?" Slat looked puzzled.

"It's a long story. Remind me to tell you about it some time. Now, what are you doing here?"

"I had a call at the station from Mr. Tom Stewart. He said to tell you the Navy is on the way back to Holy Loch. A message from 'Flag' at the Admiralty gave the order. At the moment, no one knows who gave the command."

Falk immediately thought of Koski and the others in the lighthouse. Had the Special Forces moved in to protect them?

Constable Slat continued. "I checked the office and the old hangar here at the airstrip. That mechanic has cleared out, but I found this." He handed Falk a paper bag.

Falk opened the bag and removed a sliver of wood about two inches long. Stencilled on the wood were four letters in Cyrillic script. "What is it?"

"I'm not sure. I was searching through an assortment of rubbish in the old hangar, and I kicked an empty box out of my way, and I saw that sticking up in the earthen floor. The SAS team had been through earlier, and I was just double-checking. I'd intended to check the place out when I was up here the other day, talking to your mechanic, but a call came through on my cell and I went back to the office. What do you think it is?"

"At first guess something from a Russian box maybe." Both men stared at each other for a moment. "Damn! Those guys we lost at the ferry. They could have hidden out in the hangar and picked up arms and ammo there. They could be on their way to take out the lighthouse."

Slat looked shocked. "Take out the lighthouse. Why?"

"Never mind. I've got to get over to the island right away." Falk ran toward the hangar that held his copter, Slat puffing along beside him. First the Navy got orders to return to port from an unknown source and then suspected terrorists slip past the SAS at the ferry. It all began to fall into place.

The hangar door was locked with a sturdy padlock. Falk turned to the constable. "Did you see any keys in the office when you were checking it out? I've got to get in right now."

"Not that I recall."

"We'll have to break in. Come on, let's see what we can find." They headed back to the old hangar, and, as the darkness fell, the first large drops of rain pelted them from a sullen sky. Falk knew he faced a dangerous mission when he flew to the island. Now he would have to perform a risky night landing on a rocky and treacherous terrain. He was thankful for the brief daylight reconnaissance he and Koski had performed a few days ago.

Slat had a flashlight switched on as soon as they entered the gloomy hangar. "Over there." He pointed the beam across the interior to a far wall. "I recall seeing some old iron rods. We can pry the padlock off with one of those." They took one each and walked back to the helicopter hangar. Slat was right. The iron bars, used in the hands of Slat, pried and snapped the hasp off the door without any problem.

"First time I've ever had help from the law in breaking and entering, Slat."

"Aye, and no doubt the last." Together they slid the heavy door aside and entered. "Over here." Again, Slat turned on his flashlight and walked to a bank of light switches and began throwing each one on. The bright overhead lamps soon lit the inside of the hangar, and there in the center of the hangar was Falk's helicopter, its orange and yellow radial catching the light as if lit by neon. Falk walked around the aircraft and began a preflight check. He paid special attention to the powerful spotlight slung beneath the nose. He was going to need every lumen of illumination when he made his final approach to Flangenan Island. Satisfied with the outside check, Falk swung open the door and climbed into the pilot's seat. He checked the control panel, then running his hands lightly over the flight controls, he was assured the "feel" was right.

"Okay, Constable, with your help we can wheel this beauty out and get her warmed up." Together, they had the helicopter outside in a matter of minutes.

"What are my chances of going with you out to the lighthouse?" Slat asked. "I might come in handy."

Falk thought for a moment. "I could use someone to stay with the copter after we land. You sure you want to go? It's not going to be a picnic."

Slat's heart jumped. He was going to see action. Perhaps there was still a chance he would have a story to tell his grandchildren one day.

"Aye, I'm sure."

"Then climb in and put on the earphones you'll see hanging beside the seat." As Falk again took his position at the controls and fired up the engine, the blades began their slow rotation, spinning faster by the second until they swished through the air with their own peculiar and somewhat frightening sound. Slat had secured himself in with his seatbelt and was adjusting his headset when Falk's voice crackled through to him. "Read me, okay?"

Slat turned toward Falk and nodded with his thumbs up.

"Reach up on the left side of the earphones. You'll find a microphone. Swing it into position, then we can talk."

"How's that?" Slat asked as he adjusted the microphone.

"Loud and clear. Sit back and try to relax. Here we go."

It was the first time Slat had ever been in a helicopter and at the very first separation of the aircraft from the ground he felt elated. The rush of air and the upward and horizontal movement as they sped across the airstrip with the rain slashing across the Perspex bubble surrounding them was fantastic. Falk gained altitude, bucking the wind gusts from the Atlantic as he set his course for Flangenan.

"Are you armed, Constable Slat?"

"No, sir, against regulations."

"Have you ever been trained in the use of hand weapons?"

"Aye, I served in the army back when we had to do our time. I've done a wee bit of hunting on the moors, and I know enough to keep out of trouble."

"Good. Reach beneath your seat. You'll find a metal box. Slide it out, will you?"

Slate did so. Placing the box on his knees, he opened the lid.

"That's a 9mm Smith and Wesson 669. It has a twelve round capacity. Any problems?" Falk asked.

"No problem."

"Fine. The weapon is cocked and loaded, and the safety is on. Check the location of the safety and remember it. You might have to find it in the dark." Falk touched the weapon he'd taken from Abu Scha. It was in his suit jacket pocket. Quickly, he removed the automatic and placed it in an outside pocket of his flight suit. Then, squinting ahead into the blackness of the rainy night, expertly piloted the small aircraft through the approaching rainstorm. They would be arriving over their destination in a few minutes.

Chapter 73

Swale and Jock were eating shared rations with their captors beneath a plastic ground sheet as the rain, now steady, trickled into the shallow trench they shared with two of the Special Service men. Jock leaned back against the muddy wall. "If I dinna get a real drink soon, I'll die. A mon needs a wee dram every day to stay alive."

Swale smiled. "You had enough to drink in that cellar you were living in to last the rest of your life."

"Aye, if I die tonight, and I dinna intend to."

Swale asked one of the soldiers what the plan was now that their communications were out. Did they sit and wait for back up? If their headquarters tried to make contact and got no results, what happened next? The man explained that when a six-man team is dropped on a target, they are a self-contained unit, expected to take care of their objective and make their own way back to their company. But, in this case, the objective being to protect a lighthouse on a small island, it had been arranged that when the meetings were over and the Navy returned to remove the scientists, the Special Service men would simply show up and return with the Navy. If there were a need to protect the scientists in any action against possible a terrorist attack, they would show up and take care of the problem.

"So we're prisoners until the Navy gets back, right?"

"That's what the Sarge said." The soldier adjusted his night vision binoculars and scanned the lighthouse. He'd said all he was going to.

"Listen," Swale said. The two soldiers had heard it also, the unmistakable sound of a low flying helicopter.

"Two o'clock." One of the soldiers called as a stab of brilliant white light cut through the rain and jerkily moved from side to side. The glare finally settled in a fixed downward shaft of light as the aircraft swung around the outer edge of the island, moving ever nearer to the lighthouse as it lowered closer to the rocky ground. "That crazy bastard is going to try and land in this weather at night." No one spoke as they watched the searchlight beaming down; the helicopter itself could not be seen, obliterated by the swirling rain. Swale heard the metallic rasp of automatic weapons being cocked. "Hold your fire. Wait for the Sarge's whistle. Let the silly bugger land or crash, or whatever happens first."

Then Swale remembered that Falk had said he'd be back around dusk. Could this be him? Suddenly, a figure in the helicopter's bubble appeared silhouetted for a split second against the beam of light. It was the Special Services Sergeant.

"Sergeant, the pilot of that helicopter is the head security agent in charge of the scientists' detail. Agent Joe Falk."

"Says who?"

"He's due back here tonight. He's been on the mainland and he could have news about the communications breakdown."

"If he flies that fucking copter any closer to the lighthouse in this weather and tries to land, he'll be an ex-security agent when he ploughs into the ground."

No one spoke as they watched the helicopter's beam cutting down from the sky, and the roar of the engines as the copter circled lower and lower, seeking a spot that would afford a safe landing.

Chapter 74

Koski and Tanner crowded close together, straining to see out of one of the windows of the lighthouse.

"That's him. That's Joe! He's back," Koski loudly announced to all who heard her.

"He can't land in this weather in the dark. It's madness," Tanner muttered.

Chapter 75

McLean and his men had made their landing before the rain had started. As darkness fell, they had advanced in the direction of the lighthouse. Each man covered his boots with a pair of thick woollen socks to lessen the chance of leather scraping on rock being heard. With the clatter of the helicopter, McLean signalled his men to disperse, and they vanished like a stream of cockroaches under light. McLean was certain the aircraft was looking for them when the searchlight came on. "Stay still. Let him make his passes. We'll wait for it to land. Once on the ground, we'll take it out."

"If he makes a landing in this rain and wind," one of the men said.

"It's not military," McLean replied. "I can tell by the engine sound. It could be the small civilian copter from the air strip."

Together they watched in silence as the aircraft made another attempt at a landing as a gust of wind tossed it perilously close to the lighthouse; the pilot obviously wrestling with the controls to avoid being flung against the cylindrical structure.

Chapter 76

When the wind calmed for a few seconds, Falk made his decision; it had to be now.

The small helicopter dropped toward the ground, as if sliding down its own beam of light, and lit on the wooden pier that jutted out to sea. Falk had made a wise choice. The day he and Zas had come ashore, he had noticed how sturdy and well-constructed the pier had looked. Now, as the copter sat firmly in place, its rotors winding down, Falk gave last minute instructions to Slat. "At the end of the pier you'll find coils of rope. Secure the copter, tie down the front and back, and tie a couple of hitches to the skids. And stay here on the pier." Falk removed his earphones, opened the door, slid out, and quickly ran along the pier and up to the front door of the lighthouse as it opened to him.

Koski flung her arms around his neck, and for a few seconds they remained entwined. "Thank God, you made it," she gasped.

Falk shut the door and slid the bolts across. "You okay?"

"I'm fine. But we have big problems, Joe."

Chapter 77

The man next to McLean whispered, "We can move down there and take that copter out with no problem." Nonetheless, a new thought had entered McLean's devious mind. He checked his watch. Their attack was due to start in fifteen minutes. He'd let the helicopter remain where it was. If, after they had the documents and the helicopter from Abu Scha could not make a landing, or it crashed on landing, he would force the pilot to fly him out. He'd also make sure the informer never left the island.

"Leave it where it is," McLean ordered. "I want three rocket propelled grenades directly on the lighthouse. At least one RPG to blast open the front door. Then we move in."

Chapter 78

As Falk learned what had happened inside the lighthouse, the sergeant of the Special Forces Team turned as one of his scouts silently appeared in the shallow trench. "We've got company, boss. We sighted a group proceeding toward the lighthouse, ten o'clock from this position and 700 yards down slope."

Adjusting his night vision binoculars, the NCO saw a slight movement, but only fleetingly. "They're good. Did you get a count?"

"Not sure. I'd guess four to six."

"Right, you take these two back to the pipe and don't let them out of your sight." The Sergeant indicated Swale and Jock huddled in the trench. "Try and escape and you'll be shot, understand?" Both men nodded dismally, water running off their heads and shoulders.

He snapped orders to the remaining soldier to alert the others and await his signal. Three blasts on his whistle. Then move in on the unknown invaders.

The three explosions of the RPGs smashing against the stone sides of the lighthouse changed the sergeant's plans.

"Bloody hell. Whoever that is down there just blew the fucking door of the lighthouse off its hinges."

Chapter 79

Constable Slat almost fell off the pier when the three RPGs went off. He reacted by ducking automatically against the side of the helicopter. Then the sputtering cough of automatic gunfire and orange-red flashes coming from beyond the lighthouse announced clearly that they were under fire. Still keeping low, Slat opened the co-pilot's door, reached in and retrieved his "Bobby" helmet, then, feeling fully dressed, scuttled along the pier toward the lighthouse with his newly acquired 9mm held at the ready. Anyone seeing him, raincoat flapping in the wind, and holding his helmet with one hand, would have wondered how in the hell a country copper got himself into such a situation. In his own mind, Constable Slat was charging the beaches at Normandy.

Chapter 80

Luckily, when the front door blew apart there was no one in the area to be injured. Falk had everyone up on the second level. He had seen to it that they pulled the meeting room table across the top of the stone staircase and piled chairs and whatever else that would make some sort of barricade. He knew there was a team of SAS men in the area, and the attack would certainly bring them running on the double. All they had to do was keep their heads down and wait.

One occupant of the besieged lighthouse knew it would only be a matter of time before being spirited away from the island. Assignment completed. Years of research by three of the top scientists in the world, and the results of three days seeking the final agreement on how the awesome power of solar energy and High Frequency Active Auroral power could be harnessed, controlled, and used as a boon to mankind. On the other hand, the traitor mused, as had been decided in Syria, it could be harnessed for modern warfare.

Chapter 81

When Tom Stewart learned that the Royal Navy had broken off its patrol and was heading back to base at Holy Loch, he knew Koski and Falk had a serious problem. *Cerberus,* as usual, through discrete and unknown methods, had been fully aware of all facets of the pre-arranged signals between the lighthouse and the Royal navy. Now, as his computer operator gave him the news, Stewart had the operator hook up with the British Admiralty, Flag Signals office, Whitehall, London. Within two minutes, he was assured that yes, a message had been sent, relieving HMS Exeter and Ajax from security patrol in the Outer Hebrides and reordered a return to base. When Stewart's operator asked on whose orders was the message transmitted, he was told to stand by.

Drumming his fingers on his desk in anxious anticipation of an answer he felt he knew already, Stewart was aware that the outcome of the entire operation could well mean everyone involved on the island could be killed, despite the small force of Special Service troops he had arranged to be in place. Abu Scha was dead but his plan was still going into action.

The computer operator at his desk across the room broke Stewart's train of thought.

"Better take a look at this, sir." Stewart snapped on his desktop that was always either on, or in the sleep mode. Now he saw the message from the Admiralty to the cover name being used by *Cerberus* for the Secret meetings.

To: U.S. Department of Naval Logistics. Washington D.C.

GO TO SECURE PHONE RED687. DO NOT USE COMPUTER FOR FURTHER DISCUSSION ON THIS SUBJECT. OUT.

The screen went blank as Stewart picked up his secure phone and tapped in the sixteen digits.

Chapter 82

"Get back into the room, stay away from the windows." Falk's voice carried clearly and everyone quickly obeyed. "There's an allied Special Service team on the island. They'll move in on whoever's out there. Into the room, fast."

Falk bolted the door shut and turned to Koski, keeping his voice low. "What happened to the code exchange? Where's the Navy?" Two windows blew out as a hail of automatic fire from outside raked the walls of the lighthouse.

"Long story, Joe," Koski said. "We're on our own."

Falk scanned the room. Tanner and the commander were standing together, the metal tube between them on the floor. He turned to Koski, about to ask what it was they had between them.

She spoke before he had a chance. "The entire results of the meetings are in that tube and neither of them want it out of their sight." A thunderous explosion rocked the building as another RPG smashed into the thick concrete, narrowly missing entering one of the glassless windows. The sound of automatic gunfire increased as the Special Service team engaged McLean's men.

"If they get a bead on the empty window frame and lob a grenade in here, we'll all be blown to hell." Tanner's words had a hard edge to them, emphasizing their fragile protection.

"Doctor Clayton and Koski secured the cellar. We could get down there and wait it out," Courtney suggested.

"There's a damn big hole where the front door was," the commander rasped. "We could all be killed trying to get down there."

"Wait here," Falk commanded. "I'm going to check it out." He opened the door and was out before anyone could argue. From behind the barricade of furniture, he cautiously peered down onto the lower level. Smoke still layered the air and hung close to the floor. Outside he could see the yellow flashes of flame from bursts of automatic gunfire. Falk had his weapon ready, although it would be of little use against the weaponry he was listening to, when suddenly a black figure spun through the door and flattened itself against an inside wall. Instinctively, Falk was about to fire at the intruder when he recognized the shape of Constable Slat's high crowned helmet.

"Slat, up here." The constable looked up, saw Falk, and gave a wave of recognition. "Stay there, I'm coming down."

Seconds later, he crouched beside Slat who was the first to speak.

"The fire fight has swung away from the lighthouse. There's another group up on the slope." He pointed into the darkness. "I was pinned down, thought the shrapnel and pieces of the lighthouse from that last RPG were going to take me out. I decided I'd better get inside while I could."

"Special Service team," Falk said quickly. They made a HAHO drop several hours ago and have been dug in waiting in case they were needed."

"Somebody was thinking ahead," Slat muttered.

"Now it's time for more thinking. I have a roomful of people up there." Falk pointed up the stairs. "I've got to get them to a place of safety until the Navy arrives."

"When will that be?"

"Soon, I hope." Falk crossed the area and pulled back the carpet to reveal the trap door.

"What's that?"

"That, Constable, is where our Scottish friend, the old man who used to live here, Jock, I believe his name is, was hiding out when I found him. He damn near killed me."

"Aye, well, old Jock was known to have a short temper."

"I'm going to split up the group—three in the cellar and three in the radio room. Keep an eye on the doorway while I sort them out upstairs." Just before he turned to leave, Falk grinned. "Enough adventure for you, Slat?"

"Aye, sure enough. Next time I'll be more careful what I wish for," said the old constable.

Slat edged to the gaping doorway and squinted into the darkness. It had stopped raining and the gunfire was now down to sporadic bursts. Despite the freezing cold, sweat soaked his thick regulation police shirt, and he grinned into the darkness.

Chapter 83

A camouflaged soldier ushered Swale and Jock to the pipe, ordered them into the first few feet and told them to sit with their backs to the cold iron pipe.

"Don't move. You'll live or die by following orders. Understand?" the soldier asked.

Swale and Jock nodded in unison, watching as the soldier faded from the entrance. Neither of them doubted his word.

"If that wee soldier thinks I'm going to sit here on my arse waiting for him, he's wrong," Jock said. "I need a drink and know where to find one."

Without answering, Swale got to his feet. They'd been freed from their restraints for the sake of freedom of movement in case they, too, became part of the fire fight.

"Come on, then." Swale reached down to Jock and pulled him to his feet. Together they moved down the pipe toward the secret door.

Once, when he was a kid, Swale had been playing hide and seek in the cellar of an old fruit market in London. He and his friends loved it down there among the fruit crates and the various smells, even the wetness beneath their feet was the juice from oranges, plums, cherries, currants, red and black grapes, and nectarines. Stacks of crates, some full, others empty, stood in long orderly rows. The only illumination was from 40-watt light bulbs suspended from a low arched ceiling. The brick walls were whitewashed, adding a sense of eeriness to the huge cellar, heightening the excitement the kids felt when they trespassed on the property, for it was, after all, a forbidden playground. Now, as Swale stumbled through the darkness, he recalled his nervous excitement of so long ago. This time, the seekers would not tag him and laugh shrilly with delight. They would kill him.

Chapter 84

"I'll take those plans." Jenner's voice was strong as he indicated the metal tube between Tanner and the commander. "It's obvious neither of you trust the other, so I'll be the guardian." Jenner spoke the words as Falk re-entered the room.

Damn it, Falk thought, *will they never stop arguing? They're worse than kids.* "I'll take it," he snapped. He crossed the room and took the metal tube. "Listen to me. There are two places in the lighthouse that offer the best security." Falk pointed at Tanner and the commander and snapped a crisp order. "Mr. Tanner, Professor Teesdale, and Doctor Clayton, down to the cellar. Commander, you and Doctor Jenner and Ms. Spencer will go with Agent Koski and remain in the radio room."

"You said Special Forces were out there," Courtney flared.

"They are. And all being well, they'll have taken care of whoever was trying to get in for these." Falk tapped the metal tube. "Until I'm positive we're safe, these stay with me. Now, let's move."

Chapter 85

When the withering fire from the hidden Special Service team hit and killed two of McLean's team, he didn't panic. He simply faded into the blackness, carrying two RPGs and his AK47 and moved closer toward the lighthouse as his remaining men returned fire, trying to defend themselves against a cunning adversary that had seemingly appeared from nowhere.

McLean knew the helicopter was due at any time. The storm had passed, and the wind had died down—good signs. He'd have to gamble that whoever was engaging his men in a fire fight didn't decide to shoot his copter down when it made its appearance. It was a chance he had to take. On the other hand, was it?

McLean had been a street fighter since the age of eleven. The monotonous rows of back-to-back brick houses, narrow alleys, and streets of Bogside in Belfast had been his training ground. His mentors were the meanest and hardest of the IRA.

He could now see the gaping hole where the lighthouse door had once been. He would have been inside by now if it hadn't been for the surprise attack. A sense born of harsh experience signalled to him. *Special Service bastards. Fucking SAS!* For a moment, the hatred he had harbored since he was a child welled inside him. Quickly, he forced himself to be calm. If the SAS were on the island, it was no longer a secret that the meeting was a target. They'd walked into an ambush.

McLean knew he had to make a decision. He could make it back to the Zodiac and quietly push out to sea, lose himself amid the waves, and make a landing on an empty shore miles away. Then what? Spend the rest of his life looking over his shoulder with both the Syrians and the SAS after him. He shrugged deeper into his wet coat and leaned against the wall. On the other hand, he could wait and see if the helicopter came for him, get his contact out of the lighthouse, deliver the plans, and collect a million dollars. He decided to wait.

Chapter 86

Stewart hung up the secure phone in disbelief. The report he'd been given fortified the fact that the person in the lighthouse, the informer, had been well briefed. According to the message, Flag Communications in London had gone through the tapes from the recording computers at an ultra-secret location near Jodel Bank's Astro Communications in England, a location that routinely monitored and recorded every word and sound transmitted by satellite, computer e-mails, radio transmissions, and phone conversations worldwide. What had once been but a dream was today an actuality in the British world of electronic eavesdropping. Flag had traced the signal sent to the HMS Ajax and Exeter, verifying it was transmitted from an airstrip on the Island of Tiree.

Unbeknown to Stewart, the mechanic had made the transmission, using secret frequencies and procedures supplied to Abu Scha's terrorist organization by an unknown someone who was privy to the security arrangements at the international meeting in the lighthouse.

Stewart smiled. By involving Falk and Koski in the meeting, he had placed them in the right place at the right time. The last piece of information he had received from London proved without a doubt that the English did indeed have a top secret piece of intelligence gathering hardware, something often spoken of as a far distant possibility in intelligence circles around the world. The British Signal Interceptor, in the twenty-first century, was as important as their wartime wonder of the early forties: radar. Now, *Cerberus* was one step closer to stealing the secret. Whoever had been able to get hold of the frequencies and sell them to Abu Scha could surely be able to obtain other pieces of the puzzle. And that person was in the lighthouse with nowhere to run. Falk must find the unknown informant at all costs, along with the SOLAR/ HAARP agreements.

Chapter 87

Jock squeezed into the cellar and went straight to his supply of Scotch. It was pitch black, and Swale could hear him rattling among the bottles, then the unmistakable squeak of a cork being removed, followed by the steady glug, glug of a tipped bottle held to the lips.

"Light a lamp, man. I can't see a damn thing in here," Swale complained. It was three glugs later before Jock answered.

"Hold your horses. I canna find the matches."

"Didn't have a problem finding the booze though, did you?"

"Ah, here they are." Swale heard the rattle of a match box, followed by the sudden flare as Jock lifted the glass chimney off the oil lamp and touched the match to the wick. A column of black smoke went toward the ceiling and then lessened as the wick was trimmed.

"There ye are, laddie, all the comforts of home." He rummaged in a cardboard box and came up with a can of baked beans. "Would ye join me in a bite to eat?"

Before Swale could answer, they heard the sound of the trap door being opened. Jock reached to where he usually kept his revolver. "Ach. That damned Yank took it with him."

Falk came down the ladder, the document case slung on his

shoulder. When he saw Swale and the Scot, he called up to the others. "Stay back from the entrance with Constable Slat; I'll have to make room down here." Turning to Swale, he said, "What the hell happened to you two?" He started to unscrew the cap on the document tube.

Pointing to Jock, Swale said, "Well, ol' Jock here needed some refreshment, so here we are."

Jock was busy taking the top off the can of beans with an old fashioned can opener.

"The Special Service guys," Falk said, "they could be back any moment." He glanced toward the brick door.

"Things were pretty busy when I last saw them," Swale said. Jock, spooning mouthfuls of beans into his mouth, some of them falling into his beard, didn't seem to miss a word.

"I'm putting three members of the meeting down here for safety." He slid the papers out of the tube and looked around the room. "I need a safe place to stash these," he said softly.

Swale pointed to the filthy, unmade bunk. "Over there. Under the straw mattress on the bunk. I doubt anyone will go near that."

Jock glared, but continued to spoon his beans and swig his whisky.

Falk slid all the papers under the disgustingly dirty paillasse. Swale was right. No one would want to touch the squalid bed.

"We have to find a way to signal for help. The Navy should have been here by now."

Jock took a long swig. "Ye seem to forget where ye are. This is a lighthouse, mon. This is what these places were built for. We can send a light."

Falk and Swale exchanged glances. It made sense.

"I've enough oil stored away to get a good fire started. We

can throw in these two oil burners." The surly Scott jabbed a grimy finger at the table lamps. "Ye get your people down here and we'll go up to the lantern room. I'll show you what an old fashioned lighthouse keeper can do to get those old lenses reflecting."

"Right," Falk replied. "I'll go with Jock. You stay, Swale. Remember, there's still an informer in our midst." Falk glanced once again around the room. "Don't let anyone get near those papers. Okay, Jock, we'll leave one lamp here." He picked up the unlit lamp and shook it. "Needs topping up; where's the oil?"

Jock rummaged in the small adjoining room he'd been hiding in when Falk had first found him, what seemed like a month ago, but was really, just a few days ago. He came out carrying a five gallon drum. "Lead on McDuff; lead on."

Falk, still carrying the now empty tube, went up the ladder, then reached down and hauled the oil drum up after him.

Chapter 88

Tanner, the Professor, and Kevin were crouched against the wall under the watchful eye of Slat. "Okay, Constable, Mr. Swale will take care of them." Falk watched as they descended into the cellar, then replaced the trap door and headed up the stairs, Jock and Slat in tow.

Koski looked up as the door to the radio room opened, and Falk said, "We're going to start a fire in the lantern room. Jock says we can send out a light that will be seen for miles. We need anything that will burn. Tables, chairs; if it'll burn, we want it." Jock, already heading up the last rungs into the lens room, reached back for the oil drum as Falk pushed the container toward him.

"Where did he come from?" Koski asked, upon seeing the old Scot again.

"Swale and Jock made it back. They were in the cellar. I left Swale in charge of Tanner, Doctor Clayton, and the Professor. This gentleman is Constable Slate, the lone constable we talked about a few days ago. Help him collect anything that will burn and get it up to us fast."

Jock had found the body of Zas and took the blanket off of the corpse. "I'm nah a heathen, but we need this to get the grime off the lenses." He ripped the blanket into hand size pieces. "We'll need all hands to get them clean, laddie, tell them below to get up here now."

Within minutes, willing hands were wiping and rubbing away the dirt of ages from the once pristine glass, now cracked, and in places, chipped and brown spotted. "I've polished this lens hundreds of times over the years. I never dreamed I would see ma glass in such bad condition. But it will be grand to see the prisms come back to life, even for a wee short time. And they will."

The lens was mounted in bronze fittings reaching a total size of eight feet in diameter and fifteen feet high. Falk noticed the workmanship for the first time.

"Aye, she's a Fresnal lens from a French furnace in St. Gobain. 1,024 separate prisms. When she was first installed, the five ton light was delicately balanced on heavy bronze rollers, and my father could rotate the lens with his little finger." As Jock spoke and polished, pieces of wood and furniture were being hauled up and placed into the old original oil containers.

Finally, Jock announced the pile as high enough to light. But he ordered them to continue fetching anything that would burn; they had to keep the fire as bright as possible.

"We could get the furniture out of the bunkers," Koski suggested. "There is plenty in the kitchen and the bedrooms."

"Can't take the chance, Koski. Not until we know it's safe to go outside," Falk grunted as he heaved one last piece into place on the pile.

"I'll go and scout around," Slat said.

"Better not. You stay with Koski and keep the fires going. Once I see the fire is under control, I'll take a quick look around down below."

"Pass me the oil." Jock, astride the rim above the oil containers, slid a bottle out of his pocket and took a long swig before carefully replacing his beloved malt back into his pocket.

Unscrewing the cap off the container, Falk passed up the five gallons of oil. "Take it easy up there, old timer. We need you to operate this contraption."

Chapter 89

McLean had caught sight of movement inside the lighthouse. Pressing back against the wall, he watched as a lone figure cautiously approached the broken entrance and peered into the night. The battle was still in progress, although now moving away from the lighthouse as McLean's two remaining men attempted a fighting retreat back to the cove, seeking the safety of their Zodiacs in hope of making an escape. The man McLean watched moved back from the entrance, deeper into the building until McLean could no longer see him. For a moment he toyed with the idea of firing a grenade into the lighthouse, then charging in behind the explosion. His fingers curled in readiness around the trigger of the RPG. Once again, his natural animal cunning took over. Those inside had had time to regroup and make decisions on how to defend the lighthouse. If he entered like a fool, he could die like one within seconds.

His eyes were now accustomed to the darkness, and he could see part way into the structure. There was more movement in there. He could see a clump of darkness moving but remaining inside. What were they doing? Slowly he eased forward, getting closer, one foot at a time, the AK47 slung across his chest in the ready-to-fire position. He had released the safety catch long ago. He was ready. He was almost at the entrance when he lowered himself to the ground and slithered closer using his elbows and toes to move forward. He could hear the murmur of voices and snatches of a conversation. "Constable...take...of them."

Then he heard the clatter of footsteps running up the stairs. To McLean, it sounded as if someone had given orders to take care of someone, then a group had gone back up the stairs. Were they guards, ordered to remain on the lower floor while the others had gone up to reinforce the higher parts of the lighthouse?

Whatever the case was, he had to make a move and enter the place, find the informer, get out, and take the helicopter pilot with him. He rose to his feet and began to enter when he heard loud voices. They were not attempting to keep quiet; he could hear every word now, along with the sounds of moving objects being pushed and lifted. Whatever it was they were doing was being carried out in a fast and organized manner.

McLean slowly moved inside, his senses tuned for the slightest move from the ground floor. Now inside the building, he could see a group of figures moving what appeared to have been a hastily erected barrier. He remained still, silent, and unmoving until the last piece had been moved higher up into the lighthouse. Finally, there was silence, no one moving on the next level. Staying close to the wall, he went up, gradually, every nerve alive and tense. He crossed the first floor landing and preceded up the stairs, his eyes fixed on the green painted door ahead. As he neared, he could again hear voices and the sounds of activity from beyond the door.

Chapter 90

Jock took the oil drum and started to pour the contents over the pile of combustibles. He emptied the container and threw it into the unlit pyre. His eyes were ablaze with the excitement of once again being able to control a light in his beloved lantern room.

"Jock, get on with it. We have to hurry," Falk said.

"Aye, and I will." He climbed down from the rail, reached into his pocket, and removed a box of matches. "Stand away, back against the walls. It'll go off with a roar, and I dinna want any of ye burnt to a crisp."

"No one is going to be burnt, my friend. But unless you toss those matches over here, you will be shot dead."

Jock stood transfixed at the words, then slowly tossed the matches to the commander standing a few feet from him with a 9mm automatic aimed directly at him.

Jock was by no means the only person in the lantern room shocked at what had happened in the last few seconds.

"What the hell is going on, commander?" Falk roared.

"I would like you all to stand against the wall." The commander indicated with the barrel of his weapon which wall. "And Falk, kindly push the document tube toward me. Use your foot and do it slowly."

Falk carried out the order, never taking his eyes off the commander's weapon. "So, you're the informer."

The commander nodded. "Afraid so, old boy. I've waited a long time for this."

He scooped up the document tube with one hand, never taking his eyes off the group against the wall.

"Whatever your plan is, you'll never get away with it, Commander."

"I think I will. The plan is bigger than just me. There are others involved."

McLean, outside of the door, had been able to hear what was going on for the last few minutes, ever since the commander had started to give orders. Now, he slowly turned the doorknob and eased the door ajar. No one noticed. They were still staring in disbelief at the commander.

"I'm to be taken from here to the mainland…"

McLean could not have written a better entrance line. Pushing the door open, he stepped inside the lantern room.

"Luck of the Irish is still with me." He looked at the commander, who, at that moment, was as surprised as anyone in the room. "And I'm the man to take you to the mainland, mister. Tell me the name of the man we're going to be meeting."

"Abu Scha. I didn't hear your helicopter land."

"There's one waiting outside." McLean looked at the others. "Which one of you flew the copter in here before the shooting?"

"He did." The commander pointed at Falk.

"Fine, now I need a hostage to make things safe and sound." He walked slowly around the room, never taking his eyes off of the two women.

"The man who's going to fly the helicopter is an American agent," the commander offered. "That's his partner, next to the tall blonde."

"What does the blonde do?"

"She's one of the government mediators."

McLean moved next to the commander. "Then the American would have more of a vested interest in seeing his partner didn't get hurt." He nodded to Koski. "You're now my official hostage. If he does as he's told, you'll live."

The commander shook the document tube. "I have the documents in here. Let's go." Suddenly his face changed and the smile faded from his pompous face. "Wait." He shook the tube again. Falk knew at once what had happened.

Unscrewing the cap from the container, the commander tipped it upside down and shook vigorously. Thrusting his hand down inside the tube, he desperately searched for the documents. His face reddened as he glared at Falk. "What did you do with them, Falk?"

"I've no idea what you're talking about, Commander."

"Liar! I had everything in here: the plans, the agreement, and every piece of paperwork from the last three days. I risked my life for the damn things."

Falk's voice cut across the room. "And turned traitor to your country in doing so, Commander."

The commander blinked several times. "My country turned on me, Mr. Falk. I dedicated my life to my country and what good did it do? My home was sold to some dark skinned Arab whose only claim to living in my home, in my country, was he had the money to do so. I had to sell Blaydon Hall, an ancestral home that had been in the family for four hundred years. Owned and cared for by men who, when asked, went off to fight wars for England with no questions asked and served King, Queen, and country and, in many cases, died. I had to sell because of exorbitant inheritance taxes that I could not pay from the measly monies I was paid in all the years of my service. No one cared. I was of the generation who would soon die and be forgotten. There are less of us every day, and when we are gone, there will be no one to inform the young people what it was really like to live in a country that made one proud. A country, small as it is, that was once recognized worldwide for fair play, law, and justice. Look at it now. A melting pot of different nationalities, each group distrusting the next. Fights and riots, unrest and unhappiness covered and hidden by bad sounds called music. Add to that, politicians who are hell bent to sell Britain's last vestiges of honor to the EU. Dim witted, dumbed-down, poorly educated kids who have never been taught the importance of history and patriotism, but who can reel off reams of words sung in Rap songs and name every fast food place in their town. Call me a traitor. Perhaps I am. When I deliver the papers, I'll be able to buy back my home and live the last few remaining years of my life as I once remembered English life to be." Taking a deep breath, his voice still quivering from his outburst, he continued. "I'm prepared to kill everyone in this room unless you tell me where the papers are."

Falk knew he meant every word. "I hid them down in the cellar."

McLean motioned with his AK47. "Lead the way, Mr. Agent, and when we get to the bottom of the stairs, stand with your backs to the wall."

It was a dispirited group that filed down from the lens room under the watchful eyes of McLean and the commander. Falk noticed that the sound of gunfire had faded into the distance, and except for an occasional stutter of automatic weapons, all was quiet. Had all of the Special Service team gone after McLean's men? Was it possible that one or two of the men, who had parachuted onto the island to defend the lighthouse, could be close by and appear at any moment to change the tide of events in their favor?

Once on the bottom level, McLean told the commander to go with Falk, keep whoever was down there at the point of his automatic and, without hesitation, shoot anyone who made a wrong move.

"He has Swale, an armed agent down there," the commander said.

"Then advise him, Agent Falk, that if there is any attempt to play hero, there will be two people shot up here. Now move. You have one minute to be back with the papers."

Falk lifted the trap door and called down to Swale, explaining their position as he climbed down into the cellar.

Falk went directly to the bunk and removed the papers, talking quickly to Swale as he did so. "When I go topside, get everyone into the pipe. That guy up there might try anything. Once you hear us take off, get back up the stairs and start the fire. Jock has everything ready. Koski is a hostage to guarantee I do everything he says. When the rescue party arrives, tell them I've flown to the mainland. And I think the location is going to be close to the farm I was taken to by Abu Scha. It's near a small village called Clatch."

"Thirty seconds, Falk." McLean's Irish-Belfast twang grated down to him. "Get back up here or I'll pop one of these folks."

The commander grabbed the documents from Falk as soon as he returned and made a fast count. They were all there. McLean backed toward the entrance with Koski at his side. He'd disarmed her in the lantern room and now held her own weapon against her head. "I don't want any of you back up there lighting fires, so for your own safety, I suggest you get in the cellar." One by one, they obeyed and went down the ladder. The commander replaced the trapdoor and joined McLean.

"Keep these two covered," ordered McLean. "I want to be sure no one goes back up those stairs. Sliding the RPG from his shoulder, he loaded one of the two grenades and waved them outside. As if on a second thought, he calmly lifted the trapdoor, fired the grenade down into the cellar and walked out of the shattered doorway. Twenty feet from the entrance, he reloaded, turned, and aimed the last grenade at the concrete stairway. The grenade hissed across the short distance and slammed into the stairs with a roar. At such a short range, the blast took out the stairs and part of the wall, leaving the second story hanging thirty feet above the floor.

It was still dark as McLean and the commander hustled Falk and Koski down to the pier. The commander, intent on getting away from the island, completely forgot there was an outside ladder curling up to the lantern room. McLean never even knew there was one.

After releasing the tie-downs, Falk sat at the controls, Koski and the commander in the small back seats. In the co-pilot's seat, McLean rammed the document tube between his knees. Falk wound up the engine in preparation for take off. Watching the gauges for correct engine heat, it seemed like forever to Falk as the needle slowly edged up to the needed mark. His eyes flicked across the remaining dials, and he saw he was low on gas. If they ran into a storm or a strong head wind, they would have to make a forced landing.

"Get this thing airborne, Falk; I have a rendezvous to make." McLean's harsh voice came through the earphones. Falk was about to report they were low on fuel and then changed his mind. The less McLean knew, the better.

As the helicopter lifted off the pier, it gathered speed as the nose pushed forward and the peculiar feeling of weightlessness swept over them. Falk watched the island fall away beneath them as he made a turn that would keep the lighthouse from the possible view of McLean seeing the black iron stairway on the outside of the white tower.

Falk glanced at the barrel of the automatic being thrust hard against Koski's side and knew this man would not hesitate to kill her. This caused his mind to re-run the training he and countless other agents had received at Quantico over the years.

Remain calm and make no foolish moves.

The sky was clear and moonlight now shone across the sea like a silver path leading to the mainland. Within minutes they were passing over the cliffs of Tiree. He could see one or two lights glimmering in the village and then they were across the island and over the open sea, heading for the mainland.

"Fly on compass bearing of NNE until we pass over Oban, then east for three minutes," McLean droned. "Then northeast for twelve minutes at an air speed of ninety-seven mph. At the twelve-minute mark, lower to an altitude of three hundred feet and decrease air speed to sixty mph. You will circle until I tell you where to set down."

Falk's hunch was right; he would be over the area near Clatch and the position Abu Scha had been going in search of his connection to Norway. But both McLean and the commander apparently had no idea Abu Scha was going nowhere.

Chapter 91

Everyone in the pipe ducked at the thunderous roar of the

grenade crashing into the cellar. The ground shook and flakes of rust fell from the wet iron interior. Swale had quickly carried out Falk's orders, going from the cellar to the pipe. Kevin, the last person through the brick door, had just made it.

"Everyone okay?" Swale called in the darkness. "Call out your name." All five answered. "We might be unable to get back through the cellar and out the trap door. In fact, there's a good chance there might not be a cellar. I'll check it out. Constable Slat is in charge; stay here until I report back."

The small door from the pipe to the cellar still worked. As he opened it, acrid smoke poured through into the pipe. Swale still had a flashlight in his back pocket, quickly removed it, and snapped it on, the beam cutting through the dust and smoke. He checked the walls; they seemed to be in one piece, except for great chunks that had been ripped by the shrapnel of the grenade. There was a crater in the middle of the stone floor where the grenade had made its initial impact. The wooden table and chairs were gone, along with the bunk bed. Had they remained in the cellar, they would have been blown to pieces. Skirting the crater, Swale discovered the wooden ladder still firmly affixed to the wall. He decided they could make it through and back up to the lens room.

Once everyone was assembled in the cellar, Swale attempted to open the trap door. It wouldn't give an inch. Finally, after the combined efforts of Swale, Jock, and Kevin, the trap door was forced opened enough for them to climb out into the wreckage of the first floor. It would soon be dawn and in the half light, they saw the damage that had been wrought.

"This entire place could fall down! Look at the stairs and wall. It's almost all gone," Courtney exclaimed.

"Let's just hope the wall stays up long enough for us to get to the lantern room and light the fire," Swale urged. "We can use the outside stairs. C'mon."

Clattering up the iron staircase in the pre-dawn darkness, they could see the first faint streaks of light in the east.

Within minutes, they were inside the lantern room.

"If we don't get the fire reflecting off the lenses while it's still dark enough to be noticed, we'll waste our time," Swale muttered. "Light her up, Jock."

The first match went out before landing on the stack. The second landed on the wood but nothing happened. The flame flickered and went out.

Jock cursed in Gaelic, took the box of matches, pulled one match part way out of the box, closed the box so the match jutted from it like a small cannon. Then, scraping that match to flame, waited until he was certain it was burning well and beginning to singe the box, then slowly walked to the waiting pyre and laid the box, now beginning to smoke in the center of the heap and stepped back. WHOOSH! A sheet of flame leapt skyward, the heat causing those standing too close to the lens to move back quickly.

"Bloody hell!" Swale shaded his eyes against the glare and heat. "Somebody should be able to see that in broad daylight."

"Aye, and they will, laddie, ha na fear. The old girl knows how to reflect, I can tell you."

Jock was right. The fire was now growing in strength and the reflectors were gathering every flicker and flame and intensifying the light a thousand times. "A toast to Flangenan Light. She burns bright once again." He took a long swig and passed the bottle to Kevin. "Take a wee dram for luck and pass it round." So, the bottle was passed around as the fire burned bright and heat filled the once cold room at the top of the born-again lighthouse.

Chapter 92

Tanner had refused to drink. He was thinking of his return to the States and another failed mission. Not his fault, but nonetheless he was part of a failed government project. He had worked beside the man who was the cause of his failure. Commander Harris, OBE —that bombastic little limey.

While everyone was celebrating the light, two of the Special Service men, a US Navy Seal and the SAS sergeant, entered the room.

The professor saw them first. "I say, seems the beam of light has done its job. We have company already." He pointed to the two men.

Swale looked at the men and shrugged. "Sorry, we couldn't wait for you."

Chapter 93

McLean's voice was filled with tension. "Lower, Falk. Keep her steady." They were over craggy hills of purple heather, and it was already light enough for Falk to recognize a few landmarks, one of them being the road into Clatch where he'd hitched the ride on the tractor.

Easing the helicopter slightly east and banking as he made a circle of the area below, he caught a glimpse of the old farmhouse and knew he was in the area of swampland and bogs. Not an ideal location to land a plane, or even a helicopter, for that matter.

Again, the voice of McLean crackled over the headset. "Lower, Falk. See where the road comes over the hill, next to that cairn, just east of the small tarn."

Falk knew tarn meant lake and saw it at once. The land

around it looked green and soggy as he lowered toward it. He glanced at the gas gauge; it was flickering close to empty. He only had a few more minutes of fuel left.

At that moment, McLean leaned forward and saw the gas gauge. "Take her up higher, right now. We have to stay airborne as long as possible. Also, we need to lighten our load to conserve fuel." He reached over and placed the barrel of his gun into the commander's ear. "Time for you to leave us, old man."

The commander acted as if he had no intention of losing his chance to regain his birthright or the money promised him. Despite the gun, as Falk pulled the controls back to gain height, the commander swung his arm up, grasped McLean's wrist, and pulled hard. McLean, taken by the audacity of such an act, was off guard for a split second, but that was all that was needed.

Falk kept the nose up and Koski managed a quick, vicious karate chop across the side of McLean's neck, causing him to momentarily blackout. Next, she rammed her elbow into the commander's nose, breaking it; he collapsed, groaning, completely disoriented.

Koski chopped McLean's wrist and his gun fell to the floor. Falk saw his chance and, reaching across, unsnapped the seat belt from McLean, flipped the catch on the side cockpit door, banked sharply to the right, and pushed him out of the aircraft. McLean, still clutching the document tube, never made a sound as he fell.

He turned over three times before smashing face down into the bog at the edge of the tarn, the document tube hugged to his chest. Circling once, Falk saw that the body was already sinking out of sight, the swamp taking another victim to its ghastly depths.

Koski turned away from the ugly sight as the commander rubbed his bloody nose as he started to regain consciousness. Falk retrieved the automatic from the floor and passed it back over his shoulder to Koski, shouting, "If he attempts anything, shoot him."

"Gladly," Koski said with a grim glare.

Turning toward Oban, he radioed his position and asked for help. Out of gas, he had to make an emergency landing as best he could.

Chapter 94

Less than an hour after the last flicker of light had reflected off the lenses, a Royal Navy pinnace tied up at the jetty. They carried the news that Falk and Koski had been able to overcome their attackers and were safe in Oban where everyone would be meeting later that day. The authorities had taken the commander to an undisclosed location; there were no other details at the moment. A full debriefing would be held in Oban.

As they walked toward the jetty, Courtney and Kevin stopped and looked back at the lighthouse. Jock and Swale were talking, standing beside the broken front entrance.

"Jock said he was staying at the lighthouse." Courtney shook her head in disbelief. "I would have thought he'd want to get back home after all this."

"It's his home, Courtney. This is where he wants to be. Swale suggested to me that we get together, talk to the powers that be, and see if we can arrange for him to move back in on a permanent basis. You know, as a way of saying thanks for all his help," Kevin said.

"I'll second that. Now, about that island you mentioned, the one with lots of sun and very little clothing?"

"You mean with the champagne cooling in the sea?"

"That's the place."

They stepped into the pinnace and sat together in the stern.

"It's an ideal place to be in late October, perfect weather."

"Not too many tourists?" Courtney asked.

"None at all. There would be just the two of us, except for a very old couple who look after the place."

"What place is this?"

"Used to belong to a movie actor. I bought the island from him, including the house. Wanna go?"

The Navy boat was ready to move with Swale and Slat the last to scurry on board. Slat waved to Jock as the lines were cast off, and the boat moved slowly away from the jetty.

"October is a long time to wait, Kevin," Courtney said.

"There will be plenty of meetings between now and then. Did you ever know of a three-government pact to ever stop checking up on each other? There'll be meetings in Tel-Aviv, London, and Washington until the project is finished. And at the rate governments move, we can make at least three meetings on the island for ourselves in between the official ones."

Chapter 95

Jenner and the professor were sitting together, deep in conversation. Tanner sat alone, scowling into the distance.

The debriefing dinner was a somber affair. No bagpipes and laughter here. Koski and Falk had been congratulated on their fine work in thwarting the commander's escape.

Swale was recognized for his ability to keep everyone together during the ordeal and also after McLean's attempt to kill them in the cellar.

Questions from Courtney in reference to the outcome with the commander were politely turned aside on the grounds that, due to the gravity of the matter, it was not possible at this time to reveal any details.

"Most likely, they'll put him in the Bloody Tower and shoot him," Swale whispered to Kevin.

Koski heard him, grinned, and rolled her eyes. "Do they still do that?"

"In England they do. Wish we had the same rules," Falk replied.

"I feel sorry for him," Courtney said. "That speech he made about all the years of service to his country and his home being sold out from under him."

Tanner said, "He's dangerous. People like him have to be removed. Bombastic little bastard."

Chapter 96

"Tom Stewart wants to see us. He's making a stopover at the Tahoe-Truckee airport on his way to Sacramento." Falk hung up the phone and leaned back in his swivel chair. Two months had passed since he and Koski had arrived back home after the Scottish assignment.

Koski asked, "Another assignment?"

"He didn't say, just said to meet him at the airport and he'd buy us dinner. Next morning, he has a meeting in Sacramento. He's using a company plane."

Koski crossed the room and sat facing Falk across the desk.

She knew what Falk meant when he said "company plane." Stewart, as usual, was on *Cerberus* business.

"Well, he won't have to be a big spender to buy us dinner at Tahoe-Truckee airport."

Falk laughed. "He told me to make reservations in Truckee."

"Alright, that's more like it."

Chapter 97

Stewart looked around the dining room of well-known restaurant in Truckee. "Certainly looks Western."

"Yep, they serve a great steak. You do eat steak, don't you, Mr. Stewart?" Koski asked.

"Yes, I do. In addition, due to the circumstances and the assignments you have worked on for the company, I think you should call me Tom. Except under certain conditions where protocol is called for."

The waiter came with their drinks, and Stewart waited until he'd left before continuing.

"As usual, you both did an outstanding job on the meetings. Everyone has returned to their own countries and is back at work, despite the loss of the documents. The three scientists have made a recap of their three day meeting. At last word, all was proceeding fine."

Falk asked, "And the commander?"

"Yes, well, his case is a little different." Stewart sipped his drink, set it down, and began. "The Arab gentleman who purchased the commander's old home, Blaydon Hall in Sussex, decided the Hall wasn't what he really wanted and put the place up for sale."

Koski and Falk exchanged glances.

"You might wonder what significance this has to do with our day to day operations at *Cerberus*. Well, for one thing, the fine old home is now part of the *Cerberus* organization. Anyone asking about the new owners will be told an American Pop artist has purchased the estate and that she demands total privacy. A security system par excellence has been mounted to ensure her privacy. Of course, *Cerberus* will have installed its necessary electronic equipment and other special needs, prior to any leak about the Hall changing hands."

"Why does *Cerberus* need a place like that?" Falk asked.

"For one thing, a listening post. After we arranged the 'death' of the commander in his wild dash for freedom, we were able to spirit him away and keep him under wraps. We made a deal. If he connected us with his man in the British Signal Interceptor department, we would pay him what he would have received from Abu Scha. He agreed. Now, bit by bit, we are getting feedback from his man on how to develop our own system that will enable us to also listen in to any communications around the world."

"You mean you paid the commander and let him go free?" Koski said.

"We paid him, yes. Not to worry, we know where he is at all times. We made certain of that. Now, let's enjoy a good meal."

As they drove back to Reno, Koski said, "Joe, you were right when you said there might be more to our assignment at the lighthouse than we thought. Stewart masterminded a way to steal Britain's Signal Inceptor, pay off the commander, and assure that *Cerberus* had a direct line from the secret location in Britain to Blaydon Hall, which is now a listening post and God knows what else for *Cerberus*."

Chapter 98

Early April and the gardens were beginning to come to life. A hint of summer rode a breeze blowing softly over the wide green lawns to the lake. A figure stood alone gazing across the grounds, both hands atop the stone balustrade leading to the wide curving steps that had, over the last three hundred years, lead many a fine gathering of crowned heads and high society into the gardens to participate in parties, fetes, weddings, and celebrations held at Blaydon Hall.

A smile played the corners of his mouth as he softly quoted a Latin motto carved into the stonework of the fireplace in the great room of the hall. "*Good Fortune is the Comrade of Virtue.*" Commander Harris turned and slowly crossed to the French windows of the house and entered his ancestral home.

Lawyers are being murdered by laser-driven arrows. The FBI believes that someone is training Native Americans to take over the US economic system. Joe Falk and Susan Koski are assigned to find the hired killer and The Fox, the real force behind the killings.
GREAT SOUTHWEST BOOK FESTIVAL AWARD
AMAZON KINDLE GENRE BESTSELLER
Now included in THE COMPLETE KOSKI & FALK Volume I.

A 700-year-old prayer book, a key and a faded blueprint came to light and begin a search for Nazi Herman Goering's treasure. In modern day Vienna, American agents Koski and Falk must locate the treasure and the Judas List—a compendium of individuals and organizations that financed WWII, and intend to bring about the Fourth Reich.

PACIFIC RIM BOOK FESTIVAL AWARD
Now included in THE COMPLETE KOSKI & FALK Volume I.

Jamul, an adored American pop singer, dreams of a grand show of Islamic Jihad power, intending to use a biological weapon to eradicate religious leaders at an Easter service at the Hollywood Bowl. Cerberus agents Joe Falk and Susan Koski must stop the next brutal terrorist attack on American soil.

LOS ANGELES BOOK FESTIVAL AWARD
Now included in THE COMPLETE KOSKI & FALK Volume I.

A stolen weapon of mass destruction hidden years ago on board the Queen Mary has remained there undisturbed. Up to now. Agents Falk and Koski are called in to evacuate the ship and somehow locate the bomb. Risking their lives to locate the weapon, they discover that a Girl Scout has strayed from her group during evacuation and is hiding in the ship.

PACIFIC RIM BOOK FESTIVAL AWARD
Now included in THE COMPLETE KOSKI & FALK Volume II.

Koski and Falk come up against what very well may prove to be their most complex and dangerous case yet: The Quantum Death Machine. Each faces mortal peril, while, at the same time, their smoldering relationship begins to heat up.

AMSTERDAM BOOK FESTIVAL AWARD
Now included in THE COMPLETE KOSKI & FALK Volume II.

Published after QUANTUM DEATH, its prequel:

Long-ignored computer genius Kate Keenan has designed a computer program that will put Hollywood and Bollywood out of business. Suddenly everyone wants her…and her program. To stay alive, Kate goes into hiding, barely keeping ahead of a lethal hoard of pursuers with only one thing in mind: *Finding Kate* and possessing or destroying the program.

Now included in THE COMPLETE KOSKI & FALK Volume II.

"We chose the place for its neutrality. The Brits opted for its inaccessibility and the Israelis agreed because of its impregnability," Agent Joseph Falk's voice crackled in the earphones of fellow Agent Susan Koski as she swept her binoculars across the vastness of the dark green sea below to focus on the jagged black rock that comprised the home of Flangenan Lighthouse, a lighthouse clinging tenaciously to the rocky outcroppings three miles west of Tiree Island for over one hundred years. Then she spied a concrete bunker recently added to the west curve of the lighthouse, and yet another built into the east face of the rock cliff...

Now included in THE COMPLETE KOSKI & FALK Volume II.

From a little known address within the Vatican, operation "Eternity" is launched, ultimately redefining the world's intelligence services and their strategic plan for global cooperation. It all begins with a humble Pope with a different plan for this and the next world. "68 VIA CONDOTTI: Eternity Ltd." is the third of five Kate Keenan Special Assignment books in a serialized read not unlike watching a 1950s movie serial. A simple realization in the mind of God's Hand on Earth ultimately reaches beyond this time and world.

CHANG THE MAGIC CAT is a rollicking, adventurous screenplay-novel set in merry old England. It follows Chang, the wise, mystical, magical, all-knowing cat through his adventures with bumbling humans as they search to discover the rightful heir to Briersly Manor.

About the Author

A. G. Hayes studied television writing at UCLA. He has published short fiction for CBS TV and other television production companies. He lives in the Sierra Nevada Foothills and spends his time writing and traveling to nearly every part of the world. He has used personal experiences gained during service with the British intelligence in Eastern Europe and the Middle East to enrich the characters of his protagonist teams. He is the multi-award-winning author of *Who's Killing All the Lawyers* (Savant 2011), *The Judas List* (Savant 2012), *Imminent Danger* (Savant 2013), *The Chemical Factor* (Savant 2015), *Quantum Death* (Savant 2016) and *Finding Kate* (Savant 2016), *The Solar Triangle* (Savant 2017) and *68 Via Condotti: Book One - Eternity Ltd.* (Savant 2019) as well as the delightful vaudeville-style screenplay-novel, *CHANG the Magic Cat* (Aignos 2017).

If you enjoyed *The Complete Koski & Falk,* consider these other works from Savant Books and Publications:

Essay, Essay, Essay by Yasuo Kobachi

Aloha from Coffee Island by Walter Miyanari

Footprints, Smiles and Little White Lies by Daniel S. Janik

The Illustrated Middle Earth by Daniel S. Janik

Last and Final Harvest by Daniel S. Janik

A Whale's Tale by Daniel S. Janik

Tropic of California by R. Page Kaufman

Tropic of California (companion music CD) by R. Page Kaufman

The Village Curtain by Tony Tame

Dare to Love in Oz by William Maltese

The Interzone by Tatsuyuki Kobayashi

Today I Am a Man by Larry Rodness

The Bahrain Conspiracy by Bentley Gates

Called Home by Gloria Schumann

Kanaka Blues by Mike Farris

First Breath edited by Z. M. Oliver

Poor Rich by Jean Blasiar

The Jumper Chronicles by W. C. Peever

William Maltese's Flicker by William Maltese

My Unborn Child by Orest Stocco

Last Song of the Whales by Four Arrows

Perilous Panacea by Ronald Klueh

Falling but Fulfilled by Zachary M. Oliver

Mythical Voyage by Robin Ymer

Hello, Norma Jean by Sue Dolleris

Richer by Jean Blasiar

Manifest Intent by Mike Farris

Charlie No Face by David B. Seaburn

Number One Bestseller by Brian Morley

My Two Wives and Three Husbands by S. Stanley Gordon

In Dire Straits by Jim Currie

Wretched Land by Mila Komarnisky

Chan Kim by Ilan Herman

Who's Killing All the Lawyers? by A. G. Hayes

Ammon's Horn by G. Amati

Wavelengths edited by Zachary M. Oliver

Almost Paradise by Laurie Hanan

Communion by Jean Blasiar and Jonathan Marcantoni

The Oil Man by Leon Puissegur

Random Views of Asia from the Mid-Pacific by William E. Sharp

The Isla Vista Crucible by Reilly Ridgell

Blood Money by Scott Mastro

In the Himalayan Nights by Anoop Chandola

On My Behalf by Helen Doan

Traveler's Rest by Jonathan Marcantoni

Keys in the River by Tendai Mwanaka

Chimney Bluffs by David B. Seaburn

The Loons by Sue Dolleris

Light Surfer by David Allan Williams

The Judas List by A. G. Hayes

The Path of the Templar by W. C. Peever

The Desperate Cycle by Tony Tame

Shutterbug by Buz Sawyer

Blessed are the Peacekeepers by Tom Donnelly and Mike Munger

The Bellwether Messages edited by D. S. Janik

The Turtle Dances by Daniel S. Janik

The Lazarus Conspiracies by Richard Rose

Purple Haze by George B. Hudson

Imminent Danger by A. G. Hayes

Lullaby Moon (CD) by Malia Elliott of Leon & Malia

Volutions edited by Suzanne Langford

In the Eyes of the Son by Hans Brinckmann

The Hanging of Dr. Hanson by Bentley Gates

Flight of Destiny by Francis Powell

Elaine of Corbenic by Tima Z. Newman

Ballerina Birdies by Marina Yamamoto

More More Time by David B. Seabird

Crazy Like Me by Erin Lee

Cleopatra Unconquered by Helen R. Davis

Valedictory by Daniel Scott

The Chemical Factor by A. G. Hayes

Quantum Death by A. G. Hayes and Raymond Gaynor

Big Heaven by Charlotte Hebert

Captain Riddle's Treasure by GV Rama Rao

All Things Await by Seth Clabough

Tsunami Libido by Cate Burns

Finding Kate by A. G. Hayes

The Adventures of Purple Head, Buddha Monkey and Sticky Feet
by Erik and Forest Bracht

In the Shadows of My Mind by Andrew Massie

The Gumshoe by Richard Rose

In Search of Somatic Therapy by Setsuko Tsuchiya

Cereus by Z. Roux

The Solar Triangle by A. G. Hayes

Shadow and Light edited by Helen R. Davis

A Real Daughter by Lynne McKelvey

StoryTeller by Nicholas Bylotas

Bo Henry at Three Forks by Daniel Bradford

Kindred edited by Gary "Doc" Krinberg
Cleopatra Victorious by Helen R. Davis
Navel of the Sea by Elizabeth McKague
Entwined edited by Gary "Doc" Krinberg

Coming Soon
Truth and Tell Travel the Solar System by Helen R. Davis
Honeymoon Forever: Find Love, Keep Love by R. Page Kaufman
Leon and Malia's Island Music (music CD)

and from our *avant garde* imprint, Aignos Publishing:

The Dark Side of Sunshine by Paul Guzzo
Happy that it's Not True by Carlos Aleman
Cazadores de Libros Perdidos by German William Cabasssa
Barber [Spanish]
The Desert and the City by Derek Bickerton
The Overnight Family Man by Paul Guzzo
There is No Cholera in Zimbabwe by Zachary M. Oliver
John Doe by Buz Sawyers
The Piano Tuner's Wife by Jean Yamasaki Toyama
Nuno by Carlos Aleman
An Aura of Greatness by Brendan P. Burns
Polonio Pass by Doc Krinberg
Iwana by Alvaro Leiva
University and King by Jeffrey Ryan Long
The Surreal Adventures of Dr. Mingus by Jesus Richard Felix
Rodriguez
Letters by Buz Sawyers
In the Heart of the Country by Derek Bickerton

El Camino De Regreso by Maricruz Acuna [Spanish]

Diego in Two Places by Carlos Aleman

Prepositions by Jean Yamasaki Toyama

Deep Slumber of Dogs by Doc Krinberg

Saddam's Parrot by Jim Currie

Beneath Them by Natalie Roers

Chang the Magic Cat by A. G. Hayes

Illegal by E. M. Duesel

Island Wildlife: Exiles, Expats and Exotic Others by Robert
Friedman

The Winter Spider by Doc Krinberg

The Princess in My Head by J. G. Matheny

Comic Crusaders by Richard Rose

I'll Remember by Clif Mc Crady

Coming Soon:

The City and The Desert by Derek Bickerton

Till Then Our Written Love Will Have To Do by Cheryl R. Woods

The Edge of Madness by Raymond Gaynor

Aignos Publishing | an imprint of Savant Books and Publications
http://www.savantbooksandpublications.com

www.ingramcontent.com/pod-product-compliance
Lightning Source LLC
Chambersburg PA
CBHW070339030726
47504CB00001B/7